The Collected Supernatural and Weird Fiction of Nathaniel Hawthorne Volume 1

The Collected
Supernatural and Weird
Fiction of
Nathaniel Hawthorne
Volume 1

Including One Novel 'The House of the Seven
Gables', One Novelette 'Rappaccini's Daughter',
and Fifteen Short Stories
of the Strange and Unusual

Nathaniel Hawthorne

LEONAUR

*The Collected
Supernatural and Weird
Fiction of
Nathaniel Hawthorne
Volume 1
Including One Novel 'The House of the Seven Gables',
One Novelette 'Rappaccini's Daughter',
and Fifteen Short Stories of the Strange and Unusual*
by Nathaniel Hawthorne

FIRST EDITION

Leonaur is an imprint
of Oakpast Ltd

Copyright in this form © 2011 Oakpast Ltd

ISBN: 978-0-85706-799-9 (hardcover)
ISBN: 978-0-85706-800-2 (softcover)

http://www.leonaur.com

Publisher's Notes

Contents

The House of the Seven Gables

1: THE OLD PYNCHEON FAMILY

Halfway down a by-street of one of our New England towns stands a rusty wooden house, with seven acutely peaked gables, facing towards various points of the compass, and a huge, clustered chimney in the midst. The street is Pyncheon Street; the house is the old Pyncheon House; and an elm-tree, of wide circumference, rooted before the door, is familiar to every town-born child by the title of the Pyncheon Elm. On my occasional visits to the town aforesaid, I seldom failed to turn down Pyncheon Street, for the sake of passing through the shadow of these two antiquities,—the great elm-tree and the weather-beaten edifice.

The aspect of the venerable mansion has always affected me like a human countenance, bearing the traces not merely of outward storm and sunshine, but expressive also, of the long lapse of mortal life, and accompanying vicissitudes that have passed within. Were these to be worthily recounted, they would form a narrative of no small interest and instruction, and possessing, moreover, a certain remarkable unity, which might almost seem the result of artistic arrangement. But the story would include a chain of events extending over the better part of two centuries, and, written out with reasonable amplitude, would fill a bigger folio volume, or a longer series of duodecimos, than could prudently be appropriated to the annals of all New England during a similar period. It consequently becomes imperative to make short work with most of the traditionary lore of which the old

Pyncheon House, otherwise known as the House of the Seven Gables, has been the theme.

With a brief sketch, therefore, of the circumstances amid which the foundation of the house was laid, and a rapid glimpse at its quaint exterior, as it grew black in the prevalent east wind,—pointing, too, here and there, at some spot of more verdant mossiness on its roof and walls,—we shall commence the real action of our tale at an epoch not very remote from the present day. Still, there will be a connection with the long past—a reference to forgotten events and personages, and to manners, feelings, and opinions, almost or wholly obsolete—which, if adequately translated to the reader, would serve to illustrate how much of old material goes to make up the freshest novelty of human life. Hence, too, might be drawn a weighty lesson from the little-regarded truth, that the act of the passing generation is the germ which may and must produce good or evil fruit in a far-distant time; that, together with the seed of the merely temporary crop, which mortals term expediency, they inevitably sow the acorns of a more enduring growth, which may darkly overshadow their posterity.

The House of the Seven Gables, antique as it now looks, was not the first habitation erected by civilized man on precisely the same spot of ground. Pyncheon Street formerly bore the humbler appellation of Maule's Lane, from the name of the original occupant of the soil, before whose cottage-door it was a cow-path. A natural spring of soft and pleasant water—a rare treasure on the sea-girt peninsula where the Puritan settlement was made—had early induced Matthew Maule to build a hut, shaggy with thatch, at this point, although somewhat too remote from what was then the centre of the village. In the growth of the town, however, after some thirty or forty years, the site covered by this rude hovel had become exceedingly desirable in the eyes of a prominent and powerful personage, who asserted plausible claims to the proprietorship of this and a large adjacent tract of land, on the strength of a grant from the legislature.

Colonel Pyncheon, the claimant, as we gather from whatever traits of him are preserved, was characterized by an iron energy of purpose. Matthew Maule, on the other hand, though an obscure man, was stubborn in the defence of what he considered his right; and, for several years, he succeeded in protecting the acre or two of earth which, with his own toil, he had hewn out of the primeval forest, to be his garden ground and homestead. No written record of this dispute is known to be in existence. Our acquaintance with the whole subject is derived chiefly from tradition. It would be bold, therefore, and possibly unjust, to venture a decisive opinion as to its merits; although it appears to have been at least a matter of doubt, whether Colonel Pyncheon's claim were not unduly stretched, in order to make it cover the small metes and bounds of Matthew Maule.

What greatly strengthens such a suspicion is the fact that this controversy between two ill-matched antagonists—at a period, moreover, laud it as we may, when personal influence had far more weight than now—remained for years undecided, and came to a close only with the death of the party occupying the disputed soil. The mode of his death, too, affects the mind differently, in our day, from what it did a century and a half ago. It was a death that blasted with strange horror the humble name of the dweller in the cottage, and made it seem almost a religious act to drive the plough over the little area of his habitation, and obliterate his place and memory from among men.

Old Matthew Maule, in a word, was executed for the crime of witchcraft. He was one of the martyrs to that terrible delusion, which should teach us, among its other morals, that the influential classes, and those who take upon themselves to be leaders of the people, are fully liable to all the passionate error that has ever characterized the maddest mob. Clergymen, judges, statesmen,—the wisest, calmest, holiest persons of their day stood in the inner circle round about the gallows, loudest to applaud the work of blood, latest to confess themselves miserably deceived. If any one part of their proceedings can be said to deserve less blame than another, it was the singular indiscrimination with which they persecuted, not merely the poor and aged, as in former judicial massacres, but people of all ranks; their own equals, brethren, and wives.

Amid the disorder of such various ruin, it is not strange that a man of inconsiderable note, like Maule, should have trodden the martyr's path to the hill of execution almost unremarked in the throng of his fellow sufferers. But, in after days, when the frenzy of that hideous epoch had subsided, it was remembered how loudly Colonel Pyncheon had joined in the general cry, to purge the land from witchcraft; nor did it fail to be whispered, that there was an invidious acrimony in the zeal with which he had sought the condemnation of Matthew Maule. It was well known that the victim had recognized the bitterness of personal enmity in his persecutor's conduct towards him, and that he declared himself hunted to death for his spoil.

At the moment of execution—with the halter about his neck, and while Colonel Pyncheon sat on horseback, grimly gazing at the scene Maule had addressed him from the scaffold, and uttered a prophecy, of which history, as well as fireside tradition, has preserved the very words. "God," said the dying man, pointing his finger, with a ghastly look, at the undismayed countenance of his enemy,—"God will give him blood to drink!" After the reputed wizard's death, his humble homestead had fallen an easy spoil into Colonel Pyncheon's grasp. When it was understood, however, that the colonel intended to erect a family mansion-spacious, ponderously framed of oaken timber, and calculated to endure for many generations of his posterity over the spot first covered by the log-built hut of Matthew Maule, there was much shaking of the head among the village gossips.

Without absolutely expressing a doubt whether the stalwart Puritan had acted as a man of conscience and integrity throughout the proceedings which have been sketched, they, nevertheless, hinted that he was about to build his house over an unquiet grave. His home would include the home of the dead and buried wizard, and would thus afford the ghost of the latter a kind of privilege to haunt its new apartments, and the chambers into which future bridegrooms were to lead their brides, and where children of the Pyncheon blood were to be born. The terror and ugliness of Maule's crime, and the wretchedness of his punishment, would darken the freshly plastered walls, and infect them early with the scent of an old and melancholy house. Why, then,—while so much of the soil around him was bestrewn with the virgin forest leaves,—why should Colonel Pyncheon prefer a site that had already been accurst?

But the Puritan soldier and magistrate was not a man to be turned aside from his well-considered scheme, either by dread of the wizard's ghost, or by flimsy sentimentalities of any kind, however specious. Had he been told of a bad air, it might have moved him somewhat; but he was ready to encounter an evil spirit on his own ground. Endowed with commonsense, as massive and hard as blocks of granite, fastened together by stern rigidity of purpose, as with iron clamps, he followed out his original design, probably without so much as imagining an objection to it. On the score of delicacy, or any scrupulousness which a finer sensibility might have taught him, the colonel, like most of his breed and generation, was impenetrable. He therefore dug his cellar, and laid the deep foundations of his mansion, on the square of earth whence Matthew Maule, forty years before, had first swept away the fallen leaves.

It was a curious, and, as some people thought, an ominous fact, that, very soon after the workmen began their operations, the spring of water, above mentioned, entirely lost the deliciousness of its pristine quality. Whether its sources were disturbed by the depth of the new cellar, or whatever subtler cause might lurk at the bottom, it is certain that the water of Maule's Well, as it continued to be called, grew hard and brackish. Even such we find it now; and any old woman of the neighbourhood will certify that it is productive of intestinal mischief to those who quench their thirst there.

The reader may deem it singular that the head carpenter of the new edifice was no other than the son of the very man from whose dead gripe the property of the soil had been wrested. Not improbably he was the best workman of his time; or, perhaps, the colonel thought it expedient, or was impelled by some better feeling, thus openly to cast aside all animosity against the race of his fallen antagonist. Nor was it out of keeping with the general coarseness and matter-of-fact character of the age, that the son should be willing to earn an honest penny, or, rather, a weighty amount of sterling pounds, from the purse of his father's deadly enemy. At all events, Thomas Maule became the architect of the House of the Seven Gables, and performed his duty so faithfully that the timber framework fastened by his hands still holds together.

Thus the great house was built. Familiar as it stands in the writer's recollection,—for it has been an object of curiosity with him from boyhood, both as a specimen of the best and stateliest architecture of a long past epoch, and as the scene of events more full of human interest, perhaps, than those of a gray feudal castle,—familiar as it stands, in its rusty old age, it is therefore only the more difficult to imagine the bright novelty with which it first caught the sunshine. The impression of its actual state, at this distance of a hundred and sixty years, darkens inevitably through the picture which we would fain give of its appearance on the morning when the Puritan magnate bade all the town to be his guests.

A ceremony of consecration, festive as well as religious, was now to be performed. A prayer and discourse from the Rev. Mr. Higginson, and the outpouring of a psalm from the general throat of the community, was to be made acceptable to the grosser sense by ale, cider, wine, and brandy, in copious effusion, and, as some authorities aver, by an ox, roasted whole, or at least, by the weight and substance of an ox, in more manageable joints and sirloins. The carcass of a deer, shot within twenty miles, had supplied material for the vast circumference of a pasty. A codfish of sixty pounds, caught in the bay, had been dissolved into the rich liquid of a chowder. The chimney of the new house, in short, belching forth its kitchen smoke, impregnated the whole air with the scent of meats, fowls, and fishes, spicily concocted with odoriferous herbs, and onions in abundance. The mere smell of such festivity, making its way to everybody's nostrils, was at once an invitation and an appetite.

Maule's Lane, or Pyncheon Street, as it were now more decorous to call it, was thronged, at the appointed hour, as with a congregation on its way to church. All, as they approached, looked upward at the imposing edifice, which was henceforth to assume its rank among the habitations of mankind. There it rose, a little withdrawn from the line of the street, but in pride, not modesty. Its whole visible exterior was ornamented with quaint figures, conceived in the grotesqueness of a Gothic fancy, and drawn or stamped in the glittering plaster, composed of lime, pebbles, and bits of glass, with which the woodwork of the walls was overspread.

On every side the seven gables pointed sharply towards the sky, and presented the aspect of a whole sisterhood of edifices, breathing through the spiracles of one great chimney. The many lattices, with their small, diamond-shaped panes, admitted the sunlight into hall and chamber, while, nevertheless, the second story, projecting far over the base, and itself retiring beneath the third, threw a shadowy and thoughtful gloom into the lower rooms. Carved globes of wood were affixed under the jutting stories. Little spiral rods of iron beautified each of the seven peaks.

On the triangular portion of the gable, that fronted next the street, was a dial, put up that very morning, and on which the sun was still marking the passage of the first bright hour in a history that was not destined to be all so bright. All around were scattered shavings, chips, shingles, and broken halves of bricks; these, together with the lately turned earth, on which the grass had not begun to grow, contributed to the impression of strangeness and novelty proper to a house that had yet its place to make among men's daily interests.

The principal entrance, which had almost the breadth of a church-door, was in the angle between the two front gables, and was covered by an open porch, with benches beneath its shelter. Under this arched doorway, scraping their feet on the unworn threshold, now trod the clergymen, the elders, the magistrates, the deacons, and whatever of aristocracy there was in town or county. Thither, too, thronged the plebeian classes as freely as their betters, and in larger number. Just within the entrance, however, stood two serving-men, pointing some of the guests to the neighbourhood of the kitchen and ushering others into the statelier rooms,—hospitable alike to all, but still with a scrutinizing regard to the high or low degree of each. Velvet garments sombre but rich, stiffly plaited ruffs and bands, embroidered gloves, venerable beards, the mien and countenance of authority, made it easy to distinguish the gentleman of worship, at that period, from the tradesman, with his plodding air, or the labourer, in his leathern jerkin, stealing awe-stricken into the house which he had perhaps helped to build.

One inauspicious circumstance there was, which awakened a hardly concealed displeasure in the breasts of a few of the more punctilious visitors. The founder of this stately mansion—a gentleman noted for the square and ponderous courtesy of his demeanour, ought surely to have stood in his own hall, and to have offered the first welcome to so many eminent personages as here presented themselves in honour of his solemn festival. He was as yet invisible; the most favoured of the guests had not beheld him.

This sluggishness on Colonel Pyncheon's part became still more unaccountable, when the second dignitary of the province made his appearance, and found no more ceremonious a reception. The lieutenant-governor, although his visit was one of the anticipated glories of the day, had alighted from his horse, and assisted his lady from her side-saddle, and crossed the Colonel's threshold, without other greeting than that of the principal domestic.

This person—a gray-headed man, of quiet and most respectful deportment—found it necessary to explain that his master still remained in his study, or private apartment; on entering which, an hour before, he had expressed a wish on no account to be disturbed.

"Do not you see, fellow," said the high-sheriff of the county, taking the servant aside, "that this is no less a man than the lieutenant-governor? Summon Colonel Pyncheon at once! I know that he received letters from England this morning; and, in the perusal and consideration of them, an hour may have passed away without his noticing it. But he will be ill-pleased, I judge, if you suffer him to neglect the courtesy due to one of our chief rulers, and who may be said to represent King William, in the absence of the governor himself. Call your master instantly."

"Nay, please your worship," answered the man, in much perplexity, but with a backwardness that strikingly indicated the hard and severe character of Colonel Pyncheon's domestic rule; "my master's orders were exceeding strict; and, as your worship knows, he permits of no discretion in the obedience of those who owe him service. Let who list open yonder door; I dare not, though the governor's own voice should bid me do it!"

"Pooh, pooh, master high sheriff!" cried the lieutenant-governor, who had overheard the foregoing discussion, and felt himself high enough in station to play a little with his dignity. "I will take the matter into my own hands. It is time that the good Colonel came forth to greet his friends; else we shall be apt to suspect that he has taken a sip too much of his Canary wine, in his extreme deliberation which cask it were best to broach in honor of the day! But since he is so much behindhand, I will give him a remembrancer myself!"

Accordingly, with such a tramp of his ponderous riding-boots as might of itself have been audible in the remotest of the seven gables, he advanced to the door, which the servant pointed out, and made its new panels re-echo with a loud, free knock. Then, looking round, with a smile, to the spectators, he awaited a response. As none came, however, he knocked again, but with the same unsatisfactory result as at first. And now, being a trifle choleric in his temperament, the lieutenant-governor uplifted the heavy hilt of his sword, wherewith he so beat and banged upon the door, that, as some of the bystanders whispered, the racket might have disturbed the dead. Be that as it might, it seemed to

15

produce no awakening effect on Colonel Pyncheon. When the sound subsided, the silence through the house was deep, dreary, and oppressive, notwithstanding that the tongues of many of the guests had already been loosened by a surreptitious cup or two of wine or spirits.

"Strange, forsooth!—very strange!" cried the lieutenant-governor, whose smile was changed to a frown. "But seeing that our host sets us the good example of forgetting ceremony, I shall likewise throw it aside, and make free to intrude on his privacy."

He tried the door, which yielded to his hand, and was flung wide open by a sudden gust of wind that passed, as with a loud sigh, from the outermost portal through all the passages and apartments of the new house. It rustled the silken garments of the ladies, and waved the long curls of the gentlemen's wigs, and shook the window-hangings and the curtains of the bedchambers; causing everywhere a singular stir, which yet was more like a hush. A shadow of awe and half-fearful anticipation—nobody knew wherefore, nor of what—had all at once fallen over the company.

They thronged, however, to the now open door, pressing the lieutenant-governor, in the eagerness of their curiosity, into the room in advance of them. At the first glimpse they beheld nothing extraordinary: a handsomely furnished room, of moderate size, somewhat darkened by curtains; books arranged on shelves; a large map on the wall, and likewise a portrait of Colonel Pyncheon, beneath which sat the original colonel himself, in an oaken elbow-chair, with a pen in his hand. Letters, parchments, and blank sheets of paper were on the table before him. He appeared to gaze at the curious crowd, in front of which stood the lieutenant-governor; and there was a frown on his dark and massive countenance, as if sternly resentful of the boldness that had impelled them into his private retirement.

A little boy—the colonel's grandchild, and the only human being that ever dared to be familiar with him—now made his way among the guests, and ran towards the seated figure; then pausing halfway, he began to shriek with terror. The company, tremulous as the leaves of a tree, when all are shaking together, drew nearer, and perceived that there was an unnatural distortion in the fixedness of Colonel Pyncheon's stare; that there was blood on his ruff, and that his hoary beard was saturated with it. It was too late to give assistance. The iron-hearted Puritan, the relentless persecutor, the grasping and strong-willed man was dead! Dead, in his new house! There is a tradition, only worth alluding to as lending a tinge of superstitious awe to a scene perhaps gloomy enough without it, that a voice spoke loudly among the guests, the tones of which were like those of old Matthew Maule, the executed wizard,—"God hath given him blood to drink!"

Thus early had that one guest,—the only guest who is certain, at one time or another, to find his way into every human dwelling,—thus early had Death stepped across the threshold of the House of the Seven Gables!

Colonel Pyncheon's sudden and mysterious end made a vast deal of noise in its day. There were many rumours, some of which have vaguely drifted down to the present time, how that appearances indicated violence; that there were the marks of fingers on his throat, and the print of a bloody hand on his plaited ruff; and that his peaked beard was dishevelled, as if it had been fiercely clutched and pulled. It was averred, likewise, that the lattice window, near the colonel's chair, was open; and that, only a few minutes before the fatal occurrence, the figure of a man had been seen clambering over the garden fence, in the rear of the house.

But it were folly to lay any stress on stories of this kind, which are sure to spring up around such an event as that now related, and which, as in the present case, sometimes prolong themselves for ages afterwards, like the toadstools that indicate where the fallen and buried trunk of a tree has long since mouldered into the earth. For our own part, we allow them just as little credence as to that other fable of the skeleton hand which the lieutenant-governor was said to have seen at the colonel's throat, but which vanished away, as he advanced farther into the room.

Certain it is, however, that there was a great consultation and dispute of doctors over the dead body. One,—John Swinnerton by name,—who appears to have been a man of eminence, upheld it, if we have rightly understood his terms of art, to be a case of apoplexy. His professional brethren, each for himself, adopted various hypotheses, more or less plausible, but all dressed out in a perplexing mystery of phrase, which, if it do not show a bewilderment of mind in these erudite physicians, certainly causes it in the unlearned peruser of their opinions. The coroner's jury sat upon the corpse, and, like sensible men, returned an unassailable verdict of "Sudden Death!"

It is indeed difficult to imagine that there could have been a serious suspicion of murder, or the slightest grounds for implicating any particular individual as the perpetrator. The rank, wealth, and eminent character of the deceased must have insured the strictest scrutiny into every ambiguous circumstance. As none such is on record, it is safe to assume that none existed. Tradition,—which sometimes brings down truth that history has let slip, but is oftener the wild babble of the time, such as was formerly spoken at the fireside and now congeals in newspapers,— tradition is responsible for all contrary averments.

In Colonel Pyncheon's funeral sermon, which was printed, and is still extant, the Rev. Mr. Higginson enumerates, among the many felicities of his distinguished parishioner's earthly career, the happy seasonableness of his death. His duties all performed,—the highest prosperity attained,—his race and future generations fixed on a stable basis, and with a stately roof to shelter them for centuries to come,—what other upward step remained for this good man to take, save the final step from earth to the golden gate of heaven! The pious clergyman surely would not have uttered words like these had he in the least suspected that the colonel had been thrust into the other world with the clutch of violence upon his throat.

The family of Colonel Pyncheon, at the epoch of his death, seemed destined to as fortunate a permanence as can anywise

18

consist with the inherent instability of human affairs. It might fairly be anticipated that the progress of time would rather increase and ripen their prosperity, than wear away and destroy it. For, not only had his son and heir come into immediate enjoyment of a rich estate, but there was a claim through an Indian deed, confirmed by a subsequent grant of the General Court, to a vast and as yet unexplored and unmeasured tract of Eastern lands. These possessions—for as such they might almost certainly be reckoned—comprised the greater part of what is now known as Waldo County, in the state of Maine, and were more extensive than many a dukedom, or even a reigning prince's territory, on European soil. When the pathless forest that still covered this wild principality should give place—as it inevitably must, though perhaps not till ages hence—to the golden fertility of human culture, it would be the source of incalculable wealth to the Pyncheon blood.

Had the colonel survived only a few weeks longer, it is probable that his great political influence, and powerful connections at home and abroad, would have consummated all that was necessary to render the claim available. But, in spite of good Mr. Higginson's congratulatory eloquence, this appeared to be the one thing which Colonel Pyncheon, provident and sagacious as he was, had allowed to go at loose ends. So far as the prospective territory was concerned, he unquestionably died too soon. His son lacked not merely the father's eminent position, but the talent and force of character to achieve it: he could, therefore, effect nothing by dint of political interest; and the bare justice or legality of the claim was not so apparent, after the colonel's decease, as it had been pronounced in his lifetime. Some connecting link had slipped out of the evidence, and could not anywhere be found.

Efforts, it is true, were made by the Pyncheons, not only then, but at various periods for nearly a hundred years afterwards, to obtain what they stubbornly persisted in deeming their right. But, in course of time, the territory was partly regranted to more favoured individuals, and partly cleared and occupied by actual settlers. These last, if they ever heard of the Pyncheon title, would have laughed at the idea of any man's asserting a right— on the strength of mouldy parchments, signed with the faded autographs of governors and legislators long dead and forgotten—to the lands which they or their fathers had wrested from the wild hand of nature by their own sturdy toil. This impalpable claim, therefore, resulted in nothing more solid than to cherish, from generation to generation, an absurd delusion of family importance, which all along characterized the Pyncheons. It caused the poorest member of the race to feel as if he inherited a kind of nobility, and might yet come into the possession of princely wealth to support it.

In the better specimens of the breed, this peculiarity threw an ideal grace over the hard material of human life, without stealing away any truly valuable quality. In the baser sort, its effect was to increase the liability to sluggishness and dependence, and induce the victim of a shadowy hope to remit all self-effort, while awaiting the realization of his dreams. Years and years after their claim had passed out of the public memory, the Pyncheons were accustomed to consult the colonel's ancient map, which had been projected while Waldo County was still an unbroken wilderness. Where the old land surveyor had put down woods, lakes, and rivers, they marked out the cleared spaces, and dotted the villages and towns, and calculated the progressively increasing value of the territory, as if there were yet a prospect of its ultimately forming a princedom for themselves.

In almost every generation, nevertheless, there happened to be some one descendant of the family gifted with a portion of the hard, keen sense, and practical energy, that had so remarkably distinguished the original founder. His character, indeed, might be traced all the way down, as distinctly as if the Colonel himself, a little diluted, had been gifted with a sort of intermittent immortality on earth. At two or three epochs, when the fortunes of the family were low, this representative of hereditary qualities had made his appearance, and caused the traditionary gossips of the town to whisper among themselves, "Here is the old Pyncheon come again! Now the Seven Gables will be new-shingled!"

From father to son, they clung to the ancestral house with singular tenacity of home attachment. For various reasons, however, and from impressions often too vaguely founded to be put on paper, the writer cherishes the belief that many, if not most, of the successive proprietors of this estate were troubled with doubts as to their moral right to hold it. Of their legal tenure there could be no question; but old Matthew Maule, it is to be feared, trode downward from his own age to a far later one, planting a heavy footstep, all the way, on the conscience of a Pyncheon. If so, we are left to dispose of the awful query, whether each inheritor of the property—conscious of wrong, and failing to rectify it—did not commit anew the great guilt of his ancestor, and incur all its original responsibilities. And supposing such to be the case, would it not be a far truer mode of expression to say of the Pyncheon family, that they inherited a great misfortune, than the reverse?

We have already hinted that it is not our purpose to trace down the history of the Pyncheon family, in its unbroken connection with the House of the Seven Gables; nor to show, as in a magic picture, how the rustiness and infirmity of age gathered over the venerable house itself. As regards its interior life, a large, dim looking-glass used to hang in one of the rooms, and was fabled to contain within its depths all the shapes that had ever been reflected there,—the old colonel himself, and his many descendants, some in the garb of antique babyhood, and others in the bloom of feminine beauty or manly prime, or saddened with the wrinkles of frosty age. Had we the secret of that mirror, we would gladly sit down before it, and transfer its revelations to our page.

But there was a story, for which it is difficult to conceive any foundation, that the posterity of Matthew Maule had some connection with the mystery of the looking-glass, and that, by what appears to have been a sort of mesmeric process, they could make its inner region all alive with the departed Pyncheons;

not as they had shown themselves to the world, nor in their better and happier hours, but as doing over again some deed of sin, or in the crisis of life's bitterest sorrow. The popular imagination, indeed, long kept itself busy with the affair of the old Puritan Pyncheon and the wizard Maule; the curse which the latter flung from his scaffold was remembered, with the very important addition, that it had become a part of the Pyncheon inheritance. If one of the family did but gurgle in his throat, a bystander would be likely enough to whisper, between jest and earnest, "He has Maule's blood to drink!"

The sudden death of a Pyncheon, about a hundred years ago, with circumstances very similar to what have been related of the colonel's exit, was held as giving additional probability to the received opinion on this topic. It was considered, moreover, an ugly and ominous circumstance, that Colonel Pyncheon's picture—in obedience, it was said, to a provision of his will— remained affixed to the wall of the room in which he died. Those stern, immitigable features seemed to symbolize an evil influence, and so darkly to mingle the shadow of their presence with the sunshine of the passing hour, that no good thoughts or purposes could ever spring up and blossom there. To the thoughtful mind there will be no tinge of superstition in what we figuratively express, by affirming that the ghost of a dead progenitor—perhaps as a portion of his own punishment—is often doomed to become the Evil Genius of his family.

The Pyncheons, in brief, lived along, for the better part of two centuries, with perhaps less of outward vicissitude than has attended most other New England families during the same period of time. Possessing very distinctive traits of their own, they nevertheless took the general characteristics of the little community in which they dwelt; a town noted for its frugal, discreet, well-ordered, and home-loving inhabitants, as well as for the somewhat confined scope of its sympathies; but in which, be it said, there are odder individuals, and, now and then, stranger occurrences, than one meets with almost anywhere else. During the Revolution, the Pyncheon of that epoch, adopting the royal side, became a refugee; but repented, and made his reappearance, just at the point of time to preserve the House of the Seven Gables from confiscation.

For the last seventy years the most noted event in the Pyncheon annals had been likewise the heaviest calamity that ever befell the race; no less than the violent death—for so it was adjudged—of one member of the family by the criminal act of another. Certain circumstances attending this fatal occurrence had brought the deed irresistibly home to a nephew of the deceased Pyncheon. The young man was tried and convicted of the crime; but either the circumstantial nature of the evidence, and possibly some lurking doubts in the breast of the executive, or, lastly—an argument of greater weight in a republic than it could have been under a monarchy,—the high respectability and political influence of the criminal's connections, had availed to mitigate his doom from death to perpetual imprisonment. This sad affair had chanced about thirty years before the action of our story commences. Latterly, there were rumours (which few believed, and only one or two felt greatly interested in) that this long-buried man was likely, for some reason or other, to be summoned forth from his living tomb.

It is essential to say a few words respecting the victim of this now almost forgotten murder. He was an old bachelor, and possessed of great wealth, in addition to the house and real estate which constituted what remained of the ancient Pyncheon property. Being of an eccentric and melancholy turn of mind, and greatly given to rummaging old records and hearkening to old traditions, he had brought himself, it is averred, to the conclusion that Matthew Maule, the wizard, had been foully wronged out of his homestead, if not out of his life.

Such being the case, and he, the old bachelor, in possession of the ill-gotten spoil,—with the black stain of blood sunken deep into it, and still to be scented by conscientious nostrils,—the question occurred, whether it were not imperative upon him, even at this late hour, to make restitution to Maule's posterity. To a man living so much in the past, and so little in the present, as the secluded and antiquarian old bachelor, a century and a half seemed not so vast a period as to obviate the propriety of substituting right for wrong. It was the belief of those who knew him best, that he would positively have taken the very singular step of giving up the House of the Seven Gables to the representative of Matthew Maule, but for the unspeakable tumult which a suspicion of the old gentleman's project awakened among his Pyncheon relatives.

Their exertions had the effect of suspending his purpose; but it was feared that he would perform, after death, by the operation of his last will, what he had so hardly been prevented from doing in his proper lifetime. But there is no one thing which men so rarely do, whatever the provocation or inducement, as to bequeath patrimonial property away from their own blood. They may love other individuals far better than their relatives,— they may even cherish dislike, or positive hatred, to the latter; but yet, in view of death, the strong prejudice of propinquity revives, and impels the testator to send down his estate in the line marked out by custom so immemorial that it looks like nature. In all the Pyncheons, this feeling had the energy of disease. It was too powerful for the conscientious scruples of the old bachelor; at whose death, accordingly, the mansion-house, together with most of his other riches, passed into the possession of his next legal representative.

This was a nephew, the cousin of the miserable young man who had been convicted of the uncle's murder. The new heir, up to the period of his accession, was reckoned rather a dissipated youth, but had at once reformed, and made himself an exceedingly respectable member of society. In fact, he showed more of the Pyncheon quality, and had won higher eminence in the world, than any of his race since the time of the original Puritan. Applying himself in earlier manhood to the study of the law, and having a natural tendency towards office, he had attained, many years ago, to a judicial situation in some inferior court, which gave him for life the very desirable and imposing title of judge. Later, he had engaged in politics, and served a part of two terms in Congress, besides making a considerable figure in both branches of the State legislature.

Judge Pyncheon was unquestionably an honour to his race. He had built himself a country-seat within a few miles of his native town, and there spent such portions of his time as could be spared from public service in the display of every grace and virtue—as a newspaper phrased it, on the eve of an election—befitting the Christian, the good citizen, the horticulturist, and the gentleman.

There were few of the Pyncheons left to sun themselves in the glow of the judge's prosperity. In respect to natural increase, the breed had not thriven; it appeared rather to be dying out. The only members of the family known to be extant were, first, the judge himself, and a single surviving son, who was now travelling in Europe; next, the thirty years' prisoner, already alluded to, and a sister of the latter, who occupied, in an extremely retired manner, the House of the Seven Gables, in which she had a life-estate by the will of the old bachelor. She was understood to be wretchedly poor, and seemed to make it her choice to remain so; inasmuch as her affluent cousin, the judge, had repeatedly offered her all the comforts of life, either in the old mansion or his own modern residence. The last and youngest Pyncheon was a little country-girl of seventeen, the daughter of another of the judge's cousins, who had married a young woman of no family or property, and died early and in poor circumstances. His widow had recently taken another husband.

As for Matthew Maule's posterity, it was supposed now to be extinct. For a very long period after the witchcraft delusion, however, the Maules had continued to inhabit the town where their progenitor had suffered so unjust a death. To all appearance, they were a quiet, honest, well-meaning race of people, cherishing no malice against individuals or the public for the wrong which had been done them; or if, at their own fireside, they transmitted from father to child any hostile recollection of the wizard's fate and their lost patrimony, it was never acted upon, nor openly expressed.

Nor would it have been singular had they ceased to remember that the House of the Seven Gables was resting its heavy framework on a foundation that was rightfully their own. There is something so massive, stable, and almost irresistibly imposing in the exterior presentment of established rank and great possessions, that their very existence seems to give them a right to exist; at least, so excellent a counterfeit of right, that few poor and humble men have moral force enough to question it, even in their secret minds. Such is the case now, after so many ancient prejudices have been overthrown; and it was far more so in ante-Revolutionary days, when the aristocracy could venture to be proud, and the low were content to be abased.

Thus the Maules, at all events, kept their resentments within their own breasts. They were generally poverty-stricken; always plebeian and obscure; working with unsuccessful diligence at handicrafts; labouring on the wharves, or following the sea, as sailors before the mast; living here and there about the town, in hired tenements, and coming finally to the almshouse as the natural home of their old age. At last, after creeping, as it were, for such a length of time along the utmost verge of the opaque puddle of obscurity, they had taken that downright plunge which, sooner or later, is the destiny of all families, whether princely or plebeian. For thirty years past, neither town-record, nor gravestone, nor the directory, nor the knowledge or memory of man, bore any trace of Matthew Maule's descendants. His blood might possibly exist elsewhere; here, where its lowly current could be traced so far back, it had ceased to keep an onward course.

So long as any of the race were to be found, they had been marked out from other men—not strikingly, nor as with a sharp line, but with an effect that was felt rather than spoken of—by an hereditary character of reserve. Their companions, or those who endeavoured to become such, grew conscious of a circle round about the Maules, within the sanctity or the spell of which, in spite of an exterior of sufficient frankness and good-fellowship, it was impossible for any man to step. It was this indefinable peculiarity, perhaps, that, by insulating them from human aid, kept them always so unfortunate in life. It certainly operated to prolong in their case, and to confirm to them as their only inheritance, those feelings of repugnance and superstitious terror with which the people of the town, even after awakening from their frenzy, continued to regard the memory of the reputed witches.

The mantle, or rather the ragged cloak, of old Matthew Maule had fallen upon his children. They were half believed to inherit mysterious attributes; the family eye was said to possess strange power. Among other good-for-nothing properties and privileges, one was especially assigned them,—that of exercising an influence over people's dreams. The Pyncheons, if all stories were true, haughtily as they bore themselves in the noonday streets of their native town, were no better than bond-servants to these plebeian Maules, on entering the topsy-turvy commonwealth of sleep. Modern psychology, it may be, will endeavour to reduce these alleged necromancies within a system, instead of rejecting them as altogether fabulous.

A descriptive paragraph or two, treating of the seven-gabled mansion in its more recent aspect, will bring this preliminary chapter to a close. The street in which it upreared its venerable peaks has long ceased to be a fashionable quarter of the town; so that, though the old edifice was surrounded by habitations of modern date, they were mostly small, built entirely of wood, and typical of the most plodding uniformity of common life. Doubtless, however, the whole story of human existence may be latent in each of them, but with no picturesqueness, externally, that can attract the imagination or sympathy to seek it there. But as for the old structure of our story, its white-oak frame, and its boards, shingles, and crumbling plaster, and even the huge, clustered chimney in the midst, seemed to constitute only the least and meanest part of its reality.

So much of mankind's varied experience had passed there,— so much had been suffered, and something, too, enjoyed,—that the very timbers were oozy, as with the moisture of a heart. It was itself like a great human heart, with a life of its own, and full of rich and sombre reminiscences.

The deep projection of the second story gave the house such a meditative look, that you could not pass it without the idea that it had secrets to keep, and an eventful history to moralize upon. In front, just on the edge of the unpaved sidewalk, grew the Pyncheon Elm, which, in reference to such trees as one usually meets with, might well be termed gigantic. It had been planted by a great-grandson of the first Pyncheon, and, though now four-score years of age, or perhaps nearer a hundred, was still in its strong and broad maturity, throwing its shadow from side to side of the street, overtopping the seven gables, and sweeping the whole black roof with its pendant foliage. It gave beauty to the old edifice, and seemed to make it a part of nature. The street having been widened about forty years ago, the front gable was now precisely on a line with it.

On either side extended a ruinous wooden fence of open lattice-work, through which could be seen a grassy yard, and, especially in the angles of the building, an enormous fertility of burdocks, with leaves, it is hardly an exaggeration to say, two or three feet long. Behind the house there appeared to be a garden, which undoubtedly had once been extensive, but was now in-fringed upon by other enclosures, or shut in by habitations and outbuildings that stood on another street. It would be an omis-sion, trifling, indeed, but unpardonable, were we to forget the green moss that had long since gathered over the projections of the windows, and on the slopes of the roof nor must we fail to direct the reader's eye to a crop, not of weeds, but flower-shrubs, which were growing aloft in the air, not a great way from the chimney, in the nook between two of the gables. They were called Alice's Posies.

The tradition was, that a certain Alice Pyncheon had flung up the seeds, in sport, and that the dust of the street and the decay of the roof gradually formed a kind of soil for them, out of which they grew, when Alice had long been in her grave. However the flowers might have come there, it was both sad and sweet to observe how Nature adopted to herself this desolate, decaying, gusty, rusty old house of the Pyncheon family; and how the ever-returning Summer did her best to gladden it with tender beauty, and grew melancholy in the effort.

There is one other feature, very essential to be noticed, but which, we greatly fear, may damage any picturesque and romantic impression which we have been willing to throw over our sketch of this respectable edifice. In the front gable, under the impending brow of the second story, and contiguous to the street, was a shop-door, divided horizontally in the midst, and with a window for its upper segment, such as is often seen in dwellings of a somewhat ancient date. This same shop-door had been a subject of no slight mortification to the present occupant of the august Pyncheon House, as well as to some of her predecessors. The matter is disagreeably delicate to handle; but, since the reader must needs be let into the secret, he will please to understand, that, about a century ago, the head of the Pyncheons found himself involved in serious financial difficulties.

The fellow (gentleman, as he styled himself) can hardly have been other than a spurious interloper; for, instead of seeking office from the king or the royal governor, or urging his hereditary claim to Eastern lands, he bethought himself of no better avenue to wealth than by cutting a shop-door through the side of his ancestral residence. It was the custom of the time, indeed, for merchants to store their goods and transact business in their own dwellings. But there was something pitifully small in this old Pyncheon's mode of setting about his commercial operations; it was whispered, that, with his own hands, all beruffled as they were, he used to give change for a shilling, and would turn a half-penny twice over, to make sure that it was a good one. Beyond all question, he had the blood of a petty huckster in his veins, through whatever channel it may have found its way there.

Immediately on his death, the shop-door had been locked, bolted, and barred, and, down to the period of our story, had probably never once been opened. The old counter, shelves, and other fixtures of the little shop remained just as he had left them.

It used to be affirmed, that the dead shop-keeper, in a white wig, a faded velvet coat, an apron at his waist, and his ruffles carefully turned back from his wrists, might be seen through the chinks of the shutters, any night of the year, ransacking his till, or poring over the dingy pages of his day-book. From the look of unutterable woe upon his face, it appeared to be his doom to spend eternity in a vain effort to make his accounts balance.

And now—in a very humble way, as will be seen—we proceed to open our narrative.

2: THE LITTLE SHOP-WINDOW

It still lacked half an hour of sunrise, when Miss Hepzibah Pyncheon—we will not say awoke, it being doubtful whether the poor lady had so much as closed her eyes during the brief night of midsummer—but, at all events, arose from her solitary pillow, and began what it would be mockery to term the adornment of her person. Far from us be the indecorum of assisting, even in imagination, at a maiden lady's toilet! Our story must therefore await Miss Hepzibah at the threshold of her chamber; only presuming, meanwhile, to note some of the heavy sighs that laboured from her bosom, with little restraint as to their lugubrious depth and volume of sound, inasmuch as they could be audible to nobody save a disembodied listener like ourself.

The Old Maid was alone in the old house. Alone, except for a certain respectable and orderly young man, an artist in the daguerreotype line, who, for about three months back, had been a lodger in a remote gable,—quite a house by itself, indeed,—with locks, bolts, and oaken bars on all the intervening doors. Inaudible, consequently, were poor Miss Hepzibah's gusty sighs. Inaudible the creaking joints of her stiffened knees, as she knelt down by the bedside. And inaudible, too, by mortal ear, but heard with all-comprehending love and pity in the farthest heaven, that almost agony of prayer—now whispered, now a groan, now a struggling silence—wherewith she besought the Divine assistance through the day!

Evidently, this is to be a day of more than ordinary trial to

Miss Hepzibah, who, for above a quarter of a century gone by, has dwelt in strict seclusion, taking no part in the business of life, and just as little in its intercourse and pleasures. Not with such fervour prays the torpid recluse, looking forward to the cold, sunless, stagnant calm of a day that is to be like innumerable yesterdays.

The maiden lady's devotions are concluded. Will she now issue forth over the threshold of our story? Not yet, by many moments. First, every drawer in the tall, old-fashioned bureau is to be opened, with difficulty, and with a succession of spasmodic jerks then, all must close again, with the same fidgety reluctance. There is a rustling of stiff silks; a tread of backward and forward footsteps to and fro across the chamber. We suspect Miss Hepzibah, moreover, of taking a step upward into a chair, in order to give heedful regard to her appearance on all sides, and at full length, in the oval, dingy-framed toilet-glass, that hangs above her table. Truly! well, indeed! who would have thought it! Is all this precious time to be lavished on the matutinal repair and beautifying of an elderly person, who never goes abroad, whom nobody ever visits, and from whom, when she shall have done her utmost, it were the best charity to turn one's eyes another way?

Now she is almost ready. Let us pardon her one other pause; for it is given to the sole sentiment, or, we might better say,—heightened and rendered intense, as it has been, by sorrow and seclusion,—to the strong passion of her life. We heard the turning of a key in a small lock; she has opened a secret drawer of an escritoire, and is probably looking at a certain miniature, done in Malbone's most perfect style, and representing a face worthy of no less delicate a pencil. It was once our good fortune to see this picture. It is a likeness of a young man, in a silken dressing-gown of an old fashion, the soft richness of which is well adapted to the countenance of reverie, with its full, tender lips, and beautiful eyes, that seem to indicate not so much capacity of thought, as gentle and voluptuous emotion.

Of the possessor of such features we shall have a right to ask nothing, except that he would take the rude world easily, and make himself happy in it. Can it have been an early lover of Miss Hepzibah? No; she never had a lover—poor thing, how could she?—nor ever knew, by her own experience, what love technically means. And yet, her undying faith and trust, her fresh remembrance, and continual devotedness towards the original of that miniature, have been the only substance for her heart to feed upon.

She seems to have put aside the miniature, and is standing again before the toilet-glass. There are tears to be wiped off. A few more footsteps to and fro; and here, at last,—with another pitiful sigh, like a gust of chill, damp wind out of a long-closed vault, the door of which has accidentally been set, ajar—here comes Miss Hepzibah Pyncheon! Forth she steps into the dusky, time-darkened passage; a tall figure, clad in black silk, with a long and shrunken waist, feeling her way towards the stairs like a near-sighted person, as in truth she is.

The sun, meanwhile, if not already above the horizon, was ascending nearer and nearer to its verge. A few clouds, floating high upward, caught some of the earliest light, and threw down its golden gleam on the windows of all the houses in the street, not forgetting the House of the Seven Gables, which—many such sunrises as it had witnessed—looked cheerfully at the present one. The reflected radiance served to show, pretty distinctly, the aspect and arrangement of the room which Hepzibah entered, after descending the stairs. It was a low-studded room, with a beam across the ceiling, panelled with dark wood, and having a large chimney-piece, set round with pictured tiles, but now closed by an iron fire-board, through which ran the funnel of a modern stove.

There was a carpet on the floor, originally of rich texture, but so worn and faded in these latter years that its once brilliant figure had quite vanished into one indistinguishable hue. In the way of furniture, there were two tables: one, constructed with perplexing intricacy and exhibiting as many feet as a centipede; the other, most delicately wrought, with four long and slender legs, so apparently frail that it was almost incredible what a length of time the ancient tea-table had stood upon them. Half a dozen chairs stood about the room, straight and stiff, and so ingeniously contrived for the discomfort of the human person that they were irksome even to sight, and conveyed the ugliest possible idea of the state of society to which they could have been adapted.

One exception there was, however, in a very antique elbow-chair, with a high back, carved elaborately in oak, and a roomy depth within its arms, that made up, by its spacious comprehensiveness, for the lack of any of those artistic curves which abound in a modern chair.

As for ornamental articles of furniture, we recollect but two, if such they may be called. One was a map of the Pyncheon territory at the eastward, not engraved, but the handiwork of some skilful old draughtsman, and grotesquely illuminated with pictures of Indians and wild beasts, among which was seen a lion; the natural history of the region being as little known as its geography, which was put down most fantastically awry. The other adornment was the portrait of old Colonel Pyncheon, at two thirds length, representing the stern features of a Puritanic-looking personage, in a skull-cap, with a laced band and a grizzly beard; holding a Bible with one hand, and in the other uplifting an iron sword-hilt. The latter object, being more successfully depicted by the artist, stood out in far greater prominence than the sacred volume.

Face to face with this picture, on entering the apartment, Miss Hepzibah Pyncheon came to a pause; regarding it with a singular scowl, a strange contortion of the brow, which, by people who did not know her, would probably have been interpreted as an expression of bitter anger and ill-will. But it was no such thing. She, in fact, felt a reverence for the pictured visage, of which only a far-descended and time-stricken virgin could be susceptible; and this forbidding scowl was the innocent result of her near-sightedness, and an effort so to concentrate her powers of vision as to substitute a firm outline of the object instead of a vague one.

We must linger a moment on this unfortunate expression of poor Hepzibah's brow. Her scowl,—as the world, or such part of it as sometimes caught a transitory glimpse of her at the window, wickedly persisted in calling it,—her scowl had done Miss Hepzibah a very ill office, in establishing her character as an ill-tempered old maid; nor does it appear improbable that, by often gazing at herself in a dim looking-glass, and perpetually encountering her own frown with its ghostly sphere, she had been led to interpret the expression almost as unjustly as the world did. "How miserably cross I look!" she must often have whispered to herself; and ultimately have fancied herself so, by a sense of inevitable doom. But her heart never frowned. It was naturally tender, sensitive, and full of little tremors and palpitations; all of which weaknesses it retained, while her visage was growing so perversely stern, and even fierce. Nor had Hepzibah ever any hardihood, except what came from the very warmest nook in her affections.

All this time, however, we are loitering faintheartedly on the threshold of our story. In very truth, we have an invincible reluctance to disclose what Miss Hepzibah Pyncheon was about to do.

It has already been observed, that, in the basement story of the gable fronting on the street, an unworthy ancestor, nearly a century ago, had fitted up a shop. Ever since the old gentleman retired from trade, and fell asleep under his coffin-lid, not only the shop-door, but the inner arrangements, had been suffered to remain unchanged; while the dust of ages gathered inch-deep over the shelves and counter, and partly filled an old pair of scales, as if it were of value enough to be weighed. It treasured itself up, too, in the half-open till, where there still lingered a base sixpence, worth neither more nor less than the hereditary pride which had here been put to shame. Such had been the state and condition of the little shop in old Hepzibah's childhood, when she and her brother used to play at hide-and-seek in its forsaken precincts. So it had remained, until within a few days past.

But now, though the shop-window was still closely curtained from the public gaze, a remarkable change had taken place in its interior. The rich and heavy festoons of cobweb, which it had cost a long ancestral succession of spiders their life's labour to spin and weave, had been carefully brushed away from the ceiling. The counter, shelves, and floor had all been scoured, and the latter was overstrewn with fresh blue sand. The brown scales, too, had evidently undergone rigid discipline, in an unavailing effort to rub off the rust, which, alas! had eaten through and through their substance. Neither was the little old shop any longer empty of merchantable goods. A curious eye, privileged to take an account of stock and investigate behind the counter, would have discovered a barrel, yea, two or three barrels and half *ditto*,— one containing flour, another apples, and a third, perhaps, Indian meal.

There was likewise a square box of pine-wood, full of soap in bars; also, another of the same size, in which were tallow candles, ten to the pound. A small stock of brown sugar, some white beans and split peas, and a few other commodities of low price, and such as are constantly in demand, made up the bulkier portion of the merchandise. It might have been taken for a ghostly or phantasmagoric reflection of the old shop-keeper Pyncheon's shabbily provided shelves, save that some of the articles were of a description and outward form which could hardly have been known in his day. For instance, there was a glass pickle-jar, filled with fragments of Gibraltar rock; not, indeed, splinters of the veritable stone foundation of the famous fortress, but bits of delectable candy, neatly done up in white paper. Jim Crow, moreover, was seen executing his world-renowned dance, in gingerbread.

A party of leaden dragoons were galloping along one of the shelves, in equipments and uniform of modern cut; and there were some sugar figures, with no strong resemblance to the humanity of any epoch, but less unsatisfactorily representing our own fashions than those of a hundred years ago. Another phenomenon, still more strikingly modern, was a package of Lucifer matches, which, in old times, would have been thought actually to borrow their instantaneous flame from the nether fires of Tophet.

In short, to bring the matter at once to a point, it was incontrovertibly evident that somebody had taken the shop and fixtures of the long-retired and forgotten Mr. Pyncheon, and was about to renew the enterprise of that departed worthy, with a different set of customers. Who could this bold adventurer be? And, of all places in the world, why had he chosen the House of the Seven Gables as the scene of his commercial speculations?

We return to the elderly maiden. She at length withdrew her eyes from the dark countenance of the colonel's portrait, heaved a sigh,—indeed, her breast was a very cave of Aolus that morning,—and stept across the room on tiptoe, as is the customary gait of elderly women. Passing through an intervening passage, she opened a door that communicated with the shop, just now so elaborately described. Owing to the projection of the upper story—and still more to the thick shadow of the Pyncheon Elm, which stood almost directly in front of the gable—the twilight, here, was still as much akin to night as morning. Another heavy sigh from Miss Hepzibah! After a moment's pause on the threshold, peering towards the window with her near-sighted scowl, as if frowning down some bitter enemy, she suddenly projected herself into the shop. The haste, and, as it were, the galvanic impulse of the movement, were really quite startling.

Nervously—in a sort of frenzy, we might almost say—she began to busy herself in arranging some children's playthings, and other little wares, on the shelves and at the shop-window. In the aspect of this dark-arrayed, pale-faced, ladylike old figure there was a deeply tragic character that contrasted irreconcilably with the ludicrous pettiness of her employment. It seemed a queer anomaly, that so gaunt and dismal a personage should take a toy in hand; a miracle, that the toy did not vanish in her grasp; a miserably absurd idea, that she should go on perplexing her stiff and sombre intellect with the question how to tempt little boys into her premises! Yet such is undoubtedly her object. Now she places a gingerbread elephant against the window, but with so tremulous a touch that it tumbles upon the floor, with the dismemberment of three legs and its trunk; it has ceased to be an elephant, and has become a few bits of musty gingerbread.

There, again, she has upset a tumbler of marbles, all of which roll different ways, and each individual marble, devil-directed, into the most difficult obscurity that it can find. Heaven help our poor old Hepzibah, and forgive us for taking a ludicrous view of her position! As her rigid and rusty frame goes down upon its hands and knees, in quest of the absconding marbles, we positively feel so much the more inclined to shed tears of sympathy, from the very fact that we must needs turn aside and laugh at her. For here,—and if we fail to impress it suitably upon the reader, it is our own fault, not that of the theme, here is one of the truest points of melancholy interest that occur in ordinary life.

It was the final throe of what called itself old gentility. A lady—who had fed herself from childhood with the shadowy food of aristocratic reminiscences, and whose religion it was that a lady's hand soils itself irremediably by doing aught for bread,—this born lady, after sixty years of narrowing means, is fain to step down from her pedestal of imaginary rank. Poverty, treading closely at her heels for a lifetime, has come up with her at last. She must earn her own food, or starve! And we have stolen upon Miss Hepzibah Pyncheon, too irreverently, at the instant of time when the patrician lady is to be transformed into the plebeian woman.

In this republican country, amid the fluctuating waves of our social life, somebody is always at the drowning-point. The tragedy is enacted with as continual a repetition as that of a popular drama on a holiday, and, nevertheless, is felt as deeply, perhaps, as when an hereditary noble sinks below his order. More deeply; since, with us, rank is the grosser substance of wealth and a splendid establishment, and has no spiritual existence after the death of these, but dies hopelessly along with them. And, therefore, since we have been unfortunate enough to introduce our heroine at so inauspicious a juncture, we would entreat for a mood of due solemnity in the spectators of her fate.

Let us behold, in poor Hepzibah, the immemorial, lady— two hundred years old, on this side of the water, and thrice as many on the other,—with her antique portraits, pedigrees, coats of arms, records and traditions, and her claim, as joint heiress, to that princely territory at the eastward, no longer a wilderness, but a populous fertility,—born, too, in Pyncheon Street, under the Pyncheon Elm, and in the Pyncheon House, where she has spent all her days,—reduced. Now, in that very house, to be the hucksteress of a cent-shop.

This business of setting up a petty shop is almost the only resource of women, in circumstances at all similar to those of our unfortunate recluse. With her near-sightedness, and those tremulous fingers of hers, at once inflexible and delicate, she could not be a seamstress; although her sampler, of fifty years gone by, exhibited some of the most recondite specimens of ornamental needlework. A school for little children had been often in her thoughts; and, at one time, she had begun a review of her early studies in the New England Primer, with a view to prepare herself for the office of instructress.

But the love of children had never been quickened in Hepzibah's heart, and was now torpid, if not extinct; she watched the little people of the neighbourhood from her chamber-window, and doubted whether she could tolerate a more intimate acquaintance with them. Besides, in our day, the very ABC has become a science greatly too abstruse to be any longer taught by pointing a pin from letter to letter. A modern child could teach old Hepzibah more than old Hepzibah could teach the child. So—with many a cold, deep heart-quake at the idea of at last coming into sordid contact with the world, from which she had so long kept aloof, while every added day of seclusion had rolled another stone against the cavern door of her hermitage— the poor thing bethought herself of the ancient shop-window, the rusty scales, and dusty till.

She might have held back a little longer; but another circumstance, not yet hinted at, had somewhat hastened her decision. Her humble preparations, therefore, were duly made, and the enterprise was now to be commenced. Nor was she entitled to complain of any remarkable singularity in her fate; for, in the town of her nativity, we might point to several little shops of a similar description, some of them in houses as ancient as that of the Seven Gables; and one or two, it may be, where a decayed gentlewoman stands behind the counter, as grim an image of family pride as Miss Hepzibah Pyncheon herself.

It was overpoweringly ridiculous,—we must honestly confess it,—the deportment of the maiden lady while setting her shop in order for the public eye. She stole on tiptoe to the window, as cautiously as if she conceived some bloody-minded villain to be watching behind the elm-tree, with intent to take her life. Stretching out her long, lank arm, she put a paper of pearl-buttons, a jew's-harp, or whatever the small article might be, in its destined place, and straightway vanished back into the dusk, as if the world need never hope for another glimpse of her.

It might have been fancied, indeed, that she expected to minister to the wants of the community unseen, like a disembodied divinity or enchantress, holding forth her bargains to the reverential and awe-stricken purchaser in an invisible hand. But Hepzibah had no such flattering dream. She was well aware that she must ultimately come forward, and stand revealed in her proper individuality; but, like other sensitive persons, she could not bear to be observed in the gradual process, and chose rather to flash forth on the world's astonished gaze at once.

The inevitable moment was not much longer to be delayed. The sunshine might now be seen stealing down the front of the opposite house, from the windows of which came a reflected gleam, struggling through the boughs of the elm-tree, and enlightening the interior of the shop more distinctly than heretofore. The town appeared to be waking up. A baker's cart had already rattled through the street, chasing away the latest vestige of night's sanctity with the jingle-jangle of its dissonant bells. A milkman was distributing the contents of his cans from door to door; and the harsh peal of a fisherman's conch shell was heard far off, around the corner. None of these tokens escaped Hepzibah's notice. The moment had arrived. To delay longer would be only to lengthen out her misery. Nothing remained, except to take down the bar from the shop-door, leaving the entrance free—more than free—welcome, as if all were household friends—to every passer-by, whose eyes might be attracted by the commodities at the window.

This last act Hepzibah now performed, letting the bar fall with what smote upon her excited nerves as a most astounding clatter. Then—as if the only barrier betwixt herself and the world had been thrown down, and a flood of evil consequences would come tumbling through the gap—she fled into the inner parlour, threw herself into the ancestral elbow-chair, and wept.

Our miserable old Hepzibah! It is a heavy annoyance to a writer, who endeavours to represent nature, its various attitudes and circumstances, in a reasonably correct outline and true colouring, that so much of the mean and ludicrous should be hopelessly mixed up with the purest pathos which life anywhere supplies to him. What tragic dignity, for example, can be wrought into a scene like this! How can we elevate our history of retribution for the sin of long ago, when, as one of our most prominent figures, we are compelled to introduce—not a young and lovely woman, nor even the stately remains of beauty, storm-shattered by affliction—but a gaunt, sallow, rusty-jointed maiden, in a long-waisted silk gown, and with the strange horror of a turban on her head!

Her visage is not even ugly. It is redeemed from insignificance only by the contraction of her eyebrows into a near-sighted scowl. And, finally, her great life-trial seems to be, that, after sixty years of idleness, she finds it convenient to earn comfortable bread by setting up a shop in a small way. Nevertheless, if we look through all the heroic fortunes of mankind, we shall find this same entanglement of something mean and trivial with whatever is noblest in joy or sorrow. Life is made up of marble and mud.

And, without all the deeper trust in a comprehensive sympathy above us, we might hence be led to suspect the insult of a sneer, as well as an immitigable frown, on the iron countenance of fate. What is called poetic insight is the gift of discerning, in this sphere of strangely mingled elements, the beauty and the majesty which are compelled to assume a garb so sordid.

3: The First Customer

Miss Hepzibah Pyncheon sat in the oaken elbow-chair, with her hands over her face, giving way to that heavy down-sinking of the heart which most persons have experienced, when the image of hope itself seems ponderously moulded of lead, on the eve of an enterprise at once doubtful and momentous. She was suddenly startled by the tinkling alarum—high, sharp, and irregular—of a little bell. The maiden lady arose upon her feet, as pale as a ghost at cock-crow; for she was an enslaved spirit, and this the talisman to which she owed obedience.

This little bell,—to speak in plainer terms,—being fastened over the shop-door, was so contrived as to vibrate by means of a steel spring, and thus convey notice to the inner regions of the house when any customer should cross the threshold. Its ugly and spiteful little din (heard now for the first time, perhaps, since Hepzibah's periwigged predecessor had retired from trade) at once set every nerve of her body in responsive and tumultuous vibration. The crisis was upon her! Her first customer was at the door!

Without giving herself time for a second thought, she rushed into the shop, pale, wild, desperate in gesture and expression, scowling portentously, and looking far better qualified to do fierce battle with a housebreaker than to stand smiling behind the counter, bartering small wares for a copper recompense. Any ordinary customer, indeed, would have turned his back and fled. And yet there was nothing fierce in Hepzibah's poor old heart; nor had she, at the moment, a single bitter thought against the world at large, or one individual man or woman. She wished them all well, but wished, too, that she herself were done with them, and in her quiet grave.

The applicant, by this time, stood within the doorway. Coming freshly, as he did, out of the morning light, he appeared to have brought some of its cheery influences into the shop along with him. It was a slender young man, not more than one or two and twenty years old, with rather a grave and thoughtful expression for his years, but likewise a springy alacrity and vigor. These qualities were not only perceptible, physically, in his make and motions, but made themselves felt almost immediately in his character. A brown beard, not too silken in its texture, fringed his chin, but as yet without completely hiding it; he wore a short moustache, too, and his dark, high-featured countenance looked all the better for these natural ornaments.

As for his dress, it was of the simplest kind; a summer sack of cheap and ordinary material, thin chequered pantaloons, and a straw hat, by no means of the finest braid. Oak Hall might have supplied his entire equipment. He was chiefly marked as a gentleman—if such, indeed, he made any claim to be—by the rather remarkable whiteness and nicety of his clean linen.

He met the scowl of old Hepzibah without apparent alarm, as having heretofore encountered it and found it harmless.

"So, my dear Miss Pyncheon," said the daguerreotypist,—for it was that sole other occupant of the seven-gabled mansion,— "I am glad to see that you have not shrunk from your good purpose. I merely look in to offer my best wishes, and to ask if I can assist you any further in your preparations."

People in difficulty and distress, or in any manner at odds with the world, can endure a vast amount of harsh treatment, and perhaps be only the stronger for it; whereas they give way at once before the simplest expression of what they perceive to be genuine sympathy. So it proved with poor Hepzibah; for, when she saw the young man's smile,—looking so much the brighter on a thoughtful face,—and heard his kindly tone, she broke first into a hysteric giggle and then began to sob.

"Ah, Mr. Holgrave," cried she, as soon as she could speak,

"I never can go through with it! Never, never, never! I wish I were dead, and in the old family tomb, with all my forefathers! With my father, and my mother, and my sister! Yes, and with my brother, who had far better find me there than here! The world is too chill and hard,—and I am too old, and too feeble, and too hopeless!"

"Oh, believe me, Miss Hepzibah," said the young man quietly, "these feelings will not trouble you any longer, after you are once fairly in the midst of your enterprise. They are unavoidable at this moment, standing, as you do, on the outer verge of your long seclusion, and peopling the world with ugly shapes, which you will soon find to be as unreal as the giants and ogres of a child's story-book. I find nothing so singular in life, as that everything appears to lose its substance the instant one actually grapples with it. So it will be with what you think so terrible."

"But I am a woman!" said Hepzibah piteously. "I was going to say, a lady,—but I consider that as past."

"Well; no matter if it be past!" answered the artist, a strange gleam of half-hidden sarcasm flashing through the kindliness of his manner. "Let it go! You are the better without it. I speak frankly, my dear Miss Pyncheon!—for are we not friends? I look upon this as one of the fortunate days of your life. It ends an epoch and begins one. Hitherto, the life-blood has been gradually chilling in your veins as you sat aloof, within your circle of gentility, while the rest of the world was fighting out its battle with one kind of necessity or another. Henceforth, you will at least have the sense of healthy and natural effort for a purpose, and of lending your strength be it great or small—to the united struggle of mankind. This is success,—all the success that anybody meets with!"

"It is natural enough, Mr. Holgrave, that you should have ideas like these," rejoined Hepzibah, drawing up her gaunt figure with slightly offended dignity. "You are a man, a young man, and brought up, I suppose, as almost everybody is nowadays, with a view to seeking your fortune. But I was born a lady, and have always lived one; no matter in what narrowness of means, always a lady."

"But I was not born a gentleman; neither have I lived like one," said Holgrave, slightly smiling; "so, my dear madam, you will hardly expect me to sympathize with sensibilities of this kind; though, unless I deceive myself, I have some imperfect comprehension of them. These names of gentleman and lady had a meaning, in the past history of the world, and conferred privileges, desirable or otherwise, on those entitled to bear them. In the present—and still more in the future condition of society-they imply, not privilege, but restriction!"

"These are new notions," said the old gentlewoman, shaking her head. "I shall never understand them; neither do I wish it."

"We will cease to speak of them, then," replied the artist, with a friendlier smile than his last one, "and I will leave you to feel whether it is not better to be a true woman than a lady. Do you really think, Miss Hepzibah, that any lady of your family has ever done a more heroic thing, since this house was built, than you are performing in it today? Never; and if the Pyncheons had always acted so nobly, I doubt whether an old wizard Maule's anathema, of which you told me once, would have had much weight with Providence against them."

"Ah!—no, no!" said Hepzibah, not displeased at this allusion to the sombre dignity of an inherited curse. "If old Maule's ghost, or a descendant of his, could see me behind the counter to-day, he would call it the fulfilment of his worst wishes. But I thank you for your kindness, Mr. Holgrave, and will do my utmost to be a good shop-keeper."

"Pray do" said Holgrave, "and let me have the pleasure of being your first customer. I am about taking a walk to the seashore, before going to my rooms, where I misuse Heaven's blessed sunshine by tracing out human features through its agency. A few of those biscuits, dipt in sea-water, will be just what I need for breakfast. What is the price of half a dozen?"

"Let me be a lady a moment longer," replied Hepzibah, with a manner of antique stateliness to which a melancholy smile lent a kind of grace. She put the biscuits into his hand, but rejected the compensation. "A Pyncheon must not, at all events under her forefathers' roof, receive money for a morsel of bread from her only friend!"

Holgrave took his departure, leaving her, for the moment, with spirits not quite so much depressed. Soon, however, they had subsided nearly to their former dead level. With a beating heart, she listened to the footsteps of early passengers, which now began to be frequent along the street. Once or twice they seemed to linger; these strangers, or neighbours, as the case might be, were looking at the display of toys and petty commodities in Hepzibah's shop-window. She was doubly tortured; in part, with a sense of overwhelming shame that strange and unloving eyes should have the privilege of gazing, and partly because the idea occurred to her, with ridiculous importunity, that the window was not arranged so skilfully, nor nearly to so much advantage, as it might have been.

It seemed as if the whole fortune or failure of her shop might depend on the display of a different set of articles, or substituting a fairer apple for one which appeared to be specked. So she made the change, and straightway fancied that everything was spoiled by it; not recognizing that it was the nervousness of the juncture, and her own native squeamishness as an old maid, that wrought all the seeming mischief.

Anon, there was an encounter, just at the doorstep, betwixt two labouring men, as their rough voices denoted them to be. After some slight talk about their own affairs, one of them chanced to notice the shop-window, and directed the other's attention to it.

"See here!" cried he; "what do you think of this? Trade seems to be looking up in Pyncheon Street!"

"Well, well, this is a sight, to be sure!" exclaimed the other. "In the old Pyncheon House, and underneath the Pyncheon Elm! Who would have thought it? Old Maid Pyncheon is setting up a cent-shop!"

"Will she make it go, think you, Dixey?" said his friend. "I don't call it a very good stand. There's another shop just round the corner."

"Make it go!" cried Dixey, with a most contemptuous expression, as if the very idea were impossible to be conceived. "Not a bit of it! Why, her face—I've seen it, for I dug her garden for her one year—her face is enough to frighten the Old Nick himself, if he had ever so great a mind to trade with her. People can't stand it, I tell you! She scowls dreadfully, reason or none, out of pure ugliness of temper."

"Well, that's not so much matter," remarked the other man. "These sour-tempered folks are mostly handy at business, and know pretty well what they are about. But, as you say, I don't think she'll do much. This business of keeping cent-shops is overdone, like all other kinds of trade, handicraft, and bodily labour. I know it, to my cost! My wife kept a cent-shop three months, and lost five dollars on her outlay."

"Poor business!" responded Dixey, in a tone as if he were shaking his head,— "poor business."

For some reason or other, not very easy to analyze, there had hardly been so bitter a pang in all her previous misery about the matter as what thrilled Hepzibah's heart on overhearing the above conversation. The testimony in regard to her scowl was frightfully important; it seemed to hold up her image wholly relieved from the false light of her self-partialities, and so hideous that she dared not look at it. She was absurdly hurt, moreover, by the slight and idle effect that her setting up shop—an event of such breathless interest to herself—appeared to have upon the public, of which these two men were the nearest representatives. A glance; a passing word or two; a coarse laugh; and she was doubtless forgotten before they turned the corner. They cared nothing for her dignity, and just as little for her degradation.

Then, also, the augury of ill-success, uttered from the sure wisdom of experience, fell upon her half-dead hope like a clod into a grave. The man's wife had already tried the same experiment, and failed! How could the born lady—the recluse of half a lifetime, utterly unpractised in the world, at sixty years of age,—how could she ever dream of succeeding, when the hard, vulgar, keen, busy, hackneyed New England woman had lost five dollars on her little outlay! Success presented itself as an impossibility, and the hope of it as a wild hallucination.

Some malevolent spirit, doing his utmost to drive Hepzibah mad, unrolled before her imagination a kind of panorama, representing the great thoroughfare of a city all astir with customers. So many and so magnificent shops as there were! Groceries, toy-shops, drygoods stores, with their immense panes of plate-glass, their gorgeous fixtures, their vast and complete assortments of merchandise, in which fortunes had been invested; and those noble mirrors at the farther end of each establishment, doubling all this wealth by a brightly burnished vista of unrealities! On one side of the street this splendid bazaar, with a multitude of perfumed and glossy salesmen, smirking, smiling, bowing, and measuring out the goods.

On the other, the dusky old House of the Seven Gables, with the antiquated shop-window under its projecting story, and Hepzibah herself, in a gown of rusty black silk, behind the counter, scowling at the world as it went by! This mighty contrast thrust itself forward as a fair expression of the odds against which she was to begin her struggle for a subsistence. Success? Preposterous! She would never think of it again! The house might just as well be buried in an eternal fog while all other houses had the sunshine on them; for not a foot would ever cross the threshold, nor a hand so much as try the door!

But, at this instant, the shop-bell, right over her head, tinkled as if it were bewitched. The old gentlewoman's heart seemed to be attached to the same steel spring, for it went through a series of sharp jerks, in unison with the sound. The door was thrust open, although no human form was perceptible on the other side of the half-window. Hepzibah, nevertheless, stood at a gaze, with her hands clasped, looking very much as if she had summoned up an evil spirit, and were afraid, yet resolved, to hazard the encounter.

"Heaven help me!" she groaned mentally. "Now is my hour of need!"

The door, which moved with difficulty on its creaking and rusty hinges, being forced quite open, a square and sturdy little urchin became apparent, with cheeks as red as an apple. He was clad rather shabbily (but, as it seemed, more owing to his mother's carelessness than his father's poverty), in a blue apron, very wide and short trousers, shoes somewhat out at the toes, and a chip hat, with the frizzles of his curly hair sticking through its crevices. A book and a small slate, under his arm, indicated that he was on his way to school. He stared at Hepzibah a moment, as an elder customer than himself would have been likely enough to do, not knowing what to make of the tragic attitude and queer scowl wherewith she regarded him.

"Well, child," said she, taking heart at sight of a personage so little formidable,—"well, my child, what did you wish for?"

"That Jim Crow there in the window," answered the urchin, holding out a cent, and pointing to the gingerbread figure that had attracted his notice, as he loitered along to school; "the one that has not a broken foot."

So Hepzibah put forth her lank arm, and, taking the effigy from the shop-window, delivered it to her first customer.

"No matter for the money," said she, giving him a little push towards the door; for her old gentility was contumaciously squeamish at sight of the copper coin, and, besides, it seemed such pitiful meanness to take the child's pocket-money in exchange for a bit of stale gingerbread. "No matter for the cent. You are welcome to Jim Crow."

The child, staring with round eyes at this instance of liberality, wholly unprecedented in his large experience of cent-shops, took the man of gingerbread, and quitted the premises. No sooner had he reached the sidewalk (little cannibal that he was!) than Jim Crow's head was in his mouth. As he had not been careful to shut the door, Hepzibah was at the pains of closing it after him, with a pettish ejaculation or two about the troublesomeness of young people, and particularly of small boys. She had just placed another representative of the renowned Jim Crow at the window, when again the shop-bell tinkled clam-

orously, and again the door being thrust open, with its characteristic jerk and jar, disclosed the same sturdy little urchin who,
precisely two minutes ago, had made his exit. The crumbs and
discoloration of the cannibal feast, as yet hardly consummated,
were exceedingly visible about his mouth.

"What is it now, child?" asked the maiden lady rather impatiently; "did you come back to shut the door?"

"No," answered the urchin, pointing to the figure that had
just been put up; "I want that other Jim Crow."

"Well, here it is for you," said Hepzibah, reaching it down;
but recognizing that this pertinacious customer would not quit
her on any other terms, so long as she had a gingerbread figure
in her shop, she partly drew back her extended hand, "Where is
the cent?"

The little boy had the cent ready, but, like a true-born Yankee,
would have preferred the better bargain to the worse. Looking
somewhat chagrined, he put the coin into Hepzibah's hand, and
departed, sending the second Jim Crow in quest of the former
one. The new shop-keeper dropped the first solid result of her
commercial enterprise into the till. It was done! The sordid stain
of that copper coin could never be washed away from her palm.
The little schoolboy, aided by the impish figure of the negro
dancer, had wrought an irreparable ruin. The structure of ancient aristocracy had been demolished by him, even as if his
childish gripe had torn down the seven-gabled mansion.

Now let Hepzibah turn the old Pyncheon portraits with
their faces to the wall, and take the map of her Eastern territory
to kindle the kitchen fire, and blow up the flame with the empty
breath of her ancestral traditions! What had she to do with ancestry? Nothing; no more than with posterity! No lady, now, but
simply Hepzibah Pyncheon, a forlorn old maid, and keeper of
a cent-shop!

Nevertheless, even while she paraded these ideas somewhat
ostentatiously through her mind, it is altogether surprising
what a calmness had come over her. The anxiety and misgivings which had tormented her, whether asleep or in melancholy

day-dreams, ever since her project began to take an aspect of solidity, had now vanished quite away. She felt the novelty of her position, indeed, but no longer with disturbance or affright. Now and then, there came a thrill of almost youthful enjoyment. It was the invigorating breath of a fresh outward atmosphere, after the long torpor and monotonous seclusion of her life. So wholesome is effort! So miraculous the strength that we do not know of!

The healthiest glow that Hepzibah had known for years had come now in the dreaded crisis, when, for the first time, she had put forth her hand to help herself. The little circlet of the schoolboy's copper coin—dim and lustreless though it was, with the small services which it had been doing here and there about the world—had proved a talisman, fragrant with good, and deserving to be set in gold and worn next her heart. It was as potent, and perhaps endowed with the same kind of efficacy, as a galvanic ring! Hepzibah, at all events, was indebted to its subtile operation both in body and spirit; so much the more, as it inspired her with energy to get some breakfast, at which, still the better to keep up her courage, she allowed herself an extra spoonful in her infusion of black tea.

Her introductory day of shop-keeping did not run on, however, without many and serious interruptions of this mood of cheerful vigour. As a general rule, Providence seldom vouchsafes to mortals any more than just that degree of encouragement which suffices to keep them at a reasonably full exertion of their powers. In the case of our old gentlewoman, after the excitement of new effort had subsided, the despondency of her whole life threatened, ever and anon, to return. It was like the heavy mass of clouds which we may often see obscuring the sky, and making a gray twilight everywhere, until, towards nightfall, it yields temporarily to a glimpse of sunshine. But, always, the envious cloud strives to gather again across the streak of celestial azure.

Customers came in, as the forenoon advanced, but rather slowly; in some cases, too, it must be owned, with little satisfaction either to themselves or Miss Hepzibah; nor, on the whole, with an aggregate of very rich emolument to the till. A little girl, sent by her mother to match a skein of cotton thread, of a peculiar hue, took one that the near-sighted old lady pronounced extremely like, but soon came running back, with a blunt and cross message, that it would not do, and, besides, was very rotten! Then, there was a pale, care-wrinkled woman, not old but haggard, and already with streaks of gray among her hair, like silver ribbons; one of those women, naturally delicate, whom you at once recognize as worn to death by a brute—probably a drunken brute—of a husband, and at least nine children.

She wanted a few pounds of flour, and offered the money, which the decayed gentlewoman silently rejected, and gave the poor soul better measure than if she had taken it. Shortly afterwards, a man in a blue cotton frock, much soiled, came in and bought a pipe, filling the whole shop, meanwhile, with the hot odour of strong drink, not only exhaled in the torrid atmosphere of his breath, but oozing out of his entire system, like an inflammable gas. It was impressed on Hepzibah's mind that this was the husband of the care-wrinkled woman. He asked for a paper of tobacco; and as she had neglected to provide herself with the article, her brutal customer dashed down his newly-bought pipe and left the shop, muttering some unintelligible words, which had the tone and bitterness of a curse. Hereupon Hepzibah threw up her eyes, unintentionally scowling in the face of Providence!

No less than five persons, during the forenoon, inquired for ginger-beer, or root-beer, or any drink of a similar brewage, and, obtaining nothing of the kind, went off in an exceedingly bad humour. Three of them left the door open, and the other two pulled it so spitefully in going out that the little bell played the very deuce with Hepzibah's nerves. A round, bustling, fire-ruddy housewife of the neighbourhood burst breathless into the shop, fiercely demanding yeast; and when the poor gentlewoman, with her cold shyness of manner, gave her hot customer to understand that she did not keep the article, this very capable housewife took upon herself to administer a regular rebuke.

"A cent-shop, and no yeast!" quoth she; "That will never do! Who ever heard of such a thing? Your loaf will never rise, no more than mine will today. You had better shut up shop at once."

"Well," said Hepzibah, heaving a deep sigh, "perhaps I had!"

Several times, moreover, besides the above instance, her lady-like sensibilities were seriously infringed upon by the familiar, if not rude, tone with which people addressed her. They evidently considered themselves not merely her equals, but her patrons and superiors. Now, Hepzibah had unconsciously flattered herself with the idea that there would be a gleam or halo, of some kind or other, about her person, which would insure an obeisance to her sterling gentility, or, at least, a tacit recognition of it.

On the other hand, nothing tortured her more intolerably than when this recognition was too prominently expressed. To one or two rather officious offers of sympathy, her responses were little short of acrimonious; and, we regret to say, Hepzibah was thrown into a positively unchristian state of mind by the suspicion that one of her customers was drawn to the shop, not by any real need of the article which she pretended to seek, but by a wicked wish to stare at her. The vulgar creature was determined to see for herself what sort of a figure a mildewed piece of aristocracy, after wasting all the bloom and much of the decline of her life apart from the world, would cut behind a counter. In this particular case, however mechanical and innocuous it might be at other times, Hepzibah's contortion of brow served her in good stead.

"I never was so frightened in my life!" said the curious customer, in describing the incident to one of her acquaintances. "She's a real old vixen, take my word of it! She says little, to be sure; but if you could only see the mischief in her eye!"

On the whole, therefore, her new experience led our decayed gentlewoman to very disagreeable conclusions as to the temper and manners of what she termed the lower classes, whom heretofore she had looked down upon with a gentle and pitying complaisance, as herself occupying a sphere of unquestionable superiority. But, unfortunately, she had likewise to struggle against a bitter emotion of a directly opposite kind: a sentiment of virulence, we mean, towards the idle aristocracy to which it had so recently been her pride to belong.

When a lady, in a delicate and costly summer garb, with a floating veil and gracefully swaying gown, and, altogether, an ethereal lightness that made you look at her beautifully slippered feet, to see whether she trod on the dust or floated in the air,—when such a vision happened to pass through this retired street, leaving it tenderly and delusively fragrant with her passage, as if a bouquet of tea-roses had been borne along,—then again, it is to be feared, old Hepzibah's scowl could no longer vindicate itself entirely on the plea of near-sightedness.

"For what end," thought she, giving vent to that feeling of hostility which is the only real abasement of the poor in presence of the rich,—"for what good end, in the wisdom of Providence, does that woman live? Must the whole world toil, that the palms of her hands may be kept white and delicate?"

Then, ashamed and penitent, she hid her face.

"May God forgive me!" said she.

Doubtless, God did forgive her. But, taking the inward and outward history of the first half-day into consideration, Hepzibah began to fear that the shop would prove her ruin in a moral and religious point of view, without contributing very essentially towards even her temporal welfare.

4: A Day Behind the Counter

Towards noon, Hepzibah saw an elderly gentleman, large and portly, and of remarkably dignified demeanour, passing slowly along on the opposite side of the white and dusty street. On coming within the shadow of the Pyncheon Elm, he stopt, and (taking off his hat, meanwhile, to wipe the perspiration from his brow) seemed to scrutinize, with especial interest, the dilapidated and rusty-visaged House of the Seven Gables. He himself, in a very different style, was as well worth looking at as the house.

53

No better model need be sought, nor could have been found, of a very high order of respectability, which, by some indescribable magic, not merely expressed itself in his looks and gestures, but even governed the fashion of his garments, and rendered them all proper and essential to the man.

Without appearing to differ, in any tangible way, from other people's clothes, there was yet a wide and rich gravity about them that must have been a characteristic of the wearer, since it could not be defined as pertaining either to the cut or material. His gold-headed cane, too,—a serviceable staff, of dark polished wood,—had similar traits, and, had it chosen to take a walk by itself, would have been recognized anywhere as a tolerably adequate representative of its master. This character—which showed itself so strikingly in everything about him, and the effect of which we seek to convey to the reader—went no deeper than his station, habits of life, and external circumstances.

One perceived him to be a personage of marked influence and authority; and, especially, you could feel just as certain that he was opulent as if he had exhibited his bank account, or as if you had seen him touching the twigs of the Pyncheon Elm, and, Midas-like, transmuting them to gold.

In his youth, he had probably been considered a handsome man; at his present age, his brow was too heavy, his temples too bare, his remaining hair too gray, his eye too cold, his lips too closely compressed, to bear any relation to mere personal beauty. He would have made a good and massive portrait; better now, perhaps, than at any previous period of his life, although his look might grow positively harsh in the process of being fixed upon the canvas. The artist would have found it desirable to study his face, and prove its capacity for varied expression; to darken it with a frown,—to kindle it up with a smile.

While the elderly gentleman stood looking at the Pyncheon House, both the frown and the smile passed successively over his countenance. His eye rested on the shop-window, and putting up a pair of gold-bowed spectacles, which he held in his hand, he minutely surveyed Hepzibah's little arrangement of toys and commodities. At first it seemed not to please him,—nay, to cause him exceeding displeasure,—and yet, the very next moment, he smiled. While the latter expression was yet on his lips, he caught a glimpse of Hepzibah, who had involuntarily bent forward to the window; and then the smile changed from acrid and disagreeable to the sunniest complacency and benevolence. He bowed, with a happy mixture of dignity and courteous kindliness, and pursued his way.

"There he is!" said Hepzibah to herself, gulping down a very bitter emotion, and, since she could not rid herself of it, trying to drive it back into her heart. "What does he think of it, I wonder? Does it please him? Ah! he is looking back!"

The gentleman had paused in the street, and turned himself half about, still with his eyes fixed on the shop-window. In fact, he wheeled wholly round, and commenced a step or two, as if designing to enter the shop; but, as it chanced, his purpose was anticipated by Hepzibah's first customer, the little cannibal of Jim Crow, who, staring up at the window, was irresistibly attracted by an elephant of gingerbread. What a grand appetite had this small urchin!—Two Jim Crows immediately after breakfast!—and now an elephant, as a preliminary whet before dinner. By the time this latter purchase was completed, the elderly gentleman had resumed his way, and turned the street corner.

"Take it as you like, Cousin Jaffrey," muttered the maiden lady, as she drew back, after cautiously thrusting out her head, and looking up and down the street,—"Take it as you like! You have seen my little shop-window. Well!—what have you to say?—is not the Pyncheon House my own, while I'm alive?"

After this incident, Hepzibah retreated to the back parlour, where she at first caught up a half-finished stocking, and began knitting at it with nervous and irregular jerks; but quickly finding herself at odds with the stitches, she threw it aside, and walked hurriedly about the room. At length she paused before the portrait of the stern old Puritan, her ancestor, and the founder of the house. In one sense, this picture had almost faded into the canvas, and hidden itself behind the duskiness of age;

in another, she could not but fancy that it had been growing more prominent and strikingly expressive, ever since her earliest familiarity with it as a child.

For, while the physical outline and substance were darkening away from the beholder's eye, the bold, hard, and, at the same time, indirect character of the man seemed to be brought out in a kind of spiritual relief. Such an effect may occasionally be observed in pictures of antique date. They acquire a look which an artist (if he have anything like the complacency of artists nowadays) would never dream of presenting to a patron as his own characteristic expression, but which, nevertheless, we at once recognize as reflecting the unlovely truth of a human soul. In such cases, the painter's deep conception of his subject's inward traits has wrought itself into the essence of the picture, and is seen after the superficial coloring has been rubbed off by time.

While gazing at the portrait, Hepzibah trembled under its eye. Her hereditary reverence made her afraid to judge the character of the original so harshly as a perception of the truth compelled her to do. But still she gazed, because the face of the picture enabled her—at least, she fancied so—to read more accurately, and to a greater depth, the face which she had just seen in the street.

"This is the very man!" murmured she to herself. "Let Jaffrey Pyncheon smile as he will, there is that look beneath! Put on him a skull-cap, and a band, and a black cloak, and a Bible in one hand and a sword in the other,—then let Jaffrey smile as he might,—nobody would doubt that it was the old Pyncheon come again. He has proved himself the very man to build up a new house! Perhaps, too, to draw down a new curse!"

Thus did Hepzibah bewilder herself with these fantasies of the old time. She had dwelt too much alone,—too long in the Pyncheon House,—until her very brain was impregnated with the dry-rot of its timbers. She needed a walk along the noonday street to keep her sane.

By the spell of contrast, another portrait rose up before her, painted with more daring flattery than any artist would have ventured upon, but yet so delicately touched that the likeness remained perfect. Malbone's miniature, though from the same original, was far inferior to Hepzibah's air-drawn picture, at which affection and sorrowful remembrance wrought together. Soft, mildly, and cheerfully contemplative, with full, red lips, just on the verge of a smile, which the eyes seemed to herald by a gentle kindling-up of their orbs! Feminine traits, moulded inseparably with those of the other sex! The miniature, likewise, had this last peculiarity; so that you inevitably thought of the original as resembling his mother, and she a lovely and lovable woman, with perhaps some beautiful infirmity of character, that made it all the pleasanter to know and easier to love her.

"Yes," thought Hepzibah, with grief of which it was only the more tolerable portion that welled up from her heart to her eyelids, "they persecuted his mother in him! He never was a Pyncheon!"

But here the shop-bell rang; it was like a sound from a remote distance,—so far had Hepzibah descended into the sepulchral depths of her reminiscences. On entering the shop, she found an old man there, a humble resident of Pyncheon Street, and whom, for a great many years past, she had suffered to be a kind of familiar of the house. He was an immemorial personage, who seemed always to have had a white head and wrinkles, and never to have possessed but a single tooth, and that a half-decayed one, in the front of the upper jaw. Well advanced as Hepzibah was, she could not remember when Uncle Venner, as the neighbourhood called him, had not gone up and down the street, stooping a little and drawing his feet heavily over the gravel or pavement.

But still there was something tough and vigorous about him, that not only kept him in daily breath, but enabled him to fill a place which would else have been vacant in the apparently crowded world. To go of errands with his slow and shuffling gait, which made you doubt how he ever was to arrive anywhere; to saw a small household's foot or two of firewood, or knock to pieces an old barrel, or split up a pine board for kindling-stuff;

in summer, to dig the few yards of garden ground appertaining to a low-rented tenement, and share the produce of his labour at the halves; in winter, to shovel away the snow from the sidewalk, or open paths to the woodshed, or along the clothes-line; such were some of the essential offices which Uncle Venner performed among at least a score of families.

Within that circle, he claimed the same sort of privilege, and probably felt as much warmth of interest, as a clergyman does in the range of his parishioners. Not that he laid claim to the tithe pig; but, as an analogous mode of reverence, he went his rounds, every morning, to gather up the crumbs of the table and overflowings of the dinner-pot, as food for a pig of his own.

In his younger days—for, after all, there was a dim tradition that he had been, not young, but younger—Uncle Venner was commonly regarded as rather deficient, than otherwise, in his wits. In truth he had virtually pleaded guilty to the charge, by scarcely aiming at such success as other men seek, and by taking only that humble and modest part in the intercourse of life which belongs to the alleged deficiency. But now, in his extreme old age,—whether it were that his long and hard experience had actually brightened him, or that his decaying judgment rendered him less capable of fairly measuring himself,—the venerable man made pretensions to no little wisdom, and really enjoyed the credit of it.

There was likewise, at times, a vein of something like poetry in him; it was the moss or wall-flower of his mind in its small dilapidation, and gave a charm to what might have been vulgar and commonplace in his earlier and middle life. Hepzibah had a regard for him, because his name was ancient in the town and had formerly been respectable. It was a still better reason for awarding him a species of familiar reverence that Uncle Venner was himself the most ancient existence, whether of man or thing, in Pyncheon Street, except the House of the Seven Gables, and perhaps the elm that overshadowed it.

This patriarch now presented himself before Hepzibah, clad in an old blue coat, which had a fashionable air, and must have accrued to him from the cast-off wardrobe of some dashing clerk. As for his trousers, they were of tow-cloth, very short in the legs, and bagging down strangely in the rear, but yet having a suitableness to his figure which his other garment entirely lacked. His hat had relation to no other part of his dress, and but very little to the head that wore it. Thus Uncle Venner was a miscellaneous old gentleman, partly himself, but, in good measure, somebody else; patched together, too, of different epochs; an epitome of times and fashions.

"So, you have really begun trade," said he,—"really begun trade! Well, I'm glad to see it. Young people should never live idle in the world, nor old ones neither, unless when the rheumatise gets hold of them. It has given me warning already; and in two or three years longer, I shall think of putting aside business and retiring to my farm. That's yonder,—the great brick house, you know,—the workhouse, most folks call it; but I mean to do my work first, and go there to be idle and enjoy myself. And I'm glad to see you beginning to do your work, Miss Hepzibah!"

"Thank you, Uncle Venner" said Hepzibah, smiling; for she always felt kindly towards the simple and talkative old man. Had he been an old woman, she might probably have repelled the freedom, which she now took in good part. "It is time for me to begin work, indeed! Or, to speak the truth, I have just begun when I ought to be giving it up."

"Oh, never say that, Miss Hepzibah!" answered the old man. "You are a young woman yet. Why, I hardly thought myself younger than I am now, it seems so little while ago since I used to see you playing about the door of the old house, quite a small child! Oftener, though, you used to be sitting at the threshold, and looking gravely into the street; for you had always a grave kind of way with you,—a grown-up air, when you were only the height of my knee. It seems as if I saw you now; and your grandfather with his red cloak, and his white wig, and his cocked hat, and his cane, coming out of the house, and stepping so grandly up the street!

"Those old gentlemen that grew up before the Revolution

used to put on grand airs. In my young days, the great man of the town was commonly called King; and his wife, not Queen to be sure, but Lady. Nowadays, a man would not dare to be called King; and if he feels himself a little above common folks, he only stoops so much the lower to them. I met your cousin, the judge, ten minutes ago; and, in my old tow-cloth trousers, as you see, the judge raised his hat to me, I do believe! At any rate, the judge bowed and smiled!"

"Yes," said Hepzibah, with something bitter stealing unawares into her tone; "my cousin Jaffrey is thought to have a very pleasant smile!"

"And so he has" replied Uncle Venner. "And that's rather remarkable in a Pyncheon; for, begging your pardon, Miss Hepzibah, they never had the name of being an easy and agreeable set of folks. There was no getting close to them. But now, Miss Hepzibah, if an old man may be bold to ask, why don't Judge Pyncheon, with his great means, step forward, and tell his cousin to shut up her little shop at once? It's for your credit to be doing something, but it's not for the judge's credit to let you!"

"We won't talk of this, if you please, Uncle Venner," said Hepzibah coldly. "I ought to say, however, that, if I choose to earn bread for myself, it is not Judge Pyncheon's fault. Neither will he deserve the blame," added she more kindly, remembering Uncle Venner's privileges of age and humble familiarity, "if I should, by and by, find it convenient to retire with you to your farm."

"And it's no bad place, either, that farm of mine!" cried the old man cheerily, as if there were something positively delightful in the prospect. "No bad place is the great brick farm-house, especially for them that will find a good many old cronies there, as will be my case. I quite long to be among them, sometimes, of the winter evenings; for it is but dull business for a lonesome elderly man, like me, to be nodding, by the hour together, with no company but his air-tight stove. Summer or winter, there's a great deal to be said in favour of my farm!

"And, take it in the autumn, what can be pleasanter than to spend a whole day on the sunny side of a barn or a wood-pile, chatting with somebody as old as one's self; or, perhaps, idling away the time with a natural-born simpleton, who knows how to be idle, because even our busy Yankees never have found out how to put him to any use? Upon my word, Miss Hepzibah, I doubt whether I've ever been so comfortable as I mean to be at my farm, which most folks call the workhouse. But you,— you're a young woman yet,—you never need go there! Something still better will turn up for you. I'm sure of it!"

Hepzibah fancied that there was something peculiar in her venerable friend's look and tone; insomuch, that she gazed into his face with considerable earnestness, endeavouring to discover what secret meaning, if any, might be lurking there. Individuals whose affairs have reached an utterly desperate crisis almost invariably keep themselves alive with hopes, so much the more airily magnificent as they have the less of solid matter within their grasp whereof to mould any judicious and moderate expectation of good.

Thus, all the while Hepzibah was perfecting the scheme of her little shop, she had cherished an unacknowledged idea that some harlequin trick of fortune would intervene in her favour. For example, an uncle—who had sailed for India fifty years before, and never been heard of since—might yet return, and adopt her to be the comfort of his very extreme and decrepit age, and adorn her with pearls, diamonds, and Oriental shawls and turbans, and make her the ultimate heiress of his unreckonable riches. Or the member of Parliament, now at the head of the English branch of the family,—with which the elder stock, on this side of the Atlantic, had held little or no intercourse for the last two centuries,—this eminent gentleman might invite Hepzibah to quit the ruinous House of the Seven Gables, and come over to dwell with her kindred at Pyncheon Hall.

But, for reasons the most imperative, she could not yield to his request. It was more probable, therefore, that the descendants of a Pyncheon who had emigrated to Virginia, in some past generation, and became a great planter there,—hearing of Hepzibah's destitution, and impelled by the splendid generosity

of character with which their Virginian mixture must have enriched the New England blood,—would send her a remittance
of a thousand dollars, with a hint of repeating the favour annually. Or,—and, surely, anything so undeniably just could not be
beyond the limits of reasonable anticipation,—the great claim
to the heritage of Waldo County might finally be decided in
favour of the Pyncheons; so that, instead of keeping a cent-shop,
Hepzibah would build a palace, and look down from its highest
tower on hill, dale, forest, field, and town, as her own share of the
ancestral territory.

These were some of the fantasies which she had long dreamed
about; and, aided by these, Uncle Venner's casual attempt at encouragement kindled a strange festal glory in the poor, bare,
melancholy chambers of her brain, as if that inner world were
suddenly lighted up with gas. But either he knew nothing of
her castles in the air,—as how should he?—or else her earnest
scowl disturbed his recollection, as it might a more courageous
man's. Instead of pursuing any weightier topic, Uncle Venner
was pleased to favour Hepzibah with some sage counsel in her
shop-keeping capacity.

"Give no credit!"—these were some of his golden maxims,—
"Never take paper-money. Look well to your change! Ring the
silver on the four-pound weight! Shove back all English half-
pence and base copper tokens, such as are very plenty about
town! At your leisure hours, knit children's woollen socks and
mittens! Brew your own yeast, and make your own ginger-
beer!"

And while Hepzibah was doing her utmost to digest the hard
little pellets of his already uttered wisdom, he gave vent to his
final, and what he declared to be his all-important advice, as
follows:—

"Put on a bright face for your customers, and smile pleasantly
as you hand them what they ask for! A stale article, if you dip it
in a good, warm, sunny smile, will go off better than a fresh one
that you've scowled upon."

To this last apothegm poor Hepzibah responded with a sigh

so deep and heavy that it almost rustled Uncle Venner quite away, like a withered leaf,—as he was,—before an autumnal gale. Recovering himself, however, he bent forward, and, with a good deal of feeling in his ancient visage, beckoned her nearer to him.

"When do you expect him home?" whispered he.

"Whom do you mean?" asked Hepzibah, turning pale.

"Ah!—You don't love to talk about it," said Uncle Venner. "Well, well! we'll say no more, though there's word of it all over town. I remember him, Miss Hepzibah, before he could run alone!"

During the remainder of the day, poor Hepzibah acquitted herself even less creditably, as a shop-keeper, than in her earlier efforts. She appeared to be walking in a dream; or, more truly, the vivid life and reality assumed by her emotions made all outward occurrences unsubstantial, like the teasing phantasms of a half-conscious slumber. She still responded, mechanically, to the frequent summons of the shop-bell, and, at the demand of her customers, went prying with vague eyes about the shop, proffering them one article after another, and thrusting aside—perversely, as most of them supposed—the identical thing they asked for. There is sad confusion, indeed, when the spirit thus flits away into the past, or into the more awful future, or, in any manner, steps across the spaceless boundary betwixt its own region and the actual world; where the body remains to guide itself as best it may, with little more than the mechanism of animal life.

It is like death, without death's quiet privilege,—its freedom from mortal care. Worst of all, when the actual duties are comprised in such petty details as now vexed the brooding soul of the old gentlewoman. As the animosity of fate would have it, there was a great influx of custom in the course of the afternoon. Hepzibah blundered to and fro about her small place of business, committing the most unheard-of errors: now stringing up twelve, and now seven, tallow-candles, instead of ten to the pound; selling ginger for Scotch snuff, pins for needles, and needles for pins; misreckoning her change, sometimes to the public detriment, and much oftener to her own; and thus she went on, doing her utmost to bring chaos back again, until, at the close of the day's labour, to her inexplicable astonishment, she found the money-drawer almost destitute of coin. After all her painful traffic, the whole proceeds were perhaps half a dozen coppers, and a questionable ninepence which ultimately proved to be copper likewise.

At this price, or at whatever price, she rejoiced that the day had reached its end. Never before had she had such a sense of the intolerable length of time that creeps between dawn and sunset, and of the miserable irksomeness of having aught to do, and of the better wisdom that it would be to lie down at once, in sullen resignation, and let life, and its toils and vexations, trample over one's prostrate body as they may! Hepzibah's final operation was with the little devourer of Jim Crow and the elephant, who now proposed to eat a camel. In her bewilderment, she offered him first a wooden dragoon, and next a handful of marbles; neither of which being adapted to his else omnivorous appetite, she hastily held out her whole remaining stock of natural history in gingerbread, and huddled the small customer out of the shop. She then muffled the bell in an unfinished stocking, and put up the oaken bar across the door.

During the latter process, an omnibus came to a stand-still under the branches of the elm-tree. Hepzibah's heart was in her mouth. Remote and dusky, and with no sunshine on all the intervening space, was that region of the Past whence her only guest might be expected to arrive! Was she to meet him now?

Somebody, at all events, was passing from the farthest interior of the omnibus towards its entrance. A gentleman alighted; but it was only to offer his hand to a young girl whose slender figure, nowise needing such assistance, now lightly descended the steps, and made an airy little jump from the final one to the sidewalk. She rewarded her cavalier with a smile, the cheery glow of which was seen reflected on his own face as he re-entered the vehicle. The girl then turned towards the House of the Seven Gables, to the door of which, meanwhile,—not the shop-door, but the antique portal,—the omnibus-man had carried a light trunk and a bandbox. First giving a sharp rap of the old iron knocker, he left his passenger and her luggage at the door-step, and departed.

"Who can it be?" thought Hepzibah, who had been screwing her visual organs into the acutest focus of which they were capable. "The girl must have mistaken the house." She stole softly into the hall, and, herself invisible, gazed through the dusty sidelights of the portal at the young, blooming, and very cheerful face which presented itself for admittance into the gloomy old mansion. It was a face to which almost any door would have opened of its own accord.

The young girl, so fresh, so unconventional, and yet so orderly and obedient to common rules, as you at once recognized her to be, was widely in contrast, at that moment, with everything about her. The sordid and ugly luxuriance of gigantic weeds that grew in the angle of the house, and the heavy projection that overshadowed her, and the time-worn framework of the door,—none of these things belonged to her sphere. But, even as a ray of sunshine, fall into what dismal place it may, instantaneously creates for itself a propriety in being there, so did it seem altogether fit that the girl should be standing at the threshold. It was no less evidently proper that the door should swing open to admit her. The maiden lady herself, sternly inhospitable in her first purposes, soon began to feel that the door ought to be shoved back, and the rusty key be turned in the reluctant lock.

"Can it be Phoebe?" questioned she within herself. "It must be little Phoebe; for it can be nobody else,—and there is a look of her father about her, too! But what does she want here? And how like a country cousin, to come down upon a poor body in this way, without so much as a day's notice, or asking whether she would be welcome! Well; she must have a night's lodging, I suppose; and tomorrow the child shall go back to her mother."

Phoebe, it must be understood, was that one little offshoot of the Pyncheon race to whom we have already referred, as a native of a rural part of New England, where the old fashions and feelings of relationship are still partially kept up. In her own circle, it was regarded as by no means improper for kinsfolk to visit one another without invitation, or preliminary and ceremonious warning. Yet, in consideration of Miss Hepzibah's recluse way of life, a letter had actually been written and despatched, conveying information of Phoebe's projected visit. This epistle, for three or four days past, had been in the pocket of the penny-postman, who, happening to have no other business in Pyncheon Street, had not yet made it convenient to call at the House of the Seven Gables.

"No—she can stay only one night," said Hepzibah, unbolting the door. "If Clifford were to find her here, it might disturb him!"

5: MAY AND NOVEMBER

Phoebe Pyncheon slept, on the night of her arrival, in a chamber that looked down on the garden of the old house. It fronted towards the east, so that at a very seasonable hour a glow of crimson light came flooding through the window, and bathed the dingy ceiling and paper-hangings in its own hue. There were curtains to Phoebe's bed; a dark, antique canopy, and ponderous festoons of a stuff which had been rich, and even magnificent, in its time; but which now brooded over the girl like a cloud, making a night in that one corner, while elsewhere it was beginning to be day.

The morning light, however, soon stole into the aperture at the foot of the bed, betwixt those faded curtains. Finding the new guest there,—with a bloom on her cheeks like the morning's own, and a gentle stir of departing slumber in her limbs, as when an early breeze moves the foliage,—the dawn kissed her brow. It was the caress which a dewy maiden—such as the Dawn is, immortally—gives to her sleeping sister, partly from the impulse of irresistible fondness, and partly as a pretty hint that it is time now to unclose her eyes.

At the touch of those lips of light, Phoebe quietly awoke, and, for a moment, did not recognize where she was, nor how those heavy curtains chanced to be festooned around her. Nothing, indeed, was absolutely plain to her, except that it was now early morning, and that, whatever might happen next, it was proper, first of all, to get up and say her prayers. She was the more inclined to devotion from the grim aspect of the chamber and its furniture, especially the tall, stiff chairs; one of which stood close by her bedside, and looked as if some old-fashioned personage had been sitting there all night, and had vanished only just in season to escape discovery.

When Phoebe was quite dressed, she peeped out of the window, and saw a rosebush in the garden. Being a very tall one, and of luxuriant growth, it had been propped up against the side of the house, and was literally covered with a rare and very beautiful species of white rose. A large portion of them, as the girl afterwards discovered, had blight or mildew at their hearts; but, viewed at a fair distance, the whole rosebush looked as if it had been brought from Eden that very summer, together with the mould in which it grew.

The truth was, nevertheless, that it had been planted by Alice Pyncheon,—she was Phoebe's great-great-grand-aunt,—in soil which, reckoning only its cultivation as a garden-plat, was now unctuous with nearly two hundred years of vegetable decay. Growing as they did, however, out of the old earth, the flowers still sent a fresh and sweet incense up to their Creator; nor could it have been the less pure and acceptable because Phoebe's young breath mingled with it, as the fragrance floated past the window. Hastening down the creaking and carpetless staircase, she found her way into the garden, gathered some of the most perfect of the roses, and brought them to her chamber.

Little Phoebe was one of those persons who possess, as their exclusive patrimony, the gift of practical arrangement. It is a kind of natural magic that enables these favoured ones to bring out the hidden capabilities of things around them; and particularly to give a look of comfort and habitableness to any place which, for however brief a period, may happen to be their home. A wild hut of underbrush, tossed together by wayfarers through the primitive forest, would acquire the home aspect by one night's lodging of such a woman, and would retain it long after her quiet figure had disappeared into the surrounding shade.

No less a portion of such homely witchcraft was requisite to reclaim, as it were, Phoebe's waste, cheerless, and dusky chamber, which had been untenanted so long—except by spiders, and mice, and rats, and ghosts—that it was all overgrown with the desolation which watches to obliterate every trace of man's happier hours. What was precisely Phoebe's process we find it impossible to say. She appeared to have no preliminary design, but gave a touch here and another there; brought some articles of furniture to light and dragged others into the shadow; looped up or let down a window-curtain; and, in the course of half an hour, had fully succeeded in throwing a kindly and hospitable smile over the apartment. No longer ago than the night before, it had resembled nothing so much as the old maid's heart; for there was neither sunshine nor household fire in one nor the other, and, save for ghosts and ghostly reminiscences, not a guest, for many years gone by, had entered the heart or the chamber.

There was still another peculiarity of this inscrutable charm. The bedchamber, no doubt, was a chamber of very great and varied experience, as a scene of human life: the joy of bridal nights had throbbed itself away here; new immortals had first drawn earthly breath here; and here old people had died. But—whether it were the white roses, or whatever the subtile influence might be—a person of delicate instinct would have known at once that it was now a maiden's bedchamber, and had been purified of all former evil and sorrow by her sweet breath and happy thoughts. Her dreams of the past night, being such cheerful ones, had exorcised the gloom, and now haunted the chamber in its stead.

After arranging matters to her satisfaction, Phoebe emerged from her chamber, with a purpose to descend again into the garden. Besides the rosebush, she had observed several other species of flowers growing there in a wilderness of neglect, and obstructing one another's development (as is often the parallel case in human society) by their uneducated entanglement and confusion. At the head of the stairs, however, she met Hepzibah, who, it being still early, invited her into a room which she would probably have called her *boudoir*, had her education embraced any such French phrase. It was strewn about with a few old books, and a work-basket, and a dusty writing-desk; and had, on one side, a large black article of furniture, of very strange appearance, which the old gentlewoman told Phoebe was a harpsichord. It looked more like a coffin than anything else; and, indeed,—not having been played upon, or opened, for years,—there must have been a vast deal of dead music in it, stifled for want of air. Human finger was hardly known to have touched its chords since the days of Alice Pyncheon, who had learned the sweet accomplishment of melody in Europe.

Hepzibah bade her young guest sit down, and, herself taking a chair nearby, looked as earnestly at Phoebe's trim little figure as if she expected to see right into its springs and motive secrets.

"Cousin Phoebe," said she, at last, "I really can't see my way clear to keep you with me."

These words, however, had not the inhospitable bluntness with which they may strike the reader; for the two relatives, in a talk before bedtime, had arrived at a certain degree of mutual understanding. Hepzibah knew enough to enable her to appreciate the circumstances (resulting from the second marriage of the girl's mother) which made it desirable for Phoebe to establish herself in another home. Nor did she misinterpret Phoebe's character, and the genial activity pervading it,—one of the most valuable traits of the true New England woman,—which had impelled her forth, as might be said, to seek her fortune, but with a self-respecting purpose to confer as much benefit as she could anywise receive. As one of her nearest kindred, she had naturally betaken herself to Hepzibah, with no idea of forcing herself on her cousin's protection, but only for a visit of a week or two, which might be indefinitely extended, should it prove for the happiness of both.

To Hepzibah's blunt observation, therefore, Phoebe replied as frankly, and more cheerfully.

"Dear cousin, I cannot tell how it will be," said she. "But I really think we may suit one another much better than you suppose."

"You are a nice girl,—I see it plainly," continued Hepzibah; "and it is not any question as to that point which makes me hesitate. But, Phoebe, this house of mine is but a melancholy place for a young person to be in. It lets in the wind and rain, and the snow, too, in the garret and upper chambers, in wintertime, but it never lets in the sunshine. And as for myself, you see what I am,—a dismal and lonesome old woman (for I begin to call myself old, Phoebe), whose temper, I am afraid, is none of the best, and whose spirits are as bad as can be! I cannot make your life pleasant, Cousin Phoebe, neither can I so much as give you bread to eat."

"You will find me a cheerful little body" answered Phoebe, smiling, and yet with a kind of gentle dignity, "and I mean to earn my bread. You know I have not been brought up a Pyncheon. A girl learns many things in a New England village."

"Ah! Phoebe," said Hepzibah, sighing, "your knowledge would do but little for you here! And then it is a wretched thought that you should fling away your young days in a place like this. Those cheeks would not be so rosy after a month or two. Look at my face!" and, indeed, the contrast was very striking,—"you see how pale I am! It is my idea that the dust and continual decay of these old houses are unwholesome for the lungs."

"There is the garden,—the flowers to be taken care of," observed Phoebe. "I should keep myself healthy with exercise in the open air."

"And, after all, child," exclaimed Hepzibah, suddenly rising, as if to dismiss the subject, "it is not for me to say who shall be a guest or inhabitant of the old Pyncheon House. Its master is coming."

"Do you mean Judge Pyncheon?" asked Phoebe in surprise.

"Judge Pyncheon!" answered her cousin angrily. "He will hardly cross the threshold while I live! No, no! But, Phoebe, you shall see the face of him I speak of."

She went in quest of the miniature already described, and returned with it in her hand. Giving it to Phoebe, she watched her features narrowly, and with a certain jealousy as to the mode in which the girl would show herself affected by the picture.

"How do you like the face?" asked Hepzibah.

"It is handsome!—it is very beautiful!" said Phoebe admiringly. "It is as sweet a face as a man's can be, or ought to be. It has something of a child's expression,—and yet not childish,—only one feels so very kindly towards him! He ought never to suffer anything. One would bear much for the sake of sparing him toil or sorrow. Who is it, Cousin Hepzibah?"

"Did you never hear," whispered her cousin, bending towards her, "of Clifford Pyncheon?"

"Never. I thought there were no Pyncheons left, except yourself and our cousin Jaffrey," answered Phoebe. "And yet I seem to have heard the name of Clifford Pyncheon. Yes!—from my father or my mother; but has he not been a long while dead?"

"Well, well, child, perhaps he has!" said Hepzibah with a sad, hollow laugh; "but, in old houses like this, you know, dead people are very apt to come back again! We shall see. And, Cousin Phoebe, since, after all that I have said, your courage does not fail you, we will not part so soon. You are welcome, my child, for the present, to such a home as your kinswoman can offer you."

With this measured, but not exactly cold assurance of a hospitable purpose, Hepzibah kissed her cheek.

They now went below stairs, where Phoebe—not so much assuming the office as attracting it to herself, by the magnetism of innate fitness—took the most active part in preparing breakfast. The mistress of the house, meanwhile, as is usual with persons of her stiff and unmalleable cast, stood mostly aside; willing to lend her aid, yet conscious that her natural inaptitude would be likely to impede the business in hand. Phoebe and the fire that boiled the teakettle were equally bright, cheerful, and efficient, in their respective offices. Hepzibah gazed forth from her habitual sluggishness, the necessary result of long solitude, as from another sphere.

She could not help being interested, however, and even amused, at the readiness with which her new inmate adapted herself to the circumstances, and brought the house, moreover, and all its rusty old appliances, into a suitableness for her purposes. Whatever she did, too, was done without conscious effort, and with frequent outbreaks of song, which were exceedingly pleasant to the ear. This natural tunefulness made Phoebe seem like a bird in a shadowy tree; or conveyed the idea that the stream of life warbled through her heart as a brook sometimes warbles through a pleasant little dell. It betokened the cheeriness of an active temperament, finding joy in its activity, and, therefore, rendering it beautiful; it was a New England trait,—the stern old stuff of Puritanism with a gold thread in the web.

Hepzibah brought out some old silver spoons with the family crest upon them, and a china tea-set painted over with grotesque figures of man, bird, and beast, in as grotesque a landscape. These pictured people were odd humourists, in a world of their own,—a world of vivid brilliancy, so far as colour went, and still unfaded, although the teapot and small cups were as ancient as the custom itself of tea-drinking.

"Your great-great-great-great-grandmother had these cups, when she was married," said Hepzibah to Phoebe. "She was a Davenport, of a good family. They were almost the first teacups ever seen in the colony; and if one of them were to be broken, my heart would break with it. But it is nonsense to speak so about a brittle teacup, when I remember what my heart has gone through without breaking."

The cups—not having been used, perhaps, since Hepzibah's youth—had contracted no small burden of dust, which Phoebe washed away with so much care and delicacy as to satisfy even the proprietor of this invaluable china.

"What a nice little housewife you are!" exclaimed the latter, smiling, and at the same time frowning so prodigiously that the smile was sunshine under a thunder-cloud. "Do you do other things as well? Are you as good at your book as you are at washing teacups?"

"Not quite, I am afraid," said Phoebe, laughing at the form of Hepzibah's question. "But I was schoolmistress for the little children in our district last summer, and might have been so still."

"Ah! 'tis all very well!" observed the maiden lady, drawing herself up. "But these things must have come to you with your mother's blood. I never knew a Pyncheon that had any turn for them."

It is very queer, but not the less true, that people are generally quite as vain, or even more so, of their deficiencies than of their available gifts; as was Hepzibah of this native inapplicability, so to speak, of the Pyncheons to any useful purpose. She regarded it as an hereditary trait; and so, perhaps, it was, but unfortunately a morbid one, such as is often generated in families that remain long above the surface of society.

Before they left the breakfast-table, the shop-bell rang sharply, and Hepzibah set down the remnant of her final cup of tea, with a look of sallow despair that was truly piteous to behold. In cases of distasteful occupation, the second day is generally worse than the first. We return to the rack with all the soreness of the preceding torture in our limbs. At all events, Hepzibah had fully satisfied herself of the impossibility of ever becoming wonted to this peevishly obstreperous little bell. Ring as often as it might, the sound always smote upon her nervous system rudely and suddenly. And especially now, while, with her crested teaspoons and antique china, she was flattering herself with ideas of gentility, she felt an unspeakable disinclination to confront a customer.

"Do not trouble yourself, dear cousin!" cried Phoebe, starting lightly up. "I am shop-keeper today."

"You, child!" exclaimed Hepzibah. "What can a little country girl know of such matters?"

"Oh, I have done all the shopping for the family at our village store," said Phoebe. "And I have had a table at a fancy fair, and made better sales than anybody. These things are not to be learnt; they depend upon a knack that comes, I suppose," added she, smiling, "with one's mother's blood. You shall see that I am as nice a little saleswoman as I am a housewife!"

The old gentlewoman stole behind Phoebe, and peeped from the passageway into the shop, to note how she would manage her undertaking. It was a case of some intricacy. A very ancient woman, in a white short gown and a green petticoat, with a string of gold beads about her neck, and what looked like a nightcap on her head, had brought a quantity of yarn to barter for the commodities of the shop. She was probably the very last person in town who still kept the time-honored spinning-wheel in constant revolution. It was worthwhile to hear the croaking and hollow tones of the old lady, and the pleasant voice of Phoebe, mingling in one twisted thread of talk; and still better to contrast their figures,—so light and bloomy,—so decrepit and dusky,—with only the counter betwixt them, in one sense, but more than threescore years, in another. As for the bargain, it was wrinkled slyness and craft pitted against native truth and sagacity.

"Was not that well done?" asked Phoebe, laughing, when the customer was gone.

"Nicely done, indeed, child!" answered Hepzibah. "I could not have gone through with it nearly so well. As you say, it must be a knack that belongs to you on the mother's side."

It is a very genuine admiration, that with which persons too shy or too awkward to take a due part in the bustling world regard the real actors in life's stirring scenes; so genuine, in fact, that the former are usually fain to make it palatable to their self-love, by assuming that these active and forcible qualities are incompatible with others, which they choose to deem higher and more important. Thus, Hepzibah was well content to acknowledge Phoebe's vastly superior gifts as a shop-keeper'—she listened, with compliant ear, to her suggestion of various methods whereby the influx of trade might be increased, and rendered profitable, without a hazardous outlay of capital.

She consented that the village maiden should manufacture yeast, both liquid and in cakes; and should brew a certain kind of beer, nectareous to the palate, and of rare stomachic virtues; and, moreover, should bake and exhibit for sale some little spice-cakes, which whosoever tasted would longingly desire to taste again. All such proofs of a ready mind and skilful handiwork were highly acceptable to the aristocratic hucksteress, so long as she could murmur to herself with a grim smile, and a half-natural sigh, and a sentiment of mixed wonder, pity, and growing affection:—

"What a nice little body she is! If she only could be a lady; too—but that's impossible! Phoebe is no Pyncheon. She takes everything from her mother!"

As to Phoebe's not being a lady, or whether she were a lady or no, it was a point, perhaps, difficult to decide, but which could hardly have come up for judgment at all in any fair and healthy mind. Out of New England, it would be impossible to meet with a person combining so many ladylike attributes with so many others that form no necessary (if compatible) part of the character. She shocked no canon of taste; she was admirably in keeping with herself, and never jarred against surrounding cir-cumstances. Her figure, to be sure,—so small as to be almost childlike, and so elastic that motion seemed as easy or easier to it than rest, would hardly have suited one's idea of a countess. Neither did her face—with the brown ringlets on either side, and the slightly piquant nose, and the wholesome bloom, and the clear shade of tan, and the half dozen freckles, friendly re-membrances of the April sun and breeze—precisely give us a right to call her beautiful.

But there was both lustre and depth in her eyes. She was very pretty; as graceful as a bird, and graceful much in the same way; as pleasant about the house as a gleam of sunshine falling on the floor through a shadow of twinkling leaves, or as a ray of firelight that dances on the wall while evening is drawing nigh. Instead of discussing her claim to rank among ladies, it would be preferable to regard Phoebe as the example of feminine grace and availability combined, in a state of society, if there were any such, where ladies did not exist. There it should be woman's office to move in the midst of practical affairs, and to gild them all, the very homeliest,—were it even the scouring of pots and kettles,—with an atmosphere of loveliness and joy.

Such was the sphere of Phoebe. To find the born and educated lady, on the other hand, we need look no farther than Hepzibah, our forlorn old maid, in her rustling and rusty silks, with her deeply cherished and ridiculous consciousness of long descent, her shadowy claims to princely territory, and, in the way of accomplishment, her recollections, it may be, of having formerly thrummed on a harpsichord, and walked a minuet, and worked an antique tapestry-stitch on her sampler. It was a fair parallel between new Plebeianism and old Gentility.

It really seemed as if the battered visage of the House of the Seven Gables, black and heavy-browed as it still certainly looked, must have shown a kind of cheerfulness glimmering through its dusky windows as Phoebe passed to and fro in the interior. Otherwise, it is impossible to explain how the people of the neighbourhood so soon became aware of the girl's presence. There was a great run of custom, setting steadily in, from about ten o' clock until towards noon,—relaxing, somewhat, at dinner-time, but recommencing in the afternoon, and, finally, dying away a half an hour or so before the long day's sunset.

One of the stanchest patrons was little Ned Higgins, the devourer of Jim Crow and the elephant, who to-day signalized his omnivorous prowess by swallowing two dromedaries and a locomotive. Phoebe laughed, as she summed up her aggregate of sales upon the slate; while Hepzibah, first drawing on a pair of silk gloves, reckoned over the sordid accumulation of copper coin, not without silver intermixed, that had jingled into the till.

"We must renew our stock, Cousin Hepzibah!" cried the little saleswoman. "The gingerbread figures are all gone, and so are those Dutch wooden milkmaids, and most of our other playthings. There has been constant inquiry for cheap raisins, and a great cry for whistles, and trumpets, and jew's-harps; and at least a dozen little boys have asked for molasses-candy. And we must contrive to get a peck of russet apples, late in the season as it is. But, dear cousin, what an enormous heap of copper! Positively a copper mountain!"

"Well done! well done! well done!" quoth Uncle Venner, who had taken occasion to shuffle in and out of the shop several times in the course of the day. "Here's a girl that will never end her days at my farm! Bless my eyes, what a brisk little soul!"

"Yes, Phoebe is a nice girl!" said Hepzibah, with a scowl of austere approbation. "But, Uncle Venner, you have known the family a great many years. Can you tell me whether there ever was a Pyncheon whom she takes after?"

"I don't believe there ever was," answered the venerable man. "At any rate, it never was my luck to see her like among them, nor, for that matter, anywhere else. I've seen a great deal of the world, not only in people's kitchens and backyards but at the street-corners, and on the wharves, and in other places where my business calls me; and I'm free to say, Miss Hepzibah, that I never knew a human creature do her work so much like one of God's angels as this child Phoebe does!"

Uncle Venner's eulogium, if it appear rather too high-strained for the person and occasion, had, nevertheless, a sense in which it was both subtle and true. There was a spiritual quality in Phoebe's activity. The life of the long and busy day—spent in occupations that might so easily have taken a squalid and ugly aspect—had been made pleasant, and even lovely, by the spontaneous grace with which these homely duties seemed to bloom out of her character; so that labor, while she dealt with it, had the easy and flexible charm of play. Angels do not toil, but let their good works grow out of them; and so did Phoebe.

The two relatives—the young maid and the old one—found time before nightfall, in the intervals of trade, to make rapid advances towards affection and confidence. A recluse, like Hepzibah, usually displays remarkable frankness, and at least temporary affability, on being absolutely cornered, and brought to the point of personal intercourse; like the angel whom Jacob wrestled with, she is ready to bless you when once overcome.

The old gentlewoman took a dreary and proud satisfaction in leading Phoebe from room to room of the house, and recounting the traditions with which, as we may say, the walls were lugubriously frescoed. She showed the indentations made by the lieutenant-governor's sword-hilt in the door-panels of the apartment where old Colonel Pyncheon, a dead host, had received his affrighted visitors with an awful frown. The dusky terror of that frown, Hepzibah observed, was thought to be lingering ever since in the passageway. She bade Phoebe step into one of the tall chairs, and inspect the ancient map of the Pyncheon territory at the eastward.

In a tract of land on which she laid her finger, there existed a silver mine, the locality of which was precisely pointed out in some memoranda of Colonel Pyncheon himself, but only to be made known when the family claim should be recognized by government. Thus it was for the interest of all New England that the Pyncheons should have justice done them. She told, too, how that there was undoubtedly an immense treasure of English guineas hidden somewhere about the house, or in the cellar, or possibly in the garden.

"If you should happen to find it, Phoebe," said Hepzibah, glancing aside at her with a grim yet kindly smile, "we will tie up the shop-bell for good and all!"

"Yes, dear cousin," answered Phoebe; "but, in the mean time, I hear somebody ringing it!"

When the customer was gone, Hepzibah talked rather vaguely, and at great length, about a certain Alice Pyncheon, who had been exceedingly beautiful and accomplished in her lifetime, a hundred years ago. The fragrance of her rich and delightful character still lingered about the place where she had lived, as a dried rose-bud scents the drawer where it has withered and perished. This lovely Alice had met with some great and mysterious calamity, and had grown thin and white, and gradually faded out of the world.

But, even now, she was supposed to haunt the House of the Seven Gables, and, a great many times,—especially when one of the Pyncheons was to die,—she had been heard playing sadly and beautifully on the harpsichord. One of these tunes, just as it had sounded from her spiritual touch, had been written down by an amateur of music; it was so exquisitely mournful that nobody, to this day, could bear to hear it played, unless when a great sorrow had made them know the still profounder sweetness of it.

"Was it the same harpsichord that you showed me?" inquired Phoebe.

"The very same," said Hepzibah. "It was Alice Pyncheon's harpsichord. When I was learning music, my father would never let me open it. So, as I could only play on my teacher's instrument, I have forgotten all my music long ago."

Leaving these antique themes, the old lady began to talk about the daguerreotypist, whom, as he seemed to be a well-meaning and orderly young man, and in narrow circumstances, she had permitted to take up his residence in one of the seven gables. But, on seeing more of Mr. Holgrave, she hardly knew what to make of him. He had the strangest companions imaginable; men with long beards, and dressed in linen blouses, and other such new-fangled and ill-fitting garments; reformers, temperance lecturers, and all manner of cross-looking philanthropists; community-men, and come-outers, as Hepzibah believed, who acknowledged no law, and ate no solid food, but lived on the scent of other people's cookery, and turned up their noses at the fare.

As for the daguerreotypist, she had read a paragraph in a penny paper, the other day, accusing him of making a speech full of wild and disorganizing matter, at a meeting of his *banditti*-like associates. For her own part, she had reason to believe that he practised animal magnetism, and, if such things were in fashion nowadays, should be apt to suspect him of studying the Black Art up there in his lonesome chamber.

"But, dear cousin," said Phoebe, "if the young man is so dangerous, why do you let him stay? If he does nothing worse, he may set the house on fire!"

"Why, sometimes," answered Hepzibah, "I have seriously made it a question, whether I ought not to send him away. But, with all his oddities, he is a quiet kind of a person, and has such a way of taking hold of one's mind, that, without exactly liking him (for I don't know enough of the young man), I should be sorry to lose sight of him entirely. A woman clings to slight acquaintances when she lives so much alone as I do."

"But if Mr. Holgrave is a lawless person!" remonstrated Phoebe, a part of whose essence it was to keep within the limits of law.

"Oh!" said Hepzibah carelessly,—for, formal as she was, still, in her life's experience, she had gnashed her teeth against human law,—"I suppose he has a law of his own!"

6: MAULE'S WELL

After an early tea, the little country-girl strayed into the garden. The enclosure had formerly been very extensive, but was now contracted within small compass, and hemmed about, partly by high wooden fences, and partly by the outbuildings of houses that stood on another street. In its centre was a grass-plat, surrounding a ruinous little structure, which showed just enough of its original design to indicate that it had once been a summer-house. A hop-vine, springing from last year's root, was beginning to clamber over it, but would be long in covering the roof with its green mantle. Three of the seven gables either fronted or looked sideways, with a dark solemnity of aspect, down into the garden.

The black, rich soil had fed itself with the decay of a long period of time; such as fallen leaves, the petals of flowers, and the stalks and seed—vessels of vagrant and lawless plants, more useful after their death than ever while flaunting in the sun. The evil of these departed years would naturally have sprung up again, in such rank weeds (symbolic of the transmitted vices of society) as are always prone to root themselves about human dwellings. Phoebe saw, however, that their growth must have been checked by a degree of careful labour, bestowed daily and systematically on the garden.

The white double rosebush had evidently been propped up anew against the house since the commencement of the season; and a pear-tree and three damson-trees, which, except a row of currant-bushes, constituted the only varieties of fruit, bore marks of the recent amputation of several superfluous or defective limbs. There were also a few species of antique and hereditary flowers, in no very flourishing condition, but scrupulously weeded; as if some person, either out of love or curiosity, had been anxious to bring them to such perfection as they were capable of attaining.

The remainder of the garden presented a well-selected assortment of esculent vegetables, in a praiseworthy state of advancement. Summer squashes almost in their golden blossom; cucumbers, now evincing a tendency to spread away from the main stock, and ramble far and wide; two or three rows of string-beans and as many more that were about to festoon themselves on poles; tomatoes, occupying a site so sheltered and sunny that the plants were already gigantic, and promised an early and abundant harvest.

Phoebe wondered whose care and toil it could have been that had planted these vegetables, and kept the soil so clean and orderly. Not surely her cousin Hepzibah's, who had no taste nor spirits for the lady-like employment of cultivating flowers, and—with her recluse habits, and tendency to shelter herself within the dismal shadow of the house—would hardly have come forth under the speck of open sky to weed and hoe among the fraternity of beans and squashes.

It being her first day of complete estrangement from rural objects, Phoebe found an unexpected charm in this little nook of grass, and foliage, and aristocratic flowers, and plebeian vegetables. The eye of Heaven seemed to look down into it pleasantly, and with a peculiar smile, as if glad to perceive that nature, elsewhere overwhelmed, and driven out of the dusty town, had here been able to retain a breathing-place. The spot acquired a somewhat wilder grace, and yet a very gentle one, from the fact that a pair of robins had built their nest in the pear-tree, and were making themselves exceedingly busy and happy in the dark intricacy of its boughs.

Bees, too,—strange to say,—had thought it worth their while to come hither, possibly from the range of hives beside some farmhouse miles away. How many aerial voyages might they have made, in quest of honey, or honey-laden, betwixt dawn and sunset! Yet, late as it now was, there still arose a pleasant hum out of one or two of the squash-blossoms, in the depths of which these bees were plying their golden labour. There was one other object in the garden which Nature might fairly claim as her inalienable property, in spite of whatever man could do to render it his own. This was a fountain, set round with a rim of old mossy stones, and paved, in its bed, with what appeared to be a sort of mosaic-work of variously coloured pebbles.

The play and slight agitation of the water, in its upward gush, wrought magically with these variegated pebbles, and made a continually shifting apparition of quaint figures, vanishing too suddenly to be definable. Thence, swelling over the rim of moss-grown stones, the water stole away under the fence, through what we regret to call a gutter, rather than a channel. Nor must we forget to mention a hen-coop of very reverend antiquity that stood in the farther corner of the garden, not a great way from the fountain. It now contained only Chanticleer, his two wives, and a solitary chicken. All of them were pure specimens of a breed which had been transmitted down as an heirloom in the Pyncheon family, and were said, while in their prime, to have attained almost the size of turkeys, and, on the score of delicate flesh, to be fit for a prince's table.

In proof of the authenticity of this legendary renown, Hepzibah could have exhibited the shell of a great egg, which an ostrich need hardly have been ashamed of. Be that as it might, the hens were now scarcely larger than pigeons, and had a queer, rusty, withered aspect, and a gouty kind of movement, and a sleepy and melancholy tone throughout all the variations of their clucking and cackling. It was evident that the race had degenerated, like many a noble race besides, in consequence of too strict a watchfulness to keep it pure. These feathered people had existed too long in their distinct variety; a fact of which the present representatives, judging by their lugubrious deportment, seemed to be aware.

They kept themselves alive, unquestionably, and laid now and then an egg, and hatched a chicken; not for any pleasure of their own, but that the world might not absolutely lose what had once been so admirable a breed of fowls. The distinguishing mark of the hens was a crest of lamentably scanty growth, in these latter days, but so oddly and wickedly analogous to Hepzibah's turban, that Phoebe—to the poignant distress of her conscience, but inevitably—was led to fancy a general resemblance betwixt these forlorn bipeds and her respectable relative.

The girl ran into the house to get some crumbs of bread, cold potatoes, and other such scraps as were suitable to the accommodating appetite of fowls. Returning, she gave a peculiar call, which they seemed to recognize. The chicken crept through the pales of the coop and ran, with some show of liveliness, to her feet; while Chanticleer and the ladies of his household regarded her with queer, sidelong glances, and then croaked one to another, as if communicating their sage opinions of her character. So wise, as well as antique, was their aspect, as to give colour to the idea, not merely that they were the descendants of a time-honoured race, but that they had existed, in their individual capacity, ever since the House of the Seven Gables was founded, and were somehow mixed up with its destiny. They were a species of tutelary sprite, or Banshee; although winged and feathered differently from most other guardian angels.

"Here, you odd little chicken!" said Phoebe; "here are some nice crumbs for you!"

The chicken, hereupon, though almost as venerable in appearance as its mother—possessing, indeed, the whole antiquity of its progenitors in miniature,—mustered vivacity enough to flutter upward and alight on Phoebe's shoulder.

"That little fowl pays you a high compliment!" said a voice

behind Phoebe.

Turning quickly, she was surprised at sight of a young man, who had found access into the garden by a door opening out of another gable than that whence she had emerged. He held a hoe in his hand, and, while Phoebe was gone in quest of the crumbs, had begun to busy himself with drawing up fresh earth about the roots of the tomatoes.

"The chicken really treats you like an old acquaintance," continued he in a quiet way, while a smile made his face pleasanter than Phoebe at first fancied it. "Those venerable personages in the coop, too, seem very affably disposed. You are lucky to be in their good graces so soon! They have known me much longer, but never honour me with any familiarity, though hardly a day passes without my bringing them food. Miss Hepzibah, I suppose, will interweave the fact with her other traditions, and set it down that the fowls know you to be a Pyncheon!"

"The secret is," said Phoebe, smiling, "that I have learned how to talk with hens and chickens."

"Ah, but these hens," answered the young man,—"these hens of aristocratic lineage would scorn to understand the vulgar language of a barn-yard fowl. I prefer to think—and so would Miss Hepzibah—that they recognize the family tone. For you are a Pyncheon?"

"My name is Phoebe Pyncheon," said the girl, with a manner of some reserve; for she was aware that her new acquaintance could be no other than the daguerreotypist, of whose lawless propensities the old maid had given her a disagreeable idea. "I did not know that my cousin Hepzibah's garden was under another person's care."

"Yes," said Holgrave, "I dig, and hoe, and weed, in this black old earth, for the sake of refreshing myself with what little nature and simplicity may be left in it, after men have so long sown and reaped here. I turn up the earth by way of pastime. My sober occupation, so far as I have any, is with a lighter material. In short, I make pictures out of sunshine; and, not to be too much dazzled with my own trade, I have prevailed with Miss Hepzibah to let me lodge in one of these dusky gables. It is like a bandage over one's eyes, to come into it. But would you like to see a specimen of my productions?"

"A daguerreotype likeness, do you mean?" asked Phoebe with less reserve; for, in spite of prejudice, her own youthfulness sprang forward to meet his. "I don't much like pictures of that sort,—they are so hard and stern; besides dodging away from the eye, and trying to escape altogether. They are conscious of looking very unamiable, I suppose, and therefore hate to be seen."

"If you would permit me," said the artist, looking at Phoebe, "I should like to try whether the daguerreotype can bring out disagreeable traits on a perfectly amiable face. But there certainly is truth in what you have said. Most of my likenesses do look unamiable; but the very sufficient reason, I fancy, is, because the originals are so. There is a wonderful insight in Heaven's broad and simple sunshine. While we give it credit only for depicting the merest surface, it actually brings out the secret character with a truth that no painter would ever venture upon, even could he detect it. There is, at least, no flattery in my humble line of art. Now, here is a likeness which I have taken over and over again, and still with no better result. Yet the original wears, to common eyes, a very different expression. It would gratify me to have your judgment on this character."

He exhibited a daguerreotype miniature in a morocco case. Phoebe merely glanced at it, and gave it back.

"I know the face," she replied; "for its stern eye has been following me about all day. It is my Puritan ancestor, who hangs yonder in the parlour. To be sure, you have found some way of copying the portrait without its black velvet cap and gray beard, and have given him a modern coat and satin cravat, instead of his cloak and band. I don't think him improved by your alterations."

"You would have seen other differences had you looked a little longer," said Holgrave, laughing, yet apparently much struck. "I can assure you that this is a modern face, and one which you will very probably meet. Now, the remarkable point is, that the original wears, to the world's eye,—and, for aught I know, to his most intimate friends,—an exceedingly pleasant countenance, indicative of benevolence, openness of heart, sunny good-humour, and other praiseworthy qualities of that cast. The sun, as you see, tells quite another story, and will not be coaxed out of it, after half a dozen patient attempts on my part. Here we have the man, sly, subtle, hard, imperious, and, withal, cold as ice. Look at that eye! Would you like to be at its mercy? At that mouth! Could it ever smile? And yet, if you could only see the benign smile of the original! It is so much the more unfortunate, as he is a public character of some eminence, and the likeness was intended to be engraved."

"Well, I don't wish to see it anymore," observed Phoebe, turning away her eyes. "It is certainly very like the old portrait. But my cousin Hepzibah has another picture,—a miniature. If the original is still in the world, I think he might defy the sun to make him look stern and hard."

"You have seen that picture, then!" exclaimed the artist, with an expression of much interest. "I never did, but have a great curiosity to do so. And you judge favourably of the face?"

"There never was a sweeter one," said Phoebe. "It is almost too soft and gentle for a man's."

"Is there nothing wild in the eye?" continued Holgrave, so earnestly that it embarrassed Phoebe, as did also the quiet freedom with which he presumed on their so recent acquaintance. "Is there nothing dark or sinister anywhere? Could you not conceive the original to have been guilty of a great crime?"

"It is nonsense," said Phoebe a little impatiently, "for us to talk about a picture which you have never seen. You mistake it for some other. A crime, indeed! Since you are a friend of my cousin Hepzibah's, you should ask her to show you the picture."

"It will suit my purpose still better to see the original," replied the daguerreotypist coolly. "As to his character, we need not discuss its points; they have already been settled by a competent tribunal, or one which called itself competent. But, stay! Do not go yet, if you please! I have a proposition to make you."

Phoebe was on the point of retreating, but turned back, with some hesitation; for she did not exactly comprehend his manner, although, on better observation, its feature seemed rather to be lack of ceremony than any approach to offensive rudeness. There was an odd kind of authority, too, in what he now proceeded to say, rather as if the garden were his own than a place to which he was admitted merely by Hepzibah's courtesy.

"If agreeable to you," he observed, "it would give me pleasure to turn over these flowers, and those ancient and respectable fowls, to your care. Coming fresh from country air and occupations, you will soon feel the need of some such out-of-door employment. My own sphere does not so much lie among flowers. You can trim and tend them, therefore, as you please; and I will ask only the least trifle of a blossom, now and then, in exchange for all the good, honest kitchen vegetables with which I propose to enrich Miss Hepzibah's table. So we will be fellow-labourers, somewhat on the community system."

Silently, and rather surprised at her own compliance, Phoebe accordingly betook herself to weeding a flower-bed, but busied herself still more with cogitations respecting this young man, with whom she so unexpectedly found herself on terms approaching to familiarity. She did not altogether like him. His character perplexed the little country-girl, as it might a more practised observer; for, while the tone of his conversation had generally been playful, the impression left on her mind was that of gravity, and, except as his youth modified it, almost sternness. She rebelled, as it were, against a certain magnetic element in the artist's nature, which he exercised towards her, possibly without being conscious of it.

After a little while, the twilight, deepened by the shadows of the fruit-trees and the surrounding buildings, threw an obscurity over the garden.

"There," said Holgrave, "it is time to give over work! That last stroke of the hoe has cut off a beanstalk. Goodnight, Miss Phoebe Pyncheon! Any bright day, if you will put one of those rosebuds in your hair, and come to my rooms in Central Street, I will seize the purest ray of sunshine, and make a picture of the flower and its wearer." He retired towards his own solitary gable, but turned his head, on reaching the door, and called to Phoebe, with a tone which certainly had laughter in it, yet which seemed to be more than half in earnest.

"Be careful not to drink at Maule's well!" said he. "Neither drink nor bathe your face in it!"

"Maule's well!" answered Phoebe. "Is that it with the rim of mossy stones? I have no thought of drinking there,—but why not?"

"Oh," rejoined the daguerreotypist, "because, like an old lady's cup of tea, it is water bewitched!"

He vanished; and Phoebe, lingering a moment, saw a glimmering light, and then the steady beam of a lamp, in a chamber of the gable. On returning into Hepzibah's apartment of the house, she found the low-studded parlour so dim and dusky that her eyes could not penetrate the interior. She was indistinctly aware, however, that the gaunt figure of the old gentlewoman was sitting in one of the straight-backed chairs, a little withdrawn from the window, the faint gleam of which showed the blanched paleness of her cheek, turned sideways towards a corner.

"Shall I light a lamp, Cousin Hepzibah?" she asked.

"Do, if you please, my dear child," answered Hepzibah. "But put it on the table in the corner of the passage. My eyes are weak; and I can seldom bear the lamplight on them."

What an instrument is the human voice! How wonderfully responsive to every emotion of the human soul! In Hepzibah's tone, at that moment, there was a certain rich depth and moisture, as if the words, commonplace as they were, had been steeped in the warmth of her heart. Again, while lighting the lamp in the kitchen, Phoebe fancied that her cousin spoke to her.

"In a moment, cousin!" answered the girl. "These matches just glimmer, and go out."

But, instead of a response from Hepzibah, she seemed to hear the murmur of an unknown voice. It was strangely indistinct, however, and less like articulate words than an unshaped sound, such as would be the utterance of feeling and sympathy, rather than of the intellect. So vague was it, that its impression or echo in Phoebe's mind was that of unreality. She concluded that she must have mistaken some other sound for that of the human voice; or else that it was altogether in her fancy.

She set the lighted lamp in the passage, and again entered the parlour. Hepzibah's form, though its sable outline mingled with the dusk, was now less imperfectly visible. In the remoter parts of the room, however, its walls being so ill adapted to reflect light, there was nearly the same obscurity as before.

"Cousin," said Phoebe, "did you speak to me just now?"

"No, child!" replied Hepzibah.

Fewer words than before, but with the same mysterious music in them! Mellow, melancholy, yet not mournful, the tone seemed to gush up out of the deep well of Hepzibah's heart, all steeped in its profoundest emotion. There was a tremor in it, too, that—as all strong feeling is electric—partly communicated itself to Phoebe. The girl sat silently for a moment. But soon, her senses being very acute, she became conscious of an irregular respiration in an obscure corner of the room. Her physical organization, moreover, being at once delicate and healthy, gave her a perception, operating with almost the effect of a spiritual medium, that somebody was near at hand.

"My dear cousin," asked she, overcoming an indefinable reluctance, "is there not someone in the room with us?"

"Phoebe, my dear little girl," said Hepzibah, after a moment's pause, "you were up betimes, and have been busy all day. Pray go to bed; for I am sure you must need rest. I will sit in the parlour awhile, and collect my thoughts. It has been my custom for more years, child, than you have lived!" While thus dismissing her, the maiden lady stept forward, kissed Phoebe, and pressed her to her heart, which beat against the girl's bosom with a strong, high, and tumultuous swell. How came there to be so much love in this desolate old heart, that it could afford to well over thus abundantly?

"Goodnight, cousin," said Phoebe, strangely affected by Hepzibah's manner. "If you begin to love me, I am glad!"

She retired to her chamber, but did not soon fall asleep, nor then very profoundly. At some uncertain period in the depths of night, and, as it were, through the thin veil of a dream, she was conscious of a footstep mounting the stairs heavily, but not with force and decision. The voice of Hepzibah, with a hush through it, was going up along with the footsteps; and, again, responsive to her cousin's voice, Phoebe heard that strange, vague murmur, which might be likened to an indistinct shadow of human utterance.

7: THE GUEST

When Phoebe awoke,—which she did with the early twittering of the conjugal couple of robins in the pear-tree,—she heard movements below stairs, and, hastening down, found Hepzibah already in the kitchen. She stood by a window, holding a book in close contiguity to her nose, as if with the hope of gaining an olfactory acquaintance with its contents, since her imperfect vision made it not very easy to read them. If any volume could have manifested its essential wisdom in the mode suggested, it would certainly have been the one now in Hepzibah's hand; and the kitchen, in such an event, would forthwith have streamed with the fragrance of venison, turkeys, capons, larded partridges, puddings, cakes, and Christmas pies, in all manner of elaborate mixture and concoction.

It was a cookery book, full of innumerable old fashions of English dishes, and illustrated with engravings, which represented the arrangements of the table at such banquets as it might have befitted a nobleman to give in the great hall of his castle. And, amid these rich and potent devices of the culinary art (not one of which, probably, had been tested, within the memory of any man's grandfather), poor Hepzibah was seeking for some nimble little titbit, which, with what skill she had, and such materials as were at hand, she might toss up for breakfast.

Soon, with a deep sigh, she put aside the savoury volume, and inquired of Phoebe whether old Speckle, as she called one of the hens, had laid an egg the preceding day. Phoebe ran to see, but returned without the expected treasure in her hand. At that instant, however, the blast of a fish-dealer's conch was heard, announcing his approach along the street. With energetic raps at the shop-window, Hepzibah summoned the man in, and made purchase of what he warranted as the finest mackerel in his cart, and as fat a one as ever he felt with his finger so early in the season. Requesting Phoebe to roast some coffee,—which she casually observed was the real Mocha, and so long kept that each of the small berries ought to be worth its weight in gold,—the maiden lady heaped fuel into the vast receptacle of the ancient fireplace in such quantity as soon to drive the lingering dusk out of the kitchen.

The country-girl, willing to give her utmost assistance, proposed to make an Indian cake, after her mother's peculiar method, of easy manufacture, and which she could vouch for as possessing a richness, and, if rightly prepared, a delicacy, un-equalled by any other mode of breakfast-cake. Hepzibah gladly assenting, the kitchen was soon the scene of savoury preparation. Perchance, amid their proper element of smoke, which eddied forth from the ill-constructed chimney, the ghosts of departed cook-maids looked wonderingly on, or peeped down the great breadth of the flue, despising the simplicity of the projected meal, yet ineffectually pining to thrust their shadowy hands into each inchoate dish. The half-starved rats, at any rate, stole visibly out of their hiding-places, and sat on their hind-legs, snuffing the fumy atmosphere, and wistfully awaiting an opportunity to nibble.

Hepzibah had no natural turn for cookery, and, to say the truth, had fairly incurred her present meagreness by often choos-ing to go without her dinner rather than be attendant on the ro-tation of the spit, or ebullition of the pot. Her zeal over the fire, therefore, was quite an heroic test of sentiment. It was touching, and positively worthy of tears (if Phoebe, the only spectator, except the rats and ghosts aforesaid, had not been better employed than in shedding them), to see her rake out a bed of fresh and glowing coals, and proceed to broil the mackerel. Her usually pale cheeks were all ablaze with heat and hurry. She watched the fish with as much tender care and minuteness of attention as if,—we know not how to express it otherwise,—as if her own heart were on the gridiron, and her immortal happiness were involved in its being done precisely to a turn!

Life, within doors, has few pleasanter prospects than a neatly arranged and well-provisioned breakfast-table. We come to it freshly, in the dewy youth of the day, and when our spiritual and sensual elements are in better accord than at a later period; so that the material delights of the morning meal are capable of being fully enjoyed, without any very grievous reproaches, whether gastric or conscientious, for yielding even a trifle overmuch to the animal department of our nature. The thoughts, too, that run around the ring of familiar guests have a piquancy and mirthfulness, and oftentimes a vivid truth, which more rarely find their way into the elaborate intercourse of dinner.

Hepzibah's small and ancient table, supported on its slender and graceful legs, and covered with a cloth of the richest damask, looked worthy to be the scene and centre of one of the cheerfullest of parties. The vapor of the broiled fish arose like incense from the shrine of a barbarian idol, while the fragrance of the Mocha might have gratified the nostrils of a tutelary Lar, or whatever power has scope over a modern breakfast-table. Phoebe's Indian cakes were the sweetest offering of all,—in their hue befitting the rustic altars of the innocent and golden age,—or, so brightly yellow were they, resembling some of the bread which was changed to glistening gold when Midas tried to eat it.

The butter must not be forgotten,—butter which Phoebe herself had churned, in her own rural home, and brought it to her cousin as a propitiatory gift,—smelling of clover-blossoms, and diffusing the charm of pastoral scenery through the dark-panelled parlour. All this, with the quaint gorgeousness of the old china cups and saucers, and the crested spoons, and a silver cream-jug (Hepzibah's only other article of plate, and shaped like the rudest porringer), set out a board at which the stateliest of old Colonel Pyncheon's guests need not have scorned to take his place. But the Puritan's face scowled down out of the picture, as if nothing on the table pleased his appetite.

By way of contributing what grace she could, Phoebe gathered some roses and a few other flowers, possessing either scent or beauty, and arranged them in a glass pitcher, which, having long ago lost its handle, was so much the fitter for a flower-vase. The early sunshine—as fresh as that which peeped into Eve's bower while she and Adam sat at breakfast there—came twinkling through the branches of the pear-tree, and fell quite across the table. All was now ready. There were chairs and plates for three. A chair and plate for Hepzibah,—the same for Phoebe,—but what other guest did her cousin look for?

Throughout this preparation there had been a constant tremor in Hepzibah's frame; an agitation so powerful that Phoebe could see the quivering of her gaunt shadow, as thrown by the firelight on the kitchen wall, or by the sunshine on the parlour floor. Its manifestations were so various, and agreed so little with one another, that the girl knew not what to make of it. Sometimes it seemed an ecstasy of delight and happiness. At such moments, Hepzibah would fling out her arms, and infold Phoebe in them, and kiss her cheek as tenderly as ever her mother had; she appeared to do so by an inevitable impulse, and as if her bosom were oppressed with tenderness, of which she must needs pour out a little, in order to gain breathing-room.

The next moment, without any visible cause for the change, her unwonted joy shrank back, appalled, as it were, and clothed itself in mourning; or it ran and hid itself, so to speak, in the dungeon of her heart, where it had long lain chained, while a cold, spectral sorrow took the place of the imprisoned joy, that was afraid to be enfranchised,—a sorrow as black as that was bright. She often broke into a little, nervous, hysteric laugh, more touching than any tears could be; and forthwith, as if to try which was the most touching, a gush of tears would follow; or perhaps the laughter and tears came both at once, and surrounded our poor Hepzibah, in a moral sense, with a kind of pale, dim rainbow. Towards Phoebe, as we have said, she was affectionate,—far tenderer than ever before, in their brief acquaintance, except for that one kiss on the preceding night,—yet with a continually recurring pettishness and irritability. She would speak sharply to her; then, throwing aside all the starched reserve of her ordinary manner, ask pardon, and the next instant renew the just-forgiven injury.

At last, when their mutual labour was all finished, she took Phoebe's hand in her own trembling one.

"Bear with me, my dear child," she cried; "for truly my heart is full to the brim! Bear with me; for I love you, Phoebe, though I speak so roughly. Think nothing of it, dearest child! By and by, I shall be kind, and only kind!"

"My dearest cousin, cannot you tell me what has happened?" asked Phoebe, with a sunny and tearful sympathy. "What is it that moves you so?"

"Hush! hush! He is coming!" whispered Hepzibah, hastily wiping her eyes. "Let him see you first, Phoebe; for you are young and rosy, and cannot help letting a smile break out whether or no. He always liked bright faces! And mine is old now, and the tears are hardly dry on it. He never could abide tears. There; draw the curtain a little, so that the shadow may fall across his side of the table! But let there be a good deal of sunshine, too; for he never was fond of gloom, as some people are. He has had but little sunshine in his life,—poor Clifford,—and, oh, what a black shadow. Poor, poor Clifford!"

Thus murmuring in an undertone, as if speaking rather to her own heart than to Phoebe, the old gentlewoman stepped on tiptoe about the room, making such arrangements as suggested themselves at the crisis.

Meanwhile there was a step in the passage-way, above stairs. Phoebe recognized it as the same which had passed upward, as through her dream, in the night-time. The approaching guest, whoever it might be, appeared to pause at the head of the staircase; he paused twice or thrice in the descent; he paused again at the foot. Each time, the delay seemed to be without purpose, but rather from a forgetfulness of the purpose which had set him in motion, or as if the person's feet came involuntarily to a stand-still because the motive-power was too feeble to sustain his progress. Finally, he made a long pause at the threshold of the parlour. He took hold of the knob of the door; then loosened his grasp without opening it. Hepzibah, her hands convulsively clasped, stood gazing at the entrance.

"Dear Cousin Hepzibah, pray don't look so!" said Phoebe, trembling; for her cousin's emotion, and this mysteriously reluctant step, made her feel as if a ghost were coming into the room. "You really frighten me! Is something awful going to happen?"

"Hush!" whispered Hepzibah. "Be cheerful! whatever may happen, be nothing but cheerful!"

The final pause at the threshold proved so long, that Hepzibah, unable to endure the suspense, rushed forward, threw open the door, and led in the stranger by the hand. At the first glance, Phoebe saw an elderly personage, in an old-fashioned dressing-gown of faded damask, and wearing his gray or almost white hair of an unusual length. It quite overshadowed his forehead, except when he thrust it back, and stared vaguely about the room. After a very brief inspection of his face, it was easy to conceive that his footstep must necessarily be such an one as that which, slowly and with as indefinite an aim as a child's first journey across a floor, had just brought him hitherward.

Yet there were no tokens that his physical strength might not have sufficed for a free and determined gait. It was the spirit of the man that could not walk. The expression of his countenance—while, notwithstanding it had the light of reason in it—seemed to waver, and glimmer, and nearly to die away, and feebly to recover itself again. It was like a flame which we see twinkling among half-extinguished embers; we gaze at it more intently than if it were a positive blaze, gushing vividly upward,—more intently, but with a certain impatience, as if it ought either to kindle itself into satisfactory splendour, or be at once extinguished.

For an instant after entering the room, the guest stood still, retaining Hepzibah's hand instinctively, as a child does that of the grown person who guides it. He saw Phoebe, however, and caught an illumination from her youthful and pleasant aspect, which, indeed, threw a cheerfulness about the parlour, like the circle of reflected brilliancy around the glass vase of flowers that was standing in the sunshine. He made a salutation, or, to speak nearer the truth, an ill-defined, abortive attempt at curtsy. Imperfect as it was, however, it conveyed an idea, or, at least, gave a hint, of indescribable grace, such as no practised art of external manners could have attained. It was too slight to seize upon at the instant; yet, as recollected afterwards, seemed to transfigure the whole man.

"Dear Clifford," said Hepzibah, in the tone with which one soothes a wayward infant, "this is our cousin Phoebe,—little Phoebe Pyncheon,—Arthur's only child, you know. She has come from the country to stay with us awhile; for our old house has grown to be very lonely now."

"Phoebe—Phoebe Pyncheon?—Phoebe?" repeated the guest, with a strange, sluggish, ill-defined utterance. "Arthur's child! Ah, I forget! No matter. She is very welcome!"

"Come, dear Clifford, take this chair," said Hepzibah, leading him to his place. "Pray, Phoebe, lower the curtain a very little more. Now let us begin breakfast."

The guest seated himself in the place assigned him, and looked strangely around. He was evidently trying to grapple with the present scene, and bring it home to his mind with a more satisfactory distinctness. He desired to be certain, at least, that he was here, in the low-studded, cross-beamed, oaken-panelled parlour, and not in some other spot, which had stereotyped itself into his senses. But the effort was too great to be sustained with more than a fragmentary success.

Continually, as we may express it, he faded away out of his place; or, in other words, his mind and consciousness took their departure, leaving his wasted, gray, and melancholy figure—a substantial emptiness, a material ghost—to occupy his seat at table. Again, after a blank moment, there would be a flickering taper-gleam in his eyeballs. It betokened that his spiritual part had returned, and was doing its best to kindle the heart's household fire, and light up intellectual lamps in the dark and ruinous mansion, where it was doomed to be a forlorn inhabitant.

At one of these moments of less torpid, yet still imperfect animation, Phoebe became convinced of what she had at first rejected as too extravagant and startling an idea. She saw that the person before her must have been the original of the beautiful miniature in her cousin Hepzibah's possession. Indeed, with a feminine eye for costume, she had at once identified the damask dressing-gown, which enveloped him, as the same in figure, material, and fashion, with that so elaborately represented in the picture. This old, faded garment, with all its pristine brilliancy extinct, seemed, in some indescribable way, to translate the wearer's untold misfortune, and make it perceptible to the beholder's eye.

It was the better to be discerned, by this exterior type, how worn and old were the soul's more immediate garments; that form and countenance, the beauty and grace of which had almost transcended the skill of the most exquisite of artists. It could the more adequately be known that the soul of the man must have suffered some miserable wrong, from its earthly experience. There he seemed to sit, with a dim veil of decay and ruin betwixt him and the world, but through which, at flitting intervals, might be caught the same expression, so refined, so softly imaginative, which Malbone—venturing a happy touch, with suspended breath—had imparted to the miniature! There had been something so innately characteristic in this look, that all the dusky years, and the burden of unfit calamity which had fallen upon him, did not suffice utterly to destroy it.

Hepzibah had now poured out a cup of deliciously fragrant coffee, and presented it to her guest. As his eyes met hers, he seemed bewildered and disquieted.

"Is this you, Hepzibah?" he murmured sadly; then, more apart, and perhaps unconscious that he was overheard, "How changed! how changed! And is she angry with me? Why does she bend her brow so?"

Poor Hepzibah! It was that wretched scowl which time and her near-sightedness, and the fret of inward discomfort, had rendered so habitual that any vehemence of mood invariably evoked it. But at the indistinct murmur of his words her whole face grew tender, and even lovely, with sorrowful affection; the harshness of her features disappeared, as it were, behind the warm and misty glow.

"Angry!" she repeated; "angry with you, Clifford!"

Her tone, as she uttered the exclamation, had a plaintive and really exquisite melody thrilling through it, yet without subduing a certain something which an obtuse auditor might still have mistaken for asperity. It was as if some transcendent musician should draw a soul-thrilling sweetness out of a cracked instrument, which makes its physical imperfection heard in the midst of ethereal harmony,—so deep was the sensibility that found an organ in Hepzibah's voice!

"There is nothing but love here, Clifford," she added,— "nothing but love! You are at home!"

The guest responded to her tone by a smile, which did not half light up his face. Feeble as it was, however, and gone in a moment, it had a charm of wonderful beauty. It was followed by a coarser expression; or one that had the effect of coarseness on the fine mould and outline of his countenance, because there was nothing intellectual to temper it. It was a look of appetite. He ate food with what might almost be termed voracity; and seemed to forget himself, Hepzibah, the young girl, and everything else around him, in the sensual enjoyment which the bountifully spread table afforded.

In his natural system, though high-wrought and delicately refined, a sensibility to the delights of the palate was probably inherent. It would have been kept in check, however, and even converted into an accomplishment, and one of the thousand

modes of intellectual culture, had his more ethereal characteristics retained their vigour. But as it existed now, the effect was
painful and made Phoebe droop her eyes.

In a little while the guest became sensible of the fragrance of
the yet untasted coffee. He quaffed it eagerly. The subtle essence
acted on him like a charmed draught, and caused the opaque
substance of his animal being to grow transparent, or, at least,
translucent; so that a spiritual gleam was transmitted through it,
with a clearer lustre than hitherto.

"More, more!" he cried, with nervous haste in his utterance,
as if anxious to retain his grasp of what sought to escape him.
"This is what I need! Give me more!"

Under this delicate and powerful influence he sat more erect,
and looked out from his eyes with a glance that took note of
what it rested on. It was not so much that his expression grew
more intellectual; this, though it had its share, was not the most
peculiar effect. Neither was what we call the moral nature so
forcibly awakened as to present itself in remarkable prominence.
But a certain fine temper of being was now not brought out in
full relief, but changeably and imperfectly betrayed, of which it
was the function to deal with all beautiful and enjoyable things.
In a character where it should exist as the chief attribute, it
would bestow on its possessor an exquisite taste, and an enviable
susceptibility of happiness.

Beauty would be his life; his aspirations would all tend toward it; and, allowing his frame and physical organs to be in
consonance, his own developments would likewise be beautiful.
Such a man should have nothing to do with sorrow; nothing
with strife; nothing with the martyrdom which, in an infinite
variety of shapes, awaits those who have the heart, and will, and
conscience, to fight a battle with the world. To these heroic tem-
pers, such martyrdom is the richest meed in the world's gift. To
the individual before us, it could only be a grief, intense in due
proportion with the severity of the infliction.

He had no right to be a martyr; and, beholding him so fit to
be happy and so feeble for all other purposes, a generous, strong,

and noble spirit would, methinks, have been ready to sacrifice what little enjoyment it might have planned for itself,—it would have flung down the hopes, so paltry in its regard,—if thereby the wintry blasts of our rude sphere might come tempered to such a man.

Not to speak it harshly or scornfully, it seemed Clifford's nature to be a Sybarite. It was perceptible, even there, in the dark old parlour, in the inevitable polarity with which his eyes were attracted towards the quivering play of sunbeams through the shadowy foliage. It was seen in his appreciating notice of the vase of flowers, the scent of which he inhaled with a zest almost peculiar to a physical organization so refined that spiritual ingredients are moulded in with it. It was betrayed in the unconscious smile with which he regarded Phoebe, whose fresh and maidenly figure was both sunshine and flowers,—their essence, in a prettier and more agreeable mode of manifestation.

Not less evident was this love and necessity for the Beautiful, in the instinctive caution with which, even so soon, his eyes turned away from his hostess, and wandered to any quarter rather than come back. It was Hepzibah's misfortune,—not Clifford's fault. How could he,—so yellow as she was, so wrinkled, so sad of mien, with that odd uncouthness of a turban on her head, and that most perverse of scowls contorting her brow,—how could he love to gaze at her? But, did he owe her no affection for so much as she had silently given? He owed her nothing. A nature like Clifford's can contract no debts of that kind. It is—we say it without censure, nor in diminution of the claim which it indefeasibly possesses on beings of another mould—it is always selfish in its essence; and we must give it leave to be so, and heap up our heroic and disinterested love upon it so much the more, without a recompense.

Poor Hepzibah knew this truth, or, at least, acted on the instinct of it. So long estranged from what was lovely as Clifford had been, she rejoiced—rejoiced, though with a present sigh, and a secret purpose to shed tears in her own chamber that he had brighter objects now before his eyes than her aged and uncomely features. They never possessed a charm; and if they had, the canker of her grief for him would long since have destroyed it.

The guest leaned back in his chair. Mingled in his countenance with a dreamy delight, there was a troubled look of effort and unrest. He was seeking to make himself more fully sensible of the scene around him; or, perhaps, dreading it to be a dream, or a play of imagination, was vexing the fair moment with a struggle for some added brilliancy and more durable illusion.

"How pleasant!—How delightful!" he murmured, but not as if addressing any one. "Will it last? How balmy the atmosphere through that open window! An open window! How beautiful that play of sunshine! Those flowers, how very fragrant! That young girl's face, how cheerful, how blooming!—a flower with the dew on it, and sunbeams in the dewdrops! Ah! this must be all a dream! A dream! A dream! But it has quite hidden the four stone walls!"

Then his face darkened, as if the shadow of a cavern or a dungeon had come over it; there was no more light in its expression than might have come through the iron grates of a prison-window—still lessening, too, as if he were sinking farther into the depths. Phoebe (being of that quickness and activity of temperament that she seldom long refrained from taking a part, and generally a good one, in what was going forward) now felt herself moved to address the stranger.

"Here is a new kind of rose, which I found this morning in the garden," said she, choosing a small crimson one from among the flowers in the vase. "There will be but five or six on the bush this season. This is the most perfect of them all; not a speck of blight or mildew in it. And how sweet it is!—sweet like no other rose! One can never forget that scent!"

"Ah!—let me see!—let me hold it!" cried the guest, eagerly seizing the flower, which, by the spell peculiar to remembered odours, brought innumerable associations along with the fragrance that it exhaled. "Thank you! This has done me good. I remember how I used to prize this flower,—long ago, I suppose, very long ago!—or was it only yesterday? It makes me feel young again! Am I young? Either this remembrance is singularly distinct, or this consciousness strangely dim! But how kind of the fair young girl! Thank you! Thank you!"

The favourable excitement derived from this little crimson rose afforded Clifford the brightest moment which he enjoyed at the breakfast-table. It might have lasted longer, but that his eyes happened, soon afterwards, to rest on the face of the old Puritan, who, out of his dingy frame and lustreless canvas, was looking down on the scene like a ghost, and a most ill-tempered and ungenial one. The guest made an impatient gesture of the hand, and addressed Hepzibah with what might easily be recognized as the licensed irritability of a petted member of the family.

"Hepzibah!—Hepzibah!" cried he with no little force and distinctness, "why do you keep that odious picture on the wall? Yes, yes!—that is precisely your taste! I have told you, a thousand times, that it was the evil genius of the house!—my evil genius particularly! Take it down, at once!"

"Dear Clifford," said Hepzibah sadly, "you know it cannot be!"

"Then, at all events," continued he, still speaking with some energy, "pray cover it with a crimson curtain, broad enough to hang in folds, and with a golden border and tassels. I cannot bear it! It must not stare me in the face!"

"Yes, dear Clifford, the picture shall be covered," said Hepzibah soothingly. "There is a crimson curtain in a trunk above stairs,—a little faded and moth-eaten, I'm afraid,—but Phoebe and I will do wonders with it."

"This very day, remember" said he; and then added, in a low, self-communing voice, "Why should we live in this dismal house at all? Why not go to the South of France?—to Italy?— Paris, Naples, Venice, Rome? Hepzibah will say we have not the means. A droll idea that!"

He smiled to himself, and threw a glance of fine sarcastic meaning towards Hepzibah.

But the several moods of feeling, faintly as they were marked, through which he had passed, occurring in so brief an interval of time, had evidently wearied the stranger. He was probably accustomed to a sad monotony of life, not so much flowing in a stream, however sluggish, as stagnating in a pool around his feet. A slumberous veil diffused itself over his countenance, and had an effect, morally speaking, on its naturally delicate and elegant outline, like that which a brooding mist, with no sunshine in it, throws over the features of a landscape. He appeared to become grosser,—almost cloddish. If aught of interest or beauty—even ruined beauty—had heretofore been visible in this man, the beholder might now begin to doubt it, and to accuse his own imagination of deluding him with whatever grace had flickered over that visage, and whatever exquisite lustre had gleamed in those filmy eyes.

Before he had quite sunken away, however, the sharp and peevish tinkle of the shop-bell made itself audible. Striking most disagreeably on Clifford's auditory organs and the characteristic sensibility of his nerves, it caused him to start upright out of his chair.

"Good heavens, Hepzibah! what horrible disturbance have we now in the house?" cried he, wreaking his resentful impatience—as a matter of course, and a custom of old—on the one person in the world that loved him. "I have never heard such a hateful clamour! Why do you permit it? In the name of all dissonance, what can it be?"

It was very remarkable into what prominent relief—even as if a dim picture should leap suddenly from its canvas—Clifford's character was thrown by this apparently trifling annoyance. The secret was, that an individual of his temper can always be pricked more acutely through his sense of the beautiful and harmonious than through his heart. It is even possible—for similar cases have often happened—that if Clifford, in his foregoing life, had enjoyed the means of cultivating his taste to its utmost perfectibility, that subtile attribute might, before this period, have completely eaten out or filed away his affections. Shall we venture to pronounce, therefore, that his long and black calamity may not have had a redeeming drop of mercy at the bottom?

"Dear Clifford, I wish I could keep the sound from your ears," said Hepzibah, patiently, but reddening with a painful suffusion of shame. "It is very disagreeable even to me. But, do you know, Clifford, I have something to tell you? This ugly noise,— pray run, Phoebe, and see who is there!—this naughty little tinkle is nothing but our shop-bell!"

"Shop-bell!" repeated Clifford, with a bewildered stare.

"Yes, our shop-bell," said Hepzibah, a certain natural dignity, mingled with deep emotion, now asserting itself in her manner. "For you must know, dearest Clifford, that we are very poor. And there was no other resource, but either to accept assistance from a hand that I would push aside (and so would you!) were it to offer bread when we were dying for it,—no help, save from him, or else to earn our subsistence with my own hands! Alone, I might have been content to starve. But you were to be given back to me! Do you think, then, dear Clifford," added she, with a wretched smile, "that I have brought an irretrievable disgrace on the old house, by opening a little shop in the front gable? Our great-great-grandfather did the same, when there was far less need! Are you ashamed of me?"

"Shame! Disgrace! Do you speak these words to me, Hepzibah?" said Clifford,—not angrily, however; for when a man's spirit has been thoroughly crushed, he may be peevish at small offences, but never resentful of great ones. So he spoke with only a grieved emotion. "It was not kind to say so, Hepzibah! What shame can befall me now?"

And then the unnerved man—he that had been born for enjoyment, but had met a doom so very wretched—burst into a woman's passion of tears. It was but of brief continuance, however; soon leaving him in a quiescent, and, to judge by his countenance, not an uncomfortable state. From this mood, too, he partially rallied for an instant, and looked at Hepzibah with a smile, the keen, half-derisory purport of which was a puzzle to her.

"Are we so very poor, Hepzibah?" said he.

Finally, his chair being deep and softly cushioned, Clifford fell asleep. Hearing the more regular rise and fall of his breath (which, however, even then, instead of being strong and full, had a feeble kind of tremor, corresponding with the lack of vigour in his character),—hearing these tokens of settled slumber, Hepzibah seized the opportunity to peruse his face more attentively than she had yet dared to do. Her heart melted away in tears; her profoundest spirit sent forth a moaning voice, low, gentle, but inexpressibly sad. In this depth of grief and pity she felt that there was no irreverence in gazing at his altered, aged, faded, ruined face. But no sooner was she a little relieved than her conscience smote her for gazing curiously at him, now that he was so changed; and, turning hastily away, Hepzibah let down the curtain over the sunny window, and left Clifford to slumber there.

8: THE PYNCHEON OF TODAY

Phoebe, on entering the shop, beheld there the already familiar face of the little devourer—if we can reckon his mighty deeds aright—of Jim Crow, the elephant, the camel, the dromedaries, and the locomotive. Having expended his private fortune, on the two preceding days, in the purchase of the above unheard-of luxuries, the young gentleman's present errand was on the part of his mother, in quest of three eggs and half a pound of raisins. These articles Phoebe accordingly supplied, and, as a mark of gratitude for his previous patronage, and a slight super-added morsel after breakfast, put likewise into his hand a whale!

The great fish, reversing his experience with the prophet of Nineveh, immediately began his progress down the same red pathway of fate whither so varied a caravan had preceded him. This remarkable urchin, in truth, was the very emblem of old Father Time, both in respect of his all-devouring appetite for men and things, and because he, as well as Time, after ingulfing thus much of creation, looked almost as youthful as if he had been just that moment made.

After partly closing the door, the child turned back, and mumbled something to Phoebe, which, as the whale was but half disposed of, she could not perfectly understand.

"What did you say, my little fellow?" asked she.

"Mother wants to know" repeated Ned Higgins more distinctly, "how Old Maid Pyncheon's brother does? Folks say he has got home."

"My cousin Hepzibah's brother?" exclaimed Phoebe, surprised at this sudden explanation of the relationship between Hepzibah and her guest. "Her brother! And where can he have been?"

The little boy only put his thumb to his broad snub-nose, with that look of shrewdness which a child, spending much of his time in the street, so soon learns to throw over his features, however unintelligent in themselves. Then as Phoebe continued to gaze at him, without answering his mother's message, he took his departure.

As the child went down the steps, a gentleman ascended them, and made his entrance into the shop. It was the portly, and, had it possessed the advantage of a little more height, would have been the stately figure of a man considerably in the decline of life, dressed in a black suit of some thin stuff, resembling broadcloth as closely as possible. A gold-headed cane, of rare Oriental wood, added materially to the high respectability of his aspect, as did also a neckcloth of the utmost snowy purity, and the conscientious polish of his boots. His dark, square countenance, with its almost shaggy depth of eyebrows, was naturally impressive, and would, perhaps, have been rather stern, had not the gentleman considerately taken upon himself to mitigate the harsh effect by a look of exceeding good-humour and benevolence.

Owing, however, to a somewhat massive accumulation of animal substance about the lower region of his face, the look was, perhaps, unctuous rather than spiritual, and had, so to speak, a kind of fleshly effulgence, not altogether so satisfactory as he doubtless intended it to be. A susceptible observer, at any rate, might have regarded it as affording very little evidence of the general benignity of soul whereof it purported to be the outward reflection. And if the observer chanced to be ill-natured, as well as acute and susceptible, he would probably suspect that the smile on the gentleman's face was a good deal akin to the shine on his boots, and that each must have cost him and his boot-black, respectively, a good deal of hard labor to bring out and preserve them.

As the stranger entered the little shop, where the projection of the second story and the thick foliage of the elm-tree, as well as the commodities at the window, created a sort of gray medium, his smile grew as intense as if he had set his heart on counteracting the whole gloom of the atmosphere (besides any moral gloom pertaining to Hepzibah and her inmates) by the unassisted light of his countenance. On perceiving a young rose-bud of a girl, instead of the gaunt presence of the old maid, a look of surprise was manifest. He at first knit his brows; then smiled with more unctuous benignity than ever.

"Ah, I see how it is!" said he in a deep voice,—a voice which, had it come from the throat of an uncultivated man, would have been gruff, but, by dint of careful training, was now sufficiently agreeable,—"I was not aware that Miss Hepzibah Pyncheon had commenced business under such favourable auspices. You are her assistant, I suppose?"

"I certainly am," answered Phoebe, and added, with a little air of lady-like assumption (for, civil as the gentleman was, he evidently took her to be a young person serving for wages), "I am a cousin of Miss Hepzibah, on a visit to her."

"Her cousin?—and from the country? Pray pardon me, then," said the gentleman, bowing and smiling, as Phoebe never had been bowed to nor smiled on before; "in that case, we must be better acquainted; for, unless I am sadly mistaken, you are my own little kinswoman likewise! Let me see,—Mary?—Dolly?—Phoebe?—yes, Phoebe is the name! Is it possible that you are Phoebe Pyncheon, only child of my dear cousin and classmate, Arthur? Ah, I see your father now, about your mouth! Yes, yes! we must be better acquainted! I am your kinsman, my dear.

Surely you must have heard of Judge Pyncheon?"

As Phoebe curtsied in reply, the judge bent forward, with the pardonable and even praiseworthy purpose—considering the nearness of blood and the difference of age—of bestowing on his young relative a kiss of acknowledged kindred and natural affection. Unfortunately (without design, or only with such instinctive design as gives no account of itself to the intellect) Phoebe, just at the critical moment, drew back; so that her highly respectable kinsman, with his body bent over the counter and his lips protruded, was betrayed into the rather absurd predicament of kissing the empty air. It was a modern parallel to the case of Ixion embracing a cloud, and was so much the more ridiculous as the judge prided himself on eschewing all airy matter, and never mistaking a shadow for a substance.

The truth was,—and it is Phoebe's only excuse,—that, although Judge Pyncheon's glowing benignity might not be absolutely unpleasant to the feminine beholder, with the width of a street, or even an ordinary-sized room, interposed between, yet it became quite too intense, when this dark, full-fed physiognomy (so roughly bearded, too, that no razor could ever make it smooth) sought to bring itself into actual contact with the object of its regards. The man, the sex, somehow or other, was entirely too prominent in the judge's demonstrations of that sort. Phoebe's eyes sank, and, without knowing why, she felt herself blushing deeply under his look. Yet she had been kissed before, and without any particular squeamishness, by perhaps half a dozen different cousins, younger as well as older than this dark-browned, grisly-bearded, white-neck-clothed, and unctuously-benevolent judge! Then, why not by him?

On raising her eyes, Phoebe was startled by the change in Judge Pyncheon's face. It was quite as striking, allowing for the difference of scale, as that betwixt a landscape under a broad sunshine and just before a thunder-storm; not that it had the passionate intensity of the latter aspect, but was cold, hard, immitigable, like a day-long brooding cloud.

"Dear me! what is to be done now?" thought the country-girl to herself. "He looks as if there were nothing softer in him than a rock, nor milder than the east wind! I meant no harm! Since he is really my cousin, I would have let him kiss me, if I could!"

Then, all at once, it struck Phoebe that this very Judge Pyncheon was the original of the miniature which the daguerreotypist had shown her in the garden, and that the hard, stern, relentless look, now on his face, was the same that the sun had so inflexibly persisted in bringing out. Was it, therefore, no momentary mood, but, however skilfully concealed, the settled temper of his life? And not merely so, but was it hereditary in him, and transmitted down, as a precious heirloom, from that bearded ancestor, in whose picture both the expression and, to a singular degree, the features of the modern judge were shown as by a kind of prophecy?

A deeper philosopher than Phoebe might have found something very terrible in this idea. It implied that the weaknesses and defects, the bad passions, the mean tendencies, and the moral diseases which lead to crime are handed down from one generation to another, by a far surer process of transmission than human law has been able to establish in respect to the riches and honors which it seeks to entail upon posterity.

But, as it happened, scarcely had Phoebe's eyes rested again on the judge's countenance than all its ugly sternness vanished; and she found herself quite overpowered by the sultry, dog-day heat, as it were, of benevolence, which this excellent man diffused out of his great heart into the surrounding atmosphere,— very much like a serpent, which, as a preliminary to fascination, is said to fill the air with his peculiar odour.

"I like that, Cousin Phoebe!" cried he, with an emphatic nod of approbation. "I like it much, my little cousin! You are a good child, and know how to take care of yourself. A young girl— especially if she be a very pretty one—can never be too chary of her lips."

"Indeed, sir," said Phoebe, trying to laugh the matter off, "I did not mean to be unkind."

Nevertheless, whether or no it were entirely owing to the in-auspicious commencement of their acquaintance, she still acted under a certain reserve, which was by no means customary to her frank and genial nature. The fantasy would not quit her, that the original Puritan, of whom she had heard so many som-bre traditions,—the progenitor of the whole race of New Eng-land Pyncheons, the founder of the House of the Seven Gables, and who had died so strangely in it,—had now stept into the shop. In these days of off-hand equipment, the matter was easily enough arranged.

On his arrival from the other world, he had merely found it necessary to spend a quarter of an hour at a barber's, who had trimmed down the Puritan's full beard into a pair of griz-zled whiskers, then, patronizing a ready-made clothing estab-lishment, he had exchanged his velvet doublet and sable cloak, with the richly worked band under his chin, for a white collar and cravat, coat, vest, and pantaloons; and lastly, putting aside his steel-hilted broadsword to take up a gold-headed cane, the Colonel Pyncheon of two centuries ago steps forward as the judge of the passing moment!

Of course, Phoebe was far too sensible a girl to entertain this idea in any other way than as matter for a smile. Possibly, also, could the two personages have stood together before her eye, many points of difference would have been perceptible, and per-haps only a general resemblance. The long lapse of intervening years, in a climate so unlike that which had fostered the ancestral Englishman, must inevitably have wrought important changes in the physical system of his descendant. The judge's volume of muscle could hardly be the same as the colonel's; there was un-doubtedly less beef in him.

Though looked upon as a weighty man among his contem-poraries in respect of animal substance, and as favoured with a remarkable degree of fundamental development, well adapting him for the judicial bench, we conceive that the modern Judge Pyncheon, if weighed in the same balance with his ancestor, would have required at least an old-fashioned fifty-six to keep the scale in *equilibrio*. Then the judge's face had lost the ruddy English hue that showed its warmth through all the duskiness of the Colonel's weather-beaten cheek, and had taken a sallow shade, the established complexion of his countrymen. If we mistake not, moreover, a certain quality of nervousness had become more or less manifest, even in so solid a specimen of Puritan descent as the gentleman now under discussion.

As one of its effects, it bestowed on his countenance a quicker mobility than the old Englishman's had possessed, and keener vivacity, but at the expense of a sturdier something, on which these acute endowments seemed to act like dissolving acids. This process, for aught we know, may belong to the great system of human progress, which, with every ascending footstep, as it diminishes the necessity for animal force, may be destined gradually to spiritualize us, by refining away our grosser attributes of body. If so, Judge Pyncheon could endure a century or two more of such refinement as well as most other men.

The similarity, intellectual and moral, between the judge and his ancestor appears to have been at least as strong as the resemblance of mien and feature would afford reason to anticipate. In old Colonel Pyncheon's funeral discourse the clergyman absolutely canonized his deceased parishioner, and opening, as it were, a *vista* through the roof of the church, and thence through the firmament above, showed him seated, harp in hand, among the crowned choristers of the spiritual world. On his tombstone, too, the record is highly eulogistic; nor does history, so far as he holds a place upon its page, assail the consistency and uprightness of his character.

So also, as regards the Judge Pyncheon of today, neither clergyman, nor legal critic, nor inscriber of tombstones, nor historian of general or local politics, would venture a word against this eminent person's sincerity as a Christian, or respectability as a man, or integrity as a judge, or courage and faithfulness as the often-tried representative of his political party. But, besides these cold, formal, and empty words of the chisel that inscribes, the voice that speaks, and the pen that writes, for the public eye and for distant time,—and which inevitably lose much of their truth and freedom by the fatal consciousness of so doing,—there were traditions about the ancestor, and private diurnal gossip about the judge, remarkably accordant in their testimony. It is often instructive to take the woman's, the private and domestic, view of a public man; nor can anything be more curious than the vast discrepancy between portraits intended for engraving and the pencil-sketches that pass from hand to hand behind the original's back.

For example: tradition affirmed that the Puritan had been greedy of wealth; the judge, too, with all the show of liberal expenditure, was said to be as close-fisted as if his gripe were of iron. The ancestor had clothed himself in a grim assumption of kindliness, a rough heartiness of word and manner, which most people took to be the genuine warmth of nature, making its way through the thick and inflexible hide of a manly character. His descendant, in compliance with the requirements of a nicer age, had etherealized this rude benevolence into that broad benignity of smile wherewith he shone like a noonday sun along the streets, or glowed like a household fire in the drawing-rooms of his private acquaintance.

The Puritan—if not belied by some singular stories, murmured, even at this day, under the narrator's breath—had fallen into certain transgressions to which men of his great animal development, whatever their faith or principles, must continue liable, until they put off impurity, along with the gross earthly substance that involves it. We must not stain our page with any contemporary scandal, to a similar purport, that may have been whispered against the judge. The Puritan, again, an autocrat in his own household, had worn out three wives, and, merely by the remorseless weight and hardness of his character in the conjugal relation, had sent them, one after another, broken-hearted, to their graves.

Here the parallel, in some sort, fails. The judge had wedded but a single wife, and lost her in the third or fourth year of their marriage. There was a fable, however,—for such we choose to consider it, though, not impossibly, typical of Judge Pyncheon's marital deportment,—that the lady got her death-blow in the honeymoon, and never smiled again, because her husband compelled her to serve him with coffee every morning at his bedside, in token of fealty to her liege-lord and master.

But it is too fruitful a subject, this of hereditary resemblances,—the frequent recurrence of which, in a direct line, is truly unaccountable, when we consider how large an accumulation of ancestry lies behind every man at the distance of one or two centuries. We shall only add, therefore, that the Puritan—so, at least, says chimney-corner tradition, which often preserves traits of character with marvellous fidelity—was bold, imperious, relentless, crafty; laying his purposes deep, and following them out with an inveteracy of pursuit that knew neither rest nor conscience; trampling on the weak, and, when essential to his ends, doing his utmost to beat down the strong. Whether the judge in any degree resembled him, the further progress of our narrative may show.

Scarcely any of the items in the above-drawn parallel occurred to Phoebe, whose country birth and residence, in truth, had left her pitifully ignorant of most of the family traditions, which lingered, like cobwebs and incrustations of smoke, about the rooms and chimney-corners of the House of the Seven Gables. Yet there was a circumstance, very trifling in itself, which impressed her with an odd degree of horror. She had heard of the anathema flung by Maule, the executed wizard, against Colonel Pyncheon and his posterity,—that God would give them blood to drink,—and likewise of the popular notion, that this miraculous blood might now and then be heard gurgling in their throats.

The latter scandal—as became a person of sense, and, more especially, a member of the Pyncheon family—Phoebe had set down for the absurdity which it unquestionably was. But ancient superstitions, after being steeped in human hearts and embodied in human breath, and passing from lip to ear in manifold repetition, through a series of generations, become imbued with an effect of homely truth. The smoke of the domestic hearth has scented them through and through. By long transmission among household facts, they grow to look like them, and have such a familiar way of making themselves at home that their influence is usually greater than we suspect.

Thus it happened, that when Phoebe heard a certain noise in Judge Pyncheon's throat,—rather habitual with him, not altogether voluntary, yet indicative of nothing, unless it were a slight bronchial complaint, or, as some people hinted, an apoplectic symptom,—when the girl heard this queer and awkward ingurgitation (which the writer never did hear, and therefore cannot describe), she very foolishly started, and clasped her hands.

Of course, it was exceedingly ridiculous in Phoebe to be discomposed by such a trifle, and still more unpardonable to show her discomposure to the individual most concerned in it. But the incident chimed in so oddly with her previous fancies about the Colonel and the judge, that, for the moment, it seemed quite to mingle their identity.

"What is the matter with you, young woman?" said Judge Pyncheon, giving her one of his harsh looks. "Are you afraid of anything?"

"Oh, nothing, sir—nothing in the world!" answered Phoebe, with a little laugh of vexation at herself. "But perhaps you wish to speak with my cousin Hepzibah. Shall I call her?"

"Stay a moment, if you please," said the judge, again beaming sunshine out of his face. "You seem to be a little nervous this morning. The town air, Cousin Phoebe, does not agree with your good, wholesome country habits. Or has anything happened to disturb you?—anything remarkable in Cousin Hepzibah's family?— An arrival, eh? I thought so! No wonder you are out of sorts, my little cousin. To be an inmate with such a guest may well startle an innocent young girl!"

"You quite puzzle me, sir," replied Phoebe, gazing inquiringly at the judge. "There is no frightful guest in the house, but only a poor, gentle, childlike man, whom I believe to be Cousin Hepzibah's brother. I am afraid (but you, sir, will know better than I) that he is not quite in his sound senses; but so mild and quiet he seems to be, that a mother might trust her baby with him; and I think he would play with the baby as if he were only a few years older than itself. He startle me!—Oh, no indeed!"

"I rejoice to hear so favourable and so ingenuous an account of my cousin Clifford," said the benevolent judge. "Many years ago, when we were boys and young men together, I had a great affection for him, and still feel a tender interest in all his concerns. You say, Cousin Phoebe, he appears to be weak minded. Heaven grant him at least enough of intellect to repent of his past sins!"

"Nobody, I fancy," observed Phoebe, "can have fewer to repent of."

"And is it possible, my dear," rejoined the judge, with a commiserating look, "that you have never heard of Clifford Pyncheon?—that you know nothing of his history? Well, it is all right; and your mother has shown a very proper regard for the good name of the family with which she connected herself. Believe the best you can of this unfortunate person, and hope the best! It is a rule which Christians should always follow, in their judgments of one another; and especially is it right and wise among near relatives, whose characters have necessarily a degree of mutual dependence. But is Clifford in the parlour? I will just step in and see."

"Perhaps, sir, I had better call my cousin Hepzibah," said Phoebe; hardly knowing, however, whether she ought to obstruct the entrance of so affectionate a kinsman into the private regions of the house. "Her brother seemed to be just falling asleep after breakfast; and I am sure she would not like him to be disturbed. Pray, sir, let me give her notice!"

But the judge showed a singular determination to enter unannounced; and as Phoebe, with the vivacity of a person whose movements unconsciously answer to her thoughts, had stepped towards the door, he used little or no ceremony in putting her aside.

"No, no, Miss Phoebe!" said Judge Pyncheon in a voice as

deep as a thunder-growl, and with a frown as black as the cloud whence it issues. "Stay you here! I know the house, and know my cousin Hepzibah, and know her brother Clifford likewise.— nor need my little country cousin put herself to the trouble of announcing me!"—in these latter words, by the bye, there were symptoms of a change from his sudden harshness into his previous benignity of manner. "I am at home here, Phoebe, you must recollect, and you are the stranger. I will just step in, therefore, and see for myself how Clifford is, and assure him and Hepzibah of my kindly feelings and best wishes. It is right, at this juncture, that they should both hear from my own lips how much I desire to serve them. Ha! here is Hepzibah herself!"

Such was the case. The vibrations of the judge's voice had reached the old gentlewoman in the parlour, where she sat, with face averted, waiting on her brother's slumber. She now issued forth, as would appear, to defend the entrance, looking, we must needs say, amazingly like the dragon which, in fairy tales, is wont to be the guardian over an enchanted beauty. The habitual scowl of her brow was undeniably too fierce, at this moment, to pass itself off on the innocent score of near-sightedness; and it was bent on Judge Pyncheon in a way that seemed to confound, if not alarm him, so inadequately had he estimated the moral force of a deeply grounded antipathy. She made a repelling gesture with her hand, and stood a perfect picture of prohibition, at full length, in the dark frame of the doorway. But we must betray Hepzibah's secret, and confess that the native timorousness of her character even now developed itself in a quick tremor, which, to her own perception, set each of her joints at variance with its fellows.

Possibly, the judge was aware how little true hardihood lay behind Hepzibah's formidable front. At any rate, being a gentleman of steady nerves, he soon recovered himself, and failed not to approach his cousin with outstretched hand; adopting the sensible precaution, however, to cover his advance with a smile, so broad and sultry, that, had it been only half as warm as it looked, a trellis of grapes might at once have turned purple under its summer-like exposure. It may have been his purpose, indeed, to melt poor Hepzibah on the spot, as if she were a figure of yellow wax.

"Hepzibah, my beloved cousin, I am rejoiced!" exclaimed the judge most emphatically. "Now, at length, you have something to live for. Yes, and all of us, let me say, your friends and kindred, have more to live for than we had yesterday. I have lost no time in hastening to offer any assistance in my power towards making Clifford comfortable. He belongs to us all. I know how much he requires,—how much he used to require,—with his delicate taste, and his love of the beautiful. Anything in my house,— pictures, books, wine, luxuries of the table,—he may command them all! It would afford me most heartfelt gratification to see him! Shall I step in, this moment?"

"No," replied Hepzibah, her voice quivering too painfully to allow of many words. "He cannot see visitors!"

"A visitor, my dear cousin!—do you call me so?" cried the judge, whose sensibility, it seems, was hurt by the coldness of the phrase. "Nay, then, let me be Clifford's host, and your own likewise. Come at once to my house. The country air, and all the conveniences,—I may say luxuries,—that I have gathered about me, will do wonders for him. And you and I, dear Hepzibah, will consult together, and watch together, and labour together, to make our dear Clifford happy. Come! why should we make more words about what is both a duty and a pleasure on my part? Come to me at once!"

On hearing these so hospitable offers, and such generous recognition of the claims of kindred, Phoebe felt very much in the mood of running up to Judge Pyncheon, and giving him, of her own accord, the kiss from which she had so recently shrunk away. It was quite otherwise with Hepzibah; the judge's smile seemed to operate on her acerbity of heart like sunshine upon vinegar, making it ten times sourer than ever.

"Clifford," said she,—still too agitated to utter more than an abrupt sentence,—"Clifford has a home here!"

"May Heaven forgive you, Hepzibah," said Judge Pyncheon,—

reverently lifting his eyes towards that high court of equity to which he appealed,—"if you suffer any ancient prejudice or animosity to weigh with you in this matter. I stand here with an open heart, willing and anxious to receive yourself and Clifford into it. Do not refuse my good offices,—my earnest propositions for your welfare! They are such, in all respects, as it behooves your nearest kinsman to make. It will be a heavy responsibility, cousin, if you confine your brother to this dismal house and stifled air, when the delightful freedom of my country-seat is at his command."

"It would never suit Clifford," said Hepzibah, as briefly as before.

"Woman!" broke forth the judge, giving way to his resentment, "what is the meaning of all this? Have you other resources? Nay, I suspected as much! Take care, Hepzibah, take care! Clifford is on the brink of as black a ruin as ever befell him yet! But why do I talk with you, woman as you are? Make way!—I must see Clifford!"

Hepzibah spread out her gaunt figure across the door, and seemed really to increase in bulk; looking the more terrible, also, because there was so much terror and agitation in her heart. But Judge Pyncheon's evident purpose of forcing a passage was interrupted by a voice from the inner room; a weak, tremulous, wailing voice, indicating helpless alarm, with no more energy for self-defence than belongs to a frightened infant.

"Hepzibah, Hepzibah!" cried the voice; "go down on your knees to him! Kiss his feet! Entreat him not to come in! Oh, let him have mercy on me! Mercy! mercy!"

For the instant, it appeared doubtful whether it were not the judge's resolute purpose to set Hepzibah aside, and step across the threshold into the parlour, whence issued that broken and miserable murmur of entreaty. It was not pity that restrained him, for, at the first sound of the enfeebled voice, a red fire kindled in his eyes, and he made a quick pace forward, with something inexpressibly fierce and grim darkening forth, as it were, out of the whole man. To know Judge Pyncheon was to see him

118

at that moment. After such a revelation, let him smile with what sultriness he would, he could much sooner turn grapes purple, or pumpkins yellow, than melt the iron-branded impression out of the beholder's memory. And it rendered his aspect not the less, but more frightful, that it seemed not to express wrath or hatred, but a certain hot fellness of purpose, which annihilated everything but itself.

Yet, after all, are we not slandering an excellent and amiable man? Look at the judge now! He is apparently conscious of having erred, in too energetically pressing his deeds of loving-kindness on persons unable to appreciate them. He will await their better mood, and hold himself as ready to assist them then as at this moment. As he draws back from the door, an all-comprehensive benignity blazes from his visage, indicating that he gathers Hepzibah, little Phoebe, and the invisible Clifford, all three, together with the whole world besides, into his immense heart, and gives them a warm bath in its flood of affection.

"You do me great wrong, dear Cousin Hepzibah!" said he, first kindly offering her his hand, and then drawing on his glove preparatory to departure. "Very great wrong! But I forgive it, and will study to make you think better of me. Of course, our poor Clifford being in so unhappy a state of mind, I cannot think of urging an interview at present. But I shall watch over his welfare as if he were my own beloved brother; nor do I at all despair, my dear cousin, of constraining both him and you to acknowledge your injustice. When that shall happen, I desire no other revenge than your acceptance of the best offices in my power to do you."

With a bow to Hepzibah, and a degree of paternal benevolence in his parting nod to Phoebe, the judge left the shop, and went smiling along the street. As is customary with the rich, when they aim at the honors of a republic, he apologized, as it were, to the people, for his wealth, prosperity, and elevated station, by a free and hearty manner towards those who knew him; putting off the more of his dignity in due proportion with the humbleness of the man whom he saluted, and thereby proving a haughty consciousness of his advantages as irrefragably as if he had marched forth preceded by a troop of lackeys to clear the way. On this particular forenoon, so excessive was the warmth of Judge Pyncheon's kindly aspect, that (such, at least, was the rumour about town) an extra passage of the water-carts was found essential, in order to lay the dust occasioned by so much extra sunshine!

No sooner had he disappeared than Hepzibah grew deadly white, and, staggering towards Phoebe, let her head fall on the young girl's shoulder.

"O Phoebe!" murmured she, "that man has been the horror of my life! Shall I never, never have the courage,—will my voice never cease from trembling long enough to let me tell him what he is?"

"Is he so very wicked?" asked Phoebe. "Yet his offers were surely kind!"

"Do not speak of them,—he has a heart of iron!" rejoined Hepzibah. "Go, now, and talk to Clifford! Amuse and keep him quiet! It would disturb him wretchedly to see me so agitated as I am. There, go, dear child, and I will try to look after the shop."

Phoebe went accordingly, but perplexed herself, meanwhile, with queries as to the purport of the scene which she had just witnessed, and also whether judges, clergymen, and other characters of that eminent stamp and respectability, could really, in any single instance, be otherwise than just and upright men. A doubt of this nature has a most disturbing influence, and, if shown to be a fact, comes with fearful and startling effect on minds of the trim, orderly, and limit-loving class, in which we find our little country-girl. Dispositions more boldly speculative may derive a stern enjoyment from the discovery, since there must be evil in the world, that a high man is as likely to grasp his share of it as a low one.

A wider scope of view, and a deeper insight, may see rank, dignity, and station, all proved illusory, so far as regards their claim to human reverence, and yet not feel as if the universe were thereby tumbled headlong into chaos. But Phoebe, in order to keep the universe in its old place, was fain to smother, in some degree, her own intuitions as to Judge Pyncheon's character. And as for her cousin's testimony in disparagement of it, she concluded that Hepzibah's judgment was embittered by one of those family feuds which render hatred the more deadly by the dead and corrupted love that they intermingle with its native poison.

9: Clifford and Phoebe

Truly was there something high, generous, and noble in the native composition of our poor old Hepzibah! Or else,—and it was quite as probably the case,—she had been enriched by poverty, developed by sorrow, elevated by the strong and solitary affection of her life, and thus endowed with heroism, which never could have characterized her in what are called happier circumstances. Through dreary years Hepzibah had looked forward—for the most part despairingly, never with any confidence of hope, but always with the feeling that it was her brightest possibility—to the very position in which she now found herself. In her own behalf, she had asked nothing of Providence but the opportunity of devoting herself to this brother, whom she had so loved,—so admired for what he was, or might have been,—and to whom she had kept her faith, alone of all the world, wholly, unfalteringly, at every instant, and throughout life.

And here, in his late decline, the lost one had come back out of his long and strange misfortune, and was thrown on her sympathy, as it seemed, not merely for the bread of his physical existence, but for everything that should keep him morally alive. She had responded to the call. She had come forward,—our poor, gaunt Hepzibah, in her rusty silks, with her rigid joints, and the sad perversity of her scowl,—ready to do her utmost; and with affection enough, if that were all, to do a hundred times as much! There could be few more tearful sights,—and Heaven forgive us if a smile insist on mingling with our conception of it!—few sights with truer pathos in them, than Hepzibah presented on that first afternoon.

How patiently did she endeavour to wrap Clifford up in her great, warm love, and make it all the world to him, so that he should retain no torturing sense of the coldness and dreariness without! Her little efforts to amuse him! How pitiful, yet magnanimous, they were!

Remembering his early love of poetry and fiction, she unlocked a bookcase, and took down several books that had been excellent reading in their day. There was a volume of Pope, with the *Rape of the Lock* in it, and another of the *Tatler*, and an odd one of *Dryden's Miscellanies,* all with tarnished gilding on their covers, and thoughts of tarnished brilliancy inside. They had no success with Clifford. These, and all such writers of society, whose new works glow like the rich texture of a just-woven carpet, must be content to relinquish their charm, for every reader, after an age or two, and could hardly be supposed to retain any portion of it for a mind that had utterly lost its estimate of modes and manners.

Hepzibah then took up Rasselas, and began to read of the Happy Valley, with a vague idea that some secret of a contented life had there been elaborated, which might at least serve Clifford and herself for this one day. But the Happy Valley had a cloud over it. Hepzibah troubled her auditor, moreover, by innumerable sins of emphasis, which he seemed to detect, without any reference to the meaning; nor, in fact, did he appear to take much note of the sense of what she read, but evidently felt the tedium of the lecture, without harvesting its profit. His sister's voice, too, naturally harsh, had, in the course of her sorrowful lifetime, contracted a kind of croak, which, when it once gets into the human throat, is as ineradicable as sin.

In both sexes, occasionally, this lifelong croak, accompanying each word of joy or sorrow, is one of the symptoms of a settled melancholy; and wherever it occurs, the whole history of misfortune is conveyed in its slightest accent. The effect is as if the voice had been dyed black; or,—if we must use a more moderate simile,—this miserable croak, running through all the variations of the voice, is like a black silken thread, on which the crystal beads of speech are strung, and whence they take their hue. Such voices have put on mourning for dead hopes; and they ought to die and be buried along with them!

Discerning that Clifford was not gladdened by her efforts, Hepzibah searched about the house for the means of more exhilarating pastime. At one time, her eyes chanced to rest on Alice Pyncheon's harpsichord. It was a moment of great peril; for,—despite the traditionary awe that had gathered over this instrument of music, and the dirges which spiritual fingers were said to play on it,—the devoted sister had solemn thoughts of thrumming on its chords for Clifford's benefit, and accompanying the performance with her voice. Poor Clifford! Poor Hepzibah! Poor harpsichord! All three would have been miserable together. By some good agency,—possibly, by the unrecognized interposition of the long-buried Alice herself,—the threatening calamity was averted.

But the worst of all—the hardest stroke of fate for Hepzibah to endure, and perhaps for Clifford, too was his invincible distaste for her appearance. Her features, never the most agreeable, and now harsh with age and grief, and resentment against the world for his sake; her dress, and especially her turban; the queer and quaint manners, which had unconsciously grown upon her in solitude,—such being the poor gentlewoman's outward characteristics, it is no great marvel, although the mournfullest of pities, that the instinctive lover of the Beautiful was fain to turn away his eyes.

There was no help for it. It would be the latest impulse to die within him. In his last extremity, the expiring breath stealing faintly through Clifford's lips, he would doubtless press Hepzibah's hand, in fervent recognition of all her lavished love, and close his eyes,—but not so much to die, as to be constrained to look no longer on her face! Poor Hepzibah! She took counsel with herself what might be done, and thought of putting ribbons on her turban; but, by the instant rush of several guardian angels, was withheld from an experiment that could hardly have proved less than fatal to the beloved object of her anxiety.

To be brief, besides Hepzibah's disadvantages of person, there was an uncouthness pervading all her deeds; a clumsy something, that could but ill adapt itself for use, and not at all for ornament. She was a grief to Clifford, and she knew it. In this extremity, the antiquated virgin turned to Phoebe. No grovelling jealousy was in her heart. Had it pleased Heaven to crown the heroic fidelity of her life by making her personally the medium of Clifford's happiness, it would have rewarded her for all the past, by a joy with no bright tints, indeed, but deep and true, and worth a thousand gayer ecstasies. This could not be. She therefore turned to Phoebe, and resigned the task into the young girl's hands. The latter took it up cheerfully, as she did everything, but with no sense of a mission to perform, and succeeding all the better for that same simplicity.

By the involuntary effect of a genial temperament, Phoebe soon grew to be absolutely essential to the daily comfort, if not the daily life, of her two forlorn companions. The grime and sordidness of the House of the Seven Gables seemed to have vanished since her appearance there; the gnawing tooth of the dry-rot was stayed among the old timbers of its skeleton frame; the dust had ceased to settle down so densely, from the antique ceilings, upon the floors and furniture of the rooms below,—or, at any rate, there was a little housewife, as light-footed as the breeze that sweeps a garden walk, gliding hither and thither to brush it all away. The shadows of gloomy events that haunted the else lonely and desolate apartments; the heavy, breathless scent which death had left in more than one of the bedchambers, ever since his visits of long ago,—these were less powerful than the purifying influence scattered throughout the atmosphere of the household by the presence of one youthful, fresh, and thoroughly wholesome heart.

There was no morbidness in Phoebe; if there had been, the old Pyncheon House was the very locality to ripen it into incurable disease. But now her spirit resembled, in its potency, a minute quantity of ottar of rose in one of Hepzibah's huge, iron-bound trunks, diffusing its fragrance through the various articles of linen and wrought-lace, kerchiefs, caps, stockings, folded dresses, gloves, and whatever else was treasured there. As every article in the great trunk was the sweeter for the rose-scent, so did all the thoughts and emotions of Hepzibah and Clifford, sombre as they might seem, acquire a subtle attribute of happiness from Phoebe's intermixture with them. Her activity of body, intellect, and heart impelled her continually to perform the ordinary little toils that offered themselves around her, and to think the thought proper for the moment, and to sympathize,—now with the twittering gayety of the robins in the pear-tree, and now to such a depth as she could with Hepzibah's dark anxiety, or the vague moan of her brother. This facile adaptation was at once the symptom of perfect health and its best preservative.

A nature like Phoebe's has invariably its due influence, but is seldom regarded with due honor. Its spiritual force, however, may be partially estimated by the fact of her having found a place for herself, amid circumstances so stern as those which surrounded the mistress of the house; and also by the effect which she produced on a character of so much more mass than her own. For the gaunt, bony frame and limbs of Hepzibah, as compared with the tiny lightsomeness of Phoebe's figure, were perhaps in some fit proportion with the moral weight and substance, respectively, of the woman and the girl.

To the guest,—to Hepzibah's brother,—or Cousin Clifford, as Phoebe now began to call him,—she was especially necessary. Not that he could ever be said to converse with her, or often manifest, in any other very definite mode, his sense of a charm in her society. But if she were a long while absent he became pettish and nervously restless, pacing the room to and fro with the uncertainty that characterized all his movements; or else would sit broodingly in his great chair, resting his head on his hands, and evincing life only by an electric sparkle of ill-humour, whenever Hepzibah endeavoured to arouse him. Phoebe's presence, and the contiguity of her fresh life to his blighted one, was usually all that he required.

Indeed, such was the native gush and play of her spirit, that she was seldom perfectly quiet and undemonstrative, any more than a fountain ever ceases to dimple and warble with its flow. She possessed the gift of song, and that, too, so naturally, that you would as little think of inquiring whence she had caught it, or what master had taught her, as of asking the same questions about a bird, in whose small strain of music we recognize the voice of the Creator as distinctly as in the loudest accents of his thunder. So long as Phoebe sang, she might stray at her own will about the house.

Clifford was content, whether the sweet, airy homeliness of her tones came down from the upper chambers, or along the passageway from the shop, or was sprinkled through the foliage of the pear-tree, inward from the garden, with the twinkling sunbeams. He would sit quietly, with a gentle pleasure gleaming over his face, brighter now, and now a little dimmer, as the song happened to float near him, or was more remotely heard. It pleased him best, however, when she sat on a low footstool at his knee.

It is perhaps remarkable, considering her temperament, that Phoebe oftener chose a strain of pathos than of gayety. But the young and happy are not ill pleased to temper their life with a transparent shadow. The deepest pathos of Phoebe's voice and song, moreover, came sifted through the golden texture of a cheery spirit, and was somehow so interfused with the quality thence acquired, that one's heart felt all the lighter for having wept at it. Broad mirth, in the sacred presence of dark misfortune, would have jarred harshly and irreverently with the solemn symphony that rolled its undertone through Hepzibah's and her brother's life. Therefore, it was well that Phoebe so often chose sad themes, and not amiss that they ceased to be so sad while she was singing them.

Becoming habituated to her companionship, Clifford readily showed how capable of imbibing pleasant tints and gleams of cheerful light from all quarters his nature must originally have been. He grew youthful while she sat by him. A beauty,— not precisely real, even in its utmost manifestation, and which a painter would have watched long to seize and fix upon his canvas, and, after all, in vain,—beauty, nevertheless, that was not a mere dream, would sometimes play upon and illuminate his face. It did more than to illuminate; it transfigured him with an expression that could only be interpreted as the glow of an exquisite and happy spirit.

That gray hair, and those furrows,—with their record of infinite sorrow so deeply written across his brow, and so compressed, as with a futile effort to crowd in all the tale, that the whole inscription was made illegible,—these, for the moment, vanished. An eye at once tender and acute might have beheld in the man some shadow of what he was meant to be. *Anon*, as age came stealing, like a sad twilight, back over his figure, you would have felt tempted to hold an argument with Destiny, and affirm, that either this being should not have been made mortal, or mortal existence should have been tempered to his qualities. There seemed no necessity for his having drawn breath at all; the world never wanted him; but, as he had breathed, it ought always to have been the balmiest of summer air. The same perplexity will invariably haunt us with regard to natures that tend to feed exclusively upon the Beautiful, let their earthly fate be as lenient as it may.

Phoebe, it is probable, had but a very imperfect comprehension of the character over which she had thrown so beneficent a spell. Nor was it necessary. The fire upon the hearth can gladden a whole semicircle of faces round about it, but need not know the individuality of one among them all. Indeed, there was something too fine and delicate in Clifford's traits to be perfectly appreciated by one whose sphere lay so much in the Actual as Phoebe's did. For Clifford, however, the reality, and simplicity, and thorough homeliness of the girl's nature were as powerful a charm as any that she possessed. Beauty, it is true, and beauty almost perfect in its own style, was indispensable.

Had Phoebe been coarse in feature, shaped clumsily, of a harsh voice, and uncouthly mannered, she might have been rich with all good gifts, beneath this unfortunate exterior, and still, so long as she wore the guise of woman, she would have shocked Clifford, and depressed him by her lack of beauty. But nothing more beautiful—nothing prettier, at least—was ever made than Phoebe. And, therefore, to this man,—whose whole poor and impalpable enjoyment of existence heretofore, and until both his heart and fancy died within him, had been a dream,—whose images of women had more and more lost their warmth and substance, and been frozen, like the pictures of secluded artists, into the chillest ideality,—to him, this little figure of the cheeriest household life was just what he required to bring him back into the breathing world.

Persons who have wandered, or been expelled, out of the common track of things, even were it for a better system, desire nothing so much as to be led back. They shiver in their loneliness, be it on a mountain-top or in a dungeon. Now, Phoebe's presence made a home about her,—that very sphere which the outcast, the prisoner, the potentate,—the wretch beneath mankind, the wretch aside from it, or the wretch above it,—instinctively pines after,—a home! She was real! Holding her hand, you felt something; a tender something; a substance, and a warm one: and so long as you should feel its grasp, soft as it was, you might be certain that your place was good in the whole sympathetic chain of human nature. The world was no longer a delusion.

By looking a little further in this direction, we might suggest an explanation of an often-suggested mystery. Why are poets so apt to choose their mates, not for any similarity of poetic endowment, but for qualities which might make the happiness of the rudest handicraftsman as well as that of the ideal craftsman of the spirit? Because, probably, at his highest elevation, the poet needs no human intercourse; but he finds it dreary to descend, and be a stranger.

There was something very beautiful in the relation that grew up between this pair, so closely and constantly linked together, yet with such a waste of gloomy and mysterious years from his birthday to hers. On Clifford's part it was the feeling of a man naturally endowed with the liveliest sensibility to feminine influence, but who had never quaffed the cup of passionate love, and knew that it was now too late. He knew it, with the instinctive delicacy that had survived his intellectual decay. Thus, his sentiment for Phoebe, without being paternal, was not less chaste than if she had been his daughter. He was a man, it is true, and recognized her as a woman.

She was his only representative of womankind. He took unfailing note of every charm that appertained to her sex, and saw the ripeness of her lips, and the virginal development of her bosom. All her little womanly ways, budding out of her like blossoms on a young fruit-tree, had their effect on him, and sometimes caused his very heart to tingle with the keenest thrills of pleasure. At such moments,—for the effect was seldom more than momentary,—the half-torpid man would be full of harmonious life, just as a long-silent harp is full of sound, when the musician's fingers sweep across it.

But, after all, it seemed rather a perception, or a sympathy, than a sentiment belonging to himself as an individual. He read Phoebe as he would a sweet and simple story; he listened to her as if she were a verse of household poetry, which God, in requital of his bleak and dismal lot, had permitted some angel, that most pitied him, to warble through the house. She was not an actual fact for him, but the interpretation of all that he lacked on earth brought warmly home to his conception; so that this mere symbol, or life-like picture, had almost the comfort of reality.

But we strive in vain to put the idea into words. No adequate expression of the beauty and profound pathos with which it impresses us is attainable. This being, made only for happiness, and heretofore so miserably failing to be happy,—his tendencies so hideously thwarted, that, some unknown time ago, the delicate springs of his character, never morally or intellectually strong, had given way, and he was now imbecile,—this poor, forlorn voyager from the Islands of the Blest, in a frail bark, on a tempestuous sea, had been flung, by the last mountain-wave of his shipwreck, into a quiet harbour.

There, as he lay more than half lifeless on the strand, the fra-

129

grance of an earthly rose-bud had come to his nostrils, and, as odours will, had summoned up reminiscences or visions of all the living and breathing beauty amid which he should have had his home. With his native susceptibility of happy influences, he inhales the slight, ethereal rapture into his soul, and expires!

And how did Phoebe regard Clifford? The girl's was not one of those natures which are most attracted by what is strange and exceptional in human character. The path which would best have suited her was the well-worn track of ordinary life; the companions in whom she would most have delighted were such as one encounters at every turn. The mystery which enveloped Clifford, so far as it affected her at all, was an annoyance, rather than the piquant charm which many women might have found in it. Still, her native kindliness was brought strongly into play, not by what was darkly picturesque in his situation, nor so much, even, by the finer graces of his character, as by the simple appeal of a heart so forlorn as his to one so full of genuine sympathy as hers.

She gave him an affectionate regard, because he needed so much love, and seemed to have received so little. With a ready tact, the result of ever-active and wholesome sensibility, she discerned what was good for him, and did it. Whatever was morbid in his mind and experience she ignored; and thereby kept their intercourse healthy, by the incautious, but, as it were, heaven-directed freedom of her whole conduct. The sick in mind, and, perhaps, in body, are rendered more darkly and hopelessly so by the manifold reflection of their disease, mirrored back from all quarters in the deportment of those about them; they are compelled to inhale the poison of their own breath, in infinite repetition. But Phoebe afforded her poor patient a supply of purer air.

She impregnated it, too, not with a wild-flower scent,—for wildness was no trait of hers,—but with the perfume of garden-roses, pinks, and other blossoms of much sweetness, which nature and man have consented together in making grow from summer to summer, and from century to century. Such a flower was Phoebe in her relation with Clifford, and such the delight that he inhaled from her.

Yet, it must be said, her petals sometimes drooped a little, in consequence of the heavy atmosphere about her. She grew more thoughtful than heretofore. Looking aside at Clifford's face, and seeing the dim, unsatisfactory elegance and the intellect almost quenched, she would try to inquire what had been his life. Was he always thus? Had this veil been over him from his birth?—this veil, under which far more of his spirit was hidden than revealed, and through which he so imperfectly discerned the actual world,—or was its gray texture woven of some dark calamity? Phoebe loved no riddles, and would have been glad to escape the perplexity of this one.

Nevertheless, there was so far a good result of her meditations on Clifford's character, that, when her involuntary conjectures, together with the tendency of every strange circumstance to tell its own story, had gradually taught her the fact, it had no terrible effect upon her. Let the world have done him what vast wrong it might, she knew Cousin Clifford too well—or fancied so—ever to shudder at the touch of his thin, delicate fingers.

Within a few days after the appearance of this remarkable inmate, the routine of life had established itself with a good deal of uniformity in the old house of our narrative. In the morning, very shortly after breakfast, it was Clifford's custom to fall asleep in his chair; nor, unless accidentally disturbed, would he emerge from a dense cloud of slumber or the thinner mists that flitted to and fro, until well towards noonday. These hours of drowsihead were the season of the old gentlewoman's attendance on her brother, while Phoebe took charge of the shop; an arrangement which the public speedily understood, and evinced their decided preference of the younger shopwoman by the multiplicity of their calls during her administration of affairs.

Dinner over, Hepzibah took her knitting-work,—a long stocking of gray yarn, for her brother's winter wear,—and with a sigh, and a scowl of affectionate farewell to Clifford, and a gesture enjoining watchfulness on Phoebe, went to take her seat behind the counter. It was now the young girl's turn to be the nurse,—the guardian, the playmate,—or whatever is the fitter phrase,—of the gray-haired man.

10: THE PYNCHEON GARDEN

Clifford, except for Phoebe's more active instigation would ordinarily have yielded to the torpor which had crept through all his modes of being, and which sluggishly counselled him to sit in his morning chair till eventide. But the girl seldom failed to propose a removal to the garden, where Uncle Venner and the daguerreotypist had made such repairs on the roof of the ruinous arbour, or summer-house, that it was now a sufficient shelter from sunshine and casual showers. The hop-vine, too, had begun to grow luxuriantly over the sides of the little edifice, and made an interior of verdant seclusion, with innumerable peeps and glimpses into the wider solitude of the garden.

Here, sometimes, in this green play-place of flickering light, Phoebe read to Clifford. Her acquaintance, the artist, who appeared to have a literary turn, had supplied her with works of fiction, in pamphlet form,—and a few volumes of poetry, in altogether a different style and taste from those which Hepzibah selected for his amusement. Small thanks were due to the books, however, if the girl's readings were in any degree more successful than her elderly cousin's. Phoebe's voice had always a pretty music in it, and could either enliven Clifford by its sparkle and gayety of tone, or soothe him by a continued flow of pebbly and brook-like cadences.

But the fictions—in which the country-girl, unused to works of that nature, often became deeply absorbed—interested her strange auditor very little, or not at all. Pictures of life, scenes of passion or sentiment, wit, humour, and pathos, were all thrown away, or worse than thrown away, on Clifford; either because he lacked an experience by which to test their truth, or because his own griefs were a touch-stone of reality that few feigned emotions could withstand. When Phoebe broke into a peal of merry laughter at what she read, he would now and then laugh for sympathy, but oftener respond with a troubled, questioning look. If a tear—a maiden's sunshiny tear over imaginary woe—dropped upon some melancholy page, Clifford either took it as a token of actual calamity, or else grew peevish, and angrily motioned her to close the volume. And wisely too! Is not the world sad enough, in genuine earnest, without making a pastime of mock sorrows?

With poetry it was rather better. He delighted in the swell and subsidence of the rhythm, and the happily recurring rhyme. Nor was Clifford incapable of feeling the sentiment of poetry,—not, perhaps, where it was highest or deepest, but where it was most flitting and ethereal. It was impossible to foretell in what exquisite verse the awakening spell might lurk; but, on raising her eyes from the page to Clifford's face, Phoebe would be made aware, by the light breaking through it, that a more delicate intelligence than her own had caught a lambent flame from what she read. One glow of this kind, however, was often the precursor of gloom for many hours afterward; because, when the glow left him, he seemed conscious of a missing sense and power, and groped about for them, as if a blind man should go seeking his lost eyesight.

It pleased him more, and was better for his inward welfare, that Phoebe should talk, and make passing occurrences vivid to his mind by her accompanying description and remarks. The life of the garden offered topics enough for such discourse as suited Clifford best. He never failed to inquire what flowers had bloomed since yesterday. His feeling for flowers was very exquisite, and seemed not so much a taste as an emotion; he was fond of sitting with one in his hand, intently observing it, and looking from its petals into Phoebe's face, as if the garden flower were the sister of the household maiden.

Not merely was there a delight in the flower's perfume, or pleasure in its beautiful form, and the delicacy or brightness of its hue; but Clifford's enjoyment was accompanied with a perception of life, character, and individuality, that made him love these blossoms of the garden, as if they were endowed with sentiment and intelligence. This affection and sympathy for flowers is almost exclusively a woman's trait. Men, if endowed with it by nature, soon lose, forget, and learn to despise it, in their contact with coarser things than flowers. Clifford, too, had long forgotten it; but found it again now, as he slowly revived from the chill torpor of his life.

It is wonderful how many pleasant incidents continually came to pass in that secluded garden-spot when once Phoebe had set herself to look for them. She had seen or heard a bee there, on the first day of her acquaintance with the place. And often,—almost continually, indeed,—since then, the bees kept coming thither, Heaven knows why, or by what pertinacious desire, for far-fetched sweets, when, no doubt, there were broad clover-fields, and all kinds of garden growth, much nearer home than this.

Thither the bees came, however, and plunged into the squash-blossoms, as if there were no other squash-vines within a long day's flight, or as if the soil of Hepzibah's garden gave its productions just the very quality which these laborious little wizards wanted, in order to impart the Hymettus odour to their whole hive of New England honey. When Clifford heard their sunny, buzzing murmur, in the heart of the great yellow blossoms, he looked about him with a joyful sense of warmth, and blue sky, and green grass, and of God's free air in the whole height from earth to heaven. After all, there need be no question why the bees came to that one green nook in the dusty town. God sent them thither to gladden our poor Clifford. They brought the rich summer with them, in requital of a little honey.

When the bean-vines began to flower on the poles, there was one particular variety which bore a vivid scarlet blossom. The daguerreotypist had found these beans in a garret, over one of the seven gables, treasured up in an old chest of drawers by some horticultural Pyncheon of days gone by, who doubtless meant to sow them the next summer, but was himself first sown in Death's garden-ground. By way of testing whether there were still a living germ in such ancient seeds, Holgrave had planted some of them; and the result of his experiment was a splendid row of bean-vines, clambering, early, to the full height of the poles, and arraying them, from top to bottom, in a spiral profusion of red blossoms.

And, ever since the unfolding of the first bud, a multitude of humming-birds had been attracted thither. At times, it seemed as if for every one of the hundred blossoms there was one of these tiniest fowls of the air,—a thumb's bigness of burnished plumage, hovering and vibrating about the bean-poles. It was with indescribable interest, and even more than childish delight, that Clifford watched the humming-birds. He used to thrust his head softly out of the arbor to see them the better; all the while, too, motioning Phoebe to be quiet, and snatching glimpses of the smile upon her face, so as to heap his enjoyment up the higher with her sympathy. He had not merely grown young;— he was a child again.

Hepzibah, whenever she happened to witness one of these fits of miniature enthusiasm, would shake her head, with a strange mingling of the mother and sister, and of pleasure and sadness, in her aspect. She said that it had always been thus with Clifford when the humming-birds came,—always, from his babyhood,— and that his delight in them had been one of the earliest tokens by which he showed his love for beautiful things. And it was a wonderful coincidence, the good lady thought, that the artist should have planted these scarlet-flowering beans—which the humming-birds sought far and wide, and which had not grown in the Pyncheon garden before for forty years—on the very summer of Clifford's return.

Then would the tears stand in poor Hepzibah's eyes, or overflow them with a too abundant gush, so that she was fain to betake herself into some corner, lest Clifford should espy her agitation. Indeed, all the enjoyments of this period were provocative of tears. Coming so late as it did, it was a kind of Indian summer, with a mist in its balmiest sunshine, and decay and death in its gaudiest delight. The more Clifford seemed to taste the happiness of a child, the sadder was the difference to be recognized.

With a mysterious and terrible Past, which had annihilated his memory, and a blank Future before him, he had only this visionary and impalpable

Now, which, if you once look closely at it, is nothing. He himself, as was perceptible by many symptoms, lay darkly behind his pleasure, and knew it to be a baby-play, which he was to toy and trifle with, instead of thoroughly believing. Clifford saw, it may be, in the mirror of his deeper consciousness, that he was an example and representative of that great class of people whom an inexplicable Providence is continually putting at cross-purposes with the world: breaking what seems its own promise in their nature; withholding their proper food, and setting poison before them for a banquet; and thus—when it might so easily, as one would think, have been adjusted otherwise—making their existence a strangeness, a solitude, and torment.

All his life long, he had been learning how to be wretched, as one learns a foreign tongue; and now, with the lesson thoroughly by heart, he could with difficulty comprehend his little airy happiness. Frequently there was a dim shadow of doubt in his eyes. "Take my hand, Phoebe," he would say, "and pinch it hard with your little fingers! Give me a rose, that I may press its thorns, and prove myself awake by the sharp touch of pain!" Evidently, he desired this prick of a trifling anguish, in order to assure himself, by that quality which he best knew to be real, that the garden, and the seven weather-beaten gables, and Hepzibah's scowl, and Phoebe's smile, were real likewise. Without this signet in his flesh, he could have attributed no more substance to them than to the empty confusion of imaginary scenes with which he had fed his spirit, until even that poor sustenance was exhausted.

The author needs great faith in his reader's sympathy; else he must hesitate to give details so minute, and incidents apparently so trifling, as are essential to make up the idea of this garden-life. It was the Eden of a thunder-smitten Adam, who had fled for refuge thither out of the same dreary and perilous wilderness into which the original Adam was expelled.

One of the available means of amusement, of which Phoebe made the most in Clifford's behalf, was that feathered society, the hens, a breed of whom, as we have already said, was an immemorial heirloom in the Pyncheon family. In compliance with a whim of Clifford, as it troubled him to see them in confinement, they had been set at liberty, and now roamed at will about the garden; doing some little mischief, but hindered from escape by buildings on three sides, and the difficult peaks of a wooden fence on the other.

They spent much of their abundant leisure on the margin of Maule's well, which was haunted by a kind of snail, evidently a titbit to their palates; and the brackish water itself, however nauseous to the rest of the world, was so greatly esteemed by these fowls, that they might be seen tasting, turning up their heads, and smacking their bills, with precisely the air of wine-bibbers round a probationary cask. Their generally quiet, yet often brisk, and constantly diversified talk, one to another, or sometimes in soliloquy,—as they scratched worms out of the rich, black soil, or pecked at such plants as suited their taste,—had such a domestic tone, that it was almost a wonder why you could not establish a regular interchange of ideas about household matters, human and gallinaceous.

All hens are well worth studying for the piquancy and rich variety of their manners; but by no possibility can there have been other fowls of such odd appearance and deportment as these ancestral ones. They probably embodied the traditionary peculiarities of their whole line of progenitors, derived through an unbroken succession of eggs; or else this individual Chanticleer and his two wives had grown to be humourists, and a little crack-brained withal, on account of their solitary way of life, and out of sympathy for Hepzibah, their lady-patroness.

Queer, indeed, they looked! Chanticleer himself, though stalking on two stilt-like legs, with the dignity of interminable descent in all his gestures, was hardly bigger than an ordinary partridge; his two wives were about the size of quails; and as for the one chicken, it looked small enough to be still in the egg, and, at the same time, sufficiently old, withered, wizened, and experienced, to have been founder of the antiquated race. Instead of being the youngest of the family, it rather seemed to have aggregated into itself the ages, not only of these living specimens of the breed, but of all its forefathers and foremothers, whose united excellences and oddities were squeezed into its little body. Its mother evidently regarded it as the one chicken of the world, and as necessary, in fact, to the world's continuance, or, at any rate, to the equilibrium of the present system of affairs, whether in church or state.

No lesser sense of the infant fowl's importance could have justified, even in a mother's eyes, the perseverance with which she watched over its safety, ruffling her small person to twice its proper size, and flying in everybody's face that so much as looked towards her hopeful progeny. No lower estimate could have vindicated the indefatigable zeal with which she scratched, and her unscrupulousness in digging up the choicest flower or vegetable, for the sake of the fat earthworm at its root. Her nervous cluck, when the chicken happened to be hidden in the long grass or under the squash-leaves; her gentle croak of satisfaction, while sure of it beneath her wing; her note of ill-concealed fear and obstreperous defiance, when she saw her arch-enemy, a neighbour's cat, on the top of the high fence,—one or other of these sounds was to be heard at almost every moment of the day. By degrees, the observer came to feel nearly as much interest in this chicken of illustrious race as the mother-hen did.

Phoebe, after getting well acquainted with the old hen, was sometimes permitted to take the chicken in her hand, which was quite capable of grasping its cubic inch or two of body. While she curiously examined its hereditary marks,—the peculiar speckle of its plumage, the funny tuft on its head, and a knob on each of its legs,—the little biped, as she insisted, kept giving her a sagacious wink. The daguerreotypist once whispered her that these marks betokened the oddities of the Pyncheon family, and that the chicken itself was a symbol of the life of the old house, embodying its interpretation, likewise, although an unintelligible one, as such clews generally are. It was a feathered riddle; a mystery hatched out of an egg, and just as mysterious as if the egg had been addle!

The second of Chanticleer's two wives, ever since Phoebe's arrival, had been in a state of heavy despondency, caused, as it afterwards appeared, by her inability to lay an egg. One day, however, by her self-important gait, the sideways turn of her head, and the cock of her eye, as she pried into one and another nook of the garden,—croaking to herself, all the while, with inexpressible complacency,—it was made evident that this identical hen, much as mankind undervalued her, carried something about her person the worth of which was not to be estimated either in gold or precious stones.

Shortly after, there was a prodigious cackling and gratulation of Chanticleer and all his family, including the wizened chicken, who appeared to understand the matter quite as well as did his sire, his mother, or his aunt. That afternoon Phoebe found a diminutive egg,—not in the regular nest, it was far too precious to be trusted there,—but cunningly hidden under the currant-bushes, on some dry stalks of last year's grass. Hepzibah, on learning the fact, took possession of the egg and appropriated it to Clifford's breakfast, on account of a certain delicacy of flavour, for which, as she affirmed, these eggs had always been famous. Thus unscrupulously did the old gentlewoman sacrifice the continuance, perhaps, of an ancient feathered race, with no better end than to supply her brother with a dainty that hardly filled the bowl of a tea-spoon!

It must have been in reference to this outrage that Chanticleer, the next day, accompanied by the bereaved mother of the egg, took his post in front of Phoebe and Clifford, and delivered himself of a harangue that might have proved as long as his own pedigree, but for a fit of merriment on Phoebe's part. Hereupon, the offended fowl stalked away on his long stilts, and utterly withdrew his notice from Phoebe and the rest of human nature, until she made her peace with an offering of spice-cake, which, next to snails, was the delicacy most in favour with his aristocratic taste.

We linger too long, no doubt, beside this paltry rivulet of life that flowed through the garden of the Pyncheon House. But we deem it pardonable to record these mean incidents and poor delights, because they proved so greatly to Clifford's benefit. They had the earth-smell in them, and contributed to give him health and substance. Some of his occupations wrought less desirably upon him. He had a singular propensity, for example, to hang over Maule's well, and look at the constantly shifting phantasmagoria of figures produced by the agitation of the water over the mosaic-work of coloured pebbles at the bottom.

He said that faces looked upward to him there,—beautiful faces, arrayed in bewitching smiles,—each momentary face so fair and rosy, and every smile so sunny, that he felt wronged at its departure, until the same flitting witchcraft made a new one. But sometimes he would suddenly cry out, "The dark face gazes at me!" and be miserable the whole day afterwards. Phoebe, when she hung over the fountain by Clifford's side, could see nothing of all this,—neither the beauty nor the ugliness,—but only the coloured pebbles, looking as if the gush of the waters shook and disarranged them.

And the dark face, that so troubled Clifford, was no more than the shadow thrown from a branch of one of the damson-trees, and breaking the inner light of Maule's well. The truth was, however, that his fancy—reviving faster than his will and judgment, and always stronger than they—created shapes of loveliness that were symbolic of his native character, and now and then a stern and dreadful shape that typified his fate.

On Sundays, after Phoebe had been at church,—for the girl had a church-going conscience, and would hardly have been at ease had she missed either prayer, singing, sermon, or benediction,—after church-time, therefore, there was, ordinarily, a sober little festival in the garden. In addition to Clifford, Hepzibah, and Phoebe, two guests made up the company. One was the artist Holgrave, who, in spite of his consociation with reformers, and his other queer and questionable traits, continued to hold an elevated place in Hepzibah's regard.

The other, we are almost ashamed to say, was the venerable Uncle Venner, in a clean shirt, and a broadcloth coat, more respectable than his ordinary wear, inasmuch as it was neatly patched on each elbow, and might be called an entire garment, except for a slight inequality in the length of its skirts. Clifford, on several occasions, had seemed to enjoy the old man's intercourse, for the sake of his mellow, cheerful vein, which was like the sweet flavor of a frost-bitten apple, such as one picks up under the tree in December.

A man at the very lowest point of the social scale was easier and more agreeable for the fallen gentleman to encounter than a person at any of the intermediate degrees; and, moreover, as Clifford's young manhood had been lost, he was fond of feeling himself comparatively youthful, now, in apposition with the patriarchal age of Uncle Venner. In fact, it was sometimes observable that Clifford half wilfully hid from himself the consciousness of being stricken in years, and cherished visions of an earthly future still before him; visions, however, too indistinctly drawn to be followed by disappointment—though, doubtless, by depression—when any casual incident or recollection made him sensible of the withered leaf.

So this oddly composed little social party used to assemble under the ruinous arbour. Hepzibah—stately as ever at heart, and yielding not an inch of her old gentility, but resting upon it so much the more, as justifying a princess-like condescension—exhibited a not ungraceful hospitality. She talked kindly to the vagrant artist, and took sage counsel—lady as she was—with the wood-sawyer, the messenger of everybody's petty errands, the patched philosopher. And Uncle Venner, who had studied the world at street-corners, and other posts equally well adapted for just observation, was as ready to give out his wisdom as a town-pump to give water.

"Miss Hepzibah, ma'am," said he once, after they had all been cheerful together, "I really enjoy these quiet little meetings of a Sabbath afternoon. They are very much like what I expect to have after I retire to my farm!"

"Uncle Venner" observed Clifford in a drowsy, inward tone, "is always talking about his farm. But I have a better scheme for him, by and by. We shall see!"

"Ah, Mr. Clifford Pyncheon!" said the man of patches, "you may scheme for me as much as you please; but I'm not going to give up this one scheme of my own, even if I never bring it really to pass. It does seem to me that men make a wonderful mistake in trying to heap up property upon property. If I had done so, I should feel as if Providence was not bound to take care of me; and, at all events, the city wouldn't be! I'm one of those people who think that infinity is big enough for us all—and eternity long enough."

"Why, so they are, Uncle Venner," remarked Phoebe after a pause; for she had been trying to fathom the profundity and appositeness of this concluding apothegm. "But for this short life of ours, one would like a house and a moderate garden-spot of one's own."

"It appears to me," said the daguerreotypist, smiling, "that Uncle Venner has the principles of Fourier at the bottom of his wisdom; only they have not quite so much distinctness in his mind as in that of the systematizing Frenchman."

"Come, Phoebe," said Hepzibah, "it is time to bring the currants."

And then, while the yellow richness of the declining sunshine still fell into the open space of the garden, Phoebe brought out a loaf of bread and a china bowl of currants, freshly gathered from the bushes, and crushed with sugar. These, with water,—but not from the fountain of ill omen, close at hand,—constituted all the entertainment. Meanwhile, Holgrave took some pains to establish an intercourse with Clifford, actuated, it might seem, entirely by an impulse of kindliness, in order that the present hour might be cheerfuller than most which the poor recluse had spent, or was destined yet to spend.

Nevertheless, in the artist's deep, thoughtful, all-observant eyes, there was, now and then, an expression, not sinister, but questionable; as if he had some other interest in the scene than a stranger, a youthful and unconnected adventurer, might be supposed to have. With great mobility of outward mood, however, he applied himself to the task of enlivening the party; and with so much success, that even dark-hued Hepzibah threw off one tint of melancholy, and made what shift she could with the remaining portion. Phoebe said to herself,—"How pleasant he can be!" As for Uncle Venner, as a mark of friendship and approbation, he readily consented to afford the young man his countenance in the way of his profession,—not metaphorically, be it understood, but literally, by allowing a daguerreotype of his face, so familiar to the town, to be exhibited at the entrance of Holgrave's studio.

Clifford, as the company partook of their little banquet, grew to be the gayest of them all. Either it was one of those up-quivering flashes of the spirit, to which minds in an abnormal state are liable, or else the artist had subtly touched some chord that made musical vibration. Indeed, what with the pleasant summer evening, and the sympathy of this little circle of not unkindly souls, it was perhaps natural that a character so susceptible as Clifford's should become animated, and show itself readily responsive to what was said around him. But he gave out his own thoughts, likewise, with an airy and fanciful glow; so that they glistened, as it were, through the arbour, and made their escape among the interstices of the foliage. He had been as cheerful, no doubt, while alone with Phoebe, but never with such tokens of acute, although partial intelligence.

But, as the sunlight left the peaks of the Seven Gables, so did the excitement fade out of Clifford's eyes. He gazed vaguely and mournfully about him, as if he missed something precious, and missed it the more drearily for not knowing precisely what it was.

"I want my happiness!" at last he murmured hoarsely and indistinctly, hardly shaping out the words. "Many, many years have I waited for it! It is late! It is late! I want my happiness!"

Alas, poor Clifford! You are old, and worn with troubles that ought never to have befallen you. You are partly crazy and partly imbecile; a ruin, a failure, as almost everybody is,—though some in less degree, or less perceptibly, than their fellows. Fate has no happiness in store for you; unless your quiet home in the old family residence with the faithful Hepzibah, and your long summer afternoons with Phoebe, and these Sabbath festivals with Uncle Venner and the daguerreotypist, deserve to be called happiness! Why not? If not the thing itself, it is marvellously like it, and the more so for that ethereal and intangible quality which causes it all to vanish at too close an introspection. Take it, therefore, while you may. Murmur not,—question not,—but make the most of it!

11: THE ARCHED WINDOW

From the inertness, or what we may term the vegetative character, of his ordinary mood, Clifford would perhaps have been content to spend one day after another, interminably,— or, at least, throughout the summer-time,—in just the kind of life described in the preceding pages. Fancying, however, that it might be for his benefit occasionally to diversify the scene, Phoebe sometimes suggested that he should look out upon the life of the street. For this purpose, they used to mount the staircase together, to the second story of the house, where, at the termination of a wide entry, there was an arched window, of uncommonly large dimensions, shaded by a pair of curtains. It opened above the porch, where there had formerly been a balcony, the balustrade of which had long since gone to decay, and been removed.

At this arched window, throwing it open, but keeping himself in comparative obscurity by means of the curtain, Clifford had an opportunity of witnessing such a portion of the great world's movement as might be supposed to roll through one of the retired streets of a not very populous city. But he and Phoebe made a sight as well worth seeing as any that the city could exhibit. The pale, gray, childish, aged, melancholy, yet often simply cheerful, and sometimes delicately intelligent aspect of Clifford, peering from behind the faded crimson of the curtain,—watching the monotony of every-day occurrences with a kind of inconsequential interest and earnestness, and, at every petty throb of his sensibility, turning for sympathy to the eyes of the bright young girl!

If once he were fairly seated at the window, even Pyncheon Street would hardly be so dull and lonely but that, somewhere or other along its extent, Clifford might discover matter to occupy his eye, and titillate, if not engross, his observation. Things familiar to the youngest child that had begun its outlook at existence seemed strange to him. A cab; an omnibus, with its populous interior, dropping here and there a passenger, and picking up another, and thus typifying that vast rolling vehicle, the world, the end of whose journey is everywhere and nowhere; these objects he followed eagerly with his eyes, but forgot them before the dust raised by the horses and wheels had settled along their track.

As regarded novelties (among which cabs and omnibuses were to be reckoned), his mind appeared to have lost its proper gripe and retentiveness. Twice or thrice, for example, during the sunny hours of the day, a water-cart went along by the Pyncheon House, leaving a broad wake of moistened earth, instead of the white dust that had risen at a lady's lightest footfall; it was like a summer shower, which the city authorities had caught and tamed, and compelled it into the commonest routine of their convenience. With the water-cart Clifford could never grow familiar; it always affected him with just the same surprise as at first. His mind took an apparently sharp impression from it, but lost the recollection of this perambulatory shower, before its next reappearance, as completely as did the street itself, along which the heat so quickly strewed white dust again. It was the same with the railroad.

Clifford could hear the obstreperous howl of the steam-devil, and, by leaning a little way from the arched window, could catch a glimpse of the trains of cars, flashing a brief transit across the extremity of the street. The idea of terrible energy thus forced upon him was new at every recurrence, and seemed to affect him as disagreeably, and with almost as much surprise, the hundredth time as the first.

Nothing gives a sadder sense of decay than this loss or suspension of the power to deal with unaccustomed things, and to keep up with the swiftness of the passing moment. It can merely be a suspended animation; for, were the power actually to perish, there would be little use of immortality. We are less than ghosts, for the time being, whenever this calamity befalls us.

Clifford was indeed the most inveterate of conservatives. All the antique fashions of the street were dear to him; even such as were characterized by a rudeness that would naturally have annoyed his fastidious senses. He loved the old rumbling and jolting carts, the former track of which he still found in his long-buried remembrance, as the observer of to-day finds the wheel-tracks of ancient vehicles in Herculaneum. The butcher's cart, with its snowy canopy, was an acceptable object; so was the fish-cart, heralded by its horn; so, likewise, was the countryman's cart of vegetables, plodding from door to door, with long pauses of the patient horse, while his owner drove a trade in turnips, carrots, summer-squashes, string-beans, green peas, and new potatoes, with half the housewives of the neighbourhood.

The baker's cart, with the harsh music of its bells, had a pleasant effect on Clifford, because, as few things else did, it jingled the very dissonance of yore. One afternoon a scissor-grinder chanced to set his wheel a-going under the Pyncheon Elm, and just in front of the arched window. Children came running with their mothers' scissors, or the carving-knife, or the paternal razor, or anything else that lacked an edge (except, indeed, poor Clifford's wits), that the grinder might apply the article to his magic wheel, and give it back as good as new.

Round went the busily revolving machinery, kept in motion by the scissor-grinder's foot, and wore away the hard steel against the hard stone, whence issued an intense and spiteful prolongation of a hiss as fierce as those emitted by Satan and his compeers in Pandemonium, though squeezed into smaller compass. It was an ugly, little, venomous serpent of a noise, as ever did petty violence to human ears. But Clifford listened with rapturous delight. The sound, however disagreeable, had very brisk life in it, and, together with the circle of curious children watching the revolutions of the wheel, appeared to give him a more vivid sense of active, bustling, and sunshiny existence than he had attained in almost any other way. Nevertheless, its charm lay chiefly in the past; for the scissor-grinder's wheel had hissed in his childish ears.

He sometimes made doleful complaint that there were no stage-coaches nowadays. And he asked in an injured tone what had become of all those old square-topped chaises, with wings sticking out on either side, that used to be drawn by a plough-horse, and driven by a farmer's wife and daughter, peddling whortle-berries and blackberries about the town. Their disappearance made him doubt, he said, whether the berries had not left off growing in the broad pastures and along the shady country lanes.

But anything that appealed to the sense of beauty, in however humble a way, did not require to be recommended by these old associations. This was observable when one of those Italian boys (who are rather a modern feature of our streets) came along with his barrel-organ, and stopped under the wide and cool shadows of the elm. With his quick professional eye he took note of the two faces watching him from the arched window, and, opening his instrument, began to scatter its melodies abroad.

He had a monkey on his shoulder, dressed in a Highland plaid; and, to complete the sum of splendid attractions wherewith he presented himself to the public, there was a company of little figures, whose sphere and habitation was in the mahogany case of his organ, and whose principle of life was the music which the Italian made it his business to grind out. In all their variety of occupation,—the cobbler, the blacksmith, the soldier, the lady with her fan, the toper with his bottle, the milk-maid sitting by her cow—this fortunate little society might truly be said to enjoy a harmonious existence, and to make life literally a dance.

The Italian turned a crank; and, behold! every one of these small individuals started into the most curious vivacity. The cobbler wrought upon a shoe; the blacksmith hammered his iron, the soldier waved his glittering blade; the lady raised a tiny breeze with her fan; the jolly toper swigged lustily at his bottle; a scholar opened his book with eager thirst for knowledge, and turned his head to and fro along the page; the milkmaid energetically drained her cow; and a miser counted gold into his strong-box,—all at the same turning of a crank. Yes; and, moved by the self-same impulse, a lover saluted his mistress on her lips! Possibly some cynic, at once merry and bitter, had desired to signify, in this pantomimic scene, that we mortals, whatever our business or amusement,—however serious, however trifling,—all dance to one identical tune, and, in spite of our ridiculous activity, bring nothing finally to pass. For the most remarkable aspect of the affair was, that, at the cessation of the music, everybody was petrified at once, from the most extravagant life into a dead torpor.

Neither was the cobbler's shoe finished, nor the blacksmith's iron shaped out; nor was there a drop less of brandy in the toper's bottle, nor a drop more of milk in the milkmaid's pail, nor one additional coin in the miser's strong-box, nor was the scholar a page deeper in his book. All were precisely in the same condition as before they made themselves so ridiculous by their haste to toil, to enjoy, to accumulate gold, and to become wise. Saddest of all, moreover, the lover was none the happier for the maiden's granted kiss! But, rather than swallow this last too acrid ingredient, we reject the whole moral of the show.

The monkey, meanwhile, with a thick tail curling out into preposterous prolixity from beneath his tartans, took his station at the Italian's feet. He turned a wrinkled and abominable little visage to every passer-by, and to the circle of children that soon gathered round, and to Hepzibah's shop-door, and upward to the arched window, whence Phoebe and Clifford were looking down. Every moment, also, he took off his Highland bonnet, and performed a bow and scrape. Sometimes, moreover, he made personal application to individuals, holding out his small black palm, and otherwise plainly signifying his excessive desire for whatever filthy lucre might happen to be in anybody's pocket.

The mean and low, yet strangely man-like expression of his wilted countenance; the prying and crafty glance, that showed him ready to gripe at every miserable advantage; his enormous tail (too enormous to be decently concealed under his gabardine), and the deviltry of nature which it betokened,—take this monkey just as he was, in short, and you could desire no better image of the Mammon of copper coin, symbolizing the grossest form of the love of money. Neither was there any possibility of satisfying the covetous little devil. Phoebe threw down a whole handful of cents, which he picked up with joyless eagerness, handed them over to the Italian for safekeeping, and immediately recommenced a series of pantomimic petitions for more.

Doubtless, more than one New-Englander—or, let him be of what country he might, it is as likely to be the case—passed by, and threw a look at the monkey, and went on, without imagining how nearly his own moral condition was here exemplified. Clifford, however, was a being of another order. He had taken childish delight in the music, and smiled, too, at the figures which it set in motion. But, after looking awhile at the long-tailed imp, he was so shocked by his horrible ugliness, spiritual as well as physical, that he actually began to shed tears; a weakness which men of merely delicate endowments, and destitute of the fiercer, deeper, and more tragic power of laughter, can hardly avoid, when the worst and meanest aspect of life happens to be presented to them.

Pyncheon Street was sometimes enlivened by spectacles of more imposing pretensions than the above, and which brought the multitude along with them. With a shivering repugnance at the idea of personal contact with the world, a powerful impulse still seized on Clifford, whenever the rush and roar of the human tide grew strongly audible to him. This was made evident, one day, when a political procession, with hundreds of flaunting banners, and drums, fifes, clarions, and cymbals, reverberating between the rows of buildings, marched all through town, and trailed its length of trampling footsteps, and most infrequent uproar, past the ordinarily quiet House of the Seven Gables. As a mere object of sight, nothing is more deficient in picturesque features than a procession seen in its passage through narrow streets.

The spectator feels it to be fool's play, when he can distinguish the tedious commonplace of each man's visage, with the perspiration and weary self-importance on it, and the very cut of his pantaloons, and the stiffness or laxity of his shirt-collar, and the dust on the back of his black coat. In order to become majestic, it should be viewed from some vantage point, as it rolls its slow and long array through the centre of a wide plain, or the stateliest public square of a city; for then, by its remoteness, it melts all the petty personalities, of which it is made up, into one broad mass of existence,—one great life,—one collected body of mankind, with a vast, homogeneous spirit animating it. But, on the other hand, if an impressible person, standing alone over the brink of one of these processions, should behold it, not in its atoms, but in its aggregate,—as a mighty river of life, massive in its tide, and black with mystery, and, out of its depths, calling to the kindred depth within him,—then the contiguity would add to the effect. It might so fascinate him that he would hardly be restrained from plunging into the surging stream of human sympathies.

So it proved with Clifford. He shuddered; he grew pale; he threw an appealing look at Hepzibah and Phoebe, who were with him at the window. They comprehended nothing of his emotions, and supposed him merely disturbed by the unaccustomed tumult. At last, with tremulous limbs, he started up, set his foot on the window-sill, and in an instant more would have been in the unguarded balcony. As it was, the whole procession might have seen him, a wild, haggard figure, his gray locks floating in the wind that waved their banners; a lonely being, estranged from his race, but now feeling himself man again, by virtue of the irrepressible instinct that possessed him.

Had Clifford attained the balcony, he would probably have leaped into the street; but whether impelled by the species of terror that sometimes urges its victim over the very precipice which he shrinks from, or by a natural magnetism, tending towards the great centre of humanity, it were not easy to decide. Both impulses might have wrought on him at once.

But his companions, affrighted by his gesture,—which was that of a man hurried away in spite of himself,—seized Clifford's garment and held him back. Hepzibah shrieked. Phoebe, to whom all extravagance was a horror, burst into sobs and tears.

"Clifford, Clifford! are you crazy?" cried his sister.

"I hardly know, Hepzibah," said Clifford, drawing a long breath. "Fear nothing,—it is over now,—but had I taken that plunge, and survived it, methinks it would have made me another man!"

Possibly, in some sense, Clifford may have been right. He needed a shock; or perhaps he required to take a deep, deep plunge into the ocean of human life, and to sink down and be covered by its profoundness, and then to emerge, sobered, invigorated, restored to the world and to himself. Perhaps again, he required nothing less than the great final remedy—death!

A similar yearning to renew the broken links of brotherhood with his kind sometimes showed itself in a milder form; and once it was made beautiful by the religion that lay even deeper than itself. In the incident now to be sketched, there was a touching recognition, on Clifford's part, of God's care and love towards him,—towards this poor, forsaken man, who, if any mortal could, might have been pardoned for regarding himself as thrown aside, forgotten, and left to be the sport of some fiend, whose playfulness was an ecstasy of mischief.

It was the Sabbath morning; one of those bright, calm Sabbaths, with its own hallowed atmosphere, when Heaven seems to diffuse itself over the earth's face in a solemn smile, no less sweet than solemn. On such a Sabbath morn, were we pure enough to be its medium, we should be conscious of the earth's natural worship ascending through our frames, on whatever spot of ground we stood. The church-bells, with various tones, but all in harmony, were calling out and responding to one another,— "It is the Sabbath!—The Sabbath!—Yea; the Sabbath!"—and over the whole city the bells scattered the blessed sounds, now slowly, now with livelier joy, now one bell alone, now all the bells together, crying earnestly,—"It is the Sabbath!"—and flinging their accents afar off, to melt into the air and pervade it with the holy word. The air with God's sweetest and tenderest sunshine in it, was meet for mankind to breathe into their hearts, and send it forth again as the utterance of prayer.

Clifford sat at the window with Hepzibah, watching the neighbours as they stepped into the street. All of them, however unspiritual on other days, were transfigured by the Sabbath influence; so that their very garments—whether it were an old man's decent coat well brushed for the thousandth time, or a little boy's first sack and trousers finished yesterday by his mother's needle—had somewhat of the quality of ascension-robes.

Forth, likewise, from the portal of the old house stepped Phoebe, putting up her small green sunshade, and throwing upward a glance and smile of parting kindness to the faces at the arched window. In her aspect there was a familiar gladness, and a holiness that you could play with, and yet reverence it as much as ever. She was like a prayer, offered up in the homeliest beauty of one's mother-tongue. Fresh was Phoebe, moreover, and airy and sweet in her apparel; as if nothing that she wore—neither her gown, nor her small straw bonnet, nor her little kerchief, any more than her snowy stockings—had ever been put on before; or, if worn, were all the fresher for it, and with a fragrance as if they had lain among the rosebuds.

The girl waved her hand to Hepzibah and Clifford, and went up the street; a religion in herself, warm, simple, true, with a substance that could walk on earth, and a spirit that was capable of heaven.

"Hepzibah," asked Clifford, after watching Phoebe to the

corner, "do you never go to church?"

"No, Clifford!" she replied,—"not these many, many years!"

"Were I to be there," he rejoined, "it seems to me that I could pray once more, when so many human souls were praying all around me!"

She looked into Clifford's face, and beheld there a soft natural effusion; for his heart gushed out, as it were, and ran over at his eyes, in delightful reverence for God, and kindly affection for his human brethren. The emotion communicated itself to Hepzibah. She yearned to take him by the hand, and go and kneel down, they two together,—both so long separate from the world, and, as she now recognized, scarcely friends with Him above,—to kneel down among the people, and be reconciled to God and man at once.

"Dear brother," said she earnestly, "let us go! We belong nowhere. We have not a foot of space in any church to kneel upon; but let us go to some place of worship, even if we stand in the broad aisle. Poor and forsaken as we are, some pew-door will be opened to us!"

So Hepzibah and her brother made themselves, ready—as ready as they could in the best of their old-fashioned garments, which had hung on pegs, or been laid away in trunks, so long that the dampness and mouldy smell of the past was on them,—made themselves ready, in their faded bettermost, to go to church. They descended the staircase together,—gaunt, sallow Hepzibah, and pale, emaciated, age-stricken Clifford! They pulled open the front door, and stepped across the threshold, and felt, both of them, as if they were standing in the presence of the whole world, and with mankind's great and terrible eye on them alone. The eye of their Father seemed to be withdrawn, and gave them no encouragement. The warm sunny air of the street made them shiver. Their hearts quaked within them at the idea of taking one step farther.

"It cannot be, Hepzibah!—it is too late," said Clifford with deep sadness. "We are ghosts! We have no right among human beings,—no right anywhere but in this old house, which has a

153

curse on it, and which, therefore, we are doomed to haunt! And, besides," he continued, with a fastidious sensibility, inalienably characteristic of the man, "it would not be fit nor beautiful to go! It is an ugly thought that I should be frightful to my fellow-beings, and that children would cling to their mothers' gowns at sight of me!"

They shrank back into the dusky passage-way, and closed the door. But, going up the staircase again, they found the whole interior of the house tenfold more dismal, and the air closer and heavier, for the glimpse and breath of freedom which they had just snatched. They could not flee; their jailer had but left the door ajar in mockery, and stood behind it to watch them stealing out. At the threshold, they felt his pitiless gripe upon them. For, what other dungeon is so dark as one's own heart! What jailer so inexorable as one's self!

But it would be no fair picture of Clifford's state of mind were we to represent him as continually or prevailingly wretched. On the contrary, there was no other man in the city, we are bold to affirm, of so much as half his years, who enjoyed so many lightsome and griefless moments as himself. He had no burden of care upon him; there were none of those questions and contingencies with the future to be settled which wear away all other lives, and render them not worth having by the very process of providing for their support. In this respect he was a child,—a child for the whole term of his existence, be it long or short. Indeed, his life seemed to be standing still at a period little in advance of childhood, and to cluster all his reminiscences about that epoch; just as, after the torpor of a heavy blow, the sufferer's reviving consciousness goes back to a moment considerably behind the accident that stupefied him.

He sometimes told Phoebe and Hepzibah his dreams, in which he invariably played the part of a child, or a very young man. So vivid were they, in his relation of them, that he once held a dispute with his sister as to the particular figure or print of a chintz morning-dress which he had seen their mother wear, in the dream of the preceding night. Hepzibah, piquing herself

154

on a woman's accuracy in such matters, held it to be slightly different from what Clifford described; but, producing the very gown from an old trunk, it proved to be identical with his remembrance of it.

Had Clifford, every time that he emerged out of dreams so lifelike, undergone the torture of transformation from a boy into an old and broken man, the daily recurrence of the shock would have been too much to bear. It would have caused an acute agony to thrill from the morning twilight, all the day through, until bedtime; and even then would have mingled a dull, inscrutable pain and pallid hue of misfortune with the visionary bloom and adolescence of his slumber. But the nightly moonshine interwove itself with the morning mist, and enveloped him as in a robe, which he hugged about his person, and seldom let realities pierce through; he was not often quite awake, but slept open-eyed, and perhaps fancied himself most dreaming then.

Thus, lingering always so near his childhood, he had sympathies with children, and kept his heart the fresher thereby, like a reservoir into which rivulets were pouring not far from the fountain-head. Though prevented, by a subtile sense of propriety, from desiring to associate with them, he loved few things better than to look out of the arched window and see a little girl driving her hoop along the sidewalk, or schoolboys at a game of ball. Their voices, also, were very pleasant to him, heard at a distance, all swarming and intermingling together as flies do in a sunny room.

Clifford would, doubtless, have been glad to share their sports. One afternoon he was seized with an irresistible desire to blow soap-bubbles; an amusement, as Hepzibah told Phoebe apart, that had been a favourite one with her brother when they were both children. Behold him, therefore, at the arched window, with an earthen pipe in his mouth! Behold him, with his gray hair, and a wan, unreal smile over his countenance, where still hovered a beautiful grace, which his worst enemy must have acknowledged to be spiritual and immortal, since it had survived so long! Behold him, scattering airy spheres abroad from the window into the street!

Little impalpable worlds were those soap-bubbles, with the big world depicted, in hues bright as imagination, on the nothing of their surface. It was curious to see how the passers-by regarded these brilliant fantasies, as they came floating down, and made the dull atmosphere imaginative about them. Some stopped to gaze, and perhaps, carried a pleasant recollection of the bubbles onward as far as the street-corner; some looked angrily upward, as if poor Clifford wronged them by setting an image of beauty afloat so near their dusty pathway. A great many put out their fingers or their walking-sticks to touch, withal; and were perversely gratified, no doubt, when the bubble, with all its pictured earth and sky scene, vanished as if it had never been.

At length, just as an elderly gentleman of very dignified presence happened to be passing, a large bubble sailed majestically down, and burst right against his nose! He looked up,—at first with a stern, keen glance, which penetrated at once into the obscurity behind the arched window,—then with a smile which might be conceived as diffusing a dog-day sultriness for the space of several yards about him.

"Aha, Cousin Clifford!" cried Judge Pyncheon. "What! Still blowing soap-bubbles!"

The tone seemed as if meant to be kind and soothing, but yet had a bitterness of sarcasm in it. As for Clifford, an absolute palsy of fear came over him. Apart from any definite cause of dread which his past experience might have given him, he felt that native and original horror of the excellent judge which is proper to a weak, delicate, and apprehensive character in the presence of massive strength. Strength is incomprehensible by weakness, and, therefore, the more terrible. There is no greater bugbear than a strong-willed relative in the circle of his own connections.

12: THE DAGUERREOTYPIST

It must not be supposed that the life of a personage naturally so active as Phoebe could be wholly confined within the precincts of the old Pyncheon House. Clifford's demands upon her time were usually satisfied, in those long days, considerably earlier than sunset. Quiet as his daily existence seemed, it nevertheless drained all the resources by which he lived. It was not physical exercise that overwearied him,—for except that he sometimes wrought a little with a hoe, or paced the garden-walk, or, in rainy weather, traversed a large unoccupied room,—it was his tendency to remain only too quiescent, as regarded any toil of the limbs and muscles.

But, either there was a smouldering fire within him that consumed his vital energy, or the monotony that would have dragged itself with benumbing effect over a mind differently situated was no monotony to Clifford. Possibly, he was in a state of second growth and recovery, and was constantly assimilating nutriment for his spirit and intellect from sights, sounds, and events which passed as a perfect void to persons more practised with the world. As all is activity and vicissitude to the new mind of a child, so might it be, likewise, to a mind that had undergone a kind of new creation, after its long-suspended life.

Be the cause what it might, Clifford commonly retired to rest, thoroughly exhausted, while the sunbeams were still melting through his window-curtains, or were thrown with late lustre on the chamber wall. And while he thus slept early, as other children do, and dreamed of childhood, Phoebe was free to follow her own tastes for the remainder of the day and evening.

This was a freedom essential to the health even of a character so little susceptible of morbid influences as that of Phoebe. The old house, as we have already said, had both the dry-rot and the damp-rot in its walls; it was not good to breathe no other atmosphere than that. Hepzibah, though she had her valuable and redeeming traits, had grown to be a kind of lunatic by imprisoning herself so long in one place, with no other company than a single series of ideas, and but one affection, and one bitter sense of wrong.

Clifford, the reader may perhaps imagine, was too inert to operate morally on his fellow-creatures, however intimate and exclusive their relations with him. But the sympathy or magnetism among human beings is more subtile and universal than we think; it exists, indeed, among different classes of organized life, and vibrates from one to another. A flower, for instance, as Phoebe herself observed, always began to droop sooner in Clifford's hand, or Hepzibah's, than in her own; and by the same law, converting her whole daily life into a flower fragrance for these two sickly spirits, the blooming girl must inevitably droop and fade much sooner than if worn on a younger and happier breast.

Unless she had now and then indulged her brisk impulses, and breathed rural air in a suburban walk, or ocean breezes along the shore,—had occasionally obeyed the impulse of Nature, in New England girls, by attending a metaphysical or philosophical lecture, or viewing a seven-mile panorama, or listening to a concert,—had gone shopping about the city, ransacking entire depots of splendid merchandise, and bringing home a ribbon,—had employed, likewise, a little time to read the Bible in her chamber, and had stolen a little more to think of her mother and her native place—unless for such moral medicines as the above, we should soon have beheld our poor Phoebe grow thin and put on a bleached, unwholesome aspect, and assume strange, shy ways, prophetic of old-maidenhood and a cheerless future.

Even as it was, a change grew visible; a change partly to be regretted, although whatever charm it infringed upon was repaired by another, perhaps more precious. She was not so constantly gay, but had her moods of thought, which Clifford, on the whole, liked better than her former phase of unmingled cheerfulness; because now she understood him better and more delicately, and sometimes even interpreted him to himself. Her eyes looked larger, and darker, and deeper; so deep, at some silent moments, that they seemed like Artesian wells, down, down, into the infinite. She was less girlish than when we first beheld her alighting from the omnibus; less girlish, but more a woman.

The only youthful mind with which Phoebe had an opportunity of frequent intercourse was that of the daguerreotypist. Inevitably, by the pressure of the seclusion about them, they had been brought into habits of some familiarity. Had they met under different circumstances, neither of these young persons would have been likely to bestow much thought upon the other, unless, indeed, their extreme dissimilarity should have proved a principle of mutual attraction. Both, it is true, were characters proper to New England life, and possessing a common ground, therefore, in their more external developments; but as unlike, in their respective interiors, as if their native climes had been at world-wide distance.

During the early part of their acquaintance, Phoebe had held back rather more than was customary with her frank and simple manners from Holgrave's not very marked advances. Nor was she yet satisfied that she knew him well, although they almost daily met and talked together, in a kind, friendly, and what seemed to be a familiar way.

The artist, in a desultory manner, had imparted to Phoebe something of his history. Young as he was, and had his career terminated at the point already attained, there had been enough of incident to fill, very creditably, an autobiographic volume. A romance on the plan of Gil Blas, adapted to American society and manners, would cease to be a romance. The experience of many individuals among us, who think it hardly worth the telling, would equal the vicissitudes of the Spaniard's earlier life; while their ultimate success, or the point whither they tend, may be incomparably higher than any that a novelist would imagine for his hero.

Holgrave, as he told Phoebe somewhat proudly, could not boast of his origin, unless as being exceedingly humble, nor of his education, except that it had been the scantiest possible, and obtained by a few winter-months' attendance at a district school. Left early to his own guidance, he had begun to be self-dependent while yet a boy; and it was a condition aptly suited to his natural force of will. Though now but twenty-two years old (lacking some months, which are years in such a life), he had already been, first, a country schoolmaster; next, a salesman in a country store; and, either at the same time or afterwards, the political editor of a country newspaper.

He had subsequently travelled New England and the Middle States, as a peddler, in the employment of a Connecticut manufactory of cologne-water and other essences. In an episodical way he had studied and practised dentistry, and with very flattering success, especially in many of the factory-towns along our inland streams. As a supernumerary official, of some kind or other, aboard a packet-ship, he had visited Europe, and found means, before his return, to see Italy, and part of France and Germany. At a later period he had spent some months in a community of Fourierists. Still more recently he had been a public lecturer on Mesmerism, for which science (as he assured Phoebe, and, indeed, satisfactorily proved, by putting Chanticleer, who happened to be scratching nearby, to sleep) he had very remarkable endowments.

His present phase, as a daguerreotypist, was of no more importance in his own view, nor likely to be more permanent, than any of the preceding ones. It had been taken up with the careless alacrity of an adventurer, who had his bread to earn. It would be thrown aside as carelessly, whenever he should choose to earn his bread by some other equally digressive means. But what was most remarkable, and, perhaps, showed a more than common poise in the young man, was the fact that, amid all these personal vicissitudes, he had never lost his identity. Homeless as he had been,—continually changing his whereabout, and, therefore, responsible neither to public opinion nor to individuals,—putting off one exterior, and snatching up another, to be soon shifted for a third,—he had never violated the innermost man, but had carried his conscience along with him.

It was impossible to know Holgrave without recognizing this to be the fact. Hepzibah had seen it. Phoebe soon saw it likewise, and gave him the sort of confidence which such a certainty inspires. She was startled, however, and sometimes repelled,—not by any doubt of his integrity to whatever law he acknowledged, but by a sense that his law differed from her own. He made her uneasy, and seemed to unsettle everything around her, by his lack of reverence for what was fixed, unless, at a moment's warning, it could establish its right to hold its ground.

Then, moreover, she scarcely thought him affectionate in his nature. He was too calm and cool an observer. Phoebe felt his eye, often; his heart, seldom or never. He took a certain kind of interest in Hepzibah and her brother, and Phoebe herself. He studied them attentively, and allowed no slightest circumstance of their individualities to escape him. He was ready to do them whatever good he might; but, after all, he never exactly made common cause with them, nor gave any reliable evidence that he loved them better in proportion as he knew them more. In his relations with them, he seemed to be in quest of mental food, not heart-sustenance. Phoebe could not conceive what interested him so much in her friends and herself, intellectually, since he cared nothing for them, or, comparatively, so little, as objects of human affection.

Always, in his interviews with Phoebe, the artist made especial inquiry as to the welfare of Clifford, whom, except at the Sunday festival, he seldom saw.

"Does he still seem happy?" he asked one day.

"As happy as a child," answered Phoebe; "but—like a child, too—very easily disturbed."

"How disturbed?" inquired Holgrave. "By things without, or by thoughts within?"

"I cannot see his thoughts! How should I?" replied Phoebe with simple piquancy. "Very often his humour changes without any reason that can be guessed at, just as a cloud comes over the sun. Latterly, since I have begun to know him better, I feel it to be not quite right to look closely into his moods. He has had such a great sorrow, that his heart is made all solemn and sacred by it. When he is cheerful,—when the sun shines into his mind,—then I venture to peep in, just as far as the light reaches, but no further. It is holy ground where the shadow falls!"

"How prettily you express this sentiment!" said the artist. "I can understand the feeling, without possessing it. Had I your opportunities, no scruples would prevent me from fathoming

Clifford to the full depth of my plummet-line!"

"How strange that you should wish it!" remarked Phoebe involuntarily. "What is Cousin Clifford to you?"

"Oh, nothing,—of course, nothing!" answered Holgrave with a smile. "Only this is such an odd and incomprehensible world! The more I look at it, the more it puzzles me, and I begin to suspect that a man's bewilderment is the measure of his wisdom. Men and women, and children, too, are such strange creatures, that one never can be certain that he really knows them; nor ever guess what they have been from what he sees them to be now. Judge Pyncheon! Clifford! What a complex riddle—a complexity of complexities—do they present! It requires intuitive sympathy, like a young girl's, to solve it. A mere observer, like myself (who never have any intuitions, and am, at best, only subtile and acute), is pretty certain to go astray."

The artist now turned the conversation to themes less dark than that which they had touched upon. Phoebe and he were young together; nor had Holgrave, in his premature experience of life, wasted entirely that beautiful spirit of youth, which, gushing forth from one small heart and fancy, may diffuse itself over the universe, making it all as bright as on the first day of creation. Man's own youth is the world's youth; at least, he feels as if it were, and imagines that the earth's granite substance is something not yet hardened, and which he can mould into whatever shape he likes.

So it was with Holgrave. He could talk sagely about the world's old age, but never actually believed what he said; he was a young man still, and therefore looked upon the world—that gray-bearded and wrinkled profligate, decrepit, without being venerable—as a tender stripling, capable of being improved into all that it ought to be, but scarcely yet had shown the remotest promise of becoming. He had that sense, or inward prophecy,—which a young man had better never have been born than not to have, and a mature man had better die at once than utterly to relinquish,—that we are not doomed to creep on forever in the old bad way, but that, this very now, there are the harbingers abroad of a golden era, to be accomplished in his own lifetime. It seemed to Holgrave,—as doubtless it has seemed to the hopeful of every century since the epoch of Adam's grandchildren,—that in this age, more than ever before, the moss-grown and rotten Past is to be torn down, and lifeless institutions to be thrust out of the way, and their dead corpses buried, and everything to begin anew.

As to the main point,—may we never live to doubt it!—as to the better centuries that are coming, the artist was surely right. His error lay in supposing that this age, more than any past or future one, is destined to see the tattered garments of Antiquity exchanged for a new suit, instead of gradually renewing themselves by patchwork; in applying his own little life-span as the measure of an interminable achievement; and, more than all, in fancying that it mattered anything to the great end in view whether he himself should contend for it or against it. Yet it was well for him to think so. This enthusiasm, infusing itself through the calmness of his character, and thus taking an aspect of settled thought and wisdom, would serve to keep his youth pure, and make his aspirations high.

And when, with the years settling down more weightily upon him, his early faith should be modified by inevitable experience, it would be with no harsh and sudden revolution of his sentiments. He would still have faith in man's brightening destiny, and perhaps love him all the better, as he should recognize his helplessness in his own behalf; and the haughty faith, with which he began life, would be well bartered for a far humbler one at its close, in discerning that man's best directed effort accomplishes a kind of dream, while God is the sole worker of realities.

Holgrave had read very little, and that little in passing through the thoroughfare of life, where the mystic language of his books was necessarily mixed up with the babble of the multitude, so that both one and the other were apt to lose any sense that might have been properly their own. He considered himself a thinker, and was certainly of a thoughtful turn, but, with his own path to discover, had perhaps hardly yet reached the point where an educated man begins to think. The true value of his character lay in that deep consciousness of inward strength, which made all his past vicissitudes seem merely like a change of garments; in that enthusiasm, so quiet that he scarcely knew of its existence, but which gave a warmth to everything that he laid his hand on; in that personal ambition, hidden—from his own as well as other eyes—among his more generous impulses, but in which lurked a certain efficacy, that might solidify him from a theorist into the champion of some practicable cause.

Altogether in his culture and want of culture,—in his crude, wild, and misty philosophy, and the practical experience that counteracted some of its tendencies; in his magnanimous zeal for man's welfare, and his recklessness of whatever the ages had established in man's behalf; in his faith, and in his infidelity; in what he had, and in what he lacked,—the artist might fitly enough stand forth as the representative of many compeers in his native land.

His career it would be difficult to prefigure. There appeared to be qualities in Holgrave, such as, in a country where everything is free to the hand that can grasp it, could hardly fail to put some of the world's prizes within his reach. But these matters are delightfully uncertain. At almost every step in life, we meet with young men of just about Holgrave's age, for whom we anticipate wonderful things, but of whom, even after much and careful inquiry, we never happen to hear another word. The effervescence of youth and passion, and the fresh gloss of the intellect and imagination, endow them with a false brilliancy, which makes fools of themselves and other people. Like certain chintzes, calicoes, and ginghams, they show finely in their first newness, but cannot stand the sun and rain, and assume a very sober aspect after washing-day.

But our business is with Holgrave as we find him on this particular afternoon, and in the arbor of the Pyncheon garden. In that point of view, it was a pleasant sight to behold this young man, with so much faith in himself, and so fair an appearance of admirable powers,—so little harmed, too, by the many tests

164

that had tried his metal,—it was pleasant to see him in his kindly intercourse with Phoebe. Her thought had scarcely done him justice when it pronounced him cold; or, if so, he had grown warmer now.

Without such purpose on her part, and unconsciously on his, she made the House of the Seven Gables like a home to him, and the garden a familiar precinct. With the insight on which he prided himself, he fancied that he could look through Phoebe, and all around her, and could read her off like a page of a child's story-book. But these transparent natures are often deceptive in their depth; those pebbles at the bottom of the fountain are farther from us than we think. Thus the artist, whatever he might judge of Phoebe's capacity, was beguiled, by some silent charm of hers, to talk freely of what he dreamed of doing in the world. He poured himself out as to another self. Very possibly, he forgot Phoebe while he talked to her, and was moved only by the inevitable tendency of thought, when rendered sympathetic by enthusiasm and emotion, to flow into the first safe reservoir which it finds. But, had you peeped at them through the chinks of the garden-fence, the young man's earnestness and heightened colour might have led you to suppose that he was making love to the young girl!

At length, something was said by Holgrave that made it apposite for Phoebe to inquire what had first brought him acquainted with her cousin Hepzibah, and why he now chose to lodge in the desolate old Pyncheon House. Without directly answering her, he turned from the Future, which had heretofore been the theme of his discourse, and began to speak of the influences of the Past. One subject, indeed, is but the reverberation of the other.

"Shall we never, never get rid of this Past?" cried he, keeping up the earnest tone of his preceding conversation. "It lies upon the Present like a giant's dead body In fact, the case is just as if a young giant were compelled to waste all his strength in carrying about the corpse of the old giant, his grandfather, who died a long while ago, and only needs to be decently buried. Just think a moment, and it will startle you to see what slaves we are to by-gone times,—to Death, if we give the matter the right word!"

"But I do not see it," observed Phoebe.

"For example, then," continued Holgrave: "a dead man, if he happens to have made a will, disposes of wealth no longer his own; or, if he die intestate, it is distributed in accordance with the notions of men much longer dead than he. A dead man sits on all our judgment-seats; and living judges do but search out and repeat his decisions. We read in dead men's books! We laugh at dead men's jokes, and cry at dead men's pathos! We are sick of dead men's diseases, physical and moral, and die of the same remedies with which dead doctors killed their patients! We worship the living Deity according to dead men's forms and creeds. Whatever we seek to do, of our own free motion, a dead man's icy hand obstructs us! Turn our eyes to what point we may, a dead man's white, immitigable face encounters them, and freezes our very heart! And we must be dead ourselves before we can begin to have our proper influence on our own world, which will then be no longer our world, but the world of an-other generation, with which we shall have no shadow of a right to interfere. I ought to have said, too, that we live in dead men's houses; as, for instance, in this of the Seven Gables!"

"And why not," said Phoebe, "so long as we can be comfort-able in them?"

"But we shall live to see the day, I trust," went on the artist, "when no man shall build his house for posterity. Why should he? He might just as reasonably order a durable suit of clothes,—leather, or gutta-percha, or whatever else lasts longest,—so that his great-grandchildren should have the benefit of them, and cut precisely the same figure in the world that he himself does. If each generation were allowed and expected to build its own houses, that single change, comparatively unimportant in itself, would imply almost every reform which society is now suffer-ing for. I doubt whether even our public edifices—our capitols, state-houses, court-houses, city-hall, and churches,—ought to be built of such permanent materials as stone or brick. It were better that they should crumble to ruin once in twenty years, or thereabouts, as a hint to the people to examine into and reform the institutions which they symbolize."

"How you hate everything old!" said Phoebe in dismay. "It makes me dizzy to think of such a shifting world!"

"I certainly love nothing mouldy," answered Holgrave. "Now, this old Pyncheon House! Is it a wholesome place to live in, with its black shingles, and the green moss that shows how damp they are?—its dark, low-studded rooms—its grime and sordidness, which are the crystallization on its walls of the human breath, that has been drawn and exhaled here in discontent and anguish? The house ought to be purified with fire,—purified till only its ashes remain!"

"Then why do you live in it?" asked Phoebe, a little piqued.

"Oh, I am pursuing my studies here; not in books, however," replied Holgrave. "The house, in my view, is expressive of that odious and abominable Past, with all its bad influences, against which I have just been declaiming. I dwell in it for a while, that I may know the better how to hate it. By the bye, did you ever hear the story of Maule, the wizard, and what happened between him and your immeasurably great-grandfather?"

"Yes, indeed!" said Phoebe; "I heard it long ago, from my father, and two or three times from my cousin Hepzibah, in the month that I have been here. She seems to think that all the calamities of the Pyncheons began from that quarrel with the wizard, as you call him. And you, Mr. Holgrave look as if you thought so too! How singular that you should believe what is so very absurd, when you reject many things that are a great deal worthier of credit!"

"I do believe it," said the artist seriously; "not as a superstition, however, but as proved by unquestionable facts, and as exemplifying a theory. Now, see: under those seven gables, at which we now look up,—and which old Colonel Pyncheon meant to be the house of his descendants, in prosperity and happiness, down to an epoch far beyond the present,—under that roof, through a portion of three centuries, there has been perpetual remorse of conscience, a constantly defeated hope, strife amongst kindred, various misery, a strange form of death, dark suspicion, unspeakable disgrace,—all, or most of which calamity I have the means of tracing to the old Puritan's inordinate desire to plant and endow a family. To plant a family!

"This idea is at the bottom of most of the wrong and mischief which men do. The truth is, that, once in every half-century, at longest, a family should be merged into the great, obscure mass of humanity, and forget all about its ancestors. Human blood, in order to keep its freshness, should run in hidden streams, as the water of an aqueduct is conveyed in subterranean pipes. In the family existence of these Pyncheons, for instance,—forgive me Phoebe, but I cannot think of you as one of them,—in their brief New England pedigree, there has been time enough to infect them all with one kind of lunacy or another."

"You speak very unceremoniously of my kindred," said Phoebe, debating with herself whether she ought to take offence.

"I speak true thoughts to a true mind!" answered Holgrave, with a vehemence which Phoebe had not before witnessed in him. "The truth is as I say! Furthermore, the original perpetrator and father of this mischief appears to have perpetuated himself, and still walks the street,—at least, his very image, in mind and body,—with the fairest prospect of transmitting to posterity as rich and as wretched an inheritance as he has received! Do you remember the daguerreotype, and its resemblance to the old portrait?"

"How strangely in earnest you are!" exclaimed Phoebe, looking at him with surprise and perplexity; half alarmed and partly inclined to laugh. "You talk of the lunacy of the Pyncheons; is it contagious?"

"I understand you!" said the artist, colouring and laughing. "I believe I am a little mad. This subject has taken hold of my mind with the strangest tenacity of clutch since I have lodged in yonder old gable. As one method of throwing it off, I have put an incident of the Pyncheon family history, with which I happen to be acquainted, into the form of a legend, and mean to publish it in a magazine."

"Do you write for the magazines?" inquired Phoebe.

"Is it possible you did not know it?" cried Holgrave. "Well, such is literary fame! Yes. Miss Phoebe Pyncheon, among the multitude of my marvellous gifts I have that of writing stories; and my name has figured, I can assure you, on the covers of Graham and Godey, making as respectable an appearance, for aught I could see, as any of the canonized bead-roll with which it was associated. In the humorous line, I am thought to have a very pretty way with me; and as for pathos, I am as provocative of tears as an onion. But shall I read you my story?"

"Yes, if it is not very long," said Phoebe,—and added laughingly,—"nor very dull."

As this latter point was one which the daguerreotypist could not decide for himself, he forthwith produced his roll of manuscript, and, while the late sunbeams gilded the seven gables, began to read.

13: Alice Pyncheon

There was a message brought, one day, from the worshipful Gervayse Pyncheon to young Matthew Maule, the carpenter, desiring his immediate presence at the House of the Seven Gables.

"And what does your master want with me?" said the carpenter to Mr. Pyncheon's black servant. "Does the house need any repair? Well it may, by this time; and no blame to my father who built it, neither! I was reading the old Colonel's tombstone, no longer ago than last Sabbath; and, reckoning from that date, the house has stood seven-and-thirty years. No wonder if there should be a job to do on the roof."

"Don't know what massa wants," answered Scipio. "The house is a berry good house, and old Colonel Pyncheon think so too, I reckon;—else why the old man haunt it so, and frighten a poor nigga, As he does?"

"Well, well, friend Scipio; let your master know that I'm

coming," said the carpenter with a laugh. "For a fair, workman-like job, he'll find me his man. And so the house is haunted, is it? It will take a tighter workman than I am to keep the spirits out of the Seven Gables. Even if the Colonel would be quiet," he added, muttering to himself, "my old grandfather, the wizard, will be pretty sure to stick to the Pyncheons as long as their walls hold together."

"What's that you mutter to yourself, Matthew Maule?" asked Scipio. "And what for do you look so black at me?"

"No matter, darky," said the carpenter. "Do you think no-body is to look black but yourself? Go tell your master I'm coming; and if you happen to see Mistress Alice, his daughter, give Matthew Maule's humble respects to her. She has brought a fair face from Italy,—fair, and gentle, and proud,—has that same Alice Pyncheon!"

"He talk of Mistress Alice!" cried Scipio, as he returned from his errand. "The low carpenter-man! He no business so much as to look at her a great way off!"

This young Matthew Maule, the carpenter, it must be ob-served, was a person little understood, and not very generally liked, in the town where he resided; not that anything could be alleged against his integrity, or his skill and diligence in the handicraft which he exercised. The aversion (as it might justly be called) with which many persons regarded him was partly the result of his own character and deportment, and partly an inheritance.

He was the grandson of a former Matthew Maule, one of the early settlers of the town, and who had been a famous and terrible wizard in his day. This old reprobate was one of the suf-ferers when Cotton Mather, and his brother ministers, and the learned judges, and other wise men, and Sir William Phipps, the sagacious governor, made such laudable efforts to weaken the great enemy of souls, by sending a multitude of his adher-ents up the rocky pathway of Gallows Hill. Since those days, no doubt, it had grown to be suspected that, in consequence of an unfortunate overdoing of a work praiseworthy in itself, the proceedings against the witches had proved far less acceptable to the Beneficent Father than to that very Arch Enemy whom they were intended to distress and utterly overwhelm.

It is not the less certain, however, that awe and terror brooded over the memories of those who died for this horrible crime of witchcraft. Their graves, in the crevices of the rocks, were supposed to be incapable of retaining the occupants who had been so hastily thrust into them. Old Matthew Maule, especially, was known to have as little hesitation or difficulty in rising out of his grave as an ordinary man in getting out of bed, and was as often seen at midnight as living people at noonday. This pestilent wizard (in whom his just punishment seemed to have wrought no manner of amendment) had an inveterate habit of haunting a certain mansion, styled the House of the Seven Gables, against the owner of which he pretended to hold an unsettled claim for ground-rent.

The ghost, it appears,—with the pertinacity which was one of his distinguishing characteristics while alive,—insisted that he was the rightful proprietor of the site upon which the house stood. His terms were, that either the aforesaid ground-rent, from the day when the cellar began to be dug, should be paid down, or the mansion itself given up; else he, the ghostly creditor, would have his finger in all the affairs of the Pyncheons, and make everything go wrong with them, though it should be a thousand years after his death. It was a wild story, perhaps, but seemed not altogether so incredible to those who could remember what an inflexibly obstinate old fellow this wizard Maule had been.

Now, the wizard's grandson, the young Matthew Maule of our story, was popularly supposed to have inherited some of his ancestor's questionable traits. It is wonderful how many absurdities were promulgated in reference to the young man. He was fabled, for example, to have a strange power of getting into people's dreams, and regulating matters there according to his own fancy, pretty much like the stage-manager of a theatre.

There was a great deal of talk among the neighbours, particularly the petticoated ones, about what they called the witch-craft of Maule's eye. Some said that he could look into people's minds; others, that, by the marvellous power of this eye, he could draw people into his own mind, or send them, if he pleased, to do errands to his grandfather, in the spiritual world; oth-ers, again, that it was what is termed an Evil Eye, and possessed the valuable faculty of blighting corn, and drying children into mummies with the heartburn. But, after all, what worked most to the young carpenter's disadvantage was, first, the reserve and sternness of his natural disposition, and next, the fact of his not being a church-communicant, and the suspicion of his holding heretical tenets in matters of religion and polity.

After receiving Mr. Pyncheon's message, the carpenter merely tarried to finish a small job, which he happened to have in hand, and then took his way towards the House of the Seven Gables. This noted edifice, though its style might be getting a little out of fashion, was still as respectable a family residence as that of any gentleman in town. The present owner, Gervayse Pyncheon, was said to have contracted a dislike to the house, in conse-quence of a shock to his sensibility, in early childhood, from the sudden death of his grandfather. In the very act of running to climb Colonel Pyncheon's knee, the boy had discovered the old Puritan to be a corpse. On arriving at manhood, Mr. Pyncheon had visited England, where he married a lady of fortune, and had subsequently spent many years, partly in the mother coun-try, and partly in various cities on the continent of Europe.

During this period, the family mansion had been consigned to the charge of a kinsman, who was allowed to make it his home for the time being, in consideration of keeping the premises in thorough repair. So faithfully had this contract been fulfilled, that now, as the carpenter approached the house, his practised eye could detect nothing to criticise in its condition. The peaks of the seven gables rose up sharply; the shingled roof looked thoroughly water-tight; and the glittering plaster-work entirely covered the exterior walls, and sparkled in the October sun, as if it had been new only a week ago.

The house had that pleasant aspect of life which is like the cheery expression of comfortable activity in the human countenance. You could see, at once, that there was the stir of a large family within it. A huge load of oak-wood was passing through the gateway, towards the outbuildings in the rear; the fat cook— or probably it might be the housekeeper—stood at the side door, bargaining for some turkeys and poultry which a countryman had brought for sale. Now and then a maid-servant, neatly dressed, and now the shining sable face of a slave, might be seen bustling across the windows, in the lower part of the house.

At an open window of a room in the second story, hanging over some pots of beautiful and delicate flowers,—exotics, but which had never known a more genial sunshine than that of the New England autumn,—was the figure of a young lady, an exotic, like the flowers, and beautiful and delicate as they. Her presence imparted an indescribable grace and faint witchery to the whole edifice. In other respects, it was a substantial, jolly-looking mansion, and seemed fit to be the residence of a patriarch, who might establish his own headquarters in the front gable and assign one of the remainder to each of his six children, while the great chimney in the centre should symbolize the old fellow's hospitable heart, which kept them all warm, and made a great whole of the seven smaller ones.

There was a vertical sundial on the front gable; and as the carpenter passed beneath it, he looked up and noted the hour.

"Three o'clock!" said he to himself. "My father told me that dial was put up only an hour before the old colonel's death. How truly it has kept time these seven-and-thirty years past! The shadow creeps and creeps, and is always looking over the shoulder of the sunshine!"

It might have befitted a craftsman, like Matthew Maule, on being sent for to a gentleman's house, to go to the back door, where servants and work-people were usually admitted; or at least to the side entrance, where the better class of tradesmen made application. But the carpenter had a great deal of pride and stiffness in his nature; and, at this moment, moreover, his heart was bitter with the sense of hereditary wrong, because he considered the great Pyncheon House to be standing on soil which should have been his own.

On this very site, beside a spring of delicious water, his grandfather had felled the pine-trees and built a cottage, in which children had been born to him; and it was only from a dead man's stiffened fingers that Colonel Pyncheon had wrested away the title-deeds. So young Maule went straight to the principal entrance, beneath a portal of carved oak, and gave such a peal of the iron knocker that you would have imagined the stern old wizard himself to be standing at the threshold.

Black Scipio answered the summons in a prodigious, hurry; but showed the whites of his eyes in amazement on beholding only the carpenter.

"Lord-a-mercy, what a great man he be, this carpenter fellow!" mumbled Scipio, down in his throat. "Anybody think he beat on the door with his biggest hammer!"

"Here I am!" said Maule sternly. "Show me the way to your master's parlour."

As he stept into the house, a note of sweet and melancholy music thrilled and vibrated along the passage-way, proceeding from one of the rooms above stairs. It was the harpsichord which Alice Pyncheon had brought with her from beyond the sea. The fair Alice bestowed most of her maiden leisure between flowers and music, although the former were apt to droop, and the melodies were often sad. She was of foreign education, and could not take kindly to the New England modes of life, in which nothing beautiful had ever been developed.

As Mr. Pyncheon had been impatiently awaiting Maule's arrival, black Scipio, of course, lost no time in ushering the carpenter into his master's presence. The room in which this gentleman sat was a parlour of moderate size, looking out upon the garden of the house, and having its windows partly shadowed by the foliage of fruit-trees. It was Mr. Pyncheon's peculiar apartment, and was provided with furniture, in an elegant and costly style, principally from Paris; the floor (which was unusual at that day) being covered with a carpet, so skilfully and richly wrought that it seemed to glow as with living flowers. In one corner stood a marble woman, to whom her own beauty was the sole and sufficient garment.

Some pictures—that looked old, and had a mellow tinge diffused through all their artful splendour—hung on the walls. Near the fireplace was a large and very beautiful cabinet of ebony, inlaid with ivory; a piece of antique furniture, which Mr. Pyncheon had bought in Venice, and which he used as the treasure-place for medals, ancient coins, and whatever small and valuable curiosities he had picked up on his travels. Through all this variety of decoration, however, the room showed its original characteristics; its low stud, its cross-beam, its chimney-piece, with the old-fashioned Dutch tiles; so that it was the emblem of a mind industriously stored with foreign ideas, and elaborated into artificial refinement, but neither larger, nor, in its proper self, more elegant than before.

There were two objects that appeared rather out of place in this very handsomely furnished room. One was a large map, or surveyor's plan, of a tract of land, which looked as if it had been drawn a good many years ago, and was now dingy with smoke, and soiled, here and there, with the touch of fingers. The other was a portrait of a stern old man, in a Puritan garb, painted roughly, but with a bold effect, and a remarkably strong expression of character.

At a small table, before a fire of English sea-coal, sat Mr. Pyncheon, sipping coffee, which had grown to be a very favourite beverage with him in France. He was a middle-aged and really handsome man, with a wig flowing down upon his shoulders; his coat was of blue velvet, with lace on the borders and at the button-holes; and the firelight glistened on the spacious breadth of his waistcoat, which was flowered all over with gold. On the entrance of Scipio, ushering in the carpenter, Mr. Pyncheon turned partly round, but resumed his former position, and proceeded deliberately to finish his cup of coffee, without immediate notice of the guest whom he had summoned to his presence. It was not that he intended any rudeness or improper neglect,—which, indeed, he would have blushed to be guilty of,—but it never occurred to him that a person in Maule's station had a claim on his courtesy, or would trouble himself about it one way or the other.

The carpenter, however, stepped at once to the hearth, and turned himself about, so as to look Mr. Pyncheon in the face.

"You sent for me," said he. "Be pleased to explain your business, that I may go back to my own affairs."

"Ah! excuse me," said Mr. Pyncheon quietly. "I did not mean to tax your time without a recompense. Your name, I think, is Maule,—Thomas or Matthew Maule,—a son or grandson of the builder of this house?"

"Matthew Maule," replied the carpenter,—"son of him who built the house,—grandson of the rightful proprietor of the soil."

"I know the dispute to which you allude," observed Mr. Pyncheon with undisturbed equanimity. "I am well aware that my grandfather was compelled to resort to a suit at law, in order to establish his claim to the foundation-site of this edifice. We will not, if you please, renew the discussion. The matter was settled at the time, and by the competent authorities,—equitably, it is to be presumed,—and, at all events, irrevocably. Yet, singularly enough, there is an incidental reference to this very subject in what I am now about to say to you. And this same inveterate grudge,—excuse me, I mean no offence,—this irritability, which you have just shown, is not entirely aside from the matter."

"If you can find anything for your purpose, Mr. Pyncheon," said the carpenter, "in a man's natural resentment for the wrongs done to his blood, you are welcome to it."

"I take you at your word, Goodman Maule," said the owner of the Seven Gables, with a smile, "and will proceed to suggest a mode in which your hereditary resentments—justifiable or otherwise—may have had a bearing on my affairs. You have heard, I suppose, that the Pyncheon family, ever since my grandfather's days, have been prosecuting a still unsettled claim to a very large extent of territory at the Eastward?"

"Often," replied Maule,—and it is said that a smile came over his face,—"very often,—from my father!"

"This claim," continued Mr. Pyncheon, after pausing a moment, as if to consider what the carpenter's smile might mean, "appeared to be on the very verge of a settlement and full allowance, at the period of my grandfather's decease. It was well known, to those in his confidence, that he anticipated neither difficulty nor delay. Now, Colonel Pyncheon, I need hardly say, was a practical man, well acquainted with public and private business, and not at all the person to cherish ill-founded hopes, or to attempt the following out of an impracticable scheme. It is obvious to conclude, therefore, that he had grounds, not apparent to his heirs, for his confident anticipation of success in the matter of this Eastern claim. In a word, I believe,—and my legal advisers coincide in the belief, which, moreover, is authorized, to a certain extent, by the family traditions,—that my grandfather was in possession of some deed, or other document, essential to this claim, but which has since disappeared."

"Very likely," said Matthew Maule,—and again, it is said, there was a dark smile on his face,—"but what can a poor carpenter have to do with the grand affairs of the Pyncheon family?"

"Perhaps nothing," returned Mr. Pyncheon, "possibly much!"

Here ensued a great many words between Matthew Maule and the proprietor of the Seven Gables, on the subject which the latter had thus broached. It seems (although Mr. Pyncheon had some hesitation in referring to stories so exceedingly absurd in their aspect) that the popular belief pointed to some mysterious connection and dependence, existing between the family of the Maules and these vast unrealized possessions of the Pyncheons. It was an ordinary saying that the old wizard, hanged though he was, had obtained the best end of the bargain in his contest with Colonel Pyncheon; inasmuch as he had got possession of the great Eastern claim, in exchange for an acre or two of garden-ground.

A very aged woman, recently dead, had often used the metaphorical expression, in her fireside talk, that miles and miles of the Pyncheon lands had been shovelled into Maule's grave; which, by the bye, was but a very shallow nook, between two rocks, near the summit of Gallows Hill. Again, when the lawyers were making inquiry for the missing document, it was a by-word that it would never be found, unless in the wizard's skeleton hand. So much weight had the shrewd lawyers assigned to these fables, that (but Mr. Pyncheon did not see fit to inform the carpenter of the fact) they had secretly caused the wizard's grave to be searched. Nothing was discovered, however, except that, unaccountably, the right hand of the skeleton was gone.

Now, what was unquestionably important, a portion of these popular rumors could be traced, though rather doubtfully and indistinctly, to chance words and obscure hints of the executed wizard's son, and the father of this present Matthew Maule. And here Mr. Pyncheon could bring an item of his own personal evidence into play. Though but a child at the time, he either remembered or fancied that Matthew's father had had some job to perform on the day before, or possibly the very morning of the colonel's decease, in the private room where he and the carpenter were at this moment talking. Certain papers belonging to Colonel Pyncheon, as his grandson distinctly recollected, had been spread out on the table.

Matthew Maule understood the insinuated suspicion.

"My father," he said,—but still there was that dark smile, making a riddle of his countenance,—"my father was an honester man than the bloody old colonel! Not to get his rights back again would he have carried off one of those papers!"

"I shall not bandy words with you," observed the foreign-bred Mr. Pyncheon, with haughty composure. "Nor will it become me to resent any rudeness towards either my grandfather or myself. A gentleman, before seeking intercourse with a person of your station and habits, will first consider whether the urgency of the end may compensate for the disagreeableness of the means. It does so in the present instance."

He then renewed the conversation, and made great pecuniary offers to the carpenter, in case the latter should give information leading to the discovery of the lost document, and the consequent success of the Eastern claim. For a long time Matthew Maule is said to have turned a cold ear to these propositions. At last, however, with a strange kind of laugh, he inquired whether Mr. Pyncheon would make over to him the old wizard's homestead-ground, together with the House of the Seven Gables, now standing on it, in requital of the documentary evidence so urgently required.

The wild, chimney-corner legend (which, without copying all its extravagances, my narrative essentially follows) here gives an account of some very strange behaviour on the part of Colonel Pyncheon's portrait. This picture, it must be understood, was supposed to be so intimately connected with the fate of the house, and so magically built into its walls, that, if once it should be removed, that very instant the whole edifice would come thundering down in a heap of dusty ruin.

All through the foregoing conversation between Mr. Pyncheon and the carpenter, the portrait had been frowning, clenching its fist, and giving many such proofs of excessive discomposure, but without attracting the notice of either of the two colloquists. And finally, at Matthew Maule's audacious suggestion of a transfer of the seven-gabled structure, the ghostly portrait is averred to have lost all patience, and to have shown itself on the point of descending bodily from its frame. But such incredible incidents are merely to be mentioned aside.

"Give up this house!" exclaimed Mr. Pyncheon, in amazement at the proposal. "Were I to do so, my grandfather would not rest quiet in his grave!"

"He never has, if all stories are true," remarked the carpenter composedly. "But that matter concerns his grandson more than it does Matthew Maule. I have no other terms to propose."

Impossible as he at first thought it to comply with Maule's conditions, still, on a second glance, Mr. Pyncheon was of opinion that they might at least be made matter of discussion. He himself had no personal attachment for the house, nor any pleasant associations connected with his childish residence in it. On the contrary, after seven-and-thirty years, the presence of his dead grandfather seemed still to pervade it, as on that morning when the affrighted boy had beheld him, with so ghastly an aspect, stiffening in his chair. His long abode in foreign parts, moreover, and familiarity with many of the castles and ancestral halls of England, and the marble palaces of Italy, had caused him to look contemptuously at the House of the Seven Gables, whether in point of splendour or convenience.

It was a mansion exceedingly inadequate to the style of living which it would be incumbent on Mr. Pyncheon to support, after realizing his territorial rights. His steward might deign to occupy it, but never, certainly, the great landed proprietor himself. In the event of success, indeed, it was his purpose to return to England; nor, to say the truth, would he recently have quitted that more congenial home, had not his own fortune, as well as his deceased wife's, begun to give symptoms of exhaustion. The Eastern claim once fairly settled, and put upon the firm basis of actual possession, Mr. Pyncheon's property—to be measured by miles, not acres—would be worth an earldom, and would reasonably entitle him to solicit, or enable him to purchase, that elevated dignity from the British monarch. Lord Pyncheon!—or the Earl of Waldo!—how could such a magnate be expected to contract his grandeur within the pitiful compass of seven shingled gables?

In short, on an enlarged view of the business, the carpenter's terms appeared so ridiculously easy that Mr. Pyncheon could scarcely forbear laughing in his face. He was quite ashamed, after the foregoing reflections, to propose any diminution of so moderate a recompense for the immense service to be rendered.

"I consent to your proposition, Maule!" cried he. "Put me in possession of the document essential to establish my rights, and the House of the Seven Gables is your own!"

According to some versions of the story, a regular contract to the above effect was drawn up by a lawyer, and signed and sealed in the presence of witnesses. Others say that Matthew Maule was contented with a private written agreement, in which Mr. Pyncheon pledged his honour and integrity to the fulfilment of the terms concluded upon. The gentleman then ordered wine, which he and the carpenter drank together, in confirmation of their bargain.

During the whole preceding discussion and subsequent formalities, the old Puritan's portrait seems to have persisted in its shadowy gestures of disapproval; but without effect, except that, as Mr. Pyncheon set down the emptied glass, he thought he beheld his grandfather frown.

"This sherry is too potent a wine for me; it has affected my brain already," he observed, after a somewhat startled look at the picture. "On returning to Europe, I shall confine myself to the more delicate vintages of Italy and France, the best of which will not bear transportation."

"My Lord Pyncheon may drink what wine he will, and wherever he pleases," replied the carpenter, as if he had been privy to Mr. Pyncheon's ambitious projects. "But first, sir, if you desire tidings of this lost document, I must crave the favour of a little talk with your fair daughter Alice."

"You are mad, Maule!" exclaimed Mr. Pyncheon haughtily; and now, at last, there was anger mixed up with his pride. "What can my daughter have to do with a business like this?"

Indeed, at this new demand on the carpenter's part, the proprietor of the Seven Gables was even more thunder-struck than at the cool proposition to surrender his house. There was, at least, an assignable motive for the first stipulation; there appeared to be none whatever for the last. Nevertheless, Matthew Maule sturdily insisted on the young lady being summoned, and even gave her father to understand, in a mysterious kind of explanation,—which made the matter considerably darker than it looked before,—that the only chance of acquiring the requisite knowledge was through the clear, crystal medium of a pure and virgin intelligence, like that of the fair Alice.

Not to encumber our story with Mr. Pyncheon's scruples,

whether of conscience, pride, or fatherly affection, he at length ordered his daughter to be called. He well knew that she was in her chamber, and engaged in no occupation that could not readily be laid aside; for, as it happened, ever since Alice's name had been spoken, both her father and the carpenter had heard the sad and sweet music of her harpsichord, and the airier melancholy of her accompanying voice.

So Alice Pyncheon was summoned, and appeared. A portrait of this young lady, painted by a Venetian artist, and left by her father in England, is said to have fallen into the hands of the present Duke of Devonshire, and to be now preserved at Chatsworth; not on account of any associations with the original, but for its value as a picture, and the high character of beauty in the countenance.

If ever there was a lady born, and set apart from the world's vulgar mass by a certain gentle and cold stateliness, it was this very Alice Pyncheon. Yet there was the womanly mixture in her; the tenderness, or, at least, the tender capabilities. For the sake of that redeeming quality, a man of generous nature would have forgiven all her pride, and have been content, almost, to lie down in her path, and let Alice set her slender foot upon his heart. All that he would have required was simply the acknowledgment that he was indeed a man, and a fellow-being, moulded of the same elements as she.

As Alice came into the room, her eyes fell upon the carpenter, who was standing near its centre, clad in green woollen jacket, a pair of loose breeches, open at the knees, and with a long pocket for his rule, the end of which protruded; it was as proper a mark of the artisan's calling as Mr. Pyncheon's full-dress sword of that gentleman's aristocratic pretensions. A glow of artistic approval brightened over Alice Pyncheon's face; she was struck with admiration—which she made no attempt to conceal—of the remarkable comeliness, strength, and energy of Maule's figure. But that admiring glance (which most other men, perhaps, would have cherished as a sweet recollection all through life) the carpenter never forgave. It must have been the devil himself that made Maule so subtile in his preception.

"Does the girl look at me as if I were a brute beast?" thought he, setting his teeth. "She shall know whether I have a human spirit; and the worse for her, if it prove stronger than her own!"

"My father, you sent for me," said Alice, in her sweet and harp-like voice. "But, if you have business with this young man, pray let me go again. You know I do not love this room, in spite of that Claude, with which you try to bring back sunny recollections."

"Stay a moment, young lady, if you please!" said Matthew Maule. "My business with your father is over. With yourself, it is now to begin!"

Alice looked towards her father, in surprise and inquiry.

"Yes, Alice," said Mr. Pyncheon, with some disturbance and confusion. "This young man—his name is Matthew Maule—professes, so far as I can understand him, to be able to discover, through your means, a certain paper or parchment, which was missing long before your birth. The importance of the document in question renders it advisable to neglect no possible, even if improbable, method of regaining it. You will therefore oblige me, my dear Alice, by answering this person's inquiries, and complying with his lawful and reasonable requests, so far as they may appear to have the aforesaid object in view. As I shall remain in the room, you need apprehend no rude nor unbecoming deportment, on the young man's part; and, at your slightest wish, of course, the investigation, or whatever we may call it, shall immediately be broken off."

"Mistress Alice Pyncheon," remarked Matthew Maule, with the utmost deference, but yet a half-hidden sarcasm in his look and tone, "will no doubt feel herself quite safe in her father's presence, and under his all-sufficient protection."

"I certainly shall entertain no manner of apprehension, with my father at hand," said Alice with maidenly dignity. "Neither do I conceive that a lady, while true to herself, can have aught to fear from whomsoever, or in any circumstances!"

Poor Alice! By what unhappy impulse did she thus put herself at once on terms of defiance against a strength which she could not estimate?

"Then, Mistress Alice," said Matthew Maule, handing a chair,—gracefully enough, for a craftsman, "will it please you only to sit down, and do me the favour (though altogether beyond a poor carpenter's deserts) to fix your eyes on mine!"

Alice complied, She was very proud. Setting aside all advantages of rank, this fair girl deemed herself conscious of a power—combined of beauty, high, unsullied purity, and the preservative force of womanhood—that could make her sphere impenetrable, unless betrayed by treachery within. She instinctively knew, it may be, that some sinister or evil potency was now striving to pass her barriers; nor would she decline the contest. So Alice put woman's might against man's might; a match not often equal on the part of woman.

Her father meanwhile had turned away, and seemed absorbed in the contemplation of a landscape by Claude, where a shadowy and sun-streaked *vista* penetrated so remotely into an ancient wood, that it would have been no wonder if his fancy had lost itself in the picture's bewildering depths. But, in truth, the picture was no more to him at that moment than the blank wall against which it hung. His mind was haunted with the many and strange tales which he had heard, attributing mysterious if not supernatural endowments to these Maules, as well the grandson here present as his two immediate ancestors.

Mr. Pyncheon's long residence abroad, and intercourse with men of wit and fashion,—courtiers, worldings, and free-thinkers,—had done much towards obliterating the grim Puritan superstitions, which no man of New England birth at that early period could entirely escape. But, on the other hand, had not a whole community believed Maule's grandfather to be a wizard? Had not the crime been proved? Had not the wizard died for it? Had he not bequeathed a legacy of hatred against the Pyncheons to this only grandson, who, as it appeared, was now about to exercise a subtle influence over the daughter of his enemy's house? Might not this influence be the same that was called witchcraft?

Turning half around, he caught a glimpse of Maule's figure in the looking-glass. At some paces from Alice, with his arms uplifted in the air, the carpenter made a gesture as if directing downward a slow, ponderous, and invisible weight upon the maiden.

"Stay, Maule!" exclaimed Mr. Pyncheon, stepping forward. "I forbid your proceeding further!"

"Pray, my dear father, do not interrupt the young man," said Alice, without changing her position. "His efforts, I assure you, will prove very harmless."

Again Mr. Pyncheon turned his eyes towards the Claude. It was then his daughter's will, in opposition to his own, that the experiment should be fully tried. Henceforth, therefore, he did but consent, not urge it. And was it not for her sake far more than for his own that he desired its success? That lost parchment once restored, the beautiful Alice Pyncheon, with the rich dowry which he could then bestow, might wed an English duke or a German reigning-prince, instead of some New England clergyman or lawyer! At the thought, the ambitious father almost consented, in his heart, that, if the devil's power were needed to the accomplishment of this great object, Maule might evoke him. Alice's own purity would be her safeguard.

With his mind full of imaginary magnificence, Mr. Pyncheon heard a half-uttered exclamation from his daughter. It was very faint and low; so indistinct that there seemed but half a will to shape out the words, and too undefined a purport to be intelligible. Yet it was a call for help!—his conscience never doubted it;—and, little more than a whisper to his ear, it was a dismal shriek, and long re-echoed so, in the region round his heart! But this time the father did not turn.

After a further interval, Maule spoke.

"Behold your daughter," said he.

Mr. Pyncheon came hastily forward. The carpenter was standing erect in front of Alice's chair, and pointing his finger towards the maiden with an expression of triumphant power, the limits of which could not be defined, as, indeed, its scope stretched vaguely towards the unseen and the infinite. Alice sat in an attitude of profound repose, with the long brown lashes drooping over her eyes.

"There she is!" said the carpenter. "Speak to her!"

"Alice! My daughter!" exclaimed Mr. Pyncheon. "My own Alice!"

She did not stir.

"Louder!" said Maule, smiling.

"Alice! Awake!" cried her father. "It troubles me to see you thus! Awake!"

He spoke loudly, with terror in his voice, and close to that delicate ear which had always been so sensitive to every discord. But the sound evidently reached her not. It is indescribable what a sense of remote, dim, unattainable distance betwixt himself and Alice was impressed on the father by this impossibility of reaching her with his voice.

"Best touch her!" said Matthew Maule "Shake the girl, and roughly, too! My hands are hardened with too much use of axe, saw, and plane,—else I might help you!"

Mr. Pyncheon took her hand, and pressed it with the earnestness of startled emotion. He kissed her, with so great a heartthrob in the kiss, that he thought she must needs feel it. Then, in a gust of anger at her insensibility, he shook her maiden form with a violence which, the next moment, it affrighted him to remember. He withdrew his encircling arms, and Alice—whose figure, though flexible, had been wholly impassive—relapsed into the same attitude as before these attempts to arouse her. Maule having shifted his position, her face was turned towards him slightly, but with what seemed to be a reference of her very slumber to his guidance.

Then it was a strange sight to behold how the man of conventionalities shook the powder out of his periwig; how the reserved and stately gentleman forgot his dignity; how the gold-embroidered waistcoat flickered and glistened in the firelight with the convulsion of rage, terror, and sorrow in the human heart that was beating under it.

"Villain!" cried Mr. Pyncheon, shaking his clenched fist at Maule. "You and the fiend together have robbed me of my daughter. Give her back, spawn of the old wizard, or you shall climb Gallows Hill in your grandfather's footsteps!"

"Softly, Mr. Pyncheon!" said the carpenter with scornful composure. "Softly, an' it please your worship, else you will spoil those rich lace-ruffles at your wrists! Is it my crime if you have sold your daughter for the mere hope of getting a sheet of yellow parchment into your clutch? There sits Mistress Alice quietly asleep. Now let Matthew Maule try whether she be as proud as the carpenter found her awhile since."

He spoke, and Alice responded, with a soft, subdued, inward acquiescence, and a bending of her form towards him, like the flame of a torch when it indicates a gentle draught of air. He beckoned with his hand, and, rising from her chair,—blindly, but undoubtingly, as tending to her sure and inevitable centre,—the proud Alice approached him. He waved her back, and, retreating, Alice sank again into her seat.

"She is mine!" said Matthew Maule. "Mine, by the right of the strongest spirit!"

In the further progress of the legend, there is a long, grotesque, and occasionally awe-striking account of the carpenter's incantations (if so they are to be called), with a view of discovering the lost document. It appears to have been his object to convert the mind of Alice into a kind of telescopic medium, through which Mr. Pyncheon and himself might obtain a glimpse into the spiritual world. He succeeded, accordingly, in holding an imperfect sort of intercourse, at one remove, with the departed personages in whose custody the so much valued secret had been carried beyond the precincts of earth.

During her trance, Alice described three figures as being present to her spiritualized perception. One was an aged, dignified, stern-looking gentleman, clad as for a solemn festival in grave and costly attire, but with a great blood-stain on his richly wrought band; the second, an aged man, meanly dressed, with a dark and malign countenance, and a broken halter about his neck; the third, a person not so advanced in life as the former two, but beyond the middle age, wearing a coarse woollen tunic and leather breeches, and with a carpenter's rule sticking out of his side pocket. These three visionary characters possessed a mutual knowledge of the missing document.

One of them, in truth,—it was he with the blood-stain on his band,—seemed, unless his gestures were misunderstood, to hold the parchment in his immediate keeping, but was prevented by his two partners in the mystery from disburdening himself of the trust. Finally, when he showed a purpose of shouting forth the secret loudly enough to be heard from his own sphere into that of mortals, his companions struggled with him, and pressed their hands over his mouth; and forthwith—whether that he were choked by it, or that the secret itself was of a crimson hue—there was a fresh flow of blood upon his band. Upon this, the two meanly dressed figures mocked and jeered at the much-abashed old dignitary, and pointed their fingers at the stain.

At this juncture, Maule turned to Mr. Pyncheon.

"It will never be allowed," said he. "The custody of this secret, that would so enrich his heirs, makes part of your grandfather's retribution. He must choke with it until it is no longer of any value. And keep you the House of the Seven Gables! It is too dear bought an inheritance, and too heavy with the curse upon it, to be shifted yet awhile from the Colonel's posterity."

Mr. Pyncheon tried to speak, but—what with fear and passion—could make only a gurgling murmur in his throat. The carpenter smiled.

"Aha, worshipful sir!—so you have old Maule's blood to drink!" said he jeeringly.

"Fiend in man's shape! why dost thou keep dominion over my child?" cried Mr. Pyncheon, when his choked utterance could make way. "Give me back my daughter. Then go thy ways; and may we never meet again!"

"Your daughter!" said Matthew Maule. "Why, she is fairly mine! Nevertheless, not to be too hard with fair Mistress Alice, I will leave her in your keeping; but I do not warrant you that she shall never have occasion to remember Maule, the carpenter."

He waved his hands with an upward motion; and, after a few repetitions of similar gestures, the beautiful Alice Pyncheon awoke from her strange trance. She awoke without the slightest recollection of her visionary experience; but as one losing herself in a momentary reverie, and returning to the consciousness of actual life, in almost as brief an interval as the down-sinking flame of the hearth should quiver again up the chimney. On recognizing Matthew Maule, she assumed an air of somewhat cold but gentle dignity, the rather, as there was a certain peculiar smile on the carpenter's visage that stirred the native pride of the fair Alice. So ended, for that time, the quest for the lost title-deed of the Pyncheon territory at the Eastward; nor, though often subsequently renewed, has it ever yet befallen a Pyncheon to set his eye upon that parchment.

But, alas for the beautiful, the gentle, yet too haughty Alice! A power that she little dreamed of had laid its grasp upon her maiden soul. A will, most unlike her own, constrained her to do its grotesque and fantastic bidding. Her father as it proved, had martyred his poor child to an inordinate desire for measuring his land by miles instead of acres. And, therefore, while Alice Pyncheon lived, she was Maule's slave, in a bondage more humiliating, a thousand-fold, than that which binds its chain around the body. Seated by his humble fireside, Maule had but to wave his hand; and, wherever the proud lady chanced to be,—whether in her chamber, or entertaining her father's stately guests, or worshipping at church,—whatever her place or occupation, her spirit passed from beneath her own control, and bowed itself to Maule. "Alice, laugh!"—the carpenter, beside his hearth, would say; or perhaps intensely will it, without a spoken word.

And, even were it prayer-time, or at a funeral, Alice must break into wild laughter. "Alice, be sad!"—and, at the instant, down would come her tears, quenching all the mirth of those around her like sudden rain upon a bonfire. "Alice, dance."—and dance she would, not in such court-like measures as she had

189

learned abroad, but some high-paced jig, or hop-skip rigadoon, befitting the brisk lasses at a rustic merry-making. It seemed to be Maule's impulse, not to ruin Alice, nor to visit her with any black or gigantic mischief, which would have crowned her sorrows with the grace of tragedy, but to wreak a low, ungenerous scorn upon her. Thus all the dignity of life was lost. She felt herself too much abased, and longed to change natures with some worm!

One evening, at a bridal party (but not her own; for, so lost from self-control, she would have deemed it sin to marry), poor Alice was beckoned forth by her unseen despot, and constrained, in her gossamer white dress and satin slippers, to hasten along the street to the mean dwelling of a labouring-man. There was laughter and good cheer within; for Matthew Maule, that night, was to wed the labourer's daughter, and had summoned proud Alice Pyncheon to wait upon his bride. And so she did; and when the twain were one, Alice awoke out of her enchanted sleep. Yet, no longer proud,—humbly, and with a smile all steeped in sadness,—she kissed Maule's wife, and went her way.

It was an inclement night; the southeast wind drove the mingled snow and rain into her thinly sheltered bosom; her satin slippers were wet through and through, as she trod the muddy sidewalks. The next day a cold; soon, a settled cough; *anon*, a hectic cheek, a wasted form, that sat beside the harpsichord, and filled the house with music! Music in which a strain of the heavenly choristers was echoed! Oh; joy! For Alice had borne her last humiliation! Oh, greater joy! For Alice was penitent of her one earthly sin, and proud no more!

The Pyncheons made a great funeral for Alice. The kith and kin were there, and the whole respectability of the town besides. But, last in the procession, came Matthew Maule, gnashing his teeth, as if he would have bitten his own heart in twain,—the darkest and woefullest man that ever walked behind a corpse! He meant to humble Alice, not to kill her; but he had taken a woman's delicate soul into his rude gripe, to play with—and she was dead!

Holgrave, plunging into his tale with the energy and absorption natural to a young author, had given a good deal of action to the parts capable of being developed and exemplified in that manner. He now observed that a certain remarkable drowsiness (wholly unlike that with which the reader possibly feels himself affected) had been flung over the senses of his auditress. It was the effect, unquestionably, of the mystic gesticulations by which he had sought to bring bodily before Phoebe's perception the figure of the mesmerizing carpenter. With the lids drooping over her eyes,—now lifted for an instant, and drawn down again as with leaden weights,—she leaned slightly towards him, and seemed almost to regulate her breath by his.

Holgrave gazed at her, as he rolled up his manuscript, and recognized an incipient stage of that curious psychological condition which, as he had himself told Phoebe, he possessed more than an ordinary faculty of producing. A veil was beginning to be muffled about her, in which she could behold only him, and live only in his thoughts and emotions. His glance, as he fastened it on the young girl, grew involuntarily more concentrated; in his attitude there was the consciousness of power, investing his hardly mature figure with a dignity that did not belong to its physical manifestation.

It was evident, that, with but one wave of his hand and a corresponding effort of his will, he could complete his mastery over Phoebe's yet free and virgin spirit: he could establish an influence over this good, pure, and simple child, as dangerous, and perhaps as disastrous, as that which the carpenter of his legend had acquired and exercised over the ill-fated Alice.

To a disposition like Holgrave's, at once speculative and active, there is no temptation so great as the opportunity of acquiring empire over the human spirit; nor any idea more seductive to a young man than to become the arbiter of a young girl's destiny. Let us, therefore,—whatever his defects of nature and education, and in spite of his scorn for creeds and institutions,—concede to the daguerreotypist the rare and high quality of reverence for another's individuality. Let us allow him integrity, also, forever after to be confided in; since he forbade himself to twine that one link more which might have rendered his spell over Phoebe indissoluble.

He made a slight gesture upward with his hand.

"You really mortify me, my dear Miss Phoebe!" he exclaimed, smiling half-sarcastically at her. "My poor story, it is but too evident, will never do for Godey or Graham! Only think of your falling asleep at what I hoped the newspaper critics would pronounce a most brilliant, powerful, imaginative, pathetic, and original winding up! Well, the manuscript must serve to light lamps with;—if, indeed, being so imbued with my gentle dullness, it is any longer capable of flame!"

"Me asleep! How can you say so?" answered Phoebe, as unconscious of the crisis through which she had passed as an infant of the precipice to the verge of which it has rolled. "No, no! I consider myself as having been very attentive; and, though I don't remember the incidents quite distinctly, yet I have an impression of a vast deal of trouble and calamity,—so, no doubt, the story will prove exceedingly attractive."

By this time the sun had gone down, and was tinting the clouds towards the zenith with those bright hues which are not seen there until sometime after sunset, and when the horizon has quite lost its richer brilliancy. The moon, too, which had long been climbing overhead, and unobtrusively melting its disk into the azure,—like an ambitious demagogue, who hides his aspiring purpose by assuming the prevalent hue of popular sentiment,—now began to shine out, broad and oval, in its middle pathway. These silvery beams were already powerful enough to change the character of the lingering daylight. They softened and embellished the aspect of the old house; although the shadows fell deeper into the angles of its many gables, and lay brooding under the projecting story, and within the half-open door.

With the lapse of every moment, the garden grew more picturesque; the fruit-trees, shrubbery, and flower-bushes had a dark obscurity among them. The commonplace characteristics—which, at noontide, it seemed to have taken a century of sordid life to accumulate—were now transfigured by a charm of romance. A hundred mysterious years were whispering among the leaves, whenever the slight sea-breeze found its way thither and stirred them. Through the foliage that roofed the little summer-house the moonlight flickered to and fro, and fell silvery white on the dark floor, the table, and the circular bench, with a continual shift and play, according as the chinks and wayward crevices among the twigs admitted or shut out the glimmer.

So sweetly cool was the atmosphere, after all the feverish day, that the summer eve might be fancied as sprinkling dews and liquid moonlight, with a dash of icy temper in them, out of a silver vase. Here and there, a few drops of this freshness were scattered on a human heart, and gave it youth again, and sympathy with the eternal youth of nature. The artist chanced to be one on whom the reviving influence fell. It made him feel—what he sometimes almost forgot, thrust so early as he had been into the rude struggle of man with man—how youthful he still was.

"It seems to me," he observed, "that I never watched the coming of so beautiful an eve, and never felt anything so very much like happiness as at this moment. After all, what a good world we live in! How good, and beautiful! How young it is, too, with nothing really rotten or age-worn in it! This old house, for example, which sometimes has positively oppressed my breath with its smell of decaying timber! And this garden, where the black mould always clings to my spade, as if I were a sexton delving in a graveyard!

"Could I keep the feeling that now possesses me, the garden would every day be virgin soil, with the earth's first freshness in the flavor of its beans and squashes; and the house!—it would be like a bower in Eden, blossoming with the earliest roses that God ever made. Moonlight, and the sentiment in man's heart responsive to it, are the greatest of renovators and reformers. And all other reform and renovation, I suppose, will prove to be no better than moonshine!"

"I have been happier than I am now; at least, much gayer,"

said Phoebe thoughtfully. "Yet I am sensible of a great charm in this brightening moonlight; and I love to watch how the day, tired as it is, lags away reluctantly, and hates to be called yesterday so soon. I never cared much about moonlight before. What is there, I wonder, so beautiful in it, tonight?"

"And you have never felt it before?" inquired the artist, looking earnestly at the girl through the twilight.

"Never," answered Phoebe; "and life does not look the same, now that I have felt it so. It seems as if I had looked at everything, hitherto, in broad daylight, or else in the ruddy light of a cheerful fire, glimmering and dancing through a room. Ah, poor me!" she added, with a half-melancholy laugh. "I shall never be so merry as before I knew Cousin Hepzibah and poor Cousin Clifford. I have grown a great deal older, in this little time. Older, and, I hope, wiser, and,—not exactly sadder,—but, certainly, with not half so much lightness in my spirits! I have given them my sunshine, and have been glad to give it; but, of course, I cannot both give and keep it. They are welcome, notwithstanding!"

"You have lost nothing, Phoebe, worth keeping, nor which it was possible to keep," said Holgrave after a pause. "Our first youth is of no value; for we are never conscious of it until after it is gone. But sometimes—always, I suspect, unless one is exceedingly unfortunate—there comes a sense of second youth, gushing out of the heart's joy at being in love; or, possibly, it may come to crown some other grand festival in life, if any other such there be. This bemoaning of one's self (as you do now) over the first, careless, shallow gayety of youth departed, and this profound happiness at youth regained,—so much deeper and richer than that we lost,—are essential to the soul's development. In some cases, the two states come almost simultaneously, and mingle the sadness and the rapture in one mysterious emotion."

"I hardly think I understand you," said Phoebe.

"No wonder," replied Holgrave, smiling; "for I have told you a secret which I hardly began to know before I found myself giving it utterance. Remember it, however; and when the truth becomes clear to you, then think of this moonlight scene!"

"It is entirely moonlight now, except only a little flush of faint crimson, upward from the west, between those buildings," remarked Phoebe. "I must go in. Cousin Hepzibah is not quick at figures, and will give herself a headache over the day's accounts, unless I help her."

But Holgrave detained her a little longer.

"Miss Hepzibah tells me," observed he, "that you return to the country in a few days."

"Yes, but only for a little while," answered Phoebe; "for I look upon this as my present home. I go to make a few arrangements, and to take a more deliberate leave of my mother and friends. It is pleasant to live where one is much desired and very useful; and I think I may have the satisfaction of feeling myself so here."

"You surely may, and more than you imagine," said the artist. "Whatever health, comfort, and natural life exists in the house is embodied in your person. These blessings came along with you, and will vanish when you leave the threshold. Miss Hepzibah, by secluding herself from society, has lost all true relation with it, and is, in fact, dead; although she galvanizes herself into a semblance of life, and stands behind her counter, afflicting the world with a greatly-to-be-deprecated scowl. Your poor cousin Clifford is another dead and long-buried person, on whom the governor and council have wrought a necromantic miracle. I should not wonder if he were to crumble away, some morning, after you are gone, and nothing be seen of him more, except a heap of dust. Miss Hepzibah, at any rate, will lose what little flexibility she has. They both exist by you."

"I should be very sorry to think so," answered Phoebe gravely. "But it is true that my small abilities were precisely what they needed; and I have a real interest in their welfare,—an odd kind of motherly sentiment,—which I wish you would not laugh at! And let me tell you frankly, Mr. Holgrave, I am sometimes puzzled to know whether you wish them well or ill."

"Undoubtedly," said the daguerreotypist, "I do feel an interest in this antiquated, poverty-stricken old maiden lady, and this degraded and shattered gentleman,—this abortive lover of the beautiful. A kindly interest, too, helpless old children that they are! But you have no conception what a different kind of heart mine is from your own. It is not my impulse, as regards these two individuals, either to help or hinder; but to look on, to analyze, to explain matters to myself, and to comprehend the drama which, for almost two hundred years, has been dragging its slow length over the ground where you and I now tread.

"If permitted to witness the close, I doubt not to derive a moral satisfaction from it, go matters how they may. There is a conviction within me that the end draws nigh. But, though Providence sent you hither to help, and sends me only as a privileged and meet spectator, I pledge myself to lend these unfortunate beings whatever aid I can!"

"I wish you would speak more plainly," cried Phoebe, perplexed and displeased; "and, above all, that you would feel more like a Christian and a human being! How is it possible to see people in distress without desiring, more than anything else, to help and comfort them? You talk as if this old house were a theatre; and you seem to look at Hepzibah's and Clifford's misfortunes, and those of generations before them, as a tragedy, such as I have seen acted in the hall of a country hotel, only the present one appears to be played exclusively for your amusement. I do not like this. The play costs the performers too much, and the audience is too cold-hearted."

"You are severe," said Holgrave, compelled to recognize a degree of truth in the piquant sketch of his own mood.

"And then," continued Phoebe, "what can you mean by your conviction, which you tell me of, that the end is drawing near? Do you know of any new trouble hanging over my poor relatives? If so, tell me at once, and I will not leave them!"

"Forgive me, Phoebe!" said the daguerreotypist, holding out his hand, to which the girl was constrained to yield her own. "I am somewhat of a mystic, it must be confessed. The tendency is in my blood, together with the faculty of mesmerism, which might have brought me to Gallows Hill, in the good old times of witchcraft. Believe me, if I were really aware of any secret, the disclosure of which would benefit your friends,—who are my own friends, likewise,—you should learn it before we part. But I have no such knowledge."

"You hold something back!" said Phoebe.

"Nothing,—no secrets but my own," answered Holgrave. "I can perceive, indeed, that Judge Pyncheon still keeps his eye on Clifford, in whose ruin he had so large a share. His motives and intentions, however are a mystery to me. He is a determined and relentless man, with the genuine character of an inquisitor; and had he any object to gain by putting Clifford to the rack, I verily believe that he would wrench his joints from their sockets, in order to accomplish it. But, so wealthy and eminent as he is,—so powerful in his own strength, and in the support of society on all sides,—what can Judge Pyncheon have to hope or fear from the imbecile, branded, half-torpid Clifford?"

"Yet," urged Phoebe, "you did speak as if misfortune were impending!"

"Oh, that was because I am morbid!" replied the artist. "My mind has a twist aside, like almost everybody's mind, except your own. Moreover, it is so strange to find myself an inmate of this old Pyncheon House, and sitting in this old garden—(hark, how Maule's well is murmuring!)—that, were it only for this one circumstance, I cannot help fancying that Destiny is arranging its fifth act for a catastrophe."

"There!" cried Phoebe with renewed vexation; for she was by nature as hostile to mystery as the sunshine to a dark corner. "You puzzle me more than ever!"

"Then let us part friends!" said Holgrave, pressing her hand. "Or, if not friends, let us part before you entirely hate me. You, who love everybody else in the world!"

"Goodbye, then," said Phoebe frankly. "I do not mean to be angry a great while, and should be sorry to have you think so. There has Cousin Hepzibah been standing in the shadow of the doorway, this quarter of an hour past! She thinks I stay too long in the damp garden. So, goodnight, and goodbye."

On the second morning thereafter, Phoebe might have been

seen, in her straw bonnet, with a shawl on one arm and a little carpet-bag on the other, bidding *adieu* to Hepzibah and Cousin Clifford. She was to take a seat in the next train of cars, which would transport her to within half a dozen miles of her country village.

The tears were in Phoebe's eyes; a smile, dewy with affectionate regret, was glimmering around her pleasant mouth. She wondered how it came to pass, that her life of a few weeks, here in this heavy-hearted old mansion, had taken such hold of her, and so melted into her associations, as now to seem a more important centre-point of remembrance than all which had gone before. How had Hepzibah—grim, silent, and irresponsive to her overflow of cordial sentiment—contrived to win so much love? And Clifford,—in his abortive decay, with the mystery of fearful crime upon him, and the close prison-atmosphere yet lurking in his breath,—how had he transformed himself into the simplest child, whom Phoebe felt bound to watch over, and be, as it were, the providence of his unconsidered hours! Everything, at that instant of farewell, stood out prominently to her view. Look where she would, lay her hand on what she might, the object responded to her consciousness, as if a moist human heart were in it.

She peeped from the window into the garden, and felt herself more regretful at leaving this spot of black earth, vitiated with such an age-long growth of weeds, than joyful at the idea of again scenting her pine forests and fresh clover-fields. She called Chanticleer, his two wives, and the venerable chicken, and threw them some crumbs of bread from the breakfast-table. These being hastily gobbled up, the chicken spread its wings, and alighted close by Phoebe on the window-sill, where it looked gravely into her face and vented its emotions in a croak. Phoebe bade it be a good old chicken during her absence, and promised to bring it a little bag of buckwheat.

"Ah, Phoebe!" remarked Hepzibah, "you do not smile so naturally as when you came to us! Then, the smile chose to shine out; now, you choose it should. It is well that you are going back, for a little while, into your native air. There has been too much weight on your spirits. The house is too gloomy and lonesome; the shop is full of vexations; and as for me, I have no faculty of making things look brighter than they are. Dear Clifford has been your only comfort!"

"Come hither, Phoebe," suddenly cried her cousin Clifford, who had said very little all the morning. "Close!—closer!—and look me in the face!"

Phoebe put one of her small hands on each elbow of his chair, and leaned her face towards him, so that he might peruse it as carefully as he would. It is probable that the latent emotions of this parting hour had revived, in some degree, his bedimmed and enfeebled faculties. At any rate, Phoebe soon felt that, if not the profound insight of a seer, yet a more than feminine delicacy of appreciation, was making her heart the subject of its regard. A moment before, she had known nothing which she would have sought to hide. Now, as if some secret were hinted to her own consciousness through the medium of another's perception, she was fain to let her eyelids droop beneath Clifford's gaze. A blush, too,—the redder, because she strove hard to keep it down,—ascended bigger and higher, in a tide of fitful progress, until even her brow was all suffused with it.

"It is enough, Phoebe," said Clifford, with a melancholy smile. "When I first saw you, you were the prettiest little maiden in the world; and now you have deepened into beauty. Girlhood has passed into womanhood; the bud is a bloom! Go, now—I feel lonelier than I did."

Phoebe took leave of the desolate couple, and passed through the shop, twinkling her eyelids to shake off a dew-drop; for—considering how brief her absence was to be, and therefore the folly of being cast down about it—she would not so far acknowledge her tears as to dry them with her handkerchief. On the doorstep, she met the little urchin whose marvellous feats of gastronomy have been recorded in the earlier pages of our narrative. She took from the window some specimen or other of natural history,—her eyes being too dim with moisture to inform her accurately whether it was a rabbit or a hippopotamus,—put it into the child's hand as a parting gift, and went her way.

Old Uncle Venner was just coming out of his door, with a wood-horse and saw on his shoulder; and, trudging along the street, he scrupled not to keep company with Phoebe, so far as their paths lay together; nor, in spite of his patched coat and rusty beaver, and the curious fashion of his tow-cloth trousers, could she find it in her heart to outwalk him.

"We shall miss you, next Sabbath afternoon," observed the street philosopher. "It is unaccountable how little while it takes some folks to grow just as natural to a man as his own breath; and, begging your pardon, Miss Phoebe (though there can be no offence in an old man's saying it), that's just what you've grown to me! My years have been a great many, and your life is but just beginning; and yet, you are somehow as familiar to me as if I had found you at my mother's door, and you had blossomed, like a running vine, all along my pathway since. Come back soon, or I shall be gone to my farm; for I begin to find these wood-sawing jobs a little too tough for my back-ache."

"Very soon, Uncle Venner," replied Phoebe.

"And let it be all the sooner, Phoebe, for the sake of those poor souls yonder," continued her companion. "They can never do without you, now,—never, Phoebe; never—no more than if one of God's angels had been living with them, and making their dismal house pleasant and comfortable! Don't it seem to you they'd be in a sad case, if, some pleasant summer morning like this, the angel should spread his wings, and fly to the place he came from? Well, just so they feel, now that you're going home by the railroad! They can't bear it, Miss Phoebe; so be sure to come back!"

"I am no angel, Uncle Venner," said Phoebe, smiling, as she offered him her hand at the street-corner. "But, I suppose, people never feel so much like angels as when they are doing what little good they may. So I shall certainly come back!"

Thus parted the old man and the rosy girl; and Phoebe took the wings of the morning, and was soon flitting almost as rapidly away as if endowed with the aerial locomotion of the angels to whom Uncle Venner had so graciously compared her.

15: THE SCOWL AND SMILE

Several days passed over the Seven Gables, heavily and drearily enough. In fact (not to attribute the whole gloom of sky and earth to the one inauspicious circumstance of Phoebe's departure), an easterly storm had set in, and indefatigably apply itself to the task of making the black roof and walls of the old house look more cheerless than ever before. Yet was the outside not half so cheerless as the interior. Poor Clifford was cut off, at once, from all his scanty resources of enjoyment. Phoebe was not there; nor did the sunshine fall upon the floor.

The garden, with its muddy walks, and the chill, dripping foliage of its summer-house, was an image to be shuddered at. Nothing flourished in the cold, moist, pitiless atmosphere, drifting with the brackish scud of sea-breezes, except the moss along the joints of the shingle-roof, and the great bunch of weeds, that had lately been suffering from drought, in the angle between the two front gables.

As for Hepzibah, she seemed not merely possessed with the east wind, but to be, in her very person, only another phase of this gray and sullen spell of weather; the East-Wind itself, grim and disconsolate, in a rusty black silk gown, and with a turban of cloud-wreaths on its head. The custom of the shop fell off, because a story got abroad that she soured her small beer and other damageable commodities, by scowling on them. It is, perhaps, true that the public had something reasonably to complain of in her deportment; but towards Clifford she was neither ill-tempered nor unkind, nor felt less warmth of heart than always, had it been possible to make it reach him.

The inutility of her best efforts, however, palsied the poor old gentlewoman. She could do little else than sit silently in a corner of the room, when the wet pear-tree branches, sweeping across the small windows, created a noonday dusk, which Hepzibah unconsciously darkened with her woebegone aspect.

It was no fault of Hepzibah's. Everything—even the old chairs and tables, that had known what weather was for three or four such lifetimes as her own—looked as damp and chill as if the present were their worst experience. The picture of the Puritan Colonel shivered on the wall. The house itself shivered, from every attic of its seven gables down to the great kitchen fireplace, which served all the better as an emblem of the mansion's heart, because, though built for warmth, it was now so comfortless and empty.

Hepzibah attempted to enliven matters by a fire in the parlour. But the storm demon kept watch above, and, whenever a flame was kindled, drove the smoke back again, choking the chimney's sooty throat with its own breath. Nevertheless, during four days of this miserable storm, Clifford wrapt himself in an old cloak, and occupied his customary chair. On the morning of the fifth, when summoned to breakfast, he responded only by a broken-hearted murmur, expressive of a determination not to leave his bed. His sister made no attempt to change his purpose. In fact, entirely as she loved him, Hepzibah could hardly have borne any longer the wretched duty—so impracticable by her few and rigid faculties—of seeking pastime for a still sensitive, but ruined mind, critical and fastidious, without force or volition. It was at least something short of positive despair, that today she might sit shivering alone, and not suffer continually a new grief, and unreasonable pang of remorse, at every fitful sigh of her fellow sufferer.

But Clifford, it seemed, though he did not make his appearance below stairs, had, after all, bestirred himself in quest of amusement. In the course of the forenoon, Hepzibah heard a note of music, which (there being no other tuneful contrivance in the House of the Seven Gables) she knew must proceed from Alice Pyncheon's harpsichord. She was aware that Clifford, in his youth, had possessed a cultivated taste for music, and a considerable degree of skill in its practice. It was difficult, however, to conceive of his retaining an accomplishment to which daily exercise is so essential, in the measure indicated by the sweet, airy, and delicate, though most melancholy strain, that now stole upon her ear.

Nor was it less marvellous that the long-silent instrument should be capable of so much melody. Hepzibah involuntarily thought of the ghostly harmonies, prelusive of death in the family, which were attributed to the legendary Alice. But it was, perhaps, proof of the agency of other than spiritual fingers, that, after a few touches, the chords seemed to snap asunder with their own vibrations, and the music ceased.

But a harsher sound succeeded to the mysterious notes; nor was the easterly day fated to pass without an event sufficient in itself to poison, for Hepzibah and Clifford, the balmiest air that ever brought the humming-birds along with it. The final echoes of Alice Pyncheon's performance (or Clifford's, if his we must consider it) were driven away by no less vulgar a dissonance than the ringing of the shop-bell. A foot was heard scraping itself on the threshold, and thence somewhat ponderously stepping on the floor.

Hepzibah delayed a moment, while muffling herself in a faded shawl, which had been her defensive armour in a forty years' warfare against the east wind. A characteristic sound, however,— neither a cough nor a hem, but a kind of rumbling and reverberating spasm in somebody's capacious depth of chest;—impelled her to hurry forward, with that aspect of fierce faint-heartedness so common to women in cases of perilous emergency. Few of her sex, on such occasions, have ever looked so terrible as our poor scowling Hepzibah. But the visitor quietly closed the shop-door behind him, stood up his umbrella against the counter, and turned a visage of composed benignity, to meet the alarm and anger which his appearance had excited.

Hepzibah's presentiment had not deceived her. It was no other than Judge Pyncheon, who, after in vain trying the front door, had now effected his entrance into the shop.

"How do you do, Cousin Hepzibah?—and how does this most inclement weather affect our poor Clifford?" began the judge; and wonderful it seemed, indeed, that the easterly storm was not put to shame, or, at any rate, a little mollified, by the genial benevolence of his smile. "I could not rest without calling to ask, once more, whether I can in any manner promote his comfort, or your own."

"You can do nothing," said Hepzibah, controlling her agitation as well as she could. "I devote myself to Clifford. He has every comfort which his situation admits of."

"But allow me to suggest, dear cousin," rejoined the judge, "you err,—in all affection and kindness, no doubt, and with the very best intentions,—but you do err, nevertheless, in keeping your brother so secluded. Why insulate him thus from all sympathy and kindness? Clifford, alas! has had too much of solitude. Now let him try society,—the society, that is to say, of kindred and old friends. Let me, for instance, but see Clifford, and I will answer for the good effect of the interview."

"You cannot see him," answered Hepzibah. "Clifford has kept his bed since yesterday."

"What! How! Is he ill?" exclaimed Judge Pyncheon, starting with what seemed to be angry alarm; for the very frown of the old Puritan darkened through the room as he spoke. "Nay, then, I must and will see him! What if he should die?"

"He is in no danger of death," said Hepzibah,—and added, with bitterness that she could repress no longer, "none; unless he shall be persecuted to death, now, by the same man who long ago attempted it!"

"Cousin Hepzibah," said the judge, with an impressive earnestness of manner, which grew even to tearful pathos as he proceeded, "is it possible that you do not perceive how unjust, how unkind, how unchristian, is this constant, this long-continued bitterness against me, for a part which I was constrained by duty and conscience, by the force of law, and at my own peril, to act? What did I do, in detriment to Clifford, which it was possible to leave undone? How could you, his sister,—if, for your never-ending sorrow, as it has been for mine, you had known what I did,—have, shown greater tenderness? And do you think, cousin, that it has cost me no pang?—that it has left no anguish in my bosom, from that day to this, amidst all the prosperity with which Heaven has blessed me?—or that I do not now rejoice, when it is deemed consistent with the dues of public justice and the welfare of society that this dear kinsman, this early friend, this nature so delicately and beautifully constituted,—so unfortunate, let us pronounce him, and forbear to say, so guilty,—that our own Clifford, in fine, should be given back to life, and its possibilities of enjoyment?

"Ah, you little know me, Cousin Hepzibah! You little know this heart! It now throbs at the thought of meeting him! There lives not the human being (except yourself,—and you not more than I) who has shed so many tears for Clifford's calamity. You behold some of them now. There is none who would so delight to promote his happiness! Try me, Hepzibah!—try me, Cousin!—try the man whom you have treated as your enemy and Clifford's!—try Jaffrey Pyncheon, and you shall find him true, to the heart's core!"

"In the name of Heaven," cried Hepzibah, provoked only to intenser indignation by this outgush of the inestimable tenderness of a stern nature,—"in God's name, whom you insult, and whose power I could almost question, since he hears you utter so many false words without palsying your tongue,—give over, I beseech you, this loathsome pretence of affection for your victim! You hate him! Say so, like a man! You cherish, at this moment, some black purpose against him in your heart! Speak it out, at once!—or, if you hope so to promote it better, hide it till you can triumph in its success! But never speak again of your love for my poor brother. I cannot bear it! It will drive me beyond a woman's decency! It will drive me mad! Forbear! Not another word! It will make me spurn you!"

For once, Hepzibah's wrath had given her courage. She had spoken. But, after all, was this unconquerable distrust of Judge Pyncheon's integrity, and this utter denial, apparently, of his claim to stand in the ring of human sympathies,—were they founded in any just perception of his character, or merely the offspring of a woman's unreasonable prejudice, deduced from nothing?

The judge, beyond all question, was a man of eminent respectability. The church acknowledged it; the state acknowledged it. It was denied by nobody. In all the very extensive sphere of those who knew him, whether in his public or private capacities, there was not an individual—except Hepzibah, and some lawless mystic, like the daguerreotypist, and, possibly, a few political opponents—who would have dreamed of seriously disputing his claim to a high and honourable place in the world's regard. Nor (we must do him the further justice to say) did Judge Pyncheon himself, probably, entertain many or very frequent doubts, that his enviable reputation accorded with his deserts.

His conscience, therefore, usually considered the surest witness to a man's integrity,—his conscience, unless it might be for the little space of five minutes in the twenty-four hours, or, now and then, some black day in the whole year's circle,—his conscience bore an accordant testimony with the world's laudatory voice. And yet, strong as this evidence may seem to be, we should hesitate to peril our own conscience on the assertion, that the judge and the consenting world were right, and that poor Hepzibah with her solitary prejudice was wrong. Hidden from mankind,—forgotten by himself, or buried so deeply under a sculptured and ornamented pile of ostentatious deeds that his daily life could take no note of it,—there may have lurked some evil and unsightly thing. Nay, we could almost venture to say, further, that a daily guilt might have been acted by him, continually renewed, and reddening forth afresh, like the miraculous blood-stain of a murder, without his necessarily and at every moment being aware of it.

Men of strong minds, great force of character, and a hard texture of the sensibilities, are very capable of falling into mistakes of this kind. They are ordinarily men to whom forms are of paramount importance. Their field of action lies among the external phenomena of life. They possess vast ability in grasping, and arranging, and appropriating to themselves, the big, heavy, solid unrealities, such as gold, landed estate, offices of trust and emolument, and public honours. With these materials, and with deeds of goodly aspect, done in the public eye, an individual of this class builds up, as it were, a tall and stately edifice, which, in the view of other people, and ultimately in his own view, is no other than the man's character, or the man himself.

Behold, therefore, a palace! Its splendid halls and suites of spacious apartments are floored with a mosaic-work of costly marbles; its windows, the whole height of each room, admit the sunshine through the most transparent of plate-glass; its high cornices are gilded, and its ceilings gorgeously painted; and a lofty dome—through which, from the central pavement, you may gaze up to the sky, as with no obstructing medium be-tween—surmounts the whole. With what fairer and nobler em-blem could any man desire to shadow forth his character?

Ah! but in some low and obscure nook,—some narrow closet on the ground-floor, shut, locked and bolted, and the key flung away,—or beneath the marble pavement, in a stagnant water-puddle, with the richest pattern of mosaic-work above,—may lie a corpse, half decayed, and still decaying, and diffusing its death-scent all through the palace! The inhabitant will not be conscious of it, for it has long been his daily breath! Neither will the visitors, for they smell only the rich odours which the master sedulously scatters through the palace, and the incense which they bring, and delight to burn before him! Now and then, perchance, comes in a seer, before whose sadly gifted eye the whole structure melts into thin air, leaving only the hidden nook, the bolted closet, with the cobwebs festooned over its forgotten door, or the deadly hole under the pavement, and the decaying corpse within.

Here, then, we are to seek the true emblem of the man's character, and of the deed that gives whatever reality it possesses to his life. And, beneath the show of a marble palace, that pool of stagnant water, foul with many impurities, and, perhaps, tinged with blood,—that secret abomination, above which, possibly, he may say his prayers, without remembering it,—is this man's mis-erable soul!

To apply this train of remark somewhat more closely to Judge

Pyncheon. We might say (without in the least imputing crime to a personage of his eminent respectability) that there was enough of splendid rubbish in his life to cover up and paralyze a more active and subtile conscience than the judge was ever troubled with.

The purity of his judicial character, while on the bench; the faithfulness of his public service in subsequent capacities; his devotedness to his party, and the rigid consistency with which he had adhered to its principles, or, at all events, kept pace with its organized movements; his remarkable zeal as president of a Bible society; his unimpeachable integrity as treasurer of a widow's and orphan's fund; his benefits to horticulture, by producing two much esteemed varieties of the pear and to agriculture, through the agency of the famous Pyncheon bull; the cleanliness of his moral deportment, for a great many years past; the severity with which he had frowned upon, and finally cast off, an expensive and dissipated son, delaying forgiveness until within the final quarter of an hour of the young man's life; his prayers at morning and eventide, and graces at meal-time; his efforts in furtherance of the temperance cause; his confining himself, since the last attack of the gout, to five diurnal glasses of old sherry wine; the snowy whiteness of his linen, the polish of his boots, the handsomeness of his gold-headed cane, the square and roomy fashion of his coat, and the fineness of its material, and, in general, the studied propriety of his dress and equipment; the scrupulousness with which he paid public notice, in the street, by a bow, a lifting of the hat, a nod, or a motion of the hand, to all and sundry of his acquaintances, rich or poor; the smile of broad benevolence wherewith he made it a point to gladden the whole world,—what room could possibly be found for darker traits in a portrait made up of lineaments like these?

This proper face was what he beheld in the looking-glass. This admirably arranged life was what he was conscious of in the progress of every day. Then might not he claim to be its result and sum, and say to himself and the community, "Behold Judge Pyncheon there"?

And allowing that, many, many years ago, in his early and reckless youth, he had committed some one wrong act,—or that, even now, the inevitable force of circumstances should occasionally make him do one questionable deed among a thousand praiseworthy, or, at least, blameless ones,—would you characterize the judge by that one necessary deed, and that half-forgotten act, and let it overshadow the fair aspect of a lifetime? What is there so ponderous in evil, that a thumb's bigness of it should outweigh the mass of things not evil which were heaped into the other scale! This scale and balance system is a favourite one with people of Judge Pyncheon's brotherhood.

A hard, cold man, thus unfortunately situated, seldom or never looking inward, and resolutely taking his idea of himself from what purports to be his image as reflected in the mirror of public opinion, can scarcely arrive at true self-knowledge, except through loss of property and reputation. Sickness will not always help him do it; not always the death-hour!

But our affair now is with Judge Pyncheon as he stood confronting the fierce outbreak of Hepzibah's wrath. Without premeditation, to her own surprise, and indeed terror, she had given vent, for once, to the inveteracy of her resentment, cherished against this kinsman for thirty years.

Thus far the judge's countenance had expressed mild forbearance,—grave and almost gentle deprecation of his cousin's unbecoming violence,—free and Christian-like forgiveness of the wrong inflicted by her words. But when those words were irrevocably spoken, his look assumed sternness, the sense of power, and immitigable resolve; and this with so natural and imperceptible a change, that it seemed as if the iron man had stood there from the first, and the meek man not at all. The effect was as when the light, vapory clouds, with their soft colouring, suddenly vanish from the stony brow of a precipitous mountain, and leave there the frown which you at once feel to be eternal.

Hepzibah almost adopted the insane belief that it was her old Puritan ancestor, and not the modern judge, on whom she had just been wreaking the bitterness of her heart. Never did a man show stronger proof of the lineage attributed to him than Judge Pyncheon, at this crisis, by his unmistakable resemblance to the picture in the inner room.

"Cousin Hepzibah," said he very calmly, "it is time to have done with this."

"With all my heart!" answered she. "Then, why do you persecute us any longer? Leave poor Clifford and me in peace. Neither of us desires anything better!"

"It is my purpose to see Clifford before I leave this house," continued the judge. "Do not act like a madwoman, Hepzibah! I am his only friend, and an all-powerful one. Has it never occurred to you,—are you so blind as not to have seen,—that, without not merely my consent, but my efforts, my representations, the exertion of my whole influence, political, official, personal, Clifford would never have been what you call free? Did you think his release a triumph over me? Not so, my good cousin; not so, by any means! The furthest possible from that! No; but it was the accomplishment of a purpose long entertained on my part. I set him free!"

"You!" answered Hepzibah. "I never will believe it! He owed his dungeon to you; his freedom to God's providence!"

"I set him free!" reaffirmed Judge Pyncheon, with the calmest composure. "And I came hither now to decide whether he shall retain his freedom. It will depend upon himself. For this purpose, I must see him."

"Never!—it would drive him mad!" exclaimed Hepzibah, but with an irresoluteness sufficiently perceptible to the keen eye of the judge; for, without the slightest faith in his good intentions, she knew not whether there was most to dread in yielding or resistance. "And why should you wish to see this wretched, broken man, who retains hardly a fraction of his intellect, and will hide even that from an eye which has no love in it?"

"He shall see love enough in mine, if that be all!" said the judge, with well-grounded confidence in the benignity of his aspect. "But, Cousin Hepzibah, you confess a great deal, and very much to the purpose. Now, listen, and I will frankly explain my reasons for insisting on this interview. At the death, thirty years since, of our Uncle Jaffrey, it was found,—I know not whether the circumstance ever attracted much of your attention, among the sadder interests that clustered round that event,—but it was found that his visible estate, of every kind, fell far short of any estimate ever made of it. He was supposed to be immensely rich.

"Nobody doubted that he stood among the weightiest men of his day. It was one of his eccentricities, however,—and not altogether a folly, neither,—to conceal the amount of his property by making distant and foreign investments, perhaps under other names than his own, and by various means, familiar enough to capitalists, but unnecessary here to be specified. By Uncle Jaffrey's last will and testament, as you are aware, his entire property was bequeathed to me, with the single exception of a life interest to yourself in this old family mansion, and the strip of patrimonial estate remaining attached to it."

"And do you seek to deprive us of that?" asked Hepzibah, unable to restrain her bitter contempt. "Is this your price for ceasing to persecute poor Clifford?"

"Certainly not, my dear cousin!" answered the judge, smiling benevolently. "On the contrary, as you must do me the justice to own, I have constantly expressed my readiness to double or treble your resources, whenever you should make up your mind to accept any kindness of that nature at the hands of your kinsman. No, no! But here lies the gist of the matter. Of my uncle's unquestionably great estate, as I have said, not the half—no, not one third, as I am fully convinced—was apparent after his death. Now, I have the best possible reasons for believing that your brother Clifford can give me a clew to the recovery of the remainder."

"Clifford!—Clifford know of any hidden wealth? Clifford have it in his power to make you rich?" cried the old gentlewoman, affected with a sense of something like ridicule at the idea. "Impossible! You deceive yourself! It is really a thing to laugh at!"

"It is as certain as that I stand here!" said Judge Pyncheon, striking his gold-headed cane on the floor, and at the same time stamping his foot, as if to express his conviction the more forcibly by the whole emphasis of his substantial person. "Clifford told me so himself!"

"No, no!" exclaimed Hepzibah incredulously. "You are dreaming, Cousin Jaffrey."

"I do not belong to the dreaming class of men," said the judge quietly. "Some months before my uncle's death, Clifford boasted to me of the possession of the secret of incalculable wealth. His purpose was to taunt me, and excite my curiosity. I know it well. But, from a pretty distinct recollection of the particulars of our conversation, I am thoroughly convinced that there was truth in what he said. Clifford, at this moment, if he chooses,—and choose he must!—can inform me where to find the schedule, the documents, the evidences, in whatever shape they exist, of the vast amount of Uncle Jaffrey's missing property. He has the secret. His boast was no idle word. It had a directness, an emphasis, a particularity, that showed a backbone of solid meaning within the mystery of his expression."

"But what could have been Clifford's object," asked Hepzibah, "in concealing it so long?"

"It was one of the bad impulses of our fallen nature," replied the judge, turning up his eyes. "He looked upon me as his enemy. He considered me as the cause of his overwhelming disgrace, his imminent peril of death, his irretrievable ruin. There was no great probability, therefore, of his volunteering information, out of his dungeon, that should elevate me still higher on the ladder of prosperity. But the moment has now come when he must give up his secret."

"And what if he should refuse?" inquired Hepzibah. "Or,— as I steadfastly believe,—what if he has no knowledge of this wealth?"

"My dear cousin," said Judge Pyncheon, with a quietude which he had the power of making more formidable than any violence, "since your brother's return, I have taken the precaution (a highly proper one in the near kinsman and natural guardian of an individual so situated) to have his deportment and habits constantly and carefully overlooked. Your neighbours have been eye-witnesses to whatever has passed in the garden. The butcher, the baker, the fish-monger, some of the customers of your shop, and many a prying old woman, have told me several of the secrets of your interior.

"A still larger circle—I myself, among the rest—can testify to his extravagances at the arched window. Thousands beheld him, a week or two ago, on the point of flinging himself thence into the street. From all this testimony, I am led to apprehend—reluctantly, and with deep grief—that Clifford's misfortunes have so affected his intellect, never very strong, that he cannot safely remain at large. The alternative, you must be aware,—and its adoption will depend entirely on the decision which I am now about to make,—the alternative is his confinement, probably for the remainder of his life, in a public asylum for persons in his unfortunate state of mind."

"You cannot mean it!" shrieked Hepzibah.

"Should my cousin Clifford," continued Judge Pyncheon, wholly undisturbed, "from mere malice, and hatred of one whose interests ought naturally to be dear to him,—a mode of passion that, as often as any other, indicates mental disease,—should he refuse me the information so important to myself, and which he assuredly possesses, I shall consider it the one needed jot of evidence to satisfy my mind of his insanity. And, once sure of the course pointed out by conscience, you know me too well, Cousin Hepzibah, to entertain a doubt that I shall pursue it."

"O Jaffrey,—Cousin Jaffrey," cried Hepzibah mournfully, not passionately, "it is you that are diseased in mind, not Clifford! You have forgotten that a woman was your mother!—that you have had sisters, brothers, children of your own!—or that there ever was affection between man and man, or pity from one man to another, in this miserable world! Else, how could you have dreamed of this? You are not young, Cousin Jaffrey!—no, nor middle-aged,—but already an old man! The hair is white upon

213

your head! How many years have you to live? Are you not rich enough for that little time? Shall you be hungry,—shall you lack clothes, or a roof to shelter you,—between this point and the grave? No! but, with the half of what you now possess, you could revel in costly food and wines, and build a house twice as splendid as you now inhabit, and make a far greater show to the world,—and yet leave riches to your only son, to make him bless the hour of your death!

"Then, why should you do this cruel, cruel thing?—so mad a thing, that I know not whether to call it wicked! Alas, Cousin Jaffrey, this hard and grasping spirit has run in our blood these two hundred years. You are but doing over again, in another shape, what your ancestor before you did, and sending down to your posterity the curse inherited from him!"

"Talk sense, Hepzibah, for Heaven's sake!" exclaimed the judge, with the impatience natural to a reasonable man, on hearing anything so utterly absurd as the above, in a discussion about matters of business. "I have told you my determination. I am not apt to change. Clifford must give up his secret, or take the consequences. And let him decide quickly; for I have several affairs to attend to this morning, and an important dinner engagement with some political friends."

"Clifford has no secret!" answered Hepzibah. "And God will not let you do the thing you meditate!"

"We shall see," said the unmoved judge. "Meanwhile, choose whether you will summon Clifford, and allow this business to be amicably settled by an interview between two kinsmen, or drive me to harsher measures, which I should be most happy to feel myself justified in avoiding. The responsibility is altogether on your part."

"You are stronger than I," said Hepzibah, after a brief consideration; "and you have no pity in your strength! Clifford is not now insane; but the interview which you insist upon may go far to make him so. Nevertheless, knowing you as I do, I believe it to be my best course to allow you to judge for yourself as to the improbability of his possessing any valuable secret. I will call

214

Clifford. Be merciful in your dealings with him!—be far more merciful than your heart bids you be!—for God is looking at you, Jaffrey Pyncheon!"

The judge followed his cousin from the shop, where the foregoing conversation had passed, into the parlour, and flung himself heavily into the great ancestral chair. Many a former Pyncheon had found repose in its capacious arms: rosy children, after their sports; young men, dreamy with love; grown men, weary with cares; old men, burdened with winters,—they had mused, and slumbered, and departed to a yet profounder sleep. It had been a long tradition, though a doubtful one, that this was the very chair, seated in which the earliest of the judge's New England forefathers—he whose picture still hung upon the wall—had given a dead man's silent and stern reception to the throng of distinguished guests.

From that hour of evil omen until the present, it may be,—though we know not the secret of his heart,—but it may be that no wearier and sadder man had ever sunk into the chair than this same Judge Pyncheon, whom we have just beheld so immitigably hard and resolute. Surely, it must have been at no slight cost that he had thus fortified his soul with iron. Such calmness is a mightier effort than the violence of weaker men. And there was yet a heavy task for him to do. Was it a little matter—a trifle to be prepared for in a single moment, and to be rested from in another moment,—that he must now, after thirty years, encounter a kinsman risen from a living tomb, and wrench a secret from him, or else consign him to a living tomb again?

"Did you speak?" asked Hepzibah, looking in from the threshold of the parlour; for she imagined that the judge had uttered some sound which she was anxious to interpret as a relenting impulse. "I thought you called me back."

"No, no" gruffly answered Judge Pyncheon with a harsh frown, while his brow grew almost a black purple, in the shadow of the room. "Why should I call you back? Time flies! Bid Clifford come to me!"

The judge had taken his watch from his vest pocket and now

held it in his hand, measuring the interval which was to ensue before the appearance of Clifford.

16: Clifford's Chamber

Never had the old house appeared so dismal to poor Hepzibah as when she departed on that wretched errand. There was a strange aspect in it. As she trode along the foot-worn passages, and opened one crazy door after another, and ascended the creaking staircase, she gazed wistfully and fearfully around. It would have been no marvel, to her excited mind, if, behind or beside her, there had been the rustle of dead people's garments, or pale visages awaiting her on the landing-place above. Her nerves were set all ajar by the scene of passion and terror through which she had just struggled. Her colloquy with Judge Pyncheon, who so perfectly represented the person and attributes of the founder of the family, had called back the dreary past. It weighed upon her heart.

Whatever she had heard, from legendary aunts and grandmothers, concerning the good or evil fortunes of the Pyncheons,— stories which had heretofore been kept warm in her remembrance by the chimney-corner glow that was associated with them,—now recurred to her, sombre, ghastly, cold, like most passages of family history, when brooded over in melancholy mood. The whole seemed little else but a series of calamity, reproducing itself in successive generations, with one general hue, and varying in little, save the outline. But Hepzibah now felt as if the judge, and Clifford, and herself,—they three together,— were on the point of adding another incident to the annals of the house, with a bolder relief of wrong and sorrow, which would cause it to stand out from all the rest.

Thus it is that the grief of the passing moment takes upon itself an individuality, and a character of climax, which it is destined to lose after a while, and to fade into the dark gray tissue common to the grave or glad events of many years ago. It is but for a moment, comparatively, that anything looks strange or startling,—a truth that has the bitter and the sweet in it.

But Hepzibah could not rid herself of the sense of something unprecedented at that instant passing and soon to be accomplished. Her nerves were in a shake. Instinctively she paused before the arched window, and looked out upon the street, in order to seize its permanent objects with her mental grasp, and thus to steady herself from the reel and vibration which affected her more immediate sphere. It brought her up, as we may say, with a kind of shock, when she beheld everything under the same appearance as the day before, and numberless preceding days, except for the difference between sunshine and sullen storm.

Her eyes travelled along the street, from doorstep to doorstep, noting the wet sidewalks, with here and there a puddle in hollows that had been imperceptible until filled with water. She screwed her dim optics to their acutest point, in the hope of making out, with greater distinctness, a certain window, where she half saw, half guessed, that a tailor's seamstress was sitting at her work. Hepzibah flung herself upon that unknown woman's companionship, even thus far off. Then she was attracted by a chaise rapidly passing, and watched its moist and glistening top, and its splashing wheels, until it had turned the corner, and refused to carry any further her idly trifling, because appalled and overburdened, mind.

When the vehicle had disappeared, she allowed herself still another loitering moment; for the patched figure of good Uncle Venner was now visible, coming slowly from the head of the street downward, with a rheumatic limp, because the east wind had got into his joints. Hepzibah wished that he would pass yet more slowly, and befriend her shivering solitude a little longer. Anything that would take her out of the grievous present, and interpose human beings betwixt herself and what was nearest to her,—whatever would defer for an instant the inevitable errand on which she was bound,—all such impediments were welcome. Next to the lightest heart, the heaviest is apt to be most playful.

Hepzibah had little hardihood for her own proper pain, and far less for what she must inflict on Clifford. Of so slight a nature, and so shattered by his previous calamities, it could not well

217

be short of utter ruin to bring him face to face with the hard, relentless man who had been his evil destiny through life. Even had there been no bitter recollections, nor any hostile interest now at stake between them, the mere natural repugnance of the more sensitive system to the massive, weighty, and unimpressible one, must, in itself, have been disastrous to the former. It would be like flinging a porcelain vase, with already a crack in it, against a granite column.

Never before had Hepzibah so adequately estimated the powerful character of her cousin Jaffrey,—powerful by intellect, energy of will, the long habit of acting among men, and, as she believed, by his unscrupulous pursuit of selfish ends through evil means. It did but increase the difficulty that Judge Pyncheon was under a delusion as to the secret which he supposed Clifford to possess. Men of his strength of purpose and customary sagacity, if they chance to adopt a mistaken opinion in practical matters, so wedge it and fasten it among things known to be true, that to wrench it out of their minds is hardly less difficult than pulling up an oak.

Thus, as the judge required an impossibility of Clifford, the latter, as he could not perform it, must needs perish. For what, in the grasp of a man like this, was to become of Clifford's soft poetic nature, that never should have had a task more stubborn than to set a life of beautiful enjoyment to the flow and rhythm of musical cadences! Indeed, what had become of it already? Broken! Blighted! All but annihilated! Soon to be wholly so!

For a moment, the thought crossed Hepzibah's mind, whether Clifford might not really have such knowledge of their deceased uncle's vanished estate as the judge imputed to him. She remembered some vague intimations, on her brother's part, which—if the supposition were not essentially preposterous—might have been so interpreted. There had been schemes of travel and residence abroad, daydreams of brilliant life at home, and splendid castles in the air, which it would have required boundless wealth to build and realize. Had this wealth been in her power, how gladly would Hepzibah have bestowed it all upon her iron-hearted kinsman, to buy for Clifford the freedom and seclusion of the desolate old house! But she believed that her brother's schemes were as destitute of actual substance and purpose as a child's pictures of its future life, while sitting in a little chair by its mother's knee. Clifford had none but shadowy gold at his command; and it was not the stuff to satisfy Judge Pyncheon!

Was there no help in their extremity? It seemed strange that there should be none, with a city round about her. It would be so easy to throw up the window, and send forth a shriek, at the strange agony of which everybody would come hastening to the rescue, well understanding it to be the cry of a human soul, at some dreadful crisis! But how wild, how almost laughable, the fatality,—and yet how continually it comes to pass, thought Hepzibah, in this dull delirium of a world,—that whosoever, and with however kindly a purpose, should come to help, they would be sure to help the strongest side!

Might and wrong combined, like iron magnetized, are endowed with irresistible attraction. There would be Judge Pyncheon,—a person eminent in the public view, of high station and great wealth, a philanthropist, a member of Congress and of the church, and intimately associated with whatever else bestows good name,—so imposing, in these advantageous lights, that Hepzibah herself could hardly help shrinking from her own conclusions as to his hollow integrity. The judge, on one side! And who, on the other? The guilty Clifford! Once a byword! Now, an indistinctly remembered ignominy!

Nevertheless, in spite of this perception that the judge would draw all human aid to his own behalf, Hepzibah was so unaccustomed to act for herself, that the least word of counsel would have swayed her to any mode of action. Little Phoebe Pyncheon would at once have lighted up the whole scene, if not by any available suggestion, yet simply by the warm vivacity of her character. The idea of the artist occurred to Hepzibah. Young and unknown, mere vagrant adventurer as he was, she had been conscious of a force in Holgrave which might well adapt him to be the champion of a crisis. With this thought in her mind, she unbolted a door, cobwebbed and long disused, but which had served as a former medium of communication between her own part of the house and the gable where the wandering daguerreotypist had now established his temporary home.

He was not there. A book, face downward, on the table, a roll of manuscript, a half-written sheet, a newspaper, some tools of his present occupation, and several rejected daguerreotypes, conveyed an impression as if he were close at hand. But, at this period of the day, as Hepzibah might have anticipated, the artist was at his public rooms. With an impulse of idle curiosity, that flickered among her heavy thoughts, she looked at one of the daguerreotypes, and beheld Judge Pyncheon frowning at her. Fate stared her in the face. She turned back from her fruitless quest, with a heartsinking sense of disappointment.

In all her years of seclusion, she had never felt, as now, what it was to be alone. It seemed as if the house stood in a desert, or, by some spell, was made invisible to those who dwelt around, or passed beside it; so that any mode of misfortune, miserable accident, or crime might happen in it without the possibility of aid. In her grief and wounded pride, Hepzibah had spent her life in divesting herself of friends; she had wilfully cast off the support which God has ordained his creatures to need from one another; and it was now her punishment, that Clifford and herself would fall the easier victims to their kindred enemy.

Returning to the arched window, she lifted her eyes,—scowling, poor, dim-sighted Hepzibah, in the face of Heaven!—and strove hard to send up a prayer through the dense gray pavement of clouds. Those mists had gathered, as if to symbolize a great, brooding mass of human trouble, doubt, confusion, and chill indifference, between earth and the better regions. Her faith was too weak; the prayer too heavy to be thus uplifted. It fell back, a lump of lead, upon her heart.

It smote her with the wretched conviction that Providence intermeddled not in these petty wrongs of one individual to his fellow, nor had any balm for these little agonies of a solitary soul; but shed its justice, and its mercy, in a broad, sunlike sweep,

220

over half the universe at once. Its vastness made it nothing. But Hepzibah did not see that, just as there comes a warm sunbeam into every cottage window, so comes a lovebeam of God's care and pity for every separate need.

At last, finding no other pretext for deferring the torture that she was to inflict on Clifford,—her reluctance to which was the true cause of her loitering at the window, her search for the artist, and even her abortive prayer,—dreading, also, to hear the stern voice of Judge Pyncheon from below stairs, chiding her delay,—she crept slowly, a pale, grief-stricken figure, a dismal shape of woman, with almost torpid limbs, slowly to her brother's door, and knocked!

There was no reply.

And how should there have been? Her hand, tremulous with the shrinking purpose which directed it, had smitten so feebly against the door that the sound could hardly have gone inward. She knocked again. Still no response! Nor was it to be wondered at. She had struck with the entire force of her heart's vibration, communicating, by some subtle magnetism, her own terror to the summons. Clifford would turn his face to the pillow, and cover his head beneath the bedclothes, like a startled child at midnight. She knocked a third time, three regular strokes, gentle, but perfectly distinct, and with meaning in them; for, modulate it with what cautious art we will, the hand cannot help playing some tune of what we feel upon the senseless wood.

Clifford returned no answer.

"Clifford! Dear brother!" said Hepzibah. "Shall I come in?"

A silence.

Two or three times, and more, Hepzibah repeated his name, without result; till, thinking her brother's sleep unwontedly profound, she undid the door, and entering, found the chamber vacant. How could he have come forth, and when, without her knowledge? Was it possible that, in spite of the stormy day, and worn out with the irksomeness within doors he had betaken himself to his customary haunt in the garden, and was now shivering under the cheerless shelter of the summer-house?

She hastily threw up a window, thrust forth her turbaned head and the half of her gaunt figure, and searched the whole garden through, as completely as her dim vision would allow.

She could see the interior of the summer-house, and its circular seat, kept moist by the droppings of the roof. It had no occupant. Clifford was not thereabouts; unless, indeed, he had crept for concealment (as, for a moment, Hepzibah fancied might be the case) into a great, wet mass of tangled and broad-leaved shadow, where the squash-vines were clambering tumultuously upon an old wooden framework, set casually aslant against the fence. This could not be, however; he was not there; for, while Hepzibah was looking, a strange grimalkin stole forth from the very spot, and picked his way across the garden. Twice he paused to snuff the air, and then anew directed his course towards the parlour window.

Whether it was only on account of the stealthy, prying manner common to the race, or that this cat seemed to have more than ordinary mischief in his thoughts, the old gentlewoman, in spite of her much perplexity, felt an impulse to drive the animal away, and accordingly flung down a window stick. The cat stared up at her, like a detected thief or murderer, and, the next instant, took to flight. No other living creature was visible in the garden. Chanticleer and his family had either not left their roost, disheartened by the interminable rain, or had done the next wisest thing, by seasonably returning to it. Hepzibah closed the window.

But where was Clifford? Could it be that, aware of the presence of his Evil Destiny, he had crept silently down the staircase, while the judge and Hepzibah stood talking in the shop, and had softly undone the fastenings of the outer door, and made his escape into the street? With that thought, she seemed to behold his gray, wrinkled, yet childlike aspect, in the old-fashioned garments which he wore about the house; a figure such as one sometimes imagines himself to be, with the world's eye upon him, in a troubled dream. This figure of her wretched brother would go wandering through the city, attracting all eyes, and everybody's wonder and repugnance, like a ghost, the more to be shuddered at because visible at noontide.

To incur the ridicule of the younger crowd, that knew him not,—the harsher scorn and indignation of a few old men, who might recall his once familiar features! To be the sport of boys, who, when old enough to run about the streets, have no more reverence for what is beautiful and holy, nor pity for what is sad,—no more sense of sacred misery, sanctifying the human shape in which it embodies itself,—than if Satan were the father of them all! Goaded by their taunts, their loud, shrill cries, and cruel laughter,—insulted by the filth of the public ways, which they would fling upon him,—or, as it might well be, distracted by the mere strangeness of his situation, though nobody should afflict him with so much as a thoughtless word,—what wonder if Clifford were to break into some wild extravagance which was certain to be interpreted as lunacy? Thus Judge Pyncheon's fiendish scheme would be ready accomplished to his hands!

Then Hepzibah reflected that the town was almost completely water-girdled. The wharves stretched out towards the centre of the harbour, and, in this inclement weather, were deserted by the ordinary throng of merchants, labourers, and sea-faring men; each wharf a solitude, with the vessels moored stem and stern, along its misty length. Should her brother's aimless footsteps stray thitherward, and he but bend, one moment, over the deep, black tide, would he not bethink himself that here was the sure refuge within his reach, and that, with a single step, or the slightest overbalance of his body, he might be forever beyond his kinsman's gripe? Oh, the temptation! To make of his ponderous sorrow a security! To sink, with its leaden weight upon him, and never rise again!

The horror of this last conception was too much for Hepzibah. Even Jaffrey Pyncheon must help her now She hastened down the staircase, shrieking as she went.

"Clifford is gone!" she cried. "I cannot find my brother. Help, Jaffrey Pyncheon! Some harm will happen to him!"

She threw open the parlour-door. But, what with the shade

of branches across the windows, and the smoke-blackened ceiling, and the dark oak-panelling of the walls, there was hardly so much daylight in the room that Hepzibah's imperfect sight could accurately distinguish the judge's figure. She was certain, however, that she saw him sitting in the ancestral arm-chair, near the centre of the floor, with his face somewhat averted, and looking towards a window. So firm and quiet is the nervous system of such men as Judge Pyncheon, that he had perhaps stirred not more than once since her departure, but, in the hard composure of his temperament, retained the position into which accident had thrown him.

"I tell you, Jaffrey," cried Hepzibah impatiently, as she turned from the parlour-door to search other rooms, "my brother is not in his chamber! You must help me seek him!"

But Judge Pyncheon was not the man to let himself be startled from an easy-chair with haste ill-befitting either the dignity of his character or his broad personal basis, by the alarm of an hysteric woman. Yet, considering his own interest in the matter, he might have bestirred himself with a little more alacrity.

"Do you hear me, Jaffrey Pyncheon?" screamed Hepzibah, as she again approached the parlour-door, after an ineffectual search elsewhere. "Clifford is gone."

At this instant, on the threshold of the parlour, emerging from within, appeared Clifford himself! His face was preternaturally pale; so deadly white, indeed, that, through all the glimmering indistinctness of the passageway, Hepzibah could discern his features, as if a light fell on them alone. Their vivid and wild expression seemed likewise sufficient to illuminate them; it was an expression of scorn and mockery, coinciding with the emotions indicated by his gesture.

As Clifford stood on the threshold, partly turning back, he pointed his finger within the parlour, and shook it slowly as though he would have summoned, not Hepzibah alone, but the whole world, to gaze at some object inconceivably ridiculous. This action, so ill-timed and extravagant,—accompanied, too, with a look that showed more like joy than any other kind of excitement,—compelled Hepzibah to dread that her stern kins-man's ominous visit had driven her poor brother to absolute insanity. Nor could she otherwise account for the judge's quies-cent mood than by supposing him craftily on the watch, while Clifford developed these symptoms of a distracted mind.

"Be quiet, Clifford!" whispered his sister, raising her hand to impress caution. "Oh, for Heaven's sake, be quiet!"

"Let him be quiet! What can he do better?" answered Clif-ford, with a still wilder gesture, pointing into the room which he had just quitted. "As for us, Hepzibah, we can dance now!—we can sing, laugh, play, do what we will! The weight is gone, Hepzibah! It is gone off this weary old world, and we may be as light-hearted as little Phoebe herself."

And, in accordance with his words, he began to laugh, still pointing his finger at the object, invisible to Hepzibah, within the parlour. She was seized with a sudden intuition of some hor-rible thing. She thrust herself past Clifford, and disappeared into the room; but almost immediately returned, with a cry choking in her throat. Gazing at her brother with an affrighted glance of inquiry, she beheld him all in a tremor and a quake, from head to foot, while, amid these commoted elements of passion or alarm, still flickered his gusty mirth.

"My God! what is to become of us?" gasped Hepzibah.

"Come!" said Clifford in a tone of brief decision, most unlike what was usual with him. "We stay here too long! Let us leave the old house to our cousin Jaffrey! He will take good care of it!"

Hepzibah now noticed that Clifford had on a cloak,—a gar-ment of long ago,—in which he had constantly muffled him-self during these days of easterly storm. He beckoned with his hand, and intimated, so far as she could comprehend him, his purpose that they should go together from the house. There are chaotic, blind, or drunken moments, in the lives of persons who lack real force of character,—moments of test, in which courage would most assert itself,—but where these individuals, if left to themselves, stagger aimlessly along, or follow implicitly whatever guidance may befall them, even if it be a child's. No matter how preposterous or insane, a purpose is a Godsend to them. Hepzibah had reached this point.

Unaccustomed to action or responsibility,—full of horror at what she had seen, and afraid to inquire, or almost to imagine, how it had come to pass,—affrighted at the fatality which seemed to pursue her brother,—stupefied by the dim, thick, stifling atmosphere of dread which filled the house as with a death-smell, and obliterated all definiteness of thought,—she yielded without a question, and on the instant, to the will which Clifford expressed. For herself, she was like a person in a dream, when the will always sleeps. Clifford, ordinarily so destitute of this faculty, had found it in the tension of the crisis.

"Why do you delay so?" cried he sharply. "Put on your cloak and hood, or whatever it pleases you to wear! No matter what; you cannot look beautiful nor brilliant, my poor Hepzibah! Take your purse, with money in it, and come along!"

Hepzibah obeyed these instructions, as if nothing else were to be done or thought of. She began to wonder, it is true, why she did not wake up, and at what still more intolerable pitch of dizzy trouble her spirit would struggle out of the maze, and make her conscious that nothing of all this had actually happened. Of course it was not real; no such black, easterly day as this had yet begun to be; Judge Pyncheon had not talked with, her. Clifford had not laughed, pointed, beckoned her away with him; but she had merely been afflicted—as lonely sleepers often are—with a great deal of unreasonable misery, in a morning dream!

"Now—now—I shall certainly awake!" thought Hepzibah, as she went to and fro, making her little preparations. "I can bear it no longer I must wake up now!"

But it came not, that awakening moment! It came not, even when, just before they left the house, Clifford stole to the parlour-door, and made a parting obeisance to the sole occupant of the room.

"What an absurd figure the old fellow cuts now!" whispered he to Hepzibah. "Just when he fancied he had me completely under his thumb! Come, come; make haste! or he will start up, like Giant Despair in pursuit of Christian and Hopeful, and catch us yet!"

As they passed into the street, Clifford directed Hepzibah's attention to something on one of the posts of the front door. It was merely the initials of his own name, which, with somewhat of his characteristic grace about the forms of the letters, he had cut there when a boy. The brother and sister departed, and left Judge Pyncheon sitting in the old home of his forefathers, all by himself; so heavy and lumpish that we can liken him to nothing better than a defunct nightmare, which had perished in the midst of its wickedness, and left its flabby corpse on the breast of the tormented one, to be gotten rid of as it might!

17: THE FLIGHT OF TWO OWLS

Summer as it was, the east wind set poor Hepzibah's few remaining teeth chattering in her head, as she and Clifford faced it, on their way up Pyncheon Street, and towards the centre of the town. Not merely was it the shiver which this pitiless blast brought to her frame (although her feet and hands, especially, had never seemed so death-a-cold as now), but there was a moral sensation, mingling itself with the physical chill, and causing her to shake more in spirit than in body. The world's broad, bleak atmosphere was all so comfortless! Such, indeed, is the impression which it makes on every new adventurer, even if he plunge into it while the warmest tide of life is bubbling through his veins.

What, then, must it have been to Hepzibah and Clifford,— so time-stricken as they were, yet so like children in their inexperience,—as they left the doorstep, and passed from beneath the wide shelter of the Pyncheon Elm! They were wandering all abroad, on precisely such a pilgrimage as a child often meditates, to the world's end, with perhaps a sixpence and a biscuit in his pocket. In Hepzibah's mind, there was the wretched consciousness of being adrift. She had lost the faculty of self-guidance; but, in view of the difficulties around her, felt it hardly worth an effort to regain it, and was, moreover, incapable of making one.

As they proceeded on their strange expedition, she now and then cast a look sidelong at Clifford, and could not but observe that he was possessed and swayed by a powerful excitement. It was this, indeed, that gave him the control which he had at once, and so irresistibly, established over his movements. It not a little resembled the exhilaration of wine. Or, it might more fancifully be compared to a joyous piece of music, played with wild vivacity, but upon a disordered instrument. As the cracked jarring note might always be heard, and as it jarred loudest amidst the loftiest exultation of the melody, so was there a continual quake through Clifford, causing him most to quiver while he wore a triumphant smile, and seemed almost under a necessity to skip in his gait.

They met few people abroad, even on passing from the retired neighborhood of the House of the Seven Gables into what was ordinarily the more thronged and busier portion of the town. Glistening sidewalks, with little pools of rain, here and there, along their unequal surface; umbrellas displayed ostentatiously in the shop-windows, as if the life of trade had concentrated itself in that one article; wet leaves of the horse-chestnut or elm-trees, torn off untimely by the blast and scattered along the public way; an unsightly, accumulation of mud in the middle of the street, which perversely grew the more unclean for its long and laborious washing,—these were the more definable points of a very sombre picture.

In the way of movement and human life, there was the hasty rattle of a cab or coach, its driver protected by a waterproof cap over his head and shoulders; the forlorn figure of an old man, who seemed to have crept out of some subterranean sewer, and was stooping along the kennel, and poking the wet rubbish with a stick, in quest of rusty nails; a merchant or two, at the door of the post-office, together with an editor and a miscellaneous politician, awaiting a dilatory mail; a few visages of retired sea-captains at the window of an insurance office, looking out vacantly at the vacant street, blaspheming at the weather, and fretting at the dearth as well of public news as local gossip.

What a treasure-trove to these venerable *quidnuncs*, could they have guessed the secret which Hepzibah and Clifford were carrying along with them! But their two figures attracted hardly so much notice as that of a young girl, who passed at the same instant, and happened to raise her skirt a trifle too high above her ankles. Had it been a sunny and cheerful day, they could hardly have gone through the streets without making themselves obnoxious to remark. Now, probably, they were felt to be in keeping with the dismal and bitter weather, and therefore did not stand out in strong relief, as if the sun were shining on them, but melted into the gray gloom and were forgotten as soon as gone.

Poor Hepzibah! Could she have understood this fact, it would have brought her some little comfort; for, to all her other troubles,—strange to say!—there was added the womanish and old-maiden-like misery arising from a sense of unseemliness in her attire. Thus, she was fain to shrink deeper into herself, as it were, as if in the hope of making people suppose that here was only a cloak and hood, threadbare and woefully faded, taking an airing in the midst of the storm, without any wearer!

As they went on, the feeling of indistinctness and unreality kept dimly hovering round about her, and so diffusing itself into her system that one of her hands was hardly palpable to the touch of the other. Any certainty would have been preferable to this. She whispered to herself, again and again, "Am I awake?— Am I awake?" and sometimes exposed her face to the chill spatter of the wind, for the sake of its rude assurance that she was. Whether it was Clifford's purpose, or only chance, had led them thither, they now found themselves passing beneath the arched entrance of a large structure of gray stone.

Within, there was a spacious breadth, and an airy height from floor to roof, now partially filled with smoke and steam, which eddied voluminously upward and formed a mimic cloud-region over their heads. A train of cars was just ready for a start; the locomotive was fretting and fuming, like a steed impatient for a headlong rush; and the bell rang out its hasty peal, so well expressing the brief summons which life vouchsafes to us in its hurried career. Without question or delay,—with the irresistible decision, if not rather to be called recklessness, which had so strangely taken possession of him, and through him of Hepzibah,—Clifford impelled her towards the cars, and assisted her to enter. The signal was given; the engine puffed forth its short, quick breaths; the train began its movement; and, along with a hundred other passengers, these two unwonted travellers sped onward like the wind.

At last, therefore, and after so long estrangement from everything that the world acted or enjoyed, they had been drawn into the great current of human life, and were swept away with it, as by the suction of fate itself.

Still haunted with the idea that not one of the past incidents, inclusive of Judge Pyncheon's visit, could be real, the recluse of the Seven Gables murmured in her brother's ear,—

"Clifford! Clifford! Is not this a dream?"

"A dream, Hepzibah!" repeated he, almost laughing in her face. "On the contrary, I have never been awake before!"

Meanwhile, looking from the window, they could see the world racing past them. At one moment, they were rattling through a solitude; the next, a village had grown up around them; a few breaths more, and it had vanished, as if swallowed by an earthquake. The spires of meeting-houses seemed set adrift from their foundations; the broad-based hills glided away. Everything was unfixed from its age-long rest, and moving at whirlwind speed in a direction opposite to their own.

Within the car there was the usual interior life of the railroad, offering little to the observation of other passengers, but full of novelty for this pair of strangely enfranchised prisoners. It was novelty enough, indeed, that there were fifty human beings in close relation with them, under one long and narrow roof, and drawn onward by the same mighty influence that had taken their two selves into its grasp. It seemed marvellous how all these people could remain so quietly in their seats, while so much noisy strength was at work in their behalf. Some, with tickets in their hats (long travellers these, before whom lay a hundred miles of railroad), had plunged into the English scenery and adventures of pamphlet novels, and were keeping company with dukes and earls.

Others, whose briefer span forbade their devoting themselves to studies so abstruse, beguiled the little tedium of the way with penny-papers. A party of girls, and one young man, on opposite sides of the car, found huge amusement in a game of ball. They tossed it to and fro, with peals of laughter that might be measured by mile-lengths; for, faster than the nimble ball could fly, the merry players fled unconsciously along, leaving the trail of their mirth afar behind, and ending their game under another sky than had witnessed its commencement.

Boys, with apples, cakes, candy, and rolls of variously tinctured lozenges,—merchandise that reminded Hepzibah of her deserted shop,—appeared at each momentary stopping-place, doing up their business in a hurry, or breaking it short off, lest the market should ravish them away with it. New people continually entered. Old acquaintances—for such they soon grew to be, in this rapid current of affairs—continually departed. Here and there, amid the rumble and the tumult, sat one asleep. Sleep; sport; business; graver or lighter study; and the common and inevitable movement onward! It was life itself!

Clifford's naturally poignant sympathies were all aroused. He caught the color of what was passing about him, and threw it back more vividly than he received it, but mixed, nevertheless, with a lurid and portentous hue. Hepzibah, on the other hand, felt herself more apart from human kind than even in the seclusion which she had just quitted.

"You are not happy, Hepzibah!" said Clifford apart, in a tone of approach. "You are thinking of that dismal old house, and of Cousin Jaffrey"—here came the quake through him,—"and of Cousin Jaffrey sitting there, all by himself! Take my advice,— follow my example,—and let such things slip aside. Here we are,

231

in the world, Hepzibah!—in the midst of life!—in the throng of our fellow beings! Let you and I be happy! As happy as that youth and those pretty girls, at their game of ball!"

"Happy—" thought Hepzibah, bitterly conscious, at the word, of her dull and heavy heart, with the frozen pain in it,— "happy. He is mad already; and, if I could once feel myself broad awake, I should go mad too!"

If a fixed idea be madness, she was perhaps not remote from it. Fast and far as they had rattled and clattered along the iron track, they might just as well, as regarded Hepzibah's mental images, have been passing up and down Pyncheon Street. With miles and miles of varied scenery between, there was no scene for her save the seven old gable-peaks, with their moss, and the tuft of weeds in one of the angles, and the shop-window, and a customer shaking the door, and compelling the little bell to jingle fiercely, but without disturbing Judge Pyncheon!

This one old house was everywhere! It transported its great, lumbering bulk with more than railroad speed, and set itself phlegmatically down on whatever spot she glanced at. The quality of Hepzibah's mind was too unmalleable to take new impressions so readily as Clifford's. He had a winged nature; she was rather of the vegetable kind, and could hardly be kept long alive, if drawn up by the roots. Thus it happened that the relation heretofore existing between her brother and herself was changed. At home, she was his guardian; here, Clifford had become hers, and seemed to comprehend whatever belonged to their new position with a singular rapidity of intelligence. He had been startled into manhood and intellectual vigour; or, at least, into a condition that resembled them, though it might be both diseased and transitory.

The conductor now applied for their tickets; and Clifford, who had made himself the purse-bearer, put a bank-note into his hand, as he had observed others do.

"For the lady and yourself?" asked the conductor. "And how far?"

"As far as that will carry us," said Clifford. "It is no great matter. We are riding for pleasure merely."

"You choose a strange day for it, sir!" remarked a gimlet-eyed old gentleman on the other side of the car, looking at Clifford and his companion, as if curious to make them out. "The best chance of pleasure, in an easterly rain, I take it, is in a man's own house, with a nice little fire in the chimney."

"I cannot precisely agree with you," said Clifford, courteously bowing to the old gentleman, and at once taking up the clew of conversation which the latter had proffered. "It had just occurred to me, on the contrary, that this admirable invention of the railroad—with the vast and inevitable improvements to be looked for, both as to speed and convenience—is destined to do away with those stale ideas of home and fireside, and substitute something better."

"In the name of common-sense," asked the old gentleman rather testily, "what can be better for a man than his own parlour and chimney-corner?"

"These things have not the merit which many good people attribute to them," replied Clifford. "They may be said, in few and pithy words, to have ill served a poor purpose. My impression is, that our wonderfully increased and still increasing facilities of locomotion are destined to bring us around again to the nomadic state. You are aware, my dear sir,—you must have observed it in your own experience,—that all human progress is in a circle; or, to use a more accurate and beautiful figure, in an ascending spiral curve. While we fancy ourselves going straight forward, and attaining, at every step, an entirely new position of affairs, we do actually return to something long ago tried and abandoned, but which we now find etherealized, refined, and perfected to its ideal.

"The past is but a coarse and sensual prophecy of the present and the future. To apply this truth to the topic now under discussion. In the early epochs of our race, men dwelt in temporary huts, of bowers of branches, as easily constructed as a bird's-nest, and which they built,—if it should be called building, when such sweet homes of a summer solstice rather grew than were made with hands,—which Nature, we will say, assisted them to rear where fruit abounded, where fish and game were plentiful, or, most especially, where the sense of beauty was to be gratified by a lovelier shade than elsewhere, and a more exquisite arrangement of lake, wood, and hill. This life possessed a charm which, ever since man quitted it, has vanished from existence. And it typified something better than itself.

"It had its drawbacks; such as hunger and thirst, inclement weather, hot sunshine, and weary and foot-blistering marches over barren and ugly tracts, that lay between the sites desirable for their fertility and beauty. But in our ascending spiral, we escape all this. These railroads—could but the whistle be made musical, and the rumble and the jar got rid of—are positively the greatest blessing that the ages have wrought out for us. They give us wings; they annihilate the toil and dust of pilgrimage; they spiritualize travel! Transition being so facile, what can be any man's inducement to tarry in one spot?

"Why, therefore, should he build a more cumbrous habitation than can readily be carried off with him? Why should he make himself a prisoner for life in brick, and stone, and old worm-eaten timber, when he may just as easily dwell, in one sense, nowhere,—in a better sense, wherever the fit and beautiful shall offer him a home?"

Clifford's countenance glowed, as he divulged this theory; a youthful character shone out from within, converting the wrinkles and pallid duskiness of age into an almost transparent mask. The merry girls let their ball drop upon the floor, and gazed at him. They said to themselves, perhaps, that, before his hair was gray and the crow's-feet tracked his temples, this now decaying man must have stamped the impress of his features on many a woman's heart. But, alas! no woman's eye had seen his face while it was beautiful.

"I should scarcely call it an improved state of things," observed Clifford's new acquaintance, "to live everywhere and nowhere!"

"Would you not?" exclaimed Clifford, with singular energy.

234

"It is as clear to me as sunshine,—were there any in the sky,— that the greatest possible stumbling-blocks in the path of human happiness and improvement are these heaps of bricks and stones, consolidated with mortar, or hewn timber, fastened together with spike-nails, which men painfully contrive for their own torment, and call them house and home! The soul needs air; a wide sweep and frequent change of it. Morbid influences, in a thousand-fold variety, gather about hearths, and pollute the life of households. There is no such unwholesome atmosphere as that of an old home, rendered poisonous by one's defunct fore-fathers and relatives.

"I speak of what I know. There is a certain house within my familiar recollection,—one of those peaked-gable (there are sev-en of them), projecting-storied edifices, such as you occasionally see in our older towns,—a rusty, crazy, creaky, dry-rotted, dingy, dark, and miserable old dungeon, with an arched window over the porch, and a little shop-door on one side, and a great, mel-ancholy elm before it! Now, sir, whenever my thoughts recur to this seven-gabled mansion (the fact is so very curious that I must needs mention it), immediately I have a vision or im-age of an elderly man, of remarkably stern countenance, sitting in an oaken elbow-chair, dead, stone-dead, with an ugly flow of blood upon his shirt-bosom! Dead, but with open eyes! He taints the whole house, as I remember it. I could never flourish there, nor be happy, nor do nor enjoy what God meant me to do and enjoy."

His face darkened, and seemed to contract, and shrivel itself up, and wither into age.

"Never, sir!" he repeated. "I could never draw cheerful breath there!"

"I should think not," said the old gentleman, eyeing Clifford earnestly, and rather apprehensively. "I should conceive not, sir, with that notion in your head!"

"Surely not," continued Clifford; "and it were a relief to me if that house could be torn down, or burnt up, and so the earth be rid of it, and grass be sown abundantly over its foundation.

Not that I should ever visit its site again! for, sir, the farther I get away from it, the more does the joy, the lightsome freshness, the heart-leap, the intellectual dance, the youth, in short,—yes, my youth, my youth!—the more does it come back to me. No longer ago than this morning, I was old. I remember looking in the glass, and wondering at my own gray hair, and the wrinkles, many and deep, right across my brow, and the furrows down my cheeks, and the prodigious trampling of crow's-feet about my temples! It was too soon! I could not bear it! Age had no right to come! I had not lived! But now do I look old? If so, my aspect belies me strangely; for—a great weight being off my mind—I feel in the very heyday of my youth, with the world and my best days before me!"

"I trust you may find it so," said the old gentleman, who seemed rather embarrassed, and desirous of avoiding the observation which Clifford's wild talk drew on them both. "You have my best wishes for it."

"For Heaven's sake, dear Clifford, be quiet!" whispered his sister. "They think you mad."

"Be quiet yourself, Hepzibah!" returned her brother. "No matter what they think! I am not mad. For the first time in thirty years my thoughts gush up and find words ready for them. I must talk, and I will!"

He turned again towards the old gentleman, and renewed the conversation.

"Yes, my dear sir," said he, "it is my firm belief and hope that these terms of roof and hearth-stone, which have so long been held to embody something sacred, are soon to pass out of men's daily use, and be forgotten. Just imagine, for a moment, how much of human evil will crumble away, with this one change! What we call real estate—the solid ground to build a house on—is the broad foundation on which nearly all the guilt of this world rests.

"A man will commit almost any wrong,—he will heap up an immense pile of wickedness, as hard as granite, and which will weigh as heavily upon his soul, to eternal ages,—only to build a great, gloomy, dark-chambered mansion, for himself to die in, and for his posterity to be miserable in. He lays his own dead corpse beneath the underpinning, as one may say, and hangs his frowning picture on the wall, and, after thus converting himself into an evil destiny, expects his remotest great-grandchildren to be happy there. I do not speak wildly. I have just such a house in my mind's eye!"

"Then, sir," said the old gentleman, getting anxious to drop the subject, "you are not to blame for leaving it."

"Within the lifetime of the child already born," Clifford went on, "all this will be done away. The world is growing too ethereal and spiritual to bear these enormities a great while longer. To me, though, for a considerable period of time, I have lived chiefly in retirement, and know less of such things than most men,—even to me, the harbingers of a better era are unmistakable. Mesmerism, now! Will that effect nothing, think you, towards purging away the grossness out of human life?"

"All a humbug!" growled the old gentleman.

"These rapping spirits, that little Phoebe told us of, the other day," said Clifford,—"what are these but the messengers of the spiritual world, knocking at the door of substance? And it shall be flung wide open!"

"A humbug, again!" cried the old gentleman, growing more and more testy at these glimpses of Clifford's metaphysics. "I should like to rap with a good stick on the empty pates of the dolts who circulate such nonsense!"

"Then there is electricity,—the demon, the angel, the mighty physical power, the all-pervading intelligence!" exclaimed Clifford. "Is that a humbug, too? Is it a fact—or have I dreamt it— that, by means of electricity, the world of matter has become a great nerve, vibrating thousands of miles in a breathless point of time? Rather, the round globe is a vast head, a brain, instinct with intelligence! Or, shall we say, it is itself a thought, nothing but thought, and no longer the substance which we deemed it!"

"If you mean the telegraph," said the old gentleman, glancing his eye toward its wire, alongside the rail-track, "it is an excellent thing,—that is, of course, if the speculators in cotton and politics don't get possession of it. A great thing, indeed, sir, particularly as regards the detection of bank-robbers and murderers."

"I don't quite like it, in that point of view," replied Clifford. "A bank-robber, and what you call a murderer, likewise, has his rights, which men of enlightened humanity and conscience should regard in so much the more liberal spirit, because the bulk of society is prone to controvert their existence. An almost spiritual medium, like the electric telegraph, should be consecrated to high, deep, joyful, and holy missions. Lovers, day by, day—hour by hour, if so often moved to do it,—might send their heart-throbs from Maine to Florida, with some such words as these 'I love you forever!'—'My heart runs over with love!'—'I love you more than I can!' and, again, at the next message 'I have lived an hour longer, and love you twice as much!' Or, when a good man has departed, his distant friend should be conscious of an electric thrill, as from the world of happy spirits, telling him 'Your dear friend is in bliss!'

"Or, to an absent husband, should come tidings thus 'An immortal being, of whom you are the father, has this moment come from God!' and immediately its little voice would seem to have reached so far, and to be echoing in his heart. But for these poor rogues, the bank-robbers,—who, after all, are about as honest as nine people in ten, except that they disregard certain formalities, and prefer to transact business at midnight rather than 'Change-hours,—and for these murderers, as you phrase it, who are often excusable in the motives of their deed, and deserve to be ranked among public benefactors, if we consider only its result,—for unfortunate individuals like these, I really cannot applaud the enlistment of an immaterial and miraculous power in the universal world-hunt at their heels!"

"You can't, hey?" cried the old gentleman, with a hard look.

"Positively, no!" answered Clifford. "It puts them too miserably at disadvantage. For example, sir, in a dark, low, cross-beamed, panelled room of an old house, let us suppose a dead man, sitting in an armchair, with a bloodstain on his shirt-bosom,—and let us add to our hypothesis another man, issuing from the house, which he feels to be over-filled with the dead man's presence,— and let us lastly imagine him fleeing, Heaven knows whither, at the speed of a hurricane, by railroad! Now, sir, if the fugitive alight in some distant town, and find all the people babbling about that self-same dead man, whom he has fled so far to avoid the sight and thought of, will you not allow that his natural rights have been infringed? He has been deprived of his city of refuge, and, in my humble opinion, has suffered infinite wrong!"

"You are a strange man; Sir!" said the old gentleman, bringing his gimlet-eye to a point on Clifford, as if determined to bore right into him. "I can't see through you!"

"No, I'll be bound you can't!" cried Clifford, laughing. "And yet, my dear sir, I am as transparent as the water of Maule's well! But come, Hepzibah! We have flown far enough for once. Let us alight, as the birds do, and perch ourselves on the nearest twig, and consult wither we shall fly next!"

Just then, as it happened, the train reached a solitary way-station. Taking advantage of the brief pause, Clifford left the car, and drew Hepzibah along with him. A moment afterwards, the train—with all the life of its interior, amid which Clifford had made himself so conspicuous an object—was gliding away in the distance, and rapidly lessening to a point which, in another moment, vanished. The world had fled away from these two wanderers. They gazed drearily about them. At a little distance stood a wooden church, black with age, and in a dismal state of ruin and decay, with broken windows, a great rift through the main body of the edifice, and a rafter dangling from the top of the square tower.

Farther off was a farmhouse, in the old style, as venerably black as the church, with a roof sloping downward from the three-story peak, to within a man's height of the ground. It seemed uninhabited. There were the relics of a wood-pile, indeed, near the door, but with grass sprouting up among the chips and scattered logs. The small raindrops came down aslant; the wind was not turbulent, but sullen, and full of chilly moisture.

Clifford shivered from head to foot. The wild effervescence of his mood—which had so readily supplied thoughts, fantasies, and a strange aptitude of words, and impelled him to talk from the mere necessity of giving vent to this bubbling-up gush of ideas had entirely subsided. A powerful excitement had given him energy and vivacity. Its operation over, he forthwith began to sink.

"You must take the lead now, Hepzibah!" murmured he, with a torpid and reluctant utterance. "Do with me as you will!" She knelt down upon the platform where they were standing and lifted her clasped hands to the sky. The dull, gray weight of clouds made it invisible; but it was no hour for disbelief,—no juncture this to question that there was a sky above, and an Almighty Father looking from it!

"O God!"—ejaculated poor, gaunt Hepzibah,—then paused a moment, to consider what her prayer should be,—"*O God,— our Father,—are we not thy children? Have mercy on us!*"

18: GOVERNOR PYNCHEON

Judge Pyncheon, while his two relatives have fled away with such ill-considered haste, still sits in the old parlour, keeping house, as the familiar phrase is, in the absence of its ordinary occupants. To him, and to the venerable House of the Seven Gables, does our story now betake itself, like an owl, bewildered in the daylight, and hastening back to his hollow tree.

The judge has not shifted his position for a long while now. He has not stirred hand or foot, nor withdrawn his eyes so much as a hair's-breadth from their fixed gaze towards the corner of the room, since the footsteps of Hepzibah and Clifford creaked along the passage, and the outer door was closed cautiously behind their exit. He holds his watch in his left hand, but clutched in such a manner that you cannot see the dial-plate. How profound a fit of meditation! Or, supposing him asleep, how infantile a quietude of conscience, and what wholesome order in the gastric region, are betokened by slumber so entirely undisturbed with starts, cramp, twitches, muttered dreamtalk, trumpet-blasts through the nasal organ, or any slightest irregularity of breath! You must hold your own breath, to satisfy yourself whether he breathes at all.

It is quite inaudible. You hear the ticking of his watch; his breath you do not hear. A most refreshing slumber, doubtless! And yet, the judge cannot be asleep. His eyes are open! A veteran politician, such as he, would never fall asleep with wide-open eyes, lest some enemy or mischief-maker, taking him thus at unawares, should peep through these windows into his consciousness, and make strange discoveries among the reminiscences, projects, hopes, apprehensions, weaknesses, and strong points, which he has heretofore shared with nobody. A cautious man is proverbially said to sleep with one eye open. That may be wisdom. But not with both; for this were heedlessness! No, no! Judge Pyncheon cannot be asleep.

It is odd, however, that a gentleman so burdened with engagements,—and noted, too, for punctuality,—should linger thus in an old lonely mansion, which he has never seemed very fond of visiting. The oaken chair, to be sure, may tempt him with its roominess. It is, indeed, a spacious, and, allowing for the rude age that fashioned it, a moderately easy seat, with capacity enough, at all events, and offering no restraint to the judge's breadth of beam. A bigger man might find ample accommodation in it. His ancestor, now pictured upon the wall, with all his English beef about him, used hardly to present a front extending from elbow to elbow of this chair, or a base that would cover its whole cushion.

But there are better chairs than this,—mahogany, black walnut, rosewood, spring-seated and damask-cushioned, with varied slopes, and innumerable artifices to make them easy, and obviate the irksomeness of too tame an ease,—a score of such might be at Judge Pyncheon's service. Yes! in a score of drawing-rooms he would be more than welcome. Mamma would advance to meet him, with outstretched hand; the virgin daughter, elderly as he has now got to be,—an old widower, as he smilingly describes himself,—would shake up the cushion for the judge, and do her pretty utmost to make him comfortable. For the judge is a prosperous man.

He cherishes his schemes, moreover, like other people, and reasonably brighter than most others; or did so, at least, as he lay abed this morning, in an agreeable half-drowse, planning the business of the day, and speculating on the probabilities of the next fifteen years. With his firm health, and the little inroad that age has made upon him, fifteen years or twenty—yes, or perhaps five-and-twenty!—are no more than he may fairly call his own. Five-and-twenty years for the enjoyment of his real estate in town and country, his railroad, bank, and insurance shares, his United States stock,—his wealth, in short, however invested, now in possession, or soon to be acquired; together with the public honours that have fallen upon him, and the weightier ones that are yet to fall! It is good! It is excellent! It is enough!

Still lingering in the old chair! If the judge has a little time to throw away, why does not he visit the insurance office, as is his frequent custom, and sit awhile in one of their leathern-cushioned arm-chairs, listening to the gossip of the day, and dropping some deeply designed chance-word, which will be certain to become the gossip of tomorrow. And have not the bank directors a meeting at which it was the judge's purpose to be present, and his office to preside? Indeed they have; and the hour is noted on a card, which is, or ought to be, in Judge Pyncheon's right vest-pocket. Let him go thither, and loll at ease upon his moneybags! He has lounged long enough in the old chair!

This was to have been such a busy day. In the first place, the interview with Clifford. Half an hour, by the judge's reckoning, was to suffice for that; it would probably be less, but—taking into consideration that Hepzibah was first to be dealt with, and that these women are apt to make many words where a few would do much better—it might be safest to allow half an hour. Half an hour? Why, judge, it is already two hours, by your own undeviatingly accurate chronometer. Glance your eye down at it and see! Ah; he will not give himself the trouble either to bend his head, or elevate his hand, so as to bring the faithful time-keeper within his range of vision! Time, all at once, appears to have become a matter of no moment with the judge!

And has he forgotten all the other items of his memoranda? Clifford's affair arranged, he was to meet a State Street broker, who has undertaken to procure a heavy percentage, and the best of paper, for a few loose thousands which the judge happens to have by him, uninvested. The wrinkled note-shaver will have taken his railroad trip in vain. Half an hour later, in the street next to this, there was to be an auction of real estate, including a portion of the old Pyncheon property, originally belonging to Maule's garden ground.

It has been alienated from the Pyncheons these four-score years; but the judge had kept it in his eye, and had set his heart on reannexing it to the small demesne still left around the Seven Gables; and now, during this odd fit of oblivion, the fatal hammer must have fallen, and transferred our ancient patrimony to some alien possessor. Possibly, indeed, the sale may have been postponed till fairer weather. If so, will the judge make it convenient to be present, and favour the auctioneer with his bid, On the proximate occasion?

The next affair was to buy a horse for his own driving. The one heretofore his favourite stumbled, this very morning, on the road to town, and must be at once discarded. Judge Pyncheon's neck is too precious to be risked on such a contingency as a stumbling steed. Should all the above business be seasonably got through with, he might attend the meeting of a charitable society; the very name of which, however, in the multiplicity of his benevolence, is quite forgotten; so that this engagement may pass unfulfilled, and no great harm done. And if he have time, amid the press of more urgent matters, he must take measures for the renewal of Mrs. Pyncheon's tombstone, which, the sexton tells him, has fallen on its marble face, and is cracked quite in twain.

She was a praiseworthy woman enough, thinks the judge, in spite of her nervousness, and the tears that she was so oozy with, and her foolish behaviour about the coffee; and as she took her departure so seasonably, he will not grudge the second tomb-stone. It is better, at least, than if she had never needed any! The next item on his list was to give orders for some fruit-trees, of a rare variety, to be deliverable at his country-seat in the ensuing autumn. Yes, buy them, by all means; and may the peaches be luscious in your mouth, Judge Pyncheon!

After this comes something more important. A committee of his political party has besought him for a hundred or two of dol-lars, in addition to his previous disbursements, towards carrying on the fall campaign. The judge is a patriot; the fate of the coun-try is staked on the November election; and besides, as will be shadowed forth in another paragraph, he has no trifling stake of his own in the same great game. He will do what the commit-tee asks; nay, he will be liberal beyond their expectations; they shall have a check for five hundred dollars, and more anon, if it be needed. What next? A decayed widow, whose husband was Judge Pyncheon's early friend, has laid her case of destitution before him, in a very moving letter. She and her fair daughter have scarcely bread to eat. He partly intends to call on her to-day,—perhaps so—perhaps not,—accordingly as he may happen to have leisure, and a small banknote.

Another business, which, however, he puts no great weight on (it is well, you know, to be heedful, but not over-anxious, as respects one's personal health),—another business, then, was to consult his family physician. About what, for Heaven's sake? Why, it is rather difficult to describe the symptoms. A mere dimness of sight and dizziness of brain, was it?—or disagreeable choking, or stifling, or gurgling, or bubbling, in the region of the thorax, as the anatomists say?—or was it a pretty severe throbbing and kicking of the heart, rather creditable to him than otherwise, as showing that the organ had not been left out of the judge's physical contrivance? No matter what it was. The doctor prob-ably would smile at the statement of such trifles to his profes-sional ear; the judge would smile in his turn; and meeting one another's eyes, they would enjoy a hearty laugh together! But a fig for medical advice. The judge will never need it.

Pray, pray, Judge Pyncheon, look at your watch, Now! What— not a glance! It is within ten minutes of the dinner hour! It surely cannot have slipped your memory that the dinner of to-day is to be the most important, in its consequences, of all the dinners you ever ate. Yes, precisely the most important; although, in the course of your somewhat eminent career, you have been placed high towards the head of the table, at splendid banquets, and have poured out your festive eloquence to ears yet echoing with Webster's mighty organ-tones. No public dinner this, however. It is merely a gathering of some dozen or so of friends from several districts of the State; men of distinguished character and influence, assembling, almost casually, at the house of a common friend, likewise distinguished, who will make them welcome to a little better than his ordinary fare.

Nothing in the way of French cookery, but an excellent dinner, nevertheless. Real turtle, we understand, and salmon, tautog, canvas-backs, pig, English mutton, good roast beef, or dainties of that serious kind, fit for substantial country gentlemen, as these honourable persons mostly are. The delicacies of the season, in short, and flavoured by a brand of old Madeira which has been the pride of many seasons. It is the Juno brand; a glorious wine, fragrant, and full of gentle might; a bottled-up happiness, put by for use; a golden liquid, worth more than liquid gold; so rare and admirable, that veteran wine-bibbers count it among their epochs to have tasted it! It drives away the heartache, and substitutes no headache! Could the judge but quaff a glass, it might enable him to shake off the unaccountable lethargy which (for the ten intervening minutes, and five to boot, are already past) has made him such a laggard at this momentous dinner. It would all but revive a dead man! Would you like to sip it now, Judge Pyncheon?

Alas, this dinner. Have you really forgotten its true object? Then let us whisper it, that you may start at once out of the oaken chair, which really seems to be enchanted, like the one in Comus, or that in which Moll Pitcher imprisoned your own grandfather. But ambition is a talisman more powerful than witchcraft. Start up, then, and, hurrying through the streets, burst in upon the company, that they may begin before the fish is spoiled! They wait for you; and it is little for your interest that they should wait. These gentlemen—need you be told it?—have assembled, not without purpose, from every quarter of the State.

They are practised politicians, every man of them, and skilled to adjust those preliminary measures which steal from the people, without its knowledge, the power of choosing its own rulers. The popular voice, at the next gubernatorial election, though loud as thunder, will be really but an echo of what these gentlemen shall speak, under their breath, at your friend's festive board. They meet to decide upon their candidate. This little knot of subtle schemers will control the convention, and, through it, dictate to the party.

And what worthier candidate,—more wise and learned, more noted for philanthropic liberality, truer to safe principles, tried oftener by public trusts, more spotless in private character, with a larger stake in the common welfare, and deeper grounded, by hereditary descent, in the faith and practice of the Puritans,—what man can be presented for the suffrage of the people, so eminently combining all these claims to the chief-rulership as Judge Pyncheon here before us?

Make haste, then! Do your part! The meed for which you have toiled, and fought, and climbed, and crept, is ready for your grasp! Be present at this dinner!—drink a glass or two of that noble wine!—make your pledges in as low a whisper as you will!—and you rise up from table virtually governor of the glorious old State! Governor Pyncheon of Massachusetts!

And is there no potent and exhilarating cordial in a certainty like this? It has been the grand purpose of half your lifetime to obtain it. Now, when there needs little more than to signify your acceptance, why do you sit so lumpishly in your great-great-grandfather's oaken chair, as if preferring it to the gubernatorial one? We have all heard of King Log; but, in these jostling times, one of that royal kindred will hardly win the race for an elective chief-magistracy.

Well; it is absolutely too late for dinner! Turtle, salmon, tautog, woodcock, boiled turkey, South-Down mutton, pig, roast-beef, have vanished, or exist only in fragments, with lukewarm potatoes, and gravies crusted over with cold fat. The judge, had he done nothing else, would have achieved wonders with his knife and fork. It was he, you know, of whom it used to be said, in reference to his ogre-like appetite, that his Creator made him a great animal, but that the dinner-hour made him a great beast. Persons of his large sensual endowments must claim indulgence, at their feeding-time. But, for once, the judge is entirely too late for dinner! Too late, we fear, even to join the party at their wine!

The guests are warm and merry; they have given up the judge; and, concluding that the Free-Soilers have him, they will fix upon another candidate. Were our friend now to stalk in among them, with that wide-open stare, at once wild and stolid, his ungenial presence would be apt to change their cheer. Neither would it be seemly in Judge Pyncheon, generally so scrupulous in his attire, to show himself at a dinner-table with that crimson stain upon his shirt-bosom. By the bye, how came it there? It is an ugly sight, at any rate; and the wisest way for the judge is to button his coat closely over his breast, and, taking his horse and chaise from the livery stable, to make all speed to his own house. There, after a glass of brandy and water, and a mutton-chop, a beefsteak, a broiled fowl, or some such hasty little dinner and supper all in one, he had better spend the evening by the fireside. He must toast his slippers a long while, in order to get rid of the chilliness which the air of this vile old house has sent curdling through his veins.

Up, therefore, Judge Pyncheon, up! You have lost a day. But tomorrow will be here *anon*. Will you rise, betimes, and make the most of it? Tomorrow. Tomorrow! Tomorrow. We, that are alive, may rise betimes tomorrow. As for him that has died to-day, his morrow will be the resurrection morn.

Meanwhile the twilight is glooming upward out of the corners of the room. The shadows of the tall furniture grow deeper, and at first become more definite; then, spreading wider, they lose their distinctness of outline in the dark gray tide of oblivion, as it were, that creeps slowly over the various objects, and the one human figure sitting in the midst of them. The gloom has not entered from without; it has brooded here all day, and now, taking its own inevitable time, will possess itself of everything. The judge's face, indeed, rigid and singularly white, refuses to melt into this universal solvent.

Fainter and fainter grows the light. It is as if another double-handful of darkness had been scattered through the air. Now it is no longer gray, but sable. There is still a faint appearance at the window; neither a glow, nor a gleam, nor a glimmer,—any phrase of light would express something far brighter than this doubtful perception, or sense, rather, that there is a window there. Has it yet vanished? No!—yes!—not quite! And there is still the swarthy whiteness,—we shall venture to marry these ill-agreeing words,—the swarthy whiteness of Judge Pyncheon's face.

The features are all gone: there is only the paleness of them left. And how looks it now? There is no window! There is no face! An infinite, inscrutable blackness has annihilated sight! Where is our universe? All crumbled away from us; and we, adrift in chaos, may hearken to the gusts of homeless wind, that go sighing and murmuring about in quest of what was once a world!

Is there no other sound? One other, and a fearful one. It is the ticking of the judge's watch, which, ever since Hepzibah left the room in search of Clifford, he has been holding in his hand. Be the cause what it may, this little, quiet, never-ceasing throb of Time's pulse, repeating its small strokes with such busy regularity, in Judge Pyncheon's motionless hand, has an effect of terror, which we do not find in any other accompaniment of the scene.

But, listen! That puff of the breeze was louder. It had a tone unlike the dreary and sullen one which has bemoaned itself, and afflicted all mankind with miserable sympathy, for five days past. The wind has veered about! It now comes boisterously from the northwest, and, taking hold of the aged framework of the Seven Gables, gives it a shake, like a wrestler that would try strength with his antagonist. Another and another sturdy tussle with the blast! The old house creaks again, and makes a vociferous but somewhat unintelligible bellowing in its sooty throat (the big flue, we mean, of its wide chimney), partly in complaint at the rude wind, but rather, as befits their century and a half of hostile intimacy, in tough defiance.

A rumbling kind of a bluster roars behind the fire-board. A door has slammed above stairs. A window, perhaps, has been left open, or else is driven in by an unruly gust. It is not to be conceived, before-hand, what wonderful wind-instruments are these old timber mansions, and how haunted with the strangest noises, which immediately begin to sing, and sigh, and sob, and shriek,—and to smite with sledge-hammers, airy but ponderous, in some distant chamber,—and to tread along the entries as with stately footsteps, and rustle up and down the staircase, as with silks miraculously stiff,—whenever the gale catches the house with a window open, and gets fairly into it.

Would that we were not an attendant spirit here! It is too awful! This clamour of the wind through the lonely house; the judge's quietude, as he sits invisible; and that pertinacious ticking of his watch!

As regards Judge Pyncheon's invisibility, however, that matter will soon be remedied. The northwest wind has swept the sky clear. The window is distinctly seen. Through its panes, moreover, we dimly catch the sweep of the dark, clustering foliage outside, fluttering with a constant irregularity of movement, and letting in a peep of starlight, now here, now there. Oftener than any other object, these glimpses illuminate the judge's face. But here comes more effectual light.

Observe that silvery dance upon the upper branches of the pear-tree, and now a little lower, and now on the whole mass of boughs, while, through their shifting intricacies, the moonbeams fall aslant into the room. They play over the judge's figure and show that he has not stirred throughout the hours of darkness. They follow the shadows, in changeful sport, across his unchanging features. They gleam upon his watch. His grasp conceals the dial-plate,—but we know that the faithful hands have met; for one of the city clocks tells midnight.

A man of sturdy understanding, like Judge Pyncheon, cares no more for twelve o'clock at night than for the corresponding hour of noon. However just the parallel drawn, in some of the preceding pages, between his Puritan ancestor and himself, it fails in this point. The Pyncheon of two centuries ago, in common with most of his contemporaries, professed his full belief in spiritual ministrations, although reckoning them chiefly of a malignant character. The Pyncheon of tonight, who sits in yonder armchair, believes in no such nonsense.

Such, at least, was his creed, some few hours since. His hair will not bristle, therefore, at the stories which—in times when chimney-corners had benches in them, where old people sat poking into the ashes of the past, and raking out traditions like live coals—used to be told about this very room of his ancestral house. In fact, these tales are too absurd to bristle even childhood's hair. What sense, meaning, or moral, for example, such as even ghost-stories should be susceptible of, can be traced in the ridiculous legend, that, at midnight, all the dead Pyncheons are bound to assemble in this parlour? And, pray, for what? Why, to see whether the portrait of their ancestor still keeps its place upon the wall, in compliance with his testamentary directions! Is it worthwhile to come out of their graves for that?

We are tempted to make a little sport with the idea. Ghost-stories are hardly to be treated seriously any longer. The family-party of the defunct Pyncheons, we presume, goes off in this wise.

First comes the ancestor himself, in his black cloak, steeple-hat, and trunk-breeches, girt about the waist with a leathern belt, in which hangs his steel-hilted sword; he has a long staff in his hand, such as gentlemen in advanced life used to carry, as much for the dignity of the thing as for the support to be derived from it. He looks up at the portrait; a thing of no substance, gazing at its own painted image! All is safe. The picture is still there. The purpose of his brain has been kept sacred thus long after the man himself has sprouted up in graveyard grass. See! he lifts his ineffectual hand, and tries the frame. All safe! But is that a smile?—is it not, rather a frown of deadly import, that darkens over the shadow of his features?

The stout colonel is dissatisfied! So decided is his look of discontent as to impart additional distinctness to his features; through which, nevertheless, the moonlight passes, and flickers on the wall beyond. Something has strangely vexed the ancestor! With a grim shake of the head, he turns away. Here come other Pyncheons, the whole tribe, in their half a dozen generations, jostling and elbowing one another, to reach the picture. We behold aged men and grandames, a clergyman with the Puritanic stiffness still in his garb and mien, and a red-coated officer of the old French war; and there comes the shop-keeping Pyncheon of a century ago, with the ruffles turned back from his wrists; and there the periwigged and brocaded gentleman of the artist's legend, with the beautiful and pensive Alice, who brings no pride out of her virgin grave.

All try the picture-frame. What do these ghostly people seek? A mother lifts her child, that his little hands may touch it! There is evidently a mystery about the picture, that perplexes these poor Pyncheons when they ought to be at rest. In a corner, meanwhile, stands the figure of an elderly man, in a leathern jerkin and breeches, with a carpenter's rule sticking out of his side pocket; he points his finger at the bearded colonel and his descendants, nodding, jeering, mocking, and finally bursting into obstreperous, though inaudible laughter.

Indulging our fancy in this freak, we have partly lost the power of restraint and guidance. We distinguish an unlooked-for figure in our visionary scene. Among those ancestral people there is a young man, dressed in the very fashion of today: he wears a dark frock-coat, almost destitute of skirts, gray pantaloons, gaiter boots of patent leather, and has a finely wrought gold chain across his breast, and a little silver-headed whalebone stick in his hand. Were we to meet this figure at noonday, we should greet him as young Jaffrey Pyncheon, the judge's only surviving child, who has been spending the last two years in foreign travel. If still in life, how comes his shadow hither? If dead, what a misfortune! The old Pyncheon property, together with the great estate acquired by the young man's father, would devolve on whom? On poor, foolish Clifford, gaunt Hepzibah, and rustic little Phoebe!

But another and a greater marvel greets us! Can we believe our eyes? A stout, elderly gentleman has made his appearance; he has an aspect of eminent respectability, wears a black coat and pantaloons, of roomy width, and might be pronounced scrupulously neat in his attire, but for a broad crimson stain across his snowy neckcloth and down his shirt-bosom. Is it the judge, or no? How can it be Judge Pyncheon? We discern his figure, as plainly as the flickering moonbeams can show us anything, still seated in the oaken chair! Be the apparition whose it may, it advances to the picture, seems to seize the frame, tries to peep behind it, and turns away, with a frown as black as the ancestral one.

The fantastic scene just hinted at must by no means be considered as forming an actual portion of our story. We were betrayed into this brief extravagance by the quiver of the moonbeams; they dance hand-in-hand with shadows, and are reflected in the looking-glass, which, you are aware, is always a kind of window or doorway into the spiritual world. We needed relief, moreover, from our too long and exclusive contemplation of that figure in the chair. This wild wind, too, has tossed our thoughts into strange confusion, but without tearing them away from their one determined centre. Yonder leaden judge sits immovably upon our soul. Will he never stir again? We shall go mad unless he stirs!

You may the better estimate his quietude by the fearlessness of a little mouse, which sits on its hind legs, in a streak of moonlight, close by Judge Pyncheon's foot, and seems to meditate a journey of exploration over this great black bulk. Ha! what has startled the nimble little mouse? It is the visage of grimalkin, outside of the window, where he appears to have posted himself for a deliberate watch. This grimalkin has a very ugly look. Is it a cat watching for a mouse, or the devil for a human soul? Would we could scare him from the window!

Thank Heaven, the night is well-nigh past! The moonbeams have no longer so silvery a gleam, nor contrast so strongly with the blackness of the shadows among which they fall. They are paler now; the shadows look gray, not black. The boisterous wind is hushed. What is the hour? Ah! the watch has at last ceased to tick; for the judge's forgetful fingers neglected to wind it up, as usual, at ten o'clock, being half an hour or so before his ordinary bedtime,—and it has run down, for the first time in five years.

But the great world-clock of Time still keeps its beat. The dreary night—for, oh, how dreary seems its haunted waste, behind us!—gives place to a fresh, transparent, cloudless morn. Blessed, blessed radiance! The daybeam—even what little of it finds its way into this always dusky parlour—seems part of the universal benediction, annulling evil, and rendering all goodness possible, and happiness attainable. Will Judge Pyncheon now rise up from his chair? Will he go forth, and receive the early sunbeams on his brow? Will he begin this new day,—which God has smiled upon, and blessed, and given to mankind,—will he begin it with better purposes than the many that have been spent amiss? Or are all the deep-laid schemes of yesterday as stubborn in his heart, and as busy in his brain, as ever?

In this latter case, there is much to do. Will the judge still insist with Hepzibah on the interview with Clifford? Will he buy a safe, elderly gentleman's horse? Will he persuade the purchaser of the old Pyncheon property to relinquish the bargain in his favour? Will he see his family physician, and obtain a medicine that shall preserve him, to be an honour and blessing to his race, until the utmost term of patriarchal longevity? Will Judge Pyncheon, above all, make due apologies to that company of honourable friends, and satisfy them that his absence from the festive board was unavoidable, and so fully retrieve himself in their good opinion that he shall yet be Governor of Massachusetts?

And all these great purposes accomplished, will he walk the streets again, with that dog-day smile of elaborate benevolence, sultry enough to tempt flies to come and buzz in it? Or will he, after the tomb-like seclusion of the past day and night, go forth a humbled and repentant man, sorrowful, gentle, seeking no profit, shrinking from worldly honour, hardly daring to love God, but bold to love his fellow man, and to do him what good he may? Will he bear about with him,—no odious grin of feigned benignity, insolent in its pretence, and loathsome in its falsehood,—but the tender sadness of a contrite heart, broken, at last, beneath its own weight of sin? For it is our belief, whatever show of honour he may have piled upon it, that there was heavy sin at the base of this man's being.

Rise up, Judge Pyncheon! The morning sunshine glimmers through the foliage, and, beautiful and holy as it is, shuns not to kindle up your face. Rise up, thou subtle, worldly, selfish, iron-hearted hypocrite, and make thy choice whether still to be subtle, worldly, selfish, iron-hearted, and hypocritical, or to tear these sins out of thy nature, though they bring the lifeblood with them! The Avenger is upon thee! Rise up, before it be too late!

What! Thou art not stirred by this last appeal? No, not a jot! And there we see a fly,—one of your common house-flies, such as are always buzzing on the window-pane,—which has smelt out Governor Pyncheon, and alights, now on his forehead, now on his chin, and now, Heaven help us! is creeping over the bridge of his nose, towards the would-be chief-magistrate's wide-open eyes! Canst thou not brush the fly away? Art thou too sluggish? Thou man, that hadst so many busy projects yesterday! Art thou too weak, that wast so powerful? Not brush away a fly? Nay, then, we give thee up!

And hark! the shop-bell rings. After hours like these latter ones, through which we have borne our heavy tale, it is good to be made sensible that there is a living world, and that even this old, lonely mansion retains some manner of connection with it. We breathe more freely, emerging from Judge Pyncheon's presence into the street before the Seven Gables.

19: ALICE'S POSIES

Uncle Venner, trundling a wheelbarrow, was the earliest person stirring in the neighbourhood the day after the storm.

Pyncheon Street, in front of the House of the Seven Gables, was a far pleasanter scene than a by-lane, confined by shabby fences, and bordered with wooden dwellings of the meaner class, could reasonably be expected to present. Nature made sweet amends, that morning, for the five unkindly days which had preceded it. It would have been enough to live for, merely to look up at the wide benediction of the sky, or as much of it as was visible between the houses, genial once more with sunshine. Every object was agreeable, whether to be gazed at in the breadth, or examined more minutely.

Such, for example, were the well-washed pebbles and gravel of the sidewalk; even the sky-reflecting pools in the centre of the street; and the grass, now freshly verdant, that crept along the base of the fences, on the other side of which, if one peeped over, was seen the multifarious growth of gardens. Vegetable productions, of whatever kind, seemed more than negatively happy, in the juicy warmth and abundance of their life. The Pyncheon Elm, throughout its great circumference, was all alive, and full of the morning sun and a sweet-tempered little breeze, which lingered within this verdant sphere, and set a thousand leafy tongues a-whispering all at once.

This aged tree appeared to have suffered nothing from the gale. It had kept its boughs unshattered, and its full complement of leaves; and the whole in perfect verdure, except a single branch, that, by the earlier change with which the elm-tree sometimes prophesies the autumn, had been transmuted to bright gold. It was like the golden branch that gained Aeneas and the Sibyl admittance into Hades.

This one mystic branch hung down before the main entrance of the Seven Gables, so nigh the ground that any passer-by might have stood on tiptoe and plucked it off. Presented at the door, it would have been a symbol of his right to enter, and be made acquainted with all the secrets of the house. So little faith is due to external appearance, that there was really an inviting aspect over the venerable edifice, conveying an idea that its history must be a decorous and happy one, and such as would be delightful for a fireside tale. Its windows gleamed cheerfully in the slanting sunlight.

The lines and tufts of green moss, here and there, seemed pledges of familiarity and sisterhood with Nature; as if this human dwelling-place, being of such old date, had established its prescriptive title among primeval oaks and whatever other objects, by virtue of their long continuance, have acquired a gracious right to be. A person of imaginative temperament, while passing by the house, would turn, once and again, and peruse it well: its many peaks, consenting together in the clustered chimney; the deep projection over its basement-storey; the arched window, imparting a look, if not of grandeur, yet of antique gentility, to the broken portal over which it opened; the luxuriance of gigantic burdocks, near the threshold; he would note all these characteristics, and be conscious of something deeper than he saw.

He would conceive the mansion to have been the residence of the stubborn old Puritan, Integrity, who, dying in some forgotten generation, had left a blessing in all its rooms and chambers, the efficacy of which was to be seen in the religion, honesty, moderate competence, or upright poverty and solid happiness, of his descendants, to this day.

One object, above all others, would take root in the imaginative observer's memory. It was the great tuft of flowers,—weeds, you would have called them, only a week ago,—the tuft of crimson-spotted flowers, in the angle between the two front gables. The old people used to give them the name of Alice's Posies, in remembrance of fair Alice Pyncheon, who was believed to have brought their seeds from Italy. They were flaunting in rich beauty and full bloom today, and seemed, as it were, a mystic expression that something within the house was consummated.

It was but little after sunrise, when Uncle Venner made his appearance, as aforesaid, impelling a wheelbarrow along the street. He was going his matutinal rounds to collect cabbage-leaves, turnip-tops, potato-skins, and the miscellaneous refuse of the dinner-pot, which the thrifty housewives of the neighbour-hood were accustomed to put aside, as fit only to feed a pig. Uncle Venner's pig was fed entirely, and kept in prime order, on these eleemosynary contributions; insomuch that the patched philosopher used to promise that, before retiring to his farm, he would make a feast of the portly grunter, and invite all his neighbours to partake of the joints and spare-ribs which they had helped to fatten.

Miss Hepzibah Pyncheon's housekeeping had so greatly im-proved, since Clifford became a member of the family, that her share of the banquet would have been no lean one; and Uncle Venner, accordingly, was a good deal disappointed not to find the large earthen pan, full of fragmentary eatables, that ordinarily awaited his coming at the back doorstep of the Seven Gables.

"I never knew Miss Hepzibah so forgetful before," said the patriarch to himself. "She must have had a dinner yesterday,—no question of that! She always has one, nowadays. So where's the pot-liquor and potato-skins, I ask? Shall I knock, and see if she's stirring yet? No, no,—'t won't do! If little Phoebe was about the house, I should not mind knocking; but Miss Hepzibah, likely as not, would scowl down at me out of the window, and look cross, even if she felt pleasantly. So, I'll come back at noon."

With these reflections, the old man was shutting the gate of the little back-yard. Creaking on its hinges, however, like every other gate and door about the premises, the sound reached the ears of the occupant of the northern gable, one of the windows of which had a side-view towards the gate.

"Good-morning, Uncle Venner!" said the daguerreotypist,

leaning out of the window. "Do you hear nobody stirring?"

"Not a soul," said the man of patches. "But that's no wonder. 'Tis barely half an hour past sunrise, yet. But I'm really glad to see you, Mr. Holgrave! There's a strange, lonesome look about this side of the house; so that my heart misgave me, somehow or other, and I felt as if there was nobody alive in it. The front of the house looks a good deal cheerier; and Alice's Posies are blooming there beautifully; and if I were a young man, Mr. Holgrave, my sweetheart should have one of those flowers in her bosom, though I risked my neck climbing for it! Well, and did the wind keep you awake last night?"

"It did, indeed!" answered the artist, smiling. "If I were a believer in ghosts,—and I don't quite know whether I am or not,—I should have concluded that all the old Pyncheons were running riot in the lower rooms, especially in Miss Hepzibah's part of the house. But it is very quiet now."

"Yes, Miss Hepzibah will be apt to over-sleep herself, after being disturbed, all night, with the racket," said Uncle Venner. "But it would be odd, now, wouldn't it, if the judge had taken both his cousins into the country along with him? I saw him go into the shop yesterday."

"At what hour?" inquired Holgrave.

"Oh, along in the forenoon," said the old man. "Well, well! I must go my rounds, and so must my wheelbarrow. But I'll be back here at dinner-time; for my pig likes a dinner as well as a breakfast. No meal-time, and no sort of victuals, ever seems to come amiss to my pig. Good morning to you! And, Mr. Holgrave, if I were a young man, like you, I'd get one of Alice's Posies, and keep it in water till Phoebe comes back."

"I have heard," said the daguerreotypist, as he drew in his head, "that the water of Maule's well suits those flowers best."

Here the conversation ceased, and Uncle Venner went on his way. For half an hour longer, nothing disturbed the repose of the Seven Gables; nor was there any visitor, except a carrier-boy, who, as he passed the front doorstep, threw down one of his newspapers; for Hepzibah, of late, had regularly taken it in. After

258

a while, there came a fat woman, making prodigious speed, and stumbling as she ran up the steps of the shop-door. Her face glowed with fire-heat, and, it being a pretty warm morning, she bubbled and hissed, as it were, as if all a-fry with chimney-warmth, and summer-warmth, and the warmth of her own corpulent velocity. She tried the shop-door; it was fast. She tried it again, with so angry a jar that the bell tinkled angrily back at her.

"The deuce take Old Maid Pyncheon!" muttered the irascible housewife. "Think of her pretending to set up a cent-shop, and then lying abed till noon! These are what she calls gentlefolk's airs, I suppose! But I'll either start her ladyship, or break the door down!"

She shook it accordingly, and the bell, having a spiteful little temper of its own, rang obstreperously, making its remonstrances heard,—not, indeed, by the ears for which they were intended,—but by a good lady on the opposite side of the street. She opened the window, and addressed the impatient applicant.

"You'll find nobody there, Mrs. Gubbins."

"But I must and will find somebody here!" cried Mrs. Gubbins, inflicting another outrage on the bell. "I want a half-pound of pork, to fry some first-rate flounders for Mr. Gubbins's breakfast; and, lady or not, Old Maid Pyncheon shall get up and serve me with it!"

"But do hear reason, Mrs. Gubbins!" responded the lady opposite. "She, and her brother too, have both gone to their cousin's, Judge Pyncheon's at his country-seat. There's not a soul in the house, but that young daguerreotype-man that sleeps in the north gable. I saw old Hepzibah and Clifford go away yesterday; and a queer couple of ducks they were, paddling through the mud-puddles! They're gone, I'll assure you."

"And how do you know they're gone to the judge's?" asked Mrs. Gubbins. "He's a rich man; and there's been a quarrel between him and Hepzibah this many a day, because he won't give her a living. That's the main reason of her setting up a cent-shop."

"I know that well enough," said the neighbour. "But they're gone,—that's one thing certain. And who but a blood relation, that couldn't help himself, I ask you, would take in that awful-tempered old maid, and that dreadful Clifford? That's it, you may be sure."

Mrs. Gubbins took her departure, still brimming over with hot wrath against the absent Hepzibah. For another half-hour, or, perhaps, considerably more, there was almost as much quiet on the outside of the house as within. The elm, however, made a pleasant, cheerful, sunny sigh, responsive to the breeze that was elsewhere imperceptible; a swarm of insects buzzed merrily under its drooping shadow, and became specks of light whenever they darted into the sunshine; a locust sang, once or twice, in some inscrutable seclusion of the tree; and a solitary little bird, with plumage of pale gold, came and hovered about Alice's Posies.

At last our small acquaintance, Ned Higgins, trudged up the street, on his way to school; and happening, for the first time in a fortnight, to be the possessor of a cent, he could by no means get past the shop-door of the Seven Gables. But it would not open. Again and again, however, and half a dozen other agains, with the inexorable pertinacity of a child intent upon some object important to itself, did he renew his efforts for admittance. He had, doubtless, set his heart upon an elephant; or, possibly, with Hamlet, he meant to eat a crocodile. In response to his more violent attacks, the bell gave, now and then, a moderate tinkle, but could not be stirred into clamour by any exertion of the little fellow's childish and tiptoe strength. Holding by the door-handle, he peeped through a crevice of the curtain, and saw that the inner door, communicating with the passage towards the parlour, was closed.

"Miss Pyncheon!" screamed the child, rapping on the window-pane, "I want an elephant!"

There being no answer to several repetitions of the summons, Ned began to grow impatient; and his little pot of passion quickly boiling over, he picked up a stone, with a naughty purpose to fling it through the window; at the same time blubbering and sputtering with wrath. A man—one of two who happened to be passing by—caught the urchin's arm.

"What's the trouble, old gentleman?" he asked.

"I want old Hepzibah, or Phoebe, or any of them!" answered Ned, sobbing. "They won't open the door; and I can't get my elephant!"

"Go to school, you little scamp!" said the man. "There's another cent-shop round the corner. 'T is very strange, Dixey," added he to his companion, "what's become of all these Pyncheon's! Smith, the livery-stable keeper, tells me Judge Pyncheon put his horse up yesterday, to stand till after dinner, and has not taken him away yet. And one of the judge's hired men has been in, this morning, to make inquiry about him. He's a kind of person, they say, that seldom breaks his habits, or stays out o' nights."

"Oh, he'll turn up safe enough!" said Dixey. "And as for Old Maid Pyncheon, take my word for it, she has run in debt, and gone off from her creditors. I foretold, you remember, the first morning she set up shop, that her devilish scowl would frighten away customers. They couldn't stand it!"

"I never thought she'd make it go," remarked his friend. "This business of cent-shops is overdone among the women-folks. My wife tried it, and lost five dollars on her outlay!"

"Poor business!" said Dixey, shaking his head. "Poor business!"

In the course of the morning, there were various other attempts to open a communication with the supposed inhabitants of this silent and impenetrable mansion. The man of root-beer came, in his neatly painted wagon, with a couple of dozen full bottles, to be exchanged for empty ones; the baker, with a lot of crackers which Hepzibah had ordered for her retail custom; the butcher, with a nice titbit which he fancied she would be eager to secure for Clifford. Had any observer of these proceedings been aware of the fearful secret hidden within the house, it would have affected him with a singular shape and modification of horror, to see the current of human life making this small eddy hereabouts,—whirling sticks, straws and all such tri-fles, round and round, right over the black depth where a dead corpse lay unseen!

The butcher was so much in earnest with his sweetbread of lamb, or whatever the dainty might be, that he tried every accessible door of the Seven Gables, and at length came round again to the shop, where he ordinarily found admittance.

"It's a nice article, and I know the old lady would jump at it," said he to himself. "She can't be gone away! In fifteen years that I have driven my cart through Pyncheon Street, I've never known her to be away from home; though often enough, to be sure, a man might knock all day without bringing her to the door. But that was when she'd only herself to provide for."

Peeping through the same crevice of the curtain where, only a little while before, the urchin of elephantine appetite had peeped, the butcher beheld the inner door, not closed, as the child had seen it, but ajar, and almost wide open. However it might have happened, it was the fact. Through the passage-way there was a dark *vista* into the lighter but still obscure interior of the parlour. It appeared to the butcher that he could pretty clearly discern what seemed to be the stalwart legs, clad in black pantaloons, of a man sitting in a large oaken chair, the back of which concealed all the remainder of his figure. This contemptuous tranquillity on the part of an occupant of the house, in response to the butcher's indefatigable efforts to attract notice, so piqued the man of flesh that he determined to withdraw.

"So," thought he, "there sits Old Maid Pyncheon's bloody brother, while I've been giving myself all this trouble! Why, if a hog hadn't more manners, I'd stick him! I call it demeaning a man's business to trade with such people; and from this time forth, if they want a sausage or an ounce of liver, they shall run after the cart for it!"

He tossed the titbit angrily into his cart, and drove off in a pet.

Not a great while afterwards there was a sound of music turning the corner and approaching down the street, with several intervals of silence, and then a renewed and nearer outbreak of brisk melody. A mob of children was seen moving onward, or stopping, in unison with the sound, which appeared to proceed from the centre of the throng; so that they were loosely bound together by slender strains of harmony, and drawn along captive; with ever and *anon* an accession of some little fellow in an apron and straw-hat, capering forth from door or gateway.

Arriving under the shadow of the Pyncheon Elm, it proved to be the Italian boy, who, with his monkey and show of puppets, had once before played his hurdy-gurdy beneath the arched window. The pleasant face of Phoebe—and doubtless, too, the liberal recompense which she had flung him—still dwelt in his remembrance. His expressive features kindled up, as he recognized the spot where this trifling incident of his erratic life had chanced. He entered the neglected yard (now wilder than ever, with its growth of hog-weed and burdock), stationed himself on the doorstep of the main entrance, and, opening his show-box, began to play.

Each individual of the automatic community forthwith set to work, according to his or her proper vocation: the monkey, taking off his Highland bonnet, bowed and scraped to the bystanders most obsequiously, with ever an observant eye to pick up a stray cent; and the young foreigner himself, as he turned the crank of his machine, glanced upward to the arched window, expectant of a presence that would make his music the livelier and sweeter. The throng of children stood near; some on the sidewalk; some within the yard; two or three establishing themselves on the very door-step; and one squatting on the threshold. Meanwhile, the locust kept singing in the great old Pyncheon Elm.

"I don't hear anybody in the house," said one of the children to another. "The monkey won't pick up anything here."

"There is somebody at home," affirmed the urchin on the threshold. "I heard a step!"

Still the young Italian's eye turned sidelong upward; and it really seemed as if the touch of genuine, though slight and almost playful, emotion communicated a juicier sweetness to the dry, mechanical process of his minstrelsy. These wanderers are readily responsive to any natural kindness—be it no more than a smile, or a word itself not understood, but only a warmth in it—which befalls them on the roadside of life. They remember these things, because they are the little enchantments which, for the instant,—for the space that reflects a landscape in a soap-bubble,—build up a home about them.

Therefore, the Italian boy would not be discouraged by the heavy silence with which the old house seemed resolute to clog the vivacity of his instrument. He persisted in his melodious appeals; he still looked upward, trusting that his dark, alien countenance would soon be brightened by Phoebe's sunny aspect. Neither could he be willing to depart without again beholding Clifford, whose sensibility, like Phoebe's smile, had talked a kind of heart's language to the foreigner. He repeated all his music over and over again, until his auditors were getting weary. So were the little wooden people in his show-box, and the monkey most of all. There was no response, save the singing of the locust.

"No children live in this house," said a schoolboy, at last. "Nobody lives here but an old maid and an old man. You'll get nothing here! Why don't you go along?"

"You fool, you, why do you tell him?" whispered a shrewd little Yankee, caring nothing for the music, but a good deal for the cheap rate at which it was had. "Let him play as he likes! If there's nobody to pay him, that's his own lookout!"

Once more, however, the Italian ran over his round of melodies. To the common observer—who could understand nothing of the case, except the music and the sunshine on the hither side of the door—it might have been amusing to watch the pertinacity of the street-performer. Will he succeed at last? Will that stubborn door be suddenly flung open? Will a group of joyous children, the young ones of the house, come dancing, shouting, laughing, into the open air, and cluster round the show-box, looking with eager merriment at the puppets, and tossing each a copper for long-tailed Mammon, the monkey, to pick up?

But to us, who know the inner heart of the Seven Gables as well as its exterior face, there is a ghastly effect in this repetition of light popular tunes at its door-step. It would be an ugly business, indeed, if Judge Pyncheon (who would not have cared a fig for Paganini's fiddle in his most harmonious mood) should make his appearance at the door, with a bloody shirt-bosom, and a grim frown on his swarthily white visage, and motion the foreign vagabond away! Was ever before such a grinding out of jigs and waltzes, where nobody was in the cue to dance? Yes, very often. This contrast, or intermingling of tragedy with mirth, happens daily, hourly, momently. The gloomy and desolate old house, deserted of life, and with awful Death sitting sternly in its solitude, was the emblem of many a human heart, which, nevertheless, is compelled to hear the thrill and echo of the world's gayety around it.

Before the conclusion of the Italian's performance, a couple of men happened to be passing, On their way to dinner. "I say, you young French fellow!" called out one of them,—"come away from that doorstep, and go somewhere else with your nonsense! The Pyncheon family live there; and they are in great trouble, just about this time. They don't feel musical today. It is reported all over town that Judge Pyncheon, who owns the house, has been murdered; and the city marshal is going to look into the matter. So be off with you, at once!"

As the Italian shouldered his hurdy-gurdy, he saw on the doorstep a card, which had been covered, all the morning, by the newspaper that the carrier had flung upon it, but was now shuffled into sight. He picked it up, and perceiving something written in pencil, gave it to the man to read. In fact, it was an engraved card of Judge Pyncheon's with certain pencilled memoranda on the back, referring to various businesses which it had been his purpose to transact during the preceding day. It formed a prospective epitome of the day's history; only that affairs had not turned out altogether in accordance with the programme. The card must have been lost from the judge's vest-pocket in his preliminary attempt to gain access by the main entrance of the house. Though well soaked with rain, it was still partially legible.

"Look here; Dixey!" cried the man. "This has something to do with Judge Pyncheon. See!—here's his name printed on it; and here, I suppose, is some of his handwriting."

"Let's go to the city marshal with it!" said Dixey. "It may give him just the clew he wants. After all," whispered he in his companion's ear, "it would be no wonder if the judge has gone into that door and never come out again! A certain cousin of his may have been at his old tricks. And Old Maid Pyncheon having got herself in debt by the cent-shop,—and the judge's pocket-book being well filled,—and bad blood amongst them already! Put all these things together and see what they make!"

"Hush, hush!" whispered the other. "It seems like a sin to be the first to speak of such a thing. But I think, with you, that we had better go to the city marshal."

"Yes, yes!" said Dixey. "Well!—I always said there was something devilish in that woman's scowl!"

The men wheeled about, accordingly, and retraced their steps up the street. The Italian, also, made the best of his way off, with a parting glance up at the arched window. As for the children, they took to their heels, with one accord, and scampered as if some giant or ogre were in pursuit, until, at a good distance from the house, they stopped as suddenly and simultaneously as they had set out. Their susceptible nerves took an indefinite alarm from what they had overheard. Looking back at the grotesque peaks and shadowy angles of the old mansion, they fancied a gloom diffused about it which no brightness of the sunshine could dispel.

An imaginary Hepzibah scowled and shook her finger at them, from several windows at the same moment. An imaginary Clifford—for (and it would have deeply wounded him to know it) he had always been a horror to these small people—stood behind the unreal Hepzibah, making awful gestures, in a faded dressing-gown. Children are even more apt, if possible, than grown people, to catch the contagion of a panic terror. For the rest of the day, the more timid went whole streets about, for the sake of avoiding the Seven Gables; while the bolder signalized their hardihood by challenging their comrades to race past the mansion at full speed.

It could not have been more than half an hour after the disappearance of the Italian boy, with his unseasonable melodies, when a cab drove down the street. It stopped beneath the Pyncheon Elm; the cabman took a trunk, a canvas bag, and a bandbox, from the top of his vehicle, and deposited them on the doorstep of the old house; a straw bonnet, and then the pretty figure of a young girl, came into view from the interior of the cab. It was Phoebe! Though not altogether so blooming as when she first tripped into our story,—for, in the few intervening weeks, her experiences had made her graver, more womanly, and deeper-eyed, in token of a heart that had begun to suspect its depths,—still there was the quiet glow of natural sunshine over her.

Neither had she forfeited her proper gift of making things look real, rather than fantastic, within her sphere. Yet we feel it to be a questionable venture, even for Phoebe, at this juncture, to cross the threshold of the Seven Gables. Is her healthful presence potent enough to chase away the crowd of pale, hideous, and sinful phantoms, that have gained admittance there since her departure? Or will she, likewise, fade, sicken, sadden, and grow into deformity, and be only another pallid phantom, to glide noiselessly up and down the stairs, and affright children as she pauses at the window?

At least, we would gladly forewarn the unsuspecting girl that there is nothing in human shape or substance to receive her, unless it be the figure of Judge Pyncheon, who—wretched spectacle that he is, and frightful in our remembrance, since our night-long vigil with him!—still keeps his place in the oaken chair.

Phoebe first tried the shop-door. It did not yield to her hand; and the white curtain, drawn across the window which formed the upper section of the door, struck her quick perceptive faculty as something unusual.

Without making another effort to enter here, she betook herself to the great portal, under the arched window. Finding it fastened, she knocked. A reverberation came from the emptiness within. She knocked again, and a third time; and, listening intently, fancied that the floor creaked, as if Hepzibah were coming, with her ordinary tiptoe movement, to admit her. But so dead a silence ensued upon this imaginary sound, that she began to question whether she might not have mistaken the house, familiar as she thought herself with its exterior.

Her notice was now attracted by a child's voice, at some distance. It appeared to call her name. Looking in the direction whence it proceeded, Phoebe saw little Ned Higgins, a good way down the street, stamping, shaking his head violently, making deprecatory gestures with both hands, and shouting to her at mouth-wide screech.

"No, no, Phoebe!" he screamed. "Don't you go in! There's something wicked there! Don't—don't—don't go in!"

But, as the little personage could not be induced to approach near enough to explain himself, Phoebe concluded that he had been frightened, on some of his visits to the shop, by her cousin Hepzibah; for the good lady's manifestations, in truth, ran about an equal chance of scaring children out of their wits, or compelling them to unseemly laughter. Still, she felt the more, for this incident, how unaccountably silent and impenetrable the house had become. As her next resort, Phoebe made her way into the garden, where on so warm and bright a day as the present, she had little doubt of finding Clifford, and perhaps Hepzibah also, idling away the noontide in the shadow of the arbour.

Immediately on her entering the garden gate, the family of hens half ran, half flew to meet her; while a strange grimalkin, which was prowling under the parlour window, took to his heels, clambered hastily over the fence, and vanished. The arbour was vacant, and its floor, table, and circular bench were still damp, and bestrewn with twigs and the disarray of the past storm. The growth of the garden seemed to have got quite out

268

of bounds; the weeds had taken advantage of Phoebe's absence, and the long-continued rain, to run rampant over the flowers and kitchen-vegetables. Maule's well had overflowed its stone border, and made a pool of formidable breadth in that corner of the garden.

The impression of the whole scene was that of a spot where no human foot had left its print for many preceding days,— probably not since Phoebe's departure,—for she saw a side-comb of her own under the table of the arbour, where it must have fallen on the last afternoon when she and Clifford sat there.

The girl knew that her two relatives were capable of far greater oddities than that of shutting themselves up in their old house, as they appeared now to have done. Nevertheless, with indistinct misgivings of something amiss, and apprehensions to which she could not give shape, she approached the door that formed the customary communication between the house and garden. It was secured within, like the two which she had already tried.

She knocked, however; and immediately, as if the application had been expected, the door was drawn open, by a considerable exertion of some unseen person's strength, not wide, but far enough to afford her a sidelong entrance. As Hepzibah, in order not to expose herself to inspection from without, invariably opened a door in this manner, Phoebe necessarily concluded that it was her cousin who now admitted her.

Without hesitation, therefore, she stepped across the threshold, and had no sooner entered than the door closed behind her.

20: The Flower of Eden

Phoebe, coming so suddenly from the sunny daylight, was altogether bedimmed in such density of shadow as lurked in most of the passages of the old house. She was not at first aware by whom she had been admitted. Before her eyes had adapted themselves to the obscurity, a hand grasped her own with a firm but gentle and warm pressure, thus imparting a welcome which caused her heart to leap and thrill with an indefinable shiver of enjoyment. She felt herself drawn along, not towards the parlour, but into a large and unoccupied apartment, which had formerly been the grand reception-room of the Seven Gables.

The sunshine came freely into all the uncurtained windows of this room, and fell upon the dusty floor; so that Phoebe now clearly saw—what, indeed, had been no secret, after the encounter of a warm hand with hers—that it was not Hepzibah nor Clifford, but Holgrave, to whom she owed her reception. The subtile, intuitive communication, or, rather, the vague and formless impression of something to be told, had made her yield unresistingly to his impulse. Without taking away her hand, she looked eagerly in his face, not quick to forebode evil, but unavoidably conscious that the state of the family had changed since her departure, and therefore anxious for an explanation.

The artist looked paler than ordinary; there was a thoughtful and severe contraction of his forehead, tracing a deep, vertical line between the eyebrows. His smile, however, was full of genuine warmth, and had in it a joy, by far the most vivid expression that Phoebe had ever witnessed, shining out of the New England reserve with which Holgrave habitually masked whatever lay near his heart. It was the look wherewith a man, brooding alone over some fearful object, in a dreary forest or illimitable desert, would recognize the familiar aspect of his dearest friend, bringing up all the peaceful ideas that belong to home, and the gentle current of every-day affairs. And yet, as he felt the necessity of responding to her look of inquiry, the smile disappeared.

"I ought not to rejoice that you have come, Phoebe," said he. "We meet at a strange moment!"

"What has happened!" she exclaimed. "Why is the house so deserted? Where are Hepzibah and Clifford?"

"Gone! I cannot imagine where they are!" answered Holgrave. "We are alone in the house!"

"Hepzibah and Clifford gone?" cried Phoebe. "It is not possible! And why have you brought me into this room, instead of the parlour? Ah, something terrible has happened! I must run and see!"

"No, no, Phoebe!" said Holgrave holding her back. "It is as I have told you. They are gone, and I know not whither. A terrible event has, indeed, happened, but not to them, nor, as I undoubtingly believe, through any agency of theirs. If I read your character rightly, Phoebe," he continued, fixing his eyes on hers with stern anxiety, intermixed with tenderness, "gentle as you are, and seeming to have your sphere among common things, you yet possess remarkable strength. You have wonderful poise, and a faculty which, when tested, will prove itself capable of dealing with matters that fall far out of the ordinary rule."

"Oh, no, I am very weak!" replied Phoebe, trembling. "But tell me what has happened!"

"You are strong!" persisted Holgrave. "You must be both strong and wise; for I am all astray, and need your counsel. It may be you can suggest the one right thing to do!"

"Tell me!—tell me!" said Phoebe, all in a tremble. "It oppresses,—it terrifies me,—this mystery! Anything else I can bear!"

The artist hesitated. Notwithstanding what he had just said, and most sincerely, in regard to the self-balancing power with which Phoebe impressed him, it still seemed almost wicked to bring the awful secret of yesterday to her knowledge. It was like dragging a hideous shape of death into the cleanly and cheerful space before a household fire, where it would present all the uglier aspect, amid the decorousness of everything about it. Yet it could not be concealed from her; she must needs know it.

"Phoebe," said he, "do you remember this?" He put into her hand a daguerreotype; the same that he had shown her at their first interview in the garden, and which so strikingly brought out the hard and relentless traits of the original.

"What has this to do with Hepzibah and Clifford?" asked Phoebe, with impatient surprise that Holgrave should so trifle with her at such a moment. "It is Judge Pyncheon! You have shown it to me before!"

"But here is the same face, taken within this half-hour" said the artist, presenting her with another miniature. "I had just finished it when I heard you at the door."

"This is death!" shuddered Phoebe, turning very pale. "Judge Pyncheon dead!"

"Such as there represented," said Holgrave, "he sits in the next room. The judge is dead, and Clifford and Hepzibah have vanished! I know no more. All beyond is conjecture. On returning to my solitary chamber, last evening, I noticed no light, either in the parlour, or Hepzibah's room, or Clifford's; no stir nor footstep about the house. This morning, there was the same death-like quiet. From my window, I overheard the testimony of a neighbor, that your relatives were seen leaving the house in the midst of yesterday's storm. A rumour reached me, too, of Judge Pyncheon being missed.

"A feeling which I cannot describe—an indefinite sense of some catastrophe, or consummation—impelled me to make my way into this part of the house, where I discovered what you see. As a point of evidence that may be useful to Clifford, and also as a memorial valuable to myself,—for, Phoebe, there are hereditary reasons that connect me strangely with that man's fate,—I used the means at my disposal to preserve this pictorial record of Judge Pyncheon's death."

Even in her agitation, Phoebe could not help remarking the calmness of Holgrave's demeanour. He appeared, it is true, to feel the whole awfulness of the judge's death, yet had received the fact into his mind without any mixture of surprise, but as an event preordained, happening inevitably, and so fitting itself into past occurrences that it could almost have been prophesied.

"Why have you not thrown open the doors, and called in witnesses?" inquired she with a painful shudder. "It is terrible to be here alone!"

"But Clifford!" suggested the artist. "Clifford and Hepzibah! We must consider what is best to be done in their behalf. It is a wretched fatality that they should have disappeared! Their flight will throw the worst colouring over this event of which it is susceptible. Yet how easy is the explanation, to those who know them! Bewildered and terror-stricken by the similarity of this death to a former one, which was attended with such disastrous consequences to Clifford, they have had no idea but of removing themselves from the scene. How miserably unfortunate! Had Hepzibah but shrieked aloud,—had Clifford flung wide the door, and proclaimed Judge Pyncheon's death,—it would have been, however awful in itself, an event fruitful of good consequences to them. As I view it, it would have gone far towards obliterating the black stain on Clifford's character."

"And how," asked Phoebe, "could any good come from what is so very dreadful?"

"Because," said the artist, "if the matter can be fairly considered and candidly interpreted, it must be evident that Judge Pyncheon could not have come unfairly to his end. This mode of death had been an idiosyncrasy with his family, for generations past; not often occurring, indeed, but, when it does occur, usually attacking individuals about the judge's time of life, and generally in the tension of some mental crisis, or, perhaps, in an access of wrath. Old Maule's prophecy was probably founded on a knowledge of this physical predisposition in the Pyncheon race.

"Now, there is a minute and almost exact similarity in the appearances connected with the death that occurred yesterday and those recorded of the death of Clifford's uncle thirty years ago. It is true, there was a certain arrangement of circumstances, unnecessary to be recounted, which made it possible nay, as men look at these things, probable, or even certain—that old Jaffrey Pyncheon came to a violent death, and by Clifford's hands."

"Whence came those circumstances?" exclaimed Phoebe. "He being innocent, as we know him to be!"

"They were arranged," said Holgrave,—"at least such has long been my conviction,—they were arranged after the uncle's death, and before it was made public, by the man who sits in yonder parlour. His own death, so like that former one, yet attended by none of those suspicious circumstances, seems the stroke of God upon him, at once a punishment for his wickedness, and making plain the innocence of Clifford. But this flight,—it distorts everything! He may be in concealment, near at hand. Could we but bring him back before the discovery of the judge's death, the evil might be rectified."

"We must not hide this thing a moment longer!" said Phoebe. "It is dreadful to keep it so closely in our hearts. Clifford is innocent. God will make it manifest! Let us throw open the doors, and call all the neighbourhood to see the truth!"

"You are right, Phoebe," rejoined Holgrave. "Doubtless you are right."

Yet the artist did not feel the horror, which was proper to Phoebe's sweet and order-loving character, at thus finding herself at issue with society, and brought in contact with an event that transcended ordinary rules. Neither was he in haste, like her, to betake himself within the precincts of common life. On the contrary, he gathered a wild enjoyment,—as it were, a flower of strange beauty, growing in a desolate spot, and blossoming in the wind,—such a flower of momentary happiness he gathered from his present position. It separated Phoebe and himself from the world, and bound them to each other, by their exclusive knowledge of Judge Pyncheon's mysterious death, and the counsel which they were forced to hold respecting it.

The secret, so long as it should continue such, kept them within the circle of a spell, a solitude in the midst of men, a remoteness as entire as that of an island in mid-ocean; once divulged, the ocean would flow betwixt them, standing on its widely sundered shores. Meanwhile, all the circumstances of their situation seemed to draw them together; they were like two children who go hand in hand, pressing closely to one another's side, through a shadow-haunted passage. The image of awful Death, which filled the house, held them united by his stiffened grasp.

These influences hastened the development of emotions that might not otherwise have flowered so. Possibly, indeed, it had been Holgrave's purpose to let them die in their undeveloped germs. "Why do we delay so?" asked Phoebe. "This secret takes away my breath! Let us throw open the doors!"

"In all our lives there can never come another moment like this!" said Holgrave. "Phoebe, is it all terror?—nothing but terror? Are you conscious of no joy, as I am, that has made this the only point of life worth living for?"

"It seems a sin," replied Phoebe, trembling, "to think of joy at such a time!"

"Could you but know, Phoebe, how it was with me the hour before you came!" exclaimed the artist. "A dark, cold, miserable hour! The presence of yonder dead man threw a great black shadow over everything; he made the universe, so far as my perception could reach, a scene of guilt and of retribution more dreadful than the guilt. The sense of it took away my youth. I never hoped to feel young again! The world looked strange, wild, evil, hostile; my past life, so lonesome and dreary; my future, a shapeless gloom, which I must mould into gloomy shapes! But, Phoebe, you crossed the threshold; and hope, warmth, and joy came in with you! The black moment became at once a blissful one. It must not pass without the spoken word. I love you!"

"How can you love a simple girl like me?" asked Phoebe, compelled by his earnestness to speak. "You have many, many thoughts, with which I should try in vain to sympathize. And I,—I, too,—I have tendencies with which you would sympathize as little. That is less matter. But I have not scope enough to make you happy."

"You are my only possibility of happiness!" answered Holgrave. "I have no faith in it, except as you bestow it on me!"

"And then—I am afraid!" continued Phoebe, shrinking towards Holgrave, even while she told him so frankly the doubts with which he affected her. "You will lead me out of my own quiet path. You will make me strive to follow you where it is pathless. I cannot do so. It is not my nature. I shall sink down and perish!"

"Ah, Phoebe!" exclaimed Holgrave, with almost a sigh, and a smile that was burdened with thought.

"It will be far otherwise than as you forebode. The world

owes all its onward impulses to men ill at ease. The happy man inevitably confines himself within ancient limits. I have a presentiment that, hereafter, it will be my lot to set out trees, to make fences,—perhaps, even, in due time, to build a house for another generation,—in a word, to conform myself to laws and the peaceful practice of society. Your poise will be more powerful than any oscillating tendency of mine."

"I would not have it so!" said Phoebe earnestly.

"Do you love me?" asked Holgrave. "If we love one another, the moment has room for nothing more. Let us pause upon it, and be satisfied. Do you love me, Phoebe?"

"You look into my heart," said she, letting her eyes drop. "You know I love you!"

And it was in this hour, so full of doubt and awe, that the one miracle was wrought, without which every human existence is a blank. The bliss which makes all things true, beautiful, and holy shone around this youth and maiden. They were conscious of nothing sad nor old. They transfigured the earth, and made it Eden again, and themselves the two first dwellers in it. The dead man, so close beside them, was forgotten. At such a crisis, there is no death; for immortality is revealed anew, and embraces everything in its hallowed atmosphere.

But how soon the heavy earth-dream settled down again!

"Hark!" whispered Phoebe. "Somebody is at the street door!"

"Now let us meet the world!" said Holgrave. "No doubt, the rumour of Judge Pyncheon's visit to this house, and the flight of Hepzibah and Clifford, is about to lead to the investigation of the premises. We have no way but to meet it. Let us open the door at once."

But, to their surprise, before they could reach the street door,—even before they quitted the room in which the foregoing interview had passed,—they heard footsteps in the farther passage. The door, therefore, which they supposed to be securely locked,—which Holgrave, indeed, had seen to be so, and at which Phoebe had vainly tried to enter,—must have been opened from without. The sound of footsteps was not harsh, bold, decided, and intrusive, as the gait of strangers would naturally be, making authoritative entrance into a dwelling where they knew themselves unwelcome. It was feeble, as of persons either weak or weary; there was the mingled murmur of two voices, familiar to both the listeners.

"Can it be?" whispered Holgrave.

"It is they!" answered Phoebe. "Thank God!—thank God!"

And then, as if in sympathy with Phoebe's whispered ejaculation, they heard Hepzibah's voice more distinctly.

"Thank God, my brother, we are at home!"

"Well!—Yes!—thank God!" responded Clifford. "A dreary home, Hepzibah! But you have done well to bring me hither! Stay! That parlour door is open. I cannot pass by it! Let me go and rest me in the arbor, where I used,—oh, very long ago, it seems to me, after what has befallen us,—where I used to be so happy with little Phoebe!"

But the house was not altogether so dreary as Clifford imagined it. They had not made many steps,—in truth, they were lingering in the entry, with the listlessness of an accomplished purpose, uncertain what to do next,—when Phoebe ran to meet them. On beholding her, Hepzibah burst into tears. With all her might, she had staggered onward beneath the burden of grief and responsibility, until now that it was safe to fling it down. Indeed, she had not energy to fling it down, but had ceased to uphold it, and suffered it to press her to the earth. Clifford appeared the stronger of the two.

"It is our own little Phoebe!—Ah! and Holgrave with, her" exclaimed he, with a glance of keen and delicate insight, and a smile, beautiful, kind, but melancholy. "I thought of you both, as we came down the street, and beheld Alice's Posies in full bloom. And so the flower of Eden has bloomed, likewise, in this old, darksome house today."

21: THE DEPARTURE

The sudden death of so prominent a member of the social

world as the Honourable Judge Jaffrey Pyncheon created a sensation (at least, in the circles more immediately connected with the deceased) which had hardly quite subsided in a fortnight.

It may be remarked, however, that, of all the events which constitute a person's biography, there is scarcely one—none, certainly, of anything like a similar importance—to which the world so easily reconciles itself as to his death. In most other cases and contingencies, the individual is present among us, mixed up with the daily revolution of affairs, and affording a definite point for observation.

At his decease, there is only a vacancy, and a momentary eddy,—very small, as compared with the apparent magnitude of the ingurgitated object,—and a bubble or two, ascending out of the black depth and bursting at the surface. As regarded Judge Pyncheon, it seemed probable, at first blush, that the mode of his final departure might give him a larger and longer posthumous vogue than ordinarily attends the memory of a distinguished man. But when it came to be understood, on the highest professional authority, that the event was a natural, and—except for some unimportant particulars, denoting a slight idiosyncrasy—by no means an unusual form of death, the public, with its customary alacrity, proceeded to forget that he had ever lived. In short, the honourable judge was beginning to be a stale subject before half the country newspapers had found time to put their columns in mourning, and publish his exceedingly eulogistic obituary.

Nevertheless, creeping darkly through the places which this excellent person had haunted in his lifetime, there was a hidden stream of private talk, such as it would have shocked all decency to speak loudly at the street-corners. It is very singular, how the fact of a man's death often seems to give people a truer idea of his character, whether for good or evil, than they have ever possessed while he was living and acting among them. Death is so genuine a fact that it excludes falsehood, or betrays its emptiness; it is a touchstone that proves the gold, and dishonours the baser metal. Could the departed, whoever he may be, return in a week after his decease, he would almost invariably find himself at a higher or lower point than he had formerly occupied, on the scale of public appreciation.

But the talk, or scandal, to which we now allude, had reference to matters of no less old a date than the supposed murder, thirty or forty years ago, of the late Judge Pyncheon's uncle. The medical opinion with regard to his own recent and regretted decease had almost entirely obviated the idea that a murder was committed in the former case. Yet, as the record showed, there were circumstances irrefragably indicating that some person had gained access to old Jaffrey Pyncheon's private apartments, at or near the moment of his death. His desk and private drawers, in a room contiguous to his bedchamber, had been ransacked; money and valuable articles were missing; there was a bloody hand-print on the old man's linen; and, by a powerfully welded chain of deductive evidence, the guilt of the robbery and apparent murder had been fixed on Clifford, then residing with his uncle in the House of the Seven Gables.

Whencesoever originating, there now arose a theory that undertook so to account for these circumstances as to exclude the idea of Clifford's agency. Many persons affirmed that the history and elucidation of the facts, long so mysterious, had been obtained by the daguerreotypist from one of those mesmerical seers who, nowadays, so strangely perplex the aspect of human affairs, and put everybody's natural vision to the blush, by the marvels which they see with their eyes shut.

According to this version of the story, Judge Pyncheon, exemplary as we have portrayed him in our narrative, was, in his youth, an apparently irreclaimable scapegrace. The brutish, the animal instincts, as is often the case, had been developed earlier than the intellectual qualities, and the force of character, for which he was afterwards remarkable. He had shown himself wild, dissipated, addicted to low pleasures, little short of ruffianly in his propensities, and recklessly expensive, with no other resources than the bounty of his uncle. This course of conduct had alienated the old bachelor's affection, once strongly fixed upon him.

Now it is averred,—but whether on authority available in a court of justice, we do not pretend to have investigated,—that the young man was tempted by the devil, one night, to search his uncle's private drawers, to which he had unsuspected means of access. While thus criminally occupied, he was startled by the opening of the chamber-door. There stood old Jaffrey Pyncheon, in his nightclothes! The surprise of such a discovery, his agitation, alarm, and horror, brought on the crisis of a disorder to which the old bachelor had an hereditary liability; he seemed to choke with blood, and fell upon the floor, striking his temple a heavy blow against the corner of a table. What was to be done? The old man was surely dead! Assistance would come too late! What a misfortune, indeed, should it come too soon, since his reviving consciousness would bring the recollection of the ignominious offence which he had beheld his nephew in the very act of committing!

But he never did revive. With the cool hardihood that always pertained to him, the young man continued his search of the drawers, and found a will, of recent date, in favour of Clifford,—which he destroyed,—and an older one, in his own favour, which he suffered to remain. But before retiring, Jaffrey bethought himself of the evidence, in these ransacked drawers, that someone had visited the chamber with sinister purposes. Suspicion, unless averted, might fix upon the real offender. In the very presence of the dead man, therefore, he laid a scheme that should free himself at the expense of Clifford, his rival, for whose character he had at once a contempt and a repugnance.

It is not probable, be it said, that he acted with any set purpose of involving Clifford in a charge of murder. Knowing that his uncle did not die by violence, it may not have occurred to him, in the hurry of the crisis, that such an inference might be drawn. But, when the affair took this darker aspect, Jaffrey's previous steps had already pledged him to those which remained. So craftily had he arranged the circumstances, that, at Clifford's trial, his cousin hardly found it necessary to swear to anything false, but only to withhold the one decisive explanation, by refraining to state what he had himself done and witnessed.

Thus Jaffrey Pyncheon's inward criminality, as regarded Clifford, was, indeed, black and damnable; while its mere outward show and positive commission was the smallest that could possibly consist with so great a sin. This is just the sort of guilt that a man of eminent respectability finds it easiest to dispose of. It was suffered to fade out of sight or be reckoned a venial matter, in the Honourable Judge Pyncheon's long subsequent survey of his own life. He shuffled it aside, among the forgotten and forgiven frailties of his youth, and seldom thought of it again.

We leave the judge to his repose. He could not be styled fortunate at the hour of death. Unknowingly, he was a childless man, while striving to add more wealth to his only child's inheritance. Hardly a week after his decease, one of the Cunard steamers brought intelligence of the death, by cholera, of Judge Pyncheon's son, just at the point of embarkation for his native land. By this misfortune Clifford became rich; so did Hepzibah; so did our little village maiden, and, through her, that sworn foe of wealth and all manner of conservatism,—the wild reformer,—Holgrave!

It was now far too late in Clifford's life for the good opinion of society to be worth the trouble and anguish of a formal vindication. What he needed was the love of a very few; not the admiration, or even the respect, of the unknown many. The latter might probably have been won for him, had those on whom the guardianship of his welfare had fallen deemed it advisable to expose Clifford to a miserable resuscitation of past ideas, when the condition of whatever comfort he might expect lay in the calm of forgetfulness. After such wrong as he had suffered, there is no reparation.

The pitiable mockery of it, which the world might have been ready enough to offer, coming so long after the agony had done its utmost work, would have been fit only to provoke bitterer laughter than poor Clifford was ever capable of. It is a truth (and it would be a very sad one but for the higher hopes which it suggests) that no great mistake, whether acted or endured, in our mortal sphere, is ever really set right. Time, the continual vicissitude of circumstances, and the invariable inopportunity of death, render it impossible. If, after long lapse of years, the right seems to be in our power, we find no niche to set it in. The better remedy is for the sufferer to pass on, and leave what he once thought his irreparable ruin far behind him.

The shock of Judge Pyncheon's death had a permanently invigorating and ultimately beneficial effect on Clifford. That strong and ponderous man had been Clifford's nightmare. There was no free breath to be drawn, within the sphere of so malevolent an influence. The first effect of freedom, as we have witnessed in Clifford's aimless flight, was a tremulous exhilaration. Subsiding from it, he did not sink into his former intellectual apathy. He never, it is true, attained to nearly the full measure of what might have been his faculties. But he recovered enough of them partially to light up his character, to display some outline of the marvellous grace that was abortive in it, and to make him the object of no less deep, although less melancholy interest than heretofore. He was evidently happy. Could we pause to give another picture of his daily life, with all the appliances now at command to gratify his instinct for the Beautiful, the garden scenes, that seemed so sweet to him, would look mean and trivial in comparison.

Very soon after their change of fortune, Clifford, Hepzibah, and little Phoebe, with the approval of the artist, concluded to remove from the dismal old House of the Seven Gables, and take up their abode, for the present, at the elegant country-seat of the late Judge Pyncheon. Chanticleer and his family had already been transported thither, where the two hens had forthwith begun an indefatigable process of egg-laying, with an evident design, as a matter of duty and conscience, to continue their illustrious breed under better auspices than for a century past. On the day set for their departure, the principal personages of our story, including good Uncle Venner, were assembled in the parlour.

"The country-house is certainly a very fine one, so far as the plan goes," observed Holgrave, as the party were discussing their future arrangements. "But I wonder that the late judge—being so opulent, and with a reasonable prospect of transmitting his wealth to descendants of his own—should not have felt the propriety of embodying so excellent a piece of domestic architecture in stone, rather than in wood. Then, every generation of the family might have altered the interior, to suit its own taste and convenience; while the exterior, through the lapse of years, might have been adding venerableness to its original beauty, and thus giving that impression of permanence which I consider essential to the happiness of any one moment."

"Why," cried Phoebe, gazing into the artist's face with infinite amazement, "how wonderfully your ideas are changed! A house of stone, indeed! It is but two or three weeks ago that you seemed to wish people to live in something as fragile and temporary as a bird's-nest!"

"Ah, Phoebe, I told you how it would be!" said the artist, with a half-melancholy laugh. "You find me a conservative already! Little did I think ever to become one. It is especially unpardonable in this dwelling of so much hereditary misfortune, and under the eye of yonder portrait of a model conservative, who, in that very character, rendered himself so long the evil destiny of his race."

"That picture!" said Clifford, seeming to shrink from its stern glance. "Whenever I look at it, there is an old dreamy recollection haunting me, but keeping just beyond the grasp of my mind. Wealth, it seems to say!—boundless wealth!—unimaginable wealth! I could fancy that, when I was a child, or a youth, that portrait had spoken, and told me a rich secret, or had held forth its hand, with the written record of hidden opulence. But those old matters are so dim with me, nowadays! What could this dream have been?"

"Perhaps I can recall it," answered Holgrave. "See! There are a hundred chances to one that no person, unacquainted with the secret, would ever touch this spring."

"A secret spring!" cried Clifford. "Ah, I remember now! I did discover it, one summer afternoon, when I was idling and dreaming about the house, long, long ago. But the mystery escapes me."

The artist put his finger on the contrivance to which he had referred. In former days, the effect would probably have been to cause the picture to start forward. But, in so long a period of concealment, the machinery had been eaten through with rust; so that at Holgrave's pressure, the portrait, frame and all, tumbled suddenly from its position, and lay face downward on the floor. A recess in the wall was thus brought to light, in which lay an object so covered with a century's dust that it could not immediately be recognized as a folded sheet of parchment. Holgrave opened it, and displayed an ancient deed, signed with the hieroglyphics of several Indian *sagamores*, and conveying to Colonel Pyncheon and his heirs, forever, a vast extent of territory at the Eastward.

"This is the very parchment, the attempt to recover which cost the beautiful Alice Pyncheon her happiness and life," said the artist, alluding to his legend. "It is what the Pyncheons sought in vain, while it was valuable; and now that they find the treasure, it has long been worthless."

"Poor Cousin Jaffrey! This is what deceived him," exclaimed Hepzibah. "When they were young together, Clifford probably made a kind of fairy-tale of this discovery. He was always dreaming hither and thither about the house, and lighting up its dark corners with beautiful stories. And poor Jaffrey, who took hold of everything as if it were real, thought my brother had found out his uncle's wealth. He died with this delusion in his mind!"

"But," said Phoebe, apart to Holgrave, "how came you to know the secret?"

"My dearest Phoebe," said Holgrave, "how will it please you to assume the name of Maule? As for the secret, it is the only inheritance that has come down to me from my ancestors. You should have known sooner (only that I was afraid of frightening you away) that, in this long drama of wrong and retribution,

I represent the old wizard, and am probably as much a wizard as ever he was. The son of the executed Matthew Maule, while building this house, took the opportunity to construct that recess, and hide away the Indian deed, on which depended the immense land-claim of the Pyncheons. Thus they bartered their eastern territory for Maule's garden-ground."

"And now" said Uncle Venner "I suppose their whole claim is not worth one man's share in my farm yonder!"

"Uncle Venner," cried Phoebe, taking the patched philosopher's hand, "you must never talk any more about your farm! You shall never go there, as long as you live! There is a cottage in our new garden,—the prettiest little yellowish-brown cottage you ever saw; and the sweetest-looking place, for it looks just as if it were made of gingerbread,—and we are going to fit it up and furnish it, on purpose for you. And you shall do nothing but what you choose, and shall be as happy as the day is long, and shall keep Cousin Clifford in spirits with the wisdom and pleasantness which is always dropping from your lips!"

"Ah! my dear child," quoth good Uncle Venner, quite overcome, "if you were to speak to a young man as you do to an old one, his chance of keeping his heart another minute would not be worth one of the buttons on my waistcoat! And—soul alive!—that great sigh, which you made me heave, has burst off the very last of them! But, never mind! It was the happiest sigh I ever did heave; and it seems as if I must have drawn in a gulp of heavenly breath, to make it with. Well, well, Miss Phoebe! They'll miss me in the gardens hereabouts, and round by the back doors; and Pyncheon Street, I'm afraid, will hardly look the same without old Uncle Venner, who remembers it with a mowing field on one side, and the garden of the Seven Gables on the other. But either I must go to your country-seat, or you must come to my farm,—that's one of two things certain; and I leave you to choose which!"

"Oh, come with us, by all means, Uncle Venner!" said Clifford, who had a remarkable enjoyment of the old man's mellow, quiet, and simple spirit. "I want you always to be within five minutes, saunter of my chair. You are the only philosopher I ever knew of whose wisdom has not a drop of bitter essence at the bottom!"

"Dear me!" cried Uncle Venner, beginning partly to realize what manner of man he was. "And yet folks used to set me down among the simple ones, in my younger days! But I suppose I am like a Roxbury russet,—a great deal the better, the longer I can be kept. Yes; and my words of wisdom, that you and Phoebe tell me of, are like the golden dandelions, which never grow in the hot months, but may be seen glistening among the withered grass, and under the dry leaves, sometimes as late as December. And you are welcome, friends, to my mess of dandelions, if there were twice as many!"

A plain, but handsome, dark-green barouche had now drawn up in front of the ruinous portal of the old mansion-house. The party came forth, and (with the exception of good Uncle Venner, who was to follow in a few days) proceeded to take their places. They were chatting and laughing very pleasantly together; and—as proves to be often the case, at moments when we ought to palpitate with sensibility—Clifford and Hepzibah bade a final farewell to the abode of their forefathers, with hardly more emotion than if they had made it their arrangement to return thither at tea-time.

Several children were drawn to the spot by so unusual a spectacle as the barouche and pair of gray horses. Recognizing little Ned Higgins among them, Hepzibah put her hand into her pocket, and presented the urchin, her earliest and staunchest customer, with silver enough to people the Domdaniel cavern of his interior with as various a procession of quadrupeds as passed into the ark.

Two men were passing, just as the barouche drove off.

"Well, Dixey," said one of them, "what do you think of this? My wife kept a cent-shop three months, and lost five dollars on her outlay. Old Maid Pyncheon has been in trade just about as long, and rides off in her carriage with a couple of hundred thousand,—reckoning her share, and Clifford's, and Phoebe's,—

and some say twice as much! If you choose to call it luck, it is all very well; but if we are to take it as the will of Providence, why, I can't exactly fathom it!"

"Pretty good business!" quoth the sagacious Dixey,—"pretty good business!"

Maule's well, all this time, though left in solitude, was throwing up a succession of kaleidoscopic pictures, in which a gifted eye might have seen foreshadowed the coming fortunes of Hepzibah and Clifford, and the descendant of the legendary wizard, and the village maiden, over whom he had thrown love's web of sorcery. The Pyncheon Elm, moreover, with what foliage the September gale had spared to it, whispered unintelligible prophecies. And wise Uncle Venner, passing slowly from the ruinous porch, seemed to hear a strain of music, and fancied that sweet Alice Pyncheon—after witnessing these deeds, this bygone woe and this present happiness, of her kindred mortals—had given one farewell touch of a spirit's joy upon her harpsichord, as she floated heavenward from the HOUSE OF THE SEVEN GABLES!

The Great Stone Face

(A tale from *The Snow Image and Other Twice-Told Tales*)

One afternoon, when the sun was going down, a mother and her little boy sat at the door of their cottage, talking about the Great Stone Face. They had but to lift their eyes, and there it was plainly to be seen, though miles away, with the sunshine brightening all its features.

And what was the Great Stone Face?

Embosomed amongst a family of lofty mountains, there was a valley so spacious that it contained many thousand inhabitants. Some of these good people dwelt in log-huts, with the black forest all around them, on the steep and difficult hillsides. Others had their homes in comfortable farmhouses, and cultivated the rich soil on the gentle slopes or level surfaces of the valley. Others, again, were congregated into populous villages, where some wild, highland rivulet, tumbling down from its birthplace in the upper mountain region, had been caught and tamed by human cunning, and compelled to turn the machinery of cotton-factories. The inhabitants of this valley, in short, were numerous, and of many modes of life. But all of them, grown people and children, had a kind of familiarity with the Great Stone Pace, although some possessed the gift of distinguishing this grand natural phenomenon more perfectly than many of their neighbours.

The Great Stone Face, then, was a work of Nature in her mood of majestic playfulness, formed on the perpendicular side of a mountain by some immense rocks, which had been thrown together in such a position as, when viewed at a proper distance, precisely to resemble the features of the human countenance. It seemed as if an enormous giant, or a Titan, had sculptured his own likeness on the precipice. There was the broad arch of the forehead, a hundred feet in height; the nose, with its long bridge; and the vast lips, which, if they could have spoken, would have rolled their thunder accents from one end of the valley to the other. True it is, that if the spectator approached too near, he lost the outline of the gigantic visage, and could discern only a heap of ponderous and gigantic rocks, piled in chaotic ruin one upon another. Retracing his steps, however, the wondrous features would again be seen; and the farther he withdrew from them, the more like a human face, with all its original divinity intact, did they appear; until, as it grew dim in the distance, with the clouds and glorified vapor of the mountains clustering about it, the Great Stone Pace seemed positively to be alive.

It was a happy lot for children to grow up to man hood or womanhood with the Great Stone Face before their eyes, for all the features were noble, and the expression was at once grand and sweet, as if it were the glow of a vast, warm heart, that embraced all mankind in its affections, and had room for more. It was an education only to look at it. According to the belief of many people, the valley owed much of its fertility to this benign aspect that was continually beaming over it, illuminating the clouds, and infusing its tenderness into the sun shine.

As we began with saying, a mother and her little boy sat at their cottage-door, gazing at the Great Stone Face, and talking about it. The child's name was Ernest.

"Mother," said he, while the Titanic visage smiled on him, "I wish that it could speak, for it looks so very kindly that its voice must needs be pleasant. If I were to see a man with such a face, I should love him dearly."

"If an old prophecy should come to pass," answered his mother, "we may see a man, some time or other, with exactly such a face as that."

"What prophecy do you mean, dear mother?" eagerly inquired Ernest. "Pray tell me all about it!"

So his mother told him a story that her own mother had told to her, when she herself was younger than little Ernest; a story, not of things that were past, but of what was yet to come; a story, nevertheless, so very old, that even the Indians, who formerly inhabited this valley, had heard it from their forefathers, to whom, as they affirmed, it had been murmured by the mountain streams, and whispered by the wind among the treetops. The purport was, that, at some future day, a child should be born hereabouts, who was destined to become the greatest and noblest personage of his time, and whose countenance, in manhood, should bear an exact resemblance to the Great Stone Face. Not a few old-fashioned people, and young ones likewise, in the ardour of their hopes, still cherished an enduring faith in this old prophecy. But others, who had seen more of the world, had watched and waited till they were weary, and had beheld no man with such a face, nor any man that proved to be much greater or nobler than his neighbours, concluded it to be nothing but an idle tale. At all events, the great man of the prophecy had not yet appeared.

"O mother, dear mother!" cried Ernest, clapping his hands above his head, "I do hope that I shall live to see him!"

His mother was an affectionate and thoughtful woman, and felt that it was wisest not to discourage the generous hopes of her little boy. So she only said to him, "Perhaps you may."

And Ernest never forgot the story that his mother told him. It was always in his mind, whenever he looked upon the Great Stone Pace. He spent his childhood in the log-cottage where he was born, and was dutiful to his mother, and helpful to her in many things, assisting her much with his little hands, and more with his loving-heart. In this manner, from a happy yet often pensive child, he grew up to be a mild, quiet, unobtrusive boy, and sun-browned with labour in the fields, but with more intelligence brightening his aspect than is seen in many lads who have been taught at famous schools. Yet Ernest had had no teacher, save only that the Great Stone Pace became one to him.

When the toil of the day was over, he would gaze at it for hours, until he began to imagine that those vast features recognized him, and gave him a smile of kindness and encouragement, responsive to his own look of veneration. We must not take upon us to affirm that this was a mistake, although the Face may have looked no more kindly at Ernest than at all the world besides. But the secret was, that the boy's tender and confiding simplicity discerned what other people could not see; and thus the love, which was meant for all, became his peculiar portion.

About this time, there went a rumour throughout the valley, that the great man, foretold from ages long ago, who was to bear a resemblance to the Great Stone Face, had appeared at last. It seems that, many years before, a young man had migrated from the valley and settled at a distant seaport, where, after getting together a little money, he had set up as a shopkeeper. His name but I could never learn whether it was his real one, or a nickname that had grown out of his habits and success in life—was Gathergold. Being shrewd and active, and endowed by Providence with that inscrutable faculty which develops itself in what the world calls luck, he became an exceedingly rich merchant, and owner of a whole fleet of bulky-bottomed ships.

All the countries of the globe appeared to join hands for the mere purpose of adding heap after heap to the mountainous accumulation of this one man's wealth. The cold regions of the north, almost within the gloom and shadow of the Arctic Circle, sent him their tribute in the shape of furs; hot Africa sifted for him the golden sands of her rivers, and gathered up the ivory tusks of her great elephants out of the forests; the East came bringing him the rich shawls, and spices, and teas, and the effulgence of diamonds, and the gleaming purity of large pearls.

The ocean, not to be behindhand with the earth, yielded up her mighty whales, that Mr. Gathergold might sell their oil, and make a profit on it. Be the original commodity what it might, it was gold within his grasp. It might be said of him, as of Midas in the fable, that whatever he touched with his finger immediately glistened, and grew yellow, and was changed at once into sterling metal, or, which suited him still better, into piles of coin. And, when Mr. Gathergold had become so very rich that it would have taken him a hundred years only to count his wealth, he be thought himself of his native valley, and resolved to go back thither, and end his days where he was born. With this purpose in view, he sent a skilful architect to build him such a palace as should be fit for a man of his vast wealth to live in.

As I have said above, it had already been rumoured in the valley that Mr. Gathergold had turned out to be the prophetic personage so long and vainly looked for, and that his visage was the perfect and undeniable similitude of the Great Stone Face. People were the more ready to believe that this must needs be the fact, when they be held the splendid edifice that rose, as if by enchantment, on the site of his father's old weather-beaten farm-house. The exterior was of marble, so dazzlingly white that it seemed as though the whole structure might melt away in the sunshine, like those humbler ones which Mr. Gathergold, in his young play-days, before his fingers were gifted with the touch of transmutation, had been accustomed to build of snow. It had a richly ornamented *portico*, supported by tall pillars, beneath which was a lofty door, studded with silver knobs, and made of a kind of variegated wood that had been brought from beyond the sea.

The windows, from the floor to the ceiling of each stately apartment, were composed, respectively, of but one enormous pane of glass, so transparently pure that it was said to be a finer medium than even the vacant atmosphere. Hardly anybody had been permitted to see the interior of this palace; but it was re-ported, and with good semblance of truth, to be far more gor-geous than the outside, insomuch that whatever was iron or brass in other houses was silver or gold in this; and Mr. Gath-ergold's bedchamber, especially, made such a glittering appear-ance that no ordinary man would have been able to close his eyes there. But, on the other hand, Mr. Gathergold was now so inured to wealth, that perhaps he could not have closed his eyes unless where the gleam of it was certain to find its way beneath his eyelids.

In due time, the mansion was finished; next came the upholsterers, with magnificent furniture; then, a whole troop of black and white servants, the harbingers of Mr. Gathergold, who, in his own majestic person, was expected to arrive at sunset. Our friend Ernest, meanwhile, had been deeply stirred by the idea that the great man, the noble man, the man of prophecy, after so many ages of delay, was at length to be made manifest to his native valley. He knew, boy as he was, that there were a thousand ways in which Mr. Gathergold, with his vast wealth, might transform himself into an angel of beneficence, and assume a control over human affairs as wide and benignant as the smile of the Great Stone Face. Full of faith and hope, Ernest doubted not that what the people said was true, and that now he was to behold the living likeness of those wondrous features on the mountain-side. While the boy was still gazing up the valley, and fancying, as he always did, that the Great Stone Face returned his gaze and looked kindly at him, the rumbling of wheels was heard, approaching swiftly along the winding road.

"Here he comes!" cried a group of people who were assembled to witness the arrival. "Here comes the great Mr. Gathergold!"

A carriage, drawn by four horses, dashed round the turn of the road. Within it, thrust partly out of the window, appeared the physiognomy of a little old man, with a skin as yellow as if his own Midas-hand had transmuted it. He had a low forehead, small, sharp eyes, puckered about with innumerable wrinkles, and very thin lips, which he made still thinner by pressing them forcibly together.

"The very image of the Great Stone Face!" shouted the people. "Sure enough, the old prophecy is true; and here we have the great man come, at last!"

And, what greatly perplexed Ernest, they seemed actually to believe that here was the likeness which they spoke of. By the roadside there chanced to be an old beggar-woman and two little beggar-children, stragglers from some far-off region, who, as the carriage rolled on ward, held out their hands and lifted up their doleful voices, most piteously beseeching charity. A yellow claw—the very same that had clawed together so much wealth—poked itself out of the coach-window, and dropt some copper coins upon the ground; so that, though the great man's name seems to have been Gathergold, he might just as suitably have been nicknamed Scattercopper. Still, nevertheless, with an earnest shout, and evidently with as much good faith as ever, the people bellowed,—

"He is the very image of the Great Stone Face!"

But Ernest turned sadly from the wrinkled shrewdness of that sordid visage, and gazed up the valley, where, amid a gathering mist, gilded by the last sun beams, he could still distinguish those glorious features which had impressed themselves into his soul. Their aspect cheered him. What did the benign lips seem to say?

"He will come! Fear not, Ernest; the man will come!"

The years went on, and Ernest ceased to be a boy. He had grown to be a young man now. He attracted little notice from the other inhabitants of the valley; for they saw nothing remarkable in his way of life, save that, when the labour of the day was over, he still loved to go apart and gaze and meditate upon the Great Stone Face. According to their idea of the matter, it was a folly, indeed, but pardonable, inasmuch as Ernest was industrious, kind, and neighbourly, and neglected no duty for the sake of indulging this idle habit. They knew not that the Great Stone Face had become a teacher to him, and that the sentiment which was expressed in it would enlarge the young man's heart, and fill it with wider and deeper sympathies than other hearts.

They knew not that thence would come a better wisdom than could be learned from books, and a better life than could be moulded on the defaced example of other human lives. Neither did Ernest know that the thoughts and affections which came to him so naturally, in the fields and at the fireside, and wherever he communed with himself, were of a higher tone than those which all men shared with him. A simple soul,—

simple as when his mother first taught him the old prophecy,—
he beheld the marvellous features beaming adown the valley,
and still wondered that their human counterpart was so long in
making his appearance.

By this time poor Mr. Gathergold was dead and buried; and
the oddest part of the matter was, that his wealth, which was
the body and spirit of his existence, had disappeared before his
death, leaving nothing of him but a living skeleton, covered over
with a wrinkled, yellow skin. Since the melting away of his gold,
it had been very generally conceded that there was no such
striking resemblance, after all, betwixt the ignoble features of the
ruined merchant and that majestic face upon the mountain-side.
So the people ceased to honour him during his lifetime, and
quietly consigned him to forgetfulness after his decease. Once
in a while, it is true, his memory was brought up in connection
with the magnificent palace which he had built, and which had
long ago been turned into a hotel for the accommodation of
strangers, multitudes of whom came, every summer, to visit that
famous natural curiosity, the Great Stone Face. Thus, Mr. Gathergold being discredited and thrown into the shade, the man of
prophecy was yet to come.

It so happened that a native-born son of the valley, many years
before, had enlisted as a soldier, and, after a great deal of hard
fighting, had now become an illustrious commander. Whatever
he may be called in history, he was known in camps and on
the battlefield under the nickname of Old Blood-and-Thunder.
This war-worn veteran, being now infirm with age and wounds,
and weary of the turmoil of a military life, and of the roll of the
drum and the clangour of the trumpet, that had so long been
ringing in his ears, had lately signified a purpose of returning to
his native valley, hoping to find repose where he remembered to
have left it. The inhabitants, his old neighbours and their grown-
up children, were resolved to welcome the renowned warrior
with a salute of cannon and a public dinner; and all the more
enthusiastically, it being affirmed that now, at last, the likeness of
the Great Stone Face had actually appeared.

An *aid-de-camp* of Old Blood-and-Thunder, travelling through the valley, was said to have been struck with the resemblance. Moreover the schoolmates and early acquaintances of the general were ready to testify, on oath, that, to the best of their recollection, the aforesaid general had been exceedingly like the majestic image, even when a boy, only that the idea had never occurred to them at that period. Great, therefore, was the excitement throughout the valley; and many people, who had never once thought of glancing at the Great Stone Face for years before, now spent their time in gazing at it, for the sake of knowing exactly how General Blood-and-Thunder looked.

On the day of the great festival, Ernest, with all the other people of the valley, left their work, and proceeded to the spot where the sylvan banquet was prepared. As he approached, the loud voice of the Rev. Dr. Battleblast was heard, beseeching a blessing on the good things set before them, and on the distinguished friend of peace in whose honour they were assembled. The tables were arranged in a cleared space of the woods, shut in by the surrounding trees, except where a *vista* opened eastward, and afforded a distant view of the Great Stone Face. Over the general's chair, which was a relic from the home of Washington, there was an arch of verdant boughs, with the laurel profusely intermixed, and surmounted by his country's banner, beneath which he had won his victories.

Our friend Ernest raised himself on his tiptoes, in hopes to get a glimpse of the celebrated guest; but there was a mighty crowd about the tables anxious to hear the toasts and speeches, and to catch any word that might fall from the general in reply; and a volunteer company, doing duty as a guard, pricked ruthlessly with their bayonets at any particularly quiet person among the throng. So Ernest, being of an unobtrusive character, was thrust quite into the background, where he could see no more of Old Blood-and-Thunder's physiognomy than if it had been still blazing on the battlefield. To console himself, he turned towards the Great Stone Face, which, like a faithful and long-remembered friend, looked back and smiled upon him through the *vista* of the forest. Meantime, however, he could overhear the remarks of various individuals, who were comparing the features of the hero with the face on the distant mountain-side.

"'Tis the same face, to a hair!" cried one man, cutting a caper for joy.

"Wonderfully like, that's a fact!" responded another.

"Like! why, I call it Old Blood-and-Thunder himself, in a monstrous looking-glass!" cried a third. "And why not? He's the greatest man of this or any other age, beyond a doubt."

And then all three of the speakers gave a great shout, which communicated electricity to the crowd, and called forth a roar from a thousand voices, that went reverberating for miles among the mountains, until you might have supposed that the Great Stone Face had poured its thunder-breath into the cry. All these comments, and this vast enthusiasm, served the more to interest our friend; nor did he think of questioning that now, at length, the mountain-visage had found its human counterpart. It is true, Ernest had imagined that this long-looked-for personage would appear in the character of a man of peace, uttering wisdom, and doing good, and making people happy. But, taking an habitual breadth of view, with all his simplicity, he contended that Providence should choose its own method of blessing mankind, and could conceive that this great end might be effected even by a warrior and a bloody sword, should inscrutable wisdom see fit to order matters so.

"The general! the general!" was now the cry. "Hush! silence! Old Blood-and-Thunder 's going to make a speech."

Even so; for, the cloth being removed, the general's health had been drunk amid shouts of applause, and he now stood upon his feet to thank the company. Ernest saw him. There he was, over the shoulders of the crowd, from the two glittering epaulets and embroidered collar upward, beneath the arch of green boughs with intertwined laurel, and the banner drooping as if to shade his brow! And there, too, visible in the same glance, through the *vista* of the forest, appeared the Great Stone Face! And was there, indeed, such a resemblance as the crowd had testified?

Alas, Ernest could not recognize it! He beheld a war-worn and weather-beaten countenance, full of energy, and expressive of an iron will; but the gentle wisdom, the deep, broad, tender sympathies, were altogether wanting in Old Blood-and-Thunder's visage; and even if the Great Stone Face had assumed his look of stern command, the milder traits would still have tempered it.

"This is not the man of prophecy," sighed Ernest, to himself, as he made his way out of the throng. "And must the world wait longer yet?"

The mists had congregated about the distant mountain-side, and there were seen the grand and awful features of the Great Stone Face, awful but benignant, as if a mighty angel were sitting among the hills, and enrobing himself in a cloud-vesture of gold and purple. As he looked, Ernest could hardly believe but that a smile beamed over the whole visage, with a radiance still brightening, although without motion of the lips. It was probably the effect of the western sunshine, melting through the thinly diffused vapors that had swept between him and the object that he gazed at. But—as it always did—the aspect of his marvellous friend made Ernest as hopeful as if he had never hoped in vain.

"Fear not, Ernest," said his heart, even as if the Great Face were whispering him,—"fear not, Ernest; he will come."

More years sped swiftly and tranquilly away. Ernest still dwelt in his native valley, and was now a man of middle age. By imperceptible degrees, he had become known among the people. Now, as heretofore, he laboured for his bread, and was the same simple-hearted man that he had always been. But he had thought and felt so much, he had given so many of the best hours of his life to unworldly hopes for some great good to mankind, that it seemed as though he had been talking with the angels, and had imbibed a portion of their wisdom unawares. It was visible in the calm and well-considered beneficence of his daily life, the quiet stream of which had made a wide green margin all along its course.

Not a day passed by, that the world was not the better because this man, humble as he was, had lived. He never stepped aside from his own path, yet would always reach a blessing to his neighbour. Almost involuntarily, too, he had become a preacher. The pure and high simplicity of his thought, which, as one of its manifestations, took shape in the good deeds that dropped silently from his hand, flowed also forth in speech. He uttered truths that wrought upon and moulded the lives of those who heard him. His auditors, it may be, never suspected that Ernest, their own neighbour and familiar friend, was more than an ordinary man; least of all did Ernest himself suspect it; but, inevitably as the murmur of a rivulet, came thoughts out of his mouth that no other human lips had spoken.

When the people's minds had had a little time to cool, they were ready enough to acknowledge their mistake in imagining a similarity between General Blood-and-Thunder's truculent physiognomy and the benign visage on the mountain-side. But now, again, there were reports and many paragraphs in the newspapers, affirming that the likeness of the Great Stone Face had appeared upon the broad shoulders of a certain eminent statesman. He, like Mr. Gathergold and Old Blood-and-Thunder, was a native of the valley, but had left it in his early days, and taken up the trades of law and politics.

Instead of the rich man's wealth and the warrior's sword, he had but a tongue, and it was mightier than both together. So wonderfully eloquent was he, that whatever he might choose to say, his auditors had no choice but to believe him; wrong looked like right, and right like wrong; for when it pleased him, he could make a kind of illuminated fog with his mere breath, and obscure the natural daylight with it. His tongue, indeed, was a magic instrument: sometimes it rumbled like the thunder; sometimes it warbled like the sweetest music. It was the blast of war,—the song of peace; and it seemed to have a heart in it, when there was no such matter.

In good truth, he was a wondrous man; and when his tongue had acquired him all other imaginable success,—when it had been heard in halls of state, and in the courts of princes and potentates,—after it had made him known all over the world, even as a voice crying from shore to shore,—it finally persuaded his countrymen to select him for the Presidency. Before this time,—indeed, as soon as he began to grow celebrated,—his admirers had found out the resemblance between him and the Great Stone Face; and so much were they struck by it, that throughout the country this distinguished gentleman was known by the name of Old Stony Phiz. The phrase was considered as giving a highly favourable aspect to his political prospects; for, as is likewise the case with the Popedom, nobody ever becomes President without taking a name other than his own.

While his friends were doing their best to make him President, Old Stony Phiz, as he was called, set out on a visit to the valley where he was born. Of course, he had no other object that to shake hands with his fellow-citizens, and neither thought nor cared about any effect which his progress through the country might have upon the election. Magnificent preparations were made to receive the illustrious statesman; a cavalcade of horse men set forth to meet him at the boundary line of the State, and all the people left their business and gathered along the wayside to see him pass.

Among these was Ernest. Though more than once disappointed, as we have seen, he had such a hopeful and confiding nature, that he was always ready to believe in whatever seemed beautiful and good. He kept his heart continually open, and thus was sure to catch the blessing from on high, when it should come. So now again, as buoyantly as ever, he went forth to behold the likeness of the Great Stone Face.

The cavalcade came prancing along the road, with a great clattering of hoofs and a mighty cloud of dust, which rose up so dense and high that the visage of the mountain-side was completely hidden from Ernest's eyes. All the great men of the neighbourhood were there on horseback: militia officers, in uniform; the member of Congress; the sheriff of the county; the editors of news papers; and many a farmer, too, had mounted his patient steed, with his Sunday coat upon his back. It really was a very brilliant spectacle, especially as there were numerous banners flaunting over the cavalcade, on some of which were gorgeous portraits of the illustrious statesman and the Great Stone Face, smiling familiarly at one another, like two brothers. If the pictures were to be trusted, the mutual resemblance, it must be confessed, was marvellous.

We must not forget to mention that there was a band of music, which made the echoes of the mountains ring and reverberate with the loud triumph of its strains; so that airy and soul-thrilling melodies broke out among all the heights and hollows, as if every nook of his native valley had found a voice, to welcome the distinguished guest. But the grandest effect was when the far-off mountain precipice flung back the music; for then the Great Stone Face itself seemed to be swelling the triumphant chorus, in acknowledgment that, at length, the man of prophecy was come.

All this while the people were throwing up their hats and shouting, with enthusiasm so contagious that the heart of Ernest kindled up, and he likewise threw up his hat, and shouted, as loudly as the loudest, "*Huzza* for the great man! *Huzza* for Old Stony Phiz?" But as yet he had not seen him.

"Here he is, now!" cried those who stood near Ernest. "There! There! Look at Old Stony Phiz and then at the Old Man of the Mountain, and see if they are not as like as two twin-brothers!"

In the midst of all this gallant array, came an open *barouche*, drawn by four white horses; and in the *barouche*, with his massive head uncovered, sat the illustrious statesman, Old Stony Phiz himself.

"Confess it," said one of Ernest's neighbours to him, "the Great Stone Face has met its match at last!"

Now, it must be owned that, at his first glimpse of the countenance which was bowing and smiling from the *barouche*, Ernest did fancy that there was a resemblance between it and the old familiar face upon the mountain side. The brow, with its massive depth and loftiness, and all the other features, indeed, were boldly and strongly hewn, as if in emulation of a more than heroic, of a Titanic model. But the sublimity and stateliness, the grand expression of a divine sympathy, that illuminated the mountain visage, and etherealized its ponderous granite substance into spirit, might here be sought in vain. Something had been originally left out, or had departed.

And therefore the marvellously gifted states man had always a weary gloom in the deep caverns of his eyes, as of a child that has outgrown its playthings, or a man of mighty faculties and little aims, whose life, with all its high performances, was vague and empty, because no high purpose had endowed it with reality.

Still, Ernest's neighbour was thrusting his elbow into his side, and pressing him for an answer.

"Confess! confess! Is not he the very picture of your Old Man of the Mountain?"

"No!" said Ernest, bluntly, "I see little or no likeness."

"Then so much the worse for the Great Stone Face!" answered his neighbour; and again he set up a shout for Old Stony Phiz.

But Ernest turned away, melancholy, and almost despondent: for this was the saddest of his disappointments, to behold a man who might have fulfilled the prophecy, and had not willed to do so. Meantime, the cavalcade, the banners, the music, and the *barouches* swept past him, with the vociferous crowd in the rear, leaving the dust to settle down, and the Great Stone Face to be revealed again, with the grandeur that it had worn for untold centuries.

"Lo, here I am, Ernest!" the benign lips seemed to say. "I have waited longer than thou, and am not yet weary. Fear not; the man will come."

The years hurried onward, treading in their haste on one another's heels. And now they began to bring white hairs, and scatter them over the head of Ernest; they made reverend wrinkles across his forehead, end furrows in his cheeks. He was an aged man. But not in vain had he grown old: more than the white hairs on his head were the sage thoughts in his mind; his wrinkles and furrows were inscriptions that Time had graved, and in which he had written legends of wisdom that had been tested by the tenor of a life. And Ernest had ceased to be obscure. Unsought for, undesired, had come the fame which so many seek, and made him known in the great world, beyond the limits of the valley in which he had dwelt so quietly.

College professors, and even the active men of cities, came from far to see and converse with Ernest; for the report had gone abroad that this simple husbandman had ideas unlike those of other men, not gained from books, but of a higher tone,—a tranquil and familiar majesty, as if he had been talking with the angels as his daily friends. Whether it were sage, statesman, or philanthropist, Ernest received these visitors with the gentle sincerity that had characterized him from boyhood, and spoke freely with them of whatever came uppermost, or lay deepest in his heart or their own. While they talked together, his face would kindle, unawares, and shine upon them, as with a mild evening light. Pensive with the fullness of such discourse, his guests took leave and went their way; and passing up the valley, paused to look at the Great Stone Face, imagining that they had seen its likeness in a human countenance, but could not remember where.

While Ernest had been growing up and growing old, a bountiful Providence had granted a new poet to this earth. He, likewise, was a native of the valley, but had spent the greater part of his life at a distance from that romantic region, pouring out his sweet music amid the bustle and din of cities. Often, however, did the mountains which had been familiar to him in his childhood lift their snowy peaks into the clear atmosphere of his poetry. Neither was the Great Stone Face forgotten, for the poet had celebrated it in an ode, which was grand enough to have been uttered by its own majestic lips.

This man of genius, we may say, had come down from heaven with wonderful endowments. If he sang of a mountain, the eyes of all mankind beheld a mightier grandeur reposing on its breast, or soaring to its summit, than had before been seen there. If his theme were a lovely lake, a celestial smile had now been thrown over it, to gleam forever on its surface. If it were the vast old sea, even the deep immensity of its dread bosom seemed to swell the higher, as if moved by the emotions of the song. Thus the world assumed another and a better aspect from the hour that the poet blessed it with his happy eyes. The Creator had bestowed him, as the last best touch to his own handiwork. Creation was not finished till the poet came to interpret, and so complete it.

The effect was no less high and beautiful, when his human brethren were the subject of his verse. The man or woman, sordid with the common dust of life, who crossed his daily path, and the little child who played in it, were glorified if he beheld them in his mood of poetic faith. He showed the golden links of the great chain that intertwined them with an angelic kindred; he brought out the hidden traits of a celestial birth that made them worthy of such kin. Some, indeed, there were, who thought to show the soundness of their judgement by affirming that all the beauty and dignity of the natural world existed only in the poet's fancy. Let such men speak for themselves, who undoubtedly appear to have been spawned forth by Nature with a contemptuous bitterness; she having plastered them up out of her refuse stuff, after all the swine were made. As respects all things else, the poet's ideal was the truest truth.

The songs of this poet found their way to Ernest. He read them after his customary toil, seated on the bench before his cottage-door, where for such a length of time he had filled his repose with thought, by gazing at the Great Stone Face. And now as he read *stanzas* that caused the soul to thrill within him, he lifted his eyes to the vast countenance beaming on him so benignantly.

"O majestic friend," he murmured, addressing the Great Stone Face, "is not this man worthy to resemble thee?"

The Face seemed to smile, but answered not a word.

Now it happened that the poet, though he dwelt so far away, had not only heard of Ernest, but had meditated much upon his character, until he deemed nothing so desirable as to meet this man, whose untaught wisdom walked hand in hand with the noble simplicity of his life. One summer morning, therefore, he took passage by the railroad, and, in the decline of the afternoon, alighted from the cars at no great distance from Ernest's cottage. The great hotel, which had formerly been the palace of Mr. Gathergold, was close at hand, but the poet, with his carpetbag on his arm, inquired at once where Ernest dwelt, and was resolved to be accepted as his guest.

Approaching the door, he there found the good old man, holding a volume in his hand, which alternately he read, and then, with a finger between the leaves, looked lovingly at the Great Stone Face.

"Good evening," said the poet. "Can you give a traveller a night's lodging?"

"Willingly," answered Ernest; and then he added, smiling, "Methinks I never saw the Great Stone Face look so hospitably at a stranger."

The poet sat down on the bench beside him, and he and Ernest talked together. Often had the poet held intercourse with the wittiest and the wisest, but never before with a man like Ernest, whose thoughts and feelings gushed up with such a natural freedom, and who made great truths so familiar by his simple utterance of them. Angels, as had been so often said, seemed to have wrought with him at his labour in the fields; angels seemed to have sat with him by the fireside; and, dwelling with angels as friend with friends, he had imbibed the sublimity of their ideas, and imbued it with the sweet and lowly charm of household words. So thought the poet.

And Ernest, on the other hand, was moved and agitated by the living images which the poet flung out of his mind, and which peopled all the air about the cottage-door with shapes of beauty, both gay and pensive. The sympathies of these two men instructed them with a profounder sense than either could have attained alone. Their minds accorded into one strain, and made delightful music which neither of them could have claimed as all his own, nor distinguished his own share from the other's. They led one another, as it were, into a high pavilion of their thoughts, so remote, and hitherto so dim, that they had never entered it before, and so beautiful that they desired to be there always.

As Ernest listened to the poet, he imagined that the Great Stone Face was bending forward to listen too. He gazed earnestly into the poet's glowing eyes.

"Who are you, my strangely gifted guest?" he said.

The poet laid his finger on the volume that Ernest had been reading.

"You have read these poems," said he. "You know me, then,— for I wrote them."

Again, and still more earnestly than before, Ernest examined the poet's features; then turned towards the Great Stone Face; then back, with an uncertain aspect, to his guest. But his countenance fell; he shook his head, and sighed.

"Wherefore are you sad?" inquired the poet. "Because," replied Ernest, "all through life I have awaited the fulfilment of a prophecy; and, when I read these poems, I hoped that it might be fulfilled in you."

"You hoped," answered the poet, faintly smiling, "to find in me the likeness of the Great Stone Face. And you are disappointed, as formerly with Mr. Gathergold, and Old Blood-and-Thunder, and Old Stony Phiz. Yes, Ernest, it is my doom. You must add my name to the illustrious three, and record another failure of your hopes. For—in shame and sadness do I speak it, Ernest—I am not worthy to be typified by yonder benign and majestic image."

"And why?" asked Ernest. He pointed to the volume. "Are not those thoughts divine?"

"They have a strain of the Divinity," replied the poet. "You can hear in them the far-off echo of a heavenly song. But my life, dear Ernest, has not corresponded with my thought. I have had grand dreams, but they have been only dreams, because I have lived—and that, too, by my own choice—among poor and mean realities. Sometimes even—shall I dare to say it?—I lack faith in the grandeur, the beauty, and the goodness, which my own works are said to have made more evident in nature and in human life. Why, then, pure seeker of the good and true, shouldst thou hope to find me, in yonder image of the divine?"

The poet spoke sadly, and his eyes were dim with tears. So, likewise, were those of Ernest.

At the hour of sunset, as had long been his frequent custom, Ernest was to discourse to an assemblage of the neighbouring inhabitants in the open air. He and the poet, arm in arm, still talking together as they went along, proceeded to the spot. It was a small nook among the hills, with a gray precipice behind, the stern front of which was relieved by the pleasant foliage of many creeping plants, that made a tapestry for the naked rock, by hanging their festoons from all its rugged angles. At a small elevation above the ground, set in a rich framework of verdure, there appeared a niche, spacious enough to admit a human figure, with freedom for such gestures as spontaneously accompany earnest thought and genuine emotion.

Into this natural pulpit Ernest ascended, and threw a look of familiar kindness around upon his audience. They stood, or sat, or reclined upon the grass, as seemed good to each, with the departing sunshine falling obliquely over them, and mingling its subdued cheerfulness with the solemnity of a grove of ancient trees, beneath and amid the boughs of which the golden rays were constrained to pass. In another direction was seen the Great Stone Face, with the same cheer, combined with the same solemnity, in its benignant aspect.

Ernest began to speak, giving to the people of what was in his heart and mind. His words had power, because they accorded with his thoughts; and his thoughts had reality and depth, because they harmonized with the life which he had always lived. It was not mere breath that this preacher uttered; they were the words of life, because a life of good deeds and holy love was melted into them. Pearls, pure and rich, had been dissolved into this precious draught.

The poet, as he listened, felt that the being and character of Ernest were a nobler strain of poetry than he had ever written. His eyes glistening with tears, he gazed reverentially at the venerable man, and said within himself that never was there an aspect so worthy of a prophet and a sage as that mild, sweet, thoughtful countenance, with the glory of white hair diffused about it. At a distance, but distinctly to be seen, high up in the golden light of the setting sun, appeared the Great Stone Face, with hoary mists around it, like the white hairs around the brow of Ernest. Its look of grand beneficence seemed to embrace the world.

At that moment, in sympathy with a thought which he was about to utter, the face of Ernest assumed a grandeur of expression, so imbued with benevolence, that the poet, by an irresistible impulse, threw his arms aloft, and shouted,—

"Behold! Behold! Ernest is himself the likeness of the Great Stone Face!"

Then all the people looked, and saw that what the deep-sighted poet said was true. The prophecy was fulfilled. But Ernest, having finished what he had to say, took the poet's arm, and walked slowly homeward, still hoping that some wiser and better man than himself would by and by appear, bearing a resemblance to the *GREAT STONE FACE.*

Young Goodman Brown

(A tale from *Mosses From an Old Manse and Other Stories*)

Young Goodman Brown came forth at sunset into the street at Salem village; but put his head back, after crossing the threshold, to exchange a parting kiss with his young wife. And Faith, as the wife was aptly named, thrust her own pretty head into the street, letting the wind play with the pink ribbons of her cap while she called to Goodman Brown.

"Dearest heart," whispered she, softly and rather sadly, when her lips were close to his ear, "prithee put off your journey until sunrise and sleep in your own bed tonight. A lone woman is troubled with such dreams and such thoughts that she's afeard of herself sometimes. Pray tarry with me this night, dear husband, of all nights in the year."

"My love and my Faith," replied young Goodman Brown, "of all nights in the year, this one night must I tarry away from thee. My journey, as thou callest it, forth and back again, must needs be done 'twixt now and sunrise. What, my sweet, pretty wife, dost thou doubt me already, and we but three months married?"

"Then God bless you!" said Faith, with the pink ribbons; "and may you find all well when you come back."

"Amen!" cried Goodman Brown. "Say thy prayers, dear Faith, and go to bed at dusk, and no harm will come to thee."

So they parted; and the young man pursued his way until, being about to turn the corner by the meeting-house, he looked back and saw the head of Faith still peeping after him with a melancholy air, in spite of her pink ribbons.

"Poor little Faith!" thought he, for his heart smote him. "What a wretch am I to leave her on such an errand! She talks of dreams, too. Methought as she spoke there was trouble in her face, as if a dream had warned her what work is to be done to-night. But no, no; 't would kill her to think it. Well, she's a blessed angel on earth; and after this one night I'll cling to her skirts and follow her to heaven."

With this excellent resolve for the future, Goodman Brown felt himself justified in making more haste on his present evil purpose. He had taken a dreary road, darkened by all the gloomiest trees of the forest, which barely stood aside to let the narrow path creep through, and closed immediately behind. It was all as lonely as could be; and there is this peculiarity in such a solitude, that the traveller knows not who may be concealed by the innumerable trunks and the thick boughs overhead; so that with lonely footsteps he may yet be passing through an unseen multitude.

"There may be a devilish Indian behind every tree," said Goodman Brown to himself; and he glanced fearfully behind him as he added, "What if the devil himself should be at my very elbow!"

His head being turned back, he passed a crook of the road, and, looking forward again, beheld the figure of a man, in grave and decent attire, seated at the foot of an old tree. He arose at Goodman Brown's approach and walked onward side by side with him.

"You are late, Goodman Brown," said he. "The clock of the Old South was striking as I came through Boston, and that is full fifteen minutes agone."

"Faith kept me back a while," replied the young man, with a tremor in his voice, caused by the sudden appearance of his companion, though not wholly unexpected.

It was now deep dusk in the forest, and deepest in that part of it where these two were journeying. As nearly as could be discerned, the second traveller was about fifty years old, apparently in the same rank of life as Goodman Brown, and bearing a considerable resemblance to him, though perhaps more in expression than features. Still they might have been taken for father and son. And yet, though the elder person was as simply clad as the younger, and as simple in manner too, he had an indescribable air of one who knew the world, and who would not have felt abashed at the governor's dinner table or in King William's court, were it possible that his affairs should call him thither. But the only thing about him that could be fixed upon as remarkable was his staff, which bore the likeness of a great black snake, so curiously wrought that it might almost be seen to twist and wriggle itself like a living serpent. This, of course, must have been an ocular deception, assisted by the uncertain light.

"Come, Goodman Brown," cried his fellow-traveller, "this is a dull pace for the beginning of a journey. Take my staff, if you are so soon weary."

"Friend," said the other, exchanging his slow pace for a full stop, "having kept covenant by meeting thee here, it is my purpose now to return whence I came. I have scruples touching the matter thou wot'st of."

"Sayest thou so?" replied he of the serpent, smiling apart. "Let us walk on, nevertheless, reasoning as we go; and if I convince thee not thou shalt turn back. We are but a little way in the forest yet."

"Too far! too far!" exclaimed the good man, unconsciously resuming his walk. "My father never went into the woods on such an errand, nor his father before him. We have been a race of honest men and good Christians since the days of the martyrs; and shall I be the first of the name of Brown that ever took this path and kept—"

"Such company, thou wouldst say," observed the elder person, interpreting his pause. "Well said, Goodman Brown! I have been as well acquainted with your family as with ever a one among the Puritans; and that's no trifle to say. I helped your grandfather, the constable, when he lashed the Quaker woman so smartly through the streets of Salem; and it was I that brought your father a pitch-pine knot, kindled at my own hearth, to set fire to an Indian village, in King Philip's war. They were my good friends, both; and many a pleasant walk have we had along this path, and returned merrily after midnight. I would fain be friends with you for their sake."

"If it be as thou sayest," replied Goodman Brown, "I marvel they never spoke of these matters; or, verily, I marvel not, seeing that the least rumour of the sort would have driven them from New England. We are a people of prayer, and good works to boot, and abide no such wickedness."

"Wickedness or not," said the traveller with the twisted staff, "I have a very general acquaintance here in New England. The deacons of many a church have drunk the communion wine with me; the selectmen of divers towns make me their chairman; and a majority of the Great and General Court are firm supporters of my interest. The governor and I, too—But these are state secrets."

"Can this be so?" cried Goodman Brown, with a stare of amazement at his undisturbed companion. "Howbeit, I have nothing to do with the governor and council; they have their own ways, and are no rule for a simple husbandman like me. But, were I to go on with thee, how should I meet the eye of that good old man, our minister, at Salem village? Oh, his voice would make me tremble both Sabbath day and lecture day."

Thus far the elder traveller had listened with due gravity; but now burst into a fit of irrepressible mirth, shaking himself so violently that his snake-like staff actually seemed to wriggle in sympathy.

"Ha! ha! ha!" shouted he again and again; then composing himself, "Well, go on, Goodman Brown, go on; but, prithee, don't kill me with laughing."

"Well, then, to end the matter at once," said Goodman Brown, considerably nettled, "there is my wife, Faith. It would break her dear little heart; and I'd rather break my own."

"Nay, if that be the case," answered the other, "e'en go thy ways, Goodman Brown. I would not for twenty old women like the one hobbling before us that Faith should come to any harm."

As he spoke he pointed his staff at a female figure on the path, in whom Goodman Brown recognized a very pious and exemplary dame, who had taught him his catechism in youth, and was still his moral and spiritual adviser, jointly with the minister and Deacon Gookin.

"A marvel, truly, that Goody Cloyse should be so far in the wilderness at nightfall," said he. "But with your leave, friend, I shall take a cut through the woods until we have left this Christian woman behind. Being a stranger to you, she might ask whom I was consorting with and whither I was going."

"Be it so," said his fellow-traveller. "Betake you to the woods, and let me keep the path."

Accordingly the young man turned aside, but took care to watch his companion, who advanced softly along the road until he had come within a staff's length of the old dame. She, meanwhile, was making the best of her way, with singular speed for so aged a woman, and mumbling some indistinct words—a prayer, doubtless—as she went. The traveller put forth his staff and touched her withered neck with what seemed the serpent's tail.

"The devil!" screamed the pious old lady.

"Then Goody Cloyse knows her old friend?" observed the traveller, confronting her and leaning on his writhing stick.

"Ah, forsooth, and is it your worship indeed?" cried the good dame. "Yea, truly is it, and in the very image of my old gossip, Goodman Brown, the grandfather of the silly fellow that now is. But—would your worship believe it?—my broomstick hath strangely disappeared, stolen, as I suspect, by that unhanged witch, Goody Cory, and that, too, when I was all anointed with the juice of smallage, and cinquefoil, and wolf's bane."

"Mingled with fine wheat and the fat of a new-born babe," said the shape of old Goodman Brown.

"Ah, your worship knows the recipe," cried the old lady, cackling aloud. "So, as I was saying, being all ready for the meeting, and no horse to ride on, I made up my mind to foot it; for they tell me there is a nice young man to be taken into communion tonight. But now your good worship will lend me your arm, and we shall be there in a twinkling."

"That can hardly be," answered her friend. "I may not spare you my arm, Goody Cloyse; but here is my staff, if you will."

So saying, he threw it down at her feet, where, perhaps, it assumed life, being one of the rods which its owner had formerly lent to the Egyptian *magi*. Of this fact, however, Goodman Brown could not take cognizance. He had cast up his eyes in astonishment, and, looking down again, beheld neither Goody Cloyse nor the serpentine staff, but his fellow-traveller alone, who waited for him as calmly as if nothing had happened.

"That old woman taught me my catechism," said the young man; and there was a world of meaning in this simple comment.

They continued to walk onward, while the elder traveller exhorted his companion to make good speed and persevere in the path, discoursing so aptly that his arguments seemed rather to spring up in the bosom of his auditor than to be suggested by himself. As they went, he plucked a branch of maple to serve for a walking stick, and began to strip it of the twigs and little boughs, which were wet with evening dew. The moment his fingers touched them they became strangely withered and dried up as with a week's sunshine. Thus the pair proceeded, at a good free pace, until suddenly, in a gloomy hollow of the road, Goodman Brown sat himself down on the stump of a tree and refused to go any farther.

"Friend," said he, stubbornly, "my mind is made up. Not another step will I budge on this errand. What if a wretched old woman do choose to go to the devil when I thought she was going to heaven: is that any reason why I should quit my dear Faith and go after her?"

"You will think better of this by and by," said his acquaintance, composedly. "Sit here and rest yourself a while; and when you feel like moving again, there is my staff to help you along."

Without more words, he threw his companion the maple stick, and was as speedily out of sight as if he had vanished into the deepening gloom. The young man sat a few moments by the roadside, applauding himself greatly, and thinking with how clear a conscience he should meet the minister in his morning walk, nor shrink from the eye of good old Deacon Gookin. And what calm sleep would be his that very night, which was to have been spent so wickedly, but so purely and sweetly now, in the arms of Faith! Amidst these pleasant and praiseworthy meditations, Goodman Brown heard the tramp of horses along the road, and deemed it advisable to conceal himself within the verge of the forest, conscious of the guilty purpose that had brought him thither, though now so happily turned from it.

On came the hoof tramps and the voices of the riders, two grave old voices, conversing soberly as they drew near. These mingled sounds appeared to pass along the road, within a few yards of the young man's hiding-place; but, owing doubtless to the depth of the gloom at that particular spot, neither the travellers nor their steeds were visible. Though their figures brushed the small boughs by the wayside, it could not be seen that they intercepted, even for a moment, the faint gleam from the strip of bright sky athwart which they must have passed.

Goodman Brown alternately crouched and stood on tiptoe, pulling aside the branches and thrusting forth his head as far as he durst without discerning so much as a shadow. It vexed him the more, because he could have sworn, were such a thing possible, that he recognized the voices of the minister and Deacon Gookin, jogging along quietly, as they were wont to do, when bound to some ordination or ecclesiastical council. While yet within hearing, one of the riders stopped to pluck a switch.

"Of the two, reverend sir," said the voice like the deacon's, "I had rather miss an ordination dinner than tonight's meeting. They tell me that some of our community are to be here from Falmouth and beyond, and others from Connecticut and Rhode Island, besides several of the Indian powwows, who, after their fashion, know almost as much deviltry as the best of us. Moreover, there is a goodly young woman to be taken into communion."

"Mighty well, Deacon Gookin!" replied the solemn old tones of the minister. "Spur up, or we shall be late. Nothing can be done, you know, until I get on the ground."

The hoofs clattered again; and the voices, talking so strangely in the empty air, passed on through the forest, where no church had ever been gathered or solitary Christian prayed. Whither, then, could these holy men be journeying so deep into the heathen wilderness? Young Goodman Brown caught hold of a tree for support, being ready to sink down on the ground, faint and overburdened with the heavy sickness of his heart. He looked up to the sky, doubting whether there really was a heaven above him. Yet there was the blue arch, and the stars brightening in it.

"With heaven above and Faith below, I will yet stand firm against the devil!" cried Goodman Brown.

While he still gazed upward into the deep arch of the firmament and had lifted his hands to pray, a cloud, though no wind was stirring, hurried across the zenith and hid the brightening stars. The blue sky was still visible, except directly overhead, where this black mass of cloud was sweeping swiftly northward. Aloft in the air, as if from the depths of the cloud, came a confused and doubtful sound of voices. Once the listener fancied that he could distinguish the accents of towns-people of his own, men and women, both pious and ungodly, many of whom he had met at the communion table, and had seen others rioting at the tavern.

The next moment, so indistinct were the sounds, he doubted whether he had heard aught but the murmur of the old forest, whispering without a wind. Then came a stronger swell of those familiar tones, heard daily in the sunshine at Salem village, but never until now from a cloud of night There was one voice of a young woman, uttering lamentations, yet with an uncertain sorrow, and entreating for some favour, which, perhaps, it would grieve her to obtain; and all the unseen multitude, both saints and sinners, seemed to encourage her onward.

"Faith!" shouted Goodman Brown, in a voice of agony and desperation; and the echoes of the forest mocked him, crying, "Faith! Faith!" as if bewildered wretches were seeking her all through the wilderness.

The cry of grief, rage, and terror was yet piercing the night, when the unhappy husband held his breath for a response. There was a scream, drowned immediately in a louder murmur of voices, fading into far-off laughter, as the dark cloud swept away, leaving the clear and silent sky above Goodman Brown. But something fluttered lightly down through the air and caught on the branch of a tree. The young man seized it, and beheld a pink ribbon.

"My Faith is gone!" cried he, after one stupefied moment. "There is no good on earth; and sin is but a name. Come, devil; for to thee is this world given."

And, maddened with despair, so that he laughed loud and long, did Goodman Brown grasp his staff and set forth again, at such a rate that he seemed to fly along the forest path rather than to walk or run. The road grew wilder and drearier and more faintly traced, and vanished at length, leaving him in the heart of the dark wilderness, still rushing onward with the instinct that guides mortal man to evil. The whole forest was peopled with frightful sounds—the creaking of the trees, the howling of wild beasts, and the yell of Indians; while sometimes the wind tolled like a distant church bell, and sometimes gave a broad roar around the traveller, as if all Nature were laughing him to scorn. But he was himself the chief horror of the scene, and shrank not from its other horrors.

"Ha! ha! ha!" roared Goodman Brown when the wind laughed at him.

"Let us hear which will laugh loudest. Think not to frighten me with your deviltry. Come witch, come wizard, come Indian powwow, come devil himself, and here comes Goodman Brown. You may as well fear him as he fear you."

In truth, all through the haunted forest there could be nothing more frightful than the figure of Goodman Brown. On he flew among the black pines, brandishing his staff with frenzied gestures, now giving vent to an inspiration of horrid blasphemy, and now shouting forth such laughter as set all the echoes of the forest laughing like demons around him. The fiend in his own shape is less hideous than when he rages in the breast of man.

Thus sped the demoniac on his course, until, quivering among the trees, he saw a red light before him, as when the felled trunks and branches of a clearing have been set on fire, and throw up their lurid blaze against the sky, at the hour of midnight. He paused, in a lull of the tempest that had driven him onward, and heard the swell of what seemed a hymn, rolling solemnly from a distance with the weight of many voices. He knew the tune; it was a familiar one in the choir of the village meeting-house. The verse died heavily away, and was lengthened by a chorus, not of human voices, but of all the sounds of the benighted wilderness pealing in awful harmony together. Goodman Brown cried out, and his cry was lost to his own ear by its unison with the cry of the desert.

In the interval of silence he stole forward until the light glared full upon his eyes. At one extremity of an open space, hemmed in by the dark wall of the forest, arose a rock, bearing some rude, natural resemblance either to an altar or a pulpit, and surrounded by four blazing pines, their tops aflame, their stems untouched, like candles at an evening meeting. The mass of foliage that had overgrown the summit of the rock was all on fire, blazing high into the night and fitfully illuminating the whole field. Each pendent twig and leafy festoon was in a blaze. As the red light arose and fell, a numerous congregation alternately shone forth, then disappeared in shadow, and again grew, as it were, out of the darkness, peopling the heart of the solitary woods at once.

"A grave and dark-clad company," quoth Goodman Brown.

In truth they were such. Among them, quivering to and fro between gloom and splendour, appeared faces that would be seen next day at the council board of the province, and others which, Sabbath after Sabbath, looked devoutly heavenward, and benignantly over the crowded pews, from the holiest pulpits in the land. Some affirm that the lady of the governor was there. At least there were high dames well known to her, and wives of honoured husbands, and widows, a great multitude, and ancient maidens, all of excellent repute, and fair young girls, who trembled lest their mothers should espy them. Either the sudden gleams of light flashing over the obscure field bedazzled Goodman Brown, or he recognized a score of the church members of Salem village famous for their especial sanctity. Good old Deacon Gookin had arrived, and waited at the skirts of that venerable saint, his revered pastor.

But, irreverently consorting with these grave, reputable, and pious people, these elders of the church, these chaste dames and dewy virgins, there were men of dissolute lives and women of spotted fame, wretches given over to all mean and filthy vice, and suspected even of horrid crimes. It was strange to see that the good shrank not from the wicked, nor were the sinners abashed by the saints. Scattered also among their pale-faced enemies were the Indian priests, or powwows, who had often scared their native forest with more hideous incantations than any known to English witchcraft.

"But where is Faith?" thought Goodman Brown; and, as hope came into his heart, he trembled.

Another verse of the hymn arose, a slow and mournful strain, such as the pious love, but joined to words which expressed all that our nature can conceive of sin, and darkly hinted at far more. Unfathomable to mere mortals is the lore of fiends. Verse after verse was sung; and still the chorus of the desert swelled between like the deepest tone of a mighty organ; and with the final peal of that dreadful anthem there came a sound, as if the roaring wind, the rushing streams, the howling beasts, and every other voice of the unconcerted wilderness were mingling and according with the voice of guilty man in homage to the prince of all.

The four blazing pines threw up a loftier flame, and obscurely discovered shapes and visages of horror on the smoke wreaths above the impious assembly. At the same moment the fire on the rock shot redly forth and formed a glowing arch above its base, where now appeared a figure. With reverence be it spoken, the figure bore no slight similitude, both in garb and manner, to some grave divine of the New England churches.

"Bring forth the converts!" cried a voice that echoed through the field and rolled into the forest.

At the word, Goodman Brown stepped forth from the shadow of the trees and approached the congregation, with whom he felt a loathful brotherhood by the sympathy of all that was wicked in his heart. He could have well-nigh sworn that the shape of his own dead father beckoned him to advance, looking downward from a smoke wreath, while a woman, with dim features of despair, threw out her hand to warn him back. Was it his mother? But he had no power to retreat one step, nor to resist, even in thought, when the minister and good old Deacon Gookin seized his arms and led him to the blazing rock. Thither came also the slender form of a veiled female, led between Goody Cloyse, that pious teacher of the catechism, and Martha Carrier, who had received the devil's promise to be queen of hell. A rampant hag was she. And there stood the proselytes beneath the canopy of fire.

"Welcome, my children," said the dark figure, "to the communion of your race. Ye have found thus young your nature and your destiny. My children, look behind you!"

They turned; and flashing forth, as it were, in a sheet of flame, the fiend worshippers were seen; the smile of welcome gleamed darkly on every visage.

"There," resumed the sable form, "are all whom ye have reverenced from youth. Ye deemed them holier than yourselves, and shrank from your own sin, contrasting it with their lives of righteousness and prayerful aspirations heavenward. Yet here are they all in my worshipping assembly. This night it shall be granted you to know their secret deeds: how hoary-bearded elders of the church have whispered wanton words to the young maids of their households; how many a woman, eager for widows' weeds, has given her husband a drink at bedtime and let him sleep his last sleep in her bosom; how beardless youths have made haste to inherit their fathers' wealth; and how fair damsels—blush not, sweet ones—have dug little graves in the garden, and bidden me, the sole guest to an infant's funeral.

"By the sympathy of your human hearts for sin ye shall scent out all the places—whether in church, bedchamber, street, field, or forest—where crime has been committed, and shall exult to behold the whole earth one stain of guilt, one mighty blood spot. Far more than this. It shall be yours to penetrate, in every bosom, the deep mystery of sin, the fountain of all wicked arts, and which inexhaustibly supplies more evil impulses than human power—than my power at its utmost—can make manifest in deeds. And now, my children, look upon each other."

They did so; and, by the blaze of the hell-kindled torches, the wretched man beheld his Faith, and the wife her husband, trembling before that unhallowed altar.

"Lo, there ye stand, my children," said the figure, in a deep and solemn tone, almost sad with its despairing awfulness, as if his once angelic nature could yet mourn for our miserable race. "Depending upon one another's hearts, ye had still hoped that virtue were not all a dream. Now are ye undeceived. Evil is the nature of mankind. Evil must be your only happiness. Welcome again, my children, to the communion of your race."

"Welcome," repeated the fiend worshippers, in one cry of despair and triumph.

And there they stood, the only pair, as it seemed, who were yet hesitating on the verge of wickedness in this dark world. A basin was hollowed, naturally, in the rock. Did it contain water, reddened by the lurid light? or was it blood? or, perchance, a liquid flame? Herein did the shape of evil dip his hand and prepare to lay the mark of baptism upon their foreheads, that they might be partakers of the mystery of sin, more conscious of the secret guilt of others, both in deed and thought, than they could now be of their own. The husband cast one look at his pale wife, and Faith at him. What polluted wretches would the next glance show them to each other, shuddering alike at what they disclosed and what they saw!

"Faith! Faith!" cried the husband, "look up to heaven, and resist the wicked one."

Whether Faith obeyed he knew not. Hardly had he spoken when he found himself amid calm night and solitude, listening to a roar of the wind which died heavily away through the forest. He staggered against the rock, and felt it chill and damp; while a hanging twig, that had been all on fire, besprinkled his cheek with the coldest dew.

The next morning young Goodman Brown came slowly into the street of Salem village, staring around him like a bewildered man. The good old minister was taking a walk along the grave-yard to get an appetite for breakfast and meditate his sermon, and bestowed a blessing, as he passed, on Goodman Brown. He shrank from the venerable saint as if to avoid an anathema. Old Deacon Gookin was at domestic worship, and the holy words of his prayer were heard through the open window. "What God doth the wizard pray to?" quoth Goodman Brown.

Goody Cloyse, that excellent old Christian, stood in the early sunshine at her own lattice, catechizing a little girl who had brought her a pint of morning's milk. Goodman Brown snatched away the child as from the grasp of the fiend himself. Turning the corner by the meeting-house, he spied the head of Faith, with the pink ribbons, gazing anxiously forth, and bursting into such joy at sight of him that she skipped along the street and almost kissed her husband before the whole village. But Goodman Brown looked sternly and sadly into her face, and passed on without a greeting.

Had Goodman Brown fallen asleep in the forest and only dreamed a wild dream of a witch-meeting?

Be it so if you will; but, alas! it was a dream of evil omen for young Goodman Brown. A stern, a sad, a darkly meditative, a distrustful, if not a desperate man did he become from the night of that fearful dream. On the Sabbath day, when the congregation were singing a holy psalm, he could not listen because an anthem of sin rushed loudly upon his ear and drowned all the blessed strain. When the minister spoke from the pulpit with power and fervid eloquence, and, with his hand on the open Bible, of the sacred truths of our religion, and of saint-like lives and triumphant deaths, and of future bliss or misery unutterable, then did Goodman Brown turn pale, dreading lest the roof should thunder down upon the gray blasphemer and his hearers.

Often, waking suddenly at midnight, he shrank from the bosom of Faith; and at morning or eventide, when the family knelt down at prayer, he scowled and muttered to himself, and gazed sternly at his wife, and turned away. And when he had lived long, and was borne to his grave a hoary corpse, followed by Faith, an aged woman, and children and grandchildren, a goodly procession, besides neighbours not a few, they carved no hopeful verse upon his tombstone, for his dying hour was gloom.

Dr. Heidegger's Experiment
(A *Tale from Twice Told Tales* Volume 1)

That very singular man, old Dr. Heidegger, once invited four venerable friends to meet him in his study. There were three white-bearded gentlemen, Mr. Medbourne, Colonel Killigrew, and Mr. Gascoigne, and a withered gentlewoman, whose name was the Widow Wycherly. They were all melancholy old creatures, who had been unfortunate in life, and whose greatest misfortune it was that they were not long ago in their graves. Mr. Medbourne, in the vigour of his age, had been a prosperous merchant, but had lost his all by a frantic speculation, and was now little better than a mendicant.

Colonel Killigrew had wasted his best years, and his health and substance, in the pursuit of sinful pleasures, which had given birth to a brood of pains, such as the gout, and divers other torments of soul and body. Mr. Gascoigne was a ruined politician, a man of evil fame, or at least had been so till time had buried him from the knowledge of the present generation, and made him obscure instead of infamous. As for the Widow Wycherly, tradition tells us that she was a great beauty in her day; but, for a long while past, she had lived in deep seclusion, on account of certain scandalous stories which had prejudiced the gentry of the town against her.

It is a circumstance worth mentioning that each of these three old gentlemen, Mr. Medbourne, Colonel Killigrew, and Mr. Gascoigne, were early lovers of the Widow Wycherly, and had once been on the point of cutting each other's throats for her sake. And, before proceeding further, I will merely hint that Dr. Heidegger and all his four guests were sometimes thought to be a little beside themselves—as is not unfrequently the case with old people, when worried either by present troubles or woeful recollections.

"My dear old friends," said Dr. Heidegger, motioning them to be seated, "I am desirous of your assistance in one of those little experiments with which I amuse myself here in my study."

If all stories were true, Dr. Heidegger's study must have been a very curious place. It was a dim, old-fashioned chamber, festooned with cobwebs, and besprinkled with antique dust. Around the walls stood several oaken bookcases, the lower shelves of which were filled with rows of gigantic folios and black-letter *quartos*, and the upper with little parchment-covered *duodecimos*. Over the central bookcase was a bronze bust of Hippocrates, with which, according to some authorities, Dr. Heidegger was accustomed to hold consultations in all difficult cases of his practice.

In the obscurest corner of the room stood a tall and narrow oaken closet, with its door ajar, within which doubtfully appeared a skeleton. Between two of the bookcases hung a looking-glass, presenting its high and dusty plate within a tarnished gilt frame. Among many wonderful stories related of this mirror, it was fabled that the spirits of all the doctor's deceased patients dwelt within its verge, and would stare him in the face whenever he looked thitherward. The opposite side of the chamber was ornamented with the full-length portrait of a young lady, arrayed in the faded magnificence of silk, satin, and brocade, and with a visage as faded as her dress.

Above half a century ago, Dr. Heidegger had been on the point of marriage with this young lady; but, being affected with some slight disorder, she had swallowed one of her lover's prescriptions, and died on the bridal evening. The greatest curiosity of the study remains to be mentioned; it was a ponderous folio volume, bound in black leather, with massive silver clasps. There were no letters on the back, and nobody could tell the title of the book. But it was well known to be a book of magic; and once, when a chambermaid had lifted it, merely to brush away the dust, the skeleton had rattled in its closet, the picture of the young lady had stepped one foot upon the floor, and several ghastly faces had peeped forth from the mirror; while the brazen head of Hippocrates frowned, and said—"Forbear!"

Such was Dr. Heidegger's study. On the summer afternoon of our tale a small round table, as black as ebony, stood in the centre of the room, sustaining a cut-glass vase of beautiful form and elaborate workmanship. The sunshine came through the window, between the heavy festoons of two faded damask curtains, and fell directly across this vase; so that a mild splendour was reflected from it on the ashen visages of the five old people who sat around. Four champagne glasses were also on the table.

"My dear old friends," repeated Dr. Heidegger, "may I reckon on your aid in performing an exceedingly curious experiment?"

Now Dr. Heidegger was a very strange old gentleman, whose eccentricity had become the nucleus for a thousand fantastic stories. Some of these fables, to my shame be it spoken, might possibly be traced back to my own veracious self; and if any passages of the present tale should startle the reader's faith, I must be content to bear the stigma of a fiction monger.

When the doctor's four guests heard him talk of his proposed experiment, they anticipated nothing more wonderful than the murder of a mouse in an air pump, or the examination of a cobweb by the microscope, or some similar nonsense, with which he was constantly in the habit of pestering his intimates. But without waiting for a reply, Dr. Heidegger hobbled across the chamber, and returned with the same ponderous folio, bound in black leather, which common report affirmed to be a book of magic. Undoing the silver clasps, he opened the volume, and took from among its black-letter pages a rose, or what was once a rose, though now the green leaves and crimson petals had assumed one brownish hue, and the ancient flower seemed ready to crumble to dust in the doctor's hands.

"This rose, said Dr. Heidegger, with a sigh, "this same withered and crumbling flower, blossomed five and fifty years ago. It was given me by Sylvia Ward, whose portrait hangs yonder; and I meant to wear it in my bosom at our wedding. Five and fifty years it has been treasured between the leaves of this old volume. Now, would you deem it possible that this rose of half a century could ever bloom again?"

"Nonsense!" said the Widow Wycherly, with a peevish toss of her head. "You might as well ask whether an old woman's wrinkled face could ever bloom again."

"See!" answered Dr. Heidegger.

He uncovered the vase, and threw the faded rose into the water which it contained. At first, it lay lightly on the surface of the fluid, appearing to imbibe none of its moisture. Soon, however, a singular change began to be visible. The crushed and dried petals stirred, and assumed a deepening tinge of crimson, as if the flower were reviving from a deathlike slumber; the slender stalk and twigs of foliage became green; and there was the rose of half a century, looking as fresh as when Sylvia Ward had first given it to her lover. It was scarcely full blown; for some of its delicate red leaves curled modestly around its moist bosom, within which two or three dewdrops were sparkling.

"That is certainly a very pretty deception," said the doctor's friends; carelessly, however, for they had witnessed greater miracles at a conjurer's show; "pray how was it effected?"

"Did you never hear of the 'Fountain of Youth'?" asked Dr. Heidegger, "which Ponce de Leon, the Spanish adventurer, went in search of two or three centuries ago?"

"But did Ponce de Leon ever find it?" said the Widow Wycherly.

"No, answered Dr. Heidegger, "for he never sought it in the right place. The famous Fountain of Youth, if I am rightly informed, is situated in the southern part of the Floridian peninsula, not far from Lake Macaco. Its source is overshadowed by several gigantic magnolias, which, though numberless centuries old, have been kept as fresh as violets by the virtues of this wonderful water. An acquaintance of mine, knowing my curiosity in such matters, has sent me what you see in the vase."

"Ahem!" said Colonel Killigrew, who believed not a word of the doctor's story: "and what may be the effect of this fluid on the human frame?"

"You shall judge for yourself, my dear colonel," replied Dr. Heidegger; "and all of you, my respected friends, are welcome to so much of this admirable fluid as may restore to you the bloom of youth. For my own part, having had much trouble in growing old, I am in no hurry to grow young again. With your permission, therefore, I will merely watch the progress of the experiment."

While he spoke, Dr. Heidegger had been filling the four champagne glasses with the water of the Fountain of Youth. It was apparently impregnated with an effervescent gas, for little bubbles were continually ascending from the depths of the glasses, and bursting in silvery spray at the surface. As the liquor diffused a pleasant perfume, the old people doubted not that it possessed cordial and comfortable properties; and though utter sceptics as to its rejuvenescent power, they were inclined to swallow it at once. But Dr. Heidegger besought them to stay a moment.

"Before you drink, my respectable old friends," said he, "it would be well that, with the experience of a lifetime to direct you, you should draw up a few general rules for your guidance, in passing a second time through the perils of youth. Think what a sin and shame it would be, if, with your peculiar advantages, you should not become patterns of virtue and wisdom to all the young people of the age!"

The doctor's four venerable friends made him no answer, except by a feeble and tremulous laugh; so very ridiculous was the idea that, knowing how closely repentance treads behind the steps of error, they should ever go astray again.

"Drink, then," said the doctor, bowing: "I rejoice that I have so well selected the subjects of my experiment."

With palsied hands, they raised the glasses to their lips. The liquor, if it really possessed such virtues as Dr. Heidegger imputed to it, could not have been bestowed on four human beings who needed it more woefully. They looked as if they had never known what youth or pleasure was, but had been the offspring of Nature's dotage, and always the gray, decrepit, sapless, miserable creatures, who now sat stooping round the doctor's table, without life enough in their souls or bodies to be animated even by the prospect of growing young again. They drank off the water, and replaced their glasses on the table.

Assuredly there was an almost immediate improvement in the aspect of the party, not unlike what might have been produced by a glass of generous wine, together with a sudden glow of cheerful sunshine brightening over all their visages at once. There was a healthful suffusion on their cheeks, instead of the ashen hue that had made them look so corpse-like. They gazed at one another, and fancied that some magic power had really begun to smooth away the deep and sad inscriptions which Father Time had been so long engraving on their brows. The Widow Wycherly adjusted her cap, for she felt almost like a woman again.

"Give us more of this wondrous water!" cried they, eagerly. "We are younger—but we are still too old! Quick—give us more!"

"Patience, patience!" quoth Dr. Heidegger, who sat watching the experiment with philosophic coolness. "You have been a long time growing old. Surely, you might be content to grow young in half an hour! But the water is at your service."

Again he filled their glasses with the liquor of youth, enough of which still remained in the vase to turn half the old people in the city to the age of their own grandchildren. While the bubbles were yet sparkling on the brim, the doctor's four guests snatched their glasses from the table, and swallowed the contents at a single gulp. Was it delusion? even while the draught was passing down their throats, it seemed to have wrought a change on their whole systems. Their eyes grew clear and bright; a dark shade deepened among their silvery locks, they sat around the table, three gentlemen of middle age, and a woman, hardly beyond her buxom prime.

"My dear widow, you are charming!" cried Colonel Killigrew, whose eyes had been fixed upon her face, while the shadows of age were flitting from it like darkness from the crimson daybreak.

The fair widow knew, of old, that Colonel Killigrew's compliments were not always measured by sober truth; so she started up and ran to the mirror, still dreading that the ugly visage of an old woman would meet her gaze. Meanwhile, the three gentlemen behaved in such a manner as proved that the water of the Fountain of Youth possessed some intoxicating qualities; unless, indeed, their exhilaration of spirits were merely a lightsome dizziness caused by the sudden removal of the weight of years. Mr. Gascoigne's mind seemed to run on political topics, but whether relating to the past, present, or future could not easily be determined, since the same ideas and phrases have been in vogue these fifty years.

Now he rattled forth full-throated sentences about patriotism, national glory, and the people's right; now he muttered some perilous stuff or other, in a sly and doubtful whisper, so cautiously that even his own conscience could scarcely catch the secret; and now, again, he spoke in measured accents, and a deeply deferential tone, as if a royal ear were listening to his well-turned periods. Colonel Killigrew all this time had been trolling forth a jolly bottle song, and ringing his glass in symphony with the chorus, while his eyes wandered toward the buxom figure of the Widow Wycherly. On the other side of the table, Mr. Medbourne was involved in a calculation of dollars and cents, with which was strangely intermingled a project for supplying the East Indies with ice, by harnessing a team of whales to the polar icebergs.

As for the Widow Wycherly, she stood before the mirror curtseying and simpering to her own image, and greeting it as the friend whom she loved better than all the world beside. She thrust her face close to the glass, to see whether some long-remembered wrinkle or crow's foot had indeed vanished. She examined whether the snow had so entirely melted from her hair that the venerable cap could be safely thrown aside. At last, turning briskly away, she came with a sort of dancing step to the table.

"My dear old doctor," cried she, "pray favour me with another glass!"

"Certainly, my dear madam, certainly!" replied the complaisant doctor; "see! I have already filled the glasses."

There, in fact, stood the four glasses, brimful of this wonderful water, the delicate spray of which, as it effervesced from the surface, resembled the tremulous glitter of diamonds. It was now so nearly sunset that the chamber had grown duskier than ever; but a mild and moonlike splendour gleamed from within the vase, and rested alike on the four guests and on the doctor's venerable figure. He sat in a high-backed, elaborately-carved, oaken arm-chair, with a gray dignity of aspect that might have well befitted that very Father Time, whose power had never been disputed, save by this fortunate company. Even while quaffing the third draught of the Fountain of Youth, they were almost awed by the expression of his mysterious visage.

But, the next moment, the exhilarating gush of young life shot through their veins. They were now in the happy prime of youth. Age, with its miserable train of cares and sorrows and diseases, was remembered only as the trouble of a dream, from which they had joyously awoke. The fresh gloss of the soul, so early lost, and without which the world's successive scenes had been but a gallery of faded pictures, again threw its enchantment over all their prospects. They felt like new-created beings in a new-created universe.

"We are young! We are young!" they cried exultingly.

Youth, like the extremity of age, had effaced the strongly-marked characteristics of middle life, and mutually assimilated them all. They were a group of merry youngsters, almost maddened with the exuberant frolicsomeness of their years. The most singular effect of their gayety was an impulse to mock the infirmity and decrepitude of which they had so lately been the victims. They laughed loudly at their old-fashioned attire, the wide-skirted coats and flapped waist-coats of the young men, and the ancient cap and gown of the blooming girl.

One limped across the floor like a gouty grandfather; one set a pair of spectacles astride of his nose, and pretended to pore over the black-letter pages of the book of magic; a third seated himself in an armchair, and strove to imitate the venerable dignity of Dr. Heidegger. Then all shouted mirthfully, and leaped about the room. The Widow Wycherly—if so fresh a damsel could be called a widow—tripped up to the doctor's chair, with a mischievous merriment in her rosy face.

"Doctor, you dear old soul," cried she, "get up and dance with me!" And then the four young people laughed louder than ever, to think what a queer figure the poor old doctor would cut.

"Pray excuse me," answered the doctor quietly. "I am old and rheumatic, and my dancing days were over long ago. But either of these gay young gentlemen will be glad of so pretty a partner."

"Dance with me, Clara!" cried Colonel Killigrew.

"No, no, I will be her partner!" shouted Mr. Gascoigne.

"She promised me her hand, fifty years ago!" exclaimed Mr. Medbourne.

They all gathered round her. One caught both her hands in his passionate grasp—another threw his arm about her waist—the third buried his hand among the glossy curls that clustered beneath the widow's cap. Blushing, panting, struggling, chiding, laughing, her warm breath fanning each of their faces by turns, she strove to disengage herself, yet still remained in their triple embrace. Never was there a livelier picture of youthful rivalship, with bewitching beauty for the prize. Yet, by a strange deception, owing to the duskiness of the chamber, and the antique dresses which they still wore, the tall mirror is said to have reflected the figures of the three old, gray, withered grandsires, ridiculously contending for the skinny ugliness of a shrivelled grandam.

But they were young: their burning passions proved them so. Inflamed to madness by the *coquetry* of the girl-widow, who neither granted nor quite withheld her favours, the three rivals began to interchange threatening glances. Still keeping hold of the fair prize, they grappled fiercely at one another's throats. As they struggled to and fro, the table was overturned, and the vase dashed into a thousand fragments. The precious Water of Youth flowed in a bright stream across the floor, moistening the wings of a butterfly, which, grown old in the decline of summer, had alighted there to die. The insect fluttered lightly through the chamber, and settled on the snowy head of Dr. Heidegger.

"Come, come, gentlemen! come, Madam Wycherly," exclaimed the doctor, "I really must protest against this riot."

They stood still and shivered; for it seemed as if gray Time were calling them back from their sunny youth, far down into the chill and darksome vale of years. They looked at old Dr. Heidegger, who sat in his carved arm-chair, holding the rose of half a century, which he had rescued from among the fragments of the shattered vase. At the motion of his hand, the four rioters resumed their seats; the more readily, because their violent exertions had wearied them, youthful though they were.

"My poor Sylvia's rose!" ejaculated Dr. Heidegger, holding it in the light of the sunset clouds; "it appears to be fading again."

And so it was. Even while the party were looking at it, the flower continued to shrivel up, till it became as dry and fragile as when the doctor had first thrown it into the vase. He shook off the few drops of moisture which clung to its petals.

"I love it as well thus as in its dewy freshness," observed he, pressing the withered rose to his withered lips. While he spoke, the butterfly fluttered down from the doctor's snowy head, and fell upon the floor.

His guests shivered again. A strange chillness, whether of the body or spirit they could not tell, was creeping gradually over them all. They gazed at one another, and fancied that each fleeting moment snatched away a charm, and left a deepening furrow where none had been before. Was it an illusion? Had the changes of a lifetime been crowded into so brief a space, and were they now four aged people, sitting with their old friend, Dr. Heidegger?

"Are we grown old again, so soon?" cried they, dolefully.

In truth they had. The Water of Youth possessed merely a virtue more transient than that of wine. The delirium which it created had effervesced away. Yes! they were old again. With a shuddering impulse, that showed her a woman still, the widow clasped her skinny hands before her face, and wished that the coffin lid were over it, since it could be no longer beautiful.

"Yes, friends, ye are old again," said Dr. Heidegger, "and lo! the Water of Youth is all lavished on the ground. Well—I bemoan it not; for if the fountain gushed at my very doorstep, I would not stoop to bathe my lips in it—no, though its delirium were for years instead of moments. Such is the lesson ye have taught me!"

But the doctor's four friends had taught no such lesson to themselves. They resolved forthwith to make a pilgrimage to Florida, and quaff at morning, noon, and night, from the Fountain of Youth.

The Christmas Banquet

(A tale from *Mosses From an Old Manse and Other Stories*)

"I have here attempted," said Roderick, unfolding a few sheets of manuscript, as he sat with Rosina and the sculptor in the summer-house,—"I have attempted to seize hold of a personage who glides past me occasionally, in my walk through life. My former sad experience, as you know, has gifted me with some degree of insight into the gloomy mysteries of the human heart, through which I have wandered like one astray in a dark cavern, with his torch fast flickering to extinction. But this man, this class of men, is a hopeless puzzle."

"Well, but propound him," said the sculptor. "Let us have an idea of him, to begin with."

"Why, indeed," replied Roderick, "he is such being as I could conceive you to carve out of marble,! and some yet unrealized perfection of human science to endow with an exquisite mockery of intellect; but still there lacks the last inestimable touch of a divine Creator. He looks like a man; and, perchance, like a better specimen of man than you ordinarily meet. You might esteem him wise; he is capable of cultivation and refinement, and has at least an external conscience, I but the demands that spirit makes upon spirit arc precisely those to which he cannot respond. When at last you come close to him you find him chill and unsubstantial—a mere vapor."

"I believe," said Rosina, "I have a glimmering idea of what you mean."

"Then be thankful," answered her husband, smiling; "but do

not anticipate any further illumination from what I am about to read. I have here imagined such a man to be—what, probably, he never is—conscious of the deficiency in his spiritual organization. Methinks the result would be a sense of cold unreality wherewith he would go shivering through the world, longing to exchange his load of ice for any burden of real grief that fate could fling upon a human being."

Contenting himself with this preface, Roderick began to read.

In a certain old gentleman's last will and testament there appeared a bequest, which, as his final thought and deed, was singularly in keeping with a long life of melancholy eccentricity. He devised a considerable sum for establishing a fund, the interest of which was to be expended, annually forever, in preparing a Christmas Banquet for ten of the most miserable persons that could be found. It seemed not to be the testator's purpose to make these half a score of sad hearts merry, but to provide that the stem or fierce expression of human discontent should not be drowned, even for that one holy and joyful day, amid the acclamations of festal gratitude which all Christendom sends up. And he desired, likewise, to perpetuate his own remonstrance against the earthly course of Providence, and his sad and sour dissent from those systems of religion or philosophy which either find sunshine in the world or draw it down from heaven.

The task of inviting the guests, or of selecting among such as might advance their claims to partake of this dismal hospitality, was confided to the two trustees or stewards of the fund. These gentlemen, like their deceased friend, were sombre humorists, who made it their principal occupation to number the sable threads in the web of human life, and drop all the golden ones out of the reckoning. They performed their present office with integrity and judgement. The aspect of the assembled company on the day of the first festival might not, it is true, have satisfied every beholder that these were especially the individuals, chosen forth from all the world, whose griefs were worthy to stand as indicators of the mass of human suffering. Yet, after due consideration, it could not be disputed that here was a variety of hopeless discomfort, which, if it sometimes arose from causes apparently inadequate, was thereby only the shrewder imputation against the nature and mechanism of life.

The arrangements and decorations of the banquet were probably intended to signify that death in life which had been the testator's definition of existence. The hall, illuminated by torches, was hung round with curtains of deep and dusky purple, and adorned with branches of cypress and wreaths of artificial flowers, imitative of such as used to be strown over the dead. A sprig of parsley was laid by every plate. The main reservoir of wine was a sepulchral urn of silver, whence the liquor was distributed around the table in small vases, accurately copied from those that held the tears of ancient mourners.

Neither had the stewards—if it were their taste that arranged these details—forgotten the fantasy of the old Egyptians, who seated a skeleton at every festive board, and mocked their own merriment with the imperturbable grin of a death's head. Such a fearful guest, shrouded in a black mantle, sat now at the head of the table. It was whispered, I know not with what truth, that the testator himself had once walked the visible world with the machinery of that same skeleton, and that it was one of the stipulations of his will that he should thus be permitted to sit, from year to year, at the banquet which he had instituted. If so, it was perhaps covertly implied that he had cherished no hopes of bliss beyond the grave to compensate for the evils which he felt or imagined here.

And if, in their bewildered conjectures as to the purpose of earthly existence, the banqueters should throw aside the veil, and cast an inquiring glance at this figure of death, as seeking thence the solution otherwise unattainable, the only reply would be a stare of the vacant eye caverns and a grin of the skeleton jaws. Such was the response that the dead man had fancied himself to receive when he asked of Death to solve the riddle of his life; and it was his desire to repeat it when the guests of his dismal hospitality should find themselves perplexed with the same question.

"What means that wreath?" asked several of the company, while viewing the decorations of the table.

They alluded to a wreath of cypress which was held on high by a skeleton arm, protruding from within the black mantle.

"It is a crown," said one of the stewards, "not for the worthiest, but for the woefulest, when he shall prove his claim to it."

The guest earliest bidden to the festival was a man of soft and gentle character, who had not energy to struggle against the heavy despondency to which his temperament rendered him liable; and therefore with nothing outwardly to excuse him from happiness, he had spent a life of quiet misery that made his blood torpid, and weighed upon his breath, and sat like a ponderous night fiend upon every throb of his unresisting heart. His wretchedness seemed as deep as his original nature, if not identical with it.

It was the misfortune of a second guest to cherish within his bosom a diseased heart, which had become so wretchedly sore that the continual and unavoidable rubs of the world, the blow of an enemy, the careless jostle of a stranger, and even the faithful and loving touch of a friend, alike made ulcers in it. As is the habit of people thus afflicted, he found his chief employment in exhibiting these miserable sores to any who would give themselves the pain of viewing them.

A third guest was a hypochondriac, whose imagination wrought necromancy in its outward and inward world, and caused him to see monstrous faces in the household fire, and dragons in the clouds of sunset, and fiends in the guise of beautiful women, and something ugly or wicked beneath all the pleasant surfaces of nature. His neighbour at table was one who, in his early youth, had trusted mankind too much, and hoped too highly in their behalf, and, in meeting with many disappointments, had become desperately soured.

For several years back this misanthrope had employed himself in accumulating motives for hating and despising his race—such as murder, lust, treachery, ingratitude, faithlessness of trusted friends, instinctive vices of children, impurity of women, hidden guilt in men of saintlike aspect—and, in short, all manner of black realities that sought to decorate themselves with outward grace or glory. But at every atrocious fact that was added to his catalogue, at every increase of the sad knowledge which he spent his life to collect, the native impulses of the poor man's loving and confiding heart made him groan with anguish.

Next, with his heavy brow bent downward, there stole into the hall a man naturally earnest and impassioned, who, from his immemorial infancy, had felt the consciousness of a high message to the world; but, essaying to deliver it, had found either no voice or form of speech, or else no ears to listen. Therefore his whole life was a bitter questioning of himself—"Why have not men acknowledged my mission? Am I not a self-deluding fool? What business have I on earth? Where is my grave?" Throughout the festival, he quaffed frequent draughts from the sepulchral urn of wine, hoping thus to quench the celestial fire that tortured his own breast and could not benefit his race.

Then there entered, having flung away a ticket for a ball, a gay gallant of yesterday, who had found four or five wrinkles in his brow, and more gray hairs than he could well number on his head. Endowed with sense and feeling, he had nevertheless spent his youth in folly, but had reached at last that dreary point in life where Folly quits us of her own accord, leaving us to make friends with Wisdom if we can. Thus, cold and desolate, he had come to seek Wisdom at the banquet, and wondered if the skeleton were she. To eke out the company, the stewards had invited a distressed poet from his home in the almshouse, and a melancholy idiot from the street corner.

The latter had just the glimmering of sense that was sufficient to make him conscious of a vacancy, which the poor fellow, all his life long, had mistily sought to fill up with intelligence, wandering up and down the streets, and groaning miserably because his attempts were ineffectual. The only lady in the hall was one who had fallen short of absolute and perfect beauty, merely by the trilling defect of a slight east in her left eye. But this blemish, minute as it was, so shocked the pure ideal of her soul, rather than her vanity, that she passed her life in solitude, and veiled her countenance even from her own gaze. So the skeleton sat shrouded at one end of the table and this poor lady at the other.

One other guest remains to be described. He was a young man of smooth brow, fair cheek, and fashionable mien. So far as his exterior developed him, he might much more suitably have found a place at some merry Christmas table, than have been numbered among the blighted, fate-stricken, fancy-tortured set of ill-starred banqueters. Murmurs arose among the guests as they noted the glance of general scrutiny which the intruder threw over his companions. What had he to do among them? Why did not the skeleton of the dead founder of the feast unbend its rattling joints, arise, and motion the unwelcome stranger from the board?

"Shameful!" said the morbid man, while a new ulcer broke out in his heart. "He comes to mock us,—we shall be the jest of his tavern friends!—he will make a farce of our miseries, and bring it out upon the stage!"

"Oh. never mind him!" said the hypochondriac, smiling sourly. "He shall feast from yonder tureen of viper soup; and if there is a *fricassee* of scorpions on the table, pray let him have his share of it. For the dessert, he shall taste the apples of Sodom. Then, if he like our Christmas fare, let him return again next year!"

"Trouble him not," murmured the melancholy man, with gentleness. "What matters it whether the consciousness of misery come a few years sooner or later? If this youth deem himself happy now, yet let him sit with us for the sake of the wretchedness to come."

The poor idiot approached the young man with that mournful aspect of vacant inquiry which his face continually wore, and which caused people to say that he was always in search of his missing wits. After no little examination he touched the stranger's hand, but immediately drew back his own, shaking his head and shivering.

"Cold, cold, cold!" muttered the idiot.

The young man shivered too, and smiled.

"Gentlemen,—and you, madam,"—said one of the stewards of the festival, "do not conceive so ill either of our caution or judgment as to imagine that we have admitted this young stranger—Gervayse Hastings by name—without a full investigation and thoughtful balance of his claims. Trust me, not a guest at the table is better entitled to his seat."

The steward's guaranty was perforce satisfactory. The company, therefore, took their places and addressed themselves to the serious business of the feast, but were soon disturbed by the hypochondriac, who thrust back his chair complaining that a dish of stewed toads and vipers was set before him, and that there was green ditch water in his cup of wine. This mistake being amended, he quietly resumed his seat. The wine, as it flowed freely from the sepulchral urn, seemed to come imbued with all gloomy inspirations; so that its influence was not to cheer, but either to sink the revellers into a deeper melancholy or elevate their spirits to an enthusiasm of wretchedness.

The conversation was various. They told sad stories about people who might have been worthy guests at such a festival as the present. They talked of grisly incidents in human history; of strange crimes, which, if truly considered, were but convulsions of agony; of some lives that had been altogether wretched, and of others, which, wearing a general semblance of happiness, had yet been deformed sooner or later by misfortune, as by the intrusion of a grim face at a banquet; of deathbed scenes, and what dark intimations might be gathered from the words of dying men; of suicide, and whether the more eligible mode were by halter, knife, poison, drowning, gradual starvation, or the fumes of charcoal.

The majority of the guests, as is the custom with people thoroughly and profoundly sick at heart, were anxious to make their own woes the theme of discussion, and prove themselves most excellent in anguish. The misanthropist went deep into the philosophy of evil, and wandered about in the darkness, with now and then a gleam of discoloured light hovering on ghastly shapes and horrid scenery. Many a miserable thought, such as men have stumbled upon from age to age, did he now rake up again, and gloat over it as an inestimable gem, a diamond, a treasure far preferable to those bright, spiritual revelations of a better world, which are like precious stones from heaven's pavement. And then, amid his lore of wretchedness he hid his face and wept.

It was a festival at which the woeful man of Uz might suitably have been a guest, together with all, in each succeeding age. who have tasted deepest of the bitterness of life. And be it said, too, that every son or daughter of woman, however favoured with happy fortune, might, at one sad moment or another, have claimed the privilege of a stricken heart, to sit down at this table. But, throughout the feast, it was remarked that the young stranger, Gervayse Hastings, was unsuccessful in his attempts to catch its pervading spirit. At any deep, strong thought that found utterance, and which was torn out, as it were, from the saddest recesses of human consciousness, he looked mystified and bewildered; even more than the poor idiot, who seemed to grasp at such things with his earnest heart, and thus occasionally to comprehend them. The young man's conversation was of a colder and lighter kind, often brilliant, but lacking the powerful characteristics of a nature that had been developed by suffering.

"Sir," said the misanthropist, bluntly, in reply to some observation by Gervayse Hastings, "pray do not address me again. We have no right to talk together. Our minds have nothing in common. By what claim you appear at this banquet I cannot guess; but methinks, to a man who could say what you have just now said, my companions and myself must seem no more than shadows flickering on the wall. And precisely such a shadow are you to us."

The young man smiled and bowed, but drawing himself back in his chair, he buttoned his coat over his breast, as if the banqueting hall were growing chill. Again the idiot fixed his melancholy stare upon the youth and murmured, "Cold, cold, cold!"

The banquet drew to its conclusion, and the guests departed. Scarcely had they stepped across the threshold of the hall, when the scene that had there passed seemed like the vision of a sick fancy, or an exhalation from a stagnant heart Now and then, however, during the year that ensued, these melancholy people caught glimpses of one another, transient, indeed, but enough to prove that they walked the earth with the ordinary allotment of reality. Sometimes a pair of them came face to face, while stealing through the evening twilight, enveloped in their sable cloaks. Sometimes they casually met in churchyards. Once, also, it happened that two of the dismal banqueters mutually started at recognizing each other in the noonday sunshine of a crowded street, stalking there like ghosts astray. Doubtless they wondered why the skeleton did not come abroad at noonday too.

But whenever the necessity of their affairs compelled these Christmas guests into the bustling world, they were sure to encounter the young man who had so unaccountably been admitted to the festival. They saw him among the gay and fortunate; they caught the sunny sparkle of his eye: they heard the light and careless tones of his voice, and muttered to themselves with such indication as only the aristocracy of wretchedness could kindle—"The traitor! The vile impostor! Providence, in its own good time, may give him a right to feast among us!" But the young man's unabashed eye dwelt upon their gloomy figures as they passed him, seeming to say. perchance with somewhat of a sneer, "First know my secret!—then, measure your claims with mine!"

The step of Time stole onward, and soon brought merry Christmas round again, with glad and solemn worship in the churches, and sports, games, festivals, and everywhere the bright face of Joy beside the household fire. Again likewise the hall, with its curtains of dusky purple, was illuminated by the death torches gleaming on the sepulchral decorations of the banquet. The veiled skeleton sat in state, lifting the cypress wreath above its head, as the guerdon of some guest illustrious in the qualifications which there claimed precedence. As the stewards deemed the world inexhaustible in misery, and were desirous of recognizing it in all its forms, they had not seen fit to reassemble the company of the former year. New faces now threw their gloom across the table.

There was a man of nice conscience, who bore a bloodstain in his heart—the death of a fellow-creature—which, for his more exquisite torture, had chanced with such a peculiarity of circumstances, that he could not absolutely determine whether his will had entered into the deed or not. Therefore, his whole life was spent in the agony of an inward trial for murder, with a continual sifting of the details of his terrible calamity, until his mind had no longer any thought, nor his soul any emotion, disconnected with it. There was a mother, too—a mother once, but a desolation now—who, many years before, had gone out on a pleasure party, and, returning, found her infant smothered in its little bed. And ever since she had been tortured with the fantasy that her buried baby lay smothering in its coffin.

Then there was an aged lady, who had lived from time immemorial with a constant tremor quivering through her frame. It was terrible to discern her dark shadow tremulous upon the wall; her lips, likewise, were tremulous; and the expression of her eye seemed to indicate that her soul was trembling too. Owing to the bewilderment and confusion which made almost a chaos of her intellect, it was impossible to discover what dire misfortune had thus shaken her nature to its depths: so that the stewards had admitted her to the table, not from any acquaintance with her history, but on the safe testimony of her miserable aspect.

Some surprise was expressed at the presence of a bluff, red-faced gentleman, a certain Mr. Smith, who had evidently the fat of many a rich feast within him, and the habitual twinkle of whose eye betrayed a disposition to break forth into uproarious laughter for little cause or none. It turned out, however, that with the best possible flow of spirits, our poor friend was afflicted with a physical disease of the heart, which threatened instant death on the slightest cachinnatory indulgence, or even that titillation of the bodily frame produced by merry thoughts. In this dilemma he had sought admittance to the banquet, on the ostensible plea of his irksome and miserable state, but, in reality, with the hope of imbibing a life-preserving melancholy.

A married couple had been invited from a motive of bitter humour, it being well understood that they rendered each other unutterably miserable whenever they chanced to meet, and therefore must necessarily be fit associates at the festival. In contrast with these was another couple, still unmarried, who had interchanged their hearts in early life, but had been divided by circumstances as impalpable as morning mist, and kept apart so long that their spirits now found it impossible to meet. Therefore yearning for communion, yet shrinking from one another and choosing none beside, they felt themselves companionless in life, and looked upon eternity as a boundless desert.

Next to the skeleton sat a mere son of earth—a hunter of the Exchange—a gatherer of shining dust—a man whose life's record was in his ledger, and whose soul's prison house the vaults of the bank where he kept his deposits. This person had been greatly perplexed at his invitation, deeming himself one of the most fortunate men in the city; but the stewards persisted in demanding his presence, assuring him that he had no conception how miserable he was.

And now appeared a figure which we must acknowledge as our acquaintance of the former festival. It was Gervayse Hastings, whose presence had then caused so much question and criticism, and who now took his place with the composure of one whose claims were satisfactory to himself and must needs be allowed by others. Yet his easy and unruffled face betrayed no sorrow. The well-skilled beholders gazed a moment into his eyes and shook their heads, to miss the unuttered sympathy— the countersign, never to be falsified—of those whose hearts are cavern mouths, through which they descend into a region of illimitable woe and recognize other wanderers there.

"Who is this youth?" asked the man with a blood stain on his conscience. "Surely he has never gone down into the depths! I know all the aspects of those who have passed through the dark valley. By what right is he among us?"

"Ah, it is a sinful thing to come hither without a sorrow," murmured the aged lady, in accents that partook of the eternal tremor which pervaded her whole being. "Depart, young man! Your soul has never been shaken, and, therefore. I tremble so much the more to look at you."

"His soul shaken! No; I'll answer for it," said bluff Mr. Smith, pressing his hand upon his heart and making himself as melancholy as he could, for fear of a fatal explosion of laughter. "I know the lad well; he has as fair prospects as any young man about town, and has no more right among us miserable creatures than the child unborn. He never was miserable and probably never will be!"

"Our honoured guests," interposed the stewards, "pray have patience with us, and believe, at least, that our deep veneration for the sacredness of this solemnity would preclude any wilful violation of it. Receive this young man to your table. It may not be too much to say that no guest here would exchange his own heart for the one that beats within that youthful bosom!'"

"I'd call it a bargain, and gladly too," muttered Mr. Smith, with a perplexing mixture of sadness and mirthful conceit. "A plague upon their nonsense! My own heart is the only really miserable one in the company; it will certainly be the death of me at last!"

Nevertheless, as on the former occasion, the judgement of the stewards being without appeal, the company sat down. The obnoxious guest made no more attempt to obtrude his conversation on those about him, but appeared to listen to the table talk with peculiar assiduity, as if some inestimable secret, otherwise beyond his reach, might be conveyed in a casual word. And in truth, to those who could understand and value it, there was rich matter in the upgushings and outpourings of these initiated souls to whom sorrow had been a talisman, admitting them into spiritual depths which no other spell can open.

Sometimes out of the midst of densest gloom there flashed

a momentary' radiance, pure as crystal, bright as the flame of stars, and shedding such a glow upon the mysteries of life that the guests were ready to exclaim, "Surely the riddle is on the point of being solved!" At such illuminated intervals the saddest mourners felt it to be revealed that mortal griefs are but shadowy and external; no more than the sable robes voluminously shrouding a certain divine reality, and thus indicating what might otherwise be altogether invisible to mortal eye.

"Just now," remarked the trembling old woman, "I seemed to see beyond the outside. And then my everlasting tremor passed away!"

"Would that I could dwell always in these momentary gleams of light!" said the man of stricken conscience. "Then the blood stain in my heart would be washed clean away."

This strain of conversation appeared so unintelligibly absurd to good Mr. Smith, that he burst into precisely the fit of laughter which his physicians had warned him against, as likely to prove instantaneously fatal. In effect, he fell back in his chair a corpse, with a broad grin upon his face, while his ghost, perchance, remained beside it bewildered at its unpremeditated exit. This catastrophe of course broke up the festival.

"How is this? You do not tremble?" observed the tremulous old woman to Gervayse Hastings, who was gazing at the dead man with singular intentness. "Is it not awful to see him so suddenly vanish out of the midst of life—this man of flesh and blood, whose earthly nature was so warm and strong? There is a never-ending tremor in my soul, but it trembles afresh at this! And you are calm!"

"Would that he could teach me somewhat!" said Gervayse Hastings, drawing a long breath. "Men pass before me like shadows on the wall; their actions, passions, feelings, are flickerings of the light, and then they vanish! Neither the corpse, nor yonder skeleton, nor this old woman's everlasting tremor, can give me what I seek."

And then the company departed.

We cannot linger to narrate, in such detail, more circumstances of these singular festivals, which, in accordance with the founder's will, continued to be kept with the regularity of an established institution. In process of time the stewards adopted the custom of inviting, from far and near, those individuals whose misfortunes were prominent above other men's, and whose mental and moral development might, therefore, be supposed to possess a corresponding interest.

The exiled noble of the French Revolution, and the broken soldier of the Empire, were alike represented at the table. Fallen monarchs, wandering about the earth, have found places at that forlorn and miserable feast. The statesman, when his party flung him off, might, if he chose it, be once more a great man for the space of a single banquet. Aaron Burr's name appears on the record at a period when his ruin—the profoundest and most striking, with more of moral circumstance in it than that of almost any other man—was complete in his lonely age. Stephen Girard, when his wealth weighed upon him like a mountain, once sought admittance of his own accord.

It is not probable, however, that these men had any lesson to teach in the lore of discontent and misery which might not equally well have been studied in the common walks of life. Illustrious unfortunates attract a wider sympathy, not because their griefs are more intense, but because, being set on lofty pedestals, they the better serve mankind as instances and by-words of calamity.

It concerns our present purpose to say that, at each successive festival, Gervayse Hastings showed his face, gradually changing from the smooth beauty of his youth to the thoughtful comeliness of manhood, and thence to the bald impressive dignity of age. He was the only individual invariably present. Yet on every occasion there were murmurs, both from those who knew his character and position, and from them whose hearts shrank back as denying his companionship in their mystic fraternity.

"Who is this impassive man?" had been asked a hundred times. "Has he suffered? Has he sinned? There are no traces of either. Then wherefore is he here?"

"You must inquire of the stewards, or of himself," was the constant reply. "We seem to know him well here in our city, and know nothing of him but what is creditable and fortunate. Yet hither he comes, year after year, to this gloomy banquet, and sits among the guests like a marble statue. Ask yonder skeleton; perhaps that may solve the riddle."

It was in truth a wonder. The life of Gervayse Hastings was not merely a prosperous, but a brilliant one. Everything had gone well with him. He was wealthy, far beyond the expenditure that was required by habits of magnificence, a taste of rare purity and cultivation, a love of travel, a scholar's instinct to collect a splendid library, and, moreover, what seemed a magnificent liberality to the distressed. He had sought happiness, and not vainly, if a lovely and tender wife and children of fair promise could insure it. He had, besides, ascended above the limit which separates the obscure from the distinguished, and had won a stainless reputation in affairs of the widest public importance.

Not that he was a popular character, or had within him the mysterious attributes which are essential to that species of success. To the public he was a cold abstraction, wholly destitute of those rich hues of personality, that living warmth, and the peculiar faculty of stamping his own heart's impression on a multitude of hearts by which the people recognize their favourites. And it must be owned that, after his most intimate associates had done their best to know him thoroughly and love him warmly, they were startled to find how little hold he had upon their affections. They approved, they admired, but still in those moments when the human spirit most craves reality they shrank back from Gervayse Hastings, as powerless to give them what they sought. It was the feeling of distrustful regret with which we should draw back the hand after extending it, in an illusive twilight, to grasp the hand of a shadow upon the wall.

As the superficial fervency of youth decayed, this peculiar effect of Gervayse Hastings's character grew more perceptible. His children, when he extended his arms, came coldly to his knees, but never climbed them of their own accord. His wife wept secretly, and almost adjudged herself a criminal, because she shivered in the chill of his bosom. He, too, occasionally appeared not unconscious of the chillness of his moral atmosphere, and willing, if it might be so, to warm himself at a kindly fire. But age stole onward and benumbed him more and more.

As the hoarfrost began to gather on him his wife went to her grave, and was doubtless warmer there; his children either died or were scattered to different homes of their own: and old Gervayse Hastings, unscathed by grief—alone, but needing no companionship, continued his steady walk through life, and still on every Christmas day attended at the dismal banquet. His privilege as a guest had become prescriptive now. Had he claimed the head of the table, even the skeleton would have been ejected from its seat.

Finally, at the merry Christmas tide, when he had numbered fourscore years complete, this pale, high-browed, marble-featured old man once more entered the long-frequented hall, with the same impassive aspect that had called forth so much dissatisfied remark at his first attendance. Time, except in matters merely external, had done nothing for him, either of good or evil. As he took his place he threw a calm, inquiring glance around the table, as if to ascertain whether any guest had yet appeared, after so many unsuccessful banquets, who might impart to him the mystery—the deep, warm secret—the life within the life—which, whether manifested in joy or sorrow, is what gives substance to a world of shadows.

"My friends," said Gervayse Hastings, assuming a position which his long conversance with the festival caused to appear natural, "you are welcome! I drink to you all in this cup of sepulchral wine."

The guests replied courteously, but still in a manner that proved them unable to receive the old man as a member of their sad fraternity. It may be well to give the reader an idea of the present company at the banquet.

One was formerly a clergyman, enthusiastic in his profession, and apparently of the genuine dynasty of those old Puritan divines whose faith in their calling, and stern exercise of it, had placed them among the mighty of the earth. But, yielding to the speculative tendency of the age, he had gone astray from the firm foundation of an ancient faith, and wandered into a cloud region, where everything was misty and deceptive, ever mocking him with a semblance of reality, but still dissolving when he flung himself upon it for support and rest. His instinct and early training demanded something steadfast; but, looking forward, he beheld vapors piled on vapors, and behind him an impassable gulf between the man of yesterday and today, on the borders of which he paced to and fro, sometimes wringing his hands in agony, and often making his own woe a theme of scornful merriment.

This surely was a miserable man. Next there was a theorist— one of a numerous tribe, although he deemed himself unique since the creation—a theorist who had conceived a plan, by which all the wretchedness of earth, moral and physical, might be done away, and the bliss of the millennium at once accomplished. But, the incredulity of mankind debarring him from action, he was smitten with as much grief as if the whole mass of woe which he was denied the opportunity to remedy were crowded into his own bosom. A plain old man in black attracted much of the company's notice, on the supposition that he was no other than Father Miller, who, it seemed, had given himself up to despair at the tedious delay of the final conflagration.

Then there was a man distinguished for native pride and obstinacy, who, a little while before, had possessed immense wealth, and held the control of a vast moneyed interest which he had wielded in the same spirit as a despotic monarch would wield the power of his empire, carrying on a tremendous moral warfare, the roar and tremor of which was felt at every fireside in the land. At length came a crushing ruin—a total overthrow of fortune, power, and character—the effect of which on his imperious, and, in many respects, noble and lofty nature, might have entitled him to a place, not merely at our festival, but among the peers of Pandemonium.

There was a modern philanthropist, who had become so deeply sensible of the calamities of thousands and millions of his fellow-creatures, and of the impracticableness of any general measures for their relief, that he had no heart to do what little good lay immediately within his power, but contented himself with being miserable for sympathy. Near him sat a gentleman in a predicament hitherto unprecedented, but of which the present epoch probably affords numerous examples. Ever since he was of capacity to read a newspaper, this person had prided himself on his consistent adherence to one political party, but, in the confusion of these latter days, had got bewildered and knew not whereabouts his party was.

This wretched condition, so morally desolate and disheartening to a man who has long accustomed himself to merge his individualiiy in the mass of a great body, can only be conceived by such as have experienced it. His next companion was a popular orator who had lost his voice, and—as it was pretty much all that he had to lose—had fallen into a state of hopeless melancholy. The table was likewise graced by two of the gentler sex: one, a half-starved, consumptive seamstress, the representative of thousands just as wretched; the other, a woman of unemployed energy, who found herself in the world with nothing to achieve, nothing to enjoy, and nothing even to suffer. She had, therefore, driven herself to the verge of madness by dark broodings over the wrongs of her sex, and its exclusion from a proper field of action.

The roll of guests being thus complete, a side table had been set for three or four disappointed office seekers, with hearts as sick as death, whom the stewards had admitted partly because their calamities really entitled them to entrance here, and partly that they were in especial need of a good dinner. There was likewise a homeless dog, with his tail between his legs, licking up the crumbs and gnawing the fragments of the feast,—such a melancholy cur as one sometimes sees about the streets without a master, and willing to follow the first that will accept his service.

In their own way, these were as wretched a set of people as ever had assembled at the festival. There they sat, with the veiled skeleton of the founder holding aloft the cypress wreath at one end of the table, and at the other, wrapped in furs, the withered figure of Gervayse Hastings, stately, calm, and cold, impressing the company with awe, yet so little interesting their sympathy that he might have vanished into thin air without their once exclaiming, "Whither is he gone?"

"Sir," said the philanthropist, addressing the old man, "you have been so long a guest at this annual festival, and have thus been conversant with so many varieties of human affliction, that, not improbably, you have thence derived some great and important lessons. How blessed were your lot could you reveal a secret by which all this mass of woe might be removed!"

"I know of but one misfortune," answered Gervayse Hastings, quietly, "and that is my own."

"Your own!" rejoined the philanthropist. "And looking back on your serene and prosperous life, how can you claim to be the sole unfortunate of the human race?"

"You will not understand it," replied Gervayse Hastings, feebly, and with a singular inefficiency of pronunciation, and sometimes putting one word for another. "None have understood it—not even those who experience the like. It is a chilliness—a want of earnestness—a feeling as if what should be my heart were a thing of vapor—a haunting perception of unreality! Thus seeming to possess all that other men have—all that men aim at—I have really possessed nothing, neither joy nor griefs. All things, all persons—as was truly said to me at this table long and long ago—have been like shadows flickering on the wall. It was so with my wife and children—with those who seemed my friends: it is so with yourselves, whom I see now before me. Neither have I myself any real existence, but am a shadow like the rest."

"And how is it with your views of a future life?" inquired the speculative clergyman.

"Worse than with you," said the old man, in a hollow and

feeble tone; "for I cannot conceive it earnestly enough to feel either hope or fear. Mine—mine is the wetchedness! This cold heart—this unreal life! Ah! it grows colder still."

It so chanced that at this juncture the decayed ligaments of the skeleton gave way, and the dry bones fell together in a heap, thus causing the dusty wreath of cypress to drop upon the table. The attention of the company being thus diverted for a single instant from Gervayse Hastings, they perceived, on turning again towards him, that the old man had undergone a change. His shadow had ceased to flicker on the wall.

"Well, Rosina, what is your criticism?" asked Roderick as he rolled up the manuscript.

"Frankly, your success is by no means complete," replied she. "It is true, I have an idea of the character you endeavour to describe; but it is rather by dint of my own thought than your expression."

"That is unavoidable," observed the sculptor, "because the characteristics are all negative. If Gervayse Hastings could have imbibed one human grief at the gloomy banquet, the task of describing him would have been infinitely easier. Of such persons—and we do meet with these moral monsters now and then—it is difficult to conceive how they came to exist here, or what there is in them capable of existence hereafter. They seem to be on the outside of everything; and nothing wearies the soul more than an attempt to comprehend them within its grasp."

The Wedding Knell

(A tale from *Twice Told Tales* Volume 1)

There is a certain church in the city of New York which I have always regarded with peculiar interest, on account of a marriage there solemnized, under very singular circumstances, in my grandmother's girlhood. That venerable lady chanced to be a spectator of the scene, and ever after made it her favourite narrative. Whether the edifice now standing on the same site be the identical one to which she referred, I am not antiquarian enough to know; nor would it be worthwhile to correct myself, perhaps, of an agreeable error, by reading the date of its erection on the tablet over the door. It is a stately church, surrounded by an inclosure of the loveliest green, within which appear urns, pillars, obelisks, and other forms of monumental marble, the tributes of private affection, or more splendid memorials of historic dust. With such a place, though the tumult of the city rolls beneath its tower, one would be willing to connect some legendary interest.

The marriage might be considered as the result of an early engagement, though there had been two intermediate weddings on the lady's part, and forty years of celibacy on that of the gentleman. At sixty-five, Mr. Ellenwood was a shy, but not quite a secluded man; selfish, like all men who brood over their own hearts, yet manifesting on rare occasions a vein of generous sentiment; a scholar throughout life, though always an indolent one, because his studies had no definite object, either of public advantage or personal ambition; a gentleman, high bred and fastidiously delicate, yet sometimes requiring a considerable relaxation, in his behalf, of the common rules of society.

In truth, there were so many anomalies in his character, and though shrinking with diseased sensibility from public notice, it had been his fatality so often to become the topic of the day, by some wild eccentricity of conduct, that people searched his lineage for an hereditary taint of insanity. But there was no need of this. His caprices had their origin in a mind that lacked the support of an engrossing purpose, and in feelings that preyed upon themselves for want of other food. If he were mad, it was the consequence, and not the cause, of an aimless and abortive life.

The widow was as complete a contrast to her third bridegroom, in everything but age, as can well be conceived. Compelled to relinquish her first engagement, she had been united to a man of twice her own years, to whom she became an exemplary wife, and by whose death she was left in possession of a splendid fortune. A southern gentleman, considerably younger than herself, succeeded to her hand, and carried her to Charleston, where, after many uncomfortable years, she found herself again a widow. It would have been singular, if any uncommon delicacy of feeling had survived through such a life as Mrs. Dabney's; it could not but be crushed and killed by her early disappointment, the cold duty of her first marriage, the dislocation of the heart's principles, consequent on a second union and the unkindness of her southern husband, which had inevitably driven her to connect the idea of his death with that of her comfort.

To be brief, she was that wisest, but unloveliest, variety of woman, a philosopher, bearing troubles of the heart with equanimity, dispensing with all that should have been her happiness, and making the best of what remained. Sage in most matters, the widow was perhaps the more amiable for the one frailty that made her ridiculous. Being childless, she could not remain beautiful by proxy, in the person of a daughter; she therefore refused to grow old and ugly, on any consideration; she struggled with Time, and held fast her roses in spite of him, till the venerable thief appeared to have relinquished the spoil, as not worth the trouble of acquiring it.

The approaching marriage of this woman of the world with such an unworldly man as Mr. Ellenwood was announced soon after Mrs. Dabney's return to her native city. Superficial observers, and deeper ones, seemed to concur in supposing that the lady must have borne no inactive part in arranging the affair; there were considerations of expediency which she would be far more likely to appreciate than Mr. Ellenwood; and there was just the specious phantom of sentiment and romance in this late union of two early lovers which sometimes makes a fool of a woman who has lost her true feelings among the accidents of life. All the wonder was, how the gentleman, with his lack of worldly wisdom and agonizing consciousness of ridicule, could have been induced to take a measure at once so prudent and so laughable.

But while people talked the wedding-day arrived. The ceremony was to be solemnized according to the Episcopalian forms, and in open church, with a degree of publicity that attracted many spectators, who occupied the front seats of the galleries, and the pews near the altar and along the broad aisle. It had been arranged, or possibly it was the custom of the day, that the parties should proceed separately to church. By some accident the bridegroom was a little less punctual than the widow and her bridal attendants; with whose arrival, after this tedious, but necessary preface, the action of our tale may be said to commence.

The clumsy wheels of several old-fashioned coaches were heard, and the gentlemen and ladies composing the bridal party came through the church door with the sudden and gladsome effect of a burst of sunshine. The whole group, except the principal figure, was made up of youth and gayety. As they streamed up the broad aisle, while the pews and pillars seemed to brighten on either side, their steps were as buoyant as if they mistook the church for a ball-room, and were ready to dance hand in hand to the altar. So brilliant was the spectacle that few took notice of a singular phenomenon that had marked its entrance. At the moment when the bride's foot touched the threshold the bell swung heavily in the tower above her, and sent forth its deepest knell. The vibrations died away and returned with prolonged solemnity, as she entered the body of the church.

"Good heavens! what an omen," whispered a young lady to her lover.

"On my honour," replied the gentleman, "I believe the bell has the good taste to toll of its own accord. What has she to do with weddings? If you, dearest Julia, were approaching the altar the bell would ring out its merriest peal. It has only a funeral knell for her."

The bride and most of her company had been too much occupied with the bustle of entrance to hear the first boding stroke of the bell, or at least to reflect on the singularity of such a welcome to the altar. They therefore continued to advance with undiminished gayety. The gorgeous dresses of the time, the crimson velvet coats, the gold-laced hats, the hoop petticoats, the silk, satin, brocade, and embroidery, the buckles, canes, and swords, all displayed to the best advantage on persons suited to such finery, made the group appear more like a bright-coloured picture than anything real.

But by what perversity of taste had the artist represented his principal figure as so wrinkled and decayed, while yet he had decked her out in the brightest splendour of attire, as if the loveliest maiden had suddenly withered into age, and become a moral to the beautiful around her! On they went, however, and had glittered along about a third of the aisle, when another stroke of the bell seemed to fill the church with a visible gloom, dimming and obscuring the bright pageant, till it shone forth again as from a mist.

This time the party wavered, stopped, and huddled closer together, while a slight scream was heard from some of the ladies, and a confused whispering among the gentlemen. Thus tossing to and fro, they might have been fancifully compared to a splendid bunch of flowers, suddenly shaken by a puff of wind, which threatened to scatter the leaves of an old, brown, withered rose, on the same stalk with two dewy buds—such being the emblem of the widow between her fair young bridemaids. But her heroism was admirable. She had started with an irrepressible shudder, as if the stroke of the bell had fallen directly on her heart; then, recovering herself, while her attendants were yet in dismay, she took the lead, and paced calmly up the aisle. The bell continued to swing, strike, and vibrate, with the same doleful regularity as when a corpse is on its way to the tomb.

"My young friends here have their nerves a little shaken," said the widow, with a smile, to the clergyman at the altar. "But so many weddings have been ushered in with the merriest peal of the bells, and yet turned out unhappily, that I shall hope for better fortune under such different auspices."

"Madam," answered the rector, in great perplexity, "this strange occurrence brings to my mind a marriage sermon of the famous Bishop Taylor, wherein he mingles so many thoughts of mortality and future woe, that, to speak somewhat after his own rich style, he seems to hang the bridal chamber in black, and cut the wedding garment out of a coffin pall. And it has been the custom of divers nations to infuse something of sadness into their marriage ceremonies, so to keep death in mind while contracting that engagement which is life's chiefest business. Thus we may draw a sad but profitable moral from this funeral knell."

But, though the clergyman might have given his moral even a keener point, he did not fail to dispatch an attendant to inquire into the mystery, and stop those sounds, so dismally appropriate to such a marriage. A brief space elapsed, during which the silence was broken only by whispers, and a few suppressed titterings, among the wedding party and the spectators, who, after the first shock, were disposed to draw an ill-natured merriment from the affair. The young have less charity for aged follies than the old for those of youth. The widow's glance was observed to wander, for an instant, towards a window of the church, as if searching for the time-worn marble that she had dedicated to her first husband; then her eyelids dropped over their faded orbs, and her thoughts were drawn irresistibly to another grave. Two buried men, with a voice at her ear, and a cry afar off, were calling her to lie down beside them.

Perhaps, with momentary truth of feeling, she thought how much happier had been her fate, if, after years of bliss, the bell were now tolling for her funeral, and she were followed to the grave by the old affection of her earliest lover, long her husband. But why had she returned to him, when their cold hearts shrank from each other's embrace?

Still the death-bell tolled so mournfully, that the sunshine seemed to fade in the air. A whisper, communicated from those who stood nearest the windows, now spread through the church; a hearse, with a train of several coaches, was creeping along the street, conveying some dead man to the churchyard, while the bride awaited a living one at the altar. Immediately after, the footsteps of the bridegroom and his friends were heard at the door. The widow looked down the aisle, and clinched the arm of one of her bridesmaids in her bony hand with such unconscious violence, that the fair girl trembled.

"You frighten me, my dear madam!" cried she. "For Heaven's sake, what is the matter?"

"Nothing, my dear, nothing," said the widow; then, whispering close to her ear, "There is a foolish fancy that I cannot get rid of. I am expecting my bridegroom to come into the church, with my first two husbands for groomsmen!"

"Look, look!" screamed the bridesmaid. "What is here? The funeral!"

As she spoke, a dark procession paced into the church. First came an old man and woman, like chief mourners at a funeral, attired from head to foot in the deepest black, all but their pale features and hoary hair; he leaning on a staff, and supporting her decrepit form with his nerveless arm. Behind appeared another, and another pair, as aged, as black, and mournful as the first. As they drew near, the widow recognized in every face some trait of former friends, long forgotten, but now returning, as if from their old graves, to warn her to prepare a shroud; or, with purpose almost as unwelcome, to exhibit their wrinkles and infirmity, and claim her as their companion by the tokens of her own decay. Many a merry night had she danced with them, in youth. And now, in joyless age, she felt that some withered partner should request her hand, and all unite, in a dance of death, to the music of the funeral bell.

While these aged mourners were passing up the aisle, it was observed that, from pew to pew, the spectators shuddered with irrepressible awe, as some object, hitherto concealed by the intervening figures, came full in sight. Many turned away their faces; others kept a fixed and rigid stare; and a young girl giggled hysterically, and fainted with the laughter on her lips. When the spectral procession approached the altar, each couple separated, and slowly diverged, till, in the centre, appeared a form, that had been worthily ushered in with all this gloomy pomp, the death knell, and the funeral. It was the bridegroom in his shroud!

No garb but that of the grave could have befitted such a deathlike aspect; the eyes, indeed, had the wild gleam of a sepulchral lamp; all else was fixed in the stern calmness which old men wear in the coffin. The corpse stood motionless, but addressed the widow in accents that seemed to melt into the clang of the bell, which fell heavily on the air while he spoke.

"Come, my bride!" said those pale lips, "the hearse is ready. The sexton stands waiting for us at the door of the tomb. Let us be married; and then to our coffins!"

How shall the widow's horror be represented? It gave her the ghastliness of a dead man's bride. Her youthful friends stood apart, shuddering at the mourners, the shrouded bridegroom, and herself; the whole scene expressed, by the strongest imagery, the vain struggle of the gilded vanities of this world, when opposed to age, infirmity, sorrow, and death. The awestruck silence was first broken by the clergyman.

"Mr. Ellenwood," said he, soothingly, yet with somewhat of authority, "you are not well. Your mind has been agitated by the unusual circumstances in which you are placed. The ceremony must be deferred. As an old friend, let me entreat you to return home."

"Home! yes, but not without my bride," answered he, in the same hollow accents. "You deem this mockery; perhaps madness. Had I bedizened my aged and broken frame with scarlet and embroidery—had I forced my withered lips to smile at my dead heart—that might have been mockery, or madness. But now, let young and old declare, which of us has come hither without a wedding garment, the bridegroom or the bride!"

He stepped forward at a ghostly pace, and stood beside the widow, contrasting the awful simplicity of his shroud with the glare and glitter in which she had arrayed herself for this unhappy scene. None, that beheld them, could deny the terrible strength of the moral which his disordered intellect had contrived to draw.

"Cruel! cruel!" groaned the heart-stricken bride.

"Cruel!" repeated he; then, losing his deathlike composure in a wild bitterness: "Heaven judge which of us has been cruel to the other! In youth you deprived me of my happiness, my hopes, my aims; you took away all the substance of my life, and made it a dream without reality enough even to grieve at—with only a pervading gloom, through which I walked wearily, and cared not whither. But after forty years, when I have built my tomb, and would not give up the thought of resting there—no, not for such a life as we once pictured—you call me to the altar. At your summons I am here.

"But other husbands have enjoyed your youth, your beauty, your warmth of heart, and all that could be termed your life. What is there for me but your decay and death? And therefore I have bidden these funeral friends, and bespoken the sexton's deepest knell, and am come, in my shroud, to wed you, as with a burial service, that we may join our hands at the door of the sepulchre, and enter it together."

It was not frenzy; it was not merely the drunkenness of strong emotion, in a heart unused to it, that now wrought upon the bride. The stern lesson of the day had done its work; her worldliness was gone. She seized the bridegroom's hand.

"Yes!" cried she. "Let us wed, even at the door of the sepulchre! My life is gone in vanity and emptiness. But at its close there is one true feeling. It has made me what I was in youth; it makes me worthy of you. Time is no more for both of us. Let us wed for Eternity!"

With a long and deep regard, the bridegroom looked into her eyes, while a tear was gathering in his own. How strange that gush of human feeling from the frozen bosom of a corpse! He wiped away the tears even with his shroud.

"Beloved of my youth," said he, "I have been wild. The despair of my whole lifetime had returned at once, and maddened me. Forgive; and be forgiven. Yes; it is evening with us now; and we have realized none of our morning dreams of happiness. But let us join our hands before the altar, as lovers whom adverse circumstances have separated through life, yet who meet again as they are leaving it, and find their earthly affection changed into something holy as religion. And what is Time, to the married of Eternity?"

Amid the tears of many, and a swell of exalted sentiment, in those who felt aright, was solemnized the union of two immortal souls. The train of withered mourners, the hoary bridegroom in his shroud, the pale features of the aged bride, and the death-bell tolling through the whole, till its deep voice overpowered the marriage words, all marked the funeral of earthly hopes. But as the ceremony proceeded, the organ, as if stirred by the sympathies of this impressive scene, poured forth an anthem, first mingling with the dismal knell, then rising to a loftier strain, till the soul looked down upon its wo. And when the awful rite was finished, and with cold hand in cold hand, the Married of Eternity withdrew, the organ's peal of solemn triumph drowned the Wedding Knell.

Rappaccini's Daughter

(A tale from *Mosses From an Old Manse and Other Stories*)

We do not remember to have seen any translated specimens of the productions of M. de l'Aubépine—a fact the less to be wondered at, as his very name is unknown to many of his own countrymen as well as to the student of foreign literature. As a writer, he seems to occupy an unfortunate position between the Transcendentalists (who, under one name or another, have their share in all the current literature of the world) and the great body of pen-and-ink men who address the intellect and sympathies of the multitude. If not too refined, at all events too remote, too shadowy, and unsubstantial in his modes of development to suit the taste of the latter class, and yet too popular to satisfy the spiritual or metaphysical requisitions of the former, he must necessarily find himself without an audience, except here and there an individual or possibly an isolated clique.

His writings, to do them justice, are not altogether destitute of fancy and originality; they might have won him greater reputation but for an inveterate love of allegory, which is apt to invest his plots and characters with the aspect of scenery and people in the clouds, and to steal away the human warmth out of his conceptions. His fictions are sometimes historical, sometimes of the present day, and sometimes, so far as can be discovered, have little or no reference either to time or space. In any case, he generally contents himself with a very slight embroidery of outward manners,—the faintest possible counterfeit of real life,—and endeavours to create an interest by some less obvious peculiarity of the subject.

Occasionally a breath of Nature, a raindrop of pathos and tenderness, or a gleam of humour, will find its way into the midst of his fantastic imagery, and make us feel as if, after all, we were yet within the limits of our native earth. We will only add to this very cursory notice that M. de l'Aubépine's productions, if the reader chance to take them in precisely the proper point of view, may amuse a leisure hour as well as those of a brighter man; if otherwise, they can hardly fail to look excessively like nonsense.

Our author is voluminous; he continues to write and publish with as much praiseworthy and indefatigable prolixity as if his efforts were crowned with the brilliant success that so justly attends those of Eugene Sue. His first appearance was by a collection of stories in a long series of volumes entitled *Contes deux fois racontées*. The titles of some of his more recent works (we quote from memory) are as follows: *Le Voyage Céleste à Chemin de Fer*, 3 tom., 1838; *Le nouveau Père Adam et la nouvelle Mère Eve*, 2 tom., 1839; *Roderic; ou le Serpent à l'estomac*, 2 tom., 1840; *Le Culte du Feu*, a folio volume of ponderous research into the religion and ritual of the old Persian Ghebers, published in 1841; *La Soirée du Château en Espagne*, 1 tom., 8vo, 1842; and *L'Artiste du Beau; ou le Papillon Mécanique*, 5 tom., 4to, 1843.

Our somewhat wearisome perusal of this startling catalogue of volumes has left behind it a certain personal affection and sympathy, though by no means admiration, for M. de l'Aubépine; and we would fain do the little in our power towards introducing him favourably to the American public. The ensuing tale is a translation of his *Beatrice; ou la Belle Empoisonneuse*, recently published in *La Revue Anti-Aristocratique*. This journal, edited by the Comte de Bearhaven, has for some years past led the defence of liberal principles and popular rights with a faithfulness and ability worthy of all praise.

★★★★★★

A young man, named Giovanni Guasconti, came, very long ago, from the more southern region of Italy, to pursue his studies at the University of Padua. Giovanni, who had but a scanty supply of gold *ducats* in his pocket, took lodgings in a high and gloomy chamber of an old edifice which looked not unworthy to have been the palace of a Paduan noble, and which, in fact, exhibited over its entrance the armorial bearings of a family long since extinct.

The young stranger, who was not unstudied in the great poem of his country, recollected that one of the ancestors of this family, and perhaps an occupant of this very mansion, had been pictured by Dante as a partaker of the immortal agonies of his *Inferno*. These reminiscences and associations, together with the tendency to heartbreak natural to a young man for the first time out of his native sphere, caused Giovanni to sigh heavily as he looked around the desolate and ill-furnished apartment.

"HolyVirgin, *signor!*" cried old Dame Lisabetta, who, won by the youth's remarkable beauty of person, was kindly endeavouring to give the chamber a habitable air, "what a sigh was that to come out of a young man's heart! Do you find this old mansion gloomy? For the love of Heaven, then, put your head out of the window, and you will see as bright sunshine as you have left in Naples."

Guasconti mechanically did as the old woman advised, but could not quite agree with her that the Paduan sunshine was as cheerful as that of southern Italy. Such as it was, however, it fell upon a garden beneath the window and expended its fostering influences on a variety of plants, which seemed to have been cultivated with exceeding care.

"Does this garden belong to the house?" asked Giovanni.

"Heaven forbid, *signor*, unless it were fruitful of better pot herbs than any that grow there now," answered old Lisabetta. "No; that garden is cultivated by the own hands of Signor Giacomo Rappaccini, the famous doctor, who, I warrant him, has been heard of as far as Naples. It is said that he distils these plants into medicines that are as potent as a charm. Oftentimes you may see the *signor* doctor at work, and perchance the *signora*, his daughter, too, gathering the strange flowers that grow in the garden."

The old woman had now done what she could for the aspect of the chamber; and, commending the young man to the protection of the saints, took her departure.

Giovanni still found no better occupation than to look down into the garden beneath his window. From its appearance, he judged it to be one of those botanic gardens which were of earlier date in Padua than elsewhere in Italy or in the world. Or, not improbably, it might once have been the pleasure-place of an opulent family; for there was the ruin of a marble fountain in the centre, sculptured with rare art, but so woefully shattered that it was impossible to trace the original design from the chaos of remaining fragments. The water, however, continued to gush and sparkle into the sunbeams as cheerfully as ever.

A little gurgling sound ascended to the young man's window, and made him feel as if the fountain were an immortal spirit that sung its song unceasingly and without heeding the vicissitudes around it, while one century imbodied it in marble and another scattered the perishable garniture on the soil. All about the pool into which the water subsided grew various plants, that seemed to require a plentiful supply of moisture for the nourishment of gigantic leaves, and in some instances, flowers gorgeously magnificent.

There was one shrub in particular, set in a marble vase in the midst of the pool, that bore a profusion of purple blossoms, each of which had the lustre and richness of a gem; and the whole together made a show so resplendent that it seemed enough to illuminate the garden, even had there been no sunshine. Every portion of the soil was peopled with plants and herbs, which, if less beautiful, still bore tokens of assiduous care, as if all had their individual virtues, known to the scientific mind that fostered them. Some were placed in urns, rich with old carving, and others in common garden pots; some crept serpent-like along the ground or climbed on high, using whatever means of ascent was offered them. One plant had wreathed itself round a statue of Vertumnus, which was thus quite veiled and shrouded in a drapery of hanging foliage, so happily arranged that it might have served a sculptor for a study.

While Giovanni stood at the window he heard a rustling behind a screen of leaves, and became aware that a person was at work in the garden. His figure soon emerged into view, and showed itself to be that of no common labourer, but a tall, emaciated, sallow, and sickly-looking man, dressed in a scholar's garb of black. He was beyond the middle term of life, with gray hair, a thin, gray beard, and a face singularly marked with intellect and cultivation, but which could never, even in his more youthful days, have expressed much warmth of heart.

Nothing could exceed the intentness with which this scientific gardener examined every shrub which grew in his path: it seemed as if he was looking into their inmost nature, making observations in regard to their creative essence, and discovering why one leaf grew in this shape and another in that, and wherefore such and such flowers differed among themselves in hue and perfume. Nevertheless, in spite of this deep intelligence on his part, there was no approach to intimacy between himself and these vegetable existences.

On the contrary, he avoided their actual touch or the direct inhaling of their odours with a caution that impressed Giovanni most disagreeably; for the man's demeanour was that of one walking among malignant influences, such as savage beasts, or deadly snakes, or evil spirits, which, should he allow them one moment of license, would wreak upon him some terrible fatality. It was strangely frightful to the young man's imagination to see this air of insecurity in a person cultivating a garden, that most simple and innocent of human toils, and which had been alike the joy and labour of the unfallen parents of the race. Was this garden, then, the Eden of the present world? And this man, with such a perception of harm in what his own hands caused to grow,—was he the Adam?

The distrustful gardener, while plucking away the dead leaves or pruning the too luxuriant growth of the shrubs, defended his hands with a pair of thick gloves. Nor were these his only armour. When, in his walk through the garden, he came to the magnificent plant that hung its purple gems beside the marble fountain, he placed a kind of mask over his mouth and nostrils, as if all this beauty did but conceal a deadlier malice; but, finding his task still too dangerous, he drew back, removed the mask, and called loudly, but in the infirm voice of a person affected with inward disease, "Beatrice! Beatrice!"

"Here am I, my father. What would you?" cried a rich and youthful voice from the window of the opposite house—a voice as rich as a tropical sunset, and which made Giovanni, though he knew not why, think of deep hues of purple or crimson and of perfumes heavily delectable. "Are you in the garden?"

"Yes, Beatrice," answered the gardener, "and I need your help."

Soon there emerged from under a sculptured portal the figure of a young girl, arrayed with as much richness of taste as the most splendid of the flowers, beautiful as the day, and with a bloom so deep and vivid that one shade more would have been too much. She looked redundant with life, health, and energy; all of which attributes were bound down and compressed, as it were and girdled tensely, in their luxuriance, by her virgin zone. Yet Giovanni's fancy must have grown morbid while he looked down into the garden; for the impression which the fair stranger made upon him was as if here were another flower, the human sister of those vegetable ones, as beautiful as they, more beautiful than the richest of them, but still to be touched only with a glove, nor to be approached without a mask. As Beatrice came down the garden path, it was observable that she handled and inhaled the odour of several of the plants which her father had most sedulously avoided.

"Here, Beatrice," said the latter, "see how many needful offices require to be done to our chief treasure. Yet, shattered as I am, my life might pay the penalty of approaching it so closely as circumstances demand. Henceforth, I fear, this plant must be consigned to your sole charge."

"And gladly will I undertake it," cried again the rich tones of the young lady, as she bent towards the magnificent plant and opened her arms as if to embrace it. "Yes, my sister, my splendour, it shall be Beatrice's task to nurse and serve thee; and thou shalt reward her with thy kisses and perfumed breath, which to her is as the breath of life."

Then, with all the tenderness in her manner that was so strikingly expressed in her words, she busied herself with such attentions as the plant seemed to require; and Giovanni, at his lofty window, rubbed his eyes and almost doubted whether it were a girl tending her favourite flower, or one sister performing the duties of affection to another. The scene soon terminated. Whether Dr. Rappaccini had finished his labours in the garden, or that his watchful eye had caught the stranger's face, he now took his daughter's arm and retired. Night was already closing in; oppressive exhalations seemed to proceed from the plants and steal upward past the open window; and Giovanni, closing the lattice, went to his couch and dreamed of a rich flower and beautiful girl. Flower and maiden were different, and yet the same, and fraught with some strange peril in either shape.

But there is an influence in the light of morning that tends to rectify whatever errors of fancy, or even of judgment, we may have incurred during the sun's decline, or among the shadows of the night, or in the less wholesome glow of moonshine. Giovanni's first movement, on starting from sleep, was to throw open the window and gaze down into the garden which his dreams had made so fertile of mysteries. He was surprised and a little ashamed to find how real and matter-of-fact an affair it proved to be, in the first rays of the sun which gilded the dewdrops that hung upon leaf and blossom, and, while giving a brighter beauty to each rare flower, brought everything within the limits of ordinary experience.

The young man rejoiced that, in the heart of the barren city, he had the privilege of overlooking this spot of lovely and luxuriant vegetation. It would serve, he said to himself, as a symbolic language to keep him in communion with Nature. Neither the sickly and thoughtworn Dr. Giacomo Rappaccini, it is true, nor his brilliant daughter, were now visible; so that Giovanni could not determine how much of the singularity which he attributed to both was due to their own qualities and how much to his wonder-working fancy; but he was inclined to take a most rational view of the whole matter.

In the course of the day he paid his respects to Signor Pietro Baglioni, professor of medicine in the university, a physician of eminent repute to whom Giovanni had brought a letter of introduction. The professor was an elderly personage, apparently of genial nature, and habits that might almost be called jovial. He kept the young man to dinner, and made himself very agreeable by the freedom and liveliness of his conversation, especially when warmed by a flask or two of Tuscan wine. Giovanni, conceiving that men of science, inhabitants of the same city, must needs be on familiar terms with one another, took an opportunity to mention the name of Dr. Rappaccini. But the professor did not respond with so much cordiality as he had anticipated.

"Ill would it become a teacher of the divine art of medicine," said Professor Pietro Baglioni, in answer to a question of Giovanni, "to withhold due and well-considered praise of a physician so eminently skilled as Rappaccini; but, on the other hand, I should answer it but scantily to my conscience were I to permit a worthy youth like yourself, Signor Giovanni, the son of an ancient friend, to imbibe erroneous ideas respecting a man who might hereafter chance to hold your life and death in his hands. The truth is, our worshipful Dr. Rappaccini has as much science as any member of the faculty—with perhaps one single exception—in Padua, or all Italy; but there are certain grave objections to his professional character."

"And what are they?" asked the young man.

"Has my friend Giovanni any disease of body or heart, that he is so inquisitive about physicians?" said the professor, with a smile. "But as for Rappaccini, it is said of him—and I, who know the man well, can answer for its truth—that he cares infinitely more for science than for mankind. His patients are interesting to him only as subjects for some new experiment. He would sacrifice human life, his own among the rest, or whatever else was dearest to him, for the sake of adding so much as a grain of mustard seed to the great heap of his accumulated knowledge."

"Methinks he is an awful man indeed," remarked Guasconti, mentally recalling the cold and purely intellectual aspect of Rappaccini. "And yet, worshipful professor, is it not a noble spirit? Are there many men capable of so spiritual a love of science?"

"God forbid," answered the professor, somewhat testily; "at least, unless they take sounder views of the healing art than those adopted by Rappaccini. It is his theory that all medicinal virtues are comprised within those substances which we term vegetable poisons. These he cultivates with his own hands, and is said even to have produced new varieties of poison, more horribly deleterious than Nature, without the assistance of this learned person, would ever have plagued the world withal.

"That the *signor* doctor does less mischief than might be expected with such dangerous substances is undeniable. Now and then, it must be owned, he has effected, or seemed to effect, a marvellous cure; but, to tell you my private mind, Signor Giovanni, he should receive little credit for such instances of success,—they being probably the work of chance,—but should be held strictly accountable for his failures, which may justly be considered his own work."

The youth might have taken Baglioni's opinions with many grains of allowance had he known that there was a professional warfare of long continuance between him and Dr. Rappaccini, in which the latter was generally thought to have gained the advantage. If the reader be inclined to judge for himself, we refer him to certain black-letter tracts on both sides, preserved in the medical department of the University of Padua.

"I know not, most learned professor," returned Giovanni, after musing on what had been said of Rappaccini's exclusive zeal for science,—"I know not how dearly this physician may love his art; but surely there is one object more dear to him. He has a daughter."

"Aha!" cried the professor, with a laugh. "So now our friend

Giovanni's secret is out. You have heard of this daughter, whom all the young men in Padua are wild about, though not half a dozen have ever had the good hap to see her face. I know little of the Signora Beatrice save that Rappaccini is said to have instructed her deeply in his science, and that, young and beautiful as fame reports her, she is already qualified to fill a professor's chair. Perchance her father destines her for mine! Other absurd rumours there be, not worth talking about or listening to. So now, Signor Giovanni, drink off your glass of lachrymal."

Guasconti returned to his lodgings somewhat heated with the wine he had quaffed, and which caused his brain to swim with strange fantasies in reference to Dr. Rappaccini and the beautiful Beatrice. On his way, happening to pass by a florist's, he bought a fresh bouquet of flowers.

Ascending to his chamber, he seated himself near the window, but within the shadow thrown by the depth of the wall, so that he could look down into the garden with little risk of being discovered. All beneath his eye was a solitude. The strange plants were basking in the sunshine, and now and then nodding gently to one another, as if in acknowledgment of sympathy and kindred. In the midst, by the shattered fountain, grew the magnificent shrub, with its purple gems clustering all over it; they glowed in the air, and gleamed back again out of the depths of the pool, which thus seemed to overflow with coloured radiance from the rich reflection that was steeped in it.

At first, as we have said, the garden was a solitude. Soon, however,—as Giovanni had half hoped, half feared, would be the case,—a figure appeared beneath the antique sculptured portal, and came down between the rows of plants, inhaling their various perfumes as if she were one of those beings of old classic fable that lived upon sweet odours. On again beholding Beatrice, the young man was even startled to perceive how much her beauty exceeded his recollection of it; so brilliant, so vivid, was its character, that she glowed amid the sunlight, and, as Giovanni whispered to himself, positively illuminated the more shadowy intervals of the garden path.

Her face being now more revealed than on the former occasion, he was struck by its expression of simplicity and sweetness,—qualities that had not entered into his idea of her character, and which made him ask anew what manner of mortal she might be. Nor did he fail again to observe, or imagine, an analogy between the beautiful girl and the gorgeous shrub that hung its gemlike flowers over the fountain,—a resemblance which Beatrice seemed to have indulged a fantastic humour in heightening, both by the arrangement of her dress and the selection of its hues.

Approaching the shrub, she threw open her arms, as with a passionate ardour, and drew its branches into an intimate embrace—so intimate that her features were hidden in its leafy bosom and her glistening ringlets all intermingled with the flowers.

"Give me thy breath, my sister," exclaimed Beatrice; "for I am faint with common air. And give me this flower of thine, which I separate with gentlest fingers from the stem and place it close beside my heart."

With these words the beautiful daughter of Rappaccini plucked one of the richest blossoms of the shrub, and was about to fasten it in her bosom. But now, unless Giovanni's draughts of wine had bewildered his senses, a singular incident occurred. A small orange-coloured reptile, of the lizard or chameleon species, chanced to be creeping along the path, just at the feet of Beatrice. It appeared to Giovanni,—but, at the distance from which he gazed, he could scarcely have seen anything so minute,—it appeared to him, however, that a drop or two of moisture from the broken stem of the flower descended upon the lizard's head. For an instant the reptile contorted itself violently, and then lay motionless in the sunshine.

Beatrice observed this remarkable phenomenon and crossed herself, sadly, but without surprise; nor did she therefore hesitate to arrange the fatal flower in her bosom. There it blushed, and almost glimmered with the dazzling effect of a precious stone, adding to her dress and aspect the one appropriate charm which nothing else in the world could have supplied. But Giovanni, out of the shadow of his window, bent forward and shrank back, and murmured and trembled.

"Am I awake? Have I my senses?" said he to himself. "What is this being? Beautiful shall I call her, or inexpressibly terrible?"

Beatrice now strayed carelessly through the garden, approaching closer beneath Giovanni's window, so that he was compelled to thrust his head quite out of its concealment in order to gratify the intense and painful curiosity which she excited. At this moment there came a beautiful insect over the garden wall; it had, perhaps, wandered through the city, and found no flowers or verdure among those antique haunts of men until the heavy perfumes of Dr. Rappaccini's shrubs had lured it from afar. Without alighting on the flowers, this winged brightness seemed to be attracted by Beatrice, and lingered in the air and fluttered about her head.

Now, here it could not be but that Giovanni Guasconti's eyes deceived him. Be that as it might, he fancied that, while Beatrice was gazing at the insect with childish delight, it grew faint and fell at her feet; its bright wings shivered; it was dead—from no cause that he could discern, unless it were the atmosphere of her breath. Again Beatrice crossed herself and sighed heavily as she bent over the dead insect.

An impulsive movement of Giovanni drew her eyes to the window. There she beheld the beautiful head of the young man—rather a Grecian than an Italian head, with fair, regular features, and a glistening of gold among his ringlets—gazing down upon her like a being that hovered in midair. Scarcely knowing what he did, Giovanni threw down the bouquet which he had hitherto held in his hand.

"*Signora*," said he, "there are pure and healthful flowers. Wear them for the sake of Giovanni Guasconti."

"Thanks, *signor*," replied Beatrice, with her rich voice, that came forth as it were like a gush of music, and with a mirthful expression half childish and half woman-like. "I accept your gift, and would fain recompense it with this precious purple flower;

but if I toss it into the air it will not reach you. So Signor Guasconti must even content himself with my thanks."

She lifted the bouquet from the ground, and then, as if inwardly ashamed at having stepped aside from her maidenly reserve to respond to a stranger's greeting, passed swiftly homeward through the garden. But few as the moments were, it seemed to Giovanni, when she was on the point of vanishing beneath the sculptured portal, that his beautiful bouquet was already beginning to wither in her grasp. It was an idle thought; there could be no possibility of distinguishing a faded flower from a fresh one at so great a distance.

For many days after this incident the young man avoided the window that looked into Dr. Rappaccini's garden, as if something ugly and monstrous would have blasted his eyesight had he been betrayed into a glance. He felt conscious of having put himself, to a certain extent, within the influence of an unintelligible power by the communication which he had opened with Beatrice. The wisest course would have been, if his heart were in any real danger, to quit his lodgings and Padua itself at once; the next wiser, to have accustomed himself, as far as possible, to the familiar and daylight view of Beatrice—thus bringing her rigidly and systematically within the limits of ordinary experience. Least of all, while avoiding her sight, ought Giovanni to have remained so near this extraordinary being that the proximity and possibility even of intercourse should give a kind of substance and reality to the wild vagaries which his imagination ran riot continually in producing.

Guasconti had not a deep heart—or, at all events, its depths were not sounded now; but he had a quick fancy, and an ardent southern temperament, which rose every instant to a higher fever pitch. Whether or no Beatrice possessed those terrible attributes, that fatal breath, the affinity with those so beautiful and deadly flowers which were indicated by what Giovanni had witnessed, she had at least instilled a fierce and subtle poison into his system. It was not love, although her rich beauty was a madness to him; nor horror, even while he fancied her spirit to be imbued with the same baneful essence that seemed to pervade her physical frame; but a wild offspring of both love and horror that had each parent in it, and burned like one and shivered like the other.

Giovanni knew not what to dread; still less did he know what to hope; yet hope and dread kept a continual warfare in his breast, alternately vanquishing one another and starting up afresh to renew the contest. Blessed are all simple emotions, be they dark or bright! It is the lurid intermixture of the two that produces the illuminating blaze of the infernal regions.

Sometimes he endeavoured to assuage the fever of his spirit by a rapid walk through the streets of Padua or beyond its gates: his footsteps kept time with the throbbings of his brain, so that the walk was apt to accelerate itself to a race. One day he found himself arrested; his arm was seized by a portly personage, who had turned back on recognizing the young man and expended much breath in overtaking him.

"Signor Giovanni! Stay, my young friend!" cried he. "Have you forgotten me? That might well be the case if I were as much altered as yourself."

It was Baglioni, whom Giovanni had avoided ever since their first meeting, from a doubt that the professor's sagacity would look too deeply into his secrets. Endeavouring to recover himself, he stared forth wildly from his inner world into the outer one and spoke like a man in a dream.

"Yes; I am Giovanni Guasconti. You are Professor Pietro Baglioni. Now let me pass!"

"Not yet, not yet, Signor Giovanni Guasconti," said the professor, smiling, but at the same time scrutinizing the youth with an earnest glance. "What! did I grow up side by side with your father? and shall his son pass me like a stranger in these old streets of Padua? Stand still, Signor Giovanni; for we must have a word or two before we part."

"Speedily, then, most worshipful professor, speedily," said Giovanni, with feverish impatience. "Does not your worship see that I am in haste?"

Now, while he was speaking there came a man in black along the street, stooping and moving feebly like a person in inferior health. His face was all overspread with a most sickly and sallow hue, but yet so pervaded with an expression of piercing and active intellect that an observer might easily have overlooked the merely physical attributes and have seen only this wonderful energy. As he passed, this person exchanged a cold and distant salutation with Baglioni, but fixed his eyes upon Giovanni with an intentness that seemed to bring out whatever was within him worthy of notice. Nevertheless, there was a peculiar quietness in the look, as if taking merely a speculative, not a human interest, in the young man.

"It is Dr. Rappaccini!" whispered the professor when the stranger had passed. "Has he ever seen your face before?"

"Not that I know," answered Giovanni, starting at the name.

"He *has* seen you! he must have seen you!" said Baglioni, hastily. "For some purpose or other, this man of science is making a study of you. I know that look of his! It is the same that coldly illuminates his face as he bends over a bird, a mouse, or a butterfly, which, in pursuance of some experiment, he has killed by the perfume of a flower; a look as deep as Nature itself, but without Nature's warmth of love. Signor Giovanni, I will stake my life upon it, you are the subject of one of Rappaccini's experiments!"

"Will you make a fool of me?" cried Giovanni, passionately. "*That, signor* professor, were an untoward experiment."

"Patience! patience!" replied the imperturbable professor. "I tell thee, my poor Giovanni, that Rappaccini has a scientific interest in thee. Thou hast fallen into fearful hands! And the Signora Beatrice,—what part does she act in this mystery?"

But Guasconti, finding Baglioni's pertinacity intolerable, here broke away, and was gone before the professor could again seize his arm. He looked after the young man intently and shook his head.

"This must not be," said Baglioni to himself. "The youth is the son of my old friend, and shall not come to any harm from which the arcana of medical science can preserve him. Besides, it is too insufferable an impertinence in Rappaccini, thus to snatch the lad out of my own hands, as I may say, and make use of him for his infernal experiments. This daughter of his! It shall be looked to. Perchance, most learned Rappaccini, I may foil you where you little dream of it!"

Meanwhile Giovanni had pursued a circuitous route, and at length found himself at the door of his lodgings. As he crossed the threshold he was met by old Lisabetta, who smirked and smiled, and was evidently desirous to attract his attention; vainly, however, as the ebullition of his feelings had momentarily subsided into a cold and dull vacuity. He turned his eyes full upon the withered face that was puckering itself into a smile, but seemed to behold it not. The old dame, therefore, laid her grasp upon his cloak.

"*Signor! signor!*" whispered she, still with a smile over the whole breadth of her visage, so that it looked not unlike a grotesque carving in wood, darkened by centuries. "Listen, *signor!* There is a private entrance into the garden!"

"What do you say?" exclaimed Giovanni, turning quickly about, as if an inanimate thing should start into feverish life. "A private entrance into Dr. Rappaccini's garden?"

"Hush! hush! not so loud!" whispered Lisabetta, putting her hand over his mouth. "Yes; into the worshipful doctor's garden, where you may see all his fine shrubbery. Many a young man in Padua would give gold to be admitted among those flowers."

Giovanni put a piece of gold into her hand.

"Show me the way," said he.

A surmise, probably excited by his conversation with Baglioni, crossed his mind, that this interposition of old Lisabetta might perchance be connected with the intrigue, whatever were its nature, in which the professor seemed to suppose that Dr. Rappaccini was involving him. But such a suspicion, though it disturbed Giovanni, was inadequate to restrain him. The instant that he was aware of the possibility of approaching Beatrice, it seemed an absolute necessity of his existence to do so.

It mattered not whether she were angel or demon; he was irrevocably within her sphere, and must obey the law that whirled him onward, in ever-lessening circles, towards a result which he did not attempt to foreshadow; and yet, strange to say, there came across him a sudden doubt whether this intense interest on his part were not delusory; whether it were really of so deep and positive a nature as to justify him in now thrusting himself into an incalculable position; whether it were not merely the fantasy of a young man's brain, only slightly or not at all connected with his heart.

He paused, hesitated, turned half about, but again went on. His withered guide led him along several obscure passages, and finally undid a door, through which, as it was opened, there came the sight and sound of rustling leaves, with the broken sunshine glimmering among them. Giovanni stepped forth, and, forcing himself through the entanglement of a shrub that wreathed its tendrils over the hidden entrance, stood beneath his own window in the open area of Dr. Rappaccini's garden.

How often is it the case that, when impossibilities have come to pass and dreams have condensed their misty substance into tangible realities, we find ourselves calm, and even coldly self-possessed, amid circumstances which it would have been a delirium of joy or agony to anticipate! Fate delights to thwart us thus. Passion will choose his own time to rush upon the scene, and lingers sluggishly behind when an appropriate adjustment of events would seem to summon his appearance. So was it now with Giovanni.

Day after day his pulses had throbbed with feverish blood at the improbable idea of an interview with Beatrice, and of standing with her, face to face, in this very garden, basking in the Oriental sunshine of her beauty, and snatching from her full gaze the mystery which he deemed the riddle of his own existence. But now there was a singular and untimely equanimity within his breast. He threw a glance around the garden to discover if Beatrice or her father were present, and, perceiving that he was alone, began a critical observation of the plants.

The aspect of one and all of them dissatisfied him; their gorgeousness seemed fierce, passionate, and even unnatural. There was hardly an individual shrub which a wanderer, straying by himself through a forest, would not have been startled to find growing wild, as if an unearthly face had glared at him out of the thicket. Several also would have shocked a delicate instinct by an appearance of artificialness indicating that there had been such commixture, and, as it were, adultery, of various vegetable species, that the production was no longer of God's making, but the monstrous offspring of man's depraved fancy, glowing with only an evil mockery of beauty.

They were probably the result of experiment, which in one or two cases had succeeded in mingling plants individually lovely into a compound possessing the questionable and ominous character that distinguished the whole growth of the garden. In fine, Giovanni recognized but two or three plants in the collection, and those of a kind that he well knew to be poisonous. While busy with these contemplations he heard the rustling of a silken garment, and, turning, beheld Beatrice emerging from beneath the sculptured portal.

Giovanni had not considered with himself what should be his deportment; whether he should apologize for his intrusion into the garden, or assume that he was there with the privity at least, if not by the desire, of Dr. Rappaccini or his daughter; but Beatrice's manner placed him at his ease, though leaving him still in doubt by what agency he had gained admittance. She came lightly along the path and met him near the broken fountain. There was surprise in her face, but brightened by a simple and kind expression of pleasure.

"You are a connoisseur in flowers, *signor*," said Beatrice, with a smile, alluding to the bouquet which he had flung her from the window. "It is no marvel, therefore, if the sight of my father's rare collection has tempted you to take a nearer view. If he were here, he could tell you many strange and interesting facts as to the nature and habits of these shrubs; for he has spent a lifetime in such studies, and this garden is his world."

"And yourself, lady," observed Giovanni, "if fame says true,—you likewise are deeply skilled in the virtues indicated by these rich blossoms and these spicy perfumes. Would you deign to be my instructress, I should prove an apter scholar than if taught by Signor Rappaccini himself."

"Are there such idle rumours?" asked Beatrice, with the music of a pleasant laugh. "Do people say that I am skilled in my father's science of plants? What a jest is there! No; though I have grown up among these flowers, I know no more of them than their hues and perfume; and sometimes methinks I would fain rid myself of even that small knowledge. There are many flowers here, and those not the least brilliant, that shock and offend me when they meet my eye. But pray, *signor*, do not believe these stories about my science. Believe nothing of me save what you see with your own eyes."

"And must I believe all that I have seen with my own eyes?" asked Giovanni, pointedly, while the recollection of former scenes made him shrink. "No, *signora*; you demand too little of me. Bid me believe nothing save what comes from your own lips."

It would appear that Beatrice understood him. There came a deep flush to her cheek; but she looked full into Giovanni's eyes, and responded to his gaze of uneasy suspicion with a queenlike haughtiness.

"I do so bid you, *signor*," she replied. "Forget whatever you may have fancied in regard to me. If true to the outward senses, still it may be false in its essence; but the words of Beatrice Rappaccini's lips are true from the depths of the heart outward. Those you may believe."

A fervour glowed in her whole aspect and beamed upon Giovanni's consciousness like the light of truth itself; but while she spoke there was a fragrance in the atmosphere around her, rich and delightful, though evanescent, yet which the young man, from an indefinable reluctance, scarcely dared to draw into his lungs. It might be the odour of the flowers. Could it be Beatrice's breath which thus embalmed her words with a strange richness, as if by steeping them in her heart? A faintness passed like a shadow over Giovanni and flitted away; he seemed to gaze through the beautiful girl's eyes into her transparent soul, and felt no more doubt or fear.

The tinge of passion that had coloured Beatrice's manner vanished; she became gay, and appeared to derive a pure delight from her communion with the youth not unlike what the maiden of a lonely island might have felt conversing with a voyager from the civilized world. Evidently her experience of life had been confined within the limits of that garden. She talked now about matters as simple as the daylight or summer clouds, and now asked questions in reference to the city, or Giovanni's distant home, his friends, his mother, and his sisters—questions indicating such seclusion, and such lack of familiarity with modes and forms, that Giovanni responded as if to an infant. Her spirit gushed out before him like a fresh rill that was just catching its first glimpse of the sunlight and wondering at the reflections of earth and sky which were flung into its bosom.

There came thoughts, too, from a deep source, and fantasies of a gemlike brilliancy, as if diamonds and rubies sparkled upward among the bubbles of the fountain. Ever and *anon* there gleamed across the young man's mind a sense of wonder that he should be walking side by side with the being who had so wrought upon his imagination, whom he had idealized in such hues of terror, in whom he had positively witnessed such manifestations of dreadful attributes,—that he should be conversing with Beatrice like a brother, and should find her so human and so maidenlike. But such reflections were only momentary; the effect of her character was too real not to make itself familiar at once.

In this free intercourse they had strayed through the garden, and now, after many turns among its avenues, were come to the shattered fountain, beside which grew the magnificent shrub, with its treasury of glowing blossoms. A fragrance was diffused from it which Giovanni recognized as identical with that which he had attributed to Beatrice's breath, but incomparably more powerful. As her eyes fell upon it, Giovanni beheld her press her hand to her bosom as if her heart were throbbing suddenly and painfully.

"For the first time in my life," murmured she, addressing the shrub, "I had forgotten thee."

"I remember, *signora*," said Giovanni, "that you once promised to reward me with one of these living gems for the bouquet which I had the happy boldness to fling to your feet. Permit me now to pluck it as a memorial of this interview."

He made a step towards the shrub with extended hand; but Beatrice darted forward, uttering a shriek that went through his heart like a dagger. She caught his hand and drew it back with the whole force of her slender figure. Giovanni felt her touch thrilling through his fibres.

"Touch it not!" exclaimed she, in a voice of agony. "Not for thy life! It is fatal!"

Then, hiding her face, she fled from him and vanished beneath the sculptured portal. As Giovanni followed her with his eyes, he beheld the emaciated figure and pale intelligence of Dr. Rappaccini, who had been watching the scene, he knew not how long, within the shadow of the entrance.

No sooner was Guasconti alone in his chamber than the image of Beatrice came back to his passionate musings, invested with all the witchery that had been gathering around it ever since his first glimpse of her, and now likewise imbued with a tender warmth of girlish womanhood. She was human; her nature was endowed with all gentle and feminine qualities; she was worthiest to be worshipped; she was capable, surely, on her part, of the height and heroism of love. Those tokens which he had hitherto considered as proofs of a frightful peculiarity in her physical and moral system were now either forgotten, or, by the subtle sophistry of passion transmitted into a golden crown of enchantment, rendering Beatrice the more admirable by so much as she was the more unique.

Whatever had looked ugly was now beautiful; or, if incapable of such a change, it stole away and hid itself among those shapeless half ideas which throng the dim region beyond the daylight of our perfect consciousness. Thus did he spend the night, nor fell asleep until the dawn had begun to awake the slumbering flowers in Dr. Rappaccini's garden, whither Giovanni's dreams doubtless led him. Up rose the sun in his due season, and, flinging his beams upon the young man's eyelids, awoke him to a sense of pain. When thoroughly aroused, he became sensible of a burning and tingling agony in his hand—in his right hand—the very hand which Beatrice had grasped in her own when he was on the point of plucking one of the gemlike flowers. On the back of that hand there was now a purple print like that of four small fingers, and the likeness of a slender thumb upon his wrist.

Oh, how stubbornly does love,—or even that cunning semblance of love which flourishes in the imagination, but strikes no depth of root into the heart,—how stubbornly does it hold its faith until the moment comes when it is doomed to vanish into thin mist! Giovanni wrapped a handkerchief about his hand and wondered what evil thing had stung him, and soon forgot his pain in a reverie of Beatrice.

After the first interview, a second was in the inevitable course of what we call fate. A third; a fourth; and a meeting with Beatrice in the garden was no longer an incident in Giovanni's daily life, but the whole space in which he might be said to live; for the anticipation and memory of that ecstatic hour made up the remainder. Nor was it otherwise with the daughter of Rappaccini. She watched for the youth's appearance, and flew to his side with confidence as unreserved as if they had been playmates from early infancy—as if they were such playmates still. If, by any unwonted chance, he failed to come at the appointed moment, she stood beneath the window and sent up the rich sweetness of her tones to float around him in his chamber and echo and reverberate throughout his heart: "Giovanni! Giovanni! Why tarriest thou? Come down!" And down he hastened into that Eden of poisonous flowers.

But, with all this intimate familiarity, there was still a reserve in Beatrice's demeanour, so rigidly and invariably sustained that the idea of infringing it scarcely occurred to his imagination. By all appreciable signs, they loved; they had looked love with eyes that conveyed the holy secret from the depths of one soul into the depths of the other, as if it were too sacred to be whispered by the way; they had even spoken love in those gushes of passion when their spirits darted forth in articulated breath like tongues of long-hidden flame; and yet there had been no seal of lips, no clasp of hands, nor any slightest caress such as love claims and hallows.

He had never touched one of the gleaming ringlets of her hair; her garment—so marked was the physical barrier between them—had never been waved against him by a breeze. On the few occasions when Giovanni had seemed tempted to overstep the limit, Beatrice grew so sad, so stern, and withal wore such a look of desolate separation, shuddering at itself, that not a spoken word was requisite to repel him. At such times he was startled at the horrible suspicions that rose, monster-like, out of the caverns of his heart and stared him in the face; his love grew thin and faint as the morning mist, his doubts alone had substance. But, when Beatrice's face brightened again after the momentary shadow, she was transformed at once from the mysterious, questionable being whom he had watched with so much awe and horror; she was now the beautiful and unsophisticated girl whom he felt that his spirit knew with a certainty beyond all other knowledge.

A considerable time had now passed since Giovanni's last meeting with Baglioni. One morning, however, he was disagreeably surprised by a visit from the professor, whom he had scarcely thought of for whole weeks, and would willingly have forgotten still longer. Given up as he had long been to a pervading excitement, he could tolerate no companions except upon condition of their perfect sympathy with his present state of feeling. Such sympathy was not to be expected from Professor Baglioni.

The visitor chatted carelessly for a few moments about the

gossip of the city and the university, and then took up another topic.

"I have been reading an old classic author lately," said he, "and met with a story that strangely interested me. Possibly you may remember it. It is of an Indian prince, who sent a beautiful woman as a present to Alexander the Great. She was as lovely as the dawn and gorgeous as the sunset; but what especially distinguished her was a certain rich perfume in her breath—richer than a garden of Persian roses. Alexander, as was natural to a youthful conqueror, fell in love at first sight with this magnificent stranger; but a certain sage physician, happening to be present, discovered a terrible secret in regard to her."

"And what was that?" asked Giovanni, turning his eyes downward to avoid those of the professor.

"That this lovely woman," continued Baglioni, with emphasis, "had been nourished with poisons from her birth upward, until her whole nature was so imbued with them that she herself had become the deadliest poison in existence. Poison was her element of life. With that rich perfume of her breath she blasted the very air. Her love would have been poison—her embrace death. Is not this a marvellous tale?"

"A childish fable," answered Giovanni, nervously starting from his chair. "I marvel how your worship finds time to read such nonsense among your graver studies."

"By the by," said the professor, looking uneasily about him, "what singular fragrance is this in your apartment? Is it the perfume of your gloves? It is faint, but delicious; and yet, after all, by no means agreeable. Were I to breathe it long, methinks it would make me ill. It is like the breath of a flower; but I see no flowers in the chamber."

"Nor are there any," replied Giovanni, who had turned pale as the professor spoke; "nor, I think, is there any fragrance except in your worship's imagination. Odours, being a sort of element combined of the sensual and the spiritual, are apt to deceive us in this manner. The recollection of a perfume, the bare idea of it, may easily be mistaken for a present reality."

"Ay; but my sober imagination does not often play such tricks," said Baglioni; "and, were I to fancy any kind of odour, it would be that of some vile apothecary drug, wherewith my fingers are likely enough to be imbued. Our worshipful friend Rappaccini, as I have heard, tinctures his medicaments with odours richer than those of Araby. Doubtless, likewise, the fair and learned Signora Beatrice would minister to her patients with draughts as sweet as a maiden's breath; but woe to him that sips them!"

Giovanni's face evinced many contending emotions. The tone in which the professor alluded to the pure and lovely daughter of Rappaccini was a torture to his soul; and yet the intimation of a view of her character opposite to his own, gave instantaneous distinctness to a thousand dim suspicions, which now grinned at him like so many demons. But he strove hard to quell them and to respond to Baglioni with a true lover's perfect faith.

"Signor Professor," said he, "you were my father's friend; perchance, too, it is your purpose to act a friendly part towards his son. I would fain feel nothing towards you save respect and deference; but I pray you to observe, *signor*, that there is one subject on which we must not speak. You know not the Signora Beatrice. You cannot, therefore, estimate the wrong—the blasphemy, I may even say—that is offered to her character by a light or injurious word."

"Giovanni! my poor Giovanni!" answered the professor, with a calm expression of pity, "I know this wretched girl far better than yourself. You shall hear the truth in respect to the poisoner Rappaccini and his poisonous daughter; yes, poisonous as she is beautiful. Listen; for, even should you do violence to my gray hairs, it shall not silence me. That old fable of the Indian woman has become a truth by the deep and deadly science of Rappaccini and in the person of the lovely Beatrice."

Giovanni groaned and hid his face

"Her father," continued Baglioni, "was not restrained by natural affection from offering up his child in this horrible manner as the victim of his insane zeal for science; for, let us do him justice, he is as true a man of science as ever distilled his own heart in an alembic. What, then, will be your fate? Beyond a doubt you are selected as the material of some new experiment. Perhaps the result is to be death; perhaps a fate more awful still. Rappaccini, with what he calls the interest of science before his eyes, will hesitate at nothing."

"It is a dream," muttered Giovanni to himself; "surely it is a dream."

"But," resumed the professor, "be of good cheer, son of my friend. It is not yet too late for the rescue. Possibly we may even succeed in bringing back this miserable child within the limits of ordinary nature, from which her father's madness has estranged her. Behold this little silver vase! It was wrought by the hands of the renowned Benvenuto Cellini, and is well worthy to be a love gift to the fairest dame in Italy. But its contents are invaluable. One little sip of this antidote would have rendered the most virulent poisons of the Borgias innocuous. Doubt not that it will be as efficacious against those of Rappaccini. Bestow the vase, and the precious liquid within it, on your Beatrice, and hopefully await the result."

Baglioni laid a small, exquisitely wrought silver vial on the table and withdrew, leaving what he had said to produce its effect upon the young man's mind.

"We will thwart Rappaccini yet," thought he, chuckling to himself, as he descended the stairs; "but, let us confess the truth of him, he is a wonderful man—a wonderful man indeed; a vile empiric, however, in his practice, and therefore not to be tolerated by those who respect the good old rules of the medical profession."

Throughout Giovanni's whole acquaintance with Beatrice, he had occasionally, as we have said, been haunted by dark surmises as to her character; yet so thoroughly had she made herself felt by him as a simple, natural, most affectionate, and guileless creature, that the image now held up by Professor Baglioni looked as strange and incredible as if it were not in accordance with his own original conception. True, there were ugly recollections connected with his first glimpses of the beautiful girl; he could not quite forget the bouquet that withered in her grasp, and the insect that perished amid the sunny air, by no ostensible agency save the fragrance of her breath. These incidents, however, dissolving in the pure light of her character, had no longer the efficacy of facts, but were acknowledged as mistaken fantasies, by whatever testimony of the senses they might appear to be substantiated.

There is something truer and more real than what we can see with the eyes and touch with the finger. On such better evidence had Giovanni founded his confidence in Beatrice, though rather by the necessary force of her high attributes than by any deep and generous faith on his part. But now his spirit was incapable of sustaining itself at the height to which the early enthusiasm of passion had exalted it; he fell down, grovelling among earthly doubts, and defiled therewith the pure whiteness of Beatrice's image. Not that he gave her up; he did but distrust. He resolved to institute some decisive test that should satisfy him, once for all, whether there were those dreadful peculiarities in her physical nature which could not be supposed to exist without some corresponding monstrosity of soul.

His eyes, gazing down afar, might have deceived him as to the lizard, the insect, and the flowers; but if he could witness, at the distance of a few paces, the sudden blight of one fresh and healthful flower in Beatrice's hand, there would be room for no further question. With this idea he hastened to the florist's and purchased a bouquet that was still gemmed with the morning dewdrops.

It was now the customary hour of his daily interview with Beatrice. Before descending into the garden, Giovanni failed not to look at his figure in the mirror,—a vanity to be expected in a beautiful young man, yet, as displaying itself at that troubled and feverish moment, the token of a certain shallowness of feeling and insincerity of character. He did gaze, however, and said to himself that his features had never before possessed so rich a grace, nor his eyes such vivacity, nor his cheeks so warm a hue of superabundant life.

"At least," thought he, "her poison has not yet insinuated itself into my system. I am no flower to perish in her grasp."

With that thought he turned his eyes on the bouquet, which he had never once laid aside from his hand. A thrill of indefinable horror shot through his frame on perceiving that those dewy flowers were already beginning to droop; they wore the aspect of things that had been fresh and lovely yesterday. Giovanni grew white as marble, and stood motionless before the mirror, staring at his own reflection there as at the likeness of something frightful. He remembered Baglioni's remark about the fragrance that seemed to pervade the chamber. It must have been the poison in his breath!

Then he shuddered—shuddered at himself. Recovering from his stupor, he began to watch with curious eye a spider that was busily at work hanging its web from the antique cornice of the apartment, crossing and recrossing the artful system of interwoven lines—as vigorous and active a spider as ever dangled from an old ceiling. Giovanni bent towards the insect, and emitted a deep, long breath. The spider suddenly ceased its toil; the web vibrated with a tremor originating in the body of the small artisan. Again Giovanni sent forth a breath, deeper, longer, and imbued with a venomous feeling out of his heart: he knew not whether he were wicked, or only desperate. The spider made a convulsive gripe with his limbs and hung dead across the window.

"Accursed! accursed!" muttered Giovanni, addressing himself. "Hast thou grown so poisonous that this deadly insect perishes by thy breath?"

At that moment a rich, sweet voice came floating up from the garden.

"Giovanni! Giovanni! It is past the hour! Why tarriest thou? Come down!"

"Yes," muttered Giovanni again. "She is the only being whom my breath may not slay! Would that it might!"

He rushed down, and in an instant was standing before the bright and loving eyes of Beatrice. A moment ago his wrath and despair had been so fierce that he could have desired nothing so much as to wither her by a glance; but with her actual presence there came influences which had too real an existence to be at once shaken off: recollections of the delicate and benign power of her feminine nature, which had so often enveloped him in a religious calm; recollections of many a holy and passionate outgush of her heart, when the pure fountain had been unsealed from its depths and made visible in its transparency to his mental eye; recollections which, had Giovanni known how to estimate them, would have assured him that all this ugly mystery was but an earthly illusion, and that, whatever mist of evil might seem to have gathered over her, the real Beatrice was a heavenly angel.

Incapable as he was of such high faith, still her presence had not utterly lost its magic. Giovanni's rage was quelled into an aspect of sullen insensibility. Beatrice, with a quick spiritual sense, immediately felt that there was a gulf of blackness between them which neither he nor she could pass. They walked on together, sad and silent, and came thus to the marble fountain and to its pool of water on the ground, in the midst of which grew the shrub that bore gem-like blossoms. Giovanni was affrighted at the eager enjoyment—the appetite, as it were—with which he found himself inhaling the fragrance of the flowers.

"Beatrice," asked he, abruptly, "whence came this shrub?"

"My father created it," answered she, with simplicity.

"Created it! created it!" repeated Giovanni. "What mean you, Beatrice?"

"He is a man fearfully acquainted with the secrets of Nature," replied Beatrice; "and, at the hour when I first drew breath, this plant sprang from the soil, the offspring of his science, of his intellect, while I was but his earthly child. Approach it not!" continued she, observing with terror that Giovanni was drawing nearer to the shrub. "It has qualities that you little dream of. But I, dearest Giovanni,—I grew up and blossomed with the plant and was nourished with its breath. It was my sister, and I loved it with a human affection; for, alas!—hast thou not suspected it?— there was an awful doom."

Here Giovanni frowned so darkly upon her that Beatrice paused and trembled. But her faith in his tenderness reassured her, and made her blush that she had doubted for an instant.

"There was an awful doom," she continued, "the effect of my father's fatal love of science, which estranged me from all society of my kind. Until Heaven sent thee, dearest Giovanni, oh, how lonely was thy poor Beatrice!"

"Was it a hard doom?" asked Giovanni, fixing his eyes upon her.

"Only of late have I known how hard it was," answered she, tenderly. "Oh, yes; but my heart was torpid, and therefore quiet."

Giovanni's rage broke forth from his sullen gloom like a lightning flash out of a dark cloud.

"Accursed one!" cried he, with venomous scorn and anger. "And, finding thy solitude wearisome, thou hast severed me likewise from all the warmth of life and enticed me into thy region of unspeakable horror!"

"Giovanni!" exclaimed Beatrice, turning her large bright eyes upon his face. The force of his words had not found its way into her mind; she was merely thunderstruck.

"Yes, poisonous thing!" repeated Giovanni, beside himself with passion. "Thou hast done it! Thou hast blasted me! Thou hast filled my veins with poison! Thou hast made me as hateful, as ugly, as loathsome and deadly a creature as thyself—a world's wonder of hideous monstrosity! Now, if our breath be happily as fatal to ourselves as to all others, let us join our lips in one kiss of unutterable hatred, and so die!"

"What has befallen me?" murmured Beatrice, with a low moan out of her heart. "Holy Virgin, pity me, a poor heartbroken child!"

"Thou,—dost thou pray?" cried Giovanni, still with the same fiendish scorn. "Thy very prayers, as they come from thy lips, taint the atmosphere with death. Yes, yes; let us pray! Let us to church and dip our fingers in the holy water at the portal! They that come after us will perish as by a pestilence! Let us sign crosses in the air! It will be scattering curses abroad in the likeness of holy symbols!"

"Giovanni," said Beatrice, calmly, for her grief was beyond passion, "why dost thou join thyself with me thus in those terrible words? I, it is true, am the horrible thing thou namest me. But thou,—what hast thou to do, save with one other shudder at my hideous misery to go forth out of the garden and mingle with thy race, and forget there ever crawled on earth such a monster as poor Beatrice?"

"Dost thou pretend ignorance?" asked Giovanni, scowling upon her. "Behold! this power have I gained from the pure daughter of Rappaccini."

There was a swarm of summer insects flitting through the air in search of the food promised by the flower odours of the fatal garden. They circled round Giovanni's head, and were evidently attracted towards him by the same influence which had drawn them for an instant within the sphere of several of the shrubs. He sent forth a breath among them, and smiled bitterly at Beatrice as at least a score of the insects fell dead upon the ground.

"I see it! I see it!" shrieked Beatrice. "It is my father's fatal science! No, no, Giovanni; it was not I! Never! never! I dreamed only to love thee and be with thee a little time, and so to let thee pass away, leaving but thine image in mine heart; for, Giovanni, believe it, though my body be nourished with poison, my spirit is God's creature, and craves love as its daily food. But my father,— he has united us in this fearful sympathy. Yes; spurn me, tread upon me, kill me! Oh, what is death after such words as thine? But it was not I. Not for a world of bliss would I have done it."

Giovanni's passion had exhausted itself in its outburst from his lips. There now came across him a sense, mournful, and not without tenderness, of the intimate and peculiar relationship between Beatrice and himself. They stood, as it were, in an utter solitude, which would be made none the less solitary by the densest throng of human life. Ought not, then, the desert of humanity around them to press this insulated pair closer together? If they should be cruel to one another, who was there to be kind to them? Besides, thought Giovanni, might there not still be a hope of his returning within the limits of ordinary nature, and leading Beatrice, the redeemed Beatrice, by the hand? O, weak, and selfish, and unworthy spirit, that could dream of an earthly union and earthly happiness as possible, after such deep love had been so bitterly wronged as was Beatrice's love by Giovanni's blighting words! No, no; there could be no such hope. She must pass heavily, with that broken heart, across the borders of Time—she must bathe her hurts in some fount of paradise, and forget her grief in the light of immortality, and *there* be well.

But Giovanni did not know it.

"Dear Beatrice," said he, approaching her, while she shrank away as always at his approach, but now with a different impulse, "dearest Beatrice, our fate is not yet so desperate. Behold! there is a medicine, potent, as a wise physician has assured me, and almost divine in its efficacy. It is composed of ingredients the most opposite to those by which thy awful father has brought this calamity upon thee and me. It is distilled of blessed herbs. Shall we not quaff it together, and thus be purified from evil?"

"Give it me!" said Beatrice, extending her hand to receive the little silver vial which Giovanni took from his bosom. She added, with a peculiar emphasis, "I will drink; but do thou await the result."

She put Baglioni's antidote to her lips; and, at the same moment, the figure of Rappaccini emerged from the portal and came slowly towards the marble fountain. As he drew near, the pale man of science seemed to gaze with a triumphant expression at the beautiful youth and maiden, as might an artist who should spend his life in achieving a picture or a group of statuary and finally be satisfied with his success. He paused; his bent form grew erect with conscious power; he spread out his hands over them in the attitude of a father imploring a blessing upon his children; but those were the same hands that had thrown poison into the stream of their lives. Giovanni trembled. Beatrice shuddered nervously, and pressed her hand upon her heart.

"My daughter," said Rappaccini, "thou art no longer lonely

in the world. Pluck one of those precious gems from thy sister shrub and bid thy bridegroom wear it in his bosom. It will not harm him now. My science and the sympathy between thee and him have so wrought within his system that he now stands apart from common men, as thou dost, daughter of my pride and triumph, from ordinary women. Pass on, then, through the world, most dear to one another and dreadful to all besides!"

"My father," said Beatrice, feebly,—and still as she spoke she kept her hand upon her heart,—"wherefore didst thou inflict this miserable doom upon thy child?"

"Miserable!" exclaimed Rappaccini. "What mean you, foolish girl? Dost thou deem it misery to be endowed with marvellous gifts against which no power nor strength could avail an enemy—misery, to be able to quell the mightiest with a breath—misery, to be as terrible as thou art beautiful? Wouldst thou, then, have preferred the condition of a weak woman, exposed to all evil and capable of none?"

"I would fain have been loved, not feared," murmured Beatrice, sinking down upon the ground. "But now it matters not. I am going, father, where the evil which thou hast striven to mingle with my being will pass away like a dream—like the fragrance of these poisonous flowers, which will no longer taint my breath among the flowers of Eden. Farewell, Giovanni! Thy words of hatred are like lead within my heart; but they, too, will fall away as I ascend. Oh, was there not, from the first, more poison in thy nature than in mine?"

To Beatrice,—so radically had her earthly part been wrought upon by Rappaccini's skill,—as poison had been life, so the powerful antidote was death; and thus the poor victim of man's ingenuity and of thwarted nature, and of the fatality that attends all such efforts of perverted wisdom, perished there, at the feet of her father and Giovanni. Just at that moment Professor Pietro Baglioni looked forth from the window, and called loudly, in a tone of triumph mixed with horror, to the thunderstricken man of science, "Rappaccini! Rappaccini! and is *this* the upshot of your experiment!"

John Inglefield's Thanksgiving

(A tale from *The Snow Image and Other Twice-Told Tales*)

On the evening of Thanksgiving day, John Inglefield, the blacksmith, sat in his elbow-chair, among those who had been keeping festival at his board. Being the central figure of the domestic circle, the fire threw its strongest light on his massive and sturdy frame, reddening his rough visage, so that it looked like the head of an iron statue, all aglow, from his own forge, and with its features rudely fashioned on his own anvil. At John Inglefield's right hand was an empty chair. The other places round the hearth were filled by the members of the family, who all sat quietly, while, with a semblance of fantastic merriment, their shadows danced on the wall behind them.

One of the group was John Inglefield's son, who had been bred at college, and was now a student of theology at Andover. There was also a daughter of sixteen, whom nobody could look at without thinking of a rosebud almost blossomed. The only other person at the fireside was Robert Moore, formerly an apprentice of the blacksmith, but now his journeyman, and who seemed more like an own son of John Inglefield than did the pale and slender student.

Only these four had kept New England's festival beneath that roof. The vacant chair at John Inglefield's right hand was in memory of his wife, whom death had snatched from him since the previous Thanksgiving. With a feeling that few would have looked for in his rough nature, the bereaved husband had himself set the chair in its place next his own; and often did his eye glance thitherward, as if he deemed it possible that the cold grave might send back its tenant to the cheerful fireside, at least for that one evening. Thus did he cherish the grief that was dear to him. But there was another grief which he would fain have torn from his heart; or, since that could never be, have buried it too deep for others to behold, or for his own remembrance. Within the past year another member of his household had gone from him, but not to the grave. Yet they kept no vacant chair for her.

While John Inglefield and his family were sitting round the hearth with the shadows dancing behind them on the wall, the outer door was opened, and a light foot step came along the passage. The latch of the inner door was lifted by some familiar hand, and a young girl came in, wearing a cloak and hood, which she took off, and laid on the table beneath the looking-glass. Then, after gazing a moment at the fireside circle, she approached, and took the seat at John Inglefield's right hand, as if it had been reserved on purpose for her.

"Here I am, at last, father," said she. "You ate your Thanksgiving dinner without me, but I have come back to spend the evening with you."

Yes, it was Prudence Inglefield. She wore the same neat and maidenly attire which she had been accustomed to put on when the household work was over for the day, and her hair was parted from her brow, in the simple and modest fashion that became her best of all. If her cheek might otherwise have been pale, yet the glow of the fire suffused it with a healthful bloom. If she had spent the many months of her absence in guilt and infamy, yet they seemed to have left no traces on. her gentle aspect. She could not have looked less altered, had she merely stepped away from her father's fireside for half an hour, and returned while the blaze was quivering upwards from the same brands that were burning at her departure.

And to John Inglefield she was the very image of his buried wife, such as he remembered her on the first Thanksgiving which they had passed under their own roof. Therefore, though naturally a stern and rugged man, he could not speak unkindly to his sinful child, nor yet could he take her to his bosom.

"You are welcome home, Prudence," said he, glancing: sideways at her, and his voice faltered. "Your mother would have rejoiced to see you, but she has been gone from us these four mouths."

"I know it, father, I know it," replied Prudence, quickly. "And yet, when I first came in, my eyes were so dazzled by the firelight, that she seemed to be sitting in this very chair!"

By this time the other members of the family had begun to recover from their surprise, and became sensible that it was no ghost from the grave, nor vision of their vivid recollections, but Prudence, her own self. Her brother was the next that greeted her. He advanced and held out his hand affectionately, as a brother should; yet not entirely like a brother, for, with all his kindness, he was still a clergyman, and speaking to a child of sin.

"Sister Prudence," said he, earnestly, "I rejoice that a merciful Providence hath turned your steps homeward, in time for me to bid you a last farewell. In a few weeks, sister, I am to sail as a missionary to the far islands of the Pacific. There is not one of these beloved faces that I shall ever hope to behold again on this earth. O, may I see all of them—yours and all—beyond the grave!"

A shadow flitted across the girl's countenance.

"The grave is very dark, brother," answered she, withdrawing her hand somewhat hastily from his grasp. "You must look your last at me by the light of this fire."

While this was passing, the twin-girl—the rosebud that had grown on the same stem with the castaway—stood gazing at her sister, longing to fling herself upon her bosom, so that the tendrils of their hearts might intertwine again. At first she was restrained by mingled grief and shame, and by a dread that Prudence was too much changed to respond to her affection, or that her own purity would be felt as a reproach by the lost one. But, as she listened to the familiar voice, while the face grew more and more familiar, she forgot everything save that Prudence had come back. Springing forward, she would have clasped her in a close embrace. At that very instant, however, Prudence started from her chair, and held out both her hands, with a warning gesture.

"No, Mary,—no, my sister," cried she, "do not you touch me. Your bosom must not be pressed to mine!"

Mary shuddered and stood still, for she felt that something darker than the grave was between Prudence and herself, though they seemed so near each other in the light of their father's hearth, where they had grown up together. Meanwhile Prudence threw her eyes around the room, in search of one who had not yet bidden her welcome. He had withdrawn from his seat by the fire side, and was standing near the door, with his face averted, so that his features could be discerned only by the flickering shadow of the profile upon the wall. But Prudence called to him, in a cheerful and kindly tone:—

"Come, Robert," said she, "won't you shake hands with your old friend?"

Robert Moore held back for a moment, but affection struggled powerfully, and overcame his pride and resentment; he rushed towards Prudence, seized her hand, and pressed it to his bosom.

"There, there, Robert!" said she, smiling sadly, as she withdrew her hand, "you must not give me too warm a welcome."

And now, having exchanged greetings with each member of the family, Prudence again seated herself in the chair at John Inglefield's right hand. She was naturally a girl of quick and tender sensibilities, gladsome in her general mood, but with a bewitching pathos inter fused among her merriest words and deeds. It was remarked of her, too, that she had a faculty, even from childhood, of throwing her own feelings, like a spell, over her companions. Such as she had been in her days of innocence, so did she appear this evening. Her friends, in the surprise and bewilderment of her return, almost forgot that she had ever left them, or that she had forfeited any of her claims to their affection.

In the morning, perhaps, they might have looked at her with altered eyes, but by the Thanksgiving fireside they felt only that their own Prudence had come back to them, and were thankful. John Inglefield's rough visage brightened with the glow of his heart, as it grew warm and merry within him; once or twice, even, he laughed till the room rang again, yet seemed startled by the echo of his own mirth. The grave young minister became as frolicsome as a schoolboy. Mary, too, the rosebud, forgot that her twin-blossom had ever been torn from the stem, and trampled in the dust. And as for Robert Moore, he gazed at Prudence with the bashful earnestness of love new-born, while she, with sweet maiden coquetry, half smiled upon and half discouraged him.

In short, it was one of those intervals when sorrow vanishes in its own depth of shadow, and joy starts forth in transitory brightness. When the clock struck eight, Prudence poured out her father's customary draught of herb-tea, which had been steeping by the fireside ever since twilight.

"God bless you, child!" said John Inglefield, as he took the cup from her hand; "you have made your old father happy again. But we miss your mother sadly. Prudence, sadly. It seems as if she ought to be here now."

"Now, father, or never," replied Prudence.

It was now the hour for domestic worship. But while the family were making preparations for this duty, they suddenly perceived that Prudence had put on her cloak and hood, and was lifting the latch of the door.

"Prudence, Prudence! where are you going?" cried they all, with one voice.

As Prudence passed out of the door, she turned towards them, and flung back her hand with a gesture of farewell. But her face was so changed that they hardly recognized it. Sin and evil passions glowed through its comeliness, and wrought a horrible deformity; a smile gleamed in her eyes, as of triumphant mockery, at their surprise and grief.

"Daughter," cried John Inglefield, between wrath and sorrow, "stay and be your father's blessing, or take his curse with you!"

Tor an instant Prudence lingered and looked back into the fire-lighted room, while her countenance wore almost the expression as if she were struggling with a fiend, who had power to seize his victim even within the hallowed precincts of her lather's hearth. The fiend prevailed; and Prudence vanished into the outer darkness. When the family rushed to the door, they could see nothing, but heard the sound of wheels rattling over the frozen ground.

That same night, among the painted beauties at the theatre of a neighbouring city, there was one whose dissolute mirth seemed inconsistent with any sympathy for pure affections, and for the joys and griefs which are hallowed by them. Yet this was Prudence Inglefield. Her visit to the Thanksgiving fireside was the realization of one of those waking dreams in which the guilty soul will sometimes stray back to its innocence. But Sin, alas! is careful of her bond-slaves; they hear her voice, perhaps, at the holiest moment, and are constrained to go whither she summons them. The same dark power that drew Prudence Inglefield from her father's hearth—the same in its nature, though heightened then to a dread necessity—would snatch a guilty soul from the gate of heaven, and make its sin and its punishment alike eternal.

David Swan

A Fantasy

(A tale from *Twice Told Tales* Volume 1)

We can be but partially acquainted even with events which actually influence our course through life, and our final destiny. There are innumerable other events, if such they may be called, which come close upon us, yet pass away without actual results, or even betraying their near approach, by the reflection of any light or shadow across our minds. Could we know all the vicissitudes of our fortunes, life would be too full of hope and fear, exultation or disappointment, to afford us a single hour of true serenity. This idea may be illustrated by a page from the secret history of David Swan.

We have nothing to do with David, until we find him, at the age of twenty, on the high road from his native place to the city of Boston, where his uncle, a small dealer in the grocery line, was to take him behind the counter. Be it enough to say, that he was a native of New Hampshire, born of respectable parents, and had received an ordinary school education, with a classic finish by a year at Gilmanton academy. After journeying on foot, from sunrise till nearly noon of a summer's day, his weariness and the increasing heat determined him to sit down in the first convenient shade, and await the coming up of the stage coach.

As if planted on purpose for him, there soon appeared a little tuft of maples, with a delightful recess in the midst, and such a fresh bubbling spring, that it seemed never to have sparkled for any wayfarer but David Swan. Virgin or not, he kissed it with his thirsty lips, and then flung himself along the brink, pillowing his head upon some shirts and a pair of pantaloons, tied up in a striped cotton handkerchief. The sunbeams could not reach him; the dust did not yet rise from the road, after the heavy rain of yesterday; and his grassy lair suited the young man better than a bed of down. The spring murmured drowsily beside him; the branches waved dreamily across the blue sky, overhead; and a deep sleep, perchance hiding dreams within its depths, fell upon David Swan. But we are to relate events which he did not dream of.

While he lay sound asleep in the shade, other people were wide awake, and passed to and fro, a-foot, on horseback, and in all sorts of vehicles, along the sunny road by his bedchamber. Some looked neither to the right hand nor to the left, and knew not that he was there; some merely glanced that way, without admitting the slumberer among their busy thoughts; some laughed to see how soundly he slept; and several, whose hearts were brimming full of scorn, ejected their venomous superfluity on David Swan. A middle aged widow, when nobody else was near, thrust her head a little way into the recess, and vowed that the young fellow looked charming in his sleep. A temperance lecturer saw him, and wrought poor David into the texture of his evening's discourse, as an awful instance of dead drunkenness by the roadside. But, censure, praise, merriment, scorn, and indifference, were all one, or rather all nothing, to David Swan.

He had slept only a few moments, when a brown carriage, drawn by a handsome pair of horses, bowled easily along, and was brought to a standstill, nearly in front of David's resting place. A finch pin had fallen out, and permitted one of the wheels to slide off. The damage was slight, and occasioned merely a momentary alarm to an elderly merchant and his wife, who were returning to Boston in the carriage. While the coachman and a servant were replacing the wheel, the lady and gentleman sheltered themselves beneath the maple trees, and there espied the bubbling fountain, and David Swan asleep beside it. Impressed with the awe which the humblest sleeper usually sheds around him, the merchant trod as lightly as the gout would allow; and his spouse took good heed not to rustle her silk gown, lest David should start up, all of a sudden.

"How soundly he sleeps!" whispered the old gentleman. "From what a depth he draws that easy breath! Such sleep as that, brought on without an opiate, would be worth more to me than half my income; for it would suppose health, and an untroubled mind."

"And youth, besides," said the lady. "Healthy and quiet age does not sleep thus. Our slumber is no more like his, than our wakefulness."

The longer they looked, the more did this elderly couple feel interested in the unknown youth, to whom the way side and the maple shade were as a secret chamber, with the rich gloom of damask curtains brooding over him. Perceiving that a stray sunbeam glimmered down upon his face, the lady contrived to twist a branch aside, so as to intercept it. And having done this little act of kindness, she began to feel like a mother to him.

"Providence seems to have laid him here," whispered she to her husband, "and to have brought us hither to find him, after our disappointment in our cousin's son. Methinks I can see a likeness to our departed Henry. Shall we waken him?"

"To what purpose?" said the merchant, hesitating. "We know nothing of the youth's character."

"That open countenance!" replied his wife, in the same hushed voice, yet earnestly. "This innocent sleep!"

While these whispers were passing, the sleeper's heart did not throb, nor his breath become agitated, nor his features betray the least token of interest.—Yet Fortune was bending over him, just ready to let fall a burthen of gold. The old merchant had lost his only son, and had no heir to his wealth, except a distant relative, with whose conduct he was dissatisfied. In such cases, people sometimes do stranger things than to act the magician, and awaken a young man to splendour, who fell asleep in poverty.

"Shall we not waken him?" repeated the lady, persuasively.

"The coach is ready, Sir," said the servant, behind.

The old couple started, reddened, and hurried away, mutually wondering, that they should ever have dreamed of doing anything so very ridiculous. The merchant threw himself back in the carriage, and occupied his mind with the plan of a magnificent asylum for unfortunate men of business. Meanwhile, David Swan enjoyed his nap.

The carriage could not have gone above a mile or two, when a pretty young girl came along, with a tripping pace, which showed precisely how her little heart was dancing in her bosom. Perhaps it was this merry kind of motion that caused—is there any harm in saying it?—her garter to slip its knot. Conscious that the silken girth, if silk it were, was relaxing its hold, she turned aside into the shelter of the maple trees, and there found a young man asleep by the spring! Blushing, as red as any rose, that she should have intruded into a gentleman's bedchamber, and for such a purpose too, she was about to make her escape on tiptoe.

But, there was peril near the sleeper. A monster of a bee had been wandering overhead—*buzz, buzz, buzz*—now among the leaves, now flashing through the strips of sunshine, and now lost in the dark shade, till finally he appeared to be settling on the eyelid of David Swan. The sting of a bee is sometimes deadly. As free-hearted as she was innocent, the girl attacked the intruder with her handkerchief, brushed him soundly, and drove him from beneath the maple shade. How sweet a picture! This good deed accomplished, with quickened breath, and a deeper blush, she stole a glance at the youthful stranger, for whom she had been battling with a dragon in the air.

"He is handsome!" thought she, and blushed redder yet.

How could it be that no dream of bliss grew so strong within him, that, shattered by its very strength, it should part asunder, and allow him to perceive the girl among its phantoms? Why, at least, did no smile of welcome brighten upon his face? She was come, the maid whose soul, according to the old and beautiful idea, had been severed from his own, and whom, in all his vague but passionate desires, he yearned to meet. Her, only, could he love with a perfect love—him, only, could she receive into the depths of her heart—and now her image was faintly blushing in the fountain, by his side; should it pass away, its happy lustre would never gleam upon his life again.

"How sound he sleeps!" murmured the girl.

She departed, but did not trip along the road so lightly as when she came.

Now, this girl's father was a thriving country merchant in the neighbourhood, and happened, at that identical time, to be looking out for just such a young man as David Swan. Had David formed a way side acquaintance with the daughter, he would have become the father's clerk, and all else in natural succession. So here, again, had good fortune—the best of fortunes—stolen so near, that her garments brushed against him; and he knew nothing of the matter.

The girl was hardly out of sight, when two men turned aside beneath the maple shade. Both had dark faces, set off by cloth caps, which were drawn down aslant over their brows. Their dresses were shabby, yet had a certain smartness. These were a couple of rascals, who got their living by whatever the devil sent them, and now, in the interim of other business, had staked the joint profits of their next piece of villainy on a game of cards, which was to have been decided here under the trees. But, finding David asleep by the spring, one of the rogues whispered to his fellow,

"Hiss!—Do you see that bundle under his head?"

The other villain nodded, winked, and leered.

"I'll bet you a horn of brandy," said the first, "that the chap has either a pocket book, or a snug little hoard of small change, stowed away amongst his shirts. And if not there, we shall find it in his pantaloons' pocket."

"But how if he wakes?" said the other.

His companion thrust aside his waistcoat, pointed to the handle of a dirk, and nodded.

"So be it!" muttered the second villain.

They approached the unconscious David, and, while one

pointed the dagger towards his heart, the other began to search the bundle beneath his head. Their two faces, grim, wrinkled, and ghastly with guilt and fear, bent over their victim, looking horrible enough to be mistaken for fiends, should he suddenly awake. Nay, had the villains glanced aside into the spring, even they would hardly have known themselves, as reflected there. But David Swan had never worn a more tranquil aspect, even when asleep on his mother's breast.

"I must take away the bundle," whispered one.

"If he stirs, I'll strike," muttered the other.

But, at this moment, a dog, scenting along the ground, came in beneath the maple trees, and gazed alternately at each of these wicked men, and then at the quiet sleeper. He then lapped out of the fountain.

"Pshaw!" said one villain. "We can do nothing now. The dog's master must be close behind."

"Let's take a drink, and be off," the other.

The man, with the dagger, thrust back the weapon into his bosom, and drew forth a pocket pistol, but not of that kind which kills by a single discharge. It was a flask of liquor, with a block tin tumbler screwed upon the mouth. Each drank a comfortable dram, and left the spot, with so many jests, and such laughter at their unaccomplished wickedness, that they might be said to have gone on their way rejoicing. In a few hours, they had forgotten the whole affair, nor once imagined that the recording angel had written down the crime of murder against their souls, in letters as durable as eternity. As for David Swan, he still slept quietly, neither conscious of the shadow of death when it hung over him, nor of the glow of renewed life, when that a, shadow was withdrawn.

He slept, but no longer so quietly as at first. An hour's repose had snatched, from his elastic frame, the weariness with which many hours of toil had burthened it. Now, he stirred—now, moved his lips, without a sound—now, talked, in an inward tone, to the noon-day spectres of his dream. But a noise of wheels came rattling louder and louder along the road, until it dashed through the dispersing mist of David's slumber—and there was the stage coach. He started up, with all his ideas about him.

"Halloo, driver!—Take a passenger?" shouted he.

"Room on top!" answered the driver.

Up mounted David, and bowled away merrily towards Boston, without so much as a parting glance at that fountain of dreamlike vicissitude. He knew not that a phantom of Wealth had thrown a golden hue upon its waters—nor that one of Love had sighed softly to their murmur—nor that one of Death had threatened to crimson them with his blood—all, in the brief hour since he lay down to sleep. Sleeping or waking, we hear not the airy footsteps of the strange things that almost happen. Does it not argue a superintending Providence, that, while viewless and unexpected events thrust themselves continually athwart our path, there should still be regularity enough, in mortal life, to render foresight even partially available?

Drowne's Wooden Image
(A tale from *Mosses From an Old Manse and Other Stories*)

One sunshiny morning, in the good old times of the town of Boston, a young carver in wood, well known by the name of Drowne, stood contemplating a large oaken log, which it was his purpose to convert into the figure-head of a vessel. And while he discussed within his own mind what sort of shape or similitude it were well to bestow upon this excellent piece of timber, there came into Drowne's workshop a certain Captain Hunnewell, owner and commander of the good brig called the *Cynosure*, which had just returned from her first voyage to Fayal.

"Ah! that will do, Drowne, that will do!" cried the jolly captain, tapping the log with his rattan. "I bespeak this very piece of oak for the figure-head of the Cynosure. She has shown herself the sweetest craft that ever floated, and I mean to decorate her prow with the handsomest image that the skill of man can cut out of timber. And, Drowne, you are the fellow to execute it."

"You give me more credit than I deserve, Captain Hunnewell," said the carver, modestly, yet as one conscious of eminence in his art. "But, for the sake of the good brig, I stand ready to do my best. And which of these designs do you prefer? Here,"—pointing to a staring, half-length figure, in a white wig and scarlet coat,—"here is an excellent model, the likeness of our gracious king. Here is the valiant Admiral Vernon. Or, if you prefer a female figure, what say you to Britannia with the trident?"

"All very fine, Drowne; all very fine," answered the mariner.

"But as nothing like the brig ever swam the ocean, so I am determined she shall have such a figure-head as old Neptune never saw in his life. And what is more, as there is a secret in the matter, you must pledge your credit not to betray it."

"Certainly," said Drowne, marvelling, however, what possible mystery there could be in reference to an affair so open, of necessity, to the inspection of all the world as the figure-head of a vessel. "You may depend, captain, on my being as secret as the nature of the case will permit."

Captain Hunnewell then took Drowne by the button, and communicated his wishes in so low a tone that it would be unmannerly to repeat what was evidently intended for the carver's private ear. We shall, therefore, take the opportunity to give the reader a few desirable particulars about Drowne himself.

He was the first American who is known to have attempted—in a very humble line, it is true—that art in which we can now reckon so many names already distinguished, or rising to distinction. From his earliest boyhood he had exhibited a knack—for it would be too proud a word to call it genius—a knack, therefore, for the imitation of the human figure in whatever material came most readily to hand. The snows of a New England winter had often supplied him with a species of marble as dazzlingly white, at least, as the Parian or the Carrara, and if less durable, yet sufficiently so to correspond with any claims to permanent existence possessed by the boy's frozen statues.

Yet they won admiration from maturer judges than his school-fellows, and were indeed, remarkably clever, though destitute of the native warmth that might have made the snow melt beneath his hand. As he advanced in life, the young man adopted pine and oak as eligible materials for the display of his skill, which now began to bring him a return of solid silver as well as the empty praise that had been an apt reward enough for his productions of evanescent snow. He became noted for carving ornamental pump heads, and wooden urns for gate posts, and decorations, more grotesque than fanciful, for mantelpieces. No apothecary would have deemed himself in the way of obtaining custom without setting up a gilded mortar, if not a head of Galen or Hippocrates, from the skilful hand of Drowne.

But the great scope of his business lay in the manufacture of figure-heads for vessels. Whether it were the monarch himself, or some famous British admiral or general, or the governor of the province, or perchance the favourite daughter of the ship-owner, there the image stood above the prow, decked out in gorgeous colours, magnificently gilded, and staring the whole world out of countenance, as if from an innate consciousness of its own superiority. These specimens of native sculpture had crossed the sea in all directions, and been not ignobly noticed among the crowded shipping of the Thames and wherever else the hardy mariners of New England had pushed their adventures.

It must be confessed that a family likeness pervaded these respectable progeny of Drowne's skill; that the benign countenance of the king resembled those of his subjects, and that Miss Peggy Hobart, the merchant's daughter, bore a remarkable similitude to Britannia, Victory, and other ladies of the allegoric sisterhood; and, finally, that they all had a kind of wooden aspect which proved an intimate relationship with the unshaped blocks of timber in the carver's workshop. But at least there was no inconsiderable skill of hand, nor a deficiency of any attribute to render them really works of art, except that deep quality, be it of soul or intellect, which bestows life upon the lifeless and warmth upon the cold, and which, had it been present, would have made Drowne's wooden image instinct with spirit.

The captain of the *Cynosure* had now finished his instructions.

"And Drowne," said he, impressively, "you must lay aside all other business and set about this forthwith. And as to the price, only do the job in first-rate style, and you shall settle that point yourself."

"Very well, captain," answered the carver, who looked grave and somewhat perplexed, yet had a sort of smile upon his visage; "depend upon it, I'll do my utmost to satisfy you."

From that moment the men of taste about Long Wharf and the Town Dock who were wont to show their love for the arts by frequent visits to Drowne's workshop, and admiration of his wooden images, began to be sensible of a mystery in the carver's conduct. Often he was absent in the daytime. Sometimes, as might be judged by gleams of light from the shop windows, he was at work until a late hour of the evening; although neither knock nor voice, on such occasions, could gain admittance for a visitor, or elicit any word of response. Nothing remarkable, however, was observed in the shop at those late hours when it was thrown open.

A fine piece of timber, indeed, which Drowne was known to have reserved for some work of especial dignity, was seen to be gradually assuming shape. What shape it was destined ultimately to take was a problem to his friends and a point on which the carver himself preserved a rigid silence. But day after day, though Drowne was seldom noticed in the act of working upon it, this rude form began to be developed until it became evident to all observers that a female figure was growing into mimic life. At each new visit they beheld a larger pile of wooden chips and a nearer approximation to something beautiful.

It seemed as if the hamadryad of the oak had sheltered herself from the unimaginative world within the heart of her native tree, and that it was only necessary to remove the strange shapelessness that had incrusted her, and reveal the grace and loveliness of a divinity. Imperfect as the design, the attitude, the costume, and especially the face of the image still remained, there was already an effect that drew the eye from the wooden cleverness of Drowne's earlier productions and fixed it upon the tantalizing mystery of this new project.

Copley, the celebrated painter, then a young man and a resident of Boston, came one day to visit Drowne; for he had recognized so much of moderate ability in the carver as to induce him, in the dearth of professional sympathy, to cultivate his acquaintance. On entering the shop, the artist glanced at the inflexible image of king, commander, dame, and allegory, that stood around, on the best of which might have been bestowed the questionable praise that it looked as if a living man had here been changed to wood, and that not only the physical, but the intellectual and spiritual part, partook of the stolid transformation. But in not a single instance did it seem as if the wood were imbibing the ethereal essence of humanity. What a wide distinction is here! and how far the slightest portion of the latter merit have outvalued the utmost degree of the former!

"My friend Drowne;" said Copley, smiling to himself, but alluding to the mechanical and wooden cleverness that so invariably distinguished the images, "you are really a remarkable person! I have seldom met with a man in your line of business that could do so much; for one other touch might make this figure of General Wolfe, for instance, a breathing and intelligent human creature."

"You would have me think that you are praising me highly, Mr. Copley," answered Drowne, turning his back upon Wolfe's image in apparent disgust. "But there has come a light into my mind. I know what you know as well, that the one touch which you speak of as deficient is the only one that would be truly valuable, and that without it these works of mine are no better than worthless abortions. There is the same difference between them and the works of an inspired artist as between a sign-post daub and one of your best pictures."

"This is strange," cried Copley, looking him in the face, which now, as the painter fancied, had a singular depth of intelligence, though hitherto it had not given him greatly the advantage over his own family of wooden images. "What has come over you? How is it that, possessing the idea which you have now uttered, you should produce only such works as these?"

The carver smiled, but made no reply. Copley turned again to the images, conceiving that the sense of deficiency which Drowne had just expressed, and which is so rare in a merely mechanical character, must surely imply a genius, the tokens of which had heretofore been overlooked. But no; there was not a trace of it. He was about to withdraw when his eyes chanced to fall upon a half-developed figure which lay in a corner of the workshop, surrounded by scattered chips of oak. It arrested him at once.

"What is here? Who has done this?" he broke out, after contemplating it in speechless astonishment for an instant. "Here is the divine, the life-giving touch. What inspired hand is beckoning this wood to arise and live? Whose work is this?"

"No man's work," replied Drowne. "The figure lies within that block of oak, and it is my business to find it."

"Drowne," said the true artist, grasping the carver fervently by the hand, "you are a man of genius!"

As Copley departed, happening to glance backward from the threshold, he beheld Drowne bending over the half-created shape, and stretching forth his arms as if he would have embraced and drawn it to his heart; while, had such a miracle been possible, his countenance expressed passion enough to communicate warmth and sensibility to the lifeless oak.

"Strange enough!" said the artist to himself. "Who would have looked for a modern Pygmalion in the person of a Yankee mechanic!"

As yet, the image was but vague in its outward presentment; so that, as in the cloud shapes around the western sun, the observer rather felt, or was led to imagine, than really saw what was intended by it. Day by day, however, the work assumed greater precision, and settled its irregular and misty outline into distincter grace and beauty. The general design was now obvious to the common eye. It was a female figure, in what appeared to be a foreign dress; the gown being laced over the bosom, and opening in front so as to disclose a skirt or petticoat, the folds and inequalities of which were admirably represented in the oaken substance. She wore a hat of singular gracefulness, and abundantly laden with flowers, such as never grew in the rude soil of New England, but which, with all their fanciful luxuriance, had a natural truth that it seemed impossible for the most fertile imagination to have attained without copying from real prototypes.

There were several little appendages to this dress, such as a fan, a pair of earrings, a chain about the neck, a watch in the bosom, and a ring upon the finger, all of which would have been deemed beneath the dignity of sculpture. They were put on, however, with as much taste as a lovely woman might have shown in her attire, and could therefore have shocked none but a judgment spoiled by artistic rules.

The face was still imperfect; but gradually, by a magic touch, intelligence and sensibility brightened through the features, with all the effect of light gleaming forth from within the solid oak. The face became alive. It was a beautiful, though not precisely regular and somewhat haughty aspect, but with a certain piquancy about the eyes and mouth, which, of all expressions, would have seemed the most impossible to throw over a wooden countenance. And now, so far as carving went, this wonderful production was complete.

"Drowne," said Copley, who had hardly missed a single day in his visits to the carver's workshop, "if this work were in marble it would make you famous at once; nay, I would almost affirm that it would make an era in the art. It is as ideal as an antique statue, and yet as real as any lovely woman whom one meets at a fireside or in the street. But I trust you do not mean to desecrate this exquisite creature with paint, like those staring kings and admirals yonder?"

"Not paint her!" exclaimed Captain Hunnewell, who stood by; "not paint the figure-head of the *Cynosure!* And what sort of a figure should I cut in a foreign port with such an unpainted oaken stick as this over my prow! She must, and she shall, be painted to the life, from the topmost flower in her hat down to the silver spangles on her slippers."

"Mr. Copley," said Drowne, quietly, "I know nothing of marble statuary, and nothing of the sculptor's rules of art; but of this wooden image, this work of my hands, this creature of my heart,"—and here his voice faltered and choked in a very singular manner,—"of this—of her—I may say that I know something. A well-spring of inward wisdom gushed within me as I wrought upon the oak with my whole strength, and soul, and faith. Let others do what they may with marble, and adopt what rules they choose. If I can produce my desired effect by painted wood, those rules are not for me, and I have a right to disregard them."

"The very spirit of genius," muttered Copley to himself. "How otherwise should this carver feel himself entitled to transcend all rules, and make me ashamed of quoting them?"

He looked earnestly at Drowne, and again saw that expression of human love which, in a spiritual sense, as the artist could not help imagining, was the secret of the life that had been breathed into this block of wood.

The carver, still in the same secrecy that marked all his operations upon this mysterious image, proceeded to paint the habiliments in their proper colours, and the countenance with Nature's red and white. When all was finished he threw open his workshop, and admitted the towns people to behold what he had done. Most persons, at their first entrance, felt impelled to remove their hats, and pay such reverence as was due to the richly-dressed and beautiful young lady who seemed to stand in a corner of the room, with oaken chips and shavings scattered at her feet. Then came a sensation of fear; as if, not being actually human, yet so like humanity, she must therefore be something preternatural.

There was, in truth, an indefinable air and expression that might reasonably induce the query, who and from what sphere this daughter of the oak should be? The strange, rich flowers of Eden on her head; the complexion, so much deeper and more brilliant than those of our native beauties; the foreign, as it seemed, and fantastic garb, yet not too fantastic to be worn decorously in the street; the delicately-wrought embroidery of the skirt; the broad gold chain about her neck; the curious ring upon her finger; the fan, so exquisitely sculptured in open work, and painted to resemble pearl and ebony;—where could Drowne, in his sober walk of life, have beheld the vision here so matchlessly embodied!

And then her face! In the dark eyes, and around the voluptuous mouth, there played a look made up of pride, *coquetry*, and a gleam of mirthfulness, which impressed Copley with the idea that the image was secretly enjoying the perplexing admiration of himself and other beholders.

"And will you," said he to the carver, "permit this masterpiece to become the figure-head of a vessel? Give the honest captain yonder figure of Britannia—it will answer his purpose far better—and send this fairy queen to England, where, for aught I know, it may bring you a thousand pounds."

"I have not wrought it for money," said Drowne.

"What sort of a fellow is this!" thought Copley. "A Yankee, and throw away the chance of making his fortune! He has gone mad; and thence has come this gleam of genius."

There was still further proof of Drowne's lunacy, if credit were due to the rumour that he had been seen kneeling at the feet of the oaken lady, and gazing with a lover's passionate ardour into the face that his own hands had created. The bigots of the day hinted that it would be no matter of surprise if an evil spirit were allowed to enter this beautiful form, and seduce the carver to destruction.

The fame of the image spread far and wide. The inhabitants visited it so universally, that after a few days of exhibition there was hardly an old man or a child who had not become minutely familiar with its aspect. Even had the story of Drowne's wooden image ended here, its celebrity might have been prolonged for many years by the reminiscences of those who looked upon it in their childhood, and saw nothing else so beautiful in after life. But the town was now astounded by an event, the narrative of which has formed itself into one of the most singular legends that are yet to be met with in the traditionary chimney corners of the New England metropolis, where old men and women sit dreaming of the past, and wag their heads at the dreamers of the present and the future.

One fine morning, just before the departure of the *Cynosure* on her second voyage to Fayal, the commander of that gallant vessel was seen to issue from his residence in Hanover Street. He was stylishly dressed in a blue broadcloth coat, with gold lace at the seams and button-holes, an embroidered scarlet waistcoat, a triangular hat, with a loop and broad binding of gold, and wore a silver-hilted hanger at his side. But the good captain might have been arrayed in the robes of a prince or the rags of a beggar, without in either case attracting notice, while obscured by such a companion as now leaned on his arm. The people in the street started, rubbed their eyes, and either leaped aside from their path, or stood as if transfixed to wood or marble in astonishment.

"Do you see it?—do you see it?" cried one, with tremulous eagerness. "It is the very same!"

"The same?" answered another, who had arrived in town only the night before. "Who do you mean? I see only a sea-captain in his shore-going clothes, and a young lady in a foreign habit, with a bunch of beautiful flowers in her hat. On my word, she is as fair and bright a damsel as my eyes have looked on this many a day!"

"Yes; the same!—the very same!" repeated the other. "Drowne's wooden image has come to life!"

Here was a miracle indeed! Yet, illuminated by the sunshine, or darkened by the alternate shade of the houses, and with its garments fluttering lightly in the morning breeze, there passed the image along the street. It was exactly and minutely the shape, the garb, and the face which the towns-people had so recently thronged to see and admire. Not a rich flower upon her head, not a single leaf, but had had its prototype in Drowne's wooden workmanship, although now their fragile grace had become flexible, and was shaken by every footstep that the wearer made. The broad gold chain upon the neck was identical with the one represented on the image, and glistened with the motion imparted by the rise and fall of the bosom which it decorated. A real diamond sparkled on her finger. In her right hand she bore a pearl and ebony fan, which she flourished with a fantastic and bewitching *coquetry*, that was likewise expressed in all her movements as well as in the style of her beauty and the attire that so well harmonized with it.

The face with its brilliant depth of complexion had the same piquancy of mirthful mischief that was fixed upon the countenance of the image, but which was here varied and continually shifting, yet always essentially the same, like the sunny gleam upon a bubbling fountain. On the whole, there was something so airy and yet so real in the figure, and withal so perfectly did it represent Drowne's image, that people knew not whether to suppose the magic wood etherealized into a spirit or warmed and softened into an actual woman.

"One thing is certain," muttered a Puritan of the old stamp, "Drowne has sold himself to the devil; and doubtless this gay Captain Hunnewell is a party to the bargain."

"And I," said a young man who overheard him, "would almost consent to be the third victim, for the liberty of saluting those lovely lips."

"And so would I," said Copley, the painter, "for the privilege of taking her picture."

The image, or the apparition, whichever it might be, still escorted by the bold captain, proceeded from Hanover Street through some of the cross lanes that make this portion of the town so intricate, to Ann Street, thence into Dock Square, and so downward to Drowne's shop, which stood just on the water's edge. The crowd still followed, gathering volume as it rolled along. Never had a modern miracle occurred in such broad daylight, nor in the presence of such a multitude of witnesses. The airy image, as if conscious that she was the object of the murmurs and disturbance that swelled behind her, appeared slightly vexed and flustered, yet still in a manner consistent with the light vivacity and sportive mischief that were written in her countenance. She was observed to flutter her fan with such vehement rapidity that the elaborate delicacy of its workmanship gave way, and it remained broken in her hand.

Arriving at Drowne's door, while the captain threw it open, the marvellous apparition paused an instant on the threshold, assuming the very attitude of the image, and casting over the crowd that glance of sunny *coquetry* which all remembered on the face of the oaken lady. She and her cavalier then disappeared.

"Ah!" murmured the crowd, drawing a deep breath, as with one vast pair of lungs.

"The world looks darker now that she has vanished," said some of the young men.

But the aged, whose recollections dated as far back as witch times, shook their heads, and hinted that our forefathers would have thought it a pious deed to burn the daughter of the oak with fire.

"If she be other than a bubble of the elements," exclaimed Copley, "I must look upon her face again."

He accordingly entered the shop; and there, in her usual corner, stood the image, gazing at him, as it might seem, with the very same expression of mirthful mischief that had been the farewell look of the apparition when, but a moment before, she turned her face towards the crowd. The carver stood beside his creation mending the beautiful fan, which by some accident was broken in her hand. But there was no longer any motion in the lifelike image, nor any real woman in the workshop, nor even the witchcraft of a sunny shadow, that might have deluded people's eyes as it flitted along the street. Captain Hunnewell, too, had vanished. His hoarse sea-breezy tones, however, were audible on the other side of a door that opened upon the water.

"Sit down in the stern sheets, my lady," said the gallant captain. "Come, bear a hand, you lubbers, and set us on board in the turning of a minute-glass."

And then was heard the stroke of oars.

"Drowne," said Copley with a smile of intelligence, "you have been a truly fortunate man. What painter or statuary ever had such a subject! No wonder that she inspired a genius into you, and first created the artist who afterwards created her image."

Drowne looked at him with a visage that bore the traces of tears, but from which the light of imagination and sensibility, so recently illuminating it, had departed. He was again the mechanical carver that he had been known to be all his lifetime.

"I hardly understand what you mean, Mr. Copley," said he, putting his hand to his brow. "This image! Can it have been my work? Well, I have wrought it in a kind of dream; and now that I am broad awake I must set about finishing yonder figure of Admiral Vernon."

And forthwith he employed himself on the stolid countenance of one of his wooden progeny, and completed it in his own mechanical style, from which he was never known afterwards to deviate. He followed his business industriously for many years, acquired a competence, and in the latter part of his life attained to a dignified station in the church, being remembered in records and traditions as Deacon Drowne, the carver. One of his productions, an Indian chief, gilded all over, stood during the better part of a century on the cupola of the Province House, bedazzling the eyes of those who looked upward, like an angel of the sun.

Another work of the good deacon's hand—a reduced likeness of his friend Captain Hunnewell, holding a telescope and quadrant—may be seen to this day, at the corner of Broad and State streets, serving in the useful capacity of sign to the shop of a nautical instrument maker. We know not how to account for the inferiority of this quaint old figure, as compared with the recorded excellence of the Oaken Lady, unless on the supposition that in every human spirit there is imagination, sensibility, creative power, genius, which, according to circumstances, may either be developed in this world, or shrouded in a mask of dullness until another state of being.

To our friend Drowne there came a brief season of excitement, kindled by love. It rendered him a genius for that one occasion, but, quenched in disappointment, left him again the mechanical carver in wood, without the power even of appreciating the work that his own hands had wrought. Yet who can doubt that the very highest state to which a human spirit can attain, in its loftiest aspirations, is its truest and most natural state, and that Drowne was more consistent with himself when he wrought the admirable figure of the mysterious lady, than when he perpetrated a whole progeny of blockheads?

There was a rumour in Boston, about this period, that a young Portuguese lady of rank, on some occasion of political or domestic disquietude, had fled from her home in Fayal and put herself under the protection of Captain Hunnewell, on board of whose vessel, and at whose residence, she was sheltered until a change of affairs. This fair stranger must have been the original of Drowne's Wooden Image.

Endicott and the Red Cross

(A Tale from *Twice Told Tales* volume 2)

At noon of an autumnal day, more than two centuries ago, the English colours were displayed by the standard-bearer of the Salem trainband, which had mustered for martial exercise under the orders of John Endicott. It was a period, when the religious exiles were accustomed often to buckle on their armour, and practice the handling of their weapons of war. Since the first settlement of New England, its prospects had never been so dismal. The dissensions between Charles the First and his subjects were then, and for several years afterwards, confined to the floor of Parliament.

The measures of the king and ministry were rendered more tyrannically violent by an opposition, which had not yet acquired sufficient confidence in its own strength, to resist royal injustice with the sword. The bigoted and haughty primate, Laud, Archbishop of Canterbury, controlled the religious affairs of the realm, and was consequently invested with powers which might have wrought the utter ruin of the two Puritan colonies, Plymouth and Massachusetts. There is evidence on record, that our forefathers perceived their danger, but were resolved that their infant country should not fall without a struggle, even beneath the giant strength of the king's right arm.

Such was the aspect of the times, when the folds of the English banner, with the Red Cross in its field, were flung out over a company of Puritans. Their leader, the famous Endicott, was a man of stern and resolute countenance, the effect of which was heightened by a grizzled beard that swept the upper portion of his breastplate. This piece of armour was so highly polished, that the whole surrounding scene had its image in the glittering steel. The central object, in the mirrored picture, was an edifice of humble architecture, with neither steeple nor bell to proclaim it,—what nevertheless it was,—the house of prayer.

A token of the perils of the wilderness was seen in the grim head of a wolf, which had just been slain within the precincts of the town, and, according to the regular mode of claiming the bounty, was nailed on the porch of the meetinghouse. The blood was still plashing on the door-step. There happened to be visible, at the same noontide hour, so many other characteristics of the times and manners of the Puritans, that we must endeavour to represent them in a sketch, though far less vividly than they were reflected in the polished breastplate of John Endicott.

In close vicinity to the sacred edifice appeared that important engine of Puritanic authority, the whipping-post,—with the soil around it well trodden by the feet of evil-doers, who had there been disciplined. At one corner of the meetinghouse was the pillory, and at the other the stocks; and, by a singular good fortune for our sketch, the head of an Episcopalian and suspected Catholic was grotesquely encased in the former machine; while a fellow-criminal, who had boisterously quaffed a health to the king, was confined by the legs in the latter. Side by side, on the meetinghouse steps, stood a male and a female figure.

The man was a tall, lean, haggard personification of fanaticism, bearing on his breast this label,—*A WANTON GOSPELLER*,— which betokened that he had dared to give interpretations of Holy Writ, unsanctioned by the infallible judgment of the civil and religious rulers. His aspect showed no lack of zeal to maintain his heterodoxies, even at the stake. The woman wore a cleft stick on her tongue, in appropriate retribution for having wagged that unruly member against the elders of the church; and her countenance and gestures gave much cause to apprehend, that, the moment the stick should be removed a repetition of the offence would demand new ingenuity in chastising it.

The abovementioned individuals had been sentenced to undergo their various modes of ignominy, for the space of one hour at noonday. But among the crowd were several, whose punishment would be life-long; some, whose ears had been cropt, like those of puppy-dogs; others, whose cheeks had been branded with the initials of their misdemeanours; one, with his nostrils slit and seared; and another, with a halter about his neck, which he was forbidden ever to take off, or to conceal beneath his garments. Methinks he must have been grievously tempted to affix the other end of the rope to some convenient beam or bough.

There was likewise a young woman, with no mean share of beauty, whose doom it was to wear the letter A on the breast of her gown, in the eyes of all the world and her own children. And even her own children knew what that initial signified. Sporting with her infamy, the lost and desperate creature had embroidered the fatal token in scarlet cloth, with golden thread, and the nicest art of needle-work; so that the capital A might have been thought to mean Admirable, or anything rather than Adulteress.

Let not the reader argue, from any of these evidences of iniquity, that the times of the Puritans were more vicious than our own, when, as we pass along the very street of this sketch, we discern no badge of infamy on man or woman. It was the policy of our ancestors to search out even the most secret sins, and expose them to shame, without fear or favour, in the broadest light of the noonday sun. Were such the custom now, perchance we might find materials for a no less piquant sketch than the above.

Except the malefactors whom we have described, and the diseased or infirm persons, the whole male population of the town, between sixteen years and sixty, were seen in the ranks of the trainband. A few stately savages, in all the pomp and dignity of the primeval Indian, stood gazing at the spectacle. Their flint-headed arrows were but childish weapons, compared with the matchlocks of the Puritans, and would have rattled harmlessly against the steel caps and hammered iron breastplates, which enclosed each soldier in an individual fortress. The valiant John Endicott glanced with an eye of pride at his sturdy followers, and prepared to renew the martial toils of the day.

"Come, my stout hearts!" quoth he, drawing his sword. "Let us show these poor heathen that we can handle our weapons like men of might. Well for them, if they put us not to prove it in earnest!"

The iron-breasted company straightened their line, and each man drew the heavy butt of his matchlock close to his left foot, thus awaiting the orders of the captain. But, as Endicott glanced right and left along the front, he discovered a personage at some little distance, with whom it behoved him to hold a parley. It was an elderly gentleman, wearing a black cloak and band, and a high-crowned hat, beneath which was a velvet skull-cap, the whole being the garb of a Puritan minister.

This reverend person bore a staff, which seemed to have been recently cut in the forest, and his shoes were bemired, as if he had been travelling on foot through the swamps of the wilderness. His aspect was perfectly that of a pilgrim, heightened also by an apostolic dignity. Just as Endicott perceived him, he laid aside his staff, and stooped to drink at a bubbling fountain, which gushed into the sunshine about a score of yards from the corner of the meetinghouse. But, ere the good man drank, he turned his face heavenward in thankfulness, and then, holding back his gray beard with one hand, he scooped up his simple draught in the hollow of the other.

"What, ho! good Mr. Williams," shouted Endicott. "You are welcome back again to our town of peace. How does our worthy Governor Winthrop? And what news from Boston?"

"The Governor hath his health, worshipful Sir," answered Roger Williams, now resuming his staff, and drawing near. "And, for the news, here is a letter, which, knowing I was to travel hitherward today, his Excellency committed to my charge. Belike it contains tidings of much import; for a ship arrived yesterday from England."

Mr. Williams, the minister of Salem, and of course known to

all the spectators, had now reached the spot where Endicott was standing under the banner of his company, and put the governor's epistle into his hand. The broad seal was impressed with Winthrop's coat of arms. Endicott hastily unclosed the letter, and began to read; while, as his eye passed down the page, a wrathful change came over his manly countenance. The blood glowed through it, till it seemed to be kindling with an internal heat; nor was it unnatural to suppose that his breastplate would likewise become red-hot, with the angry fire of the bosom which it covered Arriving at the conclusion, he shook the letter fiercely in his hand, so that it rustled as loud as the flag above his head.

"Black tidings these, Mr. Williams," said he; "blacker never came to New England. Doubtless you know their purport?"

"Yea, truly," replied Roger Williams; "for the governor consulted, respecting this matter, with my brethren in the ministry at Boston; and my opinion was likewise asked. And his Excellency entreats you by me, that the news be not suddenly noised abroad, lest the people be stirred up unto some outbreak, and thereby give the king and the archbishop a handle against us."

"The governor is a wise man,—a wise man, and a meek and moderate," said Endicott, setting his teeth grimly. "Nevertheless, I must do according to my own best judgment. There is neither man, woman, nor child in New England, but has a concern as dear as life in these tidings; and, if John Endicott's voice be loud enough, man, woman, and child shall hear them. Soldiers, wheel into a hollow square! Ho, good people! Here are news for one and all of you."

The soldiers closed in around their captain; and he and Roger Williams stood together under the banner of the Red Cross; while the women and the aged men pressed forward, and the mothers held up their children to look Endicott in the face. A few taps of the drum gave signal for silence and attention.

"Fellow-soldiers,—fellow-exiles," began Endicott, speaking under strong excitement, yet powerfully restraining it, "wherefore did ye leave your native country? Wherefore, I say, have we left the green and fertile fields, the cottages, or, perchance, the old gray halls, where we were born and bred, the church-yards where our forefathers lie buried? Wherefore have we come hither to set up our own tombstones in a wilderness? A howling wilderness it is! The wolf and the bear meet us within halloo of our dwellings. The savage lieth in wait for us in the dismal shadow of the woods. The stubborn roots of the trees break our ploughshares, when we would till the earth. Our children cry for bread, and we must dig in the sands of the sea-shore to satisfy them. Wherefore, I say again, have we sought this country of a rugged soil and wintry sky; Was it not for the enjoyment of our civil rights? Was it not for liberty to worship God according to our conscience?"

"Call you this liberty of conscience?" interrupted a voice on the steps of the meetinghouse.

It was the Wanton Gospeller. A sad and quiet smile flitted across the mild visage of Roger Williams. But Endicott, in the excitement of the moment, shook his sword wrathfully at the culprit,—an ominous gesture from a man like him.

"What hast thou to do with conscience, thou knave?" cried he. "I said, liberty to worship God, not license to profane and ridicule him. Break not in upon my speech; or I will lay thee neck and heels till this time tomorrow! Hearken to me, friends, nor heed that accursed rhapsodist. As I was saying, we have sacrificed all things, and have come to a land whereof the old world hath scarcely heard, that we might make a new world unto ourselves, and painfully seek a path from hence to Heaven. But what think ye now? This son of a Scotch tyrant,—this grandson of a papistical and adulterous Scotch woman, whose death proved that a golden crown cloth not always save an anointed head from the block—"

"Nay, brother, nay," interposed Mr. Williams; "thy words are not meet for a secret chamber, far less for a public street."

"Hold thy peace, Roger Williams!" answered Endicott, imperiously. "My spirit is wiser than shine, for the business now in hand. I tell ye, fellow-exiles, that Charles of England, and Laud, our bitterest persecutor, arch-priest of Canterbury, are resolute to pursue us even hither. They are taking counsel, saith this letter, to send over a governor-general, in whose breast shall be deposited all the law and equity of the land. They are minded, also, to establish the idolatrous forms of English Episcopacy; so that, when Laud shall kiss the Pope's toe, as cardinal of Rome, he may deliver New England, bound hand and foot, into the power of his master!"

A deep groan from the auditors,—a sound of wrath, as well as fear and sorrow,—responded to this intelligence.

"Look ye to it, brethren," resumed Endicott, with increasing energy. "If this king and this arch-prelate have their will, we shall briefly behold a cross on the spire of this tabernacle which we have builded, and a high altar within its walls, with wax tapers burning round it at noonday. We shall hear the sacring-bell, and the voices of the Romish priests saying the mass. But think ye, Christian men, that these abominations may be suffered without a sword drawn? without a shot fired? without blood spilt, yea, on the very stairs of the pulpit?

"No,—be ye strong of hand, and stout of heart! Here we stand on our soil, which we have bought with our goods, which we have won with our swords, which we have cleared with our axes, which we have tilled with the sweat of our brows, which we have sanctified with our prayers to the God that brought us hither! Who shall enslave us here? What have we to do with this mitred prelate,—with this crowned king? What have we to do with England?"

Endicott gazed round at the excited countenances of the people, now full of his own spirit, and then turned suddenly to the standard-bearer, who stood close behind him.

"Officer, lower your banner!" said he.

The officer obeyed; and, brandishing his sword, Endicott thrust it through the cloth, and, with his left hand, rent the Red Cross completely out of the banner. He then waved the tattered ensign above his head.

"Sacrilegious wretch!" cried the high-churchman in the pillory, unable longer to restrain himself; "thou hast rejected the symbol of our holy religion!"

"Treason, treason!" roared the royalist in the stocks. "He hath defaced the King's banner!"

"Before God and man, I will avouch the deed," answered Endicott. "Beat a flourish, drummer!—shout, soldiers and people!—in honour of the ensign of New England. Neither Pope nor Tyrant hath part in it now!"

With a cry of triumph, the people gave their sanction to one of the boldest exploits which our history records. And, for ever honoured be the name of Endicott! We look back through the mist of ages, and recognize, in the rending of the Red Cross from New England's banner, the first omen of that deliverance which our fathers consummated, after the bones of the stern Puritan had lain more than a century in the dust.

Feathertop: A Moralised Legend
(A tale from *Mosses From an Old Manse and Other Stories*)

"Dickon," cried Mother Rigby, "a coal for my pipe!"

The pipe was in the old dame's mouth when she said these words. She had thrust it there after filling it with tobacco, but without stooping to light it at the hearth, where indeed there was no appearance of a fire having been kindled that morning. Forthwith, however, as soon as the order was given, there was an intense red glow out of the bowl of the pipe, and a whiff of smoke came from Mother Rigby's lips. Whence the coal came, and how brought thither by an invisible hand, I have never been able to discover.

"Good!" quoth Mother Rigby, with a nod of her head. "Thank ye, Dickon! And now for making this scarecrow. Be within call, Dickon, in case I need you again."

The good woman had risen thus early (for as yet it was scarcely sunrise) in order to set about making a scarecrow, which she intended to put in the middle of her corn-patch. It was now the latter week of May, and the crows and blackbirds had already discovered the little, green, rolled-up leaf of the Indian corn just peeping out of the soil. She was determined, therefore, to contrive as lifelike a scarecrow as ever was seen, and to finish it immediately, from top to toe, so that it should begin its sentinel's duty that very morning.

Now Mother Rigby (as everybody must have heard) was one of the most cunning and potent witches in New England, and might, with very little trouble, have made a scarecrow ugly enough to frighten the minister himself. But on this occasion, as she had awakened in an uncommonly pleasant humour, and was further dulcified by her pipe tobacco, she resolved to produce something fine, beautiful, and splendid, rather than hideous and horrible.

"I don't want to set up a hobgoblin in my own corn-patch, and almost at my own doorstep," said Mother Rigby to herself, puffing out a whiff of smoke; "I could do it if I pleased, but I'm tired of doing marvellous things, and so I'll keep within the bounds of every-day business just for variety's sake. Besides, there is no use in scaring the little children for a mile roundabout, though 'tis true I'm a witch."

It was settled, therefore, in her own mind, that the scarecrow should represent a fine gentleman of the period, so far as the materials at hand would allow. Perhaps it may be as well to enumerate the chief of the articles that went to the composition of this figure.

The most important item of all, probably, although it made so little show, was a certain broomstick, on which Mother Rigby had taken many an airy gallop at midnight, and which now served the scarecrow by way of a spinal column, or, as the unlearned phrase it, a backbone. One of its arms was a disabled flail which used to be wielded by Goodman Rigby, before his spouse worried him out of this troublesome world; the other, if I mistake not, was composed of the pudding stick and a broken rung of a chair, tied loosely together at the elbow.

As for its legs, the right was a hoe handle, and the left an undistinguished and miscellaneous stick from the woodpile. Its lungs, stomach, and other affairs of that kind were nothing better than a meal bag stuffed with straw. Thus we have made out the skeleton and entire corporosity of the scarecrow, with the exception of its head; and this was admirably supplied by a somewhat withered and shrivelled pumpkin, in which Mother Rigby cut two holes for the eyes and a slit for the mouth, leaving a bluish-coloured knob in the middle to pass for a nose. It was really quite a respectable face.

"I've seen worse ones on human shoulders, at any rate," said Mother Rigby. "And many a fine gentleman has a pumpkin head, as well as my scarecrow."

But the clothes, in this case, were to be the making of the man. So the good old woman took down from a peg an ancient plum-coloured coat of London make, and with relics of embroidery on its seams, cuffs, pocket-flaps, and button-holes, but lamentably worn and faded, patched at the elbows, tattered at the skirts, and threadbare all over. On the left breast was a round hole, whence either a star of nobility had been rent away, or else the hot heart of some former wearer had scorched it through and through.

The neighbours said that this rich garment belonged to the Black Man's wardrobe, and that he kept it at Mother Rigby's cottage for the convenience of slipping it on whenever he wished to make a grand appearance at the governor's table. To match the coat there was a velvet waistcoat of very ample size, and formerly embroidered with foliage that had been as brightly golden as the maple leaves in October, but which had now quite vanished out of the substance of the velvet. Next came a pair of scarlet breeches, once worn by the French governor of Louisbourg, and the knees of which had touched the lower step of the throne of Louis le Grand. The Frenchman had given these small-clothes to an Indian powwow, who parted with them to the old witch for a gill of strong waters, at one of their dances in the forest.

Furthermore, Mother Rigby produced a pair of silk stockings and put them on the figure's legs, where they showed as unsubstantial as a dream, with the wooden reality of the two sticks making itself miserably apparent through the holes. Lastly, she put her dead husband's wig on the bare scalp of the pumpkin, and surmounted the whole with a dusty three-cornered hat, in which was stuck the longest tail feather of a rooster.

Then the old dame stood the figure up in a corner of her cottage and chuckled to behold its yellow semblance of a visage, with its nobby little nose thrust into the air. It had a strangely self-satisfied aspect, and seemed to say, "Come look at me!"

"And you are well worth looking at, that's a fact!" quoth Mother Rigby, in admiration at her own handiwork. "I've made many a puppet since I've been a witch, but methinks this is the finest of them all. 'Tis almost too good for a scarecrow. And, by the by, I'll just fill a fresh pipe of tobacco and then take him out to the corn-patch."

While filling her pipe the old woman continued to gaze with almost motherly affection at the figure in the corner. To say the truth, whether it were chance, or skill, or downright witchcraft, there was something wonderfully human in this ridiculous shape, bedizened with its tattered finery; and as for the countenance, it appeared to shrivel its yellow surface into a grin—a funny kind of expression betwixt scorn and merriment, as if it understood itself to be a jest at mankind. The more Mother Rigby looked the better she was pleased.

"Dickon," cried she sharply, "another coal for my pipe!"

Hardly had she spoken, then, just as before, there was a red-glowing coal on the top of the tobacco. She drew in a long whiff and puffed it forth again into the bar of morning sunshine which struggled through the one dusty pane of her cottage window. Mother Rigby always liked to flavour her pipe with a coal of fire from the particular chimney corner whence this had been brought. But where that chimney corner might be, or who brought the coal from it,—further than that the invisible messenger seemed to respond to the name of Dickon,—I cannot tell.

"That puppet yonder," thought Mother Rigby, still with her eyes fixed on the scarecrow, "is too good a piece of work to stand all summer in a corn-patch, frightening away the crows and blackbirds. He's capable of better things. Why, I've danced with a worse one, when partners happened to be scarce, at our witch meetings in the forest! What if I should let him take his chance among the other men of straw and empty fellows who go bustling about the world?"

The old witch took three or four more whiffs of her pipe and smiled.

"He'll meet plenty of his brethren at every street corner!" continued she. "Well; I didn't mean to dabble in witchcraft today, further than the lighting of my pipe, but a witch I am, and a witch I'm likely to be, and there's no use trying to shirk it. I'll make a man of my scarecrow, were it only for the joke's sake!"

While muttering these words, Mother Rigby took the pipe from her own mouth and thrust it into the crevice which represented the same feature in the pumpkin visage of the scarecrow.

"Puff, darling, puff!" said she. "Puff away, my fine fellow! your life depends on it!"

This was a strange exhortation, undoubtedly, to be addressed to a mere thing of sticks, straw, and old clothes, with nothing better than a shrivelled pumpkin for a head,—as we know to have been the scarecrow's case. Nevertheless, as we must carefully hold in remembrance, Mother Rigby was a witch of singular power and dexterity; and, keeping this fact duly before our minds, we shall see nothing beyond credibility in the remarkable incidents of our story. Indeed, the great difficulty will be at once got over, if we can only bring ourselves to believe that, as soon as the old dame bade him puff, there came a whiff of smoke from the scarecrow's mouth. It was the very feeblest of whiffs, to be sure; but it was followed by another and another, each more decided than the preceding one.

"Puff away, my pet! puff away, my pretty one!" Mother Rigby kept repeating, with her pleasantest smile. "It is the breath of life to ye; and that you may take my word for."

Beyond all question the pipe was bewitched. There must have been a spell either in the tobacco or in the fiercely-glowing coal that so mysteriously burned on top of it, or in the pungently-aromatic smoke which exhaled from the kindled weed. The figure, after a few doubtful attempts at length blew forth a volley of smoke extending all the way from the obscure corner into the bar of sunshine. There it eddied and melted away among the motes of dust. It seemed a convulsive effort; for the two or three next whiffs were fainter, although the coal still glowed and threw a gleam over the scarecrow's visage.

The old witch clapped her skinny hands together, and smiled encouragingly upon her handiwork. She saw that the charm worked well. The shrivelled, yellow face, which heretofore had been no face at all, had already a thin, fantastic haze, as it were of human likeness, shifting to and fro across it; sometimes vanishing entirely, but growing more perceptible than ever with the next whiff from the pipe. The whole figure, in like manner, assumed a show of life, such as we impart to ill-defined shapes among the clouds, and half deceive ourselves with the pastime of our own fancy.

If we must needs pry closely into the matter, it may be doubted whether there was any real change, after all, in the sordid, worn-out worthless, and ill-jointed substance of the scarecrow; but merely a spectral illusion, and a cunning effect of light and shade so coloured and contrived as to delude the eyes of most men. The miracles of witchcraft seem always to have had a very shallow subtlety; and, at least, if the above explanation do not hit the truth of the process, I can suggest no better.

"Well puffed, my pretty lad!" still cried old Mother Rigby. "Come, another good stout whiff, and let it be with might and main. Puff for thy life, I tell thee! Puff out of the very bottom of thy heart, if any heart thou hast, or any bottom to it! Well done, again! Thou didst suck in that mouthful as if for the pure love of it."

And then the witch beckoned to the scarecrow, throwing so much magnetic potency into her gesture that it seemed as if it must inevitably be obeyed, like the mystic call of the loadstone when it summons the iron.

"Why lurkest thou in the corner, lazy one?" said she. "Step forth! Thou hast the world before thee!"

Upon my word, if the legend were not one which I heard on my grandmother's knee, and which had established its place among things credible before my childish judgment could analyze its probability, I question whether I should have the face to tell it now.

In obedience to Mother Rigby's word, and extending its

arm as if to reach her outstretched hand, the figure made a step forward—a kind of hitch and jerk, however, rather than a step—then tottered and almost lost its balance. What could the witch expect? It was nothing, after all, but a scarecrow stuck upon two sticks. But the strong-willed old *beldam* scowled, and beckoned, and flung the energy of her purpose so forcibly at this poor combination of rotten wood, and musty straw, and ragged garments, that it was compelled to show itself a man, in spite of the reality of things.

So it stepped into the bar of sunshine. There it stood, poor devil of a contrivance that it was!—with only the thinnest vesture of human similitude about it, through which was evident the stiff, rickety, incongruous, faded, tattered, good-for-nothing patchwork of its substance, ready to sink in a heap upon the floor, as conscious of its own unworthiness to be erect. Shall I confess the truth? At its present point of vivification, the scarecrow reminds me of some of the lukewarm and abortive characters, composed of heterogeneous materials, used for the thousandth time, and never worth using, with which romance writers (and myself, no doubt, among the rest) have so overpeopled the world of fiction.

But the fierce old hag began to get angry and show a glimpse of her diabolic nature (like a snake's head, peeping with a hiss out of her bosom), at this pusillanimous behaviour of the thing which she had taken the trouble to put together.

"Puff away, wretch!" cried she, wrathfully. "Puff, puff, puff, thou thing of straw and emptiness! thou rag or two! thou meal bag! thou pumpkin head! thou nothing! Where shall I find a name vile enough to call thee by? Puff, I say, and suck in thy fantastic life with the smoke! else I snatch the pipe from thy mouth and hurl thee where that red coal came from."

Thus threatened, the unhappy scarecrow had nothing for it but to puff away for dear life. As need was, therefore, it applied itself lustily to the pipe, and sent forth such abundant volleys of tobacco smoke that the small cottage kitchen became all vaporous. The one sunbeam struggled mistily through, and could but imperfectly define the image of the cracked and dusty window pane on the opposite wall. Mother Rigby, meanwhile, with one brown arm *akimbo* and the other stretched towards the figure, loomed grimly amid the obscurity with such port and expression as when she was wont to heave a ponderous nightmare on her victims and stand at the bedside to enjoy their agony.

In fear and trembling did this poor scarecrow puff. But its efforts, it must be acknowledged, served an excellent purpose; for, with each successive whiff, the figure lost more and more of its dizzy and perplexing tenuity and seemed to take denser substance. Its very garments, moreover, partook of the magical change, and shone with the gloss of novelty and glistened with the skilfully embroidered gold that had long ago been rent away. And, half revealed among the smoke, a yellow visage bent its lustreless eyes on Mother Rigby.

At last the old witch clinched her fist and shook it at the figure. Not that she was positively angry, but merely acting on the principle—perhaps untrue, or not the only truth, though as high a one as Mother Rigby could be expected to attain—that feeble and torpid natures, being incapable of better inspiration, must be stirred up by fear. But here was the crisis. Should she fail in what she now sought to effect, it was her ruthless purpose to scatter the miserable simulacre into its original elements.

"Thou hast a man's aspect," said she, sternly. "Have also the echo and mockery of a voice! I bid thee speak!"

The scarecrow gasped, struggled, and at length emitted a murmur, which was so incorporated with its smoky breath that you could scarcely tell whether it were indeed a voice or only a whiff of tobacco. Some narrators of this legend hold the opinion that Mother Rigby's conjurations and the fierceness of her will had compelled a familiar spirit into the figure, and that the voice was his.

"Mother," mumbled the poor stifled voice, "be not so awful with me! I would fain speak; but being without wits, what can I say?"

"Thou canst speak, darling, canst thou?" cried Mother Rigby, relaxing her grim countenance into a smile. "And what shalt thou say, quoth-a! Say, indeed! Art thou of the brotherhood of the empty skull, and demandest of me what thou shalt say? Thou shalt say a thousand things, and saying them a thousand times over, thou shalt still have said nothing! Be not afraid, I tell thee! When thou comest into the world (whither I purpose sending thee forthwith) thou shalt not lack the wherewithal to talk. Talk! Why, thou shall babble like a mill-stream, if thou wilt. Thou hast brains enough for that, I trow!"

"At your service, mother," responded the figure.

"And that was well said, my pretty one," answered Mother Rigby. "Then thou speakest like thyself, and meant nothing. Thou shalt have a hundred such set phrases, and five hundred to the boot of them. And now, darling, I have taken so much pains with thee and thou art so beautiful, that, by my troth, I love thee better than any witch's puppet in the world; and I've made them of all sorts—clay, wax, straw, sticks, night fog, morning mist, sea foam, and chimney smoke. But thou art the very best. So give heed to what I say."

"Yes, kind mother," said the figure, "with all my heart!"

"With all thy heart!" cried the old witch, setting her hands to her sides and laughing loudly. "Thou hast such a pretty way of speaking. With all thy heart! And thou didst put thy hand to the left side of thy waistcoat as if thou really hadst one!"

So now, in high good humour with this fantastic contrivance of hers, Mother Rigby told the scarecrow that it must go and play its part in the great world, where not one man in a hundred, she affirmed, was gifted with more real substance than itself. And, that he might hold up his head with the best of them, she endowed him, on the spot, with an unreckonable amount of wealth. It consisted partly of a gold mine in Eldorado, and of ten thousand shares in a broken bubble, and of half a million acres of vineyard at the North Pole, and of a castle in the air, and a chateau in Spain, together with all the rents and income therefrom accruing.

She further made over to him the cargo of a certain ship, laden with salt of Cadiz, which she herself, by her necromantic arts, had caused to founder, ten years before, in the deepest part of mid-ocean. If the salt were not dissolved, and could be brought to market, it would fetch a pretty penny among the fishermen. That he might not lack ready money, she gave him a copper farthing of Birmingham manufacture, being all the coin she had about her, and likewise a great deal of brass, which she applied to his forehead, thus making it yellower than ever.

"With that brass alone," quoth Mother Rigby, "thou canst pay thy way all over the earth. Kiss me, pretty darling! I have done my best for thee."

Furthermore, that the adventurer might lack no possible advantage towards a fair start in life, this excellent old dame gave him a token by which he was to introduce himself to a certain magistrate, member of the council, merchant, and elder of the church (the four capacities constituting but one man), who stood at the head of society in the neighbouring metropolis. The token was neither more nor less than a single word, which Mother Rigby whispered to the scarecrow, and which the scarecrow was to whisper to the merchant.

"Gouty as the old fellow is, he'll run thy errands for thee, when once thou hast given him that word in his ear," said the old witch. "Mother Rigby knows the worshipful Justice Gookin, and the worshipful Justice knows Mother Rigby!"

Here the witch thrust her wrinkled face close to the puppet's, chuckling irrepressibly, and fidgeting all through her system, with delight at the idea which she meant to communicate.

"The worshipful Master Gookin," whispered she, "hath a comely maiden to his daughter. And hark ye, my pet! Thou hast a fair outside, and a pretty wit enough of thine own. Yea, a pretty wit enough! Thou wilt think better of it when thou hast seen more of other people's wits. Now, with thy outside and thy inside, thou art the very man to win a young girl's heart. Never doubt it! I tell thee it shall be so. Put but a bold face on the matter, sigh, smile, flourish thy hat, thrust forth thy leg like a dancing-master, put thy right hand to the left side of thy waistcoat, and pretty Polly Gookin is thine own!"

All this while the new creature had been sucking in and exhaling the vapory fragrance of his pipe, and seemed now to continue this occupation as much for the enjoyment it afforded as because it was an essential condition of his existence. It was wonderful to see how exceedingly like a human being it behaved. Its eyes (for it appeared to possess a pair) were bent on Mother Rigby, and at suitable junctures it nodded or shook its head. Neither did it lack words proper for the occasion: "Really! Indeed! Pray tell me! Is it possible! Upon my word! By no means! Oh! Ah! Hem!" and other such weighty utterances as imply attention, inquiry, acquiescence, or dissent on the part of the auditor.

Even had you stood by and seen the scarecrow made, you could scarcely have resisted the conviction that it perfectly understood the cunning counsels which the old witch poured into its counterfeit of an ear. The more earnestly it applied its lips to the pipe, the more distinctly was its human likeness stamped among visible realities, the more sagacious grew its expression, the more lifelike its gestures and movements, and the more intelligibly audible its voice. Its garments, too, glistened so much the brighter with an illusory magnificence. The very pipe, in which burned the spell of all this wonderwork, ceased to appear as a smoke-blackened earthen stump, and became a meerschaum, with painted bowl and amber mouthpiece.

It might be apprehended, however, that as the life of the illusion seemed identical with the vapor of the pipe, it would terminate simultaneously with the reduction of the tobacco to ashes. But the beldam foresaw the difficulty.

"Hold thou the pipe, my precious one," said she, "while I fill it for thee again."

It was sorrowful to behold how the fine gentleman began to fade back into a scarecrow while Mother Rigby shook the ashes out of the pipe and proceeded to replenish it from her tobacco-box.

"Dickon," cried she, in her high, sharp tone, "another coal

for this pipe!"

No sooner said than the intensely red speck of fire was glow-ing within the pipe-bowl; and the scarecrow, without waiting for the witch's bidding, applied the tube to his lips and drew in a few short, convulsive whiffs, which soon, however, became regular and equable.

"Now, mine own heart's darling," quoth Mother Rigby, "whatever may happen to thee, thou must stick to thy pipe. Thy life is in it; and that, at least, thou knowest well, if thou know-est nought besides. Stick to thy pipe, I say! Smoke, puff, blow thy cloud; and tell the people, if any question be made, that it is for thy health, and that so the physician orders thee to do. And, sweet one, when thou shalt find thy pipe getting low, go apart into some corner, and (first filling thyself with smoke) cry sharply, 'Dickon, a fresh pipe of tobacco!' and, 'Dickon, another coal for my pipe!' and have it into thy pretty mouth as speedily as may be. Else, instead of a gallant gentleman in a gold-laced coat, thou wilt be but a jumble of sticks and tattered clothes, and a bag of straw, and a withered pumpkin! Now depart, my treas-ure, and good luck go with thee!"

"Never fear, mother!" said the figure, in a stout voice, and sending forth a courageous whiff of smoke, "I will thrive, if an honest man and a gentleman may!"

"Oh, thou wilt be the death of me!" cried the old witch, convulsed with laughter. "That was well said. If an honest man and a gentleman may! Thou playest thy part to perfection. Get along with thee for a smart fellow; and I will wager on thy head, as a man of pith and substance, with a brain and what they call a heart, and all else that a man should have, against any other thing on two legs. I hold myself a better witch than yesterday, for thy sake. Did not I make thee? And I defy any witch in New England to make such another! Here; take my staff along with thee!"

The staff, though it was but a plain oaken stick, immediately took the aspect of a gold-headed cane.

"That gold head has as much sense in it as thine own," said

Mother Rigby, "and it will guide thee straight to worshipful Master Gookin's door. Get thee gone, my pretty pet, my darling, my precious one, my treasure; and if any ask thy name, it is Feathertop. For thou hast a feather in thy hat, and I have thrust a handful of feathers into the hollow of thy head, and thy wig, too, is of the fashion they call Feathertop,—so be Feathertop thy name!"

And, issuing from the cottage, Feathertop strode manfully towards town. Mother Rigby stood at the threshold, well pleased to see how the sunbeams glistened on him, as if all his magnificence were real, and how diligently and lovingly he smoked his pipe, and how handsomely he walked, in spite of a little stiffness of his legs. She watched him until out of sight, and threw a witch benediction after her darling, when a turn of the road snatched him from her view.

Betimes in the forenoon, when the principal street of the neighbouring town was just at its acme of life and bustle, a stranger of very distinguished figure was seen on the sidewalk. His port as well as his garments betokened nothing short of nobility. He wore a richly-embroidered plum-coloured coat, a waistcoat of costly velvet, magnificently adorned with golden foliage, a pair of splendid scarlet breeches, and the finest and glossiest of white silk stockings. His head was covered with a peruke, so daintily powdered and adjusted that it would have been sacrilege to disorder it with a hat; which, therefore (and it was a gold-laced hat, set off with a snowy feather), he carried beneath his arm.

On the breast of his coat glistened a star. He managed his gold-headed cane with an airy grace, peculiar to the fine gentlemen of the period; and, to give the highest possible finish to his equipment, he had lace ruffles at his wrist, of a most ethereal delicacy, sufficiently avouching how idle and aristocratic must be the hands which they half concealed.

It was a remarkable point in the accoutrement of this brilliant personage that he held in his left hand a fantastic kind of a pipe, with an exquisitely painted bowl and an amber mouthpiece.

This he applied to his lips as often as every five or six paces, and inhaled a deep whiff of smoke, which, after being retained a moment in his lungs, might be seen to eddy gracefully from his mouth and nostrils.

As may well be supposed, the street was all astir to find out the stranger's name.

"It is some great nobleman, beyond question," said one of the townspeople. "Do you see the star at his breast?"

"Nay; it is too bright to be seen," said another. "Yes; he must needs be a nobleman, as you say. But by what conveyance, think you, can his lordship have voyaged or travelled hither? There has been no vessel from the old country for a month past; and if he have arrived overland from the southward, pray where are his attendants and equipage?"

"He needs no equipage to set off his rank," remarked a third. "If he came among us in rags, nobility would shine through a hole in his elbow. I never saw such dignity of aspect. He has the old Norman blood in his veins, I warrant him."

"I rather take him to be a Dutchman, or one of your high Germans," said another citizen. "The men of those countries have always the pipe at their mouths."

"And so has a Turk," answered his companion. "But, in my judgment, this stranger hath been bred at the French court, and hath there learned politeness and grace of manner, which none understand so well as the nobility of France. That gait, now! A vulgar spectator might deem it stiff—he might call it a hitch and jerk—but, to my eye, it hath an unspeakable majesty, and must have been acquired by constant observation of the deportment of the Grand Monarque. The stranger's character and office are evident enough. He is a French ambassador, come to treat with our rulers about the cession of Canada."

"More probably a Spaniard," said another, "and hence his yellow complexion; or, most likely, he is from the Havana, or from some port on the Spanish main, and comes to make investigation about the piracies which our government is thought to connive at. Those settlers in Peru and Mexico have skins as yellow as the gold which they dig out of their mines."

"Yellow or not," cried a lady, "he is a beautiful man!—so tall, so slender! such a fine, noble face, with so well-shaped a nose, and all that delicacy of expression about the mouth! And, bless me, how bright his star is! It positively shoots out flames!"

"So do your eyes, fair lady," said the stranger, with a bow and a flourish of his pipe; for he was just passing at the instant. "Upon my honor, they have quite dazzled me."

"Was ever so original and exquisite a compliment?" murmured the lady, in an ecstasy of delight.

Amid the general admiration excited by the stranger's appearance, there were only two dissenting voices. One was that of an impertinent cur, which, after snuffing at the heels of the glistening figure, put its tail between its legs and skulked into its master's back yard, vociferating an execrable howl. The other dissentient was a young child, who squalled at the fullest stretch of his lungs, and babbled some unintelligible nonsense about a pumpkin.

Feathertop meanwhile pursued his way along the street. Except for the few complimentary words to the lady, and now and then a slight inclination of the head in requital of the profound reverences of the bystanders, he seemed wholly absorbed in his pipe. There needed no other proof of his rank and consequence than the perfect equanimity with which he comported himself, while the curiosity and admiration of the town swelled almost into clamour around him. With a crowd gathering behind his footsteps, he finally reached the mansion-house of the worshipful Justice Gookin, entered the gate, ascended the steps of the front door, and knocked. In the interim, before his summons was answered, the stranger was observed to shake the ashes out of his pipe.

"What did he say in that sharp voice?" inquired one of the spectators.

"Nay, I know not," answered his friend. "But the sun dazzles my eyes strangely. How dim and faded his lordship looks all of a sudden! Bless my wits, what is the matter with me?"

"The wonder is," said the other, "that his pipe, which was out only an instant ago, should be all alight again, and with the reddest coal I ever saw. There is something mysterious about this stranger. What a whiff of smoke was that! Dim and faded did you call him? Why, as he turns about the star on his breast is all ablaze."

"It is, indeed," said his companion; "and it will go near to dazzle pretty Polly Gookin, whom I see peeping at it out of the chamber window."

The door being now opened, Feathertop turned to the crowd, made a stately bend of his body like a great man acknowledging the reverence of the meaner sort, and vanished into the house. There was a mysterious kind of a smile, if it might not better be called a grin or grimace, upon his visage; but, of all the throng that beheld him, not an individual appears to have possessed insight enough to detect the illusive character of the stranger except a little child and a cur dog.

Our legend here loses somewhat of its continuity, and, passing over the preliminary explanation between Feathertop and the merchant, goes in quest of the pretty Polly Gookin. She was a damsel of a soft, round figure, with light hair and blue eyes, and a fair, rosy face, which seemed neither very shrewd nor very simple. This young lady had caught a glimpse of the glistening stranger while standing on the threshold, and had forthwith put on a laced cap, a string of beads, her finest kerchief, and her stiffest damask petticoat in preparation for the interview. Hurrying from her chamber to the parlour, she had ever since been viewing herself in the large looking-glass and practising pretty airs—now a smile, now a ceremonious dignity of aspect, and now a softer smile than the former, kissing her hand likewise, tossing her head, and managing her fan; while within the mirror an unsubstantial little maid repeated every gesture and did all the foolish things that Polly did, but without making her ashamed of them.

In short, it was the fault of pretty Polly's ability rather than her will if she failed to be as complete an artifice as the illustrious Feathertop himself; and, when she thus tampered with her own simplicity, the witch's phantom might well hope to win her.

No sooner did Polly hear her father's gouty footsteps approaching the parlour door, accompanied with the stiff clatter of Feathertop's high-heeled shoes, than she seated herself bolt upright and innocently began warbling a song.

"Polly! daughter Polly!" cried the old merchant. "Come hither, child."

Master Gookin's aspect, as he opened the door, was doubtful and troubled.

"This gentleman," continued he, presenting the stranger, "is the Chevalier Feathertop,—nay, I beg his pardon, my Lord Feathertop,—who hath brought me a token of remembrance from an ancient friend of mine. Pay your duty to his lordship, child, and honour him as his quality deserves."

After these few words of introduction, the worshipful magistrate immediately quitted the room. But, even in that brief moment, had the fair Polly glanced aside at her father instead of devoting herself wholly to the brilliant guest, she might have taken warning of some mischief nigh at hand. The old man was nervous, fidgety, and very pale. Purposing a smile of courtesy, he had deformed his face with a sort of galvanic grin, which, when Feathertop's back was turned, he exchanged for a scowl, at the same time shaking his fist and stamping his gouty foot—an incivility which brought its retribution along with it. The truth appears to have been that Mother Rigby's word of introduction, whatever it might be, had operated far more on the rich merchant's fears than on his good will.

Moreover, being a man of wonderfully acute observation, he had noticed that these painted figures on the bowl of Feathertop's pipe were in motion. Looking more closely he became convinced that these figures were a party of little demons, each duly provided with horns and a tail, and dancing hand in hand, with gestures of diabolical merriment, round the circumference of the pipe bowl. As if to confirm his suspicions, while Master

Gookin ushered his guest along a dusky passage from his private room to the parlour, the star on Feathertop's breast had scintillated actual flames, and threw a flickering gleam upon the wall, the ceiling, and the floor.

With such sinister prognostics manifesting themselves on all hands, it is not to be marvelled at that the merchant should have felt that he was committing his daughter to a very questionable acquaintance. He cursed, in his secret soul, the insinuating elegance of Feathertop's manners, as this brilliant personage bowed, smiled, put his hand on his heart, inhaled a long whiff from his pipe, and enriched the atmosphere with the smoky vapor of a fragrant and visible sigh. Gladly would poor Master Gookin have thrust his dangerous guest into the street; but there was a constraint and terror within him. This respectable old gentleman, we fear, at an earlier period of life, had given some pledge or other to the evil principle, and perhaps was now to redeem it by the sacrifice of his daughter.

It so happened that the parlour door was partly of glass, shaded by a silken curtain, the folds of which hung a little awry. So strong was the merchant's interest in witnessing what was to ensue between the fair Polly and the gallant Feathertop that, after quitting the room, he could by no means refrain from peeping through the crevice of the curtain.

But there was nothing very miraculous to be seen; nothing—except the trifles previously noticed—to confirm the idea of a supernatural peril environing the pretty Polly. The stranger it is true was evidently a thorough and practised man of the world, systematic and self-possessed, and therefore the sort of a person to whom a parent ought not to confide a simple, young girl without due watchfulness for the result. The worthy magistrate who had been conversant with all degrees and qualities of mankind, could not but perceive every motion and gesture of the distinguished Feathertop came in its proper place; nothing had been left rude or native in him; a well-digested conventionalism had incorporated itself thoroughly with his substance and transformed him into a work of art.

Perhaps it was this peculiarity that invested him with a species of ghastliness and awe. It is the effect of anything completely and consummately artificial, in human shape, that the person impresses us as an unreality and as having hardly pith enough to cast a shadow upon the floor. As regarded Feathertop, all this resulted in a wild, extravagant, and fantastical impression, as if his life and being were akin to the smoke that curled upward from his pipe.

But pretty Polly Gookin felt not thus. The pair were now promenading the room: Feathertop with his dainty stride and no less dainty grimace, the girl with a native maidenly grace, just touched, not spoiled, by a slightly affected manner, which seemed caught from the perfect artifice of her companion. The longer the interview continued, the more charmed was pretty Polly, until, within the first quarter of an hour (as the old magistrate noted by his watch), she was evidently beginning to be in love. Nor need it have been witchcraft that subdued her in such a hurry; the poor child's heart, it may be, was so very fervent that it melted her with its own warmth as reflected from the hollow semblance of a lover.

No matter what Feathertop said, his words found depth and reverberation in her ear; no matter what he did, his action was heroic to her eye. And by this time it is to be supposed there was a blush on Polly's cheek, a tender smile about her mouth and a liquid softness in her glance; while the star kept coruscating on Feathertop's breast, and the little demons careered with more frantic merriment than ever about the circumference of his pipe bowl. O pretty Polly Gookin, why should these imps rejoice so madly that a silly maiden's heart was about to be given to a shadow! Is it so unusual a misfortune, so rare a triumph?

By and by Feathertop paused, and throwing himself into an imposing attitude, seemed to summon the fair girl to survey his figure and resist him longer if she could. His star, his embroidery, his buckles glowed at that instant with unutterable splendor; the picturesque hues of his attire took a richer depth of colouring; there was a gleam and polish over his whole presence betokening the perfect witchery of well-ordered manners. The maiden raised her eyes and suffered them to linger upon her companion with a bashful and admiring gaze. Then, as if desirous of judging what value her own simple comeliness might have side by side with so much brilliancy, she cast a glance towards the full-length looking-glass in front of which they happened to be standing. It was one of the truest plates in the world and incapable of flattery.

No sooner did the images therein reflected meet Polly's eye than she shrieked, shrank from the stranger's side, gazed at him for a moment in the wildest dismay, and sank insensible upon the floor. Feathertop likewise had looked towards the mirror, and there beheld, not the glittering mockery of his outside show, but a picture of the sordid patchwork of his real composition stripped of all witchcraft.

The wretched simulacrum! We almost pity him. He threw up his arms with an expression of despair that went further than any of his previous manifestations towards vindicating his claims to be reckoned human, for perchance the only time since this so often empty and deceptive life of mortals began its course, an illusion had seen and fully recognized itself.

Mother Rigby was seated by her kitchen hearth in the twilight of this eventful day, and had just shaken the ashes out of a new pipe, when she heard a hurried tramp along the road. Yet it did not seem so much the tramp of human footsteps as the clatter of sticks or the rattling of dry bones.

"Ha!" thought the old witch, "what step is that? Whose skeleton is out of its grave now, I wonder?"

A figure burst headlong into the cottage door. It was Feathertop! His pipe was still alight; the star still flamed upon his breast; the embroidery still glowed upon his garments; nor had he lost, in any degree or manner that could be estimated, the aspect that assimilated him with our mortal brotherhood. But yet, in some indescribable way (as is the case with all that has deluded us when once found out), the poor reality was felt beneath the cunning artifice.

"What has gone wrong?" demanded the witch. "Did yonder sniffling hypocrite thrust my darling from his door? The villain! I'll set twenty fiends to torment him till he offer thee his daughter on his bended knees!"

"No, mother," said Feathertop despondingly; "it was not that."

"Did the girl scorn my precious one?" asked Mother Rigby, her fierce eyes glowing like two coals of Tophet. "I'll cover her face with pimples! Her nose shall be as red as the coal in thy pipe! Her front teeth shall drop out! In a week hence she shall not be worth thy having!"

"Let her alone, mother," answered poor Feathertop; "the girl was half won; and methinks a kiss from her sweet lips might have made me altogether human. But," he added, after a brief pause and then a howl of self-contempt, "I've seen myself, mother! I've seen myself for the wretched, ragged, empty thing I am! I'll exist no longer!"

Snatching the pipe from his mouth, he flung it with all his might against the chimney, and at the same instant sank upon the floor, a medley of straw and tattered garments, with some sticks protruding from the heap, and a shrivelled pumpkin in the midst. The eyeholes were now lustreless; but the rudely-carved gap, that just before had been a mouth still seemed to twist itself into a despairing grin, and was so far human.

"Poor fellow!" quoth Mother Rigby, with a rueful glance at the relics of her ill-fated contrivance. "My poor, dear, pretty Feathertop! There are thousands upon thousands of coxcombs and charlatans in the world, made up of just such a jumble of worn-out, forgotten, and good-for-nothing trash as he was! Yet they live in fair repute, and never see themselves for what they are. And why should my poor puppet be the only one to know himself and perish for it?"

While thus muttering, the witch had filled a fresh pipe of tobacco, and held the stem between her fingers, as doubtful whether to thrust it into her own mouth or Feathertop's.

"Poor Feathertop!" she continued. "I could easily give him

another chance and send him forth again tomorrow. But no; his feelings are too tender, his sensibilities too deep. He seems to have too much heart to bustle for his own advantage in such an empty and heartless world. Well! well! I'll make a scarecrow of him after all. 'Tis an innocent and useful vocation, and will suit my darling well; and, if each of his human brethren had as fit a one, 't would be the better for mankind; and as for this pipe of tobacco, I need it more than he."

So saying Mother Rigby put the stem between her lips. "Dickon!" cried she, in her high, sharp tone, "another coal for my pipe!"

Earth's Holocaust

(A tale from *Mosses From an Old Manse and Other Stories*)

Once upon a time—but whether in the time past or time to come is a matter of little or no moment—this wide world had become so overburdened with an accumulation of worn-out trumpery that the inhabitants determined to rid themselves of it by a general bonfire. The site fixed upon at the representation of the insurance companies, and as being as central a spot as any other on the globe, was one of the broadest prairies of the West, where no human habitation would be endangered by the flames, and where a vast assemblage of spectators might commodiously admire the show. Having a taste for sights of this kind, and imagining, likewise, that the illumination of the bonfire might reveal some profundity of moral truth heretofore hidden in mist or darkness, I made it convenient to journey thither and be present.

At my arrival, although the heap of condemned rubbish was as yet comparatively small, the torch had already been applied. Amid that boundless plain, in the dusk of the evening, like a far off star alone in the firmament, there was merely visible one tremulous gleam, whence none could have anticipated so fierce a blaze as was destined to ensue. With every moment, however, there came foot travellers, women holding up their aprons, men on horseback, wheelbarrows, lumbering baggage wagons, and other vehicles, great and small, and from far and near laden with articles that were judged fit for nothing but to be burned.

"What materials have been used to kindle the flame?" inquired I of a bystander; for I was desirous of knowing the whole process of the affair from beginning to end.

The person whom I addressed was a grave man, fifty years old or thereabout, who had evidently come thither as a looker on. He struck me immediately as having weighed for himself the true value of life and its circumstances, and therefore as feeling little personal interest in whatever judgement the world might form of them. Before answering my question, he looked me in the face by the kindling light of the fire.

"Oh, some very dry combustibles," replied he, "and extremely suitable to the purpose—no other, in fact, than yesterday's newspapers, last month's magazines, and last year's withered leaves. Here now comes some antiquated trash that will take fire like a handful of shavings."

As he spoke some rough-looking men advanced to the verge of the bonfire, and threw in, as it appeared, all the rubbish of the herald's office—the blazonry of coat armour, the crests and devices of illustrious families, pedigrees that extended back, like lines of light, into the mist of the dark ages, together with stars, garters, and embroidered collars, each of which, as paltry a bauble as it might appear to the uninstructed eye, had once possessed vast significance, and was still, in truth, reckoned among the most precious of moral or material facts by the worshippers of the gorgeous past. Mingled with this confused heap, which was tossed into the flames by armfuls at once, were innumerable badges of knighthood, comprising those of all the European sovereignties, and Napoleon's decoration of the Legion of Honour, the ribbons of which were entangled with those of the ancient order of St. Louis.

There, too, were the medals of our own society of Cincinnati, by means of which, as history tells us, an order of hereditary knights came near *being* constituted out of the king quellers of the revolution. And besides, there were the patents of nobility of German counts and barons, Spanish grandees, and English peers, from the worm-eaten instruments signed by William the Conqueror down to the bran new parchment of the latest lord who has received his honours from the fair hand of Victoria.

At sight of the dense volumes of smoke, mingled with vivid jets of flame, that gushed and eddied forth from this immense pile of earthly distinctions, the multitude of plebeian spectators set up a joyous shout, and clapped their hands with an emphasis that made the welkin echo. That was their moment of triumph, achieved, after long ages, over creatures of the same clay and the same spiritual infirmities, who had dared to assume the privileges due only to Heaven's better workmanship. But now there rushed towards the blazing heap a gray haired man, of stately presence, wearing a coat, from the breast of which a star, or other badge of rank, seemed to have been forcibly wrenched away. He had not the tokens of intellectual power in his face; but still there was the demeanour, the habitual and almost native dignity, of one who had been born to the idea of his own social superiority, and had never felt it questioned till that moment.

"People," cried he, gazing at the ruin of what was dearest to his eyes with grief and wonder, but nevertheless with a degree of stateliness,—"people, what have you done? This fire is consuming all that marked your advance from barbarism, or that could have prevented your relapse thither. We, the men of the privileged orders, were those who kept alive from age to age the old chivalrous spirit; the gentle and generous thought; the higher, the purer, the more refined and delicate life. With the nobles, too, you cast off the poet, the painter, the sculptor—all the beautiful arts; for we were their patrons, and created the atmosphere in which they flourish. In abolishing the majestic distinctions of rank, society loses not only its grace, but its steadfastness"—

More he would doubtless have spoken; but here there arose an outcry, sportive, contemptuous, and indignant, that altogether drowned the appeal of the fallen nobleman, insomuch that, casting one look of despair at his own half-burned pedigree, he shrunk back into the crowd, glad to shelter himself under his new-found insignificance.

"Let him thank his stars that we have not flung him into the same fire!" shouted a rude figure, spurning the embers with his foot. "And henceforth let no man dare to show a piece of musty parchment as his warrant for lording it over his fellows. If he have strength of arm, well and good; it is one species of superiority. If he have wit, wisdom, courage, force of character, let these attributes do for him what they may; but from this day forward no mortal must hope for place and consideration by reckoning up the mouldy bones of his ancestors. That nonsense is done away."

"And in good time," remarked the grave observer by my side, in a low voice, however, "if no worse nonsense comes in its place; but, at all events, this species of nonsense has fairly lived out its life."

There was little space to muse or moralize over the embers of this time-honoured rubbish; for, before it was half burned out, there came another multitude from beyond the sea, bearing the purple robes of royalty, and the crowns, globes, and sceptres of emperors and kings. All these had been condemned as useless baubles, playthings at best, fit only for the infancy of the world or rods to govern and chastise it in its non-age, but with which universal manhood at its full-grown stature could no longer brook to be insulted. Into such contempt had these regal insignia now fallen that the gilded crown and tinselled robes of the player king from Drury Lane Theatre had been thrown in among the rest, doubtless as a mockery of his brother monarchs on the great stage of the world.

It was a strange sight to discern the crown jewels of England glowing and flashing in the midst of the fire. Some of them had been delivered down from the time of the Saxon princes; others were purchased with vast revenues, or perchance ravished from the dead brows of the native potentates of Hindostan; and the whole now blazed with a dazzling lustre, as if a star had fallen in that spot and been shattered into fragments. The splendour of the ruined monarchy had no reflection save in those inestimable precious stones. But enough on this subject. It were but tedious to describe how the Emperor of Austria's mantle was converted to tinder, and how the posts and pillars of the French throne became a heap of coals, which it was impossible to distinguish from those of any other wood. Let me add, however, that I noticed one of the exiled Poles stirring up the bonfire with the Czar of Russians sceptre, which he afterwards flung into the flames.

"The smell of singed garments is quite intolerable here," observed my new acquaintance, as the breeze enveloped us in the smoke of a royal wardrobe. "Let us get to windward and see what they are doing on the other side of the bonfire."

We accordingly passed around, and were just in time to witness the arrival of a vast procession of Washingtonians,—as the votaries of temperance call themselves nowadays,—accompanied by thousands of the Irish disciples of Father Mathew, with that great apostle at their head. They brought a rich contribution to the bonfire—being nothing less than all the hogsheads and barrels of liquor in the world, which they rolled before them across the prairie.

"Now, my children," cried Father Mathew, when they reached the verge of the fire, "one shove more, and the work is done. And now let us stand off and see Satan deal with his own liquor."

Accordingly, having placed their wooden vessels within reach of the flames, the procession stood off at a safe distance, and soon beheld them burst into a blaze that reached the clouds and threatened to set die sky itself on fire. And well it might; for here was the whole world's stock of spirituous liquors, which, instead of kindling a frenzied light in the eyes of individual topers as of yore, soared upwards with a bewildering gleam that startled all mankind. It was the aggregate of that fierce fire which would otherwise have scorched the hearts of millions.

Meantime numberless bottles of precious wine were flung into the blaze, which lapped up the contents as if it loved them, and grew, like other drunkards, the merrier and fiercer for what it quaffed. Never again will the insatiable thirst of the fire fiend be so pampered. Here were the treasures of famous *bon vivants*—liquors that had been tossed on ocean, and mellowed in the sun, and hoarded long in the recesses of the earth—the pale, the gold, the ruddy juice of whatever vineyards were most delicate—the entire vintage of Tokay—all mingling in one stream with the vile fluids of the common pothouse, and contributing to heighten the selfsame blaze. And while it rose in a gigantic spire that seemed to wave against the arch of the firmament and combine itself with the light of stars, the multitude gave a shout as if the broad earth were exulting in its deliverance from the curse of ages.

But the joy was not universal. Many deemed that human life would be gloomier than ever when that brief illumination should sink down. While the reformers were at work, I overheard muttered expostulations from several respectable gentlemen with red noses and wearing gouty shoes; and a ragged worthy, whose face looked like a hearth where the fire is burned out, now expressed his discontent more openly and boldly.

"What is this world good for," said the last toper, "now that we can never be jolly anymore? What is to comfort the poor man in sorrow and perplexity? How is he to keep his heart warm against the cold winds of this cheerless earth? And what do you propose to give him in exchange for the solace that you take away? How are old friends to sit together by the fireside without a cheerful glass between them? A plague upon your reformation! It is a sad world, a cold world, a selfish world, a low world, not worth an honest fellow's living in, now that good fellowship is gone forever!"

This harangue excited great mirth among the bystanders; but, preposterous as was the sentiment, I could not help commiserating the forlorn condition of the last toper, whose boon companions had dwindled away from his side, leaving the poor fellow without a soul to countenance him in sipping his liquor, nor indeed any liquor to sip. Not that this was quite the true state of the case; for I had observed him at a critical moment filch a bottle of fourth-proof brandy that fell beside the bonfire and hide it in his pocket.

The spirituous and fermented liquors being thus disposed of, the zeal of the reformers next induced them to replenish the fire with all the boxes of tea and bags of coffee in the world.

And now came the planters of Virginia, bringing their crops and tobacco. These, being cast upon the heap of inutility, aggregated it to the size of a mountain, and incensed the atmosphere with such potent fragrance that methought we should never draw pure breath again. The present sacrifice seemed to startle the lovers of the weed more than any that they had hitherto witnessed.

"Well, they've put my pipe out," said an old gentleman flinging it into the flames in a pet. "What is this world coming to? Everything rich and racy—all the spice of life—is to be condemned as useless. Now that they have kindled the bonfire, if these nonsensical reformers would fling themselves into it, all would be well enough!"

"Be patient," responded a stanch conservative; "it will come to that in the end. They will first fling us in, and finally themselves."

From the general and systematic measures of reform I now turned to consider the individual contributions to this memorable bonfire. In many instances these were of a very amusing character. One poor fellow threw in his empty purse, and another a bundle of counterfeit or insolvable bank notes. Fashionable ladies threw in their last season's bonnets, together with heaps of ribbons, yellow lace, and much other half-worn milliner's ware, all of which proved even more evanescent in the fire than it had been in the fashion. A multitude of lovers of both sexes—discarded maids or bachelors and couples mutually weary of one another—tossed in bundles of perfumed letters and enamoured sonnets.

A hack politician, being deprived of bread by the loss of office, threw in his teeth, which happened to be false ones. The Rev. Sydney Smith—having voyaged across the Atlantic for that sole purpose—came up to the bonfire with a bitter grin and threw in certain repudiated bonds, fortified though they were with the broad seal of a sovereign state. A little boy of five years old, in the premature manliness of the present epoch, threw in his playthings; a college graduate his diploma; an apothecary, ruined by the spread of homeopathy, his whole stock of drugs and medicines; a physician his library; a parson his old sermons; and a fine gentleman of the old school his code of manners, which he had formerly written down for the benefit of the next generation.

A widow, resolving on a second marriage, slyly threw in her dead husband's miniature. A young man, jilted by his mistress, would willingly have flung his own desperate heart into the flames, but could find no means to wrench it out of his bosom. An American author, whose works were neglected by the public, threw his pen and paper into the bonfire, and betook himself to some less discouraging occupation. It somewhat startled me to overhear a number of ladies, highly respectable in appearance, proposing to fling their gowns and petticoats into the flames, and assume the garb, together with the manners, duties, offices, and responsibilities, of the opposite sex.

What favour was accorded to this scheme I am unable to say, my attention being suddenly drawn to a poor, deceived, and half-delirious girl, who, exclaiming that she was the most worthless thing alive or dead, attempted to cast herself into the fire amid all that wrecked and broken trumpery of the world. A good man, however, ran to her rescue.

"Patience, my poor girl!" said he, as he drew her back from the fierce embrace of the destroying angel. "Be patient, and abide Heaven's will. So long as you possess a living soul, all may be restored to its first freshness. These things of matter and creations of human fantasy are fit for nothing but to be burned when once they have had their day; but your day is eternity!"

"Yes," said the wretched girl, whose frenzy seemed now to have sunk down into deep despondency,—"yes and the sunshine is blotted out of it!"

It was now rumoured among the spectators that all the weapons and munitions of war were to be thrown into the bonfire, with the exception of the world's stock of gunpowder, which, as the safest mode of disposing of it, had already 'been drowned in the sea. This intelligence seemed to awaken great diversity of opinion. The hopeful philanthropist esteemed it a token that the millennium was already come; while persons of another stamp, in whose view mankind was a breed of bulldogs, prophesied that all the old stoutness, fervour, nobleness, generosity, and magnanimity of the race would disappear,—these qualities, as they affirmed, requiring blood for their nourishment. They comforted themselves, however, in the belief that the proposed abolition of war was impracticable for any length of time together.

Be that as it might, numberless great guns, whose thunder had long been the voice of battle,—the artillery of the Armada, the battering trains of Marlborough, and the adverse cannon of Napoleon and Wellington,—were trundled into the midst of the fire. By the continual addition of dry combustibles, it had now waxed so intense that neither brass nor iron could withstand it. It was wonderful to behold how these terrible instruments of slaughter melted away like playthings of wax. Then the armies of the earth wheeled around the mighty furnace, with their military music playing triumphant marches, and flung in their muskets and swords. The standard-bearers, likewise, cast one look upward at their banners, all tattered with shot holes and inscribed with the names of victorious fields; and, giving them a last flourish on the breeze, they lowered them into the flame, which snatched them upward in its rush towards the clouds.

This ceremony being over, the world was left without a single weapon in its hands, except possibly a few old king's arms and rusty swords and other trophies of the Revolution in some of our state armouries. And now the drums were beaten and the trumpets brayed all together, as a prelude to the proclamation of universal and eternal peace and the announcement that glory was no longer to be won by blood, but that it would henceforth be the contention of the human race to work out the greatest mutual good, and that beneficence, in the future annals of the earth, would claim the praise of valour. The blessed tidings were accordingly promulgated, and caused infinite rejoicings among those who had stood aghast at the horror and absurdity of war.

But I saw a grim smile pass over the seared visage of a stately old commander,—by his war-worn figure and rich military dress, he might have been one of Napoleon's famous marshals,—who, with the rest of the world's soldiery, had just flung away the sword that had been familiar to his right hand for half a century.

"Ay! Ay!" grumbled he. "Let them proclaim what they please; but, in the end, we shall find that all this foolery has only made more work for the armorers and cannon founders."

"Why, sir," exclaimed I, in astonishment, "do you imagine that the human race will ever so far return on the steps of its past madness as to weld another sword or cast another cannon?"

"There will be no need," observed, with a sneer, one who neither felt benevolence nor had faith in it. "When Cain wished to slay his brother, he was at no loss for a weapon."

"We shall see," replied the veteran commander. "If I am mistaken, so much the better; but in my opinion, without pretending to philosophize about the matter, the necessity of war lies far deeper than these honest gentlemen suppose. What! is there a field for all the petty disputes of individuals? and shall there be no great law court for the settlement of national difficulties? The battlefield is the only court where such suits can be tried."

"You forget, general," rejoined I, "that, in this advanced stage of civilization. Reason and Philanthropy combined will constitute just such a tribunal as is requisite."

"Ah, I had forgotten that, indeed!" said the old warrior, as he limped away.

The fire was now to be replenished with materials that had hitherto been considered of even greater importance to the well being of society than the warlike munitions which we had already seen consumed. A body of reformers had travelled all over the earth in quest of the machinery by which the different nations were accustomed to inflict the punishment of death. A shudder passed through the multitude as these ghastly emblems were dragged forward. Even the flames seemed at first to shrink away, displaying the shape and murderous contrivance of each in a full blaze of light, which of itself was sufficient to convince mankind of the long and deadly error of human law.

Those old implements of cruelty; those horrible monsters of mechanism; those inventions which seemed to demand something worse than man's natural heart to contrive, and which had lurked in the dusky nooks of ancient prisons, the subject of terror-stricken legend,—were now brought forth to view. Headsmen's axes, with the rust of noble and royal blood upon them, and a vast collection of halters that had choked the breath of plebeian victims, were thrown in together. A shout greeted the arrival of the guillotine, which was thrust forward on the same wheels that had borne it from one to another of the bloodstained streets of Paris.

But the loudest roar of applause went up, telling the distant sky of the triumph of the earth's redemption, when the gallows made its appearance. An ill-looking fellow, however, rushed forward, and, putting himself in the path of the reformers, bellowed hoarsely, and fought with brute fury to stay their progress.

It was little matter of surprise, perhaps, that the executioner should thus do his best to vindicate and uphold the machinery by which he himself had his livelihood and worthier individuals their death; but it deserved special note that men of a far different sphere—even of that consecrated class in whose guardianship the world is apt to trust its benevolence—were found to take the hangman's view of the question.

"Stay, my brethren!" cried one of them. "You are misled by a false philanthropy; you know not what you do. The gallows is a Heaven-ordained instrument. Bear it back, then, reverently, and set it up in its old place, else the world will fall to speedy ruin and desolation!"

"Onward! onward!" shouted a leader in the reform. "Into the flames with the accursed instrument of man's blood policy! How can human law inculcate benevolence and love while it persists in setting up the gallows as its chief symbol? One heave more, good friends, and the world will be redeemed from its greatest error."

A thousand hands, that nevertheless loathed the touch, now

lent their assistance, and thrust the ominous burden far, far into the centre of the raging furnace. There its fatal and abhorred image was beheld, first black, then a red coal, then ashes.

"That was well done!" exclaimed I.

"Yes, it was well done," replied, but with less enthusiasm than I expected, the thoughtful observer who was still at my side; "well done, if the world be good enough for the measure. Death, however, is an idea that cannot easily be dispensed with in any condition between the primal innocence and that other purity and perfection which perchance we are destined to attain after travelling round the full circle; but, at all events, it is well that the experiment should now be tried."

"Too cold! too cold!" impatiently exclaimed the young and ardent leader in this triumph. "Let the heart have its voice here as well as the intellect. And as for ripeness, and as for progress, let mankind always do the highest, kindest, noblest thing that, at any given period, it has attained the perception of; and surely that thing cannot be wrong nor wrongly timed."

I know not whether it were the excitement of the scene, or whether the good people around the bonfire were really growing more enlightened every instant; but they now proceeded to measures in the full length of which I was hardly prepared to keep them company. For instance, some threw their marriage certificates into the flames, and declared themselves candidates for a higher, holier, and more comprehensive union than that which had subsisted from the birth of time under the form of the connubial tie. Others hastened to the vaults of banks and to the coffers of the rich,—all of which were open to the first comer on this fated occasion,—and brought entire bales of paper money to enliven the blaze, and tons of coin to be melted down by its intensity.

Henceforth, they said, universal benevolence, uncoined and exhaustless, was to be the golden currency of the world. At this intelligence the bankers and speculators in the stocks grew pale, and a pickpocket, who had reaped a rich harvest among the crowd, fell down in a deadly fainting fit. A few men of business burned their day-books and ledgers, the notes and obligations of their creditors, and all other evidences of debts due to themselves; while perhaps a somewhat larger number satisfied their zeal for reform with the sacrifice of any uncomfortable recollection of their own indebtment.

There was then a cry that the period was arrived when the title deeds of landed property should be given to the flames, and the whole soil of the earth revert to the public, from whom it had been wrongfully abstracted and most unequally distributed among individuals. Another party demanded that all written constitutions, set forms of government, legislative acts, statute books, and everything else on which human invention had endeavoured to stamp its arbitrary laws, should at once be destroyed, leaving the consummated world as free as the man first created.

Whether any ultimate action was taken with regard to these propositions is beyond my knowledge; for, just then, some matters were in progress that concerned my sympathies more nearly.

"See! See! What heaps of books and pamphlets!" cried a fellow, who did not seem to be a lover of literature. "Now we shall have a glorious blaze!"

"That's just the thing!" said a modern philosopher. "Now we shall get rid of the weight of dead men's thought, which has hitherto pressed so heavily on the living intellect that it has been incompetent to any effectual self-exertion. Well done, my lads! Into the fire with them! Now you are enlightening the world indeed!"

"But what is to become of the trade?" cried a frantic bookseller.

"Oh, by all means, let them accompany their merchandise," coolly observed an author. "It will be a noble funeral pile!"

The truth was, that the human race had now reached a stage of progress so far beyond what the wisest and wittiest men of former ages had ever dreamed of that it would have been a manifest absurdity to allow the earth to be any longer encumbered with their poor achievements in the literary line. Accordingly a thorough and searching investigation had swept the booksellers' shops, hawkers' stands, public, and private libraries, and even the little book-shelf by the country fireside, and had brought the world's entire mass of printed paper, bound or in sheets, to swell the already mountain bulk of our illustrious bonfire. Thick, heavy folios, containing the labours of lexicographers, commentators and encyclopaedists, were flung in, and falling among the embers with a leaden thump, smouldered away to ashes like rotten wood.

The small, richly gilt French tomes of the last age, with the hundred volumes of Voltaire among them, went off in a brilliant shower of sparkles and little jets of flame; while the current literature of the same nation burned red and blue, and threw an infernal light over the visages of the spectators, converting them all to the aspect of party-coloured fiends. A collection of German stories emitted a scent of brimstone. The English standard authors made excellent fuel, generally exhibiting the properties of sound oak logs. Milton's works, in particular, sent up a powerful blaze, gradually reddening into a coal, which promised to endure longer than almost any other material of the pile. From Shakespeare there gushed a flame of such marvellous splendour that men shaded their eyes as against the sun's meridian glory; nor even when the works of his own elucidators were flung upon him did he cease to flash forth a dazzling radiance from beneath the ponderous heap. It is my belief that he is blazing as fervidly as ever.

"Could a poet but light a lamp at that glorious flame," remarked I, "he might then consume the midnight oil to some good purpose."

"That is the very thing which modern poets have been too apt to do, or at least to attempt," answered a critic. "The chief benefit to be expected from this conflagration of past literature undoubtedly is, that writers will henceforth be compelled to light their lamps at the sun or stars."

"If they can reach so high," said I; "but that task requires a giant, who may afterwards distribute the light among inferior men. It is not everyone that can steal the fire from heaven like Prometheus; but, when once he had done the deed, a thousand hearths were kindled by it."

It amazed me much to observe how indefinite was the proportion between the physical mass of any given author and the property of brilliant and long-continued combustion. For instance, there was not a *quarto* volume of the last century—nor, indeed, of the present—that could compete in that particular with a child's little gilt-covered book, containing *Mother Goose's Melodies. The Life and Death of Tom Thumb* outlasted the biography of Marlborough. An epic, indeed a dozen of them, was converted to white ashes before the single sheet of an old ballad was half consumed. In more than one case, too, when volumes of applauded verse proved incapable of anything better than a stifling smoke, an unregarded ditty of some nameless bard—perchance in the corner of a newspaper—soared up among the stars with a flame as brilliant as their own.

Speaking of the properties of flame, methought Shelley's poetry emitted a purer light than almost any other productions of his day, contrasting beautifully with the fitful and lurid gleams and gashes of black vapor that flashed and eddied from the volumes of Lord Byron. As for Tom Moore, some of his songs diffused an odour like a burning *pastil.*

I felt particular interest in watching the combustion of American authors, and scrupulously noted by my watch the precise number of moments that changed most of them from shabbily-printed books to indistinguishable ashes. It would be invidious, however, if not perilous, to betray these awful secrets; so that I shall content myself with observing that it was not invariably the writer most frequent in the public mouth that made the most splendid appearance in the bonfire. I especially remember that a great deal of excellent inflammability was exhibited in a thin volume of poems by Ellery Channing; although, to speak the truth, there were certain portions that hissed and spluttered in a very disagreeable fashion.

A curious phenomenon occurred in reference to several writers, native as well as foreign. Their books, though of highly respectable figure, instead of bursting into a blaze, or even smouldering out their substance in smoke, suddenly melted away in a manner that proved them to be ice.

If it be no lack of modesty to mention my own works, it must here be confessed that I looked for them with fatherly interest, but in vain. Too probably they were changed to vapor by the first action of the heat; at best, I can only hope that, in their quiet way, they contributed a glimmering spark or two to the splendour of the evening.

"Alas! and woe is me!" thus bemoaned himself a heavy-looking gentleman in green spectacles. "The world is utterly ruined, and there is nothing to live for any longer. The business of my life is snatched from me. Not a volume to be had for love or money!"

"This," remarked the sedate observer beside me, "is a bookworm—one of those men who are born to gnaw dead thoughts. His clothes, you see, are covered with the dust of libraries. He has no inward fountain of ideas; and, in good earnest, now that the old stock is abolished, I do not see what is to become of the poor fellow. Have you no word of comfort for him?"

"My dear sir," said I to the desperate bookworm, "is not Nature better than a book? Is not the human heart deeper than any system of philosophy? Is not life replete with more instruction than past observers have found it possible to write down in maxims? Be of good cheer. The great book of Time is still spread wide open before us; and, if we read it aright, it will be to us a volume of eternal truth."

"Oh, my books, my books, my precious printed books! "reiterated the forlorn bookworm. "My only reality was a bound volume; and now they will not leave me even a shadowy pamphlet!"

In fact, the last remnant of the literature of all the ages was now descending upon the blazing heap in the shape of a cloud of pamphlets from the press of the *New World*. These likewise were consumed in the twinkling of an eye, leaving the earth, for the first time since the days of Cadmus, free from the plague of letters—an enviable field for the authors of the next generation.

"Well, and does anything remain to be done?" inquired I somewhat anxiously. "Unless we set fire to the earth itself, and then leap boldly off into infinite space, I know not that we can carry reform to any farther point."

"You are vastly mistaken, my good friend," said the observer. "Believe me, the fire will not be allowed to settle down without the addition of fuel that will startle many persons who have lent a willing hand thus far."

Nevertheless there appeared to be a relaxation of effort for a little time, during which, probably, the leaders of the movement were considering what should be done next. In the interval, a philosopher threw his theory into the flames,—a sacrifice which, by those who knew how to estimate it, was pronounced the most remarkable that had yet been made. The combustion, however, was by no means brilliant. Some indefatigable people, scorning to take a moment's ease, now employed themselves in collecting all the withered leaves and fallen boughs of the forest, and thereby recruited the bonfire to a greater height than ever. But this was mere by-play.

"Here comes the fresh fuel that I spoke of," said my companion.

To my astonishment, the persons who now advanced into the vacant space around the mountain fire bore surplices and other priestly garments, mitres, crosiers, and a confusion of Popish and Protestant emblems, with which it seemed their purpose to consummate the great act of faith. Crosses from the spires of old cathedrals were cast upon the heap with as little remorse as if the reverence of centuries, passing in long array beneath the lofty towers, had not looked up to them as the holiest of symbols. The font in which infants were consecrated to God, the sacramental vessels whence piety received the hallowed draught, were given to the same destruction.

Perhaps it most nearly touched my heart to see among these devoted relics fragments of the humble communion tables and undecorated pulpits which I recognized as having been torn from the meeting-houses of New England. Those simple edifices might have been permitted to retain all of sacred embellishment that their Puritan founders had bestowed, even though the mighty structure of St. Peter's had sent its spoils to the fire of this terrible sacrifice. Yet I felt that these were but the externals of religion, and might most safely be relinquished by spirits that best knew their deep significance.

"All is well," said I, cheerfully. "The wood-paths shall be the aisles of our cathedral,—the firmament itself shall be its ceiling. What needs an earthly roof between the Deity and his worshippers? Our faith can well afford to lose all the drapery that even the holiest men have thrown around it, and be only the more sublime in its simplicity."

"True," said my companion; "but will they pause here?"

The doubt implied in his question was well founded, In the general destruction of books already described, a holy volume, that stood apart from the catalogue of human literature, and yet, in one sense, was at its head, had been spared. But the Titan of innovation,—angel or fiend, double in his nature, and capable of deeds befitting both characters,—at first shaking down only the old and rotten shapes of things, had now, as it appeared, laid his terrible hand upon the main pillars which supported the whole edifice of our moral and spiritual state. The inhabitants of the earth had grown too enlightened to define their faith within a form of words, or to limit the spiritual by any analogy to our material existence. Truths which the heavens trembled at were now but a fable of the world's infancy.

Therefore, as the final sacrifice of human error, what else remained to be thrown upon the embers of that awful pile except the book which, though a celestial revelation to past ages, was bat a voice from a lower sphere as regarded the present race of man? It was done! Upon the blazing heap of falsehood and worn-out truth—things that the earth had never needed, or had

ceased to need, or had grown childishly weary of—fell the ponderous church Bible, the great old volume that had lain so long
on the cushion of the pulpit, and whence the pastor's solemn
voice had given holy utterance on so many a Sabbath day. There,
likewise, fell the family Bible, which the long-buried patriarch
had read to his children,—in prosperity or sorrow, by the fireside and in the summer shade of trees,—and had bequeathed
downward as the heirloom of generations. There fell the bosom
Bible, the little volume that had been the soul's friend of some
sorely-tried child of dust, who thence took courage, whether his
trial were for life or death, steadfastly confronting both in the
strong assurance of immortality.

All these were flung into the fierce and riotous blaze; and
then a mighty wind came roaring across the plain with a desolate howl, as if it were the angry lamentation of the earth for the
loss of heaven's sunshine; and it shook the gigantic pyramid of
flame and scattered the cinders of half-consumed abominations
around upon the spectators.

"This is terrible!" said I, feeling that my cheek grew pale, and
seeing a like change in the visages about me.

"Be of good courage yet," answered the man with whom I
had so often spoken. He continued to gaze steadily at the spectacle with a singular calmness, as if it concerned him merely as
an observer. "Be of good courage, nor yet exult too much; for
there is far less both of good and evil in the effect of this bonfire
than the world might be willing to believe."

"How can that be?" exclaimed I, impatiently. "Has it not
consumed everything? Has it not swallowed up or melted down
every human or divine appendage of our mortal state that had
substance enough to be acted on by fire? Will there be anything
left us tomorrow morning better or worse than a heap of embers and ashes?"

"Assuredly there will," said my grave friend. "Come hither
tomorrow morning, or whenever the combustible portion of
the pile shall be quite burned oat, and you will find among
the ashes everything really valuable that you have seen cast into

the flames. Trust me, the world of tomorrow will again enrich itself with the gold and diamonds which have been cast off by the world of today. Not a truth is destroyed nor buried so deep among the ashes but it will be raked up at last."

This was a strange assurance. Yet I felt inclined to credit it, the more especially as I beheld among the wallowing flames a copy of the Holy Scriptures, the pages of which, instead of being blackened into tinder, only assumed a more dazzling whiteness as the finger marks of human imperfection were purified away. Certain marginal notes and commentaries, it is true, yielded to the intensity of the fiery test, but without detriment to the smallest syllable that had flamed from the pen of inspiration.

"Yes; there is the proof of what you say," answered I, turning to the observer; "but if only what is evil can feel the action of the fire, then, surely, the conflagration has been of inestimable utility. Yet, if I understand aright, you intimate a doubt whether the world's expectation of benefit would be realized by it."

"Listen to the talk of these worthies," said he, pointing to a group in front of the blazing pile; "possibly they may teach you something useful without intending it"

The persons whom he indicated consisted of that brutal and most earthy figure who had stood forth so furiously in defence of the gallows,—the hangman, in short,—together with the last thief and the last murderer, all three of whom were clustered about the last toper. The latter was liberally passing the brandy bottle, which he had rescued from the general destruction of wines and spirits. This little convivial party seemed at the lowest pitch of despondency, as considering that the purified world must needs be utterly unlike the sphere that they had hitherto known, and therefore but a strange and desolate abode for gentlemen of their kidney.

"The best counsel for all of us is," remarked the hangman, "that, as soon as we have finished the last drop of liquor, I help you, my three friends, to a comfortable end upon the nearest tree, and then hang myself on the same bough. This is no world for us any longer."

"Poh, poh, my good fellows!" said a dark-complexioned personage, who now joined the group,—his complexion was indeed fearfully dark, and his eyes glowed with a redder light than that of the bonfire; "be not so cast down, my dear friends; you shall see good days yet. There's one thing that these wiseacres have forgotten to throw into the fire, and without which all the rest of the conflagration is just nothing at all; yes, though they had burned the earth itself to a cinder."

"And what may that be?" eagerly demanded the last murderer.

"What but the human heart itself?" said the dark-visaged stranger, with a portentous grin. "And, unless they hit upon some method of purifying that foul cavern, forth from it will reissue all the shapes of wrong and misery—the same old shapes or worse ones—which they have taken such a vast deal of trouble to consume to ashes. I have stood by this livelong night and laughed in my sleeve at the whole business. Oh, take my word for it, it will be the old world yet!"

This brief conversation supplied me with a theme for lengthened thought. How sad a truth, if true it were, that man's agelong endeavour for perfection had served only to render him the mockery of the evil principle, from the fatal circumstance of an error at the very root of the matter! The heart, the heart,—there was the little yet boundless sphere wherein existed the original wrong of which the crime and misery of this outward world were merely types.

Purify that inward sphere, and the many shapes of evil that haunt the outward, and which now seem almost our only realities, will turn to shadowy phantoms and vanish of their own accord; but if we go no deeper than the intellect, and strive, with merely that feeble instrument, to discern and rectify what is wrong, our whole accomplishment will be a dream, so unsubstantial that it matters little whether the bonfire, which I have so faithfully described, were what we choose to call a real event and a flame that would scorch the finger, or only a phosphoric radiance and a parable of my own brain.

The Snow-Image: A Childish Miracle
(A tale from *The Snow Image and Other Twice-Told Tales*)

One afternoon of a cold winter's day, when the sun shone forth with chilly brightness, after a long storm, two children asked leave of their mother to run out and play in the new-fallen snow. The elder child was a little girl, whom, because she was of a tender and modest disposition, and was thought to be very beautiful, her parents, and other people who were familiar with her, used to call Violet. But her brother was known by the style and title of Peony, on account of the ruddiness of his broad and round little phiz, which made everybody think of sunshine and great scarlet flowers. The father of these two children, a certain Mr. Lindsey, it is important to say, was an excellent but exceedingly matter-of-fact sort of man, a dealer in hardware, and was sturdily accustomed to take what is called the common-sense view of all matters that came under his consideration.

With a heart, about as tender as other people's, he had a head as hard and impenetrable, and therefore, perhaps, as empty, as one of the iron pots which it was a part of his business to sell. The mother's character, on the other hand, had a strain of poetry in it, a trait of unworldly beauty,—a delicate and dewy flower, as it were, that had survived out of her imaginative youth, and still kept itself alive amid the dusty realities of matrimony and motherhood.

So, Violet and Peony, as I began with saying, besought their mother to let them run out and play in the new snow; for, though it had looked so dreary and dismal, drifting downward out of the gray sky, it had a very cheerful aspect, now that the sun was shining on it. The children dwelt in a city, and had no wider play-place than a little garden before the house, divided by a white fence from the street, and with a pear-tree and two or three plum-trees overshadowing it, and some rose-bushes just in front of the parlour-windows. The trees and shrubs, however, were now leafless, and their twigs were enveloped in the light snow, which thus made a kind of wintry foliage, with here and there a pendent icicle for the fruit.

"Yes, Violet,—yes, my little Peony," said their kind mother; "you may go out and play in the new snow."

Accordingly, the good lady bundled up her darlings in woollen jackets and wadded sacks, and put comforters round their necks, and a pair of striped gaiters on each little pair of legs, and worsted mittens on their hands, and gave them a kiss apiece, by way of a spell to keep away Jack Frost. Forth sallied the two children, with a hop-skip-and-jump, that carried them at once into the very heart of a huge snowdrift, whence Violet emerged like a snow-bunting, while little Peony floundered out with his round face in full bloom. Then what a merry time had they!

To look at them, frolicking in the wintry garden, you would have thought that the dark and pitiless storm had been sent for no other purpose but to provide a new plaything for Violet and Peony; and that they themselves had been created, as the snow-birds were, to take delight only in the tempest, and in the white mantle which it .spread over the earth.

At last, when they had frosted one another all over with handfuls of snow, Violet, after laughing heartily at little Peony's figure, was struck with a new idea.

"You look exactly like a snow-image, Peony," said she, "if your cheeks were not so red. And that puts me in mind! Let us make an image out of snow,—an image of a little girl,—and it shall be our sister, and shall run about and play with us all winter long. Won't it be nice?"

"O, yes!" cried Peony, as plainly as he could speak, for he was but a little boy. "That will be nice! And mamma shall see it!"

"Yes," answered Violet; "mamma shall see the new little girl. But she must not make her come into the warm parlour; for, you know, our little snow-sister will not love the warmth."

And forthwith the children began this great business of making a snow-image that should run about; while their mother, who was sitting at the window and over heard some of their talk, could not help smiling at the gravity with which they set about it. They really seemed to imagine that there would be no difficulty whatever in creating a live little girl out of the snow. And, to say the truth, if miracles are ever to be wrought, it will be by putting our hands to the work in precisely such a simple and undoubting frame of mind as that in which Violet and Peony now undertook to perform one, without so much as knowing that it was a miracle.

So thought the mother; and thought, likewise, that the new snow, just fallen from heaven, would be excellent material to make new beings of, if it were not so very cold. She gazed at the children a moment longer, delighting to watch their little figures,—the girl, tall for her age, graceful and agile, and so delicately coloured that she looked like a cheerful thought, more than a physical reality; while Peony expanded in breadth rather than height, and rolled along on his short and sturdy legs as substantial as an elephant, though not quite so big. Then the mother resumed her work. What it was I forget; but she was either trimming a silken bonnet for Violet, or darning a pair of stockings for little Peony's short legs. Again, however, and again, and yet other agains, she could not help turning her head to the window to see how the children got on with their snow-image.

Indeed, it was an exceedingly pleasant sight, those bright little souls at their task! Moreover, it was really wonderful to observe how knowingly and skilfully they managed the matter. Violet assumed the chief direction, and told Peony what to do, while, with her own delicate fingers, she shaped out all the nicer parts of the snow-figure. It seemed, in fact, not so much to be made by the children, as to grow up under their hands, while they were playing and prattling about it. Their mother was quite surprised at this; and the longer she looked, the more and more surprised she grew.

"What remarkable children mine are!" thought she, smiling with a mother's pride; and, smiling at herself, too, for being so proud of them. "What other children could have made anything so like a little girl's figure out of snow at the first trial? Well;— but now I must finish Peony's new frock, for his grandfather is coming tomorrow, and I want the little fellow to look handsome."

So she took up the frock, and was soon as busily at work again with her needle as the two children with their snow-image. But still, as the needle travelled hither and thither through the scams of the dress, the mother made her toil light and happy by listening to the airy voices of Violet and Peony. They kept talking to one another all the time, their tongues being quite as active as their feet and hands. Except at intervals, she could not distinctly hear what was said, but had merely a sweet impression that they were in a most loving mood, and were enjoying themselves highly, and that the business of making the snow-image went prosperously on. Now and then, however, when Violet and Peony happened to raise their voices, the words were as audible as if they had been spoken in the very parlour, where the mother sat. O, how delightfully those words echoed in her heart, even though they meant nothing so very wise or wonderful, after all!

But you must know a mother listens with her heart, much more than with her ears; and thus she is often delighted with the trills of celestial music, when other people can hear nothing of the kind.

"Peony, Peony!" cried Violet to her brother, who had gone to another part of the garden, "bring me some of that fresh snow, Peony, from the very farthest corner, where we have not been trampling. I want it to shape our little snow-sister's bosom with. You know that part must be quite pure, just as it came out of the sky!"

"Here it is, Violet!" answered Peony, in his bluff tone,—but a very sweet tone, too,—as he came floundering through the half-trodden drifts. "Here is the snow for her little bosom. O Violet, how beau-ti-ful she begins to look!"

"Yes," said Violet, thoughtfully and quietly; "our snow-sister does look very lovely. I did not quite know, Peony, that we could make such a sweet little girl as this."

The mother, as she listened, thought how fit and delightful an incident it would be, if fairies, or, still better, if angel-children were to come from paradise, and play invisibly with her own darlings, and help them to make their snow-image, giving it the features of celestial babyhood! Violet and Peony would not be aware of their immortal playmates,—only they would see that the image grew very beautiful while they worked at it, and would think that they themselves had done it all.

"My little girl and boy deserve such playmates, if mortal children ever did!" said the mother to herself; and then she smiled again at her own motherly pride.

Nevertheless, the idea seized upon her imagination; and, ever and *anon*, she took a glimpse out of the window, half dreaming that she might see the golden-haired children of paradise sporting with her own golden-haired Violet and bright-cheeked Peony.

Now, for a few moments, there was a busy and earnest, but indistinct hum of the two children's voices, as Violet and Peony wrought together with one happy consent. Violet still seemed to be the guiding spirit, while Peony acted rather as a labourer, and brought her the snow from far and near. And yet the little urchin evidently had a proper understanding of the matter, too!

"Peony, Peony!" cried Violet; for her brother was again at the other side of the garden. "Bring me those light wreaths of snow that have rested on the lower branches of the pear-tree. You can clamber on the snowdrift, Peony, and reach them easily. I must have them to make some ringlets for our snow-sister's head!" Here they are, Violet!" answered the little boy. "Take care you do not break them. Well done! Well done! How pretty!"

"Does she not look sweetly?" said Violet, with a very satisfied tone; "and now we must have some little shining bits of ice, to make the brightness of her eyes. She is not finished yet. Mamma will see how very beautiful she is; but papa will say, 'Tush! nonsense!—come in out of the cold!'"

"Let us call mamma to look out," said Peony; and then he shouted lustily, "Mamma! mamma!! mamma!!! Look out, and see what a nice 'ittle girl we are making!"

The mother put down her work, for an instant, and looked out of the window. But it so happened that the sun—for this was one of the shortest days of the whole year—had sunken so nearly to the edge of the world, that his setting shine came obliquely into the lady's eyes. So she was dazzled, you must understand, and could not very distinctly observe what was in the garden. Still, however, through all that bright, blinding dazzle of the sun and the new snow, she beheld a small white figure in the garden, that seemed to have a wonderful deal of human likeness about it. And she saw Violet and Peony,—indeed, she looked more at them than at the image,—she saw the two children still at work; Peony bringing fresh snow, and Violet applying it to the figure as scientifically as a sculptor adds clay to his model. Indistinctly as she discerned the snow-child, the mother thought to herself that never before was there a snow-figure so cunningly made, nor ever such a dear little girl and boy to make it.

"They do everything better than other children," said she, very complacently. "No wonder they make better snow-images!"

She sat down again to her work, and made as much haste with it as possible; because twilight would soon come, and Peony's frock was not yet finished, and grandfather was expected, by railroad, pretty early in the morning. Faster and faster, therefore, went her flying fingers. The children, likewise, kept busily at work in the garden, and still the mother listened, whenever she could catch a word. She was amused to observe how their little imaginations had got mixed up with what they were doing, and were carried away by it. They seemed positively to think that the snow-child would run about and play with them.

"What a nice playmate she will be for us, all winter long!" said Violet. "I hope papa will not be afraid of her giving us a cold! Sha' n't you love her dearly, Peony?"

"O yes!" cried Peony. "And I will hug her, and she shall sit down close by me, and drink some of my warm milk!"

"O no, Peony!" answered Violet, with grave wisdom. "That will not do at all. Warm milk will not be whole some for our little snow-sister. Little snow-people, like her, eat nothing but icicles. No, no, Peony; we must not give her anything warm to drink!"

There was a minute or two of silence; for Peony, whose short legs were never weary, had gone on a pilgrimage again to the other side of the garden. All of a sudden, Violet cried out, loudly and joyfully,—

"Look here, Peony! Come quickly! A light has been shining on her cheek out of that rose-colored cloud! and the colour does not go away! Is not that beautiful!"

"Yes; it is beau-ti-ful," answered Peony, pronouncing the three syllables with deliberate accuracy. "O Violet, only look at her hair! It is all like gold!"

"O, certainly," said Violet, with tranquillity, as if it were very much a matter of course. "That colour, you know, comes from the golden clouds, that we see up there in the sky. She is almost finished now. But her lips must be made very red,—redder than her cheeks. Perhaps, Peony, it will make them red, if we both kiss them!"

Accordingly, the mother heard two smart little smacks, as if both her children were kissing the snow-image on its frozen mouth. But, as this did not seem to make the lips quite red enough, Violet next proposed that the snow-child should be invited to kiss Peony's scarlet cheek.

"Come, 'ittle snow-sister, kiss me!" cried Peony.

"There! she has kissed you," added Violet, "and now her lips are very red. And she blushed a little, too!"

"O, what a cold kiss!" cried Peony.

Just then, there came a breeze of the pure west-wind, sweeping through the garden and rattling the parlour-windows. It sounded so wintry cold, that the mother was about to tap on the window-pane with her thimbled finger, to summon the two children in, when they both cried out to her with one voice. Ths tone was not a tone of surprise, although they were evidently a good deal excited; it appeared rather as if they were very much rejoiced at some event that had now happened, but which they had been looking for, and had reckoned upon all along.

"Mamma! mamma!" We have finished our little snow, sister, and she is running about the garden with us!"

"What imaginative little beings my children are!" thought the mother, putting the last few stitches into Peony's frock. "And it is strange, too, that they make me almost as much a child as they themselves are! I can hardly help believing, now, that the snow-image has really come to life!"

"Dear mamma!" cried Violet, "pray look out and see what a sweet playmate we have!"

The mother, being thus entreated, could no longer delay to look forth from the window. The sun was now gone out of the sky, leaving, however, a rich inheritance of his brightness among those purple and golden clouds which make the sunsets of winter so magnificent. But there was not the slightest gleam or dazzle, either on the window or on the snow; so that the good lady could look all over the garden, and see everything and everybody in it. And what do you think she saw there? Violet and Peony, of course, her own two darling children. Ah, but whom or what did she see besides? Why, if you will believe me, there was a small figure of a girl, dressed all in white, with rose-tinged cheeks and ring lets of golden hue, playing about the garden with the two children!

A stranger though she was, the child seemed to be on as familiar terms with Violet and Peony, and they with her, as if all the three had been play mates during the whole of their little lives. The mother thought to herself that it must certainly be the daughter of one of the neighbours, and that, seeing Violet and Peony in the garden, the child had run across the street to play with them. So this kind lady went to the door, intending to invite the little runaway into her comfortable parlour; for, now that the sunshine was withdrawn, the atmosphere, out of doors, was already growing very cold.

But, after opening the house-door, she stood an instant on the threshold, hesitating whether she ought to ask the child to come in, or whether she should even speak to her. Indeed, she almost doubted whether it were a real child, after all, or only a light wreath of the new-fallen snow, blown hither and thither about the garden by the intensely cold west-wind. There was certainly something very singular in the aspect of the little stranger. Among all the children of the neighbourhood, the lady could remember no such face, with its pure white, and delicate rose-colour, and the golden ringlets tossing about the forehead and cheeks.

And as for her dress, which was entirely of white, and fluttering in the breeze, it was such as no reasonable woman would put upon a little girl, when sending her out to play, in the depth of winter. It made this kind and careful mother shiver only to look at those small feet, with nothing in the world on them, except a very thin pair of white slippers. Nevertheless, airily as she was clad, the child seemed to feel not the slightest inconvenience from the cold, but danced so lightly over the snow that the tips of her toes left hardly a print in its surface; while Violet could but just keep pace with her, and Peony's short legs compelled him to lag behind.

Once, in the course of their play, the strange child placed herself between Violet and Peony, and taking a hand of each, skipped merrily forward, and they along with her. Almost immediately, however, Peony pulled away his little fist, and began to rub it as if the fingers were tingling with cold; while Violet also released herself, though with less abruptness, gravely remarking that it was better not to take hold of hands. The white-robed damsel said not a word, but danced about, just as merrily as before. If Violet and Peony did not choose to play with her, she could make just as good a playmate of the brisk and cold west-wind, which kept blowing her all about the garden, and took such liberties with her, that they seemed to have been, friends for a long time. All this while, the mother stood on the threshold, wondering how a little girl could look so much like a flying snowdrift, or how a snowdrift could look so very like a little girl.

She called Violet, and whispered to her. "Violet, my darling, what is this child's name?" asked she. "Does she live near us?"

"Why, dearest mamma," answered Violet, laughing to think that her mother did not comprehend so very plain an affair, "this is our little snow-sister, whom we have just been making!"

"Yes, dear mamma," cried Peony, running to his mother, and looking up simply into her face. "This is our snow-image! Is it not a nice 'ittle child?"

At this instant a flock of snow-birds came flitting through the air. As was very natural, they avoided Violet and Peony. But,—and this looked strange,—they flew at once to the white-robed child, fluttered eagerly about her head, alighted on her shoulders, and seemed to claim her as an old acquaintance. She, on her part, was evidently as glad to see these little birds, old Winter's grandchildren, as they were to see her, and welcomed them by holding out both her hands. Here upon, they each and all tried to alight on her two palms and ten small fingers and thumbs, crowding one another off, with an immense fluttering of their tiny wings. One dear little bird nestled tenderly in her bosom; another put its bill to her lips. They were as joyous, all the while, and seemed as much in their element, as you may have seen them when sporting with a snowstorm.

Violet and Peony stood laughing at this pretty sight for they enjoyed the merry time which their new play mate was having with these small-winged visitants, almost as much as if they themselves took part in it.

"Violet," said her mother, greatly perplexed, "tell me the truth, without any jest. Who is this little girl?"

"My darling mamma," answered Violet, looking seriously into her mother's face, and apparently surprised that she should need any further explanation, "I have told you truly who she is.

It is our little snow-image, which Peony and I have been making. Peony will tell you so, as well as I."

"Yes, mamma," asseverated Peony, with much gravity in his crimson little phiz; "this is 'ittle snow-child. Is not she a nice one? But, mamma, her hand, is oh, so very cold!"

While mamma still hesitated what to think and what to do, the street-gate was thrown open, and the father of Violet and Peony appeared, wrapped in a pilot-cloth sack, with a fur cap drawn down over his ears, and the thickest of gloves upon his hands. Mr. Lindsey was a middle-aged man, with a weary and yet a happy look in his wind-flushed and frost-pinched face, as if he had been busy all the day long, and was glad to get back to his quiet home. His eyes brightened at the sight of his wife and children, although he could not help uttering a word or two of surprise, at finding the whole family in the open air, on so bleak a day, and after sunset too. He soon perceived the little white stranger, sporting to and fro in the garden, like a dancing snow-wreath, and the flock of snow-birds fluttering about her head.

"Pray, what little girl may that be?" inquired this very sensible man. "Surely her mother must be crazy, to let her go out in such bitter weather as it has been today, with only that flimsy white gown and those thin slippers!"

"My dear husband," said his wife, "I know no more about the little thing than you do. Some neighbour's child, I suppose. Our Violet and Peony," she added, laughing at herself for repeating so absurd a story, "insist that she is nothing but a snow-image, which they have been busy about in the garden, almost all the afternoon."

As she said this, the mother glanced her eyes toward the spot where the children's snow-image had been made. What was her surprise, on perceiving that there was not the slightest trace of so much labour! no image at all!—no piled up heap of snow!—nothing whatever, save the prints of little footsteps around a vacant space!

"This is very strange!" said she.

"What is strange, dear mother?" asked Violet. "Dear father,

do not you see how it is? This is our snow-image, which Peony and I have made, because we wanted another playmate. Did not we, Peony?"

"Yes, papa," said crimson Peony. "This be our 'ittle snow-sister. Is she not beau-ti-ful? But she gave me such a cold kiss!"

"Poh, nonsense, children!" cried their good, honest father, who, as we have already intimated, had an exceedingly common-sensible way of looking at matters. "Do not tell me of making live figures out of snow. Come, wife; this little stranger must not stay out in the bleak air a moment longer. We will bring her into the parlour; and you shall give her a supper of warm bread and milk, and make her as comfortable as you can. Meanwhile, I will inquire among the neighbours; or, if necessary, send the city-crier about the streets, to give notice of a lost child."

So saying, this honest and very kind-hearted man was going toward the little white damsel, with the best intentions in the world. But Violet and Peony, each seizing their father by the hand, earnestly besought him not to make her come in.

"Dear father," cried Violet, putting herself before him, "it is true what I have been telling you! This is our little snow-girl, and she cannot live any longer than while she breathes the cold west-wind. Do not make her come into the hot room!"

"Yes, father," shouted Peony, stamping his little foot, so might-ily was he in earnest, "this be nothing but our 'ittle snow-child! She will not love the hot fire!"

"Nonsense, children, nonsense, nonsense!" cried the father, half vexed, half laughing at what he considered their foolish ob-stinacy. "Run into the house, this moment! It is too late to play any longer, now. I must take care of this little girl immediately, or she will catch her death-a-cold!"

"Husband! dear husband!" said his wife, in a low voice, for she had been looking narrowly at the snow-child, and was more perplexed than ever,—"there is something very singular in all this. You will think me foolish,—but—but—may it not be that some invisible angel has been attracted by the simplicity and good faith with which our children set about their undertaking? May he not have spent an hour of his immortality in playing with those dear little souls? and so the result is what we call a miracle. No, no! Do not laugh at me; I see what a foolish thought it is!"

"My dear wife," replied the husband, laughing heartily, "you are as much a child as Violet and Peony."

And in one sense so she was, for all through life she had kept her heart full of childlike simplicity and faith, which was as pure and clear as crystal; and, looking at all matters through this transparent medium, she sometimes saw truths so profound, that other people laughed at them as nonsense and absurdity.

But now kind Mr. Lindsey had entered the garden, breaking away from his two children, who still sent their shrill voices after him, beseeching him to let the snow-child stay and enjoy herself in the cold west-wind. As he approached, the snow-birds took to flight. The little white damsel, also, fled backward, shaking her head, as if to say, "Pray, do not touch me!" and roguishly, as it appeared, leading him through the deepest of the snow. Once, the good man stumbled, and floundered down upon his face, so that, gathering himself up again, with the snow sticking to his rough pilot-cloth sack, he looked as white and wintry as a snow-image of the largest size.

Some of the neighbours, meanwhile, seeing him from their windows, wondered what could possess poor Mr. Lindsey to be running about his garden in pursuit of a snowdrift, which the west-wind was driving hither and thither! At length, after a vast deal of trouble, he chased the little stranger into a corner, where she could not possibly escape him. His wife had been looking on, and, it being nearly twilight, was wonder-struck to observe how the snow-child gleamed and sparkled, and how she seemed to shed a glow all round about her; and when driven into the corner, she positively glistened like a star! It was a frosty kind of brightness, too, like that of an icicle in the moonlight. The wife thought it strange that good Mr. Lindsey should see nothing remarkable in the snow-child's appearance.

"Come, you odd little thing!" cried the honest man, seizing

her by the hand, "I have caught you at last, and will make you comfortable in spite of yourself. We will put a nice warm pair of worsted stockings on your frozen little feet, and you shall have a good thick shawl to wrap yourself in. Your poor white nose, I am afraid, is actually frostbitten. But we will make it all right. Come along in."

And so, with a most benevolent smile on his sagacious visage, all purple as it was with the cold, this very well-meaning gentleman took the snow-child by the hand and led her towards the house. She followed him, droopingly and reluctant; for all the glow and sparkle was gone out of her figure; and whereas just before she had resembled a bright, frosty, star-gemmed evening, with a crimson gleam on the cold horizon, she now looked as dull and languid as a thaw. As kind Mr. Lindsey led her up the steps of the door, Violet and Peony looked into his face,—their eyes full of tears, which froze before they could run down their cheeks,—and again entreated him not to bring their snow-image into the house.

"Not bring her in!" exclaimed the kind-hearted man. "Why, you are crazy, my little Violet!—quite crazy, my small Peony! She is so cold, already, that her hand has almost frozen mine, in spite of my thick gloves. Would you have her freeze to death?"

His wife, as he came up the steps, had been taking another long, earnest, almost awe-stricken gaze at the little white stranger. She hardly knew whether it was a dream or no; but she could not help fancying that she saw the delicate print of Violet's fingers on the child's neck. It looked just as if, while Violet was shaping out the image, she had given it a gentle pat with her hand, and had neglected to smooth the impression quite away.

"After all, husband," said the mother, recurring to her idea that, the angels would be as much delighted to play with Violet and Peony as she herself was,—"after all, she does look strangely like a snow-image! I do believe she is made of snow!"

A puff of the west-wind blew against the snow-child, and again she sparkled like a star.

"Snow!" repeated good Mr. Lindsey, drawing the reluctant

guest over his hospitable threshold. "No wonder she looks like snow. She is half frozen, poor little thing! But a good fire will put everything to rights."

Without further talk, and always with the same best intentions, this highly benevolent and common-sensible individual led the little white damsel—drooping, drooping, drooping, more and more—out of the frosty air, and into his comfortable parlour. A Heidenberg stove, filled to the brim with intensely burning anthracite, was sending a bright gleam through the isinglass of its iron, door, and causing the vase of water on its top to fume and bubble with excitement. A warm, sultry smell was diffused throughout the room. A thermometer on the wall farthest from the stove stood at eighty degrees. The parlour was hung with red curtains, and covered with a red carpet, and looked just as warm as it felt. The difference betwixt the atmosphere here and the cold, wintry twilight out of doors, was like stepping at once from Nova Zembla to the hottest part of India, or from the North Pole into an oven. O, this was a fine place for the little white stranger!

The common-sensible man placed the snow-child on the hearth-rug, right in front of the hissing and fuming stove.

"Now she will be comfortable!" cried Mr. Lindsey, rubbing his hands and looking about him, with the pleasantest smile you ever saw. "Make yourself at home, my child."

Sad, sad and drooping, looked the little white maiden, as she stood on the hearth-rug, with the hot blast of the stove striking through her like a pestilence. Once, she threw a glance wistfully toward the windows, and caught a glimpse, through its red curtains, of the snow-covered roofs, and the stars glimmering frostily, and all the delicious intensity of the cold night. The bleak wind rattled the window-panes, as if it were summoning her to come forth. But there stood the snow-child, drooping, before the hot stove!

But the common-sensible man saw nothing amiss.

"Come, wife," said he, "let her have a pair of thick stockings and a woollen shawl or blanket directly; and tell Dora to give her some warm supper as soon as the milk boils. You, Violet and Peony, amuse your little friend. She is out of spirits, you see, at finding herself in a strange place. Tor my part, I will go around among the neighbours, and find out where she belongs."

The mother, meanwhile, had gone in search of the shawl and stockings; for her own view of the matter, however subtle and delicate, had given way, as it always did, to the stubborn materialism of her husband. Without heeding the remonstrances of his two children, who still kept murmuring that their little snow-sister did not love the warmth, good Mr. Lindsey took his departure, shutting the parlour-door carefully behind him. Turning- up the collar of his sack over his ears, he emerged from the house, and had barely reached the street-gate, when he was recalled by the screams of Violet and Peony, and the rapping of a thimbled finger against the parlour window.

"Husband! husband!" cried his wife, showing her horror-stricken face through the window-panes. "There is no need of going for the child's parents!"

"We told you so, father!" screamed Violet and Peony, as he re-entered the parlour. "You would bring her in; and now our poor—dear—beau-ti-ful little snow-sister is thawed!"

And their own sweet little faces were already dissolved in tears; so that their father, seeing what strange things occasionally happen in this every-day world, felt not a little anxious lest his children might be going to thaw too! In. the utmost perplexity, he demanded an explanation of his wife. She could only reply, that, being summoned to the parlour by the cries of Violet and Peony, she found no trace of the little white maiden, unless it were the remains of a heap of snow, which, while she was gazing at it, melted quite away upon the hearth-rug.

"And there you see all that is left of it!" added she, pointing to a pool of water, in front of the stove.

"Yes, father," said Violet, looking reproachfully at him, through her tears, "there is all that is left of our dear little snow-sister!"

"Naughty father!" cried Peony, stamping his foot, and—I shudder to say—shaking his little fist at the common-sensible man. "We told you how it would be! What for did you bring her in?"

And the Heidenberg stove, through the isinglass of its door, seemed to glare at good Mr. Lindsey, like a red-eyed demon, triumphing in the mischief which it had done!

This, you will observe, was one of those rare cases, which yet will occasionally happen, where common-sense finds itself at fault. The remarkable story of the snow-image, though to that sagacious class of people to whom good Mr. Lindsey belongs it may seem but a childish affair, is, nevertheless, capable of being moralized in various methods, greatly for their edification. One of its lessons, for instance, might be, that it behooves men, and especially men of benevolence, to consider well what they are about, and, before acting on their philanthropic purposes, to be quite sure that they comprehend the nature and all the relations of the business in hand.

What has been established as an element of good to one being may prove absolute mischief to another; even as the warmth of the parlour was proper enough for children of flesh and blood, like Violet and Peony,—though by no means very wholesome, even, for them,—but involved nothing short of annihilation to the unfortunate snow-image.

But, after all, there is no teaching anything to wise men of good Mr. Lindsey's stamp. They know everything,—O, to be sure!—everything that has been, and everything that is, and everything that, by any future possibility, can be. And, should some phenomenon of nature or providence transcend their system, they will not recognize it, even if it come to pass under their very noses.

"Wife," said Mr. Lindsey, after a fit of silence, "see what a quantity of snow the children have brought in on their feet! It has made quite a puddle here before the stove. Pray tell Dora to bring some towels and sop it up!"

Monsieur du Miroir

(A tale from *Mosses From an Old Manse and Other Stories*)

Than the gentleman above named, there is nobody, in the whole circle of my acquaintance, whom I have more attentively studied, yet of whom I have less real knowledge, beneath the surface which it pleases him to present. Being anxious to discover who and what he really is, and how connected with me, and what are to be the results to him and to myself of the joint interest which, without any choice on my part, seems to be permanently established between us,—and incited, furthermore, by the propensities of a student of human nature, though doubtful whether Monsieur du Miroir have aught of humanity but the figure,—I have determined to place a few of his remarkable points before the public, hoping to be favoured with some clew to the explanation of his character.

Nor let the reader condemn any part of the narrative as frivolous, since a subject of such grave reflection diffuses its importance through the minutest particulars; and there is no judging beforehand what odd little circumstance may do the office of a blind man's dog among the perplexities of this dark investigation; and however extraordinary, marvellous, preternatural, and utterly incredible some of the meditated disclosures may appear, I pledge my honour to maintain as sacred a regard to fact as if my testimony were given on oath and involved the dearest interests of the personage in question.

Not that there is matter for a criminal accusation against Monsieur du Miroir, nor am I the man to bring it forward if there were. The chief that I complain of is his impenetrable mystery, which is no better than nonsense if it conceal anything good, and much worse in the contrary case.

But if undue partialities could be supposed to influence me, Monsieur du Miroir might hope to profit rather than to suffer by them, for in the whole of our long intercourse we have seldom had the slightest disagreement; and, moreover, there are reasons for supposing him a near relative of mine, and consequently entitled to the best word that I can give him. He bears undisputably a strong personal resemblance to myself, and generally puts on mourning at the funerals of the family. On the other hand, his name would indicate a French descent; in which case, infinitely preferring that my blood should flow from a bold British and pure Puritan source, I beg leave to disclaim all kindred with Monsieur du Miroir. Some genealogists trace his origin to Spain, and dub him a knight of the order of the Caballeros de los Espejoz, one of whom was overthrown by Don Quixote.

But what says Monsieur du Miroir himself of his paternity and his fatherland? Not a word did he ever say about the matter; and herein, perhaps, lies one of his most especial reasons for maintaining such a vexatious mystery, that he lacks the faculty of speech to expound it. His lips are sometimes seen to move; his eyes and countenance are alive with shifting expression, as if corresponding by visible hieroglyphics to his modulated breath; and anon he will seem to pause with as satisfied an air as if he had been talking excellent sense. Good sense or bad. Monsieur du Miroir is the sole judge of his own conversational powers, never having whispered so much as a syllable that reached the ears of any other auditor. Is he really dumb? or is all the world deaf? or is it merely a piece of my friend's waggery, meant for nothing but to make fools of us? If so he has the joke all to himself.

This dumb devil which possesses Monsieur du Miroir is, I am persuaded, the sole reason that he does not make me the most flattering protestations of friendship. In many particulars— indeed, as to all his cognizable and not preternatural points, except that, once in a great while, I speak a word or two—there exists the greatest apparent sympathy between us. Such is his confidence in my taste that he goes astray from the general fashion and copies all his dresses after mine. I never try on a new garment without expecting to meet Monsieur du Miroir in one of the same pattern. He has duplicates of all my waistcoats and cravats, shirt bosoms of precisely a similar plait, and an old coat for private wear, manufactured, I suspect, by a Chinese tailor, in exact imitation of a beloved old coat of mine, with a facsimile, stitch by stitch, of a patch upon the elbow.

In truth, the singular and minute coincidences that occur, both in the accidents of the passing day and the serious events of our lives, remind me of those doubtful legends of lovers, or twin children, twins of fate, who have lived, enjoyed, suffered, and died in unison, each faithfully repeating the last tremor of the other's breath, though separated by vast tracts of sea and land. Strange to say, my incommodities belong equally to my companion, though the burden is nowise alleviated by his participation. The other morning, after a night of torment from the toothache, I met Monsieur du Miroir with such a swollen anguish in his cheek that my own pangs were redoubled, as were also his, if I might judge by a fresh contortion of his visage. All the inequalities of my spirits are communicated to him, causing the unfortunate Monsieur du Miroir to mope and scowl through a whole summer's day, or to laugh as long, for no better reason than the gay or gloomy crotchets of my brain.

Once we were joint sufferers of a three months' sickness, and met like mutual ghosts in the first days of convalescence. Whenever I have been in love, Monsieur du Miroir has looked passionate and tender; and never did my mistress discard me but this too susceptible gentleman grew lackadaisical. His temper, also, rises to blood heat, fever heat, or boiling water heat, according to the measure of any wrong which might seem to have fallen entirely on myself. I have sometimes been calmed down by the sight of my own inordinate wrath depicted on his frowning brow.

Yet, however prompt in taking up my quarrels, I cannot call to mind that he ever struck a downright blow in my behalf; nor, in fact, do I perceive that any real and tangible good has resulted from his constant interference in my affairs; so that, in my distrustful moods, I am apt to suspect Monsieur du Miroir's sympathy to be mere outward show, not a whit better nor worse than other people's sympathy. Nevertheless, as mortal man must have something in the guise of sympathy,—and whether the true metal or merely copperwashed, is of less moment,—I choose rather to content myself with Monsieur du Miroir s such as it is than to seek the sterling coin, and perhaps miss even the counterfeit.

In my age of vanities I have often seen him in the ballroom, and might again were I to seek him there. We have encountered each other at the Tremont Theatre, where, however, he took his seat neither in the dress circle, pit, nor upper regions, nor threw a single glance at the stage, though the brightest star, even Fanny Kemble herself, might be culminating there. No; this whimsical friend of mine chose to linger in the saloon, near one of the large looking-glasses which throw back their pictures of the illuminated room. He is so full of these unaccountable eccentricities that I never like to notice Monsieur du Miroir, nor to acknowledge the slightest connection with him, in places of public resort.

He, however, has no scruple about claiming my acquaintance, even when his common sense, if he had any, might teach him that I would as willingly exchange a nod with the Old Nick. It was but the other day that he got into a large brass kettle at the entrance of a hardware store, and thrust his head, the moment afterwards, into a bright, new warming pan, whence he gave me a most merciless look of recognition. He smiled, and so did I; but these childish tricks make decent people rather shy of Monsieur du Miroir, and subject him to more dead cuts than any other gentleman in town.

One of this singular person's most remarkable peculiarities is his fondness for water, wherein he excels any temperance man whatever. His pleasure, it must be owned, is not so much to drink it (in which respect a very moderate quantities will answer his occasions) as to souse himself over head and ears wherever he may meet with it. Perhaps he is a merman, or born of a mermaid's marriage with a mortal, and thus amphibious by hereditary right, like the children which the old river deities, or nymphs of fountains, gave to earthly love. When no cleaner bathing-place happened to be at hand, I have seen the foolish fellow in a horse pond.

Sometimes he refreshes himself in the trough of a town pump, without caring what the people think about him. Often, while carefully picking my way along the street after a heavy shower, I have been scandalized to see Monsieur du Miroir, in full dress, paddling from one mud puddle to another, and plunging into the filthy depths of each. Seldom have I peeped into a well without discerning this ridiculous gentleman at the bottom, whence he gazes up, as through a long telescopic tube, and probably makes discoveries among the stars by daylight. Wandering along lonesome paths or in pathless forests, when I have come to virgin fountains, of which it would have been pleasant to deem myself the first discoverer, I have started to find Monsieur du Miroir there before me.

The solitude seemed lonelier for his presence. I have leaned from a precipice that frowns over Lake George, which the French call Nature's font of sacramental water, and used it in their log churches here and their cathedrals beyond the sea, and seen him far below in that pure element. At Niagara, too, where I would gladly have forgotten both myself and him, I could not help observing my companion in the smooth water on the very verge of the cataract just above the Table Rock. Were I to reach the sources of the Nile, I should expect to meet him there. Unless he be another Ladurlad, whose garments the depths of ocean could not moisten, it is difficult to conceive how he keeps himself in any decent pickle; though I am bound to confess that his clothes seem always as dry and comfortable as my own. But, as a friend, I could wish that he would not so often expose himself in liquor.

All that I have hitherto related may be classed among those little personal oddities which agreeably diversify the surface of society, and, though they may sometimes annoy us, yet keep our daily intercourse fresher and livelier than if they were done away. By an occasional hint, however, I have endeavoured to pave the way for stranger things to come, which, had they been disclosed at once. Monsieur du Miroir might have been deemed a shadow, and myself a person of no veracity, and this truthful history a fabulous legend. But, now that the reader knows me worthy of his confidence, I will begin to make him stare.

To speak frankly, then, I could bring the most astounding proofs that Monsieur du Miroir is at least a conjurer, if not one of that unearthly tribe with whom conjurers deal. He has inscrutable methods of conveying himself from place to place with the rapidity of the swiftest steamboat or rail car. Brick walls and oaken doors and iron bolts are no impediment to his passage. Here in my chamber, for instance, as the evening deepens into night, I sit alone—the key turned and withdrawn from the lock, the keyhole stuffed with paper to keep out a peevish little blast of wind.

Yet, lonely as I seem, were I to lift one of the lamps and step five paces eastward, Monsieur du Miroir would be sure to meet me with a lamp also in his hand; and were I to take the stage-coach tomorrow, without giving him the least hint of my design, and post onward till the week's end, at whatever hotel I might find myself I should expect to share my private apartment with this inevitable Monsieur du Miroir. Or, out of a mere wayward fantasy, were I to go by moonlight and stand beside the stone font of the Shaker Spring at Canterbury, Monsieur du Miroir would set forth on the same fool's errand, and would not fail to meet me there.

Shall I heighten the reader's wonder? While writing these latter sentences, I happened to glance towards the large, round globe of one of the brass and-irons, and lo! a miniature apparition of Monsieur du Miroir, with his face widened and gro-

tesquely contorted, as if he were making fun of my amazement!
But he has played so many of these jokes that they begin to lose
their effect. Once, presumptuous that he was, he stole into the
heaven of a young lady's eyes; so that, while I gazed and was
dreaming only of herself, I found him also in my dream. Years
have so changed him since that he need never hope to enter
those heavenly orbs again.

From these veritable statements it will be readily concluded
that, had Monsieur du Miroir played such pranks in old witch
times, matters might have gone hard with him; at least, if the
constable and *posse comitatus* could have executed a warrant, or
the jailer had been cunning enough to keep him. But it has often
occurred to me as a very singular circumstance, and as betokening either a temperament morbidly suspicious or some weighty
cause of apprehension, that he never trusts himself within the
grasp even of his most intimate friend. If you step forward to
meet him, he readily advances; if you offer him your hand, he
extends his own with an air of the utmost frankness; but, though
you calculate upon a hearty shake, you do not get hold of his
little finger. Ah, this Monsieur du Miroir is a slippery fellow!

These truly are matters of special admiration. After vainly
endeavouring, by the strenuous exertion of my own wits, to gain
a satisfactory insight into the character of Monsieur du Miroir, I
had recourse to certain wise men, and also to books of abstruse
philosophy, seeking who it was that haunted me, and why. I
heard long lectures, and read huge volumes with little profit beyond the knowledge that many former instances are recorded, in
successive ages, of similar connections between ordinary mortals
and beings possessing the attributes of Monsieur du Miroir.

Some now alive, perhaps, besides myself have such attendants.
Would that Monsieur du Miroir could be persuaded to transfer his attachment to one of those, and allow some other of his
race to assume the situation that he now holds in regard to me!
If I must needs have so intrusive an intimate, who stares me in
the face in my closest privacy and follows me even to my bedchamber, I should prefer—scandal apart—the laughing bloom

of a young girl to the dark and bearded gravity of my present companion. But such desires are never to be gratified. Though the members of Monsieur du Miroir's family have been accused, perhaps justly, of visiting their friends often in splendid halls, and seldom in darksome dungeons, yet they exhibit a rare constancy to the objects of their first attachment, however unlovely in person or unamiable in disposition—however unfortunate, or even infamous, and deserted by all the world besides. So will it be with my associate.

Our fates appear inseparably blended. It is my belief, as I find him mingling with my earliest recollections, that we came into existence together, as my shadow follows me into the sunshine, and that hereafter, as heretofore, the brightness or gloom of my fortunes will shine upon or darken the face of Monsieur du Miroir. As we have been young together, and as it is now near the summer noon with both of us, so, if long life be granted, shall each count his own wrinkles on the other's brow and his white hairs on the other's head.

And when the coffin lid shall have closed over me, and that face and form, which, more truly than the lover swears it to his beloved, are the sole light of his existence,—when they shall be laid in that dark chamber, whither his swift and secret footsteps cannot bring him,—then what is to become of poor Monsieur du Miroir? Will he have the fortitude, with my other friends, to take a last look at my pale countenance? Will he walk foremost in the funeral train? Will he come often and haunt around my grave, and weed away the nettles, and plant flowers amid the verdure, and scrape the moss out of the letters of my burial stone? Will he linger where I have lived, to remind the neglectful world of one who staked much to win a name, but will not then care whether he lost or won?

Not thus will he prove his deep fidelity. Oh, what terror, if this friend of mine, after our last farewell, should step into the crowded street, or roam along our old frequented path by the still waters, or sit down in the domestic circle where our faces are most familiar and beloved! No; but when the rays of heaven shall bless me no more, nor the thoughtful lamplight gleam upon my studies, nor the cheerful fireside gladden the meditative man, then, his task fulfilled, shall this mysterious being vanish from the earth forever. He will pass to the dark realm of nothingness, but will not find me there.

There is something fearful in bearing such a relation to a creature so imperfectly known, and in the idea that, to a certain extent, all which concerns myself will be reflected in its consequences upon him. When we feel that another is to share the selfsame fortune with ourselves, we judge more severely of our prospects, and withhold our confidence from that delusive magic which appears to shed an infallibility of happiness over our own pathway. Of late years, indeed, there has been much to sadden my intercourse with Monsieur du Miroir. Had not our union been a necessary condition of our life, we must have been estranged ere now.

In early youth, when my affections were warm and free, I loved him well, and could always spend a pleasant hour in his society, chiefly because it gave me an excellent opinion of myself. Speechless as he was, Monsieur du Miroir had then a most agreeable way of calling me a handsome fellow; and I, of course, returned the compliment; so that, the more we kept each other's company, the greater coxcombs we mutually grew. But neither of us need apprehend any such misfortune now. When we chance to meet,—for it is chance oftener than design,—each glances sadly at the other's forehead, dreading wrinkles there; and at our temples, whence the hair is thinning away too early; and at the sunken eyes, which no longer shed a gladsome light over the whole face.

I involuntarily peruse him as a record of my heavy youth, which has been wasted in sluggishness for lack of hope and impulse, or equally thrown away in toil that had no wise motive and has accomplished no good end. I perceive that the tranquil gloom of a disappointed soul has darkened through his countenance, where the blackness of the future seems to mingle with the shadows of the past, giving him the aspect of a fated man. Is it too wild a thought that my fate may have assumed this image of myself, and therefore haunts me with such inevitable pertinacity, originating every act which it appears to imitate, while it deludes me by pretending to share the events of which it is merely the emblem and the prophecy? I must banish this idea, or it will throw too deep an awe round my companion. At our next meeting, especially if it be at midnight or in solitude, I fear that I shall glance aside and shudder; in which case, as Monsieur du Miroir is extremely sensitive to ill treatment, he also will avert his eyes and express horror or disgust

But no; this is unworthy of me. As of old I sought his society for the bewitching dreams of woman's love which he inspired and because I fancied a bright fortune in his aspect, so now will I hold daily and long communion with him for the sake of the stem lessons that he will teach my manhood. With folded arms we will sit face to face, and lengthen out our silent converse till a wiser cheerfulness shall have been wrought from the very texture of despondency. He will say, perhaps indignantly, that it befits only him to mourn for the decay of outward grace, which, while he possessed it, was his all. But have not you, he will ask, a treasure in reserve, to which every year may add far more value than age or death itself can snatch from that miserable clay? He will tell me that though the bloom of life has been nipped with a frost, yet the soul must not sit shivering in its cell, but bestir itself manfully, and kindle a genial warmth from its own exercise against the autumnal and the wintry atmosphere.

And I, in return, will bid him be of good cheer, nor take it amiss that I must blanch his locks and wrinkle him up like a wilted apple, since it shall be my endeavour so to beautify his face with intellect and mild benevolence that he shall profit immensely by the change. But here a smile will glimmer somewhat sadly over Monsieur du Miroir's visage.

When this subject shall have been sufficiently discussed we may take up others as important. Reflecting upon his power of following me to the remotest regions and into the deepest privacy, I will compare the attempt to escape him to the hopeless race that men sometimes run with memory, or their own hearts, or their moral selves, which, though burdened with cares enough to crush an elephant, will never be one step behind. I will be self-contemplative, as Nature bids me, and make him the picture or visible type of what I muse upon, that my mind may not wander so vaguely as heretofore, chasing its own shadow through a chaos and catching only the monsters that abide there.

Then we will turn our thoughts to the spiritual world, of the reality of which my companions shall furnish me an illustration, if not an argument; for, as we have only the testimony of the eye to Monsieur du Miroir's existence, while all the other senses would fail to inform us that such a figure stands within arm's length, wherefore should there not be beings innumerable close beside us, and filling heaven and earth with their multitude, yet of whom no corporeal perception can take cognizance?

A blind man might as reasonably deny that Monsieur du Miroir exists as we, because the Creator has hitherto withheld the spiritual perception, can therefore contend that there are no spirits. Oh, there are! And, at this moment, when the subject of which I write has grown strong within me and surrounded itself with those solemn and awful associations which might have seemed most alien to it, I could fancy that Monsieur du Miroir himself is a wanderer from the spiritual world, with nothing human except his delusive garment of visibility. Methinks I should tremble now were his wizard power of gliding through all impediments in search of me to place him suddenly before my eyes.

Ha! What is yonder? Shape of mystery, did the tremor of my heartstrings vibrate to thine own, and call thee from thy home among the dancers of the northern lights, and shadows flung from departed sunshine, and giant spectres that appear on clouds at daybreak and affright the climber of the Alps? In truth it startled me, as I threw a wary glance eastward across the chamber, to discern an unbidden guest with his eyes bent on mine. The identical *Monsieur du Miroir!* Still there he sits and returns my gaze with as much of awe and curiosity as if he, too, had spent a solitary evening in fantastic musings and made me his theme.

So inimitably does he counterfeit that I could almost doubt which of us is the visionary form, or whether each be not the other's mystery, and both twin brethren of one fate in mutually reflected spheres. O friend, canst thou not hear and answer me? Break down the barrier between us! Grasp my hand! Speak! Listen! A few words, perhaps, might satisfy the feverish yearning of my soul for some master thought that should guide me through this labyrinth of life, teaching wherefore I was born, and how to do my task on earth, and what is death. Alas! Even that unreal image should forget to ape me and smile at these vain questions. Thus do mortals deify, as it were, a mere shadow of themselves, a spectre of human reason, and ask of that to unveil the mysteries which Divine Intelligence has revealed so far as needful to our guidance, and hid the rest.

Farewell, Monsieiur du Miroir. Of you, perhaps, as of many men, it may be doubted whether you are the wiser, though your whole business is reflection.

The Great Carbuncle
(A Tale from *Twice Told Tales* Volume 1)

At nightfall, once, in the olden time, on the rugged side of one of the Crystal Hills, a party of adventurers were refreshing themselves, after a toilsome and fruitless quest for the Great Carbuncle. They had come thither, not as friends, nor partners in the enterprise, but each, save one youthful pair, impelled by his own selfish and solitary longing for this wondrous gem. Their feeling of brotherhood, however, was strong enough to induce them to contribute a mutual aid in building a rude hut of branches, and kindling a great fire of shattered pines, that had drifted down the headlong current of the Amonoosuck, on the lower bank of which they were to pass the night.

There was but one of their number, perhaps, who had become so estranged from natural sympathies, by the absorbing spell of the pursuit, as to acknowledge no satisfaction at the sight of human faces, in the remote and solitary region whither they had ascended. A vast extent of wilderness lay between them and the nearest settlement, while scant a mile above their heads, was that bleak verge, where the hills throw off their shaggy mantle of forest trees, and either robe themselves in clouds, or tower naked into the sky. The roar of the Amonoosuck would have been too awful for endurance, if only a solitary man had listened, while the mountain stream talked with the wind.

The adventurers, therefore, exchanged hospitable greetings, and welcomed one another to the hut, where each man was the host, and all were the guests of the whole company. They spread their individual supplies of food on the flat surface of a rock, and partook of a general repast; at the close of which, a sentiment of good-fellowship was perceptible among the party, though repressed by the idea, that the renewed search for the Great Carbuncle must make them strangers again, in the morning.

Seven men and one young woman, they warmed themselves together at the fire, which extended its bright wall along the whole front of their *wigwam*. As they observed the various and contrasted figures that made up the assemblage, each man looking like a caricature of himself, in the unsteady light that flickered over him, they came mutually to the conclusion, that an odder society had never met, in city or wilderness—on mountain or plain.

The eldest of the group, a tall, lean, weather-beaten man, some sixty years of age, was clad in the skins of wild animals, whose fashion of dress he did well to imitate, since the deer, the wolf, and the bear, had long been his most intimate companions. He was one of those ill-fated mortals, such as the Indians told of, whom in their early youth, the Great Carbuncle smote with a peculiar madness, and became the passionate dream of their existence. All, who visited that region, knew him as the Seeker, and by no other name. As none could remember when he first took up the search, there went a fable in the valley of the Saco, that for his inordinate lust after the Great Carbuncle, he had been condemned to wander among the mountains till the end of time, still with the same feverish hopes at sunrise—the same despair at eve.

Near this miserable Seeker sat a little elderly personage, wearing a high crowned hat, shaped somewhat like a crucible. He was from beyond the sea, a Doctor Cacaphodel, who had wilted and dried himself into a mummy, by continually stooping over charcoal furnaces, and inhaling unwholesome fumes, during his researches in chemistry and alchemy. It was told of him, whether truly or not, that, at the commencement of his studies, he had drained his body of all its richest blood, and wasted it, with other inestimable ingredients, in an unsuccessful experiment—

and had never been a well man since.

Another of the adventurers was Master Ichabod Pigsnort, a weighty merchant and selectman of Boston, and an elder of the famous Mr. Norton's church. His enemies had a ridiculous story, that Master Pigsnort was accustomed to spend a whole hour, after prayer time, every morning and evening, in wallowing naked among an immense quantity of pine-tree shillings, which were the earliest silver coinage of Massachusetts. The fourth, whom we shall notice, had no name, that his companions knew of, and was chiefly distinguished by a sneer that always contorted his thin visage, and by a prodigious pair of spectacles, which were supposed to deform and discolour the whole face of nature, to this gentleman's perception.

The fifth adventurer likewise lacked a name, which was the greater pity, as he appeared to be a poet. He was a bright-eyed man, but woefully pined away, which was no more than natural, if, as some people affirmed, his ordinary diet was fog, morning mist, and a slice of the densest cloud within his reach, sauced with moonshine, whenever he could get it. Certain it is, that the poetry, which flowed from him, had a smack of all these dainties.

The sixth of the party was a young man of haughty mien, and sat somewhat apart from the rest, wearing his plumed hat loftily among his elders, while the fire glittered on the rich embroidery of his dress, and gleamed intensely on the jewelled pommel of his sword. This was the Lord de Vere, who, when at home, was said to spend much of his time in the burial vault of his dead progenitors, rummaging their mouldy coffins in search of all the earthly pride and vain glory, that was hidden among bones and dust; so that, besides his own share, he had the collected haughtiness of his whole line of ancestry.

Lastly, there was a handsome youth in rustic garb, and by his side, a blooming little person, in whom a delicate shade of maiden reserve was just melting into the rich glow of a young wife's affection. Her name was Hannah, and her husband's Matthew; two homely names, yet well enough adapted to the simple pair, who seemed strangely out of place among the whimsical fraternity whose wits had been set agog by the Great Carbuncle.

Beneath the shelter of one hut, in the bright blaze of the same fire, sat this varied group of adventurers, all so intent upon a single object, that, of whatever else they began to speak, their closing words were sure to be illuminated with the Great Carbuncle. Several related the circumstances that brought them thither. One had listened to a traveller's tale of this marvellous stone, in his own distant country, and had immediately been seized with such a thirst for beholding it, as could only be quenched in its intensest lustre. Another, so long ago as when the famous Captain Smith visited these coasts, had seen it blazing far at sea, and had felt no rest in all the intervening years, till now that he took up the search.

A third, being encamped on a hunting expedition, full forty miles south of the White Mountains, awoke at midnight, and beheld the Great Carbuncle gleaming like a meteor, so that the shadows of the trees fell backward from it. They spoke of the innumerable attempts, which had been made to reach the spot, and of the singular fatality which had hitherto withheld success from all adventurers, though it might seem so easy to follow to its source a light that overpowered the moon, and almost matched the sun. It was observable that each smiled scornfully at the madness of every other, in anticipating better fortune than the past, yet nourished a scarcely hidden conviction, that he would himself be the favoured one.

As if to allay their too sanguine hopes, they recurred to the Indian traditions, that a spirit kept watch about the gem, and bewildered those who sought it, either by removing it from peak to peak of the higher hills, or by calling up a mist from the enchanted lake over which it hung. But these tales were deemed unworthy of credit; all professing to believe, that the search had been baffled by want of sagacity or perseverance in the adventurers, or such other causes as might naturally obstruct the passage to any given point, among the intricacies of forest, valley, and mountain.

In a pause of the conversation, the wearer of the prodigious spectacles looked round upon the party, making each individual, in turn, the object of the sneer which invariably dwelt upon his countenance.

"So, fellow-pilgrims," said he, "here we are, seven wise men and one fair damsel—who, doubtless, is as wise as any gray beard of the company: here we are, I say, all bound on the same goodly enterprise. Methinks now, it were not amiss, that each of us declare what he proposes to do with the Great Carbuncle, provided he have the good hap to clutch it. What says our friend in the bear-skin? How mean you, good Sir, to enjoy the prize which you have been seeking, the Lord knows how long? among the Crystal Hills?"

"How enjoy it!" exclaimed the aged Seeker, bitterly. "I hope for no enjoyment from it—that folly has past, long ago! I keep up the search for this accursed stone, because the vain ambition of my youth has become a fate upon me, in old age. The pursuit alone is my strength—the energy of my soul—the warmth of my blood, and the pith and marrow of my bones! Were I to turn my back upon it, I should fall down dead, on the hither side of the Notch, which is the gate-way of this mountain region. Yet, not to have my wasted life time back again, would I give up my hopes of the Great Carbuncle! Having found it, I shall bear it to a certain cavern that I wot of, and there, grasping it in my arms, lie down and die, and keep it buried with me forever."

"Oh, wretch, regardless of the interests of science!" cried Doctor Cacaphodel, with philosophic indignation. "Thou art not worthy to behold, even from afar off, the lustre of this most precious gem that ever was concocted in the laboratory of Nature. Mine is the sole purpose for which a wise man may desire the possession of the Great Carbuncle. Immediately on obtaining it—for I have a presentiment, good people, that tile prize is reserved to crown my scientific reputation—I shall return to Europe, and employ my remaining years in reducing it to its first elements. A portion of the stone will I grind to impalpable powder; other parts shall be dissolved in acids, or whatever solvents will act upon so admirable a composition; and the remainder I design to melt in the crucible, or set on fire with the blow-pipe. By these various methods, I shall gain an accurate analysis, and finally bestow the result of my labours upon the world, in a folio volume."

"Excellent!" quoth the man with the spectacles. "Nor need you hesitate, learned Sir, on account of the necessary destruction of the gem; since the perusal of your folio may teach every mother's son of us to concoct a Great Carbuncle of his own."

"But, verily," said Master Ichabod Pigsnort, "for mine own part, I object to the making of these counterfeits, as being calculated to reduce the marketable value of the true gem. I tell ye frankly, Sirs, I have an interest in keeping up the price. Here have I quitted my regular traffic, leaving my warehouse in the care of my clerks, and putting my credit to great hazard, and furthermore, have put myself to peril of death or captivity by the accursed heathen savages—and all this without daring to ask the prayers of the congregation, because the quest for the Great Carbuncle is deemed little better than a traffic with the evil one. Now think ye that I would have done this grievous wrong to my soul, body, reputation and estate, without a reasonable chance of profit?"

"Not I, pious Master Pigsnort," said the man with the spectacles.—"I never laid such a great folly to thy charge."

"Truly, I hope not," said the merchant. "Now, as touching this Great Carbuncle, I am free to own that I have never had a glimpse of it; but be it only the hundredth part so bright as people tell, it will surely outvalue the Great Mogul's best diamond, which he holds at an incalculable sum. Wherefore, I am minded to put the Great Carbuncle on ship board, and voyage with it to England, France, Spain, Italy, or into Heathendom, if Providence should send me thither, and, in a word, dispose of the gem to the best bidder among the potentates of the earth, that he may place it among his crown jewels. If any of ye have a wiser plan, let him expound it."

"That have I, thou sordid man!" exclaimed the poet. "Dost

509

thou desire nothing brighter than gold, that thou wouldst transmute all this ethereal lustre into such dross, as thou wallowest in already? For myself, hiding the jewel under my cloak, I shall hie me back to my attic chamber, in one of the darksome alleys of London. There, night and day, will I gaze upon it—my soul shall drink its radiance—it shall be diffused throughout my intellectual powers, and gleam brightly in every line of poesy that I indite. Thus, long ages after I am gone, the splendour of the Great Carbuncle will blaze around my name!"

"Well said, Master Poet!" cried he of the spectacles. "Hide it under that cloak, say'st thou? Why, it will gleam through the holes, and make thee look like a Jack o'lanthern!"

"To think!" ejaculated the Lord de Vere, rather to himself, than his companions, the best of whom he held utterly unworthy of his intercourse,—"to think that a fellow in a tattered cloak should talk of conveying the Great Carbuncle to a garret in Grub street! Have not I resolved within myself, that the whole earth contains no fitter ornament for the great hall of my ancestral castle? There shall it flame for ages, making a noonday of midnight, glittering on the suits of armour, the banners, and *escutcheons*, that hang around the wall, and keeping bright the memory of heroes. Wherefore have all other adventurers sought the prize in vain, but that I might win it, and make it a symbol of the glories of our lofty line? And never, on the diadem of the White Mountains, did the Great Carbuncle hold a place half so honoured, as is reserved for it in the hall of the de Veres!"

"It is a noble thought," said the Cynic, with an obsequious sneer. "Yet, might I presume to say so, the gem would make a rare sepulchral lamp, and would display the glories of your lordship's progenitors more truly in the ancestral vault, than in the castle hall."

"Nay forsooth," observed Matthew, the young rustic, who sat hand in hand with his bride, "the gentleman has bethought himself of a profitable use for this bright stone. Hannah here and I are seeking it for a like purpose."

"How, fellow!" exclaimed his lordship, in surprise. "What

castle hall hast thou to hang it in?"

"No castle," replied Matthew, "but as neat a cottage as any within sight of the Crystal Hills. Ye must know, friends, that Hannah and I, being wedded the last week, have taken up the search of the Great Carbuncle, because we shall need its light in the long winter evenings; and it will be such a pretty thing to show the neighbours, when they visit us. It will shine through the house, so that we may pick up a pin in any corner, and will set all the windows a-glowing, as if there were a great fire of pine knots in the chimney. And then how pleasant, when we awake in the night, to be able to see one another's faces!"

There was a general smile among the adventurers, at the simplicity of the young couple's project, in regard to this wondrous and invaluable stone, with which the greatest monarch on earth might have been proud to adorn his palace. Especially the man with spectacles, who had sneered at all the company in turn, now twisted his visage into such an expression of ill-natured mirth, that Matthew asked him, rather peevishly, what he himself meant to do with the Great Carbuncle.

"The Great Carbuncle!" answered the Cynic, with ineffable scorn. "Why, you blockhead, there is no such thing, in *rerum natura*. I have come three thousand miles, and am resolved to set my foot on every peak of these mountains, and poke my head into every chasm, for the sole purpose of demonstrating to the satisfaction of any man, one whit less an ass than thyself, that the Great Carbuncle is all a humbug!"

Vain and foolish were the motives that had brought most of the adventurers to the Crystal Hills, but none so vain, so foolish, and so impious too, as that of the scoffer with the prodigious spectacles. He was one of those wretched and evil men, whose yearnings are downward to the darkness, instead of Heavenward, and who, could they but extinguish the lights which God hath kindled for us, would count the midnight gloom their chiefest glory. As the Cynic spoke, several of the party were startled by a gleam of red splendour, that showed the huge shapes of the surrounding mountains, and the rock-bestrewn bed of the turbulent river, with an illumination unlike that of their fire, on the trunks and black boughs of the forest trees. They listened for the roll of thunder, but heard nothing, and were glad that the tempest came not near them. The stars, those dial-points of Heaven, now warned the adventurers to close their eyes on the blazing logs, and open them, in dreams, to the glow of the Great Carbuncle.

The young married couple had taken their lodgings in the furthest corner of the *wigwam*, and were separated from the rest of the party by a curtain of curiously woven twigs, such as might have hung, in deep festoons around the bridal bower of Eve. The modest little wife had wrought this piece of tapestry, while the other guests were talking. She and her husband fell asleep with hands tenderly clasped, and awoke, from visions of unearthly radiance, to meet the more blessed light of one another's eyes. They awoke at the same instant, and with one happy smile beaming over their two faces, which grew brighter, with their consciousness of the reality of life and love. But no sooner did she recollect where they were, than the bride peeped through the interstices of the leafy curtain, and saw that the outer room of the hut was deserted.

"Up, dear Matthew!" cried she, in haste. "The strange folk are all gone! Up, this very minute, or we shall lose the Great Carbuncle!"

In truth, so little did these poor young people deserve the mighty prize which had lured them thither, that they had slept peacefully all night, and till the summits of the hills were glittering with sunshine; while the other adventurers had tossed their limbs in feverish wakefulness, or dreamed of climbing precipices, and set off to realize their dreams with the earliest peep of dawn. But Matthew and Hannah, after their calm rest, were as light as two young deer, and merely stops to say their prayers, and wash themselves in a cold pool of the Amonoosuck, and then to taste a morsel of food, ere they turned their faces to the mountainside. It was a sweet emblem of conjugal affection, as they toiled up the difficult ascent, gathering strength from the mutual aid which they afforded.

After several little accidents, such as a torn robe, a lost shoe, and the entanglement of Hannah's hair in a bough, they reached the upper verge of the forest, and were now to pursue a more adventurous course. The innumerable trunks and heavy foliage of the trees had hitherto shut in their thoughts, which now shrank affrighted from the region of wind, and cloud, and naked rocks, and desolate sunshine, that rose immeasurably above them. They gazed back at the obscure wilderness which they had traversed, and longed to be buried again in its depths, rather than trust themselves to so vast and visible a solitude.

"Shall we go on?" said Matthew, throwing his arm round Hannah's waist, both to protect her, and to comfort his heart by drawing her close to it.

But the little bride, simple as she was, had a woman's love of jewels, and could not forego the hope of possessing the very brightest in the world, in spite of the perils with which it must be won.

"Let us climb a little higher," whispered she, yet tremulously, as she turned her face upward to the lonely sky.

"Come then," said Matthew, mustering his manly courage, and drawing her along with him; for she became timid again, the moment that he grew bold.

And upward, accordingly, went the pilgrims of the Great Carbuncle, now treading upon the tops and thickly interwoven branches of dwarf pines, which, by the growth of centuries, though mossy with age, had barely reached three feet in altitude. Next, they came to masses and fragments of naked rock, heaped confusedly together, like a cairn reared by giants, in memory of a giant chief. In this bleak realm of upper air, nothing breathed, nothing grew; there was no life but what was concentred in their two hearts; they had climbed so high, that Nature herself seemed no longer to keep them company. She lingered beneath them, within the verge of the forest trees, and sent a farewell glance after her children, as they strayed where her own green footprints had never been.

But soon they were to be hidden from her eye. Densely and dark, the mists began to gather below, casting black spots of shadow on the vast landscape, and sailing heavily to one centre, as if the loftiest mountain peak had summoned a council of its kindred clouds. Finally, the vapors welded themselves, as it were, into a mass, presenting the appearance of a pavement over which the wanderers might have trodden, but where they would vainly have sought an avenue to the blessed earth which they had lost.

And the lovers yearned to behold that green earth again, more intensely, alas! than, beneath a clouded sky, they had ever desired a glimpse of Heaven. They even felt it a relief to their desolation, when the mists, creeping gradually up the mountain, concealed its lonely peak, and thus annihilated, at least for them, the whole region of visible space. But they drew closer together, with a fond and melancholy gaze, dreading lest the universal cloud should snatch them from each other's sight.

Still, perhaps, they would have been resolute to climb as far and as high, between earth and heaven, as they could find foothold, if Hannah's strength had not begun to fail, and with that, her courage also. Her breath grew short. She refused to burthen her husband with her weight, but often tottered against his side, and recovered herself each time by a feebler effort. At last, she sank down on one of the rocky steps of the acclivity.

"We are lost, dear Matthew," said she, mournfully. "We shall never find our way to the earth again. And, Oh, how happy we might have been in our cottage!"

"Dear heart!—we will yet be happy there," answered Matthew. "Look! In this direction, the sunshine penetrates the dismal mist. By its aid, I can direct our course to the passage of the Notch. Let us go back, love, and dream no more of the Great Carbuncle!"

"The sun cannot be yonder," said Hannah, with despondence. "By this time, it must be noon. If there could ever be any sunshine here, it would come from above our heads."

"But, look!" repeated Matthew, in a somewhat altered tone. "It is brightening every moment. If not sunshine, what can it be?"

Nor could the young bride any longer deny, that a radiance was breaking through the mist, and changing its dim hue to a dusky red, which continually grew more vivid, as if brilliant particles were interfused with the gloom. Now, also, the cloud began to roll away from the mountain, while, as it heavily withdrew, one object after another started out of its impenetrable obscurity into sight, with precisely the effect of a new creation, before the indistinctness of the old chaos had been completely swallowed up.

As the process went on, they saw the gleaming of water close at their feet, and found themselves on the very border of a mountain lake, deep, bright, clear, and calmly beautiful, spreading from brim to brim of a basin that had been scooped out of the solid rock. A ray of glory flashed across its surface. The pilgrims looked whence it should proceed, but closed their eyes with a thrill of awful admiration, to exclude the fervid splendour that glowed from the brow of a cliff, impending over the enchanted lake. For the simple pair had reached that lake of mystery, and found the long sought shrine of the Great Carbuncle!

They threw their arms around each other, and trembled at their own success; for, as the legends of this wondrous gem rushed thick upon their memory, they felt themselves marked out by fate—and the consciousness was fearful. Often, from childhood upward, they had seen it shining like a distant star. And now that star was throwing its intensest lustre on their hearts. They seemed changed to one another's eyes, in the red brilliancy that flamed upon their cheeks, while it lent the same fire to the lake, the rocks, and sky, and to the mists which had rolled back before its power.

But, with their next glance, they beheld an object that drew their attention even from the mighty stone. At the base of the cliff, directly beneath the Great Carbuncle, appeared the figure of a man, with his arms extended in the act of climbing, and his face turned upward, as if to drink the full gush of splendour. But he stirred not, no more than if changed to marble.

"It is the Seeker," whispered Hannah, convulsively grasping her husband's arm. "Matthew, he is dead!"

"The joy of success has killed him," replied Matthew, trembling violently.—"Or perhaps the very light of the Great Carbuncle was death!"

"The Great Carbuncle," cried a peevish voice behind them. "The Great Humbug! If you have found it, prithee point it out to me."

They turned their heads, and there was the Cynic, with his prodigious spectacles set carefully on his nose, staring now at the lake, now at the rocks, now at the distant masses of vapor, now right at the Great Carbuncle itself, yet seemingly as unconscious of its light, as if all the scattered clouds were condensed about his person. Though its radiance actually threw the shadow of the unbeliever at his own feet, as he turned his back upon the glorious jewel, he would not be convinced that there was the least glimmer there.

"Where is your Great Humbug?" he repeated. "I challenge you to make me see it!"

"There," said Matthew, incensed at such perverse blindness, and turning the Cynic round towards the illuminated cliff. "Take off those abominable spectacles, and you cannot help seeing it!"

Now these coloured spectacles probably darkened the Cynic's sight, in at least as great a degree as the smoked glasses through which people gaze at an eclipse. With resolute bravado, however, he snatched them from his nose, and fixed a bold stare full upon the ruddy blaze of the Great Carbuncle. But, scarcely had he encountered it, when, with a deep, shuddering groan, he dropt his head, and pressed both hands across his miserable eyes. Thenceforth there was, in very truth, no light of the Great Carbuncle, nor any other light on earth, nor light of Heaven itself, for the poor Cynic. So long accustomed to view all objects through a medium that deprived them of every glimpse of brightness, a single flash of so glorious a phenomenon, striking upon his naked vision, had blinded him forever.

"Matthew," said Hannah, clinging to him, "let us go hence!"

Matthew saw that she was faint, and kneeling down, supported her in his arms, while he threw some of the thrillingly cold water of the enchanted lake upon her face and bosom. It revived her, but could not renovate her courage.

"Yes, dearest!" cried Matthew, pressing her tremulous form to his breast,—"we will go hence, and return to our humble cottage. The blessed sunshine, and the quiet moonlight, shall come through our window. We will kindle the cheerful glow of our hearth, at eventide, and be happy in its light. But never again will we desire more light than all the world may share with us."

"No," said his bride, "for how could we live by day, or sleep by night, in this awful blaze of the Great Carbuncle!"

Out of the hollow of their hands, they drank each a draught from the lake, which presented them its waters uncontaminated by an earthly lip. Then, lending their guidance to the blinded Cynic, who uttered not a word, and even stifled his groans in his own most wretched heart, they began to descend the mountain. Yet, as they left the shore, till then untrodden, of the Spirit's lake, they threw a farewell glance towards the cliff, and beheld the vapors gathering in dense volumes, through which the gem burned duskily.

As touching the other pilgrims of the Great Carbuncle, the legend goes on to tell, that the worshipful Master Ichabod Pigsnort soon gave up the quest, as a desperate speculation, and wisely resolved to betake himself again to his warehouse, near the town-dock, in Boston. But, as he passed through the Notch of the mountains, a war party of Indians captured our unlucky merchant, and carried him to Montreal, there holding him in bondage, till, by the payment of a heavy ransom, he had woefully subtracted from his hoard of pine-tree shillings. By his long absence, moreover, his affairs had become so disordered, that, for the rest of his life, instead of wallowing in silver, he had seldom a sixpence worth of copper.

Doctor Cacaphodel, the alchemist, returned to his laboratory with a prodigious fragment of granite, which he ground to powder, dissolved in acids, melted in the crucible, and burnt with the blow-pipe, and published the result of his experiments in one of the heaviest folios of the day. And, for all these purposes, tile gem itself could not have answered better than the granite. The poet, by a somewhat similar mistake, made prize of a great piece of ice, which he found in a sunless chasm of the mountains, and swore that it corresponded, in all points, with his idea of the Great Carbuncle.

The critics say, that, if his poetry lacked the splendour of the gem, it retained all the coldness of the ice. The Lord de Vere went back to his ancestral hall, where he contented himself with a wax-lighted chandelier, and filled, in due course of time, another coffin in the ancestral vault. As the funeral torches gleamed within that dark receptacle, there was no need of the Great Carbuncle to shew the vanity of earthly pomp.

The Cynic, having cast aside his spectacles, wandered about the world, a miserable object, and was punished with an agonizing desire of light, for the wilful blindness of his former life. The whole night long, he would lift his splendour-blasted orbs to the moon and stars; he turned his face eastward, at sunrise, as duly as a Persian idolater; he made a pilgrimage to Rome, to witness the magnificent illumination of Saint Peter's church; and finally perished in the great fire of London, into the midst of which he had thrust himself, with the desperate idea of catching one feeble ray from the blaze, that was kindling earth and heaven.

Matthew and his bride spent many peaceful years, and were fond of telling the legend of the Great Carbuncle. The tale, however, towards the close of their lengthened lives, did not meet with the full credence that had been accorded to it by those, who remembered the ancient lustre of the gem. For it is affirmed, that, from the hour when two mortals had shown themselves so simply wise, as to reject a jewel which would have dimmed all earthly things, its splendour waned. When other pilgrims reached the cliff, they found only an opaque stone, with particles of mica glittering on its surface.

There is also a tradition that, as the youthful pair departed, the gem was loosened from the forehead of the cliff, and fell into the enchanted lake, and that, at noontide, the Seeker's form may still be seen to bend over its quenchless-gleam.

Some few believe that this inestimable stone is blazing, as of old, and say that they have caught its radiance, like a flash of summer lightning, far down the valley of the Saco. And be it owned, that, many a mile from the Crystal Hills, I saw a wondrous light around their summits, and was lured, by the faith of poesy, to be the latest pilgrim of the *GREAT CARBUNCLE.*

P.'s Correspondence
(A tale from *Mosses From an Old Manse and Other Stories*)

My unfortunate friend P. has lost the thread of his life by the interposition of long intervals of partially disordered reason. The past and present are jumbled together in his mind in a manner often productive of carious results, and which will be better understood after the perusal of the following letter than from any description that I could give. The poor fellow, without once stirring from the little whitewashed, iron-grated room to which he alludes in his first paragraph, is nevertheless a great traveller, and meets in his wanderings a variety of personages who have long ceased to be visible to any eye save his own.

In my opinion, all this is not so much a delusion as a partly wilful and partly involuntary sport of the imagination, to which his disease has imparted such morbid energy that he beholds these spectral scenes and characters with no less distinctness than a play upon the stage, and with somewhat more of illusive credence. Many of his letters are in my possession, some based upon the same vagary as the present one, and others upon hypotheses not a whit short of it in absurdity.

The whole form a series of correspondence, which, should fate seasonably remove my poor friend from what is to him a world of moonshine, I promise myself a pious pleasure in editing for the public eye. P. had always a hankering after literary reputation, and has made more than one unsuccessful effort to achieve it. It would not be a little odd if, after missing his object while seeking it by the light of reason, he should prove to have stumbled upon it in his misty excursions beyond the limits of sanity.

London, February 29, 1845.

My dear Friend,—Old associations cling to the mind with astonishing tenacity. Daily custom grows up about us like a stone wall, and consolidates itself into almost as material entity as mankind's strongest architecture. It is sometimes a serious question with me whether ideas be not really visible and tangible and endowed with all the other qualities of matter. Sitting as I do at this moment in my hired apartment, writing beside the hearth, over which hangs a print of Queen Victoria, listening to the muffled roar of the world's metropolis, and with a window at but five paces distant, through which, whenever I please, I can gaze out on actual London,—with all this positive certainty as to my whereabouts, what kind of notion, do you think, is just now perplexing my brain?

Why,—would you believe it?—that all this time I am still an inhabitant of that wearisome little chamber—that whitewashed little chamber—that little chamber with its one small window, across which, from some inscrutable reason of taste or convenience, my landlord had placed a row of iron bars—that same little chamber, in short, whither your kindness has so often brought you to visit me! Will no length of time or breadth of space enfranchise me from that unlovely abode? I travel; but it seems to be like the snail, with my house upon my head. Ah, well! I am verging, I suppose, on that period of life when present scenes and events make but feeble impressions in comparison with those of yore; so that I must reconcile myself to be more and more the prisoner of Memory, who merely lets me hop about a little with her chain around my leg.

My letters of introduction have been of the utmost service, enabling me to make the acquaintance of several distinguished characters, who, until now, have seemed as remote from the sphere of my personal intercourse as the wits of Queen Anne's time or Ben Jonson's compotators at the Mermaid.

One of the first of which I availed myself was the letter to Lord Byron. I found his lordship looking much older than I had anticipated, although, considering his former irregularities of life and the various wear and tear of his constitution, not older than a man on the verge of sixty reasonably may look. But I had invested his earthly frame, in my imagination, with the poet's spiritual immortality. He wears a brown wig, very luxuriantly curled, and extending down over his forehead. The expression of his eyes is concealed by spectacles. His early tendency to obesity having increased.

Lord Byron is now enormously fat—so fat as to give the impression of a person quite overladen with his own flesh, and without sufficient vigour to diffuse his personal life through the great mass of corporeal substance which weighs upon him so cruelly. You gaze at the mortal heap; and, while it fills your eye with what purports to be Byron, you murmur within yourself, "For Heaven's sake, where is he?" Were I disposed to be caustic, I might consider this mass of earthly matter as the symbol, in a material shape, of those evil habits and carnal vices which unspiritualize man's nature and clog up his avenues of communication with the better life.

But this would be too harsh; and, besides. Lord Byron's morals have been improving while his outward man has swollen to such unconscionable circumference. Would that he were leaner; for though he did me the honour to present his hand, yet it was so puffed out with alien substance that I could not feel as if I had touched the hand that wrote Childe Harold.

On my entrance his lordship apologized for not rising to receive me on the sufficient plea that the gout for several years past had taken up its constant residence in his right foot, which accordingly was swathed in many rolls of flannel and deposited upon a cushion. The other foot was hidden in the drapery of his chair. Do you recollect whether Byron's right or left foot was the deformed one?

The noble poet's reconciliation with Lady Byron is now, as you are aware, of ten years' standing; nor does it exhibit, I am assured, any symptom of breach or fracture. They are said to be, if not a happy, at least a contented, or at all events a quiet couple, descending the slope of life with that tolerable degree of mutual support which will enable them to come easily and comfortably to the bottom. It is pleasant to reflect how entirely the poet has redeemed his youthful errors in this particular. Her ladyship's influence, it rejoices me to add, has been productive of the happiest results upon Lord Byron in a religious point of view. He now combines the most rigid tenets of Methodism with the ultra doctrines of the Puseytes; the former being perhaps due to the convictions wrought upon his mind by his noble consort, while the latter are the embroidery and picturesque illumination demanded by his imaginative character.

Much of whatever expenditure his increasing habits of thrift continue to allow him is bestowed in the reparation or beautifying of places of worship; and this nobleman, whose name was once considered a synonym of the foul fiend, is now all but canonized as a saint in many pulpits of the metropolis and elsewhere. In politics, Lord Byron is an uncompromising conservative, and loses no opportunity, whether in the House of Lords or in private circles, of denouncing and repudiating the mischievous and anarchical notions of his earlier day. Nor does he fail to visit similar sins in other people with the sincerest vengeance which his somewhat blunted pen is capable of inflicting. Southey and he are on the most intimate terms. You are aware, that some little time before the death of Moore, Byron caused that brilliant but reprehensible man to be ejected from his house.

Moore took the insult so much to heart that it is said

to have been one great cause of the fit of illness which brought him to the grave. Others pretend that the lyrist died in a very happy state of mind, singing one of his own sacred melodies, and expressing his belief that it would be heard within the gate of paradise, and gain him instant and honourable admittance. I wish he may have found it so.

I failed not, as you may suppose in the course of conversation with Lord Byron, to pay the meed of homage due to a mighty poet, by allusions to passages in Childe Harold, and Manfred, and Don Juan, which have made so large a portion of the music of my life. My words, whether apt or otherwise, were at least warm with the enthusiasm of one worthy to discourse of immortal poesy. It was evident, however, that they did not go precisely to the right spot. I could perceive that there was some mistake or other, and was not a little angry with myself, and ashamed of my abortive attempt to throw back, from my own heart to the gifted author's ear, the echo of those strains that have resounded throughout the world.

But by and by the secret peeped quietly out. Byron,—I have the information from his own lips, so that you need not hesitate to repeat it in literary circles,—Byron is preparing a new edition of his complete works, carefully corrected, expurgated, and amended, in accordance with his present creed of taste, morals, politics, and religion. It so happened that the very passages of highest inspiration to which I had alluded were among the condemned and rejected rubbish which it is his purpose to cast into the gulf of oblivion. To whisper you the truth, it appears to me that his passions having burned out, the extinction of their vivid and riotous flame has deprived Lord Byron of the illumination by which he not merely wrote, but was enabled to feel and comprehend what he had written. Positively he no longer understands his own poetry.

This became very apparent on his favouring me so far as to read a few specimens of *Don Juan* in the moralized version. Whatever is licentious, whatever disrespectful to the sacred mysteries of our faith, whatever morbidly melancholic or splenetically sportive, whatever assails settled constitutions of government or systems of society, whatever could wound the sensibility of any mortal, except a pagan, a republican, or a dissenter, has been unrelentingly blotted out, and its place supplied by unexceptionable verses in his lordship's later style. You may judge how much of the poem remains as hitherto published.

The result is not so good as might be wished; in plain terms, it is a very sad affair indeed; for, though the torches kindled in Tophet have been extinguished, they leave an abominably ill odour, and are succeeded by no glimpses of hallowed fire. It is to be hoped, nevertheless, that this attempt on Lord Byron's part to atone for his youthful errors will at length induce the Dean of Westminster, or whatever churchman is concerned, to allow Thorwaldsen's statue of the poet its due niche in the grand old Abbey. His bones, you know, when brought from Greece, were denied sepulture among those of his tuneful brethren there.

What a vile slip of the pen was that! How absurd in me to talk about burying the bones of Byron, whom I have just seen alive, and incased in a big, round bulk of flesh! But, to say the truth, a prodigiously fat man always impresses me as a kind of hobgoblin; in the very extravagance of his mortal system I find something akin to the immateriality of a ghost. And then that ridiculous old story darted into my mind, how that Byron died of fever at Missolonghi, above twenty years ago. More and more I recognize that we dwell in a world of shadows; and, for my part, I hold it hardly worth the trouble, to attempt a distinction between shadows in the mind and shadows out of it. If there be any difference, the former are rather the more substantial.

Only think of my good fortune! The venerable Robert Burns—now, if I mistake not, in his eighty-seventh year—

happens to be making a visit to London, as if on purpose to afford me an opportunity of grasping him by the hand. For upwards of twenty years past he has hardly left his quiet cottage in Ayrshire for a single night, and has only been drawn hither now by the irresistible persuasions of all the distinguished men in England. They wish to celebrate the patriarch's birthday by a festival. It will be the greatest literary triumph on record. Pray Heaven the little spirit of life within the aged bard's bosom may not be extinguished in the lustre of that hour! I have already had the honour of an introduction to him at the British Museum, where he was examining a collection of his own unpublished letters, interspersed with songs, which have escaped the notice of all his biographers.

Poh! Nonsense! What am I thinking of? How should Burns have been embalmed in biography when he is still a hearty old man?

The figure of the bard is tall and in the highest degree reverend, nor the less so that it is much bent by the burden of time. His white hair floats like a snowdrift around his face, in which are seen the furrows of intellect and passion, like the channels of headlong torrents that have foamed themselves away. The old gentleman is in excellent preservation considering his time of life. He has that crickety sort of liveliness—I mean the cricket's humour of chirping for any cause or none—which is perhaps the most favourable mood that can befall extreme old age.

Our pride forbids us to desire it for ourselves, although we perceive it to be a beneficence of nature in the case of others. I was surprised to find it in Burns. It seems as if his ardent heart and brilliant imagination had both burned down to the last embers, leaving only a little flickering flame in one comer, which keeps dancing upward and laughing all by itself, he is no longer capable of pathos. At the request of Allan Cunningham, he attempted to sing his own song to Mary in Heaven; but it was evident that the feeling of those verses, so profoundly true and so simply expressed, was entirely beyond the scope of his present sensibilities; and, when a touch of it did partially awaken him, the tears immediately gushed into his eyes and his voice broke into a tremulous cackle. And yet he but indistinctly knew wherefore he was weeping. Ah, he must not think again of Mary in Heaven until he shake off the dull impediment of time and ascend to meet her there.

Burns then began to repeat Tam O'Shanter; but was so tickled with its wit and humour—of which, however, I suspect he had but a traditionary sense—that he soon burst into a fit of chirruping laughter, succeeded by a cough, which brought this not very agreeable exhibition to a close. On the whole, I would rather not have witnessed it. It is a satisfactory idea, however, that the last forty years of the peasant poet's life have been passed in competence and perfect comfort Having been cured of his bardic improvidence for many a day past, and grown as attentive to the main chance as a canny Scotsman should be, he is now considered to be quite well off as to pecuniary circumstances. This, I suppose, is worth having lived so long for.

I took occasion to inquire of some of the countrymen of Burns in regard to the health of Sir Walter Scott. His condition, I am sorry to say, remains the same as for ten years past; it is that of a hopeless paralytic, palsied not more in body than in those nobler attributes of which the body is the instrument. And thus he vegetates from day to day and from year to year at that splendid fantasy of Abbotsford, which grew out of his brain, and became a symbol of the great romancer's tastes, feelings, studies, prejudices, and modes of intellect. Whether in verse, prose, or architecture, he could achieve but one thing, although that one in infinite variety.

There he reclines, on a couch in his library, and is said to spend whole hours of every day in dictating tales to an amanuensis,—to an imaginary amanuensis; for it is not deemed worth any one's trouble now to take down what flows from that once brilliant fancy, every image of which was formerly worth gold and capable of being coined. Yet Cunningham, who has lately seen him, assures me that there is now and then a touch of the genius,—a striking combination of incident, or a picturesque trait of character, such as no other man alive could have hit off,—a glimmer from that ruined mind, as if the sun had suddenly flashed on a half-rusted helmet in the gloom of an ancient hall. But the plots of these romances become inextricably confused; the characters melt into one another; and the tale loses itself like the course of a stream flowing through muddy and marshy ground.

For my part, I can hardly regret that Sir Walter Scott had lost his consciousness of outward things before his works went out of vogue. It was good that he should forget his fame rather than that fame should first have forgotten him. Were he still a writer, and as brilliant a one as ever, he could no longer maintain anything like the same position in literature. The world, nowadays, requires a more earnest purpose, a deeper moral, and a closer and homelier truth than he was qualified to supply it with.

Yet who can be to the present generation even what Scott has been to the past? I had expectations from a young man—one Dickens—who published a few magazine articles, very rich in humour, and not without symptoms of genuine pathos, but the poor fellow died shortly after commencing an odd series of sketches, entitled, I think, the *Pickwick Papers*. Not impossibly the world has lost more than it dreams of by the untimely death of this Mr. Dickens.

Whom do you think I met in Pall Mall the other day? You would not hit it in ten guesses. Why, no less a man than Napoleon Bonaparte, or all that is now left of him—that is to say, the skin, bones, and corporeal substance, little cocked hat, green coat, white breeches, and small sword, which are still known by his redoubtable name. He was attended only by two policemen, who walked quietly behind the phantasm of the old ex-emperor, appearing to have no duty in regard to him except to see that none of the light-fingered gentry should possess themselves of the star of the Legion of Honour.

Nobody, save myself, so much as turned to look after him; nor, it grieves me to confess, could even I contrive to muster up any tolerable interest, even by all that the warlike spirit, formerly manifested within that now decrepit shape, had wrought upon our globe. There is no surer method of annihilating the magic influence of a great renown than by exhibiting the possessor of it in the decline, the overthrow, the utter degradation of his powers,—buried beneath his own mortality,—and lacking even the qualities of sense that enable the most ordinary men to bear themselves decently in the eye of the world. This is the state to which disease, aggravated by long endurance of a tropical climate, and assisted by old age,—for he is now above seventy,—has reduced Bonaparte.

The British government has acted shrewdly in retransporting him from St. Helena to England. They should now restore him to Paris, and there let him once again review the relics of his armies. His eye is dull and rheumy; his nether lip hung down upon his chin. While I was observing him there chanced to be a little extra bustle in the street; and he, the brother of Cæsar and Hannibal,—the great captain who had veiled the world in battle smoke and tracked it round with bloody footsteps,—was seized with a nervous trembling, and claimed the protection of the two policemen by a cracked and dolorous cry. The fellows winked at one another, laughed aside, and, patting Napoleon on the back, took each an arm and led him away.

Death and fury! Ha, villain, how came you hither? *Avaunt!* or I fling my inkstand at your head. Tush, tush; it is all a mistake. Pray, my dear friend, pardon this little outbreak. The fact is, the mention of those two policemen, and their custody of Bonaparte, had called up the idea of that odious wretch—yon remember him well—who was pleased to take such gratuitous and impertinent care of my person before I quitted New England. Forthwith up rose before my mind's eye that same little whitewashed room, with the iron-grated window,—strange that it should have been iron-grated!—where, in too easy compliance with the absurd wishes of my relatives, I have wasted several good years of my life.

Positively it seemed to me that I was still sitting there, and that the keeper—not that he ever was my keeper neither, but only a kind of intrusive devil of a body servant—had just peeped in at the door. The rascal! I owe him an old grudge, and will find a time to pay it yet. Fie! fie! The mere thought of him has exceedingly discomposed me. Even now that hateful chamber—the iron-grated window, which blasted the blessed sunshine as it fell through the dusty panes and made it poison to my sold—looks more distinct to my view than does this my comfortable apartment in the heart of London. The reality—that which I know to be such—hangs like remnants of tattered scenery over the intolerably prominent illusion. Let us think of it no more.

You will be anxious to hear of Shelley. I need not say, what is known to all the world, that this celebrated poet has for many years past been reconciled to the Church of England. In his more recent works he has applied his fine powers to the vindication of the Christian faith, with an especial view to that particular development. Latterly, as you may not have heard, he has taken orders, and been inducted to a small country living in the gift of the lord chancellor. Just now, luckily for me, he has come to the metropolis to superintend the publication of a volume of discourses treating of the poetico-philosophical proofs of

Christianity on the basis of the Thirty-Nine Articles.

On my first introduction I felt no little embarrassment as to the manner of combining what I had to say to the author of Queen Mab, the Revolt of Islam, and Prometheus Unbound with such acknowledgments as might be acceptable to a Christian minister and zealous upholder of the established church. But Shelley soon placed me at my ease. Standing where he now does, and reviewing all his successive productions from a higher point, he assures me that there is a harmony, an order, a regular procession, which enables him to lay his hand upon any one of the earlier poems and say, "This is my work," with precisely the same complacency of conscience wherewithal he contemplates the volume of discourses above mentioned. They are like the successive steps of a staircase, the lowest of which, in the depth of chaos, is as essential to the support of the whole as the highest and final one resting upon the threshold of the heavens. I felt half inclined to ask him what would have been his fate had he perished on the lower steps of his staircase instead of building his way aloft into the celestial brightness.

How all this may be I neither pretend to understand nor greatly care, so long as Shelley has really climbed, as it seems he has, from a lower region to a loftier one. Without touching upon their religious merits, I consider the productions of his maturity superior, as poems, to those of his youth. They are warmer with human love, which has served as an interpreter between his mind and the multitude. The author has learned to dip his pen oftener into his heart, and has thereby avoided the faults into which a too exclusive use of fancy and intellect are wont to betray him.

Formerly his page was often little other than a concrete arrangement of crystallizations, or even of icicles, as cold as they were brilliant. Now you take it to your heart, and are conscious of a heart warmth responsive to your own.

In his private character Shelley can hardly have grown more gentle, kind, and affectionate, than his friends always represented him to be up to that disastrous night when he was drowned in the Mediterranean.

Nonsense, again—sheer nonsense! What am I babbling about? I was thinking of that old figment of his being lost in the Bay of Spezzia, and washed ashore near Via Reggio, and burned to ashes on a funeral pyre, with wine, and spices, and frankincense; while Byron stood on the beach and beheld a flame of marvellous beauty rise heavenward from the dead poet's heart, and that his fire-purified relics were finally buried near his child in Roman earth. If all this happened three and twenty years ago, how could I have met the drowned, and burned, and buried man here in London only yesterday?

Before quitting the subject, I may mention that Dr. Reginald Heber, heretofore Bishop of Calcutta, but recently translated to a see in England, called on Shelley while I was with him. They appeared to be on terms of very cordial intimacy, and are said to have a joint poem in contemplation. What a strange, incongruous dream is the life of man!

Coleridge has at last finished his poem of *Christabel*. It will be issued entire by old John Murray in the course of the present publishing season. The poet, I hear, is visited with a troublesome affection of the tongue, which has put a period, or some lesser stop, to the life-long discourse that has hitherto been flowing from his lips. He will not survive it above a month unless his accumulation of ideas be sluiced off in some other way. Wordsworth died only a week or two ago. Heaven rest his soul, and grant that he may not have completed *The Excursion!*

Methinks I am sick of everything he wrote except his *Laodamia*. It is very sad, this inconstancy of the mind to the poets whom it once worshipped. Southey is as hale as ever, and writes with his usual diligence. Old Gifford is still alive in the extremity of age, and with most pitiable decay of what little sharp and narrow intellect the devil had gifted him withal. One hates to allow such a man the privilege of growing old and infirm. It takes away our speculative license of kicking him.

Keats? No; I have not seen him except across a crowded street, with coaches, drays, horsemen, cabs, omnibuses, foot passengers, and divers other sensual obstructions intervening betwixt his small and slender figure and my eager glance. I would fain have met him on the sea-shore, or beneath a natural arch of forest trees, or the Gothic arch of an old cathedral, or among Grecian ruins, or at a glimmering fireside on the verge of evening, or at the twilight entrance of a cave, into the dreary depths of which he would have led me by the hand; anywhere, in short, save at Temple Bar, where his presence was blotted out by the porter-swollen bulks of these gross Englishmen, I stood and watched him fading away, fading away along the pavement, and could hardly tell whether he were an actual man or a thought that had slipped out of my mind and clothed itself in human form and habiliments merely to beguile me.

At one moment he put his handkerchief to his lips, and withdrew it, I am almost certain, stained with blood. You never saw anything so fragile as his person. The truth is, Keats has all his life felt the effects of that terrible bleeding at the lungs caused by the article on his *Endymion* in the *Quarterly Review*, and which so nearly brought him to the grave. Ever since he has glided about the world like a ghost, sighing a melancholy tone in the ear of here and there a friend, but never sending forth his voice to greet the multitude. I can hardly think him a great poet. The burden of a mighty genius would never have been imposed upon shoulders so physically frail and a spirit so infirmly sensitive. Great poets should have iron sinews. Yet Keats, though for so many years he has given nothing to the world, is understood to have devoted himself to the composition of an epic poem. Some passages of it have been communicated to the inner circle of his admirers, and impressed them as the loftiest strains that have been audible on earth since Milton's days. If I can obtain copies of these specimens, I will ask you to present them to James Russell Lowell, who seems to be one of the poet's most fervent and worthiest worshippers.

The information took me by surprise. I had supposed that all Keats's poetic incense, without being embodied in human language, floated up to heaven and mingled with the songs of the immortal choristers, who, perhaps, were conscious of an unknown voice among them, and thought their melody the sweeter for it. But it is not so; he has positively written a poem on the subject of Paradise Regained, though in another sense than that which presented itself to the mind of Milton. In compliance, it may be imagined, with the dogma of those who pretend that all epic possibilities in the past history of the world are exhausted, Keats has thrown his poem forward into an indefinitely remote futurity. He pictures mankind amid the closing circumstances of the time-long warfare between good and evil.

Our race is on the eve of its final triumph. Man is within the last stride of perfection; Woman, redeemed from the thraldom against which our sibyl uplifts so powerful and so sad a remonstrance, stands equal by his side, or communes for herself with angels; the Earth, sympathizing with her children's happier state, has clothed herself in such luxuriant and loving beauty as no eye ever witnessed since our first parents saw the sun rise over dewy Eden. Nor then indeed; for this is the fulfilment of what was then but a golden promise. But the picture has its shadows. There remains to mankind another peril—a last encounter with the evil principle. Should the battle go against us, we sink back into the slime and misery of ages. If we triumph—

But it demands a poet's eye to contemplate the splendour of such a consummation and not to be dazzled.

To this great work Keats is said to have brought so deep and tender a spirit of humanity that the poem has all the sweet and warm interest of a village tale no less than the grandeur which befits so high a theme. Such, at least, is the perhaps partial representation of his friends; for I have not read or heard even a single line of the performance in question. Keats, I am told, withholds it from the press, under an idea that the age has not enough of spiritual insight to receive it worthily. I do not like this distrust; it makes me distrust the poet. The universe is waiting to respond to the highest word that the best child of time and immortality can utter. If it refuse to listen, it is because he mumbles and stammers, or discourses things unseasonable and foreign to the purpose.

I visited the House of Lords the other day to hear Canning, who, you know, is now a peer, with I forget what title. He disappointed me. Time blunts both point and edge, and does great mischief to men of his order of intellect. Then I stepped into the lower house and listened to a few words from Cobbett, who looked as earthy as a real clod-hopper, or rather as if he had lain a dozen years beneath the clods. The men whom I meet nowadays often impress me thus; probably because my spirits are not very good, and lead me to think much about graves, with the long grass upon them, and weather-worn epitaphs, and dry bones of people who made noise enough in their day, but now can only clatter, clatter, clatter when the sexton's spade disturbs them.

Were it only possible to find out who are alive and who dead, it would contribute infinitely to my peace of mind. Every day of my life somebody comes and stares me in the face whom I had quietly blotted out of the tablet of living men, and trusted nevermore to be pestered with the sight or sound of him. For instance, going to Drury Lane Thea-

535

tre a few evenings since, up rose before me, in the ghost of Hamlet's father, the bodily presence of the elder Kean, who did die, or ought to have died, in some drunken fit or other, so long ago that his fame is scarcely traditionary now. His powers are quite gone; he was rather the ghost of himself than the ghost of the Danish king.

In the stage box sat several elderly and decrepit people, and among them a stately ruin of a woman on a very large scale, with a profile—for I did not see her front face—that stamped itself into my brain as a seal impresses hot wax. By the tragic gesture with which she took a pinch of snuff, I was sure it must be Mrs. Siddons. Her brother, John Kemble, sat behind—a broken-down figure, but still with a kingly majesty about him. In lieu of all former achievements. Nature enables him to look the part of Lear far better than in the meridian of his genius.

Charles Matthews was likewise there; but a paralytic affection has distorted his once mobile countenance into a most disagreeable one-sidedness, from which he could no more wrench it into proper form than he could rearrange the face of the great globe itself. It looks as if, for the joke's sake, the poor man had twisted his features into an expression at once the most ludicrous and horrible that he could contrive, and at that very moment, as a judgment for making himself so hideous, an avenging Providence had seen fit to petrify him. Since it is out of his own power. I would gladly assist him to change countenance, for his ugly visage haunts me both at noontide and night-time. Some other players of the past generation were present, but none that greatly interested me. It behooves actors, more than all other men of publicity, to vanish from the scene betimes. Being at best but painted shadows flickering on the wall, and empty sounds that echo another's thought, it is a sad disenchantment when the colours begin to fade and the voice to croak with age.

What is there new in the literary way on your side of the

water? Nothing of the kind has come under my inspection except a volume of poems published above a year ago by Dr. Channing. I did not before know that this eminent writer is a poet; nor does the volume alluded to exhibit any of the characteristics of the author's mind as displayed in his prose works; although some of the poems have a richness that is not merely of the surface, but glows still brighter the deeper and more faithfully you look into them. They seem carelessly wrought, however, like those rings and ornaments of the very purest gold, but of rude, native manufacture, which are found among the gold dust from Africa. I doubt whether the American public will accept them; it looks less to the assay of metal than to the neat and cunning manufacture.

How slowly our literature grows up! Most of our writers of promise have come to untimely ends. There was that wild fellow, John Neal, who almost turned my boyish brain with his romances; he surely has long been dead, else he never could keep himself so quiet. Bryant has gone to his last sleep, with the Thanatopsis gleaming over him like a sculptured marble sepulchre by moonlight. Halleck, who used to write queer verses in the newspapers and published a Don Juanio poem called *Fanny*, is defunct as a poet, though averred to be exemplifying the metempsychosis as a man of business. Somewhat later there was Whittier, a fiery Quaker youth, to whom the muse had perversely assigned a battle trumpet, and who got himself lynched, ten years agone, in South Carolina.

I remember, too, a lad just from college, Longfellow by name, who scattered some delicate verses to the winds, and went to Germany, and perished, I think, of intense application, at the University of Gottingen. Willis—what a pity!—was lost, if I recollect rightly, in 1833, on his voyage to Europe, whither he was going to give us sketches of the world's sunny face. If these had lived, they might, one or all of them, have grown to be famous men.

And yet there is no telling; it may be as well that they have died. I was myself a young man of promise. Oh shattered brain, oh broken spirit, where is the fulfilment of that promise? The sad truth is, that, when fate would gently disappoint the world, it takes away the hopefulest mortals in their youth; when it would laugh the world's hopes to scorn, it lets them live. Let me die upon this apothegm, for I shall never make a truer one.

What a strange substance is the human brain! Or rather,— for there is no need of generalizing the remark,—what an odd brain is mine! Would you believe it? Daily and nightly there come scraps of poetry humming in my intellectual ear—some as airy as bird notes, and some as delicately neat as parlour music, and a few as grand as organ peals— that seem just such verses as those departed poets would have written had not an inexorable destiny snatched them from their inkstands. They visit me in spirit, perhaps desiring to engage my services as the amanuensis of their posthumous productions, and thus secure the endless renown that they have forfeited by going hence too early. But I have my own business to attend to; and besides, a medical gentleman, who interests himself in some little ailments of mine, advises me not to make too free use of pen and ink. There are clerks enough out of employment who would be glad of such a job.

Goodbye! Are you alive or dead? and what are you about? Still scribbling for the Democratic? And do those infernal compositors and proof readers misprint your unfortunate productions as vilely as ever? It is too bad. Let every man manufacture his own nonsense, say I. Expect me home soon, and—to whisper you a secret—in company with the poet Campbell, who purposes to visit Wyoming and enjoy the shadow of the laurels that he planted there. Campbell is now an old man. He calls himself well, better than ever in his life, but looks strangely pale, and so shadow-like that one might almost poke a finger through his densest material. I tell him, by way of joke, that he is as dim and forlorn as Memory, though as unsubstantial as Hope.

Your true friend, P.

P. S.—Pray present my most respectful regards to our venerable and revered friend Mr. Brockden Brown. It gratifies me to learn that a complete edition of his works, in a double-columned *octavo* volume, is shortly to issue from the press at Philadelphia. Tell him that no American writer enjoys a more classic reputation on this side of the water. *Is* old Joel Barlow yet alive? Unconscionable man! Why, he must have nearly fulfilled his century. And *does* he meditate an epic on the war between Mexico and Texas with machinery contrived on the principle of the steamengine, as being the nearest to celestial agency that our epoch can boast? How can he expect ever to rise again, if, while just sinking into his grave, he persists in burdening himself with such a ponderosity of leaden verses?

LEONAUR

ALSO FROM LEONAUR
AVAILABLE IN SOFTCOVER OR HARDCOVER WITH DUST JACKET

THE COMPLETE FOUR JUST MEN: VOLUME 2 *by Edgar Wallace—The Law of the Four Just Men & The Three Just Men*—disillusioned with a world where the wicked and the abusers of power perpetually go unpunished, the Just Men set about to rectify matters according to their own standards, and retribution is dispensed on swift and deadly wings.

THE COMPLETE RAFFLES: 1 *by E. W. Hornung—The Amateur Cracksman & The Black Mask*—By turns urbane gentleman about town and accomplished cricketer, life is just too ordinary for Raffles and that sets him on a series of adventures that have long been treasured as a real antidote to the 'white knights' who are the usual heroes of the crime fiction of this period.

THE COMPLETE RAFFLES: 2 *by E. W. Hornung—A Thief in the Night & Mr Justice Raffles*—By turns urbane gentleman about town and accomplished cricketer, life is just too ordinary for Raffles and that sets him on a series of adventures that have long been treasured as a real antidote to the 'white knights' who are the usual heroes of the crime fiction of this period.

THE COLLECTED SUPERNATURAL AND WEIRD FICTION OF WILKIE COLLINS: VOLUME 1 *by Wilkie Collins*—Contains one novel 'The Haunted Hotel', one novella 'Mad Monkton', three novelettes 'Mr Percy and the Prophet', 'The Biter Bit' and 'The Dead Alive' and eight short stories to chill the blood.

THE COLLECTED SUPERNATURAL AND WEIRD FICTION OF WILKIE COLLINS: VOLUME 2 *by Wilkie Collins*—Contains one novel 'The Two Destinies', three novellas 'The Frozen deep', 'Sister Rose' and 'The Yellow Mask' and two short stories to chill the blood.

THE COLLECTED SUPERNATURAL AND WEIRD FICTION OF WILKIE COLLINS: VOLUME 3 *by Wilkie Collins*—Contains one novel 'Dead Secret,' two novelettes 'Mrs Zant and the Ghost' and 'The Nun's Story of Gabriel's Marriage' and five short stories to chill the blood.

FUNNY BONES *selected by Dorothy Scarborough*—An Anthology of Humorous Ghost Stories.

MONTEZUMA'S CASTLE AND OTHER WEIRD TALES *by Charles B. Cory*—Cory has written a superb collection of eighteen ghostly and weird stories to chill and thrill the avid enthusiast of supernatural fiction.

SUPERNATURAL BUCHAN *by John Buchan*—Stories of Ancient Spirits, Uncanny Places & Strange Creatures.

LEONAUR

ALSO FROM LEONAUR
AVAILABLE IN SOFTCOVER OR HARDCOVER WITH DUST JACKET

MR MUKERJI'S GHOSTS *by S. Mukerji*—Supernatural tales from the British Raj period by India's Ghost story collector.

KIPLINGS GHOSTS *by Rudyard Kipling*—Twelve stories of Ghosts, Hauntings, Curses, Werewolves & Magic.

THE COLLECTED SUPERNATURAL AND WEIRD FICTION OF WASHINGTON IRVING: VOLUME 1 *by Washington Irving*—Including one novel 'A History of New York', and nine short stories of the Strange and Unusual.

THE COLLECTED SUPERNATURAL AND WEIRD FICTION OF WASHINGTON IRVING: VOLUME 2 *by Washington Irving*—Including three novelettes 'The Legend of the Sleepy Hollow', 'Dolph Heyliger', 'The Adventure of the Black Fisherman' and thirty-two short stories of the Strange and Unusual.

THE COLLECTED SUPERNATURAL AND WEIRD FICTION OF JOHN KENDRICK BANGS: VOLUME 1 *by John Kendrick Bangs*—Including one novel 'Toppleton's Client or A Spirit in Exile', and ten short stories of the Strange and Unusual.

THE COLLECTED SUPERNATURAL AND WEIRD FICTION OF JOHN KENDRICK BANGS: VOLUME 2 *by John Kendrick Bangs*—Including four novellas 'A House-Boat on the Styx', 'The Pursuit of the House-Boat', 'The Enchanted Typewriter' and 'Mr. Munchausen' of the Strange and Unusual.

THE COLLECTED SUPERNATURAL AND WEIRD FICTION OF JOHN KENDRICK BANGS: VOLUME 3 *by John Kendrick Bangs*—Including twor novellas 'Olympian Nights', 'Roger Camerden: A Strange Story', and ten short stories of the Strange and Unusual.

THE COLLECTED SUPERNATURAL AND WEIRD FICTION OF MARY SHELLEY: VOLUME 1 *by Mary Shelley*—Including one novel 'Frankenstein or the Modern Prometheus', and fourteen short stories of the Strange and Unusual.

THE COLLECTED SUPERNATURAL AND WEIRD FICTION OF MARY SHELLEY: VOLUME 2 *by Mary Shelley*—Including one novel 'The Last Man', and three short stories of the Strange and Unusual.

THE COLLECTED SUPERNATURAL AND WEIRD FICTION OF AMELIA B. EDWARDS *by Amelia B. Edwards*—Contains two novelettes 'Monsieur Maurice', and 'The Discovery of the Treasure Isles', one ballad 'A Legend of Boisguilbert'and seventeen short stories to cill the blood.